VICTORIA KASMINOFF

Petals of Insanity

Dove Gray and Gold Book One

First edition

ISBN: 979-8-9888923-1-1

Cover art by George Cotronis

This book was professionally typeset on Reedsy.
Find out more at reedsy.com

To Vanessa

My main bae, ride or die, sister, foodie companion and all around best friend. You've helped me so much in life, from talking me through mental breakdowns to listening with genuine excitement to my ideas. That means the world to me as do you.

Love you!

Prologue

The Voices summoned them long ago, when the human realm's inhabitants had stopped roaming the lands, hunting and gathering, and started to domesticate the ground's offerings. The Voices had watched them grow; it was intrigued by them. The Voices had selected few primitive humans who appealed to them and offered them gifts.

"Behold, powers that no mortal has yet dreamed."

It's wordless promise, the whispering impersonation, was beautiful and terrifying.

"With these gifts, you will use them to bring comfort and certainty to your people without directly interfering. You are the foundation for belief, of hope. Their belief will sustain you and your aspect will inspire them".

Only those with weak hearts died from shock in the face of The Voices. The rest merely coward, listening in awestruck terror, and thus the gods and goddesses were crafted for the human realm, shedding their humanity in favor for godliness that was bestowed upon them.

"There are rules," The Voices warned darkly, *"head them well, obey them and all shall be as it is set to be"*.

Time flickered by and as human civilizations rose, advanced, and fought through the ages, the gods and goddesses remained frozen in a kaleidoscope of life. And as time trekked on, rising, and falling in dramatic waves, came the destruction of many civilizations. When death came to a specific empire, the deities of the people were forgotten and wrought in a dismal state of starvation before withering away into nothing but rusted memories and, ultimately, dust. Clutched with fear at the possibility of simply no longer existing, panic was thickly woven through the gods' consciousness. Dramatic flares of power and rule-breaking ensued. The gods and goddesses created creatures of horror that inspired deep fear within their worshipers; causing them to recoil and dedicate their entire mortal lives to pleasing the gods.

Blistering rage and sickly greed poisoned all the gods into an uncontrollable war. They fought each other, tricking, killing, maiming, and destroying human subordinates carelessly… cruelly. The Voices watched, they were displeased, but they waited, watching the outcome. The war continued to wage between all the gods, fighting for the complete attention of the human subjects, while trying to destroy the other gods and goddesses for supremacy. War bled to other realms, other creatures became corrupt, destroyed, ruined. Blood ran thick across the realms and every creature and the divinities perished by the thousands until finally The Voices sent *them* down.

Alien beasts that were fashioned as clever, violent and completely loyal servants to serve The Voices in any shape or form. They brutally gathered the gods and goddesses of the human realm as well as some of their creations of destruction, before tossing them into a chamber laced with bars, filth and vermin.

A hundred millenniums have trickled by and still the human realm's Gods remain in their tiny prisons. They rotted, they fumed and raved before going completely insane.

* * *

"I want out of here! I am a God! A God! *The God!*"

"When I get out of here, I shall peel your skin from your muscles, your muscle from your bones, heal you, then I shall start all over…for centuries!"

"I'll eat my own foot for just a drop of beer."

"Disgusting savage, it is wine you should pine for! Not that primitive bitter batter!"

"Let us go! And you shall receive minor crumbs of mercy as I slowly kill you if you do so right this very instance!"

"Nine hundred and nine trillion, seven hundred and fifty-two billion, eight hundred and seventy-one million…."

"I curse your family! Curse them all to be hideous and unloved! And I curse everyone's livestock! Curse all your asses to hell with all your goats!"

"Lalla, Lalla, Lalla, aut dormi, aut lacta."

The passionate, but empty threats and ramblings bounced from the moldy ceiling to the cracked floors and ultimately fell upon deaf ears.

I ignored them, always have, always did, and always would. Their sniveling wails didn't accomplish anything but tire them and fill the reigning silence. Immortals, like the raving morons I was cursed to endure, lost the concept of time. They treated years much like hours, which was wasteful. They missed the details, and it is in the details that power hides its small revelations.

But not I.

No.

I notice everything. From the spider web cracks that crept slowly downward from the ceilings to the walls. I notice all the twittering patterns, the imbecilic chattering and the pathetic noises of my fellow inmates. I notice all the different dirty scavengers that enter and identify what they eat, how they eat, from whom they eat and whom they have begun to feast upon. Despite all my attention to the minute details, I have yet to identify the chink in the armor of my cage. No guards came down to us. It was as if we were put away in a tomb, sealed off and never to be seen or heard from again. It was a theory that the years of imprisonment increased the all-consuming rage that festered within me. It believed us untamed and violent, yet they gifted us with these powers only to suppress them and lock us all away in these forgotten, decrepit tombs. However, despite the imprisonment and the high-handedness of The Voices locking them away, our power was not destroyed. It was merely stifled. I felt my power, I felt it flowing thickly threw my veins, pulsing with a heady and excitingly teasing hegemony. The reason why I… *we* are still here is because we are still remembered. Our essences, our energy still ignites the belief in enough people to sustain us. We had figured out that the more followers we had, the more strength we begot, though admittedly our power was not as it once was, and as time trickles by, we grow weaker and weaker.

My fingers twitch uncontrollably at times with the craving to conquer, to control, to create, to dominate as I once did. It was a part of our nature, part of our desire to see the weaker, the inferior, bow before us with awe at our omnipotence. It was the natural order when The Voices gave us these gifts, placing us above our own race, making our course of action inherent in our rank. The Voices didn't view it as such though. No, they condemned us and hoarded us into prisons like common filth. Rage doesn't quite cover the broad spectrum of my emotions at the betrayal… the abuse of a greater power to the lesser. I often sometimes wondered what it would be like to drive a blade in the self-righteous chests of The Voices' pets, to cut out their still throbbing hearts and hold it in my hands before squeezing…

Dark delight caressed my spine at the blood-soaked thought. I want blood. Rich, crimson blood drenched over me as bodies lay dismembered around me. Like before. Sighing a wistful longing breath from my lungs, I focused upon the prison cell directly across from me as the creature within prowled angrily, as usual, and hissed with pompous rage.

"*We need more* power. *Power! Power! We need* It's *power!*" It wailed uncharacteristically. It appeared the desperation wormed its way into the brain creating a mindless insanity. "*The Voices are weak! That is why they lock us away, forcing us to rot out a miserable existence instead of ending us!*" A long wretched scream ended the creatures ranting.

Pity. The creature managed to entertain me frequently. I snorted silently before musing on the insect's words. Why were we imprisoned instead of killed? Was it merely for the sake of punishment? I doubt it. Was it as the creature said? The Voices' power was limited over us and thus could not end us. Yet, their power was still strong enough to contain us. I followed a spider making its way slowly across the ground. I raised my bare foot and stomped on the insect, enjoying the small kill and the satisfying sound of its body being crushed under the weight of my foot. If only I could do that to The Voices. But they were one, they had more power. If only I or at least one of us had the preeminent power then The Voices …Quick as a snake striking and fierce as a starved bear on the hunt, an idea was born in the grimy cells of my confinement and rapidly cultivated into a throbbing rhythm that fueled a fragile kernel of hope.

Yes.

Yes.

That was it.

That was exactly it!

Power as The Voices have—*No*—greater power. Everyone needed greater power and I, of course, needed the greatest power over all of them to ensure authority over these slovenly idiots. I looked up right across from my cell to find a fellow prisoner's eyes bright with vile viciousness and just dull enough with a gullibility to be controllable.

Perfect.

I smiled, baring my teeth before speaking to the once power filled being in a tone of familiarity. I reeled in the creature across from me with my wrath dipped words. I excited them with sweet promises of a blood drenched reunion with The Voices and the recruitment of new worshipers. The creature smiled a nasty snarl and nodded eagerly, soaking up my intelligence like a dried-out fish. Soon, the others slowly stopped their moaning to listen and then to cheer. Living power curled around us in unison, singing its hypnotic siren wail. I nearly shout in joy at the rough caresses I received from it. Revenge shall be intoxicating as will the blood running down my hands and mouth.

Death to all and all to misery.

* * *

Death.

It blackened the colors of life and decayed beauty with its mere mention. It's a force that no one, not even *It* can stop… but death will be used, as it always was, through wars, rage, and sickness… They will master death and destroy everything… destroy everywhere.

Deep breath in. Slow. Hold. Out. Slow. Repeat.

Turning to the sounds of laughter right outside the door cut the tension that was beginning to suffocate. Touching the cool, smooth jewelry gave comfort temporarily.

Think.

Death will never cease to exist, but gods can. There will need to be interference and, of course, a plan. A plan to push the death wielding gods right off the edge of existence.

Yes. Yes.

Perhaps… yes…. And… Perfect….

Pockets of light began to peek through the consuming darkness.

More detail, more light.

Yes!

Death will never stop, neither will darkness, but many unnecessary deaths can be avoided as can the destruction of realms. And will be avoided at all costs. Even if they all turned rancid with hate towards the plan maker, the one who interferes, it will be done.

And all the unnecessary deaths will be avoided and peace will resume.

Chapter One

The metal gates screamed as they sluggishly wrenched apart to allow the clattering cab through. A seemingly long, desolate dirt road paired with overgrown grass and twisted trees led the way to a tarnished brown building that loomed against the bright, cloudless sky. Its impressive stature and the stale depressing air churned her stomach, making her sick as nerves took a hold of her insides with a steel laced grip. When the cab came to a crunching stop in front of wide double doors with sinister steps, she tried to linger but the gruff driver grunted out the price of the fair and urged her to speed it up for he had 'places to be'. Sighing in irritation that briefly dominated her trembling nerves, she gave the driver sixty dollars that her mother had reluctantly given her and waited for the change. Once she was out of the musty back seat of the old taxi the driver took off eagerly, spraying up a light cloud of dusty smoke with a few stray bits of gravel in it.

Narrowing her eyes at the back of the dingy yellow taxi, she huffed, affronted. Exhaling the remaining annoyance, she turned back around and gazed up at the dominating building. Swallowing back the butterflies that managed to flutter up from her stomach to the back of her throat, she straightened her spine, clutched her big hobo bag tightly and placed one foot in front of the other in small steps. She managed to walk directly to the red metal doors, hesitating only when her hand made contact with the icy metal handle. Was this *really* necessary? Words that she had repressed from her family suddenly roared in her ears.

"Darling girl, no one should have... episodes as you do. It's not normal."

"Accept this help, these... images are hurting you—hurting us. You know this is not normal."

"You're an utter freak in public when you get these 'things'. Which is why we never bring you around anywhere. It's a good thing you're getting professional help. You'll finally get normal."

"We tried everything when you were younger, now it is up to the professionals to help make you a normal, better person."

Gritting her teeth, she shoved the unpleasant words away. *Normal, normal, normal,* she mocked. She yanked the door open as she shoved the stinging words back into the prison within her mind. Upon stepping inside the ward, she was swept up in dizzying white blur of stone-cold people with cheery faces, talking to her as if she were a slow and fragile creature. The glassy eyed people then very politely shoved her into a room that was a smidgen bigger than a supply closet. They raided her bag while keeping up a steady stream of soft words and empty smiles. After they settled her in, taking away her floss, giving her bright white clothes and hard slippers to wear, they urged her with wide eyes to relax before granting her a moment of reprieve from their eerie presence.

She gazed about her tiny room with a frown and analytical eyes. A robust metal door that led to the shiny hallways was covered with black and red doodles ranging from happy dancing stick figures with little tops hats, to angry cuss words and meaningless lines. The walls of her room were perfectly aligned with glossy brass-colored bricks stacked upon each other politely allowing for only one small window in its strategic design. The window had a wired fence fashioned upon the dingy looking glass from the outside. The caged window allowed for patches of dull light to tease the room in a blotchy glow. It created a somewhat trapped appearance to the whole prison themed room. What also really contributed to the whole captive themed room was the frail looking metal frame with a cracker thin mattress residing under the window. Looking cheap and utterly uncomfortable with its plastic pillow and tissue thin sheets.

Sighing quietly, she looked down at the abused ceramic floors, blotched with dark colors and scratches. Scuffing her shoe against the dull surface, childishly pleased when she made her own little black streak, she made her way over to the feeble bed. It groaned and sobbed a few loud crackles in complaint under her weight as she settled herself upon the edge but, thankfully, held up.

She hugged her bag to her chest, feeling uncomfortable through and through. No one understood her. Every teen's problem, or so they had informed her. Everyone attempted to understand but she didn't play their games correctly, for they became consumed in everything that was wrong with her and never mustered up the energy to move past her flaws. She had been to more doctors than she can count on her fingers and toes. The doctors all looked at her as if she were a new species of an insect strapped down beneath their microscopes, eager to name her so they may obtain glory for the 'discovery'. Each one trying to diagnose her or prescribe her on something to be normal. Nothing had helped and now, finally, her family has shipped her to an insane asylum, where they thought she needed to be until she was considered 'cured'. Or stay there forever if proven 'incurable'.

Her mother's parting words vibrated painfully in her mind...

"You are not allowed back home until you are sane. I will not be tainted in any way by your abnormalities. We have to think about the family name, dear. I don't need people to talk about us."

Anger burned the hurt away within her. She was *not* crazy. She heard this phrase once and it went along the lines of if you were crazy then you'd be too insane to know that you were. Well, she knew *something* was wrong with her, but she knew she wasn't certifiable to be locked up in a loony bin. It was something she felt deep within her bones. She was sane, but vastly different. Was that such a horrible thing?

The big heavy door suddenly opened, giving her a slight fright as a blank faced nurse stuck her head in and smiled unconvincingly at her. "Alright Ms. Tullia Vale, you go ahead and get nice and comfortable here. Dinner is at six pm sharp tonight. We're having meatloaf and mash potatoes. I'll come by at five fifty-five to escort you to the cafeteria, okay?" She didn't wait for a response, she only smiled stiffly and left with a clinical squeak.

And that was that.

Tullia sighed, *I hate meatloaf.* She adjusted her position on the bed, thinking over everything that had transpired in the last month. She just finished her sophomore year of high school, barely. She was happy to pass her classes with the low C's she managed. Was it truly her fault that she had such a terrible attention span when most of the time she wasn't fully aware of what was taking place around her? Though she knew perfectly well what her thoughts were doing. She found she was much more interested in what her mind was doing rather than what reality offered. She was asked out for the first time in her life… only for it to turn into a lame practical joke. Her sense of self-worth took a vicious beating, but she comforted herself with the knowledge that the stink bomb they concocted for the finale, ended up in the jerk's car, dousing him, her and his 'baby'. There was no way on or out of Earth that he was getting that stench out from his custom leather seats any time soon. To top off an already dismal month, her parents found her latest habit much too disturbing, which was why she was here. In a mental ward.

Yippee.

Groaning from the depths of her soul she slowly laid back upon the bed that also groaned and wobbled dangerously under her. Propping her hands behind her head she allowed her thoughts to wander as her eyes found figures within the ceiling texture. Her mind then began to dip into magical places. Cities crafted from colorful coral within deep gorges in the ocean flooded her mind. Shining with subtle glittery light, the scales glimmered under the light swallowing water. As fast as that image swam into her mind it morphed into a scene of mountainous terrain covered lovingly with soft, white snow and ravaged by rough gouges in the land as jagged mountain and ice castles jutted up high into a starry colored heaven above. Then before she had time to see any more, a leafy green forest with tiny little homes made from springy moss were hidden within the trees and radiant jade pools of water floated into her head. It was fantastical. She was swept up within her visions… for about a whole three minutes before she was thrust back into reality and became instantly bored.

How ironic that she could entertain herself for hours on end with nothing but herself during busy days, but as soon as she had nothing to do but daydream her mind decided to take a nap. Huffing at the mockery her brain dared to tease her with, she stood up, wincing at the trembling sound that followed her from the frail bed. She eyed the brown cabinet stuffed awkwardly into one corner, making the already tiny room have an even squishier feeling. She carefully unpacked her bag and began to dot her clinical room with a few of her allowed trinkets from home. She pulled out a quilt that she had made during her freshman summer. The bright gold and silver colors swirled together upon the soft material. She pulled a ratty old stuffed Stitch doll from her backpack. She clutched it to her chest for a suspended moment, feeling the innocent love that was seeped into its plush body from her childhood days. It represented the last happy time with her family. For the doll was bought for her the last time her parents ever took her to the theater and it was filled with so much laughter, so much happiness… She placed it tenderly upon the plastic covered pillow. She then put away three pairs of sweatshirts and carefully placed her riotous flip-flops in the bottom of the closet before she folded two pairs of yoga pants and carefully hung her beloved bag in the closet.

After that task was done the hours dripped by at a tedious rate, scraping upon Tullia's spine with an obsessive persistence. Though her solitude was broken up every fifteen minutes by a random nurse poking their head through the door to check on her. It wasn't until the machine-like nurse came back to escort her to dinner did Tullia realize just how starved she was for any type of entertainment; if her overly enthusiastic response to the nurse was anything to go by. She tasted a faint whisper of surprise from the nurse, acidic and bubbly, that was blanketed by a detached professionalism that flavored the staff of the hospital. Tullia eagerly followed the nurse down the hallway where their footsteps parted the heavy curtain of silence.

"Tomorrow, after you see the doctors, I will give you a tour so you're not cooped up in the room all the time. We encourage everyone here to partake in socializing and to walk the designated walking halls for some fresh air and physical stimulation." The nurse's strong voice was startling and loud in the clinically cold hallway. Tullia didn't say anything as her enthusiasm crashed and burned in the eerie hallway. She was less than thrilled to be shown around her free ranged prison by one of the wardens. The woman droned on and on about… something. Her feelings tasted neutral with a hint of boredom. Everything tasted of ice and cardboard. Tullia swallowed. The nurse must repeat the same phrases over and over with every new patient that had the misfortune to end up here. Tullia nodded here and there whenever the woman's eyes focused on her, seeking acknowledgment to her information. Upon reaching the cafeteria, the nurse escorted her to a line where only a handful of other people were waiting. The nurse, or as Tullia began to mentally refer to her as Nurse Robot, loaded her plate with the special of the day — meatloaf and mash potatoes — and told her she'd be back in half an hour to guide her back to her room. Then she vanished, which both relieved and terrified Tullia.

Turning around, Tullia's gaze glossed over the room. There were uneven clumps of relatively normal looking people sitting throughout the area, making it a bit difficult to find a seat that wasn't next to someone. When she managed to finally spot a seat that was isolated, she quickly made her way over and sat down at a white circular table with her tray. Drawing her legs underneath her and tucking a piece of hair behind her ear, she experimentally poked at her meatloaf and potatoes. They appeared normal, but she couldn't convince her mind to accept that there *wasn't* anything wrong with it. After all, she has been infected with popular horror movies and psychiatric ward food seemed as if it would be the main star in one of those mindless films.

Her stomach rumbled in displeasure at Tullia's hesitance, insisting her to take a chance on the only nutriment offered or else dire repercussions would take place. Sighing in resignation, she scooped up what resembled soupy mash potatoes and quickly inserted it into her mouth before she could really comprehend just what she was doing. A smooth sensation.... Bit of a butter flavor…Not too bad, smooth and plain, nothing unusual… Tullia pursed her lips when a weird after flavor of chili dance upon her tongue…

Chili?…

"Hello to you!" A high voice squeaked in her ear. Tullia jumped and gave out a short scream that ended abruptly when a clammy hand slapped over her mouth. She blinked in shock and turned her head towards a strawberry blond girl with pale blue eyes and deep dimples. "No screaming or else you'll be given a warning and eventually they'll ground you to your room. Trust me, not fun. Safe, but not fun."

She slowly removed her plastic smelling hand from Tullia's mouth and beamed a radiant smile at her. Tullia gave the girl a hesitant smile as a gush of suspicion, tart, invaded her palette from the petite girl. "I'm Olivia. Or infamously known as…" She stood up, placing one foot upon the table and striking a rather heroic pose as she bellowed, "The urinate-tor!" The harsh volume made Tullia cringe slightly before Olivia dropped back down in her seat. Olivia smiled widely before leaning in closer and whispering, "'Cause I have an overactive bladder they tell me. I need to keep intensely hydrated or else they'll search for me. So, I need to drink and drink and drink and drink…" She repeated that little phrase for a solid minute, allowing Tullia to nibble experimentally upon the meatloaf. Not bad, but definitely not good. Olivia trailed off to stare at the minty green wall blankly. She then sneezed, breaking her trance. Blinking a little, her gaze then latched onto Tullia's again. Her excitement, carbonated bubbles, bloomed once more inside Tullia's mouth.

"So? Don't leave me in the dark! I am scared of it after all. Just like the salon roll rooter. I know this for a fact. Tell me what your name is?" She asked, her smile bright and her eyes flickering from intently interested to dully unfocused to roaming quickly around the room.

"Tullia Vale." She responded slowly, torn between liking the strange girl besides her and being unnerved by her.

The girl scrunched up her nose as her lips pushed out in thought, "Tullia

Vale? Sounds like a twisted tulip all tangled in a mesh veil." Tullia repressed a snarky comment that was poised ready to strike on the tip of her tongue. The girl was a patient here, clearly there would be some flaws with her social skills. Besides, based on her sincere expression and the fact that there wasn't a sour or bitter flavor in her mouth (Tullia began to figure out that when those flavors were present, it meant something mean), she was stating what she thought, not mocking Tullia. However, her name did *not* sound like a 'twisted tulip all tangled in a mesh veil'.

"Or it could sound just like Tullia Vale." She offered, jerking back when the girl cackled out a sudden, vibrating laugh.

"Like a doe, rey, mi, so, la, be, see! It does sound like that! It does!" She howled a little, then sighed, "I'm Olivia." She stuck her hand out abruptly, smiling a chap lipped grin. Tullia felt an answering smile curl her lips as she shook Olivia's hand. She tasted of pure sugar, and bubbles. It was very nice. "Anyways, enough pleasantries. It's time to get serious. What's your idiosyncrasy?"

Tullia raised her eyebrow at Olivia, amused despite her situation of eating in an insane asylum. "Idio…syncrasy?"

"Well yeah. That's why we're here, cause of our *'idiosyncrasies.'* She raised her hands up and gave Tullia a look that was smug, "Very few people have them. We're just privileged like that. Except, of course, Putty doesn't see it as such, but he don't like anything positive in life." She jerked her thumb over her right shoulder to the mumbling hunched boy a few tables down. "He's not allowed any silly putty because he likes to eat it. I call him the Devourer of the Silly Putty! Or Putty for short." She twisted around, sitting precipitously upon the smallish white seat, before screaming out in a deep throaty voice, "Yo DSP!" The boy hoarsely yelled back a guttural slur that held no audible intelligence without looking away from his plate.

"Olivia, tone it down." A firm voice grouched from the doorway. She waved at the guard, who shook his head at her. Olivia spun back around to face Tullia with a cheeky grin, "He loves me, but just doesn't show it. Too bad I can't be his friend."

"Why?"

"Well, obviously, he's in alliance with the Tey Fauh, who is in Walmart as an apology for the salon roll rooster."

A very faint taste of…something bad. Tullia was confused, "And that's bad?"

"It's the salon roll rooster. It's an interstellar mercy of the end." Olivia's face was so earnest with her babbling nonsense, Tullia ended up nodding in acceptance to whatever she said. She swallowed thickly as the expired taste of a moldy and pungent rot coated her tongue.

Insanity.

"Anyways, I'm not mad at him. It's not his fault and you know what they say, to each bee there is pollen for honey no matter the flower." Tullia frowned at her last statement, but before she could comment on it Olivia chugged right along. "This is my third visit here. Medication and therapy just isn't quite right to make me acceptably right. But Paddington believes in his fur covered butt so therefore I can cut the cheese and say please." Tullia shoved the liquid potatoes into her mouth, trying to keep up with the rambles as she smothered the horrid taste with the mediocre food. "Hey," Olivia suddenly paused, turning her head to Tullia with a heated glare, "you totally distracted me from getting an answer from you. Why are you so mean?" Tullia leaned away from the girl a bit and opened her mouth to defend against the unfair accusation, but Olivia held up her hand, "I'll forgive you, if you tell me, right now, your idiosyncrasy."

"I…I don't think I have one." She answered hesitantly.

"What!" She hollered, making Tullia cringe at the piercing sound and volume. "Everyone here knows theirs, even if they don't, they do."

Tullia scrunched up her nose in slight confusion, "Well, I don't know what to call my idiosyncrasy, it's unknown."

Olivia gasped, "You have an unidentified super idiosyncrasy? Lucky ducky duck you. Mine is schizophrenia, though it's a tentative label. Doctors are sure there is something they are missing with me. However, it's all a ruse. I know I'm really red peak's experiment." Tullia nodded again at the girl with strawberry locks and a wide, gleaming smile. She was strange and fast paced in her speech, but Tullia liked her.

Even with the bad taste in her mouth, she liked her.

Olivia ate a spoonful of mash potatoes. "So, you appeared. They shipped you up like a glass vase with dirt and here you are." Some potato pieces went flying, narrowly missing Tullia.

"My parents forced me to go." Tullia confirmed, scooting away slightly from Olivia so that she didn't get covered in a mash potato and saliva shower. "They said… I'm basically a freak and need to get better." The biting bitterness of their words that injured her heart throbbed painfully and reflected into her voice.

The rancid taste of disgust whispered across her tongue. It hurt her that her family was disgusted with her… for being her.

"Yeah, that's what they all say. Even the mad clowns and the salon roll rooster. They're watching. But I just think they're boring and don't know how to respond to people who are prepared when shown."

She didn't make any true sense, yet this was the best conversation Tullia has ever experienced so far in her life. "I wish I was normal." Tullia said with feeling, "Then I wouldn't be in here and everyone wouldn't treat me like a freak."

Olivia's eyes were sharp and intense as she looked at Tullia. She no longer tasted of a moldy milk and pungent cheese flavor, instead she tasted like fresh, cold, mint ice. "It's all a game."

"What?" Tullia was still reeling over the sudden invasion of ice and mint in her mouth from Olivia.

"Life. It's all a game. A game of adaptation. We adapt to the head bosses in charge. The fashion, the politics, the technological advancements, people's rights, people's views, and everything in-between. If you can adapt yourself to these common ideals, then you'll never find yourself outside the box and the salon roll rooster will never get you."

Stunned by the fact that her entire speech made sense, it took a few seconds for Tullia to respond, "And I want in the box?" She asked slowly, watching Olivia dip her fingers into the mash potatoes and draw tight circles with it on the table.

"Of course. Everyone wants to be unique but belong as well. You can't truly be unique unless you're outside the box, which gains negative attention and condemnation and, usually, friendlessness." Her eyes roamed over the room again, there was a sheen of perspiration upon her upper lip, "So, you want to be near the edge, still inside, but right at the cusp of the box."

Tullia eyed the girl with an intensity usually reserved for difficult math problems. "If you think this way then why are you here?" Tullia asked. "Clearly you have this down packed to where you should be out in the world instead of in here."

Olivia gave her blank smile, "I am here. Still looking. Yes. I have to be. You see, the salon roll rooster cannot get me, can't even find me. They promised me, but still never can leave any wall unturned. And I can talk to everything and anything I want. It's never too much. Too much…" She sighed, her eyes going glassy. "But if you don't like it here, then you can cover your idiosyncrasy with a mask if you can find the perfect one that fits." After a brief stillness between them at Olivia's shockingly deep words, she seemed to shake herself and flicker between a boisterous girl who could coax laughs from Tullia, to a girl who made absolutely no sense at all.

The taste of insanity was back as well.

Twenty minutes later, dinner came to a close. Many of the patients rose and left at various intervals throughout the meal; all were escorted by nurses. When Olivia's nurse came for her, she let out a tired sigh. The nurse was a tall slender man with a pretty smile and an anime-looking hair style. "Come now, Ollie. It's time to get ready for bed."

"Is the seaside clear of possums? You know the salon roll rooster employs them." Her face was sullen and suspicious.

"Yup. The coast has been possum free all day. No signs of the salon roll rooster." He swore by an uplifted hand; his smile was kind, and his eyes were dancing with concealed amusement.

Olivia reluctantly nodded to him as she rose from her seat, "Sleep underneath the bed Tulls. Remember, ain't no wind whistlin' in the moon when the stars hang sideways." Tullia crinkled her nose but smiled and waved to the girl as she flounced besides the nurse.

Her own nurse appeared exactly three minutes later, a stiffened smile on her face. "Ready?" Nodding slowly Tullia rose, clutching her tray tightly into her hands. Dinner had been a lovely distraction from the insane reality that she was currently residing in. The walk back to her room was silent and eerie. There was very little noise besides the low hum of the lights above. Upon reaching the room, the nurse instructed Tullia to gather her bedtime items. She was then escorted to a fully functional bathroom and given twenty minutes to complete her nighttime tasks. Twenty-three minutes later, Tullia was once again standing in her tiny room, all dressed for bed.

"Alright then. There is an alarm that goes off at seven-thirty for thirty seconds. I'll be back at seven forty-five sharp so you can use the bathroom and eat breakfast after which I'll give you a tour of the facility. I'll then take you to your nine-thirty appointment with Dr. Winmore. Please be ready, okay?" Nodding to the nurse and a quick smile in parting, Tullia was alone once more in the tiny room.

The night was frightening. Uneven moonlight splayed over the room in menacing shapes and cast evil looking shadows. Tullia could feel the surrounding walls crying with the tales of the insane and unstable. A scream now and again pierced the air, speeding up her heart rate with a spike of fear. The air within the suffocating room swirled thickly with emotions, rendering it alive as Tullia felt a mirage of sensations pass through her. She gasped in stale tasting air, curling up tight under her quilt as sweat leaked from her pores.

"I want something. I want... yeah. You get me! Shut up Karen, you don't matter." A small voice muttered constantly in the room next to hers.

A strong taste of rot coiled in her mouth, trying to choke her. An icy finger tailed over her spine, freezing her sweat upon her body. Tullia ducked her head underneath her quilt and began to hum tunelessly.

Swallowing, nearly gagging, she was plagued with the thick taste of insanity and madness. Try as she may to drown out the unwanted sensations and the haunting sounds, sleep was frightened away from her grasp for the entire night.

* * *

Tullia rubbed her eyes with the backs of her hands as her nurse guided her to the examination room where the doctor was said to be awaiting her. The halls were silent. The harsh artificial light eradicated any lingering shadows that may have been tempted to overstay from the night. She felt as if she were on autopilot. Her mind was dancing with tempting images of beautifully evil creatures and the terrible horrors of the previous night all morning. She didn't taste breakfast, her pallet was numb, nor did she even recall getting out of bed. The tour of the prison was gloomy. With all the patients wandering in the designated activity rooms doing nothing made Tullia feel depressed.

The nurse stopped at a heavy looking oak door. She opened the door and smiled at Tullia. "Come in."

Her body obeyed before her brain could comprehend the words. The room was bathed in bright sunlight from a massive window and stung her strained eyes. Comfy looking chairs sat right in the middle of the room and a sturdy looking desk was huddled in the corner. Official looking documents adorned the wall in a cluster along with a framed photograph of a big, full moon over the Grand Canyon.

"Ah, Ms. Vale. A pleasure," Dr. Winmore's voice startled Tullia into clashing eyes with him. His smile was generous and held a tint of a critical shadow in the corners. His brown eyes swept over her impersonally, examining. Tullia shook his thick, dry hand without a word, eyeing him right back suspiciously. The man was middle aged, thin as an asparagus sprig with a crown of thick glossy blond hair that was tamed into waves away from his tan face. His nose was too long for his face and stooped down at the end. "Please have a seat," His slow, serenity-dipped voice gently smoothed over her jittering, sleep deprived nerves. A cold flavor… minty dashed across her tongue. Tullia sat down, self-conscious when the leather seat squeaked and squealed under her frame. The doctor took a seat across from her and once the air stilled in the room, Dr. Winmore crossed his legs and leaned back, giving her a spotlight under his dark brown scrutiny.

His mouth tilted up slightly, "Please, tell me about yourself." It was a courtesy he was offering, for she knew he already read her file brimming with all her personal information and past doctor, psychologist and even psychiatric visits. He definitely read every different prescription she has taken and probably knew everything about her from the type of blood that flowed through her veins, to the birth mark that kind of looked like a strawberry on her left hip.

The knowledge made a virulent flavor rise in her.

"I don't know what you want me to talk about. You read up everything there is to know about me in my file. I'm not sure I'd like to enlighten you any further into what causes me to hallucinate and act as though I need to be put in a padded cell."

Dr. Winmore's mouth twitched and his dark eyes warmed slightly, "My dear, I'd like to create a relationship between the two of us as confidants." She didn't want to talk to him. She didn't want to even be here. A streak of rebellion and anger heated her blood and diminished her tiredness. Tullia shifted in her seat, irritated by the smooth, squeaky material, but remained silent. The doctor titled his head to the side as he laced his fingers underneath his chin. "I know it is not enjoyable to talk to a complete stranger about yourself. Especially about your problems. However, for me to help you, I must know some information that only you can provide for me. Only you can tell your story, dear."

"I'm not crazy." She all but snarled at him, "I don't want to be here." She crossed her legs and held the man's eyes.

There was a brief moment of silence before the doctor spoke, "I see. Do you know why you're here?"

"Of course, I'm not stupid." She snapped, "I was making my family look bad, because I'm 'crazy.'" She used air quotes, "Even though I'm not crazy, they wouldn't listen to me, and I was shipped here in hopes of gaining normality."

The doctor's face did not move, his flavor was ice and mint. "You sound angry."

"I am." She retorted tartly.

"Why?"

His calm indifference grated on her. "I just see things. For hours on end, I can be in a daze and do nothing but live inside my mind. I just have an overactive imagination. That's it."

"Is that it?"

Tullia shifted her eyes down. She picked at the fraying sleeves of her sweater. Why did she feel to tell him more? Damn doctor hypnosis crap. "Well, I tend to try and recreate what I see. It annoys my parents...scares them too. I also...tend... to go into my mind anywhere and become...

unresponsive."

The doctor tilted his head, "What do you mean by unresponsive?"

"I don't hear or see anyone around me." Tullia muttered, knowing how it sounded.

He made a soft sound, "And when you said you try to recreate what you see… how do you proceed to do that?"

Though the doctor's tone was neutral and his expression serene, Tullia suddenly felt embarrassed. "I… I try to write what I see. And draw. And I create…things." She summed up lamely. Really what she did was take ingredients – Apple skins, maple leaves, ground sage, sandalwood, lavender flowers, etc.—and craft tinctures, balms, poultices, smudges, and infusions. Her mother couldn't stand the scent of her creations and her father thought her a demon worshiper. She also tries to create the weapons that she sees. Gorgeous gleaming swords, massive flamethrowers, war staves, blooded daggers, poison arrows… Tullia had never been so infatuated. She tried to create her very own dagger by melting down her mother's sterling silver utensils. However, she later learned two very important thing: One, sterling silver is not a very sturdy alloy to make weapons with and two, her mother's face, a creamy honey complexion, can go a deep indigo when enraged.

"I think that's a little more than an overactive imagination." He said gently.

Tullia ignored his words. They all said that and yet they never said anything else.

"You are sixteen years old, correct?"

"Yup." The supposedly significant age. A supposed lie.

"Tell me about your family."

Tullia paused, unsure of where to start or what to say. She didn't feel as though she belonged in the Vale's upper-class life. They liked to show off for anyone and put on a show of superiority in public. It was a show Tullia was never a part of. She was always kept at home with Constance, their live-in nanny, when she was younger. Then, eventually, she was just by herself at the age of twelve. They couldn't trust her not to have an irredeemable 'scene' in front of all their posh friends. So, she was solo majority of the time. Just her and a big empty house filled with lonely items. Her mother and father were always at parties or shows or other social events. Her older sister and brothers ignored her in favor for their significant others, friends and, of course, parties.

"They are… very social." She stated, pausing, "They like to be seen."

"Do you?"

She shrugged, "Everyone does in some way."

He seemed intrigued by her answer, "Could you elaborate?"

Tullia became uncomfortable again. As much as she wanted to say she did not need to be seen by anyone… she really wanted too. "No." She thought the doctor was going to press for an answer, but he merely nodded, typing down a few notes before focusing his attention back on her.

"Tell me, when did these…visions, shall we say, begin to plague you?"

"Didn't it tell you in my folder?" She snapped, hugely annoyed that he wanted her to repeat everything she has repeated multiple times already. It never got easier, and she found she hated the looks she'd receive from people. It was a subtle judging, but it was still there.

"We're starting from scratch." He smiled once more, but this time it held a medical edge to it. "We're going to rediscover Tullia Vale as if that file did not exist. So please," he waved his hand gracefully towards her, "delve into your history as you see fit to share with me."

Inhaling deeply to expel the irritation that began to fester within. She had resisted once, and it turned out it was more painful to drag out the therapy session with refusal instead of just doing what they asked. Tullia began her tale from the beginning. Her voice rapid and a bit too high with the determination to get through everything quickly.

When she was eight, she began talking to herself in a language completely unrecognizable to the world at random times. The part that scared, but mostly annoyed, everyone was that Tullia would never recognize when she switched languages. Though everyone insisted it wasn't an actual language on earth, more of singing series of short and long vowel sounds with flurries of soft and sometimes harsh sounding grunts intermingled within. Of course, that was only one language she managed to create, others would be nasally, with rapid tongue movements and others would require her full mouth to execute the pronunciation. As time went on, she stopped speaking make-believe languages and instead developed a habit to freeze in mid-stride, mid-speech or mid-action and stare for minutes or hours straight. Though she insisted it wasn't her fault, that her mind suddenly overwhelmed her vision and hearing from what was happening in reality. 'Visions' as she liked to call them. She never told anyone what she saw, it seemed wrong, defiling almost. But the places she was taken…

A shiver went down her spine with a mixture of fright and wonder. She saw valleys of death and despair, wrought with corpses of creatures too gnarled and vicious to identify. She saw battles, blood soaked and gory as men, women and strange unrecognizable creatures fought to the death with weapons of old and magic. She saw castles of fantasy, tall and sharp against skies of rich color. She saw a variety of beings, from gentle to harsh, beautiful to ugly, and royal to poor. They were all so fantastical and yet terrifying that it often left Tullia shakily tongue tied and completely tired. Though, these flaws to her character didn't bother her family enough to send her to a hospital. They ignored them, punishing her for her seemingly pitiful acts for attention. It wasn't until Tullia began drawing symbols, writing nonsense all over every available surface, creating elixirs, and making small weapons that her family became scared. That was the moment when they sent her packing to find out just what was wrong with her and how to get it fixed. She tried to tell them that her scribbles weren't demonic or evil, they were peaceful symbols of love, harmony from… everywhere, yet nowhere known. It was the lack of a solid foundation for her argument that convinced her parents she needed professional help, as much as they dreaded to make it known that there was a problem to anyone outside the family.

Dr. Winmore nodded, typing furiously upon his tablet. She went to open her mouth to add another feature she had developed… but her words became clogged in her throat. It was her family's… vehemently negative feelings of frustration towards Tullia that drove her to bottle up this one abnormality and keep it all to herself. She… could taste the feelings of other people. It was only with strong emotions or if she was really close to that person. She always knew when her mother was jealous of others, always knew when her sister was depressed, or when her father was seething silently. They never would utter a word of their true emotions, they had a reputation to uphold after all and no one wanted to see the cracked reality, only the flawless fantasy. She tried a few times to talk her family out from their sad or angry emotional state, but they brushed her away deeming her an ignorant child with no sense of the real world. So, she would try to 'push' sweeter emotions towards them. Almost like sending positive vibes by thinking of cupcakes and ice cream. Generally, after a little while Tullia wouldn't taste their negativity anymore, though it didn't always work precisely the way she tried to make it work.

She was conditioned to never speak of her defect, so words became hard to form when she actually thought about what she could do. She couldn't form the simplest of phrases to save her life. So, it remained unknown and unrecognized to all. The doctor asked about her social life. She didn't have one. No friends, no close people she confided in, and not a single pet to love. She wasn't allowed one.

"Very good, my dear." The doctor smiled distractedly; his mood tasted like mild bubbles with a minty edge. As if he were rummaging through all the possibilities she could be labeled as. "Excuse me for one second." He stood up and made a quiet call to someone from his desk. Five minutes later her nurse came into the room. She smiled at Tullia before hurrying over to the doctor.

They don't understand, she thought sadly, watching as the two chatted quietly on the other side of the room, giving her swift, calculating glances that had her stomach sinking. *No one understands,* she forced herself to look out the massive window instead of the two medical professionals undoubtedly discussing what course of medication they should experiment with first on her. She was so tired of everyone treating her as if she were a grenade that ticked occasionally. She didn't want to take pills, she didn't want to be here and she didn't want to be observed like a new bug underneath a microscope. She slid her gaze down to her entwined fingers. She wasn't hurting anyone. She didn't exactly want to be '*normal*'. She liked her mind's whimsical notions and wild pathways. She didn't want them to go away…

Maybe just not freeze her in place, that would be nice.

Play the game. Her mind scrambled to pull together an idea… *Live on the edge of the box with your toes hanging out where no one can see.* If she could control herself, function as a 'normie' even with her idiosyncrasies then perhaps she could escape unscathed and be free. Footsteps approached her, forcing her head to lift and face the doctor and the nurse. Their smiles were gently blank. "Now, my dear, we're going to start you on some psychoanalytic therapies. Then if needs be, we will go to the psychopharmacological route. It'll all be in low doses and tweaked to be perfect for you, alright?" It was a false courtesy he offered her, for she really had no choice, but she smiled at him and murmured her agreement anyway. She was getting out of this mental ward as fast as she could.

It was time to play the game and seemingly live within the box.

Chapter Two

Lord, what the hell was that? Putrid, horrifying, and with a rank smell she gagged and darted from the bathroom right out of the motel room. She gulped in deep breaths of fresh air, hunching over to lean on her knees in weakness. That smell could be used as a weapon. She tried to replace the horrid smell with dusty, dry air before even going in the room to clean. She really wanted to keep the bowl of generic frosted flakes and fat free milk in her stomach, thank you very much. Unfortunately, the smell would not be subdued. She didn't know what was in that bathroom, but she was pretty convinced it was an alien life form that mutated while it was being mauled by an animal and shot multiple times. Sighing loudly, Tullia stood up straight and looked back at the open motel door, eyeing the seemingly innocent room with distaste. This job was hazardous, and she needed to be paid more than she was getting paid to do it. Or at least be given a hazmat suit. With one last glare at the cheap room, she ambled over and dug through her sickly-looking maid cart for a mask, gloves and bleach. If she had a blow torch, she'd opt for that instead of the watery bleach she was given. It would work better, but alas, she was deprived of that tool for her job. Something about it being 'dangerous' and completely 'unnecessary'. Obviously, the person who deemed the rules for motel cleaning has never been in a rundown motel with questionable people that leave questionable things behind for the cleaning maid, A.K.A Tullia, to find. Donning four flimsy rubber gloves and two face masks, Tullia snatched the bleach bottle before marching back into the room with a stiff spine.

Ugh, the smell still penetrated through the protection of the masks.

This was her life for the past two years. As soon as she hit adulthood, the ever glamorized and over played 18-years-old, she left home much to her parents' not so hidden relief. They had, unexpectedly, given her a going away present of a few hundred dollars to keep her from coming home for a bit longer. Of course, they spewed the sweetest sentiments that it had almost given Tullia a toothache. Their words were pretty, but then again, they always were and in the end that's all they ever amounted to. Pretty nothings. She had tasted their exhilaration at her leaving, their liberation at her decision to road trip over the country, their happiness of a *finally* empty nest. It was all champagne bubbles and sweetness over her leaving. She hit the road in her used and slightly abused, navy blue Chevrolet Hatchback. Ugliest thing on four wheels but it did get the job done nicely for transportation.

She roamed the country for a bit, looking for a place to put down desperate roots where they could flourish in peace. Sadly, nowhere seemed right. She visited the sprawling countryside to the flat barren lands to the densely forested areas, all of which were lovely for a short time until her spine tingled with the need to move on and the missing sense of rightness. She was not supposed to be there… but somewhere else. It never helped that she'd also get going when her visions became more clustered together and people started to notice she was a bit… off. When she road tripped, her visions were limited to the night. When she tried to settle down somewhere, they overtook her life. It wasn't until she hit the dry, desert domains she began to feel more at comfortable and her visions eased up on her. Then, Las Vegas sucker punched her right in the gut.

She'll never forget the first time she chugged her way into Vegas from that dark and barren highway. The sky had just dipped into shadowy colors of night and lazy stars twinkled dimly against the rich, velvet backdrop. There was a muted glow in the distance that grew brighter and brighter, casting away the shimmering stars in its glory. The Vegas lights gleamed brightly in the nestled protection of the mountains cradling the wide-awake city. The brightness, the sense of excitement, made Tullia awestruck and feel surprisingly glamorous as she drove in the city with her ugly-as-sin car. The signs were thrilling and attractive with heavy undertones of adult themes and promises of spectaculars. It was all so wildly new and shiny that Tullia stayed for a week. Which turned into a month. Which transformed into a year.

Even now, the lights were still glittery to her, the air was parched, and the city was bathed mercilessly with the sun's rays. And she loved it. She loved the masses of tourists that swarmed The Strip, she loved the twenty-four-hour service of practically everything; but most of all she loved the obliviousness of everyone. She drew absolutely no attention; no one saw her. She finally had a chance to be herself and have no one watching her, judging her over every little thing. She worked odd jobs for a year, until her 'temporary' stay at the Oasis Motel became a permanent one when the owner offered her a job as a maid and a free room to live in. It was a proposition she took with enthusiasm that slowly soured when she discovered just how nasty the cheap rooms can become after they were used by… shady people. The pay was minimum, she received the smallest motel room that lacked a window and was half painted in a jungle theme, but Tullia was thrilled at having an actual roof over her head for free rather than her car's stained one.

Dumping the entire bottle of watery bleach into the toilet, Tullia dashed out of the room once more for fresh air. She then closed the door to the room. She'd clean it later when everything had a chance to… well, somewhat dissolve… hopefully. Ideally, she'd like it to disappear and simply sparkle, but unfortunately that wasn't going to happen. Her stomach then decided to groan in demand for nourishment, regardless of the fact that she had just dealt with a type of waste mutation.

Glancing at her watch—which read four forty-eight p.m.—she began to wheel the cart back to the main office. She was officially done at seven, but quite frankly she couldn't handle all the mess made by uncaring people anymore. Besides, short of tearing down the whole motel, the rooms were forever going to be filthy with permanent stains in various areas and the permeating scent of stale lemon soap and urine in the bathrooms. Shoving the flimsy cart in the closet Tullia shut the door then headed out to her favorite place in the world. Her car whined loudly, but eventually quieted and behaved well enough so that she could drive.

One-dollar drink, a spicy chicken sandwich from McDonalds, and a whole road rage inducing thirty minutes later Tullia made it. The Las Vegas Library located across from Nevada's Natural History Museum, Heritage Park, and Cashman's Field. The plain, square building with big windows had become a welcoming sight to Tullia over the years. It was a refuge for her, a way to escape the disgusting monotony of her life. That, and she couldn't afford anything else currently with her trifling paycheck, so it was the only source of entertainment for her. She did manage to sneak into two shows at the Bellagio when she first arrived in Vegas. They were stunning, it was the closest thing she had personally witnessed that was somewhat close to something in her visions. However, she got caught the third time trying to sneak into the Jabbawockeez show, in which they even took her picture and everything to warn people not to allow her in the casino anymore.

Getting out of her car Tullia spent a few blissful hours in the library, reading books, and watching people. She never interacted with them, despite a desire to. She was awkward and didn't know how to correctly interact with anyone. She always felt their indifference or, worse, their irritation when she began to chat. She did enjoy the general flavors the library offered. They varied from sour stress to the cardboard flavor of being bored to the sweet, carbonated flavor of inspiration and joy. After much trepidation, when closing time came, Tullia drove back to the Oasis Motel. Her poor car coughed and wheezed before clunking into a noisy rest in a narrow parking space. She stopped by the front desk to record her day's event and take a complimentary muffin. Then shuffled to her room.

Tullia's tired sigh was muffled behind the stale blueberry muffin as she entered her room. She flicked on the light and quickly shut the door behind her, locking the three locks on her door. She kicked off her shoes and threw her ratty hobo bag onto the tiny table. As she tried to shove the entire muffin in her mouth, she walked to the bathroom to wash her hands. Once done with both her muffin and the cleansing of her hands she dived onto her bed. Hearing the wailing screeches of her bed frame, Tullia relaxed and snuggled down further into her scratchy sheets. This was her sanctuary she managed to snag in her less than perfect life. However, the set up was temporary. One day she would own her own little slice of heaven with internet, a TV, and a soft mattress with millions of colorful pillows all over it.

Tullia reached over to the nightstand and snagged her borrowed book from the library. The rest of the night would be the same as every other night. She'd read until her eyes drooped, then fall asleep and let the dreams of color take her away for eight or so hours. Boring, yes, but no one watched or judged. And she loved that. Besides, Tullia was cautiously hopeful. Recently, her episodes have slowed down to where she didn't have them daily anymore. Contrary to what she wanted when she was sixteen, she wanted the visions to go away. They really hinder her daily life. They mostly occurred at night in her dreams and sometimes once in the day, when her sleep wasn't good. Hope was such a fragile flower within her that maybe, *maybe*, she could actually *be* someone rather than a shade in the shadows, watching, but never partaking. If the visions never truly disappeared… well, she'd formulate a new plan. Until then, books have kept her company in her loneliest moments.

Light dimmed into a dark shade of night and still Tullia read. She flicked on a small dim light that sometime flickered by the nightstand. A world of caves and treasures had her mind whirling excitedly as she dived deeper into her novel.

A sudden heavy crash shattered the imaginary world Tullia was in. Jerking her head up, blinking heavily in a daze, she folded the corner of the page she was on and set her book aside. Frowning in the sudden quiet, she listened hard and detected unintelligible mutterings from the adjacent room. Curious, Tullia slid off the bed, scampering on tiptoes and to press her ear to the wall to better hear.

"I sent them *four*." It was a man's voice, low and horse, as if he smoked a whole pack of cigarettes and did not drink a drop of liquid for the entire day. "There were *four*. Red head, two blonds and a brunette."

Tullia furrowed her eyebrows, the sour taste of fear and the raw fishy taste of panic coated her tongue. Weary and more than a little freaked out, Tullia quickly crawled back into her bed and surrounded herself thoroughly with her blankets for protection. She hoped that the man would leave, and her peaceful night could resume. Much to her worry, as the minutes ticked by the man in the room next to hers became even more frantic and louder. *"I sent them four! I paid my dues!"* He nearly screamed; his voice mimicking crushed glassed when stepped on. His terror was a thick and slimy coating in her mouth that had Tullia swallowing frequently. Various crashes and banging could be heard, and at one point the wall vibrated with the force of something being thrown at it. *Jerk*, Tullia thought, in between spikes of panic. She threw a glare at the wall in front of her, he better not trash that room too much, she'd have to clean that tomorrow.

"I can't take it! I sent them four! I swear on my mother I sent them four…" He sobbed out and everything in Tullia's mouth went numb. She could taste his acute terror through the wall and the horrid rot of a suicidal sensation. The sickly sour and moldy flavor destroyed her palette, causing Tullia to gag. "They'll suck me dry! Feed me to the fledglings…." Tullia huddled herself deeper in her bed. Breathing hard, she gritted her teeth in an effort to ride out the nauseous flavors of the man's emotions.

The wall in front of her began to darken…

Dark red rivulets dripped unevenly down sharp chins. Pale, cold skin dully shimmered under the moonlight. Fangs long and slender protruded out of chapped lips. Eyes both soulless and inhuman contained screams in their red depths. The creature stared at her, then gave a hissing shriek before lunging…

Tullia stiffed as the vision assaulted her in broken pieces. The man next door began to escalate again, Tullia curled up tight, clutching at the sheets as tremors rolled through her body ceaselessly. There was a soft clicking sound smothered behind deep ripping sobs, then

BANG….

A loud shot rang through the night causing Tullia to jerk in fright. Silence reigned over the space as death slunk through the air. Tears filled her eyes as her body became ice cold with fright and sadness. Death suddenly coated her tongue with a pungently bitter and bloody taste. Tears broke and slid down Tullia's cheeks, hot and wet, as she mourned for the man she did not know who took his own life.

Minutes flickered by and the death of the man was still in the air, but it had evaporated from her mouth. After all, the dead cannot feel. Tullia wiped her eyes and slowly unfolded herself from her cocoon of safety. She needed to tell someone of the body, but to do that she needed to go to the office. Cell phones were far too expensive for her to afford and besides she didn't have anyone that would ever call for her anyways.

Just as Tullia had slipped on her old flip flops, the night around her became disturbingly, unnaturally still, causing the hairs on the back of her neck to stand up. She stared at her door as the sensation of dread slithered up and over her spine. There was a loud, firm knock from outside, startling her back a few paces from her door. But the knocks weren't on her door… but on her now dead neighbor's door.

Silence ensued.

Then another firm knock.

Again silence.

Then, the sudden splintering sound of wood being destroyed stung the air. Tullia flinched as her breathing became heavy and her own fear clawed up from her stomach.

Unnatural silence occurred once more.

"Stupid boy. Does he think he can escape by killing himself? He drank enough to ensure he will be risen with ease." A scratchy voice floated obtrusively into the quiet. It sounded similar to glass on a chalkboard. Her heart stuttered, then slammed into her rib cage painfully fast.

"Then punishment can last longer. How fun." The second voice was evil dipped in liquid nitrogen and sprinkled in sandpaper.

Black and red gore in sloppy piles, shrieks of pain and delight, wet sucking, soft tearing, cracking sounds...

Bile rose swiftly in the back of her throat as grisly images swarmed her vision. Gagging, Tullia stumbled back from her door and dashed to the bathroom, heaving as her muffin and McDonalds came right out. She dry-heaved a bit longer over the toilet, her stomach determined to cleanse itself of any and everything, before her entire body was a quivering mass of mush. Gasping, Tullia heaved herself up from over the porcelain throne and staggered to the sink to douse her face and the inside of her mouth with icy water. She hadn't had horror visions in a long time. They were never something she managed to get used to, they were too... *real* to be entertaining. Pulling in ragged breaths through her clenched teeth, Tullia willed her heart to slow down and her stomach to stop clenching. Swallowing against the thick mucus in her throat, she pressed her forehead on the cool counter and focused on her breathing. She inhaled deeply through her nose, tightening her entire body as she did so. She filled her lungs to the very top with air, until she felt as though they would pop, then exhaled slowly through her mouth, releasing all her tensed muscles gradually as she did so.

The one technique from her four month visit at the psychiatric ward when she was sixteen that did help her when a vision was bad, was the tension tightening of muscles in conjunction with measured breathing. It helped ground her physical reaction when her visions were affecting her physically.

Just as her heart returned to its normal rhythm there was a set of harsh knocks again...this time on her door. She stared at the door, thinking it was obviously a hallucination on her end. The knocks, hard and rattling, sounded again. Her poor heart stopped and jumped from her chest to her throat. Tullia's eyes helplessly scanned her room for a hiding place. Diving to the floor, she forced herself under her bed, pressing herself tightly against the floor, trying to become as flat as she could, and covered her mouth with her hands to muffle her heavy, terror filled breathing. Seconds past and the night remained eerily still, however Tullia felt a sinuous oil coat her tongue. They were still there.

Splintering wood startled her, she pressed her hands harder into her face as her body stiffened tightly. Her heart fluttered rapidly within her chest as fear iced her veins. Tullia strained to hear food steps or breathing, but besides the initial violent noise from the door, the air was still and silent. A small creak came from behind, dread as sharp as knives scraped up her spine. The creak transformed into a loud shriek of protesting metals as her bed flew from above her, exposing her. The heavy scent of iron, salt, and decay surrounded her before a cold hand gripped her hair and pulled her up. Screaming in pain and terror, she was jerked up until she was on the tip of her toes. She felt strands of her hair being ripped out as a heated pressure from the grip caused tears to swell within her eyes. Cold hands encircled her throat, constricting her airway, and lifted her completely off her feet. Gagging, Tullia desperately clawed at the hands that choked her. Her eyes strained to focus on the person attached to the hands hurting her… and discovered it to be a corpse's lifeless ashen face staring up at her with a drooling broken smile. A smile that showcased bloodstained pointed teeth and fangs.

Her terror intensified as the creature in cargo pants and a tank top slowly licked its cracked, dirty lips. "Well now. What a pretty piece of meat. Just what we're short on." The voice was raspy and guttural. It leaned down to peer closer at her, Tullia saw white filmed eyes scour her body hungrily. "I think you'll be a favorite flavor. You smell quite decadent, even for a fleshy."

Vampire...

Images, all drenched in blood, crowded her mind. She remembered. Any hallucinations with vampires were always the hardest to recover from when she was younger. They were ugly, walking corpses that ate humans and behaved like animals with high intelligence. Screams lodged in her throat as the creature continued to peruse her as one would a piece of meat. Black began to cloud her vision as the hands around her throat continued to tighten, before suddenly releasing her. Tullia hit the ground, her already shriveled, oxygen deprived lungs tightened painfully upon impact. However, the pain failed to register as she wheezed in deep breaths to her deprived lungs. Her chest throbbed with the forced inhalations and coughs racked her frame from the force of her gasps.

Chuckles surrounded her, causing her to tremble with consternation as fear dampened her brow. They were playing with her, it was painfully obvious, and she knew how all their games ended. She would be mangled and sucked dry by the end of the hour if she were lucky. A hand tangled painfully in her hair again and yanked her head back at an awkward angle, forcing her body to contour painfully to keep the pressure off her neck.

The creature hissed in her face. Tullia screamed in pain as the vampire smashed his forehead into her. That very instant, mind scrambling pain was quickly swathed in the black of unconsciousness. The last thought that managed to gain clarity in her mind was sad as it was horror filled.

Holy hell, I'm going to die.

Chapter Three

She crouched low, behind the wall next to the stairs. Her parents were residing in the parlor, their favorite space in their modest house. Her father had come home, a troubled look on his face and a thunderous aura. She had known it wouldn't be all smiles when he heard about what she did, but she didn't think he'd behave like she had done something illegal.

Her mother had ushered her up to bed after a rather tense dinner of nothing but silence. She was far too scared to utter a peep with the way her father had looked and the way he chomped down on his dinner. It wasn't the first time she had wished to be older and not have to live at home with her rather stuffy parents. All of her brothers were gone and that left all the attention on her.

Now she knew full and well what her father was upset about, but she wanted to know exactly what made him mad.

"I heard about what Nixie did today." Her father's grave low voice uttered out the words as if they were a curse.

Her mother made a soft sound, "Yes, I bet the whole town knows."

"Damn it, Deema." Her father cursed. Nixie covered her face in surprise, her father was extremely conservative, he hated swearing. A fluttering sound filled the air for a split second, and Nixie could see her father's wings, thin and round, fluttering in agitation. She had always liked his wings, they were simple in shape, but their color, a mossy green, was better than any other color she had seen. It was the ideal color for camouflage.

"You do realize that our daughter hunted and successfully caught a scorpion in the Everlynn Woods. Then dragged it's corpse to town and had it appraised by Cleon!"

Nixie bit her lower lip to stifle a grin. The look on Mr. Cleon's face was one she would treasure. The jaw slacked, the eyes bugged and the stuttering of bewildered awe. He was so flabbergasted; his wits were momentarily lost to him, and her prey had caught quite a nice price at market. Probably more than he intended to give her. Now she had enough money to buy a better bow than her brother's heavily used hand-me-down.

"That is how it went, yes." Her mother's tone was neutral.

"What're we gonna do with that girl?" The question went unanswered, for her father went on, "Good lord, first her hair and now this? Why did you let that girl cut her hair?" His tone was aggrieved and prickly.

Her mother's voice was frosty in her reply, "You think I allowed such a thing? Your daughter has the notion of growing up to be a tracker and long hair simply 'gets in the way.'" A brief pause, "It's all your fault to begin with, what with your sister running off and branding a guild of wayward Fairy women that go about business like men." A tsk, and her mother's needles clicked together harshly, "That's where she got the notion, she can be a hunter. She told me she's gonna track that giant wolf that's been eating all the Fae Folk, with the elite Fae guard." A short inconceivable laugh. "And of course, her brother's allowing her to tag along in their hunting trips. That just encourages it."

A deep and ugly silence reigned in the air.

Nixie laced her fingers together tightly, listening hard. A premonition that this night was going to be the biggest night of her life, caused her heart to throb in her chest.

"I think we have indulged her too much." Her father said with a heavy voice, "She loves her aunt, and I know she's not a good influence. I just can't say no to those big eyes. I didn't take a firm enough hand to her when she was younger like I did with the boys."

"Ah, well now, Nixie is the baby girl." Her mother's voice was soft, "We all got a soft spot for her."

"It's not good though Deema." A regretful murmur, and a long silence. "Well, tomorrow I will burn her pants and bow." Her father's tone was sudden and hard, and Nixie flinched at the steel threat behind the words. "I'll inform our sons to stop coddling her in their play and expeditions. I expect you to come down hard on her with her etiquette training. We will make her a proper Fairy woman, set things right as rain." A creak, and Nixie could imagine her father leaning back in his favorite worn, oak wood seat with his hand rolled spiked skullcap cigar. "Eventually, she'll see we were only lookin' out for her best interest."

A deep, suffering sigh, "Be prepared for our daughter to hate us both quite vehemently."

An inhale, slow and hard, "We can't waiver in this. I'll not have my daughter an outcast in this town. Being a proper fairy will ensure her a good future." Then the silence resumed once more between her parents. It was a resolved silence, one that her parents would see to and make Nixie miserable.

Nixie's eyes filled with tears of sorrow as her face heated with rage. She was to be a proper fairy woman, eh? She was to be decked out in lace with all curtsies and smiles as she batted her eyes at the most eligible bachelor on the market. A proper fairy woman's dream is to marry rich and to live in luxury. A proper fairy woman did not hunt, did not camp, always listened to her husband, and did not step foot outside unless allowed.

Never.

Nixie slowly crept back to her room, allowing her tears to fall easily from her eyes as her heart bled. She sat on her bed, a bed made of sown rose and peonies petals. Two flowers in which she detested, but her mother loved them and assumed she would love them for it was 'proper' for a girl to love them. She glanced over to her vanity set, a vanity that was covered in little creams and colors... and covered in dust and neglected. Her parents had bought her that stupid thing for her twelfth birthday, they had been so proud of it and so excited for her, she had faked her excitement as well.

They thought she'd suddenly be all girly at the tender age of twelve. But she still loved mud, the outdoors and boys were still... bleh. So, it sat there in the corner of her room, ignored. Nixie wandered over to it and peered at herself in the mirror.

Her skin was dark brown, and her hair was a halo of thick dark curls, her eyes were warm. Everyone told her she had a pretty face, but honesty what's a pretty face worth? Just cause you got a pretty face doesn't mean much in terms of skill.

And then there were her wings. She hated her wings. They were loud, complicated and there was simply too much of them all around her. Her wings spanned well over her head in dolly looking loops and girly curves. Her wings were colored a bright shimmering yellow that practically glowed under any hint of light. She often had to cover up her wings with moss or mud to go tracking, least not she be spotted by her prey.

Sighing deeply from her soul, Nixie flopped back on her bed, her mind in a tizzy.

Maybe... Auntie Ailsa would take her in. She sat up suddenly, a thrill spiking through her body. Auntie Ailsa never turned away any wayward girl, she fostered them. It'll be the same for her, especially since Nixie was her biological niece.

Auntie might even know someone to train her in tracking and hunting and all that. She wasn't a 'Proper Fairy' either, so she'd understand! Nixie rushed about her room on silent feet, shoving—

Tullia jerked awake by a foreign slamming sound that seemed to rattle the very space around her. She blinked heavily, before her eyes widened with clear confusion as she took in the environment around her. She was lying in a cage; a literal cage encased her body that didn't allow for much room to move. It was like a trap cage for hunting, but human sized. She wiggled, rattling the cage a little and causing the sounds to echo in the wide, dark space around her. Panic began to seize her heart as her breathing turned labored. She gripped the icy metal bars above her and tried to bend them out of shape. They didn't even buckle a little. Tullia inhaled jaggedly, terror clawing through her veins. What in the hell happened to her? Where was she? How did she get here? Pushing the questions away for a moment, Tullia inhaled deeply, multiple times to clear her fright fogged mind and began to recall events that took place before her current situation.

She was reading… there was a man next door. He killed himself.…

Death suddenly coated her tongue with a pungently bitter and bloody taste.

"Well now. What a pretty piece of meat."

"I think you'll be a favorite flavor. You smell quite decadent."

The man grinned widely down at her, showing off sharp... fangs.

Vampires.

Ice encased her spine as a sharp horror began to creep in her throat, suffocating her. Tullia swallowed the bile that rocketed up from her stomach, wincing when the action hurt, and caused her neck to throb painfully in line with the beat of her hammering heart. Jaggedly gasping in necessary oxygen to prevent passing out again, Tullia tenderly pressed her shaky fingertips to her neck. She felt her jackhammer heart at the base of her throat and smooth skin.... She let out a gust of air in relief. No wounds, thank goodness, but it felt bruised. Tullia turned her head, ignoring the throbbing pain and tried to survey her new and scary surroundings swathed in darkness. As she looked around, the horror that she had pushed back down to her stomach, clawed back up as she discovered a few things.

She was in a warehouse, with tall industrial ceilings, cement floors and thread bare walls. There were dingy windows that allowed for gaps of moonlight through, but the darkness that occupied the inside seemed to devour any light and swallow it whole. Turning her head to the other side, again ignoring the pain this action caused, she spied dark towers that seemed to go on... forever... at least from what she could make out in the smothering blackness. She squinted, trying to peer through the gloom and identify what the towers were....

She spied a pale smudge... a foot?

All the blood drained from her face and an immediate flood of emotion attacked her mouth as personal horror bubble was popped with realization.

Sour, bitter blood flavors swarmed her mouth in a rush as Tullia made out more body parts in the darkness… and more bodies. There were people inside cages like she was but some were stacked on top of each other, creating the towers, and some were tossed carelessly to the side. She could hear smothered crying, labored breathing and small rattling sounds.

Tullia coughed as the foulness of the people's emotions nauseated her. Her breathing accelerated, and her limbs started shaking.

Block it out, block it out, block it out….

Tears gathered in her eyes as the reality sunk deep within her mind, these people, like herself, had been collected by vampires… as food. She pressed her hands to her mouth, to keep from throwing up and to keep her screams of panic inside her. This raw, immobilizing, hopeless terror tore through her, leaving her hollow and shaky.

Was she going to die, by being sucked to death by a nasty corpse? The slimy fear, sour and pungent, coated her mouth insistently.

A loud bang tore through the warehouse, bouncing off the walls and causing all the emotions in the room to morph into one common feeling: dread. A tall, lanky man sauntered through the rows of cages, causally looking over them with a lazy gaze. Tullia couldn't see his face, but she felt his foreboding aura and curled into herself as much as she could. His atmosphere was black with old blood and dripping with death. The oppressive silence thickened the air, a cold sweat broke out on the back of Tullia's neck. There were other creatures that sauntered around him, silent and quiet, and had not one ounce of emotion to them.

"Where is my new lamb?" A scratchy voice carried over in the still air.

"Right there, master." Soft footsteps became closer and closer until Tullia saw a pair of shiny loafers and suite pants in front of her face. She quivered at the waves of silent menace and hunger that wafted from the men.

"Not too bad." A cold pause, then, "Take it out." She saw shadowy figures go to the foot of her cage. They rattle it roughly, jostling her and causing the cage to dig into her backside harshly. Then the bottom of her cage slid away and hands reached for her feet. Tullia panicked and tried to curl into herself to avoid those clawed hands. She had wanted out mere moments ago, now she wanted to stay in her cage that represented safety instead of confinement as it did two seconds ago. Icy hands locked on her ankles and yanked her roughly down and out of her confinement. A small squeak escaped through her lips at the crude way in which she was handled but she quickly bit her tongue, taste of sweet bubbly glee and cold danger scraped along her palette. The men that manhandled her, pulled and twisted at her until she was presented in front of their boss with bony hands latched tightly in her hair, neck, and arms. They yanked her head back to bare her jugular. She had never been more aware of the veins throbbing in her neck as her heart pounded wildly with terror.

A death pale face consumed her field of her vision. Tullia tried to shrink back from the hideous visage that smelled like a wicked cross between rotten meat and rotting fruit, but the hard hands that dug into her prevented any movement without stinging pain. This man… no, this *creature* was a master vampire. She had seen enough visions of these monsters to be aware of how their hierarchy works, what they looked like, and just how horribly cruel they tended to be. Master vampires are the oldest and strongest vampires of their festering nest. The physical characteristics are fangs that protruded through the lower lip, a skeleton face with sunken in eyes that gave off a hazy, red glow, a rail thin appearance, and a distinctive rotting aura.

The creature looming above her hit every mark on her checklist from her visions. The stinging pain assured her that visions right now. She never felt any physical pain, even during wars. Though emotionally, she'd be wrecked. Yet, during her visions she was never the main star like now, merely an observer of events with insight to the main stars' thoughts.

"How interesting." A hissing sound from the corpse, made Tullia flinch back, her heart stuttering with stress.

A master vampire was standing in front of Tullia, evaluating her like one would a piece of meat... but the fact that there was a master vampire in front of her while she's in a lucid state meant... they are real.

They exist.

Then maybe, just maybe, her other visions... they might be...real. Perhaps she wasn't mentally sick like everyone told her she was, but actually...

Maybe...

The master vampire put his face even closer to hers, breaking Tullia's almost revelation and inhaled deeply. She stopped breathing completely and it felt as if her heart ceased to beat for a suspended moment. He raised a razor-sharp fingertip and swiped it lightly across her jugular. Tullia flinched, her heart slamming against her rib cage at the sting and the feeling of blood trickling down her neck from the fresh cut. A sudden rush of ice raced through her veins. His clawed finger came away with a droplet of blood coating the side of his nail. *Her blood.*

A blackened tongue ran along the edge of the vampire's finger, she jerked with a deep disgust at his action. His ruddy eyes brightened portentously.

Oh god, she was going to get a disease from this whole thing if she didn't die a horrible death first.

"She tastes of *magic*." He seemed to vibrate with excitement before he shoved his face into her neck and ran his tongue along the cut he made on her neck. Repugnance rolled over her in violent waves. She stiffened her entire body and tried to jerk herself away, ignoring the sharp pain caused by the sharp hands restraining her. He chuckled darkly against her neck, "Yes. Magic. *Non-wiccan* magic." The hands on her tightened painfully tight, causing her to cry out involuntarily and forced tears to bubble up from her eyes.

The master vampire leaned back slightly and grinned soullessly, "She shall be preserved. The charge for a sip is a hundredfold of the price of regular cattle." His face darkened with a horrible, ugly malevolence. "Her training shall begin now. I will personally see to it." With a dismissive flick of his hand, the vampires holding Tullia dropped their hands. Tullia curled into herself and scrambled back a few feet from the nasty vampires, her eyes felt wild as she eyed all of them.

They watched her expressionlessly. She rubbed her neck, feeling dirty and needing to bath in bleach and fire.

The master vampire's small grin grew into a slash of pointy teeth and blood. "Go see to the others." Without a sound, the vampire henchman left silently. Tullia and the master vampire were left alone in a warehouse full of caged human 'cattle'.

Great way to spend an evening, she thought wearily as she scuttled back further away from the master vampire. He didn't move, only eyed her as if she were his favorite food with that dirty smirk twisting the corners of his black stained mouth. She tasted his excitement and his bloodlust.

"Wrist." He said softly.

Tullia's eyes narrowed as she shifted back, poised to run. His crusted lips curled back further over his stained teeth, he repeated, "Wrist." When Tullia simply stared at him in clueless fright, he seemed to blur... she felt a hard slap to her left cheek. Crying out, she stumbled back, staring at the creature in front of her as she cupped her face. His face never changed as he watched, and she could taste the sweet rotten bubbles of his pleasure that blossomed over the taste of blood in her mouth. He liked her pain, he enjoyed hurting her. He was excited to hurt her.

"Wrist." he said again. Tullia tenderly held her throbbing cheek. Shivers overtook her frame as panic began to cloud her thinking.

Wildly, her eyes darted, searching for an escape with anxiety clouded eyes.

Go, go go, anywhere! Go! Go! GO! Freakin' run bitch!

Panting, nearly blinded from her panic, Tullia spun and sprinted away mindlessly. A soft chilling laugh trailed behind her, scraping knives down her back. Her alarm deepened into a hysteria as she continued to run among the towers and towers of cages... with live humans in them. Her heart thudded violently in her chest, wanting to escape the endless horror show she was somehow the star of. Her breath came out in wheezing puffs as her limbs began to take on a ferocious quiver.

Go... Go... Go... Her mind chanted on a loop, becoming increasingly frantic as her hope of escape began to wither and die with each dead-end turn and more rows of stacked human livestock. She suddenly tripped over her unstable feet and hit into a tower of cages, causing wails of pain from the prisoners within. Tullia couldn't contain her own scream as she scrambled away on her hands and knees. "Sorry. Sorry. Sorry." She rasped, pressing her hands against her mouth to stifle her gasps. Tears steadily dripped down her cheeks. If she survived, she was going to need therapy and ice cream. Lots of ice cream.

"Stupid animal." A bony hand encircled her throat, before pulling her close to his corpse-like face. The master vampire bared his teeth, his incisors dripped with blackened saliva. He squeezed her throat tightly, causing Tullia to gag as air ceased to enter in her lungs. Her limbs spasmed with mind numbing trepidation. "Training will be longer than normal, because you're slow." The creature shifted his hand to grip her jaw, squeezing it just shy of snapping her jaw. She felt her jaw creak under the pressure, before the Master Vampire flung her carelessly into a stack of cages. Screams sounded upon her impact, echoing all around her. Jagged pain heated her entire backside and lungs as she coughed and gasped in air desperately.

"Present me with your wrist." The master vampire's scathing voice caused the pain in her entire body to throb. Tullia gritted her teeth against the agony and forced her trembling limbs to move. She stood slowly, breathing shallowly, as she found her footing. Once up, she held out one shaky wrist towards the master vampire. One moment he was standing a few feet away, the next he was snarling in her face as he tangled his hand into her hair, yanking her head back painfully.

"You expect me to walk to you?" He spat at her, his fangs scraped he sides of her mouth and the smell of rot overwhelmed her. "So stupid. You are nothing but an animal, you are to listen and obey your master's commands." His face curled up into a superior sneer. "You'll learn though, they all do eventually." He raised his hand high, ready to strike her...

"Listen up!" A man with sleek, long ears, long white hair and wide gray eyes barked to a restless group of soldiers. "We have infiltrated more than a hundred

nests in the past sixty years. In those years, we have not lost a single soul to the blood consumers. Today, even though we face a new and different enemy, it will be no different. I will not allow a single Fae to fall from that violent filth in which plagues our lands. We will crush its corrupted muzzle and hang its head above the Queen's mantle. We will not falter until the beast is dead and our fellow brothers and sisters are avenged."

Stomps and grunts sounded, rattling the earth and trees with battle ready energy. The man raised his head higher as the powerful thumping quieted and stillness overtook the area. His troop, a sea of serious faces, stared back at him with dedicated attention. Pride made him stand taller, this was his specialized troop he had personally handpicked, and they all were dedicated, elite and dangerous. The soldiers all had long ears, a proud trait of the of the Fae Folk and long hair of various colors that was severely tamed back into long braids. They wore light amour across their chests and on their arms, to keep their movements unhindered.

"Let us review the snippets of knowledge we have acquired on this monster." The man growled as he stood strong in front of his troop. He motioned for his second in command to step forward. She was his best warrior. Isla was the only female to join the Seelie Guard, she proved to be far more ruthless and violent than any other Fae male he had met. Even on the battlefield, her name was the softest sound on the wind.

"The fame wolf cannot die from simple wounds or even supposed fatal wounds." Her head was raised high with dignity and her voice as clear as a chime, "A stab to the stomach is equivalent to a tickle under the chin to the monstrosity. Currently, it has no documented weaknesses." She paused, allowing the seemingly hopelessness sink into the air around them. "There is also... a rumor that the wolf has an accomplice that leads him about our lands." She glanced up at him, seeking permission. He nodded. It was better if they had all the knowledge. "Fenrir, what the wolf calls himself, is said to have a... Fae guiding him in our land."

A flurry of harsh words, stunned growls, and outright disbelief cluttered the space around them.

"Enough!" Isla shouted, her voice strong and cutting, gripped the soldiers' attention. "Though unpleasant, we all must prepare to face one of our own next to the fame wolf." A small breeze sneaked in the silent area. "Remember, the fame wolf is an animal. There is no honor in dying by an animal. Therefore, use any means of defense to not get killed." He watched Isla survey the crowd, her eyes iced water under a sun that glimmered. "A wolf's strongest asset is its sense of smell, like the bloodsuckers. The goal is to remove that asset, similar to how we deal with the blood consumers." Isla paused, and looked towards him, "Commander Cuithbeart."

He nodded at her, regaining his troops attention, "As Isla said, there is no honor in dying by an animal. Since the monstrosity is not of Fae sources, and has already proven to be hostile and violent, swiftness in killing the beast is imperative."

Grim faces stared back at the commander. In the sharply crafted faces, he saw the light of understanding and the shadows of severity twist their face into hard grimness. He felt his own heart become burdened with the weight of their responsibility. "We are all that stand in the way of the fame wolf destroying the Seelie Court and the Fae Folk".

A bone chilling quiet ensued after his words were spoken.

"You are here, for you lot are the best there is in the Seelie Court. You all have shown courage, skill, and cleverness. I ask you," He raised his head higher, "Are you resolved to stay and fight the beast in the name of the Seelie Court?" Cuithbeart's voice boomed under the sky and shook the grass with his forcefulness. He waited, looking in each one of his warriors' faces, searching for fear.

He saw none.

"I am resolved." A strong voice announced.

"As I am." Another strong echo.

"Eh, today is a good day to die I suppose. I ate well at breaky."

"Aye, I want that famed wolfs fur for me lady."

"You're too ugly for any broad."

Cuithbeart's mouth curved as Isla laughed with a fierce vigor. "I am honored to be in the presence of the most elite warriors of our race." He thumped his fist over his heart. "I am humbled, to be the leader of a team as skilled and as dedicated to the protection of innocent lives as this one is. Do not falter in your intention, just because this is a different beast. Be swift, be merciless, be precise."

The troops echoed his action as the small humor became buried underneath an emotional calm that gripped everyone in the clearing. Their attention was firmly fastened on their leader in front of them.

"What are we?" Cuithbeart growled.

"Fae of the Seelie Court!" A unison roar.

"And what do Fae of the Seelie Court honor?"

"Life!"

"How do we ensure life?"

"We protect and we serve the Court!" A synchronized roar of voices shook the trees and lifted high enough to touch the sun-drenched sky.

A sharp sting on her cheek shot throughout her mind… echoing loudly and the pain… brought her back to her horrid reality. The rotted face with dead sheened eyes peered down at her gleefully. "You're not going to die, so no need to prepare for that." The master vampire threw her once more into a tower of cages. Tullia couldn't make a sound as she hit the cold ground with a muffled thud. The pain was air stealing, and her lungs were already compressed that she couldn't even utter a sound. "You're too valuable to die. Do you know how rare it is to find a *human* with lost magic enhanced blood?" His gaunt, spiny frame glided over to her. Tullia struggled to move, her body refused to respond. The vampire stepped heavily on her solar plexus, Tullia's mangled breath became thin and puffed. She clawed at his blackened feet, but she couldn't make the cold foot move an inch. "*Very rare.* Usually, it's only weak wiccan touched blood that occurs every so often and that is uncommon…. However, you possess *lost magic* in which I've encountered it only once before." He pressed his foot harder into her stomach, grinding it down so that her rib cage creaked under the pressure. Tullia saw bright stars wink in and out of her vision. The lack of air and the intensity of pain she had never experienced, never even fathomed, made her give up on breathing completely and had the strong urge to throw up began to strengthen.

Oh gosh, she was going to throw up, then drown in her throw up like that one person on that one show she couldn't remember the name of. What a horrible way to die….

"…the best blood I've ever tasted. I've learned my lesson though, to savor instead of devour." Tullia half heard the master vampire's ramble… her consciousness was beginning to take a nosedive into unconsciousness… The foot removed itself from her solar plexus, allowing for air to fill her lungs once more. Tullia inhaled raggedly, curling instinctively into herself as a hot pain spiraled throughout her body.

A cackle echoed throughout the warehouse and seemed to cause the air to drip icicles. "Get up. Let's try this yet again."

Do not falter.

Wheezing, Tullia rose to her feet slowly. Her body, stiff, swollen and throbbing.

Be swift, be merciless, be precise.

"Wrist". He hissed.

Limping, Tullia approached the master vampire and obediently extended her wrist to him. As he snatched her offered wrist in a crushing grip, Tullia's free hand shot out and dug her fingers right into his eye sockets and dragged her nails down hard over his nose. The paper white skin cracked and tore as black blood gushed from his eyes and down his face, smothering what was left of his nose.

...strongest asset is its sense of smell... remove that asset...

Check.

An unholy, alien scream ripped out from the creature's gnarled mouth as he flung her away in his pain. Tullia hit the ground yet again with a hard smack. Biting her lip to keep from crying out, she forced her body to be quick as she clumsily got to her feet.

"You wretch!" The master vampire snarled hoarsely, clawing the air wildly, hunching his body like that of a wounded animal. "You shall pay dearly for that! I'll tear your hands and feet off and feast on you till near death

over *and over and over and over…"*

Tullia slowly backed away, swallowing thickly as she carefully avoided the cages around her. The master vampire continued to scream in rage while blindly slashing the air around him. Suddenly he stopped, frozen in perfect stillness… then abruptly dropped to the floor on all fours. He put his face down to the ground and began to chuff and growl like a wild, cornered animal. Terror caused Tullia's heartbeat to pound in her chest as her body began to stiffen up with icy fear.

What in the name of God is he doing?

Move… move…. Freakin' run!

The master vampire halted, causing Tullia to stop breathing entirely. He tilted his head, opened his mouth and sucked in a deep breath. He clicked his tongue, as if relishing the stale air, before his head snapped forward in her direction. Her eyes widened as the master vampire let out a hoarse growl and began to claw his way swiftly to where she stood on all four. She stumbled, fright an ice shock to her nerves. She gripped the cages that where behind her and yanked them down as hard as she could. The tower of captive humans swayed languorously, before cascading down toward the ground. Screams of pain and terror deafened her as the cages crashed around them in a wild cacophony of horror. The master vampire's shrieks of rage were drowned beneath the humans' cries. Her body then was shot up with instant adrenaline and decided to haul ass. Once more she was running dazed and lost in the maze of towering cages, careful of her nose, restricting her breathing to mere puffs of air. Except this time, she could hear the vampire clawing its way to her from behind. Everywhere she turned it was a dead end.

Dead end. Pain.

It hurts...

Dead end. Despair.

Death is coming...

Dead end. Hopelessness.

Dear Lord...

Dead end. Panic and pain blended in an intoxicating fashion that began to cloud her mind.

Save me...

Please, please, please...

Tullia stopped and thumped her fists against her head as the emotions, rancid and cloying in her mouth, of everyone began to warp her own thought process, muddling her thoughts…

"Focus. Focus. Focus. Shut up." She whispered, trying not to submerge underneath the pressing hopelessness and the fear. Tullia panted as she hobbled around the cages, becoming more and more confused with each turn. Becoming more and more frantic with every step.

Didn't she just come this way?

She hurt.

Where the hell was the freakin' exit? Just how big was this godforsaken warehouse?

An icy grip shackled her ankle, causing Tullia to smash down hard on her knees. She jerked her head back and screamed as the master vampire's bloodied, snarled face hissed at her. His claws dug into her ankles and then her thighs before resting on her shoulders as he pinned her in place to the cold ground. His corpse like face was distorted in rage as his fangs dripped with black saliva on to her face. His breath was rot, blood and maggots… Tullia gagged.

"Stupid wench, you're not worth this much trouble. I'm going to make you wish you were never born." His voice scraped out as he widened his mouth unnaturally wide. Her terror seemed to peak, then evaporate entirely as a warm wash of numbness settled over Tullia at the knowledge that she was going to die a horrible death and there was just nothing she could do about it.

At least she did some damage to the bloodsucker before going out. She was pretty cool for that.

A loud, scrapping crash jerked the master vampire's attention away from Tullia and jolted the numbness out of her body.

Holy shit.

Heavy steps sounded as did a wet thumping sound. The master vampire hissed dangerously, his claws tearing her flesh on her shoulders. Tullia gave a short shrill scream of pain. The footsteps did not falter but they did sound closer.

With another hiss, the master vampire dragged himself off Tullia, tossing her to the side roughly and slithered towards the sound of the footsteps. Tullia heart was a jackhammer in her chest and hope, the slimy bastard, was wiggling throughout her body.

"Berserker." The master vampire hissed with utter loathing.

Tullia's curiosity, still alive and kicking, forced her to muster up enough strength to turn her head. She saw a giant man, swathed in black from head to toe with only his eyes exposed. He stood tall and confident as he held a squirming underling vampire in one hand by the neck. The man looked down at the vampire in his grip, the underling snarled at him. The man then effortlessly ripped the head of the vampire clean off with just his hands and tossed it to the side as a child would to a toy.

Tullia felt her eyes pop out of her scull at the sheer gore that was occurring as the head rolled off and stopped facing a cage. She looked back at the man bathed in darkness in a sort of stunned terror.

He would either be a kick-ass ally and help her escape, or possibly an even worse foe than the vampires. Thankfully, his current attention was on the master vampire who stood hunched like a deformed animal and snarling like one too.

"You will die here, Berserker. You think that you can defeat the master of the clan? I've lived for more than three hundred years and have acquired thousands of minions and cattle all over the world. I am the most powerful being to walk this earth!" The shrill quality to the master vampire's voice was not convincing, and the underlying panic that Tullia tasted clued her in on the fact that the three-hundred-year-old vampire was… scared. Of the ninja looking man.

"Cute." The deep voice, rumbly and cold, sent a sharp shiver down Tullia's back. If the promise of death had a voice… that man possessed it. The man pulled out two giant black axes from his back and held them in an easy grip, as if they were nothing but light weight props. He said nothing more, which seemed to aggravate the master vampire.

"Come my children!" The vampire shrieked, throwing his arms out wide, "Come to me and let us feast on the fresh blood!"

A quivering silence ensued… then a rolling wave of heat and pungent sourness filled Tullia's mouth.

"You slayed my children." It was said flatly, in more of a statement rather than a question.

The ninja man seemed to loosen his shoulders up by rolling them, "No. I slayed the vampires here."

The master vampire didn't comment further, instead he darted forward in a blurred motion and then disappeared. The man with the axes seemed to give off a wild, powerful taste before he too disappeared. A sharp clang to the left startled Tullia, a hiss from far away sounded as did another sound of clashing of metal and screams. The violent sounds occurred in various places, that Tullia very soon lost focus on them She was given a second chance at escape, and she would make it this time. Gritting her teeth, she slowly got her feet for the millionth time that horrid night. There wasn't a spot on her body that didn't ache. Even her armpits hurt.

How? How did they hurt?

Sucking in a deep breath, so that her lungs became plump with air, Tullia then held her breath as she shakily rose to her feet. She would be damned if she was going to lay down and wait for death. Gasping once she made it to her feet, she began to limp heavily in the direction she saw the ninja man come from. Well, at the least in the direction she thought he came from, based upon where he was standing.

Okay girl, you got this. You got this. You freakin' got this. You. Got. This.

Just walk forward and don't fall and keep going until you are out of this hell hole on earth. Just start moving and you are totally getting a milkshake after this.

Nodding to her mental pep talk, Tullia clenched her teeth to lock in any sounds of pain and began to move forward. It seemed to take a year to make it to the spot where the ninja man had stood. Carefully looking around, she spied a window half covered with wooden boards shining with beautiful, silver moonlight.

Giving a small happy huff, Tullia began staggering to the window. She would shove the board out, and then go through the window. Or she'd go through the window as the board came out, that seemed far more likely. Tullia was pretty confident that it wouldn't be a far fall down to the ground from the window, but she'd look out first just to be safe. She could use some of the empty cages that seemed mangled to stand on and then she could…. a heavy weight slammed into her back, sending her hurtling to the floor. She cried out in pain as her head smacked the floor with a sharp sound. Her vision went slanted, as she saw vibrations… then everything became awash in a gray tinged blur as heat wash over her face. Sharp hands gripped her hair and yanked her head back too far, baring her neck painfully.

"I'll suck you dry. There will be more, you are not special." The master vampire's, putrid breath wafted over her face, making her recoil in disgust and cause her throbbing head to become even more foggy. He pulled on her hair harder, forcing her neck back even more. She felt a few stands being ripped out from her scalp. Tullia blinked, now completely numb and stared up in silent dread as the ceiling of the warehouse came into focus. The semi rotted beams seemed fitting in this terror ridden place. She'd have been really disappointed if they were new and up to code.

So, this was the end, her limbs, deadened, her heart sluggish, her lungs compressed, her blood throbbing in her veins… She had no more energy, her strength was gone, and the pain had overtaken her body in a crushing way. She tried to scream, but her voice was strangled with an anesthetized weight of impending doom.

And what would be the point of screaming. She was done for.

Chapter Four

Death was such an ugly feeling… an ugly acceptance, she didn't want to accept. She wanted to go out slapping at the very least, but she no longer had any type of control over her body anymore. It's almost as if her body had accepted the situation before her mind was ready too. All she could do was silently stare up at rotted ceiling that contained this horror house. She closed her eyes as hot tears silently trekked down her ice-cold face.

Perhaps, if there was such a phenomenon of receiving another chance at life, she can be reborn…. unbroken.

A sharp scrape at her neck and Tullia stopped breathing entirely, hoping it would be fast and relatively painless… a gagging sound, along with muffled snapping sounds occurred before the vampire's clutch to her was violently removed. Tullia slumped forward but luckily she was numb so the meeting of her face with the frost ground was seemingly painless. Tullia opened her eyes, her vision still wonky, but she was able to make out a pair of large boots. Struggling a bit, she managed to shift her eyes up and witness the master vampire's throat being encircled by a massive hand and suspended in air. Pain filled hissing mewls ripped from the vampire's chest as he clawed at the hand. Blood dripped down from the massive fist from the vampire's throat. She could taste a faint flavor of spicy… feet?

If she had any type of muscle reflex left, she'd have gagged for the millionth time that night.

Tullia watched as the massive hand flexed then slammed the master vampire down onto the floor. The massive boot that she had seen came down forcefully on the master vampire's back, the crunch and the scream of unadorned, raw pain that came from the master vampire informed Tullia that it hurt. A lot.

Good.

Perhaps it was an ugly part in her, but she was extremely happy that the master vampire was being pinned to the ground underneath a boot like an insect. The boot, as if hearing her mental praise, stomped down harder, causing new pain filled screams to fill the air and stab her poor little ears.

She changed her mind; she just wanted the terror filled night to be over and finally get that milkshake. And some bandages.

"How many more warehouses?" The giant man asked softly, almost gently if not for the blood stain steel of the tone. Tullia forced her eyes up higher and saw the ninja masked man looming all and apposing.

Huh. He really did look like he was wearing a ninja mask that covered his entire face, save for his eyes, and he wore what looked like an all-black military combat outfit. There was a suspended moment in which the air was tense with icy expectancy and the cries of the other frightened prisoners were muffled.

The ninja man waited calmly.

The master vampire struggled underneath the man's boot, screeching and clawing wildly like a cockroach on its back. His mouth sagged unnaturally and gushed black and red fluids out from its gnarled mouth. The man increased the pressure on his back, more snapping sounds occurred, which was interesting for Tullia since she didn't think there was anything else left in the master vampire's back to be broken.

"How many?" The ninja man asked again, very gently. The vampire continued to screech and struggle, ignoring the ninja covered man entirely. The giant man seemed to give out a very slight sigh. He reached behind him and gripped one of his axes, unsheathing it from his back holster.

Her eyes widened in an awful fear. The ninja man then glanced at her. Her vision was still hazy but she thought she saw him blink, as if shocked she was still there or still alive. She shied away from his intense stare by lowering her head slightly, trying to curl into herself in the fetal position. He seemed to stare at her for a moment more, then shake his head.

"Close your eyes now, girl. This will not be a pretty sight." He ordered softly.

She didn't hesitate to follow his order. Squeezing her eyes shut tightly, she only saw blackness with striations of fuzzy whiteness due to the pressure of squeezing so hard. The sharp swing of metal, shrieking and a dull thud was the last sounds she heard before a ghastly silence overtook the area. Even the humans in the cages were silenced. Soft scuffling sounds caused small ripples in the silence. Slowly, Tullia peeled back her lids from her eyes and saw the big ninja covered man crouched about five feet away, the corpse of the master vampire behind his massive body. He was staring at her, pain still clouded her vision, yet she did manage to see the color of his eyes that glowed in the dimness. Big tawny eyes pinned fascinated on her even as they caused anxiety to flutter in her stomach. His focus on her was intense and his attention unwavering. Tullia couldn't move, she couldn't do anything much but watch him watching her and try to breath normally. The ninja man suddenly stood up, super tall and lethal, casting a massive shadow over her.

He then slowly approached her with foreboding, heavy footsteps. Her heart sank, before going cold. Her breathing, shallow and unsteady, became gasps as the giant man crouched down in front of her. A big hand reached out to her, Tullia flinched and tried to shuffle away as a thin cry escaped through her numb lips. Her battered body refused to move a single inch, though the intention was enough to engage a deep, searing throb all over. A gentle touch brushed her hair from her sweat stained forehead. Up close, she saw that she was correct; the man's face was covered with black fabric from his nose down and forehead back. The only visible part of him were his eyes, the rest of the giant's body was swathed in a black fitted, long sleeved t-shirt with multiple straps crisscrossing over his massive chest, black cargo pants with multiple pockets and big black boots. Very big boots.

Tullia stared into those eyes resignedly. Hopefully, he'd kill her fast. She didn't want to be tossed around anymore. Then, the gold glittered beautifully before she got the distinct impression of a small, sad smile. "It's alright now." This rumbling commanded every hair on her body into awareness. Tullia stiffened further. "I'll take care of you, sweetness." Tullia watched wearily, silently, as the big man gently scooped her up from the hard floor and pressed her firmly to his chest. The motion sent hot pain shooting through her body, but she didn't realize she was trembling so hard from the cold until his heat enveloped her, chasing away the chill and steadying the constant painful throb that consumed her body. She took in a shuddering breath. Tears that were locked in her throat rose swiftly to the surface as the sense of warmth and safety invaded Tullia's senses.

Salt and smoke played on her palette and seemed to bully the remaining rusty iron taste in her mouth. She swallowed multiple times to try and keep the emotion down within her.

She would not cry, she would not cry, she would not cry, she would not cry-

Hot tears dripped from her eyes and stung her cheeks as Tullia clutched onto the man as tightly as she could. Her self control melted away as her teardrops gained traction into streams that poured from her eyes.

"He's dead right?" She whispered, her voice a thin, hoarse rasp.

The man began to move through the dingy warehouse, holding her tightly to his massive chest. "Yes."

"Like, dead-dead right? Not undead dead?"

The man paused, then his tone became slightly amused, "There is no chance he will rise again. He is very much dead."

"Yay," She said weakly, then as if her damn burst, her silent tears became choking sobs. Quickly, she covered her face with her hands to stifle the racking sobs that ripped from her chest. Her scrapped hands stung, and her cheeks stung from her tears. The man made a deep, soothing sound in the back of his throat.

"Let it all out, sweetness. Nothing's going to hurt you anymore." Tension eased within her chest as she continued to sob into her hands, tasting the smoky coconut flavor of concerned awkwardness that the man was feeling, but she deserved to cry as much as she wanted.

A small crackling sound filled the air and a woman's voice suddenly began talking. "Sabin, come in Sabin."

Tullia jerked her head up in surprise, her tears on pause for the moment. A small ball of light, swirling with faint multicolored threads bobbed steadily above the man's meaty shoulder. "Calm." The man, Sabin, murmured before addressing the light ball. "Yes?"

"Status?"

Tullia sniffed, wiped her eyes and nose before looking up at… Sabin. She couldn't see much due to the black mask covering the lower part of his face, but his jaw was stiff as if he were upset, though she tasted no anger.

"Exterminated. The master is officially dead." His tone chilled the air.

The little ball of light paused, seemed to quiver slightly, then the woman's voice began firing short, hard questions. "Humans?"

"Hundreds."

"Alive?"

"Some."

"Sane?"

"Unknown."

There was a scoffing sound, "Seems we found ourselves a human blood pen. Where are the humans kept?"

His voice deepened. "Big game cages. Little bigger than a dog create."

"Those nasty-" A wordless growl. "I hate vampires. Too dead, too organized, and too bloodthirsty. Literally." The woman's voice had a soft airiness to her tone that seemed to caress the air when she spoke.

"Call clean up." Sabin commanded. "We're going to need every wiccan higher than a six on this to erase the minds of each human, if possible. We need to act fast to rehabilitate the minority."

"Not majority." It was a statement more than a question.

Sabin didn't answer and the silence said the harsh truth. Tullia tried to look around at the cages, but Sabin's shoulders proved to be solid and a perfect blockage to her vision.

"Right." The woman muttered.

Tullia watched in fascination as the light winked out just as fast as it came, leaving a very faint mist of blue. Unconsciously, she reached up and waggled her fingers where the light was right above Sabin's shoulder. The air wasn't even warm. She looked up when she felt his weighted gaze. Sabin's liquid gold eyes watched her intensely, almost trying to visibly dissect her. Tullia felt the oddest urge to blush and cover her face from his prying eyes. She sucked in her lips nervously, shrinking back slightly.

He then winked at her and that did make Tullia blush and, she had to admit, feel a little better. She casted her eyes down and noticed that her poor pajamas were bloodied, torn and dirty. She'd have to bomb them; they could not be saved in their current state. When she sighed and began to face forward, Sabin stopped walking abruptly. She jerked her head up towards him in surprise.

"Do not look." His voice was soft and rumbly, almost like he woke up from a sleep from warm sunshine. Tiny hairs quivered all over her body. Seeing the grim look in his eyes, Tullia nodded in understanding and covered her face with her hands. She also closed her eyes for good measure.

She smelled decay and rot in the air, but at the same time she could smell steel and night wind.

She couldn't hear Sabin's footsteps, but she heard a rhythmic drip of a liquid creating an eerie echo.

Drip. Drip. Drip.

Sabin's motion was smooth, though no matter how hard he tried to remain still, his movements still jostled her wounds enough to hurt. Inhaling deeply, Tullia focused on the dripping noise. It was almost hypnotic.

Drip. Drip. Drip. Drip...

...Drip. Drip. Drip. Drip. Water drops echoed within the cave, amplifying their nagging sound into the night. The ocean was calm and the air still, a beautiful night...

Drip, drip, drip...except for the annoying drips it was a serene night.

Humanoid sea creatures stood a few feet away from the entrance of a cave on a coarse sand bed. The waves lapped at their legs. They were covered from head to toe in an array of colored scales that shimmered under the bright moonlight. They had two legs, webbed claws, webbed feet, and oversized pure black eyes that seemed to have two different lids when they blinked. Deep gashes on the sides of their neck quivered like gills and they were missing their noses. Various sized fins stuck out on the sides of their heads and sprouting from their heads was what looked like fine, corn silk-like hair.

Along with the seamen stood five warrior creatures wearing spiked helmets and shoulder pads. Their chests were adorned with armor made from turtle shells and each carried two serrated blades in both hands.

There was only one female who stood in front of the soldiers. She was smaller than the others, her features more delicate, her body lithe. She wasn't dressed in armor, rather she was draped in jewels and shells. The female wore a crown pieced together with a collection of white and pink seashells and pearls. Around her neck hung a pearl choker that cascaded down in thick layers to drape over her chest. Her hips were wrapped in a net material that was intertwined with pearls and aquamarine stones.

She stood tall and stern before the mouth of the cave.

Her soldiers shifted nervously behind her. "My Queen," One of the warriors spoke, his tone strained, "if I may?" At her nod of approval, he blurted out. "Why are we meeting the Naga's king on his land? This is the Cave of Asherah, the den of the Sea Naga. Is this not an alliance pact? Should we not meet on equal territory? To hold our land form for more than a half an hour becomes..." He paused, not willing to look weak in front of his queen, "It puts us at a disadvantage." He finished.

The queen did not look back at the soldier when she replied, instead her focus was on the mouth of the cave. "We cannot allow anyone to assume our weakness, Thander. Besides, the Merrows are rumored to be quite... versatile." She turned to face her soldiers; her pale lavender face was set in a grim look. "Even to our supposed allies, the Merrows will not falter. And while land is our weakness, we will demonstrate that it is not." All the soldiers smiled, still shifting nervously, and she held her head higher. "Yes, it is uncomfortable to hold our two-legged form and to bear the weight of gravity, but we will come into this peace treaty with silent strength against our implicit limitation." She gave them a solemn look. "We are demonstrating our trust in them, in this form. The Naga will see this."

The males nodded in understanding, making her smile. These men were her personal guard, and they have demonstrated their loyalty numerous times. She trusted them more than she had trusted her family.

"I do not foresee anything going awry. But stay alert." She cautioned.

"We're always alert." A snarky reply.

Before she could utter an equal response, the sound of slithering over coarse rocks could be heard echoing from within the cave. Her men stiffened and the queen faced the cave once more, straightened tall and tightened her gills.

Calm like the deep.

Seven towering Nagas slithered out from the cave, also adorned with trident spears and armor. The Naga people had scales all over their bodies, much similar to the Merrow, but their colors were darker. A mixture of deep blues, greens and blacks only. They towered strong on their tails, long and stout, which were each tipped with a hard, black spike. They had sharp claws, serpent eyes, and poison fangs. The five-armed Naga guards trailed behind two royally decorated figures. The royal male was King Nirah. He was the largest and darkest out of all the Naga. His eyes were dark green and his face was weathered with a scattering of scares obtained from his days in battle, making him look toughened and vicious. He did not wear a crown, instead he bore the emblem of the Naga royal family on a sash that was braided around his hips. The one female in the group was smaller than the males and covered from head to tail in dark red robes that fell richly around her. Princess of the Naga. She wore a red veil and a red head dress studded in jewels. Her features were completely hidden, but the Queen of the Merrows knew what she looked like.

"Queen Sedna." King Nirah's voice was a low, clear rasp.

The Merrow Queen Sedna bowed her head in respect, "King Nirah." She looked at the female who she knew under that veil had the most beautiful ice green eyes in all the sea. "Princess Chava." The princess bowed her head meekly, though her tail waved subtly to Sedna from under the red robe. Sedna fought a smile as she forced her attention towards King Nirah.

There was a deep silence as the two groups stared at each other, assessing each other as they always did. Only the sounds of droplets could be heard in the night.

Drip. Drip. Drip. Drip.

"You should fix that leak." Sedna commented, Nirah crossed his arms over his chest. His face was ice cold.

"Not a leak." His voice was a hoarse hiss, "Nothing to fix."

Sedna didn't flinch at the veiled aggression in the Serpent King's voice. This alliance was not ideal. Bonding over a common enemy after a tragedy did not inspire warm comradery. Sedna tightened her gills once again and began what she had practiced endlessly for days until this very meeting. "King Nirah, before we begin, on behalf of the Merrows, to show our commitment to this alliance and our empathy, we would be honored if you accepted this eternal Lisianthus." Sedna motioned for one of her guards to come forward. He stopped right at her side and held out a small bundle of light violet and pink Lisianthus flowers encased in a glass box that kept them alive.

Thanks to the Fae, those grubby money hungry bastards, but they certainly knew their trade.

King Nirah stared at the flowers without a single expression.

Sedna blinked, forcing herself still as her confidence became shaken. "I did not know Queen Pandra personally. However, her adventures and battles are known and revered by many, including the Merrows. Through her stories I have become familiar with her bravery, her wit, and her kindness. I am not arrogant enough to assume you would place these flowers on her worship site in my name. However, I know that Queen Pandra loved the rare and beautiful. These flowers are indeed rare as they are beautiful and shall never perish." Sedna motioned to the flowers, "The flowers are for the memory of how Queen Pandra loved and lived... beautifully."

King Nirah looked at Sedna, then at the flowers again. He gave a sharp motion and one of his guards slithered up to gently accept the gift. The guard passed them to his king, and he stared at them for seemingly ages. His face still completely blank. Sedna chanced a look at the princess, her head was turned in the direction of where her father stood, though with the veil Sedna could not see her reaction. Though the way her body was soft and leaning towards her father, gave Sedna just enough courage to speak the last part of her speech.

"We cannot change the past, as much as we wish too, but we can exact revenge and destroy the bad blood that taints our sea." King Nirah looked up and Sedna stared him dead in the eyes. "Queen Pandra shall be avenged as will all our fellow Sea Naga and Merrows that have fallen from the monster that has terrorized us for generations. I want the next generation to know no terror."

King Nirah gave a slow blink, then a grin stretched across his craggy face, his fangs dripping with lethal poison. "Queen Sedna, I'm afraid I underestimated your political skills... and your compassion." He passed the flowers to Princess Chava, his dark green eyes fastened on Sedna, "The gift was thoughtful, your condolences are appreciated as is your thirst for the blood of the so-named Jomungandr." His smile faded, and a weighty look came into his eyes. "I want this alliance to grow beyond a defense for a common enemy. I want this alliance to hold deep rooted veins within both our communities that will grow in future generations."

Thank her Vut-kuva. She was inwardly relieved he accepted the gift.

Sedna smiled, "Time and frequent contact will strength our bond."

King Nirah grunted in agreement and withdrew his blade. "Let us finish the alliance, with a blood vow." He sliced his palm and held out his hand towards her. Thick, red blood spilled from his hand and dripped onto the rough sand bed. Sedna withdrew her own blade form her hip and mimicked the Serpent King's action. The hot sting and the blood that swelled was an oddly beautiful sight, a promising sight. They clasped hands, the king's dwarfing hers entirely, but his grip, while firm, was not crushing.

"I, Nirah, king of the Naga, swear loyalty to this alliance between the Naga and the Merrows, that will go beyond uniting for a common enemy."

Sedna tightened her gills, "I, Sedna, queen of the Merrows, swear loyalty to the alliance between the Merrows and the Naga. I swear fidelity beyond the common threat of the Jomungandr, but as an enduring alliance throughout the generations."

A deep silence engulfed the area.

"Witnessed." Sedna did not look away from the king when Princess Chava announced the documentation of the alliance.

A bubble of elation burst inside of her. An alliance was formed, they were now connected through their blood and their vows. Not even death could break the Merrows and the Naga alliance.

Their blood dripped from their clasped hands onto the sand. Silence overtook the area once more as the significance of their actions settled into the very fabric of their souls. The only sounds that could be heard in the night was the dripping sound from inside Cave Asherah.

Drip. Drip. Drip. Drip.

"Alright now, it is safe to look." A deep voice reverberated into the tail end of Tullia's vision. The Naga and the Merrows were always interesting to see. Lately, any of her visions about them have been tinged with a sorrow that often made her heart hurt almost as much as her head. Tullia slowly uncovered her face, the air stung her cuts. She surveyed the area that was drenched in moonlight. A soft, balmy breeze caressed her sweat dampened body. Desert landscape greeted her sight with a sprinkling of classic dessert brush that probably had names, but few people actually knew them. A lonely chain fence stood a few feet away with various holes and broken links.

How was there a building in the middle of the desert?

A woman, long and lean, was standing against a tall, rusted post, her hands folded in front of her, seemingly waiting. She was striking in a form fitted, long sleeved shirt, black pants, and chunky black boots. As Sabin walked closer to her, Tullia saw that her skin was the warmest shade of brown and had lush lips, big brown eyes, high cheek bones, and a shock of black curly hair.

Did she just step out of Vogue? Tullia suddenly became conscious again of her current bloodied and torn pajamas.

"Heal her, witch." Sabin demanded as he strode up to her.

The woman's dark eyes met Tullia's. Wariness, a bitter kale flavor and pity, an egg flavor, washed over her battered palette. The woman smiled softly. "Bless your heart." She pushed off the metal pole. "Come on. I'll patch her up lickety split." She touched her hand to her heart and smiled a heart stopping smile. Tullia gave her a small tight chested wave, not super thrilled that she was going to be 'patched up', but somewhat thrilled at maybe stopping a few potential diseases with disinfectant.

And maybe fire.

"Bring her over to the car."

Sabin began to move again and the motion caused a cacophony of pain from the jostling of all of her wounds. She inhaled sharply through her teeth, clenching them tightly to keep the sobs at bay.

She was going to try and be a tough bitch until she was alone then she'd be a little baby and cry until no more tears came out.

"Stay strong sweetness. The witch is going to make you feel better." The rumbly voice was a soft breath of sound, but the taste of softness and light sweetness, like cotton candy, warmed her and made it that much harder to not cry.

She swallowed thickly and kept swallowing until the tears were firmly locked down into her heart. Tullia focused forwards and noticed that Sabin had stopped by a very worn Toyota Corolla.

"Set her in the passenger's seat. I'll do as much as I can." The witch instructed, opening the driver side and slipping in.

Gently, Sabin opened the door and set her in a threadbare seat in a car that looked gutted. When he went to withdraw, Tullia found her hands clutching onto him. She looked up at him, with wide eyes, knowing her pain and fear were on display.

His gold eyes held hers, and he touched her head, very lightly with a gloved hand, "You are safe. Chandra will not cause you any harm." Tullia blinked at the glow of this massive man's eyes and the weight of the man's words. "Your discomfort will be eased."

He stared at her, until she gave a jerky nod in understanding and released him. She noticed her hands trembled slightly. She had a distinct impression of a smile and a faint taste of sugar before Sabin withdrew from her, taking all his warmth and concealed muscles away. Tullia didn't realize how much warmth he provided until she was left to be on her own. Ice seemed to spread from her fingertips up her arms and throughout her entire body. Her injuries began to throb and ache as tremors began to rack her body. Shivering, she curled into herself to try and preserve the warmth she was given. Sabin watched her for a moment before barely touching her face gently with the tips of his glove covered fingers.

"Be at peace sweetness." His gold eyes were kind, "This nightmare is now finished." It seemed more like a pledge than a causal comment, but Tullia wasn't given any time to think about his words before he withdrew his hand from her face and stood up. He gently shut the door and left her alone in the car with the… witch.

Slowly, Tullia turned to face the witch named Chandra. She tasted the smoky concern that was warm, but there was a coolness in the warmth, a distance that Tullia often felt from doctors.

She *hated* doctors.

"Okay, pumpkin." Chandra wiggled in her seat to face Tullia. "Now don't go gettin' nervous on me, okay? Nothing bad is going to happen to you. I'm gonna make you feel better." She was such a beautiful woman. Her dark skin gleamed in the pale moonlight, making her look divine and godly. Tullia nodded at her words. Chandra held out her hands, palms up and smiled, "I'm a witch, but the good kind, like the Witch of the East not the West." She wiggled her fingers playfully, Tullia gave a small smile.

Her head throbbed to the beat of her heartbeat; it was beginning to become hard to concentrate on anything. "Reason we're in a junk bucket of a car, is so I can concentrate my magic better, cause it's a smaller space. This car is also magic immune, so I won't accidentally fix the rips in the seats instead of your cuts." She gave her a gentle smile, "Just in case you're curious. Now, just relax and feel free to ask any questions at any time. You may feel a tingle, but nothing beyond that."

Tullia nodded slowly, tucking her hands to her chest.

"By the way, I don't think we've introduced ourselves. I'm Chandra." Another glamorous smile.

"Hi. I'm Tullia." She rasped out nervously. If she wasn't in pain and if the very fundamental core of who everyone made her believe she was wasn't shattered, she'd still be super nervous due to the overly beautiful person sitting next to her.

Chandra's eyes began to glow a light blue as her palms began to smoke a faint blue color and shimmer subtly. Tullia blinked, as the wisps of smoke lengthened and stretched out towards her. She felt peace and gentleness coming from the smoke and a savory calmness from Chandra. Fascinated, despite her growing nausea, Tullia reached out to touch the faint tendrils of blue. Chandra was talking, her voice low and soothing, but Tullia could only hear the sound and not make out her words. When Tullia's fingers made contact, the smoke seemed to waver, as if shy, then she felt a small pinch in the back of her throat, before the blue smoke exploded outward.

The force of the smoke bomb flung Tullia from the car, causing her to scream with fright. She gasped as her back hit the ground. Hissing in a breath she rolled onto her side to sit up but froze when she saw what her hands were underneath. Thick, lush grass surrounded her with a few dandelions that waved happily in the small, warm breeze. They both wafted with thin blue smoke. She looked around to see the grass extended a few feet all around her. Tullia looked back to the car and blinked in shock. It's once beat up appearance no longer existed. Instead, the car was glossy and looked brand spanking new as if it just came off the lot.

Tullia furrowed her eyebrows, slightly frightened, but mostly just confused. What... exactly happened?

"Are you alright?" Sabin murmured, causing her to jump a little and look up. He was crouched down besides Tullia, like a giant shadow that hovered close enough for her to feel his heat, but he did not touch her. Tullia pushed up onto her knees and looked down at the grass again. Then back at Sabin. Tullia opened her mouth to speak but Chandra ran around the car looking frazzled, ashen, and there was a faint hint of blue smoke that could be seen coming from her person.

Even slightly wild looking, she was stunning.

"We've gotta take her to the Grand High. *Stat!*" Chandra was staring intensely at Tullia, making her feel like she crawled out of the black lagoon. "She has *magic.* Magic that I've never felt before." She shoved both of her hands into her hair, slightly panting, "It was incredible, it just acted as... as an amplifier of sorts with my magic." A short, hard laugh, "She just intensified my spell one hundred-fold... unheard of from a mere human. The Grand High doesn't even have that sort of power." Her brown eyes were wide and glued to Tullia, as if she sprouted a million tiny demon horns all over her body.

Sabin didn't reply.

"This is astounding." Chandra murmured, tapping her chin in though.

"Are you sure you just didn't lose control again Chandra? It's always a dramatic event, like this occasion." Sabin rumbled softly as he arranged himself so that he was sitting next to Tullia with his long legs stretched out in front of him. He plucked a fat dandelion from the grass as he reclined himself back on his elbow. The perfect picture of ease. If ease looked like a dual ax wielding ninja lounging in magic grass.

Chandra's face darkened, and the vinegary pickle taste of irritation coated Tullia's tongue, "I don't know whether to take that as a compliment cause you think I can pack that much of a punch, or as an insult that you think I'm that much of an inexperienced witch to lose that much control."

Sabin twirled the full dandelion, he studied the flower leisurely as he replied to Chandra, "It wasn't my intention to imply either. It's important to look at all aspects of a situation and all other factors involved before concluding anything."

Chandra huffed. She ran her hands down her smooth shirt and fussed over her hair a bit. "Impossible." She pointed to the Corolla, "That car was magic resistant, put in place by the Grand High herself. No magic should be able to touch the car, all magic is supposed to be deflected, for better magic absorption. But look at it!" She made a dramatic gesture towards the car that seemed to glisten in an outdated fashion under the dark sky. "This fact alone is why I want to take her to the Grand High. She's an expert at reading magical signatures and that girl," She pointed at Tullia accusingly, "definitely has *something* in her."

Tullia felt her stomach drop and her muscle tense up. How Chandra was looking at her was identical to how her parents looked at her when she told them of her visions or hallucinations is what they liked to refer to them as. How the doctors looked at her when they couldn't figure out why she was seeing what she saw. How everyone looked at her when they found out that she was legally insane.

Abnormal.

Weird.

Wrong.

She looked down at her lap, to avoid the probing looks. Her eyes wandered over her pink pajama pants that she bought at a thrift store three years ago, searching for the hole she had in the thigh....

Pausing, Tullia surveyed her pants critically. They looked brand new. The stain that had been on them when she bought them and the frayed bottoms were newly stitched and her favorite hole in the thigh was gone. They were also perfectly clean, as if they had never been worn. Tullia ran her hands down her thighs and noticed her perfectly manicured hands. Her nails beds, once dirty and ragged and sickeningly crusted with blood, looked as if they had been meticulously groomed. Tullia followed her arm and began to inspect the visible parts of her body. She was clean, her clothes where mended, she was completely pain free, and she smelled good.

She sniffed her armpit, and a waft of a clean spring rain kissed her nostrils.

She looked down at her shirt, her Powerpuff Girl t-shirt (her favorite pajama shirt that was technically meant to be a child's nightgown) was no longer a dingy yellow white, but a sparkling white. She drew her right foot up and inspected her ankle by rotating it carefully. She twisted this ankle when she was trying to escape, but it felt perfectly fine. She looked over her skin, going as far as to pull up pants to see the skin beneath. She had no cuts or bruises or even a speck of dirt on her entire person.

She wiggled her toes, marveling at her perfectly manicured feet. She could be a foot model with her newly revived feet. Tullia continued to inspect her body, looking for any lingering evidence of her earlier abuse, but her skin was unmarred and her muscles, when she flexed them, were unhurt. She ran her fingers through her hair and brought the long dark strands in front of her face. Her ends were healthy, hydrated and glossy.

Oh gosh, that was so awesome.

"Everything check out alright, sweetness?" Tullia shot a startled glance at Sabin. He was still toying with the fat weed, but his gold eyes were fastened upon her intensely. Such eyes… Tullia gave a small nodded as she looked down again at her lap to hide her warmed face. He most likely saw the intense inspection she did of herself.

How embarrassing.

Thank goodness she didn't get too into her inspection and start stripping. She'd do that later. In private. With the bathroom mirror. What other wonders would she find?

"Sabin, with Tullia, we need to—" Chandra began, her voice pitched higher with tension but froze mid-sentence as a loud humming began to ripple over the small space. Suddenly a bright light emanated from behind them, drenching the once dark landscape in a harsh white light. Tullia whipped her head around and squinted against the brightness to see a giant multicolored door glowing in the middle of the dessert.

The blinding door seemed to quiver, then shoot out bright bursts of color that took on the shapes of… people. Tullia blinked in surprise as about a few dozen people began to emerge within the spam of four seconds. They were all dressed in what looked like latex body suits and thigh-high rubber boots, rubber gloves and face masks that mimicked bio-hazard masks.

"Crap." Chandra huffed, "The swampers are here." She snapped her fingers, a small puff of blue smoke came from her fingers, and pointed once again at Tullia, but was looking at Sabin, "You're on babysitting duty. I've gotta direct the lot of them." She gave Sabin a stern look, before striding towards the group with stomping strides, snapping out commands in her vivacious voice. Tullia watched the commotion with fascination. The 'swampers' began jogging in multiple directions towards the warehouse, some were unpacking a whole host of equipment. She peeked at the giant man lounging next to her, he was watching the group with uninterested eyes, as if he's seen it a million times before.

She turned back to the troop of witches bustling about with a numb and unsettled feeling curling inside her gut.

Witches exist and vampires are real.

What else was real? And was there a possibility that she wasn't… totally insane?

* * *

They sat in the grass together as the witches performed their part of the operation. Sabin watched the girl, Tullia from what Chandra called her, from the corner of his eye as she ran her hands gently over the grass, she sat prettily in. She was watching the commotion with dull eyes. The little minions of the Grand High were running back and forth from the warehouse, like magic imbued soldiers with gas masks on. Their job was clean up, to keep the situation from being discovered by humans and for rehabilitation… or 'peaceful passing' for any human's caught with the vampires. Sabin tried not to stare at her for long stretches of time, he noticed she'd become nervous and curl into herself a bit. She likely wasn't aware of her actions, but he noticed her physical withdrawal. A normal reaction from what she had endured.

He ran his hand over his mask mouth roughly.

The woman had gray eyes. Not tinted, no extra colors, no contacts… her eyes were pure gray like a cold dawning after a snowstorm.

It was unsettling. Right before he slayed the master vampire, an instinct that kept his old hide alive told him to look over. When he obeyed and met the one visible gray eye of the woman, illuminated just enough by the moonlight… he nearly faltered over his kill.

Something he had not done for centuries.

He glanced at her again, then quickly away. A frayed memory had slipped in front of him, of the time an oracle had once given him a prophecy.

"You look for honor and a sense of belonging, think it can be gained through the blade of your ax in the name of something." The old woman was hunched and ratty looking, her voice was steel over jagged rocks. "You think Odin will give you peace, you think he will deliver you to your true warrior's desire." Her cackle sharpened his nerves, he bared his teeth at her. A warning. She was unfazed, and continued blithely, "Your purpose, berserker is not to lend your blades to Odin." Her eyes were clouded but held a clarity that seized Sabin's attention, froze his consuming rage within him just enough for him to listen. "It is not to live in continuous war and violence. Your purpose is to foster peace and ensure harmony."

A dry chuckle had escaped his cracked lips, his entire mouth was coated with the taste of blood, causing him to spit. "Who do you think I am, you blind bat?

I am my gods will and might. I ensure peace through violence."

The oracle seemed entertained, "You are below a measly rat. But you shall rise... one day with the help of a good master." Another hideous cackle.

Such words revived the embers of his rage, melting the ice.

"Insolence. My only master is Odin."

The crow smiled, her mouth a patchwork of missing teeth. "Hmm, keep the color gray close to your breast. It shall lead to your salvation, berserker."

His rage roared within him as the oracles image began to stain a hellish red, "I will never falter from my god's will." Sabin proclaimed, slamming his fist into his chest as his fury stretched further out within him, consuming him. "I have no need for salvation."

The oracle spread her gnarled hand out, "You will. Blood of the innocent will seep through your skin and worms its way into your insides. There it'll twist and claw at you, endlessly for eternity." A statement said with such certainty, Sabin snarled wordlessly at her. "Your master with dove gray eyes, will silence your rage."

Never. His rage was his greatest weapon. "I'll kill them." His voice was far away and his head began to pound in rhythm of his heart. His breathing increased; his thoughts slowed.

A small shrug from the bony woman, a snide smile. "Hmm. Fear not, you will not meet them in this lifetime. You have yet to choke on the misery of the dead."

Snap.

He raised his ax high above his head, it glinted under the red sun...

He broke away from the memory, glancing at Tullia again; she was resting her head on her knees, still watching the witches with glazed over eyes. He had forgotten the oracle's words. The centuries of time, isolation, blood and darkness had buried much within him to the point that he was not the same person as he was brought into this world as. He had become saturated with darkness that there was not a single bright spot for him to see when he dared look inward.

He looked down at the weed he held. It surprised the hell out of him when he saw that not only was the woman, Tullia, not dead, but through the mess of black tresses hanging in her face, he could see one visible gray eye was wide and watching him. The oracle's memory rushed up at him from the abyss.

So, in accordance with the oracle's words, Tullia was to be his master. He was to be her pet. Sabin's skin crawled with the idea of being blindly devoted towards someone again. Sabin watched her from the corner of his eye, checking for the hundredth time to see if her eyes were truly gray. A bright flash from the cleanup crew, slashed across her face suddenly, washing her face in a white light and highlighting her eyes perfectly.

They were an unequivocal dove gray.

She squinted, rubbing her eyes at the assault of light and shifted positions to sit crossed legged on the grass, turning away from the offensive light. As fast as the light came, it winked out, leaving the grassy area once more encased in a soft night glow. Tullia absent-mindlessly played with her dark hair, twisting and winding strands around nimble fingers. She didn't appear to be anything… abnormal or supernatural. Perhaps a bit more beautiful in appearance than the average human woman; with her almond eyes, her round face and the sharp curves of her lips, but other than that she was simply human. Her soft face, with a cream over raspberries undertone, and her sleek hair that was the deepest moments in the night personified was a pleasant contrast to his eyes.

Doubt seeped in his dark mind. Perhaps… his memory was flawed. Perhaps the oracle was flawed in her predictions. Perhaps the memory was never a memory, but a desperate construct from his drowning mind in hopes for a purpose once more in life. His eyes slide away from her to the dying weed he held in his hand, pondering.

No one would ever be his master. He would never allow anyone that sort of power, even if it went against his need to devote.

Would it be an awful venture, to simply protect her for the rest of her natural life? He was nothing anymore, but a drifter with no hope of redemption. A murder that was forever stained with the deaths of the innocent. But she was young, she was innocent and perhaps he could use his tarnished hands to protect her, even if it was for a moment. She was so small; it was a miracle she did not suffer more serious injuries from the leeches than she already had.

An ugly slime rose within from memories of the insidious past, the betrayal, the blood, the deaths, the ignorance….

Sabin's filth rose and swirled within him, his violent rage quiver… before rallying, whispering sweet inclinations to go find more vampires to kill… to torture… to massacre… find anyone….

Sabin shoved his rage down, burying it within him through sheer will, focusing on the little weed in his hand.

Crush it.

He tossed it aside, inhaling the dry dessert air and tilting his head back to look at the star-swathed sky, breathing away his rage's upsurge. It had been centuries since he had a purpose, since his blades were used in the name of someone, but this time he would set strict rules in place for himself. He would not blindly obey; he would never ignorantly follow anyone's words. However, he was born to follow orders, he was shaped to give his utter devotion to someone. His life was meaningless unless he had a purpose, and there was no hope of redemption for him. He was a lost body, merely acting on his own with no further purpose and not much thought.

Sabin's eyes slide once more to the little woman on the grass. Her pale face emotionless, her gray eyes glazed, and her body curled protectively around herself. Rage prowled within him, but another feeling was stirred. Her sweet presence was both calming and unsettling.

He would see, he decided. He would protect her for the rest of the day; the witches would not let her be and this would give Sabin an opportunity to see the little woman with the soft face and the sweet gale scent. Perhaps, it was because she had that scent, a scent that was engraved in his childhood, that nostalgia was close to the surface for him. He thought that nostalgia within him was long dead or forever tainted, but life did manage to surprise him every now and again.

Fast movements broke him of his reflection, he snapped his head towards the motion, tensed for violence, only to marginally relax when he identified Chandra's slender form jogging over to them, her mouth set in a grim line. She eyed Tullia critically, before facing Sabin with a harsh face. She motioned with her head towards Tullia with wide eyes. Sabin silently sighed, this was her code for 'interrogation time'. He faced Tullia and began the second part of his job. A job he didn't mind when he could use his fists or blades on offenders, but very much minded when it came to verbal interrogation with victims. He positioned his body towards her, giving her enough space so she didn't feel crowded.

"Sweetness," He called, softening his voice a bit and calling her by a name he had heard long ago called in affection in his clan. She peeked shyly up at him through her lashes, her silver eyes mimicking the fullness of the moon heavy in the sky. "Can you tell me why you were brought here?"

Tullia lowered her eyes to her lap, her hands came together and began to fiddle with her pink pajama bottoms. Something stirred in Sabin, a faint flutter that ended before he could understand the feeling.

"Someone brought their problems to where I live." Her voice was soft, her small form stiff. "They ended up… dying, but their problem didn't go away. It came to me." Her words were said in a staccato rhythm.

"Are you referring to the vampires as the problem?" Chandra asked, her arms were folded, and her stance battle ready.

Tullia nodded.

"Where were you when they abducted you?" Sabin watched as she moved to toyed with the grass, still not looking at either one of them.

"I was… in my room… at the Desert Inn Motel." She seemed a bit hesitant. He opened his mouth to ask another question, but Chandra butted in once more.

"You're visiting Vegas? Do you know why they took you then?" Chandra's tone was rough as it was breathy. Sabin cut her a sharp side look, if she was going to barge in then she shouldn't have asked him to do it. It was now his job, he didn't like sharing his duties with anyone, even the jobs he didn't like. It was his to do alone. He also didn't care for the way Chandra spoke to Tullia. He didn't like Chandra's calculating eyes assessing her either, the poor girl seemed to be struggling not to wilt in anxiety under that cold stare.

"I live here." Tullia started off slowly, still refusing to look up, "The man… the man right next to my room. I… I don't think he paid the v- vampires in full. He was short one woman. Supposedly." Tullia twisted her hands together, tightly enough to turn her fingers bone white. Her eyes skittered nervously across both of their faces.

"Supposedly?" Chandra raised her eyebrow. His rage tried to stretch out within the cage he had built around the beast.

Tullia shrugged, and when she spoke again, her voice was a bare whisper, "The man… was ranting, loudly, before he… he killed himself. So, I overheard." Her face was leeched of all color, her breathing quickened and her voice became a pitch higher, but still remained soft, "I have no idea beyond that. Nothing. They broke into my room and then took me, and I woke up in a cage and then they started to hurt me. That's all. That's everything."

Chandra opened her mouth, most likely to ask more questions, but Sabin held up his hand to stop her. He saw the witch's face glide through the expression of offense, then confusion, before settling on begrudging acceptance. She knew he was ultimately in charge, and ultimately more powerful than she was. He could kill her with much effort, and retaliation from the witches wouldn't come.

Sabin looked at Tullia, who was staring hard at her hands, a severe frown on her face.

Poor thing.

"You did good. Thank you."

She looked up at him then, her dove gray eyes were dewy, her face was drawn and pinched tight with stress. Her visage was haggard, but the strength underneath was there. He saw it and he would strengthen it further and protect it. His chest seized and his entire being flooded with a vibrancy, with a drive that he had lost many centuries ago. The sensation… of purpose, of determination, of being alive forced their way through his deadened veins, brightening this sinewy darkness just a touch. Forcing his heart to pump and his mind to race with possibilities.

Instantly, Sabin decided that he was going to protect her, not just for the day but for the rest of her life. It didn't matter if she was the oracle's prophecy or not. He had not felt a semblance of emotion since his defect. Light had evaded his presence…. Until tonight he was offered but a small taste of it, and he wanted more. This woman made him feel as though he wasn't a walking corpse, but rather a man with unstained potential. Selfish as it was, he would force himself to fit into her life and he couldn't muster up a semblance of guilt. On impulse, he reached out and smoothed her hair down on top of her head down to the side of her face. Touch was grounding to some and revolting to other victims.

She jolted in surprise but did not pull away.

Her cheek looked so plush, he felt the softness through his glove and upon closer inspection her hair hinted blue hues under the moonlight. He didn't know how to comfort people, or talk to them, and he was even more inept in speaking with victims that had suffered a brutal ordeal, but she was his sensory conduit of sorts. She was the key to just a little bit of light in his bleak life. Therefore, he would put forth an effort only with her.

"You showed bravery. You did well." He complimented softly, not knowing what else to say. Her face seemed to crumble slightly, causing mild panic within him. Did he choose the wrong verbiage? However, before true concern could overcome him, she pulled herself to together with a deep inhale, her face smoothing out. She pressed the side of her face into his palm briefly, sending a delicate shock of warmth through him, before pulling back. His hand began to throb beneath his glove with the remembrance of her soft heat. Fisting his hand, he looked up at Chandra, who rubbed her eyes tiredly.

"Alright then," She began on a sigh, "Let's start over. Do you have anyone that would begin to worry about your disappearance? You were taken last night, it's been nearly a full twenty-four hours. Is there someone who would be looking for you right now?"

Dove gray eyes seemed to shutter and darken, "No."

Chandra paused, "No one? Family? Boyfriend? Friends? Co-workers? Boss?"

Sabin stiffened a little, annoyed, his rage clawed down his spine. Then became irritated at his annoyance for being of a juvenile reason. It didn't matter if there was someone who considered her theirs. Sabin overrode them and he would make it known that they were not worthy, nor did they attend to her as they should have, hence why she was abducted by the vampires. Therefore, they were no longer justified to be near her and would be removed immediately.

"No." Tullia answered again, her voice holding a sharper edge to it. She furrowed her eyebrows a bit, clearly unmoving in her answer.

"Are you sure? There's really no one? A parole officer? *A pet?*" Chandra pressed.

Tullia looked at Chandra, her eyes churning with a deep emotion and said firmly, "There's no one." Her eyes became flat, like frosted silver moons and she looked as though she were on the verge of shutting down completely if pushed any further. He didn't like that she seemed… damaged. Sabin thought she was doing very well despite the circumstances, but everyone had their breaking point. He had witnessed it repeatedly with many.

Chandra shot a concerned glance at Sabin, then gave him a motion with her eyes that said, *'fix this or I use magic'*. Normally, he'd ignore the witch's request and have her do magic; he found he didn't care enough to ever fix anything or anyone. He was a warrior, first and foremost, was born one, died one and hopefully would die one again. Being gentle and sympathetic were of a limited quantity within him, and he felt he reached the end of that reserve long ago.

However, this woman with secret eyes and glossy hair…

Leaning back once more, feigning relaxation, he thought for a moment, thought about what he always wanted after a particularly bloody battle that settled heavy on his chest. "Are you hungry then?"

Tullia's eyes jerked towards him, shimmering, with surprise. Chandra made a disgusted sound, clearly not impressed with Sabin's question. Tullia clasped her hands together and twisted them against her solar plexus. He watched her fidget with interest, they were very small and shy motions, like a small, baby animal.

She remained silent for a few minutes, Sabin rested in the cool grass while she thought, looking up at the full moon sitting low in the sky. Dawn would soon be upon them. Sabin thought back to last time he slept… three, no four days? He'd need to either sleep or restore himself. Her soft voice broke above the muted sounds of the night and the fuss of the cleanup, "I… I could eat."

And there was never an instant where Sabin could never eat. Nodding, Sabin repressed a grin as he stood up. He faced Chandra, whose face was tight with displeasure. "Chandra, conjure up a pair of shoes for her." He told her, nodding his head towards Tullia's bare feet. Nowadays, shoes were no longer optional attire.

"You can do that?" Tullia's eyes shimmered with awe, she rose to her knees, "That's amazing!" Tullia innocent excitement and her beaming face made Chandra stared at her, then give a strangled smile. Sabin didn't think anyone could resist that adorable reaction. Chandra raised her hand and flicked her fingers. A pair of plain black flip flops suddenly adorned Tullia's feet. Her gasp of surprised and the little wiggle of her feet had Sabin clenching his jaw tight to prevent a smile. Sabin nodded his thanks at the angry witch.

"Sabin." She bit out through clenched teeth. "We need to talk."

He ignored her, "Come on then, sweetness." He watched Tullia stand up and push her long black hair behind her shoulders. Her gray eyes pierced his with quiet shadows in their depths.

He felt his heart quicken and his blood rush through his veins as she walked up right next to him, it was a sensation he had once savored before a battle. But she was of no threat to him, even if she used all her strength, she would not do him any damage. She was a tiny little thing though, barely clearing his mid bicep. It appears she was not eating enough; he would need to feed her; she'd surely grow to a healthier height. He swallowed thickly, reveling in the vibrant feeling, before forcing himself to focus. "My trucks a bit away," He held out his hand to her, "Watch where you are walking, there are critters that play at night." Tullia looked around her feet as she slid her hand into his without a hesitation. He felt a jolt shoot through his hand sharply as he enfolded his hand over hers.

Odd.

He began to walk slowly, matching his pace to her shorter strides. His eyes scanned around her feet, so that she didn't step on anything that would cause her to hurt. Be it a rock or a snake or a scorpion. He'd prevent all harm.

"*Sabin!*" Chandra's voice was shrill and tight, she ran to stand in front of them. Her usually pleasant face screwed up in a tight lipped, scrunched forehead face. She placed her hands on her hips and glared at Sabin. "Cleanup is not done."

Sabin merely looked at the witch, "Indeed. Good luck with that."

Her face twisted in rage. "I should turn you into a loaf of bread then feed you to the ducks!"

Sabin walked around Chandra, she was not a threat to him. No magic wielder was. He parked east of the building. "I don't mind ducks."

He felt a blast of air hit his back and smirked lightly. He heard a short, frustrated scream, then, "We need to talk! The Grand High must know of this!

"Then tell her." He returned flatly.

"You stupid man! I'll turn you into fat squirrel and starve you!"

"That would be concerning... if it were possible." He called back. Squirrels were wiry, but he never spared them a second glance, unless he was hungry.

Another angry shriek, high and piercing, and a few vulgar profanities followed behind them. "Fine!" She shouted, "You lumbering, flatfoot, cotton swab! I'll be at your place at six a.m. You hear me! Six a.m.! You better be there! Or I *will* do something nasty to you! I swear to you, *I will!*"

Sabin ignored her. Such a fickle temper for a supposedly high-ranking witch.

"Are you sure it's okay to leave? She seems, um, really stressed." Tullia looked over her shoulder in concern.

Sabin tugged her hand so that she'd focus in front of her and not behind her. He didn't need her tripping. "She knows where to find me when she's done with clean up. She is not my keeper or your warden. Besides, we're famished." A short second of thought, before he added, "And food is always a good idea."

Tullia looked up at him, her gray eyes dancing with enigmas and a slight flash of humor. The delicate heat of her hand began to seep through his glove and travel up his palm. The night air was still and peaceful, a silent witness that seemed to swallow the ugly actions of what occurred this night. His heart remained at a fast tempo within his chest, causing him to feel invigorated and a touch youthful. The more they put distance from the warehouse full of disinfecting witches, the more Sabin found the night events to be less of a reality. He glanced at the woman by his side, her eyes were glued to the sandy floor, most likely searching for critters. He felt his lips twitch.

"You are below a measly rat... Blood of the innocent will seep through your skin and worms its way into your insides. There it'll twist and claw at you, endlessly for eternity."

He broke away from the half-formed memory, disturbed by its clarity... by its lack of age and accuracy. He was beginning to believe that the memory was a memory, and not just an ideal little mind creation. To distract himself and to get her to talk, Sabin asked, "What are you hungry for?"

There was a small silence, the sounds of their steady footsteps crunching upon the sand filled the quiet.

"What time is it?" A velvet noise complimented the tranquility. Sabin looked at the horizon. A light touch of gray blue was beginning to wisp upward. However, the rest of the sky was swathed in black and studded thickly with stars.

"Four or five am." He said.

"Then breakfast is the only appropriate venue." She gave a small hop, jumping over a twig, like a happy child would. He could feel her slowly relaxing, slowly shedding the darkness of the events of the night away. Such untainted innocence had his rage wanting to come out and crush it… crush her…

"Agreed." He said instantly, clenching his free hand and forcing his forever awakened rage away, back into its flimsy cage. It hissed, writhing and then laughed at him in mockery. It knew it could get out. His tone was even when he said, "I think there's a few diners open at this hour."

Sabin glanced at her from the corner of his eye and saw her staring at him, her throat swallowing thickly. When he turned to face her fully, she looked away and bit her bottom lip. "I don't have much money… I actually don't have any money on me right now." She giggled self-consciously, her face pinkening, "If we could stop at an ATM real quick…" Sabin stopped walking completely, forcing her in turn to stop. He stared at her now and noted the way she stopped talking and her silver eyes skittered across his covered face, then back to the ground.

"No need. I'll be paying." He stated flatly. Currency was nothing to him and it seemed shameful to allow her to pay. She was unaware of what he required for nutriment.

She frowned, braving to look at him longer than a second. "I can't accept that. You've done so much already, I'd feel—."

"No." He cut her off, and resumed walking at the tiny, stepped pace, pulling her along gently, "I will be feeding you, and you will eat and be happy about it. And you're not payin'. End of discussion."

"Discussion?" She huffed, scuttling next to him, "I'm a grown woman. I want to pay for myself, and I want to pay for you as a thanks."

"No." Sabin said again.

"But—"

"No." Quite insistent, "Enough."

A churning silence. He saw her eyeing him intensely as her cheeks went pink, "You gonna let me talk?"

He looked up at the stars, then back into gleaming eyes. "Depends." He had the immense pleasure to watch an involuntary smile curl at the corners of her pink mouth.

"Wow. This a habit to take rescues out to eat?" Her tone was light, humorous, alive.

Never. His rage did not tolerate suspended interactions too well.

"No." After a short second, he softened his answer by adding, "Now, come."

He saw Tullia give a small shake of her head and sigh. "Man of a few words I see." She gave him a slanted look. "You win."

Sabin felt a warmth in his chest, that had nothing to do with his rage's heat and a tickle of laughter in his throat. He guided her to his truck and helped her inside of it. When he shut the door, he surveyed the night drenched desert landscape.

He was looking forward to eating.

Chapter Five

She watched passively as the two witches fought to the death for the title of scroll proprietor. Surely, they both could do it; devil knows there are too many scrolls as it is. They really needed to get digital. However, it was 'tradition' to make them fight. It was 'tradition' for the Grand High—her— to spectate the boring as hell fight.

Tradition… the word grated upon her nerves and cuffed her hands.

Taking a slow sip of her lilac laced Hennessy, the Grand High rolled the liquid over her tongue, savoring it as she took in the spectators. All of them were her minions. All of them in various states of human appearances. The scene reminded her of a dirty underground fighting club that the humans liked to glorify in movies.

How mundane. How so very… average. She ran her nail lightly around the rim of her glass. She was bored with this traditional event. Tradition was quite tedious to her. However, the Elder Counsel would keel over if she dared veer away from customs, such as the scroll proprietor tournament, which then would lead to a divide and an internal war. Which was not something she wanted… yet. The Grand High sat forward as one of the contestants dealt a particularly nasty blow to the other contender, causing them to bleed fat blood droplets down the side of their head. She liked blood.

She liked the color. Liked the iron smell. Liked its entire aesthetic. She felt a small flicker ignite within her, a shifting of sorts. A slow grin curved her lips. Well, if she had to stick to the traditional route, might as well amp it up a bit with historical savagery. She stood up abruptly and the cheers stopped suddenly as did the two fighters' movements. All eyes turned her way as an expectant stillness overtook the air. They waited on her - her flock of witches - for her words of direction.

"We are in a day and age of modern advances." Her voice echoed out in strong waves. "As we strive to maintain our core values, I do believe that some traditions should be… embellished upon." She tapped her nails together and water bubbled up from within the cracks of the floor and the ceiling. The water swirled around the two fighters, encasing them in a giant water bubble. As the two fighters fumbled with a spell to help them breath under the water, the Grand High smirked before amplifying her voice. "A simple one-on-one battle in today's complexities and intricacies of society does not prove one's worth." The globe of water began to tremble violently, losing its spherical shape as darkness unfolded within the center of the water. Massive tentacles shot out in various directions and slammed against the barrier of the globe, twisting angrily at the blockage. The twisting mass of darkness shifted to reveal a gigantic, puffy red eye and a bulbous onyx head. The eye rolled, angry and confused until it landed on the two witches, who shrank back in terror as they helplessly watched the octopus take up more and more space within the confined bubble.

The Grand High clapped. "Now, whoever survives sweet Lusca…" A pause for dramatic effect, "wins." She finished. "Or if they both die then the position is still open and please submit your application to the Elders after the tournament." She flicked her fingers out and Lusca tilted up, revealing its razor-sharp beak and dove for the two quivering witches. She smiled as she watched Lusca wrap a tentacle around one witch's waist as the other one sliced a tip off another tentacle. She looked at the crowd to see them frothing with excitement, wilder and more aggressive than before.

She looked up at the booth that the Elders occupied, to see eight eyes watching her with ambiguity. *That's right, you can't say anything*, she thought with a smirk. She reclined back in her lushly pillowed chair. Tradition, she thought, may not be so bad if it's on the extreme side of savagery. It was kind of… fun.

The Grand High started laughing.

* * *

Tullia tried not to fidget in the squeaky leather seat of Sabin's truck, but it was very, very hard. Turns out it was precisely four twenty-six am, a time Tullia had never personally witnessed before. The silence between them both was comfortable and safe, and the whole ordeal seemed as if it occurred in another life. However, Tullia's mind whirled, she wanted to ask Sabin *questions*. Such as: what did he do for a living? Was he a mythical creature too? What were the witches doing in the clean up? How did find her? Was he hot in his ninja gear? What was going to happen to the humans in the cages? Who's the Grand High? Can she order two things at the restaurant? Why did he wear a mask when COVID was over? Were his axes as heavy as they looked?

Majority of her questions were rude of a stranger to ask another stranger, so Tullia refrained, but they still burned to be answered and more questions kept accumulating within her. Sabin drove down Fremont Street, the lights were dazzling and there were a few drunken people sloshing about on the street, but other than that it was relatively quiet. There was a giant lit up Denny's sign on the corner and Tullia's stomach growled in anticipation. She pressed her hands against her stomach embarrassed, but Sabin made no comment. He pulled into an underground parking lot and drove around a bit until they got a parking space by the elevators.

"A moment." He said in his night rich voice, he looked around as he pulled out what looked like a slender silver vape stick from a hidden pocket on his ninja suit.

Too wired with curiosity to be nervous, a questioned popped out from her mouth before censoring, "Is that a vape?" They always smelled deceivingly good when people would blow smoke out behind them, and it would envelope her. "What flavor it is?"

Sabin looked at her, his golden eyes glinting with a smile. "Magic." He put the vape up to his covered mouth and the tip suddenly disappeared behind his mask. He sucked in deeply from the vape before exhaling a giant cloud of white smoke in the truck. Inhaling on reflex, Tullia smelled a strange flavor that was both sweet, earthy, familiar and unfathomable. She's never smelled anything like it before in her life, but it was far from unpleasant. Purposely inhaling deeper breaths, Tullia savored the unique fragrance until the smoke thinned before disappearing entirely.

Maybe she'll get a buzz from his second-hand smoke. That'd be nice. She was feeling overly traumatized at the moment.

Tullia turned her eyes to focus on Sabin and stared at him in disbelief. He was mask-less, his face a deep sun kissed gold that held an arrangement of features that were neither beautiful nor ugly, and his hair was blonde with a short average Joe cut. He wore a casual white t-shirt and jeans, instead of his black military looking garb. Basically, he was an entirely different person, except for his golden eyes. After just one puff, Sabin causally tucked the vape in his front pocket.

Tullia gaped, shocked and more than intrigued. She waited for an explanation or at the very least an acknowledgment of his transformation. However, Sabin merely looked over at her and asked, "Ready?" As if nothing fundamentally changed.

Ready?

She became unready when he transformed. For the first time in her life, she would put the prospect of food on hold so that she could quench the thirsty question within her.

Tullia blinked, then threw her hands up in the air, banging them against the roof of his truck. Ignoring the slight throb of pain, she asked, "So you're not gonna explain this sudden transformation? This sudden make over?" He raised an eyebrow in inquiry, eyeing her hands uncertainly. Tullia to roll her eyes, then began to tick off the questions she had on her fingers. "Where'd your mask go? What happened to your ninja getup? Is that your real hair? Was that really a vape? Did it taste good? How did your appearance change? Is this your real appearance? Are you a magician?"

Verbal diarrhea occurred then. Tullia sucked in her lips to repress the other questions that began to bubble up over her tongue. She was far too wound up to feel anything else than determination and exasperation.

Sabin tilted his head to the side slightly as he regarded Tullia with a somewhat amused and somewhat surprised look at her heavy onslaught of questions. He tasted of… spiced sweetness. "It's an illusion of sorts.

Nothing what you see is real. The Grand High, the head witch of her clan, crafted this little gadget from a vape shell, thought instead of water and nicotine or marijuana, it's a dust mixture that Chandra refuses to disclose the ingredients of." He shrugged, "It would be too conspicuous if I were to go in dressed like a… *ninja* as you described." A small smile, "People are inclined to fear what they cannot see. However, I cannot remove my mask, so an illusion is necessary in order not to draw attention to myself. I still am wearing my original clothing underneath the illusion."

"Okay, what about my other questions?" Tullia demanded.

Sabin gave another small smile, "I can do some card tricks." He offered.

She gave him a deadpan look, "I don't count that as real magic."

"Then no, I am not a magician." He sounded amused and tasted of carbonation, though his face was blank.

"How did you manage to vape through your mask?"

His eyes twinkled, "Magic."

Such an ambiguous answer. She crossed her arms on a huff. "Well, then, Mr. Vague, what did it taste like?"

He was serious but sweet tartness covered her palette. "Espresso and jewels."

Feeling bold, she asked eagerly, "Can I try it?"

Sabin seemed to hesitate, which made Tullia's gut sour with embarrassment. *Right*, she was a stranger and probably viewed as someone… well not dirty but certainly not clean. "Or maybe another time?" She said lightly, trying hard to conceal the embarrassment she felt growing within her. She swished her hand around in an effort for a nonchalance air and smiled.

Sabin's look was ambiguous, but the flavor in her mouth was hickory and sweet. After a short moment, he reached in his pocket and pulled out the vape. He vigorously wiped the mouth tip with his shirt before giving it to her, "Here you go. Just suck in, slowly. And just hold it in your mouth, don't inhale it."

Tullia smiled wide and wiggled closer to him, "Got it." Excitement fizzed through her veins as she took the warmed metal tool from his big palm. "This reminds me of the time I shared a bottle of Prosecco with a homeless woman on her birthday. She told me to drink it slow, since it was my first time with alcohol."

Sabin was amused by her again, she gathered from the bubbles on her tongue. "Did it taste good?"

She tilted her head, remembering the flavor of the overbearing sweetness tinged with the burn of alcohol and the fizzy carbonation, "It was fun cause she was funny, but the drink didn't actually... taste good." She said slowly, as though she was in a confession booth.

To not like alcohol? It seemed like a dysfunction of sorts since she was at the legal age to drink. But... ugh, it tasted bad all by itself.

Sabin nodded, as if he understood, "Alcohol is an acquired taste."

She bobbed her head in agreement, looking down at the vape, savoring the humor and the warmth of the emotions swirling in the truck. After years of having a bunch of flavors randomly force their way into her mouth, she had learned to discern what flavor meant what.

Often, she had tasted other people's humor and happiness from groups, lovers, children…. a warm savory flavor. It was her favorite that she experienced.

"Will I change in appearance too?" She asked, sneaking a peak up at Sabin.

He shook his head. "No."

Tullia frowned, "Why not? It put on a whole different person for you?"

Sabin leaned his elbow against the door and rested his head against his hand. His gold eyes were bright in the dim space. "It was formulated for me. It will not react to anyone else but me.

Tullia clicked her tongue in disapproval, "That's disappointing. I was hoping it would put a real-life filter on my face to hide my eye bags and acne."

Sabin raised his eyebrow, "You have nothing that needs to be hidden."

She blinked in surprise, then felt her face go red. Sabin didn't look like he was aware of it, but his offhand compliment was equivalent to a warm hug; and Tullia did not receive many hugs in her lifetime. It was a very warm experience.

Instead of telling him that though, she pulled a face at him that said "yeah-okay-but-no". She then looked back to the vape pen and pressed the warmed metal to her lips. She drew in a deep pull… then choked as the dense smoke crawled too far down her throat, clogging her esophagus and choking her. Her eyes watered as she began to hack her brains out, smoke puffing out of her mouth with each racking cough. "I'm… gonna… die…" She gasped out as coughs consumed her once more, causing her body to convulse as if she were possessed. Sabin quickly grabbed the vape from Tullia. Then he began to pat her back in a gentle upward motion, his big hand covering a good portion of her back. He was silent as she worked through the uncontrollable choking, coughing and gagging. Seemingly years later, the racking coughs subsided, and her breathing evened out as her throat cleared up and air easily filled her lungs once more. She sat in her seat, panting, feeling flushed and slightly damp from her tears of exertion. Apparently, vaping was not instinctive and required a certain skill set that Tullia did not possess. Mortification flooded her entire being as did the faint taste of bitter coffee and an interesting blend of metal, sparkles, and sugar.

Cool. Next time she'd take his word on what something tasted like, instead of trying to do it herself. Clearing her throat, Tullia turned her face to Sabin and gave him a wobbly smile. "Kay, I can breathe now. Curiosity satisfied." She pulled a lock of her hair forward, tugging it hard.

This instant seemed much more embarrassing than being picked off the floor after being smacked around by a vampire. Probably because the vape was her decision, whereas being brutalized by a blood sucking corpse wasn't.

"Do you need another moment to compose yourself?" Sabin's deep rumble vibrated from his hand onto her shoulder and across her chest making her very aware of just how big he was, even though he was sitting in the driver's seat. His hand had stopped patting her back in favor of gently rubbing up and down her spine. It was soothing and calmed her nerves, though her embarrassment continued to rage on unperturbed.

She became uncomfortably aware of how much of a girl she was. "I'm as composed as I'll ever be. Oh, and you're right. Coffee and gems. Your description is on point." Thank God she did not hurl on him or in his truck. She would have performed hara-kiri, because the embarrassment would haunt her until the end of her days. As it was, she wasn't going to sleep peacefully for a while from the entire night's events.

"Come." Sabin said and withdrew his hand from her back. She appreciated his lack of comments towards her epic failure. Though his amusement was clear as day by the way bubbles fizzed all along her tongue.

No other incidence occurred while they made their way out of the parking garage into the Denny's or while they were ordering. Though the waitress did raise an eyebrow at the seven different dishes Sabin ordered, she jotted them all down without a word. Throughout that entire time, Tullia's embarrassment became nonexistent with the growing presence of famine within her and the symphony of smells overwhelming her nose. The Denny's on Fremont Street was an interesting blend of modern meets retro meets industrial meets Vegas. There were neon lights, an alcohol section, crisscrossing line designs on the mustard walls, bubble lights and dingy brown booths, tables and chairs. Tullia thought that a stripper pole would be a beautiful addition to really tie everything together nicely, but sadly that was absent from the decor.

Tullia glanced frequently at Sabin's imposing form sitting across the table. Even glamoured, he was still a towering presence. His frame took up the entire booth across from her, and he wasn't even sprawled out. His muscles stood out and seemed to gleam under the artificial light. Which made him seem just so… male. Even though his face was plain it almost looked like a blur in motion. She had only ever read about men like him, the three B's: Big. Broad. And bad-ass. Tullia sneaked a glance, at him, taking a sip of water. She thought men that looked like him were all fictional or photo-shopped. Even without his filter on from the vape glamour, Sabin was just massive in stature. The only thing that was disconcerting currently was his face. It seemed…. wrong. His filter face wasn't compatible with his body and if anything, he looked slightly awkward with it applied. The face mumbled ambiguous while his stature screamed 'climb me while I flex'. Tullia put her face in her hand, now that she had her faculty about her, the dawning realization that she was openly hardcore ogling him was just… just *no*.

Tullia pulled in a deep drink of her water, trying to quench all her thirsts as she forced herself to inspect the Denny's interior again. It was a bit dingy and dim, but it smelled good and was temperate. Always a bonus. It was also a not too crowded, though there were enough people in it to keep the waitresses from idling about. There was a withered old man who sat hunched over his simple plate of eggs and toast, a group of three people who looked completely smashed from the night, and two couples that were chatting quietly. The vibe of the Denny's was sluggish, hungover but harmless. Tullia looked back to Sabin to see *him* studying *her*. She quickly looked away and focused on the lethargic waitress fussing over the menu holder. Tullia touched the tip of her tongue to her upper lip in contemplation. What does one talk about with their rescuer? They were *technically* strangers connected by a single traumatic event. An event that Tullia had no desire to ever talk about and relive again, so reminiscing is off the table of conversation. Also, she may have, kinda, sort of, a slight (a huge) hero complex towards him. Though it was still developing, Tullia had read enough fantasy books to know the signs.

Internally sighing, she forced herself into a lecture on stranger danger and the ever-changing nature of humans. Nice to your face, mean behind your back. Humans also are only self-interested, so for someone to rescue her, she must have been a bonus item or an 'in the moment task' that cost nothing extra. However, she argued, she was sitting in a Denny's with said stranger. Also are witches considered humans? Or are they human but the 'extra' version? As in, they have the sauce, and humans are sauce-less? Would that be considered racist if she didn't consider them human? Was Sabin human?

She looked at Sabin who was still staring at her. She blinked in surprise then squeezed her hands together nervously under the table.

"You seem to be busy in your thoughts. Want to share?"

She shrugged, striving for nonchalance, "I'm peachy."

His look was skeptical, but he leaned back and gave her a slight smile. "Doubtful."

Tullia shot him a look, that was clearly meant to mock him, but Sabin looked unfazed.

"You must have curiosity." She sat straighter in her seat at his words, her hands lacing together in an effort to keep still. The words were like an invitation and by the way Sabin's smile widened a fraction, it was confirmed to be. "Do you have any questions? I'll answer as many of them as I can."

This was the green light she needed, and damn if she won't slam her foot down on the gas and go.

Tullia leaned forward, placing her hands on top of the table, "You killed the vampires, right?"

A firm nod. Good. Now, to go through in sequential order all the questions that had been accumulating thus far in the past two hours.

"Why are you dressed like a ninja?"

He raised his eyebrow, "Ninja? This is mercenary attire."

"Even the mask?" She twirled her finger towards his face

"Face coverings are known throughout the world." His answers lacked any type of *pizzazz* that she was hoping for, but Tullia supposed she was being a bit fantastical. I mean, did she expect him to answer in a way a hot book character would?

Jokes on him though, because short-worded answers don't discourage her.

"Uh-huh." Her tone was doubtful, "Okay, so you're a mercenary then?" She mimicked him by raising (she thinks) her eyebrow at him.

Sabin cocked his head ever so slightly, his eyes held a gleam in their golden depths. "Of sorts."

Tullia furrowed her eyebrows at the blatant evasion. "That was ambiguous."

He took a sip of his water and looked expectantly at her, waiting for more questions. She gave a huff, miffed at him.

Okay, now it seemed the joke was to be on her.

"Are there other people such as Chandra and the vampires of different… um factions?" How does one accomplish being politically correct with supposed mythological creatures?

Sabin amused grin told her she was being a bit *extra* with her wording. "Yes, there are other factions of creatures."

It took a moment for his answer to sink into her. Suddenly, a sharp crack within vibrated her entire being occurred, shifting her viewpoint and her entire mind frame began to splinter.

"Are… are shapeshifters real?" She asked hesitantly.

A nod.

"God, you're scary. All vacant like and seeing creepy things."

"Fairies?" Her heartbeat sped up.

A nod.

Think within the box. Act normal. Act normal. Act— Look at those fairies!

"Dragons?" She strove to keep her tone normal, but her lungs were having a hard time filling up with oxygen.

A nod.

"Let's try cognitive therapy this time…"

"Naga?" Her head spun as memories upon memories fought for attention.

Sabin paused, seeming to think, "They exist, just not in this realm. The same goes for a lot of other creatures."

Realms?

"It's not normal to see and believe what you do."

"There are other realms? Like, different worlds?" Tullia's voice finally became breathy with excitement as soft memories from her visions drifted by gently.

Exotic jungles.

Underwater cities.

Season changing towns.

Blue suns.

Sabin gave a nod.

Tullia looked down at the scratched tabletop. Her hands were chubby, stumpy, and pale against the dark wood. She swallowed the lump of emotional excitement that was lodged in her throat. The creatures and the places of her visions… they existed. If the vampire slaying mercenary ninja said it was true, after rescuing her from being a part of a human cattle farm, then it simply must be true. She felt as though a darkness, that had laced itself firmly in her mind, took a massive blow and loosened its tentacles a bit.

Joy surged forth within her, making her tears struggle to break though the surface. She. Would. Not. Cry.

Swallowing again to keep the tears locked tight in her chest, she inhaled deeply and focused on breathing. After a few minutes, the urge to cry dissipated and she felt as though she had some semblance of control. She looked up at Sabin with dry eyes as her foundation crumbled away and sunshine began to peak through.

Sabin didn't say anything, probably didn't know why she was becoming so tense and emotional, but he quietly watched her slowly regain her composure with gentle gilded eyes. And his quiet, but strong presence was soothing to her.

She cleared her throat, composed, and began to unleash the hoard of questions that flooded her frontal lobe mercilessly. "How many realms are there?" Her voice was thick.

Sabin eyed her, but he shrugged. "I'm not sure. Many."

"Have you been to one of them?" She asked, leaning in closer over the tiny table.

His eyes smiled. "A few."

Tullia beamed at him, and her excitement possessed her legs to kick straight out… and made violent contact with Sabin's shins.

The man didn't even flinch upon the smashing force. But Tullia's heart nearly leaped out of her throat in both embarrassment and pure horror.

"I am so sorry!" She ducked under the table to inspect his shins. She couldn't see any damage, he was wearing long pants, but surely, he'd have the beginnings of a bruise. She kicked with everything she had in her.

A wild laugh, soft, but unhindered, had Tullia peeking up to see Sabin's glamoured face creased with a broad smile. His eyes were liquid pools of gold that shimmered with mirth. Bubbles and sweetness consumed her mouth, as Sabin shook his head, still smiling. "Sweetness, your little kick was not hard enough to warrant your reaction. It was like a flower brushing up against my skin. It did not hurt."

"Oh." Tullia struggled back up to sit correctly in her seat, and mid-rise just then three waitresses came over to their table with their arms full of plated food. They gave Tullia an odd look, though not a surprised look, and hurried on.

"Okay, so here's the salted caramel and banana cream pancakes with a side of bacon." She set that down in front of Tullia gently, "And here is the loaded veggie omelet, the ham and cheese omelet, one fit slam, veggie skillet, wild Alaskan salmon, fruit bowl, and the sirloin steak." She gave a small, slightly aggrieved huff before asking, "Anything else?"

"A refill on both drinks please." The woman nodded and took their empty water glasses away.

Tullia finally managed to untwist her body enough to get back up on the booth seat, though she banged the table multiple times and the rattling of everything on the table just made it more dramatic than it needed to be. Feeling far too winded from the tiny amount of movement, she pushed her hair out of her face, and sniffed, "Well, you may be fine now, but you'll feel the pain of my cement scuffing kick tomorrow."

Sabin just grinned with his plain face, his eyes still shining, and the slight crinkling occurred in the corner. "I'll make a note of that." He grabbed his utensil and stabbed his omelet with an interesting intensity, as if he was keeping it in place.

She touched the tip of her tongue to her upper lip, savoring the perfect flavor of humor and happiness, though there was a slight edge of heat underneath it.

She looked down at her awesome little tower of pancakes. Her stomach gave a battle cry of hungry, demanding the flood gates (her mouth) to open and let the pancakes in. For the threat of her stomach eating itself was very real at that moment.

But first, a river of syrup must christen the flat little slopes.

Tullia began to cut up her pancakes into too big pieces and dowsed her entire plate in a sea of thick, sweet, and sinful syrup. She felt the judgment of eyes and looked up to find Sabin looking at her plate with a sort of unbelieving look.

Tullia gave him a dirty look. "Don't judge my syrup consumption."

Sabin's eyes clashed with her; a teasing light returned his eyes. "Moderation."

Tullia scoffed. "I will have as much syrup as I want, sir."

Sabin gave a very tiny smile. "Wouldn't pouring it in a glass be easier?"

The sweet fizz tingled on her tongue.

Tullia gave him a sarcastic smile, before shoving a piece of pancake dripping in syrup into her mouth, she crossed her eyes at him, to let him know she was in ecstasy.

The smile did not leave his face, even when the waitress dropped off their drinks, leaving them alone once more. They ate in silence for a few minutes, savoring the food that was mediocre but satisfying to an empty stomach. When the first wave of Tullia's hunger was satiated, she swallowed and asked, "So, what realms have you been too?"

She felt a gob of syrup slide down her chin. She smacked the napkin over her face, hoping she stopped the bastard in its sticky track.

Sabin took neat, but precise bites, tearing it into his food in a way that was just shy of being animalistic.

"I went to a realm named Zerzura." He said between bites.

Zerzura.

She'd seen that place. Had seen what a traveler saw when he accidentally wandered into the gorgeous oasis from a never-ending desert. She had heard him call out that name, Zerzura in a frantic and elated voice. It was a white city that was overrun with little birds. The city gleamed like glass under the unforgiving sun of the desert and around the city walls were troves of lush vegetation and colorful flowers that held a dewy appearance as if they were just rained upon. Entering through the great white arched pillars of the city's entrance, a pool of crystal-clear water gently rippled in the still air and was overtaken by brightly colored water lotuses. There were towering palm trees, potted plants, and brightly painted pottery everywhere to be seen. But there were no people. Instead, tiny little white birds hopped around on the ground, flitted over the city, nested quaintly in the windows and chirped happily to one another all throughout the city.

Tullia leaned forward, quickly swallowing her pancake. "Did you see the little birds? Aren't they cute?"

Sabin gave her a measured look. "Yes, there were white birds everywhere. They followed me everywhere too in the city."

An image rose in her mind of Sabin in his full out ninja gear trotting through the city with a tiny hoard of white birds following him. Like a big bad momma duck and the fluffy babies bumble behind him.

She giggled, taking another bite of her pancake.

"So, how'd ya get to Zerzura?" She asked around the pancake in her mouth. But she put her hands in front so that she didn't display her partially chewed food. Therefore, she was still classy.

Sabin observed Tullia with a thoughtful look. "I was contracted to find the treasure hidden there."

Tullia chewed her pancake while pushing her ultra-sweet pancake pieces around her plate, digging deep within her for patience, so she wouldn't be that person bouncing in their seating asking, *'what happens next?!'* every second.

Sabin must have picked up on her 'please-continue-or-I'll-die" vibes, for he gave her a small smile and soft bubbles popped along her tongue. "I was contracted by a wealthy man, to seek out the treasure of Zerzura based upon the passages in the Kitab al Kanuz," Sabin shrugged. "It's considered a lost book of hidden treasures of the desert. According to the book, there were treasures of kings and queens in Zerzura."

"What did it look like?" Her voice went soft, her anticipation, her expectation seizing her lungs in an anxious squeeze.

He shrugged; his eyes held a gleam in them. "The Kita al Kanuz? Old and falling apart."

Tullia slapped the table lightly, the lightness of his tease making her smile. "No! Not the book, the realm! The realm man! Zerzura."

Sabin took a sharp bite of his egg, a tiny crease of a smile on his lips.

Then his face became clinically reminiscent. "It was a most unusual place. The realm itself, behaved oddly, as though it wasn't there until it wanted to be."

Tullia furrowed her eyebrows, "What do you mean?"

Sabin's gold eyes looked like perfect pools, deep and fathomless with sparks popping up every now and then.

Sabin took another bite, swallowed, then explained, "Usually, realm openings are more stable." He paused then a sardonic grin overtook his bland glamoured face. "Or should I say less traveling. Realm entrances remain stationary. However, with Zerzura that was not the case." The smile fell away, and Sabin took two giant bites of salmon, chewed twice, swallowed then drank his entire glass of water.

"I wandered the sand sea for weeks, trying to get into Zerzura. The description in the lost book was vague and unhelpful. The only thing I saw was miles and miles of sand and nothing else." Sabin polished off three plates of food by then, and stacked them on the side, "After the third week, I was walking and nearly ran into the white stone wall that encased the city." He shook his head. "I'm still not sure how I even managed to get into the city. It just… appeared before me."

Tullia felt a smile stretch over her face, she leaned her cheek on the back of her hand, "Did you find the treasure?"

He shook his head, "No."

Tullia frowned, "You didn't? Isn't it a city of the treasures of kings and queens?"

"It is indeed called that, but I don't think it was ever a tangible treasure. I believe it was more the city itself is the treasure that any king or queen would covet." He said.

"That is so deep." Tullia said softly.

Sabin chuckled, shaking. "It's only my thoughts. The only description that was accurate was the whiteness of the city. White stone walls, white pillars, white birds. There wasn't much color, except for the plants and water."

"Well," Tullia began slowly, then her questions just poured out, "if you didn't find the treasure, then what happened? Did you get in trouble with your boss?"

She needed answers.

The flavor that penetrated her mouth was spicy and sweet bubbles. "No. I did not receive a punishment. The man already had his greedy eyes on his next treasure location, so he wasn't too put out."

"So, you went on another treasure hunt?" She took a bite of the bacon she had. It was chewy. The absolute best. "Where'd you go?"

Sabin shook his head, "No, I turned him down when he offered me a second job. I'm not too fond of treasure hunting."

Tullia tilted her head in inquiry, "Why?" Treasure hunting sounded amazing and fun and adventurous and the definition of 'living' in her mind.

Sabin stabbed a piece of pineapple, and popped it into his mouth, "Treasure is troublesome because it usually belongs to someone, and they are not too eager to give it up. Especially if that treasure is detailed in an ancient, vague script." He tipped back his empty glass of water and took a few ice pieces in his mouth. He crunched on the ice, then sucked in a breath through his teeth. "Usually, the dead are often the nastiest to retrieve treasure from. They have multiple traps and curses set upon their treasures." Sabin shook his head, as if to shake off the memories, "It's taxing."

"I see, too much for you, huh?" Tullia teased. She so would treasure hunt if she could. Going to beautiful places… seeing things…adventuring…

Indiana Jones style.

Sabin shrugged, unbothered.

Tullia giggled, feeling giddy and nearly intoxicated with bliss. This was fun. Another person had actually physically been to where she was told she was crazy for seeing. That knowledge, and the fact that vampires nearly sucked her dry, made her feel a bit bolder than she usually would be.

"Have you ever seen a Merrow?" Tullia felt her heart racing as her mind swirled with every creature that she had ever seen in her hallucinations. Naga, fairies, Light Elves, Dark Elves….

She was wondering just how much he could confirm…

He shook his head, "No."

"How about fairies?"

He shook his head again.

"Fae folk?"

Another shake of his head.

She held up her hands, mostly to calm her racing mind. "Okay," she said, feeling her heart sink just a bit in her chest. "I want to know, what an … actual myth is? Like what doesn't exist?"

"Diet pills." He said dryly, taking another bite of egg. It was impressive he packed away that much food, but then again with his stature it made sense.

She wished she could eat that much. There'd be heavy consequences if she ate like him.

Tullia glared at him for that answer, but the uncontrollable smile on her face provably lessened the intensity. Sabin gave her a slight smile again.

"I mean, what is *real* and what was purely made up by humans in all the myths of the world?"

Sabin seemed to ponder her question for a few slow minutes, taking a few bites in between, then eventually, he let out a breath. He twisted his head slightly to the side, "That's… not quite an easy question to answer. Yes, a lot of ancient human *mythology*," His tone twisted slightly, and the taste in her mouth was tart, "is indeed true, but I'm not certain all the creatures existed. The witches would know more, but their knowledge always comes at a price."

He didn't say they didn't exist, just he wasn't sure which ones existed. Tullia sat back as everything sunk in; from the night she had, to her childhood visits to the psychiatrist office, to her isolation within her own family, the labels she was forced under. She became lightheaded with both euphoria and rage. All these years, all her life she was labeled mentally disturbed and in merely five minutes that notion was shattered. In reality, she was enlightened.

Well, okay sort of crazy, at this point in life she certainly wasn't working with a full deck of cards, but she was a sprinkle of enlightenment of sorts. She just needed more information.

She looked up at Sabin, his glamour plain and odd paired with his striking eyes. "Are you a mythical creature too?" She asked softly.

She watched as Sabin's face remained completely smooth, but the taste of sweaty feet, bitterness, pure fire and salt assaulted her mouth. Sabin's tone was unruffled as he said, "I am but a mere human." His lips twisted in an ironic smile.

Tullia's heart skidded to a stop and her brain began to reprimand her as she struggled to refrain from gagging from the flavors of his emotions.

How dare she ask that.

What the hell was her problem?

So rude.

She swallowed against the cacophony of tastes from Sabin and against her inner scolding. "Sabin, I'm very sorry, that was so rude of me. I—"

Sabin held up his hand to silence her, "No offense was made." He eyed her plate, "Eat more. You are far too little."

The intensity of the flavors dulled but they remained there. Distant, but still there. Swallowing again, Tullia nodded obediently and shoved the pancake in her mouth. Once sweet, was now tasteless… and she missed the sweet fizz from Sabin.

She totally ruined the mood, which wasn't surprising.

Shoveling as much of her pancake as she could tolerate, Tullia and Sabin sat in silence for a few minutes eating. When majority of her food was gone, and her stomach threatened a revolt, Tullia ventured into questioning Sabin just once more. Though she wouldn't get carried away this time.

She'd have control over her wayward tongue.

Tullia cleared her throat, "So, um. how did you find the warehouse?" She said slowly, glancing at Sabin, "Did you know that vampires were there?"

Sabin gave her a small smile, a smile that was starting to make her heart do weird things. Like sweet. And twist. It was odd. "Vampires are menaces to any society. The witches that control Las Vegas have a special unit that hunt vampires. I was hired 'cause this was the largest nest in the last couple hundred years they had seen. Or so they told me." He shrugged, uncaring. "Once the warehouse was confirmed as a nest, I was called in to dispose of the vampires."

"Why is there a need for vampire extermination?" Tullia asked, then rolled her eyes and held up her hand as if to pause the situation. "Okay, dumb question. Let me revise, why are the witches exterminating the vampires?"

Sabin bit into a strawberry. "Vampires are self-serving creatures. They don't care for anything other than their food source, which is human blood. This threatens the secrecy of the witch community."

Tullia contemplated for a moment. "Why do the... witches want to remain a myth in today's world?" She didn't quite understand. Wouldn't it be hard to live as a secret? Besides, there are a lot of people who considered themselves wiccan. It wouldn't be considered too weird in today's times.

Sabin gave her a grim smile, "Witches are akin to the mafia... on a global scale. They have their claws in every honey pot around the world. In order to maintain that type of control, they need to remain part of the human lore."

At Tullia's shocked look, Sabin nodded with a serious expression.

"Witches are running a worldwide Mafia?" She was still suck on that.

Sabin gave a small shrug, "They call it a cultural practice."

Tullia giggled as Sabin pushed all his empty plates to the side, folding his arms in front of him. "Besides, humans," He looked at her and cocked one eyebrow, "Well, majority of humans have an innate fear of the supernatural. It would be chaos if the witches were to come out."

Sadly, she couldn't argue against Sabin's logic. There would've been a massive either witch hunt or a race to create a device for their magic control.

Tullia leaned forward, new questions tripping off her tongue. "How did you learn to fight vampires?"

Sabin shrugged, "I fought them for many years."

"How many years?"

"Many." And that was it.

It was like pulling teeth. Would it kill him, physically kill him, to add a few more words in?

She gave a hard, gusty sigh. "So, you became a vampire exterminator?"

Sabin again shrugged, glancing away.

Would it be impolite to smack him?

It probably would be. He was feeding her, and he did save her, even though she was a bonus item in his little vampire exterminating quest, it still counts because she was alive to eat. So, she decided she'd have to simply keep asking in tiny bite sized pieces. Since he liked to give bite sized answers.

Tullia chewed on her last piece of crispy bacon as she thought over the night.

"Hey, do you still have your axes on you right now?"

Sabin nodded, watching her with quiet, gold eyes.

She furrowed her eyebrows, noting the way his posture was perfectly straight, but his back did not touch the seat behind her. "Are they comfortable to wear?"

He gave her a small smile, "They are familiar, so they are a comfort."

"Why axes? Why not a sword? Or nun-chucks?"

The waitress came over, her face blank and tired. "Any dessert?"

Sabin looked at Tullia, to which she shook her head. "The pancakes were dessert." She smiled up at the waitress, but the waitress only nodded and put down the bill. After a mumbled "Take your time." She was then gone.

Sabin reached his hand in his pocket and put down a few bills. Tullia's eyes widened when she saw the three-hundred-dollar bills sitting lightly on top of the checkbook. "I was trained to use many weapons. However,

I took to the ax naturally."

Sabin stood up, "Come now, sweetness."

Tullia stood up, feeling unsettled, numb and relatively happy. The strangest emotional combination, but not one she was against.

She followed him out. A balmy breeze and shy sunlight that began to stretch out. The ending of the summer in Vegas was an exciting moment. Everyone waited for the temperature to become less blistering and perhaps only stay in the low 90's.

She looked up to the sky, squinting at the beautiful clear sky. It was odd that everything was beautiful today. Everything looked clean and fresh, when mere hours ago, in the velvet folds of the night, a horror had stained her seemingly irrevocably.

"Come now, sweetness." Sabin said softly, beside her.

Tullia turned to look at him. "Where are we going?"

Sabin gave her a full-blown baring of his teeth in his glamoured illusion. "We are going to stop by my home. I have… a *notion* that someone will be waiting for us."

His slightly aggressive and sharp tone, not to mention the spice that dashed over her tongue told her he wasn't pleased about his little feeling. But the bubbles that accompanied the heat was an excitement that was odd to Tullia. It almost seemed as though he was eager for the confrontation.

Chapter Six

The drive to Sabin's home was nice. She was the fullest she had felt in years and Sabin told her more about the realms he visited. Well, she continuously asked question after question until she was able to put together a fuller picture with Sabin's short answers. They chatted (Mostly Tullia doing all the chatting) all the way up until Sabin turned off his truck in the parking lot. Tullia looked around curiously, they were once again in an underground parking lot that was brightly flooded with giant lights, though they were unnecessary due to the bright desert sun rays stretching out to nearly every corner of Vegas.

"Come on, sweetness." Tullia followed suite and got out of Sabin's truck. She trailed behind him slightly through the full parking lot into a neatly kept courtyard with giant palm trees, a gated pool, and typical desert bushes. Looking around, Tullia was delighted by the white and turquoise theme of the apartment complex. It looked cute and cheery and old, but still charming in its own way.

Sabin led her up a set of metal stairs to the second level that looked over the courtyard with the pool glimmering invitingly under the sun. Sabin glanced back at her, his gold eyes churning, as he unlocked his door. He gave her a nod, as if to tell her to be ready, and opened the door.

Tullia jerked back in fright as Chandra stood in the doorway, glaring up at Sabin with a vicious look that spoke of torture, blood, and body bags.

Heavy heat coated her tongue accompanied by an acidic tang made the lingering sweetness of her pancake get demolished.

Sabin seemed unsurprised, his glamoured face cold and utterly emotionless. He pushed by her, clicking his tongue in disapproval, "I see you witches lack common decency."

Chandra's lips curled. "Oh, you wanna talk about manners?" she stalked in after him, "Do you know what time it is?" She bit out. She didn't let Sabin answer, instead she hissed, "It's seven thirty-two." She held out one finger as she bared her teeth, "You have deliberately kept me waiting for an hour. You have nothing in your fridge and your home is boring."

"I do not recall making a commitment to your demand." Sabin's tone, frost covered steel was the softest sound. Tullia nervously took a step in Sabin's house, noting the heavy scent of pine and male musk that was very distinctly Sabin. Swallowing the thick emotions in the room, Tullia stayed hoovering between the threshold of the door and the outside.

Is she allowed in…?

Ask if her words were spoken aloud, Sabin turned to looked at her. "Come in, Tullia. Pay no mind to the wretched wench."

"Wench?! Why you son of whore." Chandra growled.

Tullia took two more steps inside a small studio apartment that was clean, tidy, and sparse. There was a little brown wooden table with one brown chair in front of the door right next to the air conditioner. There was a massive bed a few feet behind the chair that didn't have a single pillow on it and was covered with deep green sheets with two nightstands on each side. Behind the bed, Tullia saw a closet taking up the back wall of the studio. The kitchen was diagonal to the bed and had simple white cabinets, a small refrigerator, stove and sink. There was a small strip of brown tile where the kitchen was, but the rest of the studio was covered in brown carpet.

Very quaint, very cute. Tullia thought standing awkwardly by the door, unsure of where to go next or if she should offer to take her magic flip flops off.

Chandra's gorgeous face turned towards Tullia. "Well, don't stand there now, hon. Shut the door and take a seat. We have things we need to discuss."

"I could dismember you here with little effort. This is a great insult." Sabin's tone held a slithering darkness that tasted of heavy iron and cold, cold ice.

Chandra didn't say anything, but judging by her action ready stance, she was ready for him to attack. Tullia coughed a little and padded in deeper into his home. She made her way to the bed since Chandra was blocking her way to the kitchen chair. Tullia resisted the childish urge to flop on the bed, as she habitually did on her own. She gently sat on the bed, kicked off her magic made flip flops and repressed her sigh. His bed was so soft. She hadn't sat on a soft bed in years. She sucked in both lips to keep from laying back to appreciate the full softness of the mattress. Cause that may be slightly weird and the atmosphere would dampen her full enjoyment.

To attempt to lighten the heaviness in the air, Tullia chirped, "I like your home. It's very cute."

"You mean spartan and dull." Chandra said, shifting her eyes to Tullia for a split second before going back to Sabin.

"Thank you, Tullia." Sabin said gently, the knife's edge poised in his tone. "Now, witch. Get on with what you need to say. I am busy."

She gave him a seething look, "I already told you, the Grand High needs to examine her. This is a phenomenon that cannot be ignored."

Tullia stiffened. *Examined?* She didn't want to be examined, especially since Chandra hinted at it being more of an experimental test subject situation.

Let's cut her open and see what makes her tick...

Tullia laced her fingers together nervously against her stomach. She wanted to say something, but at the same time, keeping quiet might be a good route in case of the need to escape. She looked up at Sabin, looking to see if he was—. She blinked in surprise to see his entire body stiff and his glamour gone. His black ninja mercenary gear was fully engaged and the fact that only his vibrant gold eyes were exposed, made him appear... lethal and ominous.

Was this really the same person who ate breakfast with her?

"No." A hard word from Sabin.

Tullia looked at Chandra, there were faint little wisps of blue smoke wafting from her person. She made a face of disbelief, "No? You've misunderstood. This is not a request. It is not even for you to decide. You're not even involved. It is happening with or without your consent."

"No." He said again, and the words seemed to pull the air down with its weight.

Chandra shifted, her dark eyes flashing with steel, "You have no say in this. Everything that came from the vampire nest is property of the Black Blood Coven. Including her." She nodded her head at Tullia.

Tullia's heartbeat sped up in fright as heat and iron fought along her palette. The thought of being demoted from a person to a piece of property made her self-worth take a hit. She curled into herself a little, gnawing at her lips with anxiety.

Her fate, as a person, was in this conversation and her damn vocal cords decided to seize up.

Sabin inhaled slowly, as if to summon patience, "Your words mean nothing to me. Your coven means nothing to me. Tullia is under my protection."

"You? Claiming to protect someone without any cash present?" Chandra spat, the blue little tendrils were increasing in thickness and lengthening around her.

"I'm not the same as you witches. I do not abuse those under my care."

"You don't have people." She hissed as a shot of acid scalded Tullia's tongue.

Tullia scraped her tongue on the edges of her teeth, to try and dissolve the sting.

Okay, so this conversation was all about Tullia without a single word from her. That's super great. The doom and gloom vibe that swelled up from her gut was awesome. Her stomach clenched tight with stress; her mouth was on fire from all the anger occurring… this was a perfect morning to the night she had.

Very fitting indeed.

Chandra shifted into a crouch. Her face was lined with anger, and her posture became aggressive. She opened her hands, clawing them in the air. "Hired help, should keep their mouths shut."

Sabin moved, he shifted to stand in front of Tullia so that now all she saw was his tightly clenched back and butt. Tullia sucked in her lips, well, this view wasn't terrible in the least bit she thought with a little flutter in her knotted stomach.

"And witches should be burned." He said with an ice-cold tone.

A guttural hiss of scalding rage came from Chandra, and she shifted as thin blue smoke wafted from her form, though she did not attack. Tullia looked between Sabin and Chandra with an awkward, confused and frightened mindset as they both engaged in a deadlock stare. She felt like a third wheel in this anger battle.

"Leave." Sabin murmured, and the soft word dripped and writhed with malice as it clawed the air. Blood and heat kissed her tongue as Chandra bared her teeth.

"No. The Grand High is on her way here. We *will* all wait." Chandra bit out viciously.

Sabin didn't move a muscle, his big body a statue, but his aura shifted into something that slithers in the darkness and soaks in stale blood. He was silent as he reached back and withdrew one of his black axes.

Violence in the air hung heavy and charged as Chandra held up her hands that began to spark.

Tullia shivered as the promise of gore began to saturate the stodgy air. She scraped her teeth against her bottom lip nervously and scooted back on the bed a bit, curling slightly into herself.

"You sure you want to gain the most powerful clan in the country as your enemy?" Chandra's tone was low and slightly distorted, deeper with a rasp.

Sabin, in answer, raised his giant ax up in silence.

There was a suspended moment, as the air stilled and crystallized with pugnacious frost.

Tullia looked between them and swallowed nervously. She maybe should have said something a bit sooner…. Tullia opened her mouth to attempt to ease the violence in the air, but there was a soft whisper in her ear. "Where's popcorn when you need it, am I right?" The whisper caused Tullia to stiffen, her entire stomach turned to stone, as her bladder fainted. Her lungs collapsed and pushed up all the air up her throat that ripped out of her mouth as a deafening shriek of pure terror.

Tullia's entire center of gravity lurched away from the source of the whisper, causing her being to be thrown off the bed and tumble down jarringly to the hard floor.

As Tullia's scream died an abrupt death from the floor's greeting, a peal of high-pitched laughter above her rang out. Her poor heart had leapt into her throat and Tullia was disoriented from the sudden and brutal fright. Big hands gently gripped her upper arms and swiftly hauled her to her feet. The warm hands steadied her as she swayed.

"Are you harmed?" Sabin asked in a low voice, shoving her behind his massive, ninja covered body.

"N-no." Tullia stuttered out, her limbs jerky and disorientated.

"Awe, poor baby." A chiming voice cooed mockingly.

Tullia forced her body to calm the hell down enough to regain enough of her senses. She peaked out from behind Sabin's form to see Chandra still in a defensive position with a floating woman besides her.

The woman grinned and waggled her unnaturally long, sharp looking fingers. "Heya, how you doin' over there?"

Tullia blinked, then her eyes nearly popped out of their sockets in disbelief. Then her heart sped up in excitement and wonder. This woman embodied the title 'Grand High' and actually looked like the queen of witches.

Tullia stared at the Grand High in somewhat of a starstruck manner. First the vampire's, then witches, and now the Queen of the witches...

She was in a weird place being heaven and hell.

"Your highness..." Chandra began but was swiftly silenced when the woman held up her hand...with unnaturally long fingers tipped with sharp looking nails. She stared at Tullia's pale face peeking out from behind a massive biceps. And Tullia stared right back at her.

The queen that floated with her long legs crossed as if she were merely lounging on a beach chair, was wrapped in a pair of dark blue jeans, bare feet decorated with jewels, and a shiny ivory crop top that plunged down to her navel. She had long black hair that was braided into tiny braids with tiny gold charms all throughout her locks that defied gravity too, floating as though in water around a lovely face.

The majority of the Grand High's exposed skin was a deep midnight black with thick strokes of snow white across her eyes, around her jaw, over her mouth, down her neck and in cute little spots down her bare arms that swayed gently at her waist. Her big eyes were pure black with no pupil or white sclera to be seen and out lined in a smoky gold color. She had bold features with blood red lips, and a royal forehead. Her body, that lounged in the air, was voluptuously long and seemed to exude a sensuality.

To sum up, she was drop dead gorgeous.

Her onyx eyes, seemed to shift over to look at Sabin, "Sabin," She purred with ice and venom.

"Witch." His tone was an arctic whip. The temperature took a nosedive as the continued hostility continued to hang heavy in the air.

Sabin stood unmoved with his ax raised and did not respond to the cold greet.

The Grand High tilted her head to the side, her pure obsidian eyes shifting back to look at Tullia. As her head tilted, her suspended body began to slowly tilt as well, until she was completely upside down. Her long braids were still perfectly in place around her face and her lounged position did not change. "So, it's this girl." A long, long finger flicked out to point directly at her.

"Yes." Chandra said tightly.

The Grand High's eyes glinted black, and she smiled acerbically. The silence was suffocating with sour hostility.

"Tell me, why are you coveting Black Blood property?" She asked.

"Leave, witch. I will not ask again." Sabin said coldly.

The Grand High huffed. She spun right side up, crisscrossed her legs, and leaned forward with her fists on her hips. "Such disrespect to royalty. You tickle my rage, you annoying man." She suddenly disappeared and reappeared two inches away from Sabin's face. Her smile was cutting, "Beserker, gimme the girl. She's mine." She clawed her hands near his face but did not touch him.

"No." Sabin shoved his head forward and snapped his teeth at her so violently behind his mask that the chomp echoed loudly in the room and sent the Grand High disappearing and quickly re-appearing by Chandra in a theatrical puff of blue smoke.

"Naughty, naughty. We're all grown, why can't we just talk it out." Her eyes began to glow a pale blue color and her smile twisted into something sinister, "Or hey, I'm all for testing just how magic proof you really are." She stretched out and began to emit blue smoke from her person. She ran the tip of her tongue over her top teeth.

Oh, no. This is escalating to an unsafe level. Tullia tasted tangy metal of bloodlust and the spicy heat of anger. Swallowing thickly against the distasteful flavors, her poor mouth, Tullia gathered her non-existent courage and popped out from behind Sabin.

The Grand High was an interesting blend of a mischievous child and a cruel woman. She also liked to laugh. So, cruel humor was the only appropriate venue to take. She hoped. Tullia had no idea, but if all else failed at the very least it would offer a distraction from what was pissing everyone off.

Which… was her.

"Wanna hear a joke?" Tullia asked, as Sabin shifted to cover half of her body with his. Chandra shot her an incredulous look but refocused her attention on Sabin and the Grand High merely tilted her head in curiosity. Her glowing eyes latched on Tullia intensely.

There were screams and mysteries in the seemingly soulless depths of her eyes.

"Where did Sally go during the bombing?" Tullia waited for two beats of silence then said, "*Everywhere.*"

The Grand High blinked in surprise, then her sharp smile softened into an amused sort of grin. The blue smoke ceased, and the blood lust dropped from the atmosphere as the temperature warmed. Chandra rolled her eyes and withdrew from her crouch.

"If I may introduce myself your highness," Tullia began, bowing her head slightly, "My name is Tullia."

"Hmm, it seems you are quick on the uptake. I like that." The Grand High stared at her with unblinking, wide eyes as her lush mouth pursed in consideration. "You're the magnifier, huh?"

That analyzing look and the calculating air brought back flashes of when Tullia was trapped at the asylum. It made her feel like a teen again and the volatile emotions of back then came swarming up within her.

Damaged.

Trapped.

Useless.

Sabin growled, a sound that was more animalistic than human, distorting the phantom feelings until they were too wonky to perceive.

Tullia forced her ultra-bright 'I'm-totally-sane-right-now' smile to center herself. It was a knee jerk reaction, and most people smiled back, most did not look at her.

The Grand High eyed her, ignoring Sabin, and held out her hand towards Tullia, her razor-sharp nails glinting in the dim light. "Alright then, petal." She gave an expectant look at her, "Come here. Let's see how much of punch you really pack".

Tullia looked at the Grand High's perfectly manicured and supernaturally long fingers. It was almost hypnotic, the way her collage colored hands beckoned her to take it. She reached out but Sabin shoved a rather buff arm out across her chest, pushing her back a little.

The Grand High's obsidian eyes shot to Sabin, and she bared her teeth, "You're a buzz kill."

"I am not a forgiving man. You insulted me." Sabin voice was low, blood soaked and soft.

The Grand High bared her teeth at him and rolled her eyes. The taste of spice and vinegar made her tongue recoil and her mouth produce more saliva. Nasty…

"Fine." She withdrew her hand. Clicking her nails together a wad of cash dropped at Sabin's feet. "Forgiven now? Can we move on now?"

Sabin kicked the wad of cash deeper into his home, not once glancing down at it. His ax still poised and ready for a serious chop down.

The Grand High let out a dramatic sigh, throwing her hands up in the air. "So sensitive. Fiiiine, ya big baby." She clicked her nails twice and a loud thud behind Tullia made her flinch and whip around.

On Sabin's once modest and clean table sat mounds of crisp greenbacks that might actually be taller than Tullia.

"There. Now let me do my thing. You want us gone, don't you?" Tullia looked back at the Grand High to see her no longer floating and standing long, curved and dominate with her hands on her hips.

Sabin was silent for a few beats, then he lowered his arm from blocking Tullia. "Make it quick. And no games. I will not hesitate to sever your head from your body."

The Grand High gave a brilliant smile, turning her from gorgeous to heart stopping. "You're more than welcome to try, berserker." Her hair gently moved around her, still denying gravity's existence.

Her attention moved from Sabin to Tullia once more. The dark spotlight the witch put her under made Tullia's knees quiver. The Grand High waggled her too long fingers dramatically and a wilted tulip appeared right next to her. "Come here petal. Let us begin."

She glanced up at Sabin to see his honey gold eyes flat and dangerous as he stared at the Grand High.

"Hurry now petal. I'm a busy, busy witch." The Grand High cooed. Tullia turned to face the powerful witch. She tasted of steel, ice, and hot peppers. Her hand was extended out to her. Swallowing thickly, Tullia approached the Grand High, nervous and slightly damp from sweat, and placed her hand in the hands of a powerful witch.

She gripped Tullia's hand tightly, her face serious. The Grand High's hands were surprisingly warm and soft. Her hand began to smoky light blue. "Hmm, let me see here..." Her black eyes lightened until they glowed a bright blue color. Tullia watched as very thin smoke tendrils wrapped lightly around her wrist. There was a slightly pinch in the back of Tullia's throat, before the blue smoke began to withdraw slightly from Tullia's hands, as if frightened.

"What the..." The Grand High's brow furrowed in bewilderment, before the blue wisps suddenly clutched onto Tullia's hand and forearm. Tullia felt the wisps of magic throb lightly against her wrist, as if they contained individual pulses. At Chandra's loud gasp, both Tullia and the Grand High looked up sharply. The once withered dying tulip was now one of dozens fresh tulips and multiplying rapidly by the second. The Grand High stared at the flowers, then looked at Tullia. She flicked her free hand towards the flowers, and they fell in a heap to the floor and stopped proliferating.

A silence descended over the room as they all stared at the pile of perfectly bloomed tulips.

"Fascinating." The Grand High murmured, she clenched onto Tullia's hand harder, then her glowing blue eyes turned to consume her. "Let me taste you, petal." She opened her mouth wide, and a thick cloud of blue smoke came out and darted at her face. Tullia gave a short yelp as the blue smoke engulfed her face. She tried to move away but the Grand High held her in place. The smoke seemed to drag the air down, as if it were weighted and made it hard to inhale air. Her eyes began to sting and water as she struggled to intake air. Coughing, Tullia ripped her hand out of the Grand High's grip and stagger backwards. Her vision became blurred as tears tried desperately to clear the smoke from her eyes. Panic slowly crept back into her as air remained thin around her.

"Salty." The Grand High commented.

A hard hand caught her fumbling form and pressed her against a heated wall. There was a sharp swing of metal cutting air and a hard *thwack*.

"Oh relax, you oaf. She's fine." The Grand High's voice was exasperated. Another sharp sound, and a thick, meaty sound occurred.

A short scream of pain.

"Withdraw it. Or your henchman loses more limbs." Sabin growled.

A deep sigh, "So dramatic."

Tullia opened her mouth, sucking in more of the damning smoke before coughs racked her entire frame.

"Oh, you had something sweet recently. Syrup?" The Grand High giggled, another sharp swing and a meaty chop accompanied by a scream of pain.

Tullia blink, seeing nothing but blue and smoke…She wished the smoke would go away. There was a pinch in the back of her throat then suddenly the blue cloud dissipated abruptly as it had formed. There were more growls around her and words being thrown, but coughing roughly, Tullia only felt her entire body focus on the extreme effort it took to create convulsions to expel the lingering smoke. She gradually became aware that Sabin did not press her up against a wall, but rather press her up against his solid torso.

Almost made the whole blue cloud suffocating experience worth it for this moment.

There was high-pitched laughter that dominated the space and broke through to Tullia's frontal lobe.

The Grand High was laughing hysterically. Tears were streaming down her face and was hunched over with the force of her laughter. She was floating once more, in a crossed legged pose, her eyes pure midnight black and her face twisted with unnatural humor. "A human! A mere human is carrying the lost magic." She wiped her eyes, sighing with lingering mirth, "Honestly, if irony married contrariety then cheated with absurdity, it would be you, petal." She began to giggle again, "Lost magic contained in a *human!*"

Tullia curled away from her as the taste of rot bloomed over her tongue along with fizzy bubbles. Her eyes shifted away from the queen of witches and felt her eyes nearly fall out at the sight of Chandra hunched over pale faced as a pool of blood expanded around her. Her left hand was a bloody nub, with running streams of dark red blood. Tullia's eyes widened further when the fat blood drops from what was left of her leg, dripped steadily into the carpet. Though Chandra was a true bad-ass, for she was still poised to attack, her intact hand smoking blue and her face, though lined with pain, was twisted up in a barbaric expression of violence.

Tullia's body seemed to jerk with displayed surprise at the sight of a gravely injured woman. Sabin loosened his grip on her, only to shove her behind his massive body again.

Tullia opened her mouth, to inform them both that Chandra was bleeding out, but the Grand High's voice overruled her own, "Chandra, get patched up. You are no longer needed here."

"My Queen—" She began but was silenced when the Grand High looked at her.

She shot Sabin a nasty look to which he responded, "Don't forget your butchered bits, witch."

She flipped him off before blue smoke enveloped her and then dissipated, leaving the bloody space still bloody but now absent of the cause of blood.

"Now," A silky voice murmured, "Let's have an adult chat now." Tullia looked over to the Grand High to see her still floating, but this time she was mimicking the pose one would use when sitting in a chair. Her long legs were crossed, and her arms rested on either side like arm rests. Even though she sat on no throne, she embodied a queen. Tullia pressed closer to Sabin's heat to stave off the cold that wafted from the frosty calculating eyes of the Grand High.

"You, dear petal, are drenched in lost magic. So much so, that it seeps from your pores and attracts the chthonic magic, my type of magic, and amplifies its effects." She tilted her head, tapping a sharp tipped finger against her chin. "I bet my right boob you have experienced things that are 'extra' that humans normally don't. Vision? Voices? Visits?" Tullia didn't answer the Grand High, though it was clear she wasn't expecting Tullia to participate in the conversation as she powered on. "Lost magic is beyond rare. It's only been found as traces, *traces* a total of four times in the past seven centuries. So, for a mere human to have it is… a lot of it is bizarre to say the least." The Grand High continued to assess Tullia.

"Get to the point witch." Sabin snapped out, his black ax glinting sharply as Sabin raised it slightly higher, as if warning her.

The Grand High sniggered demeaning, "The point is, I want her."

Tullia's jaw dropped as her heart fluttered in a frenzy. When an insanely attractive person says that line, it wrecks the internal regulations within the body. And this was the first time anyone said they wanted Tullia. It didn't matter what she wanted her for, which was probably for experimentation purposes, it only mattered that she wanted her.

Tullia forced her mouth closed and resisted the urge to fan herself as her cheeks heated.

"Denied." Sabin swung his ax towards the Grand High… but his blade only met air.

"This is why I do somewhat like you. Always quick to violence. I love that aspect. The rest of you though, sucks." Her melodic voice commented from behind them, and Sabin twisted, snagging Tullia's waist as he threw his blade at the Grand High.

A tinkling laugh, that came from all around them, "Now, Sabin. We've had this little discussion before."

Sabin pulled out his other ax from the holster on his back.

A deep, irritated sigh, "Look, a human having lost magic is not a good thing. It's old, powerful and not well understood. It would be best to get her checked out."

Sabin's body was thrumming with tension, but he seemed to pause, listening…. Waiting.

The Grand High continued speaking, her voice a chiming tone of ersatz innocence. "It's for her best interest really. If I can taste her lost magic, then surely other creatures will be able to get the same vibe. That's most likely why the vampires snatched her up."

No, she was just in the wrong place at the wrong time. But the master vampire knew what she contained and wanted to keep her as a prized cattle in his live stock for the rest of her life.

Sabin paused, "What is your proposed cure then witch."

Her voice sounded in a different direction, this time, above them, but Sabin's stance remained unmoved. "Me? I have no idea what to do for it. None. Not a freaking clue."

"Then you are useless." He declared and swung both of his axes up at the ceiling. Tullia stiffened with fright as she stared at the black axes embedded in the ceiling. Some plaster sprinkled down. An arm snaked around her waist and re-positioned her to that her back was pressed up against a wall and her front was pressed up against Sabin's broad back.

Though there may have been a negative about the situation she was currently in, Tullia could not see them over the broadness, the firmness, or the warmth of Sabin's back.

"Berserker, while I may not know how to cure this phenomenon, but I know of a creature that would. Which is more than you'll ever fully be able to accomplish." An acid like degradation dripped from each word she said.

"And who would she see?" Sabin asked, his voice the personification of a level four earthquake. Rumbly, powerful, and unstoppable. Tullia peaked around Sabin, to see the Grand High popped up in front of them, blue smoke wafting softly from her curvy form. Her face was creased with smug superiority.

"Why a dragon of course." She rolled her R's in a purring manner.

Sabin rolled his shoulders, "Explain."

Her curved eyebrow twitched at the command and a vinegary flavor kissed her tongue. "I'll educate you since you're dumber than a sack of soggy socks. Dragons are old as hell and do not originate from the human realm. They have knowledge of odds and ends that have been long forgotten. If they're not insane by this current time, then their knowledge could rival that of the gods."

Sabin seemed to flinch slightly at the word, "You merely prattle. Leave, witch."

The Grand High sighed dramatically, she touched her hand to her forehead, "Let me educate you and the short-sighted tank of a man." She reclined in the air, and swirled her fingers, creating 3D red glowing stick people, "You see, the incident today will travel 'round. As I have said, lost magic is rare. So rare in fact, that many creatures do not believe in its existence, it's a wet dream myth." She grinned and the 3D people went crazy, "Chthonic magic as we witches like to call it is everyday magic. Nothing special, but gets the job done. It was the same magic used by the gods of the realm."

Sabin growled, clearly not interested in a history lesson.

"However," The Grand High rolled right along, the red stick figures morphed together to flip Sabin the bird, before returning into little stick figures running around, "Every realm contains the same magic. Chthonic magic, that comes from the elements, mainly the earth. Lost magic…" She paused, seeming to think, "is a completely different beast altogether. No one knows where it comes from, no one can hold it down long enough to study it or determine its origin. But one thing that is most popularly known about lost magic is its strength and its amplification of chthonic magic. All creatures are going to want to want her to get to the magic at any cost."

The Grand High looked at Tullia's peaking form with shrewd eyes.

"You leave her alone, she'll be either be dead, drained, enslaved or entombed by one of the factions within the week." The 3D red figures began to enact different torture and enslavement acts.

The taciturnity in her voice encased Tullia's nerves in ice. The Grand High tilted her head too far left. "She's all human, with a touch of magic. A dragon would be our best bet to know what to do with her."

"I find it suspicious of you to give this information." Sabin said slowly, after a pregnant pause. More plaster dusted down from the ceiling and floated down in the space between them.

The Grand High threw her head back and laughed, a sound that glistened in the dark, "Nothing is for free, you know that well berserker." She flipped her hair, the tiny braids making a soft rustling sound. "No, I want that lost magic to be transfer to *me*."

Sabin nodded, as if her reasoning made sense, then stepped to the side so that Tullia, who was a literal wall flower was now facing the Grand High.

"Do you wish this lost magic to be gone from your person?" Tullia turned her head to look at Sabin, his golden gaze, clear and serene, was on her.

Tullia opened her mouth, but words clogged at her throat.

Sabin watched her closely, "You can say no. Do not let the witch's words sway your heart."

She looked back at the Grand High with her beautifully designed face and thought, to know that she wasn't insane, that her visions were forced upon her by an outside force that caused her to suffer throughout her life, was enough of a comfort and conviction for her. She would have been satisfied with that. However, to have the chance to live free without visions of different realms and creatures interfering with her life...? To live normally. To be able to go to school or get a decent job? To be able to watch a movie fully... to be able to simply live without interruptions.

She had lived with this supposed lost magic her entire life, been labeled insane because of it. She had learned to operate and survive with the magic hindering her in her daily life, but she was not thriving, she was just stagnated. She was living in a shady motel and worked as maid. She didn't have any friends; she didn't have anything to look forward to in life and she didn't have... a life basically.

"I want it gone." Tullia said firmly, at that end thought, staring at the Grand High.

The Grand High gave a faint smile before looking at Sabin with a haughty look. She placed her hands on her hips again, in an ultra-sassy pose.

"You heard the girl, she wants it gone." The Grand High spread her arms out, "Come here then petal. Let's not waste any time."

Tullia took one step towards her, but Sabin stayed her with a gentle hand on her shoulder.

"I will be her escort." Sabin announced in a hard voice.

The Grand High raised her eyebrow, "I'm not paying you."

"I am concerned regarding your treatment methods. You'll treat her like a pet."

"For your information, I treat animals better than most creatures, cause most people and creatures suck." There was a sense of pride in her words, along with a savory pride flavor that infiltrated Tullia's mouth.

Sabin did say anything, but the Grand High shrugged, "Whatever." She then clapped her hands together before steeping her hand in front of her full lips as a big smile bloomed over her face. She was now sitting in the air with her long legs crossed.

"Well then, let's get this little party on the road, shall we?" She opened her mouth to say more, but her head swiveled sharply to the side. His onyx eyes sharp and her face drawn tight. It was only for a moment, but when the Grand High faced them again, she seemed… annoyed.

"Hmm, we need to visit Oizz." She said, twirling one of her long braids thoughtfully. "He's got his little grubby hands in every source of information. He'll know something."

"The goblin?" Sabin asked, his tone flat.

"The goblin." She confirmed in an amused voice, "It's gonna be fun to watch him break." Dropping her braid, she began twirling her fingers and the heap of tulips began to twirl in a tiny tornado formation.

Tullia was memorized by the way in which the Grand High was manipulating the flowers to spin lazily in a delicate mini swirl. The gentle floral scent wafted pleasantly over Tullia.

"A goblin's word is what you are going to go by?" He asked dubiously.

The Grand High shrugged, "It's one way. I want to get a colloquial pulse on the situation. Word of mouth is still the most powerful spread of information." She tapped her blood red mouth playfully. "Besides, it's not like I can just google, 'where a dragon be at?' *Stupid man.*"

"Fine." Sabin said calmly. He eyed the tiny tornado of tulips. "Get rid of these flowers."

"Ah," She brushed her hand delicately through the swirl of tulips, "You don't tell a queen what to do, Berserker."

Sabin glared, though he didn't taste of any malice emotions like earlier. Rather it was more of the vinegary annoyance and bitter exasperation.

"Now then, since we've established that I am the boss of this operation, and I made the plan, it's time to go." The Grand High gave a purely evil grin as her eyes sparked viciously, "I'll give you half an hour to meet me at Oizz's Odds and Ends pawn shop in the Ghost Crescent. I must…*comfort* Chandra. She's a bit of a mess. Don't be late." The Grand High gave them a double peace sign before simply vanishing into thin air. Leaving a thin wisp of blue behind and all the Tulips stopped spinning and fell to the floor.

Sabin sighed wearily, "Alright. Let us clean up the flowers." He looked up at the ceiling, his emotions a fine blend of exhaustion and irritation. It was a very peppery vinegar flavor. "I'll get my axes and we will be off."

Chapter Seven

"And then they lived a peaceful life, and all was well within the kingdom forever." He shut the book and smiled.

"Now this one!" A young girl thrusted another book in the man's hands eagerly. The little girl had wild, long black hair, deep brown skin, small, pointed ears, sharp hazel eyes and a pouty mouth.

"Another?" The man gave out an amused huff, his eyes glittering with soft emotions. "I've already read you five! It is hours past your bedtime. Time to sleep, little one."

"No!" The girl cried out dramatically, she rolled around on her fluffy pink bed top in mock defiance. She peaked at him from under her mass of thick hair, "Just one more? Please?

The man laughed, his face crinkling in a most familiar and comforting way. His blue eyes twinkled with pleasure as the little girl crawled on his lap and frowned up at him.

"I'm not tired, besides you just got here! I only see you once a week for a few

hours. I want you to stay."

The man gathered her up in his arms and pressed her tight to his chest. "I'm sorry, Saida. Papa's very busy, you know that. I run an entire kingdom, my love."

Saida pressed her face harder into his shoulder, savoring the scent of pine, tobacco, and leather. "Then why don't I come out of this room and move into the main house, with you?"

Her father's body stilled, Saida rushed to continue, "We would be able to see each other more often, and I swear I'll be good, I'll be so good no one will say anything! I won't be picky with anything. I'll do my school perfectly, I'll be so polite people will be completely taken with me! I can be charming, I really can." She clutched at his shirt and looked up at her father's face. She felt her heart thud wildly in her chest as her eyes fill with tears. She was told she lived in a big castle but has only known her room since birth. "I want to play outside and talk to other children, please papa?"

She was a child, she knew that, but she wasn't stupid. She was being imprisoned, and she didn't know why. She wasn't allowed out of her room. Only guards, her father and her blind tutor was allowed in her room. Her father's face sagged and creased heavily into sorrow filled lines. Saida's heart clenched tight.

"I'm afraid, my darling Saida, that you are paying for a mistake that I have made years ago. For that, I am deeply sorry." He gently touched her face, before prying her hands off him, setting her aside, and standing up. "I'll bring more books next time. Keep up on your studies and eat properly. Don't be picky, I know you hate tomatoes, but they are good for you."

"Papa," Saida croaked thickly, silent tears dripping off her face and on her bed. He wouldn't look at her. He never did when he was to leave.

"You will understand one day. I promise you will." He then knocked on the door, the sound of multiple locks unlocking was a violent noise within the silence. When the door opened, he said, "Goodnight, Saida," and left without a glance back at her.

The door quickly closed, and all the locks were re-engaged, leaving Saida alone in her pretty cage.

Infused with sudden violent anger, she kicked out of her bed and threw all of her stuffed animals wildly about her room. When one of her dolls smashed into her jewels and scattered them about the floor with sharp sounds, Saida gave a harsh breath through her nose. She stood still for few minutes, quelling the anger that bubbled her blood in the midst of a now silent bedroom.

Slowly, she turned and climbed up to the only window in her room. It was a small window, that was deeply set in the wall and was difficult to look out of, but to Saida it was her only view of the outside world. She had to stack a few of her chests and a chair on top of each other in order to reach it, but it was always worth it.

Saida shoved her head in the deep space and peer out through the glass. It was dark out, the black sky studded with silver stars and a moon so full, it looked as if it were about to fall out of the sky. She slumped a little, taking in the darkened landscape of a sickening familiar view.

The view consisted of tall, bushy trees that changed colors during the season, but never went bare. They outlined the perimeter of a cobbled courtyard that was used by the guards for training purposes occasionally. The trees pushed back so far, they seemed to continue on forever.

Stillness encased that courtyard at night, so when a swift movement occurred, it startled Saida, enough to lose her footing a bit. Though she did not fall, thankfully, but when she looked back out the window, glaring as she tried to spot what was moving. She spotted a boy dashing across the courtyard with a sack over his shoulder. She watched him sprint, before coming to a sudden halt, he whipped his head to where Saida's face peered out, watching him. She blinked, startled. Surely, he could not see her that far away? He was hard to make out, the darkness seemed to encase him entirely, save for his glittering light green eyes that reflected in the nonexistent light.

She waved at him, testing to see if he could see her. He hesitated before waving back stiffly, then rapidly ducking his head and sprinting towards the tree lines, disappearing within seconds.

Gasping, Saida stood there stunned that the boy had seen her and that he had waved. So, they could see here from this window. She had been up here many times, looking out during the day and waving at the knights and ladies. Some had looked up, but she had always thought that they couldn't see her.

Now she knew they could see her; they chose to ignore her.

She slowly crawled down, thinking of the boy, thinking of how he was running at night, free and untethered. She thought about how the air must feel, how the moons glow must be simply ravishing upon one's senses. She thought about the scents that must be around him, sweet floral, refreshing grass... She crawled in bed, tucking herself in neatly and stared up at the painted ceiling.

She wanted to run at night. She wanted to go outside during the day.

Then she made herself a vow. She would get out of here, the pretty little cage her father had isolated her in. She'd find a way and she'd explore the entire world. No one, not even her beloved father, was going to keep her trapped forever.

Saida slowly began planning.

* * *

After the Grand High left, Sabin and Tullia gathered all the tulips and tied them into two bundles with rubber bands. Sabin did an impressive high jump and ripped out his axes from the ceiling. It left two deep slashes in the ceiling. Sabin had stared at it for a moment before tucking his axes on his back and moving on.

They left the bundle of tulips in front of two rooms at Sabin's direction. When she asked why, Sabin shrugged, "Seems like a waste to throw them out."

She put her hand to her heart as she tasted the coconut flavor of awkwardness and the cotton candy like flavor of a soft emotion.

So, he was a softie for flowers, huh? That was cute.

"Okay, so what is the Ghost Crescent?" Tullia asked as they drove once again down Fremont Street. The distracting vibrant lights were off, and the brilliance of the Vegas sun shinned down and made all the signs glitter in a different way, more of a faux innocent way, rather than sinful.

"It's a hidden section in Vegas for… other beings." He said slowly.

A goofy smile just dominated her face. Tullia covered her mouth with her hands, so that she didn't look like a drooling, crazed simpleton. This was so cool, Tullia thought with a type of excited wonder that she only received from awesome books. She leaned back against the seat and turned to look at Sabin's, still, covered profile. She could see the outline of a strong jaw and a relatively chiseled side profile.

To distract herself against her curiosity, Tullia asked, "What's there?"

"Different shops."

Tullia flexed her feet and folded them tightly together, to contain her jittery exhilaration.

"So, how does one go about finding the Ghost Crescent then?"

"Murals." Sabin said.

"Murals?" She repeated, confused.

Sabin's gold eyes glanced at her, and amusement was apparent in their depths. "Yes. You have to find the right mural to drive or run into."

Tullia blinked, then confirmed, "You… drive… into a certain wall with a picture on it?"

An impression of a grin as Sabin nodded, "Yes. Though you must make sure it's the right one. Or else…" He didn't finish, but he didn't need too.

Tullia gave a small squeal, "That's like Harry Potter!"

Sabin shook his head, "The witch who designed the entrance was inspired by those novels."

"Understandable, it's Harry freakin' Potter." She couldn't contain the wiggle of excitement as she turned to face Sabin, "So then…what wall are we running into?" She asked eagerly.

Sabin's eyes crinkled in the corners as he shrugged, "I don't know."

He was the master of short answers and lack of detail. It was very impressive as it was irritating. "Have you been to the Ghost Crescent before?"

Another impression of a grin, though this time it was tinted with the slight taste of tart bubbles. "A few times. The entrance, changes daily, for security purposes." Sabin glanced at Tullia, "Though, I think the witches do it to mess with people."

She furrowed her eyebrows, "What do you mean they switch?"

"The entrance moves from one mural to the other down 7th street."

"Only down 7th street?" Tullia frowned, "That seems kinda obvious though for a portal to be a mural."

He nodded, one hand on the steering wheel while the other lounged on the open window, allowing a warm breeze to filter in. "Indeed, though no human has entered through the portal without an escort."

"You can get escorts to the Ghost Crescent?" This day... Tullia has been living for this day alone. It was one of her greatest days, despite the horror night of last night. So many revelations, encounters, and wonders.

Sabin made a low sound of confirmation, "Yes. Though the rules are strict. You must be willing to have a silencer spell place on them for life and 500 million dollars in able to hire special protection within the Ghost Crescent. There are no purchases that can be made within and no photographs either."

Tullia blinked, then sat back in her seat. Not only was this the most Sabin had said in one sitting, but now she wondered if she could buy something when they were in there. "What is the point then if you can't buy anything or talk about it?"

He shrugged, seemingly uncaring, "You'd be surprised the kinds of people that tour it."

She supposed she would. People are insane, and they're not even certified in their insanity. "Have you escorted people?"

"A few times." He said vaguely.

Tullia made an O with her mouth, then asked, "So, how can you tell which mural has the portal and which ones are just walls with paint on them?"

Sabin tilted his head slightly as he drove, "I will show you."

Tullia wiggled excitedly in her seat, eager to experience a portal in real life. They drove in silence for a few more minutes before Sabin pulled around to the back of a slightly crumbling abandoned building. Tullia stared at the artwork that covered the walls.

The entire artwork was done in black and white. Giant black X's and O's were stacked on top of each other. Some X's and O's were outlined in either pink or green and clustered in a diagonal pattern. On the other side of the wall, it said "Love is a gamble…Jackpot!" with the name Chor Boogie underneath.

Parallel to the mural was a continuation of the design, only separated by a warped looking chain and a rusted metal gate. The stacked X's and O's continued on the bottom portion of the wall and the top, but in-between there was two beautifully colored eyes and a trail of black and white hearts. The first eye had a yellow smiley face as the iris and pupil while the other eye was a collection of blues and greens.

"Cool." She commented, taking in the simple, yet busy artwork.

Sabin didn't say anything, as he got out of his truck and stared at the giant mural intensely from beside his truck. He then strode up and put his face mere centimeters away from the painted X of the mural. Tullia sucked in her lips in an attempt to keep a grin off her face. But Sabin looked utterly hilarious with his face pressed so close to a wall in his not-ninja-but-mercenary get up. He honestly looked like an overgrown trick-or-treater that was put in timeout by a grouchy neighbor.

Sabin put his pointer and thumb up to pinch his chin and Tullia couldn't help it, she began to snort with amusement. After a full minute of close observation, he turned to stare at the other part of the mural that sat adjacent from where he was looking. He went just as close as he did with the other one, for just as long and with his chin still pinched in his fingers. Tullia's stifled snorts turned into uncontrollable giggles as she continued to watch him.

Sabin nodded to the wall, it was a miracle he didn't smack his head, then he turned and motioned for Tullia to come here. She cleared her throat, to expel any remaining mirth and wiped her eyes to erase the tears of humor before she stepped out of the truck. Hobbling over to Sabin, he motioned for her to get closer to the wall.

Hesitantly, she inched her face closer to the loudly colored wall. The smell of dust, aged paint, and urine wafted up to insult her nose.

"Okay." She said slowly, curling away from the wall slightly.

"Do you see the unnatural shine and slight overlapping image?" He asked.

Tullia glanced at him, then looked back at the wall. She squinted and saw the eyes seemed to be doubled, as if someone outlined, but it was slightly off.

"I think I see the double eye." She said slowly. "It looks like someone drew over it, but it's slightly off."

"You see it. That's the sign." Sabin said, then turned and traveled back to his truck. Tullia stared at the image a bit more, fascinated by the unnatural outline and the way it glistened as if it were freshly painted rather than a few years old…

The eye design was so cool…

"Come now." Sabin called.

Tullia stared a few more seconds at the 'sign' then skipped back to Sabin's truck.

"We got lucky on our first try. It's the one with the eyes." He put his arm behind her head rest and reversed his truck to face the mural.

She looked at him, then looked at the eye mural, then looked back at Sabin, "We're just going dive right through it?

Sabin glanced at her and nodded.

Tullia gripped her seat belt tightly with nervous excitement. "Are all the portals on the ground like this one?"

"Nope. Some of them are on second story walls."

Tullia blinked. "How do you enter the portal when it's up high on the building?"

Sabin shifted gears, a taste of wildness hit her tongue. "You climb, then jump."

Tullia jerked her head around to stare at Sabin. "You're kidding."

He turned to give her a deadpan look. "Security purposes." He then winked at her and slammed on the gas. His truck lurched forward and sped straight towards the wall.

Tullia's heart pounded in her throat and as the wall came closer and closer, she couldn't stop her short scream of fright that escaped her dry lips or squeezing her eyes shut while curling into herself. Sabin laughed, a deep rolling sound that hinted at a wildness underneath the rich timber.

The truck jostled, then seemed to go over uneven terrain a bit, before all was still once more.

"It's done now, sweetness." Sabin said, his voice still held a note of laughter.

Slowly, Tullia willed her eyes open just a bit into slits, before opening them wide with excitement. Her breath let out in a rush and her heart slowly crawled back into her chest, but continued to pound, but this time in delight.

Everything was loud, bright and wild. The Ghost Crescent mimicked Vegas, flashy and promising, but with an illusionary twist. Bright lights twinkled nearly blinding against a dark sky and crowded stores piled by the narrow street nearly haphazardly.

There were people... no, humanoid looking creatures with wild looking appearances mixed in other creatures that had a variety of long ears, giant eyes, wings, and claws. Tullia gave a small puff of laughter at the sight before her.

There were shops for specialty meats, elfin couture, witch brewed wines, a gremlin toy shop, and tons of restaurants that advertised authentic foods from the different realms. Floating signs bobbed above the sidewalks, decorative lanterns swayed above the streets, and swirls of color seemed to dance in-between everyone though no one really paid them any mind. It was all so polished, so enticing, so exciting….

Though, the pristine image faltered slightly in certain places when they flickered from beautifully displayed front decor to rusty to unkempt and back and forth. Though that didn't make the shops any less popular judging by the crowds.

"This place…." Tullia murmured, entranced at the visual sensory overload. She'd seen many of the creatures walking, though not all of them. Her eyes darted around, trying to take in everything at once. She didn't want to miss a single detail of this moment. "It's dark."

"It's always night in the Ghost Crescent." Sabin said.

She now fully understood why people would pay millions just to see everything here.

Sabin slammed on his breaks, causing Tullia to jerk forward and the seat belt to bite into her solar plexus. Sabin sighed as he blew on his horn at the fanged and horned creature that jay-walked right in front of his truck. The creature seemed to jump, literally, five feet in the air from fright before dashing off in a seemingly panicked sprint. The creature then hit into a light pole and fell to the ground. It didn't get up again. "Completely pissed." Sabin shook his head, continuing to drive forward. He rolled his shoulders and stiffened as he slowly crawled his truck through the narrowed streets.

"Disgusting place." Sabin muttered darkly.

Tullia sucked in her lips to keep from laughing at Sabin's disgruntled body language. He was acting like a grumpy old man out of his comfort zone.

She tapped her fingers along the window, charmed by the area despite the overwhelming aura it gave off. Sabin gave a small growl as another inebriated creature, this time a woman with long pointed ears and a giant nose, came stumbling out in front of Sabin's car.

The heat that was dousing her palate was enough to make her want to cough.

Tullia cleared her throat. "Positive vibes, positive vibes."

Sabin glanced over at her; his gold eyes unnaturally bright in the darkness. "Subtle message to be positive?"

Tullia did her best innocent face. "Was it subtle? That wasn't what I was aiming for. But as long as you got the message, then all's good."

Sabin's laugh was a burst of wild with streaks of color. It was an *amazing* laugh, if not a bit rusty. The flavor of sweet bubbles obliterated the spice from her mouth and left with an intense sugar rush. Tullia turned her head to look at him, his eyes, the only exposed part of his body, crinkled in the corners.

Like sunshine. He had sunshine eyes when he laughed.

She wished she could see his smile.

Sabin suddenly stopped laughing when he glanced at the time on his dashboard.

"All right. No more stopping." He pressed his foot down on the gas and the shot forward.

* * *

After a few turns, several instances of nearly running over a creature or two, they finally managed to find parking. Sabin parked his truck in a very sketchy parking lot, but he seemed unconcerned.

"We will need to walk the rest of the way." He said as he got out of his truck.

Tullia bit her bottom lip and pumped her arms up and down in excitement. She would get to be up close and personal in the crowd.

Sabin opened her door in the mist of her thinking of just how awesome the little trek would be.

Sabin stepped back, to allow her to step out.

"Are you gonna vape now?" She asked, as she hopped out.

"No, it's not needed here."

Sabin hooked his arm around her waist and pressed her tightly against his side. Tullia stiffened under his grip.

"Stay close. These creatures here know nothing more than tricks and treat everything as potential prey." Sabin murmured as a group of women, with fluffy white hair, curved horns and doe like faces strutted by, looking utterly ethereal in their revealing leafy green top and shiny hooves. Their eyes, dark and cold, eyed them both sharply.

Tullia swallowed under their stares and pressed closer to Sabin.

"Let's move." Then Sabin set a grueling pace.

An eternity later, Tullia was damp with sweat, panting and mentally cursing Sabin. His long legs were merciless and uncaring that she was a squished-legged human.

"Are you well?" Sabin had the audacity to ask her as she all but hunched over on the sidewalk.

"I hate you." She managed to gasp, glancing up she saw Sabin's stupid ninja mask covered face and behind him a fancy old lit up sign that said, "Oizz's Odds & Ends Pawn Shop".

"Come hate me inside." He practically picked her up and carried her through the door that made a little chiming sound.

Tullia continued to pant, she was extremely out of shape, so that little intense fast walk just destroyed her entire body. "I didn't," she gulped in air, "get to look at," a deep inhale, hunching over a little, "anything."

"There wasn't anything interesting to see." At her glare that she gave to his blatant lie she got the impression of a smile from him. "These creatures of the Ghost Crescent view humans as prey. Many of them are barely above an animal's intelligence. The witches try to limit their access with humans; however, some manage to get loose now and again. Hence some of the 'big foot' or 'aswang' sightings. You are not safe out in the open here."

Tullia looked up at him, she felt the sweat drip down the side of her temple and her hair weighed at least ten pounds heavier than before. She sighed, she had wanted to try and touch one of the lights she saw that danced in-between the creatures on the streets. She at the very least wanted to look at things, but she was so focused on not falling down and not tripping that she didn't manage to focus on anything but her feet and the sidewalk that looked exactly like Vegas's sidewalks; complete with the naughty cards littered about and dirty as all hell.

A large hand patted her back. "Don't pout, sweetness."

His nerve was something else, Tullia glared up at him again and his gold eyes were very clearly smiling. "Shut it. I still dislike you."

Sabin's stupid chuckle did not assist in calming down her annoyance towards him. "No longer hate?" Swallowing the bubbly amusement and ignoring the stupid ninja giant, Tullia focused on her breath. Once she had enough of her breath back in her lungs, she stood up from her hunched position and looked around.

There was riot of items that made her head spin with the sheer quantity. Tullia's eyes didn't know where to look first. The tiny shop seemed to be overflowing with odds and ends that begged to be explored and held the potential of being *actual* treasure. There were towering shelves full of bits and bobs that looked like they held importance, age and worth. On the wall hung rugs, musical instruments, animal heads, and gleaming weapons. There were rows of smaller standing shelves holding various books, CDs, statues, and records. There was no surface that was spared with trinkets or books. There were even piles of various flat items that stacked up to the height of the shelves. All the while deep red walls and gold trimmings encased the area, giving the shop a luxurious, expensive feel. She had the feeling you needed some serious coinage to be able to enter the shop.

"Oh my." Tullia murmured, her eyes darting everywhere, trying to take everything in. Tullia was struggling to take in everything all at once. There was simply too much to process, but her frontal lobe couldn't communicate that properly to her thalamus. She pressed her hands to the sides of her head, feeling a little lost and confused.

Sabin's solid hands gripped her shoulders and squeezed them gently. She shook startled and looked up at him with wide eyes. "It not a normal store. Do not look at everything. Only look at parts." His voice was soft and rumbling, like lazy thunder in a spring shower.

She swallowed nodding, then through the mess of her sensory, she managed to taste her breath and nearly gagged. She needed gum. STAT.

She turned to ask Sabin for some, or a puff of his little glamour vape, cause maybe that would sufficient, but Sabin spoke.

"The witch is in the back, talking to the damned goblin." There was an exasperation in his voice. "Her games are tiresome." The taste of vinegar and pickles assaulted her mouth.

Tullia nodded absently, her eyes soaking up section by section of the pawn shop.

"You can look around. Just stay in my sight."

Tullia whipped her head around at Sabin. "Thanks mom!" She cried happily with extreme exaggeration before skipping off.

A short, deep chuckle followed her. Tullia bee-lined straight to the shelve that looked like aquatic knickknacks from a fantastical realm. Upon closer inspection, the shelve held coral clusters and colorful seashells. Nothing ridiculously wild, she thought with a mild disappointment.

They all had name tags with a brief description of what the item was. Tullia eyed the blue, pink and silver shell that had an ultra-bright gleam to it, along with two other equally dazzling shells next to a name tag that said, 'Siren Shells'. The description read:

Siren shells: created by Sirens of the Thalassa Realm, who sing into a shell then seal it, trapping their voice in the shell until the shell is smashed. Once the Siren's voice is released any and all biological males within a ten-mile radius will be enslaved to the one who smashed the shell for a thirty-two-hour period. Affects biological men only. Use with caution. Fun at raves, not recommended at weddings.

Tullia tapped her lips, she ought to drop this baby in the Men Down Under show, have a bunch of oiled hunks all over her like butter on a hot sweet roll. Gently, Tullia picked up a glittering shell and pressed it to her ear. What did a siren's voice sound like? Would she even hear anything?

A soft breath, Tullia listened closely, then a seemingly cacophony of wailing moans and tinkling chimes assaulted Tullia's poor, unsuspecting ear. Jerking the shell away she frowned down at the deceptively pretty shell with disgust. That was such an ugly sound.

Putting down the shell with mild distaste, she moved on to a shelf that was adjacent from the seashells and held various sized fancy display boxes. Tullia peered into a velvet lined box with four multicolored round stones with the name tag, 'Elf Works'.

Elf Works: concoctions of various Elf dusts and herbs that when thrown explode assorted colored smoke. Side effects included: dizziness, loss of muscle movement, brain aneurysm, hair loss, heart attack, teeth loss, and swelling of the tongue. Fun at parties. Adult supervision is required. No minors allowed to purchase.

Huh. The symptoms seemed a little bit too extreme for a party favor, but then again maybe those symptoms weren't too bad for the mythical and fantastical. Shrugging and disinterested, she turned to a shelve right behind her that was overflowing with what looked like old, used records. Tilting her head curiously, Tullia began to thumb through them. There were a few records from people she had never heard of before: Nightmare Cinema, The Ants, Elvie Prester, Spandex Jimmy, Blind Cougar, Blue Cold Ice Cubes....

Tullia picked up a record of Elvie Prester that showed a woman with long pointed ears, big pink hair, and dressed up in a tight, yellow jump suit that was heavily bejeweled. Tullia squinted at the cover, trying to bridge the niggling feeling that she had seen something like this somewhere before.... why did this seem so familiar?

She turned it over to read the song selections her frown intensifying as she read some of the song names: Pink Velvet Shoes, Freezing Hate, Greyhound, I'm so Cruel, Can't Help Falling Out of Love with You...

Hold up.

Tullia flipped the record back over to stare at the woman's yellow, bejeweled jumpsuit. Big pink hair. Elvie Prester... kind of mimicked the king of rock.

She kinda resembled Elvis Presley's style and song names.

Elvis Presley.... Elvie Prester....

A slow discovering smile stretched out across her mouth. Now Tullia had the burning desire to listen to the record to confirm her hypothesis. She looked up from her intense study of the record to find Sabin across the store, still within his line of sight, staring at a bear skin rug a few feet away. Tullia wandered over, still holding the record, to stand next to him. She looked up at the beast and thought it was tragically beautiful. The bear skin was pure black, shiny, and the head was fearsome awesome. The bear's eyes seemed to gleam with a frozen rage in its dark brown depths and its upper jaw was wrinkled as it snarled, displaying gleaming, razor-sharp teeth.

She shifted her eyes away from the bear, it was beginning to make her uneasy, and looked up at Sabin. His intensity never wavered; it was almost as if he were having a staring contest with the bear.

He wouldn't win.

"Are you planning to buy it?" She asked.

Sabin glanced down at her, looked back at the bear and seemed to… deflate a little. He shook his head slightly, "No."

The flavor of heavily spiced and salty iron tickled her palate. Her mouth went dry, and her bad breath seemed to intensify. She cleared her throat, disgusted with the rancid taste in her mouth. She went to ask Sabin for a piece of gum, but the sound of a tinkling laughter had both of them turning around. The satin red door that was behind the glass counter opened and the Grand High managed to saunter while she floated out and right over the glass counter.

She looked at Tullia and grinned widely. "Come petal! Let me introduce you to Oizz. He is the owner of this upscale pawn shop and information extraordinaire."

Tullia met the bright green eyes of Oizz, a rather imposingly framed goblin. She had seen goblins now and again in her visions, though seeing one and meeting one in person are two completely different things. Oizz was stout, about five feet tall (a typical height for goblins), with gray skin; long, fat pointed ears that sagged a little on his shiny face; a wide mouth that held a crowded mess of pointed, yellow teeth. He had no hair on his head, his bald head was wrinkled, saggy and shiny. Lastly, he had a smashed nose with giant nostrils that seemed to have more height than length and black stubble that shadowed his bulging, sagging jaw.

The green eyes drilled into her, assessing her value, and causing a slimy feeling to invade her. Tullia had the urge to hide behind Sabin. He looked like a childish nightmare come to life. She forced herself to smile at him, a smile that went completely ignored. Instead, the goblin's green eyes narrowed further.

"A human?" Oizz looked at the Grand High with sharp eyes. "That's not gonna get you much in my shop."

Right then and there, Tullia did *not* like the goblin. Sabin folded his arms; his bulk pronounced, and she could taste the sharp spicy sensation of his rage. "No." Sabin said forcefully.

Oizz shrugged, uncaring, then his focus homed in on the record she was holding. "What of mine are you holdn' girl?" Tullia began to sweat, was she not supposed to touch anything? He eyed the record in her hand, before giving her a sharp look. "That's Elvie. A classic and iconic album you're holdin' there. Original and in mint condition." Tullia looked down at the record in her hand, panicked and now a light sheen of sweat coating her forehead. "Come!" The goblin boomed, startling her into looking back up at him with wide eyes. The goblin waved them to follow him as he scurried behind the counter. He pulled out a fancy looking record player and affectionately stroke it. "I'll always make time for Elvie. Give it here, girl. You'll know real music in a bit."

Timidly, Tullia approached him and handed the record over. She noticed that the goblin had neatly manicured nailed, it was at odds with his rather… greasy appearance. Almost reverently, Oizz unsheathed the record and set up it up on the record player. The classic scratchy sound of the needle touching the recorded filled the air before an upbeat tune started up. A velvet, soulful voice began to sing, "You ain't nothin' but a greyhound… runnin' all the time! You ain't nothin but a greyhound… runnin all the time! Well, you ain't never won race then you can't love me tonight!"

Tullia threw her head back and laughed, clapping her hands, "This is just like Elvis Presley's Hound Dog!"

Just female greyhound addition.

Oizz grimaced, as a rancid sweaty flavor accompanied by a strong heat interrupted her mirth covered her tongue. "No little girl don't disrespect a legend with a mere *human* pop star. Elvie was and still is the queen of rock and roll. What is this…" He waved his hand, "Elvis Presley queen of?"

Tullia looked at the goblin and blinked in confusion then said. "He's the king of rock and roll."

Oizz furrowed his eyebrows, disbelieving, before scoffing. He stopped the music and carefully re-sheathed the record. "I'm not selling this to you, you won't respect it as it should be respected."

Tullia didn't want it, but she wasn't about to say that to a seemingly temperamental goblin. He frightened her in a 'I'll-sell-your-limbs-while-you-sleep' type of way.

The Grand High's obsidian eyes seemed to dance with malice glee. "Enough pleasantries." She turned to Oizz, who seemed to stiffen all over, though his face never lost the resting scowl.

Tullia could taste his nerves, a jittery tartness of suspicion and the bitter flavor of weariness.

"Oizz, you know things." The Grand High cooed softly, deceptively, "Tell me, where can I find a dragon?"

The goblins forehead wrinkled heavily in surprise before he gave a crooked smile that was hideously smug. "A dragon? Your highness, you flatter me with your high opinion of my knowledge, but a dragon?" He shook his bulbous head. "They're practically a myth! No one's seen 'em for practically millenniums." His emotions tasted of savory self-assurance and decadent superiority. Interesting. "There hasn't been even a whisper about 'em. I'm sorry, your highness, I don't have a clue."

Tullia swallowed against the flavors; something wasn't quite… truthful with the Goblin's answer.

The Grand High tapped her nails together thoughtfully. "So, you don't know." She sighed, her little braids swishing as she tilted her head. "You disappoint me. You have your greedy little fingers in every honey pot that holds any type of information. Yet you don't know something as simple as this?"

Oizz gave a half bow and said in a regretful tone. "Your majesty, I do my best to keep up with the information that flows through the Ghost Crescent, but honest, no one's lookin' for a dragon. Dragons may have even died off at this point in the game." He shrugged. "I am just one goblin." His grin was as charmingly terrifying as it was deceitful. "I'm afraid I have nothin' to give you on the topic of dragons."

There was a beat of silence, before the bubbly flavor of excitement and a sharp bite of rotted malice hit Tullia's tongue. She snapped her head towards the Grand High. Her face was perfectly smooth, her lush lips slightly parted and her dark eyes half hooded as she stared at the goblin. She shifted forward, leaning in closer towards Oizz.

"Are you sure, Oizz." Her tone was low, practically a purr. "You don't know anything?"

Oizz's face creased with weariness, but he bowed low again. "Many apologies, your highness. I really don't have anythin'! Those bunch are lone wolfs, they don't keep in contact with anyone and tend to go into hidin' for centuries on end."

The Grand High leaned back, her eyes frosted over. "Well now," She drawled, blue smoke wafting from her fingertips ominously. "I think you're holding back on me."

Oizz's face did not change, but the sour taste of fear coated her tongue.

"Your highness, I—" He began, but the Grand High spoke over him.

"Well, I don't mind persuading you." She grinned, and it was beautifully toxic. She flicked her fingers and two photo cards appeared. One with Oizz holding a yellow frizzy haired goblin woman with green skin and dimples and another photo of Oizz kissing a goblin woman with black hair and heavily pierced ears. "I suppose it's long overdue for Fuzza, your wife, to meet Athee... your *mistress* of thirty years."

Oh snap. Tullia blinked with surprise and watched the interrogation take a turn for the classic day time soap opera. Fantasy goblin edition.

The Oizz's gray skin paled to a pastel ash. He opened his mouth a few times, though no words ever made it out. His emotion was a riot of oily fish and sour bubbles. "Your highness…" He floundered with his speech. "I beg you, they'll chop me up into bits and feed me to the kappa!"

The Grand High raised her eyebrow, the smile unwavering from her lips. "I know." She said simply, almost happily and Oizz had a high whining sound in his throat.

"I don't know where a dragon is. I swear it on my mother's grave!" The goblin cried.

"Now let's see." She clicked her nails together and a gold smartphone bobbed next to her. "I'm honestly quite impressed with you. Not only do you have the audacity to continue to lie to me…"

The goblin rambled a bunch of messy denials, but the Grand High did not pay them mind as she continued. "You've also managed to keep your affair on the DL for thirty years." The Grand High raised her eyebrows as a number appeared on the phone screen. Oizz began to quiver in pure terror. "I will admit, that is quite skillful. Or your women are simply stupid. Though I doubt that, due to your fetish of intelligence and viciousness, right?" Her eyes cut him a sharp look.

Oizz gave a hoarse, nearly hysterical laugh, his entire frame vibrated. "Well, you know. They're a riot and fun to handle." His eyes bugged between the phone and the two pictures. "Grand High, I'm beggin' ya. I don't know no one who's seen a dragon, I've never met a dragon. I haven't even heard talk of a dragon. Honest." He raised both his hands up in surrender, his eyes wide with panic.

His panicked emotions tasted fishy and an under lying acidic flavor was suspicious.

The Grand High tilted her head all the way to the side until she was upside down. "You greatly disappoint me, goblin. You're to know everything and anything. Dragons are a part of that everything that you're supposed to know." She heaved out a dramatic sigh, complete with closing her onyx eyes and shaking her head. "As compensation for ruining my morning, I'm going to ruin you."

She opened her eyes, and the gold phone began to ring.

"Oh, wait, wait, wait, wait now!" He waved his short stubby hands frantically, his jade eyes bugging nearly out of his head, "I ain't lyin'! I swear on my mother's grave! I'm being honest! I don't know where a dragon is!"

The Grand High hissed at him, her face contorting into pure horror. She spun quickly right side up and gripped Oizz's throat. The goblin began to gag as she squeezed his throat tightly with her long-clawed fingers. The taste of the goblin's fear was sour, and the anger of the Queen was fire in her mouth. *"Peasant.* You dare utter *lies* to the *Queen!"* The smart phone continued to ring. "I know you know where one is." She smiled meanly. "Naughty creatures must be punished."

Tullia gripped her hands together nervously. It seems the Grand High liked to escalate situations to the extreme. Tullia wasn't sure if she was mentally prepared for all this drama. She glanced up at Sabin, to find his standing in a relaxed posture and passively watching the forceful interaction with indifference. Tullia turned back to look at the Grand High, biting her lower lip to keep silent.

The goblin frantically kicked his legs and clawed at the Grand High's hands, his stubby claws were ineffective against the Grand High mosaic skin and steely grip.

"Mercy!" He choked out, but his plea went unheeded.

"I gave you opportunities." She grinned menacingly.

"Hello there, Tinks and Gadgets, this is Fuzza, how can help ya?" A raspy voice on the other end of the phone could be heard.

Tullia covered her mouth to muffle any type of sound she might make. The goblin's wife answered the phone.

"Hello, Fuzza? This is the Grand High of the international Black Blood Coven, you remember me."

The was a slight pause, then, "Of course, your highness. An honor to be speakin' with you. How may I help you today?" Fuzza's voice was wary, but her tone was neutral and rigidly polite. Which was understandable since the Grand High was terrifying as all hell.

The Grand High maintained a cold eye contact with Oizz while continuing to choke him with minimum effort. She spoke pleasantly to Fuzza. "I found a rather juicy piece of information that concerns you and thought to pass it along before it becomes... too late to prevent bloodshed."

"Oh? Should I prepare to get my bank broken from the Greylight Guild?"
   Fuzza's tone was laced with a dry humor and ice. The Grand High giggled, a chilling sound, as she raised her eyebrow at Oizz. His eyes bugged out, and his ash gray tongue flopped over his sausage shaped lips. His weak thrashes stopped as he put all of his energy into mouthing frantically, *"Shifters! Shifters! Shifters!"*

The Grand High sneered at him, before she answered Fuzza on the other end of the phone. "Perhaps, though it might hurt your business more if you hire assassins to kill your customers."

Oizz's body became deflated and with that Tullia could taste refreshing, almost minty relief. Even though he was still being choked.

The Grand High seemed to squeeze Oizz's throat tighter, causing the goblin to spasm, though he didn't utter a single sound. Tullia watched the violence with a sort of detachment. Perhaps if she wasn't choked nearly to death by a vampire, she'd be more… sensitive to it, but she didn't find any of the actions real. It was almost like she was watching a show, she wasn't really there, she wasn't really present.

Perhaps sleep deprivation really was messing with her mind, but she couldn't muster up the proper level of horror over what was happening. She had been through too much today to think this cruel.

"Apparently, the Gnomes from 1-800-the-Gnome, weren't too impressed with the magic imbued gardening equipment you sold them back in February. They're speaking ill of your work and as a result your ratings have dropped from the number one imbuing smith to second best in the Ghost Crescent."

There was a beat of silence before a hellish screech, *"What!"* Sounds of shattering and breaking and crashing could be heard from the phone. A flurry of distant screams could be heard from the other line. "They dare question the quality of *my* work and drag *my* business down with their false accusations!" Another shriek of rage. "No one in this realm can beat my work. Let's see 'em try and get what I do for my price and for my skill. Those lousy micro-mini totting pieces of garden sh—"

"Now, now," The Grand High interrupted, a big, sharp smile on her face, "regain yourself, Fuzza. No assassinations are allowed, the gnomes are a protected creature. However, anything nonlethal I give you my pre-approval and blessing."

"I appreciate your information, your highness. Many thanks." There was a simmering rage in Fuzza's voice, but it was tightly restrained.

"Of course. I don't like the gnomes." The Grand High's voice rumbled darkly, her eyes flashing a bright blue, before turning dark once more. "Have fun! Remember no assassins. Bye, bye." The Grand High hung up and then dropped Oizz to the floor. He coughed harshly, while gasping in deprived air. His stumpy body quivering with the force of his gulping breaths. The Grand High watched dispassionately as the goblin wheezed for a few more minutes before shakily rising to his feet, rubbing his throat tenderly and gripping the glass counter. There were darkening bruises in the shape of the Grand High's unnaturally long fingers blooming across his rippled throat.

The Grand High smiled quite meanly. "Shifters?"

Oizz rasped in thin breaths of air a few more times, before he shakily smoothed out his little gray vest with trembling fat hands. "Shifters know shifters." He croaked. "That's a fact. And the biggest, most powerful clan of shifters in this realm are from the Mabuhay clan in the Philippines. They have their spies in every corner of the world to keep tabs on the other creatures' doings and the political happenings of this and maybe other realms."

Tullia thought back to all the visions she had throughout the years. A couple for them contained people who morphed into different creatures and even different people. Though those visions mostly focused on one shifter, who constantly changed their appearance and never wore the same face twice.

The Grand High looked down at him skeptically. "Can you contact them?"

Oizz shook his head, his ears swishing sloppily against his head. "'Fraid not. They live in a remote and mysterious part of the Philippines called Biringan City. And the spies? Those shifter spies are undetectable. Rumor has it they've got a contract from rouge witch to hide 'em." He gave a shrug. "And, as the saying goes, you can't track a shifter. They track you." Oizz clasped his shaky hands together. "However, I know a guy that can get'cha to the Municipality of Gandara for half the price via portal travel."

The Grand High sneered down at the at the goblin. "I don't need your cheap transportation. Do you have a contact from this Mabuhay clan?"

Oizz put his hand on his heart as swore fervently. "No. I swear, I don't know anyone from that clan. No one does. It's a rumor going around the Hairy Turtle."

By the shrill and fervency of his tone, Tullia supposed he was desperately trying to convey his sincerity. The bitter flavor of his panic increased along her palette with a seaweed desperation.

The Grand High watched him, her face a perfect ice sculpture.

"I heard that the Mabuhay shape shifters are rumored to know where anyone is, everyone who is anyone that is. They take some humans from nearby villages and towns back to their hidden city and they're never heard from again. That rumor's not new, been around for a few years. Though no one knows why, many suspect sacrifices, but there's also a rumor on how it's to increase the shifter population, since many shifters are infertile." Oizz was rambling at this point, and he was eyeing the damning pictures nervously still floating beside the Grand High's head. "I'll bind my word to that, I'll give you an oath, I'll sign a blood document. I'll promise my son to you… so if I could just take that picture off your hands…"

The pictures suddenly disappeared, much to Oizz's salty disappointment. "Oh no, Oizz. I don't think so." The Grand High smiled evilly at him while wagging her too long fingers in his face. "You see, if I find out you sent us to a dead end, I will not only have your thirty-year infidelity known, but your shop will be hexed." His face drooped with increasing horror. "*And* I'll turn your ears into mere little stubs, like human ears."

Oizz gripped his long-pointed ears in sheer alarm. "The ears are too far! That would just be cruel! Takin' away my male pride is going too far!"

The Grand High rubbed her blood red mouth with one claw tipped finger. "Then you better be sure your information is correct."

He gave her a defensive look, still holding both his ears protectively. "I swear on my treasure vault that those lot will know at least *somethin'* on where a dragon might be. They are your best bet rather than us city folk."

The Grand High stared at Oizz with unblinking velvet night eyes. When the goblin hunched a little lower, but maintained eye contact, she snapped her head to the side abruptly, looking at Sabin and Tullia. "Have you ever been to the Philippines?"

Tullia shook her head; Sabin didn't react to her query. The Grand High beamed a smile that may just have ruined a few hearts. "How fun." She gave a snarled smile. "However," The Grand High whipped her head around to Oizz. "We will need something for our time wasted, given that you decided to play hardball."

Oizz's face seemed to shrink in on itself. "I—I can give you ten percent off one item."

There was a beat of silence before the Grand High began to smoke blue, but her smile never faltered even as a flicker of heat danced across Tullia's tongue. "I'm sure you can do much, much better, considering how you forced me to bully you. Do you understand how hard that was for me? And now you're being stingy, towards someone who was merciful on you?"

Tullia sucked in her cheeks, the Grand High's tone was callus and venom dripped steel. The pictures of him and the two women appeared next to her, flickering in and out.

His eyes bulged and his sagging jaw quivered as he gnashed his teeth. His face looked like it was contorted in physical pain as fat droplets of sweat popped up on his brow.

"I am thankful for the Grand High's mercy." A forced sentence through gritted teeth, "I'd like to show my appreciation by allowing a f-f-free item of your choice".

Tullia could taste the bitter and sour taste of his utter resistance to offer any type of free-be.

"P-pick out anyth-thin' on a low s-shelf. Low. Shelves." Oizz seemed to choke out the words.

"You're far too generous, Oizz." The Grand High clapped her hands and brightened the space with a goddess worthy smile. Then darted in the back room, leaving a trail of fine blue smoke ion her wake. Oizz gasped before quickly waddling panicked after her.

"Your highness! Not in the vault! Anything but the items in there!" The goblin's voice cracked with stress as he continued to call after her frantically.

Tullia looked at Sabin, who stood in utter stillness. "Are we allowed to pick out something too?"

Sabin's gold eyes looked down at her, and nodded. "Pick something out quickly."

Tullia whooped, fist pumped once and grinned. "I want a siren shell."

Sabin raised his eyebrows, as if surprised by her instant decision. "A siren shell?"

She waggled her eyebrows as her smile widened. "I have a plan when all this is over. It includes that siren shell, free martinis, oiled men, and a wild thirty-two hours on the Strip with a half-naked entourage."

Sabin's eyes widened then blinked a few times. "How shocking." He murmured. There were the acidic bubbles of shock and the sweetness of amusement.

At her inquiring look, an impression of a smile occurred in Sabin's eyes. "Forgive me, your attire and sweet preferences seemed innocently childlike to me."

Tullia placed a hand on her chest and swiveled one hip out. "First of all, my pajamas are completely adulty. And second, my sweet addiction is something I share with millions of adults all around the world. Your logic is greatly flawed, sir."

Sabin shook his head at her, bubbles with a sweet and sour edge of confusion. "Go grab your shell, sweetness."

Looking back at the door that the goblin and Grand High disappeared to, Tullia decided to listen. Turning quickly, she made her way over to where the shells sat, looking sparkling and enticing. She studied the shells intensely, there were only three and all of them exciting her eyes with their glossy, exotic shell designs. She picked up an opal shell that when light hit the surface a riot of shimmering pastel colors colored the shell.

Mine.

Tullia tucked the shell to her chest, claiming it, and looked around for Sabin. He was turning a small brown looking satchel like bag over in his hands. The bag screamed 'hipster' with its slight scruffy exterior and minimalist appearance. However, this bag looked so very ordinary to Tullia, it was almost agonizing to look at for the lack of visual stimulus.

"A purse?" She asked, stroking her siren's shell's smooth surface absentmindedly with her thumb.

"It's called Endlessly Empty Satchel. This is made in the realm where fairies reside."

Tullia stared at the bag, then said. "That's a pretty lame name."

Sabin nodded.

"So, it's a man purse then?"

Sabin cut her a side look. "It's a bag that never gets full."

She raised her eyebrows and made an o with her mouth. She studied the bag closely. It looked like a roughly sewn bag with no frills and an exuding incompleteness for the almost raw plainness of the bag. "So, you can keep putting things in there?"

Sabin nodded.

"That's amazing. Can anything go in there?"

He shook his head. "It is limited to objects only." He leaned over a bit, looking at the bright white sign. "It also advises against any food, animals, or creatures, apart from fairies, to go into the bag."

"I guess if it's truly an infinite bag, then that means things can get lost…" She said uncertainly, having trouble wrapping her head around the concept of a bag being able to hold literally everything. She glanced down at the price tag then gaped. *"Fifty million?"* Tullia exclaimed, scandalized. "Why is it stupidly expensive? It's an ugly bag!"

Sabin slung the satchel around his body, adjusting it across is broad chest. "It's a rare find. The fae folk are choosy in what they release to other races."

"Wow." She mused, still reeling from the price. Sabin glanced up and tucked the bag beneath his bag, hiding it.

"Hide your shell." He murmured. Tullia quickly shoved the shell in her shallow pocket of her pajama bottoms and tucked her shirt over it just as the Grand High floated out from the back room with gleaming eyes and a wide, toothy grin.

"Let's be off." She announced, she spun around to blow a very cheeky kiss to Oizz who stood, dejected, disheveled, sweaty and read eyed behind the counter. His long ears were sagging, and his skin was two shades lighter. "Thanks, Oizzy bear. You've been fun." She winked then floated out of the doors that slammed open for her.

Tullia and Sabin both followed her outside the pawn shop. Once on the balmy streets, the Grand High gave out a rather wicked laugh. Sending a few creatures skittering away fearfully.

"Ah, to crush a goblin's soul and threaten him, is simply the best." She flipped upside down and pressed her hands to her cheeks. "I was waiting for a chance to use those pictures for months." The Grand High giggled wildly, looking half insane and half adorable. She sighed, as if satisfied from the depths of her soul.

"Hoi polloi!" She suddenly exclaimed, startling Tullia as she thrusted a giant muddy looking crystal in the air for viewing. "Behold the treasure I have, singlehandedly, finessed from that greedy goblin."

It was a thick, long crystal looking stick with pointed ends that was about the height and width of Tullia's forearm. The entire stone was a collage of deep red, sandy browns, and brown tinted creams intermixed together.

It was an ugly thing.

"Wow." Tullia paused. "Is it a wand?"

"Wand?" The Grand High snorted. "That is an outdated device, petal. Similar to the pagers of the 90's for humans. No one really uses them anymore, except old bitties. No, this gorgeous device is an M.I. HQ9 Leaf Edition."

At Tullia's completely blank look, the Grand High seemed to give the impression of rolling her eyes and waved her treasure in front of Tullia's face. "M.I. is short for Magic Incubator. The HQ stands for high quality and then the nine indicates the number of these M.I.'s that were made in a batch. So, only nine of these beautiful creations were developed." The Grand High stared at the stone in lust then smiled at Tullia. "Shall I demonstrate its function?" A rolling wave of electricity sparking the air.

Tullia nodded eagerly, liking the physical excitement in the air. The Grand High clutched the M.I. tightly and her long, long hands began to smoke a pale blue. The stone emitted a low hum before it too began to smoke a little… then it caught fire. Tullia watched in fascination as the stone lit up like a match, twisting and curling like tiny little fingers grabbing air.

The Grand High gave out another witchy laugh before the smoke ceased as did the low hum from the stone. The fire winked out, but the tip of the crystal was glowing a bright blue.

"Oh," She licked her lips, staring down at the crystal with a calculated hunger. "This has such potential."

Sabin stepped closer to Tullia, hiding her with his body. Tullia glanced up at him, but he was looking around warily.

"What does the crystal do?" She asked the Grand High, feeling protected with the bulk of Sabin at her back. It was the oddest, most comforting feeling that she didn't quite know how to process. She'd always been alone, so to know someone was actually looking out for her well being right now, even though it's small and may be unnecessary, it was such a warmth she didn't know she lacked.

The Grand High looked up from petting her crystal. "This is a storage unit that keeps magic alive for centuries. Once filled up, it can be used as an emergency magic supply, all you have to do is break it. But it needs to be filled up first."

The tip of the stone continued to glow brightly. "How do you know how much it can hold?"

The Grand High displayed the crystal like a show girl on the The Price Is Right. "When the entire stone is glowing, that's when you know it's full. Usually, an M.I. this size can hold up to a three hundred regular witch reserves."

The Grand High then threw the stone in the air and clicked her nails together. The giant crystal faded away as it deceased before completely disappearing. She clapped her hands. "Well then, since the goblin was only a bit helpful, it looks like this little adventure has a second part." She smiled impishly. "We'll need to go to my coven headquarters." She tucked her long, tiny braids behind her shoulders. "Naturally, I have a first-class teleporter and, since I am generous, I will allow you both to accompany me while I travel in it."

Sabin rolled his shoulders. "The Philippines then?"

"*Duh*, keep up now, Sabin." The Grand High flicked her fingers out as she crossed her legs in the air. "The Philippines is roughly fifteen hours ahead, so we need to plan carefully and make sure we get there when food is available. I want to eat authentic Filipino street food."

Tullia glanced at Sabin, but his ninja covered face was impossible to read as was his emotions, she couldn't taste much feeling from him.

The gold phone suddenly appeared by the Grand High, and she was looking at the screen with a furrowed brow. "If it's ten a.m. now, then it's roughly about one a.m. in the Philippines." The phone disappeared suddenly. "Alright, we will leave then in ten hours to ensure everyone is open and ready to serve me food." The Grand High fixed her hair, pulling it forward to rest in front.

Tullia was totally envious of her hair, it was gorgeous. The Grand High looked thoughtful for a moment then she clapped her hands together once. "Yes, ten hours we leave." She looked at Tullia, "Come now petal, we will—"

"No." Sabin looped a hard arm around her waist and pulled her flush against his side. "You'll not take her. I don't trust you with her safety."

The Grand High gave him a stank face. "I'm not about to eat her, berserker. In case you've forgotten due to your tiny brain, I have a vested interest in the girl. Her dead won't get me what I want." At Sabin's unyielding arm around Tullia's waist, the witch threw her hands up. "Whatever. Make sure she's prepared then and be at the coven's base at five o'clock." She gave a snide look to Sabin. "You do remember where it is, right berserker?"

He shrugged. "Sure."

The Grand High gave Sabin a dirty look. "Be there on time." Then disappeared in a puff of blue smoke.

Sabin sighed. "High handed witch." He looked down at Tullia. "Let's tie up a few loose ends." He kept her pinned her to his side and made her sprint back to his truck.

<h1 style="text-align:center">Chapter Eight</h1>

❦

The city glowed from her window, creating enough illumination in her room that other light was unnecessary. Carolina took in her city, took in the shiny black high rises, the sleek metal railways, the lush rooftop gardens, the strings of multicolored lights between buildings, the floating light orbs... the vibrant pulse of her city left no corner shadowed.

Her beautiful Black City.

There was a gentle knock at her door, before it opened without waiting. "There you are lola. Why are you sitting in the dark, all alone in your room again?" She turned, to look at her complex grandchild who flounced over to where she sat. Her grandchild's appearance was nearly impossible to identify as male or female, which is the way in which their kind preferred. Her grandchild appearance was of medium height, slender, with a smooth, round face, deeply tan skin, long black hair, and deep-set dark brown eyes. Though, she knew her grandchild identified with the male gender, he enjoyed the androgynous features immensely. She watched silently as he took her hand, bowed, and pressed his forehead to her hand gently. His dark eyes stared into hers as his grip tightened on her hand.

"Is an intervention needed? You're not thinking of bad trips, are you?"

She smiled, reaching up with her free hand she patted his cheek with affection. "I am fine. I'm admiring my city, that's all." She pinched his cheek playfully. "Since when did you become a nag, Chito?"

He glared at her without heat, rubbing his pinched cheek. "Forgive me for being concerned over your health, you are an ancient rice ball, lola."

She chuckled. "Such cheek. Your mano has been contradicted by your words." Carolina stood up from her favorite chair, turning away from the sight of her beloved city and began to make her way to the door. "Come, let us get some tea and sweets. I think Lyra made Ginanggang," She paused, then continued. "at least I hope she did. She asked me what I wanted to eat today, and I said Ginanggang...."

Chito grabbed Carolina's arm with both hands. "Lola! Wait! I have something important to ask you that... I'd rather not everyone in the house know about." At her raised eyebrow, he added a low "please".

Carolina blinked at him, then sighed. She spoiled him far too much. "You and your strange privacy talks." She turned to face him, folding her hands neatly in front of her and nodded. "Go on, then."

Chito seemed to hesitate, releasing her arm in favor for tugging nervously on his silky long strands. A few minutes pasted by in silence, Carolina didn't rush her grandchild. For him to seek out a private audience with her means what he wanted to say was important to him. Therefore, it would be important to her.

Chito seemed to rally enough courage and looked Carolina in the eyes. "I wish to leave Biringan City. I want to explore the outside world."

Carolina paused; her protective instinct rose high within her, it shouted to forbid him outright. She hushed the urge, as she stared into Chito's dark eyes. Eyes that were shining earnestly with a burning desire to break free of the safety of Biringan City. She understood the need to crawl this entire earth until no crevice was undiscovered, no person unseen, no place unknown. To see what was beyond something familiar, to discover more than one's own world... Carolina recognized the need, for she had it once as well. Many, many years ago.

However.

Chito was young. Inexperienced. Soft. Sweet. He liked to change his appearance as easily as the trends of today change. Beyond that, he was not yet grounded in himself, he was unsure of who he was as a shifter. He was conflicted with how he should be and how he wanted to be. For shifters, if one is unsure in their base character, then they are truly ambiguous and truly... no one. And that was a dangerous notion of a creature that can be anyone.

In Chito's case... to allow him out in a world, where the tide of influences could tear him apart at the seams...

No, she could not bear to have her grandchild corrupted due to her negligence, as her brother was corrupted due to their father's negligence.

*The dark thoughts made her tone hard when she addressed her grandson. "I have said this time and time again, Chito. Whatever you do, think about it seven times. If you do not **think** about who you are, then you can never be who you are meant to be and, ultimately, you will be lost in this life."*

"I have found myself!" He patted his chest, his eyes wide and his posture tense "This is me. This is Chito's original form."

Carolina gave him a remorseless look. "You've taken this form for only six months and even then, you constantly shift the features. Yesterday your hair was shoulder length. Today it is nearly to your bum!" She inhaled deeply, pinching the bridge of her nose, willing her emotions to settle. Chito reminded her so much of Alab...

Chito rolled his eyes in exasperation. "Hair changes do not count, lola. Humans change their hair all the time. They even attach fake hair on their head."

Carolina shook her head. "You lack the dedication and persistence of a singular, unchanging form, which leads to the lack of commitment to your character." She pinned him with her eyes, watching as Chito swallowed nervously and squirm.

"Being a shifter is a gift, it means to be able to take the form of everything and anything. However," She raised her hand, demanding Chito's silence when his mouth opened to undoubtedly argue. "with this gift, comes burdens. If we cannot first settle into an original form we will be consumed by forces prevalent in the world." She cupped his face and softened her tone. "I need you to understand who you are. Who is Chito? I am asking you to consider this beyond physical appearance. Who. Are. You."

Chito's beautiful oak eyes blinked at her, the fog of confusion still present. Carolina sighed but smiled at her grandson. "I am old, have lived many lives over, made many mistakes." A face flashed through her mind, a face that was now forever cursed and lost. "I've seen a lot of mistakes made as well. I teach you, so you can avoid harmful errors and succeed, where I have failed."

Chito placed his hands on hers. "I know, lola. And you don't look a day over one thousand."

Carolina squeezed his face playfully. "You persevere, and you will reap the fruits of your labor. Ponder more. Know more. Understand yourself more. Then, come to me again."

His dark eyes seemed to shimmer with impatience, but he nodded in acquiescence. She could tell he was not content by her judgment.

He was going to experiment, and possibly rebel. She'd have to keep a close eye on him. "Good boy. Now then, Ginanggang."

She linked arms with her restless grandchild and led him to the kitchen.

It was not Ginanggang served, but rather belekoy. Her second favorite snack food.

* * *

Sabin drove down Las Vegas Boulevard, following the directions Tullia gave him to where she lived. She had requested to be taken to her home, so that she could get her clothes and return library books. She said they were close, and Sabin became a bit… concerned at the rough area in which she resided. Las Vegas Boulevard was an older part of town, closer to the Strip and attracted the shady wanderers. There were a few decent shops on the street, though it was not the ideal area for a young woman to be living.

He flickered a glance to Tullia. She sat leaning against the window, watching the traffic and wiggling her feet. Her long black hair slightly wild and gave her more of a tussled appearance, like that of a tiny kitten after play. A smile threatened to tilt his lips, he doubted she'd like his comparison.

"There, Oasis Motel. That's where I'm living currently." She pointed, and Sabin felt his stomach tighten as did his hands on the steering wheel. The Oasis motel looked like a rundown motel that had quite a few scandals attached to its name, mostly suicides, hauntings, prostitution, and themed rooms.

He eyed the classic desert brown tan colored building with distaste. Then his thoughts turned dark. Tullia said she had no one to call, that she was completely alone… was she a prostitute?

Sabin felt a slow burn begin in his gut. The thought of this woman, with her big gray eyes and small stature being rented out…. His rage jumped, clawing his throat, begging to annihilate anything that moved and set fire to the motel. His heart began to beat fast at the prospect of violence, his endorphins rushed, his felt his veins pulsating with the rush of sudden adrenaline. His rage grinned within, stretching. Inhaling deeply, Sabin quelled the growing rage within him through sheer, cold logic. She looked too healthy, was too soft looking, and the only substance she seemed to be addicted to was sugar.

She had to be visiting Vegas then. By herself?

"Are you visiting Vegas?" He probed as he turned into the motel parking lot.

A slight pause. "No, I've been here about one year." Her voice was quiet, her tone guarded.

He nodded and said no more. He was not one to judge others, he had no right when his soul was blackened with the dried blood of innocents. Besides, life had taken him to hiding in sewers, attics and abandoned church basements, where rats tried to pick fights with him, and the insects were so starved, they tried to nibble him in the night.

"I-I have a hard time keeping a job and apartments are super expensive." Her tone was sheepish and higher pitched than normal. He glanced over to see her hands tightly folded in her lap. "I actually work here, I'm the maid, the only maid. But I get a free room, which is nice. The rooms, well my room is nice, the others are pretty crazy." She was rambling, clearly nervous and shy. "Some rooms have mirrors, almost all around the bed. Which is kinky." She shrugged, "To each their own, right?"

He didn't know how to comfort a person. It was clear he should say something, but that something he did not know. He was better silent and in the dark, than out in the light with people. His temperament did not allow for mingling. He'd managed to tame his violent fury long ago, through isolation. Humans and creatures of various races, he noticed, due to majority being highly senseless, managed to incite his anger readily therefore he avoided associating with them for long stretches at a time.

However, since he claimed Tullia as one of his, he would make an effort.

"You need not fret. This is your home, and you've done very well by yourself."

She went utterly silent. He found a parking space next to a broken-down car and turned off his engine. He turned to look at Tullia and stilled.

His rage roared always simmering anger as easily as a freshly sharpened ax against flesh. It surprised Sabin for a moment, that his rage surged without any provocation. Or perhaps, with the provocation of her tears.

Big tears dripped from Tullia gray eyes, making them darker like heavy storm clouds and her plush mouth trembled.

"Sweetness?" He asked surprised, then his rage choked him.

Sabin inhaled deeply, forcing his lungs to expand and thought of a still lake in the dewy hours of the dawn during fall. The air would be crisp, not yet biting, and the ground under his feet would be firm, not yet frozen. The landscape around the lake would be withering in the most elegant of ways, preparing to go bare for the winter. Everything would be quiet, fresh, and barely awake. He has always loved nature in the dawn, ever since he was a boy. His father would take him at the first break of light to train and, to Sabin, it was the best part of his day. Even though his father was merciless and utterly ruthless in his teaching methods, Sabin was excited every morning.

A wandering thought passed through his remembrance, he wondered what Tullia thought of dawn.

When his rage was leashed enough for thoughts and logic to flow, he asked. "What's wrong?" He felt his veins throbbing hotly.

"I-I'm so-sorry." She stuttered, frantically wiping her face with the back of her hands. "I-I guess I'm sleep deprived. I also may be a bit hormonal. I don't know. But your w-words really hit me." She gave a wobbly smile, her nose reddening.

Sabin's hand reached out without a thought and petted her silky head as she quietly sobbed, a slight tremor wracking her petite frame. He could smell a soft almost sweet gale resinous fragrance coming from her. A nostalgic, almost melancholy feeling filled him.

A few moments went by with soft inhales and muted traffic.

Tullia inhaled a ragged breath then covered her face with her hands and groaned. "I need a tissue." She peeked at him through her fingers. "Don't look at my scrubby face. I need a moment."

A soft feeling cooled the intensity of his rage, allowing him to relax slightly. He stopped petting her, his gloved covered hand still warm, and opened his glove box and handed her a napkin.

She thanked him shyly and wiped her eyes and nose demurely. Tullia's dove gray eyes latched onto his and looked at him for a long time, as if debating something important, before she let out a heavy soul-tired sigh. Her big gray eyes seemed to shimmer in the bright Vegas sun. "Okay. Let's go."

They both got out of the truck, sunshine pouring onto them unforgiving as is a desert sun's job. He followed Tullia up to a mismanaged door. It seems that the vampires had propped it back to look closed.

She stopped in front of her door and stared at it for long, long moments. He could see her swallowing, and a fine sheen of sweat glittering from her forehead. Sabin didn't rush her. As he waited, he looked around the parking lot, to see vagrants, graffiti, litter, and rough looking individuals stalking to the rooms with shifty eyes. He slid his eyes back to Tullia, and an odd thought wandered into his head yet again.

Did nothing else ever happen to her besides the vampires while living here?

He'd find out. And he'd determine his course of action after she told him.

Tullia's smokey eyes suddenly looked up at him, they were wide and intense. "I don't have my key."

Sabin glanced at the propped-up door in the doorway and then back to her.

Sabin nodded and stepped up close to the door, then slipped his hand through the gap between the door and the frame and slide then entire door to the side.

The room was tiny. Even for a woman as petite as Tullia, the room barely offered more than a few steps in each direction. There wasn't a separate area for the bathroom and the bedroom, it was more like a flat… just minus the kitchen and shrink it down by three times the normal size on all sides. The walls were the color of stained grease, the carpet was torn and grimy looking and the bed was smaller than a twin. There was no TV and only one beaten up chair and a wobbly looking nightstand in the room. There was a large scuffed up piece of luggage propped up next to the bed.

He felt a tugging at his lips when he saw the massive collection of books stacked on the nightstand, strewn all over the chair, a few piled on the sink and about three stacks near and on the nightstand.

His lips quirked up. She was quite well read it seemed.

Sabin turned to look at Tullia. She didn't go in, instead she stood stiff in the doorway, looking at the room with a tense face and her hands in tight fists by her side. Five minutes passed by and the unforgiving sun of the late afternoon bared down upon them, showing no sympathy from the intense heat.

"It's hot." Tullia commented, her voice was pitched slightly higher.

"Indeed." Sabin folded his arms.

Another five minutes passed by.

"Damn it." Tullia huffed, then shook her hands and began to jog in place. "Okay, okay, okay, okay, okay, okay, okay, okay, okay, this is my space… my bitch…" She chanted before running inside her room with a face set for war and a hissing sound.

Sabin stood stunned, then his lips did more than simply twitch. What an amusing girl, he thought as he followed her in. Tullia fluttered around her room; her face thunderous as she began to furiously tidy up. She was in the bathroom area, gathering a few items jerkily and shoving them into a tiny silver bag. Sabin glanced at the mountains of books.

"You have a lot of books." He commented, his eyes roamed over a few titles. There was *Then There Were None*, *The Glass Castle*, *The Green Mile*, and then there were a ton of books with half naked men on them…. He looked at her with a raised eyebrow.

"Yeah, they're just for decoration though, I don't actually read them, cause who reads books nowadays?" Her biting sarcasm tugged at Sabin's lips. "Actually, I need to return them to the library before we go. I don't want to get any late fees."

He nodded and began to gather the books and stack them together.

"But," Tullia said as she turned to face him, a frown on her lips, and multiple items in her hands that Sabin didn't recognize. "I don't want to return them." She eyed her troves of books greedily, before heaving a sigh with her entire body. "But I guess it's not going to be a short adventure. Darn it!" She stomped. "I haven't read all of them yet."

At her cute little huff Sabin chuckled, a rusty sound clanging in his chest. "I'm sure you can borrow them again."

"Yeah," She seemed to purse her lips, still looking at all her books. She was pouting, he thought with amusement. "Okay, can we put them in your truck and drop them off before we go to the Grand High's house?"

"Yes." And he started to gather books in his arms. By his third trip, he had mostly cleared out all her borrowed books from her room. It confused him slightly on why she would borrow so many at once. He wondered if she actually did read them all or if some were for decoration. When he entered in her room once more, he paused.

This girl was entertaining.

She was kneeling on top of her suitcase, wiggling so furiously she was in danger of toppling over, all while trying to zip it up. He smiled and grabbed the remaining bit of books from her room. It took a total of twenty minutes for Tullia's tiny room to become completely bare; for her to change from her pajamas; go to the management office to quit; and say goodbye to a front desk clerk named Linda. Once they were back in his truck they stopped at the library, dropped off all twenty-seven of Tullia's books then made a quick stop at to eat.

Tullia was still sipping on her milkshake as Sabin pulled up to his home.

"So, how long do you think this little excursion of finding a dragon will take?" She asked, practically skipping next to him as they made their way to his front door.

"Don't know." He opened and unlocked the door. It was strange to him to be going on a hunting trip to find a dragon in the first place with a witch. He'd be tested with the witch's presence.

She made a soft sound, following him into his home.

"It won't take me long. Make yourself comfy."

Tullia saluted him and pranced to sit at his kitchen table.

Sabin strode into his bathroom, he dug around in the forever bag and gently pulled out Tullia's siren's shell. Carefully, he placed it on his sink them threw the bag into the tub. He felt the filth covering it when he first touched it and needed to scrub it clean before he could store anything in there.

He inhaled a deep puff from his glamour pen, then as he exhaled the smoke, rolled up his sleeves.

He used an entire bottle of soap on the bag, until the water ran clear once more.

Then pulled out a few cleansing bombs that he stole from the swampers, during a different clean up mission. He dropped three down in the bag, then quickly closed it. There were three muffled blasts that jiggled the bag. When he opened the bag once more, a fresh scent of linen and lemons wafted up and a little bit of white smoke.

Satisfied, Sabin lightly wiped the outside of the bag and nodded at the clean gleam. He rolled down his sleeves, picked up the bag and Tullia's siren's shell. His house was quiet and still. Walking out he looked over to the kitchen table to see Tullia slumped over the table, fast asleep.

His lips twitched and he found himself walking over to peer at her sleeping form. It was an odd thing, many people do not look different when they sleep, only vulnerable to kill. With Tullia she seemed to become smaller, and he noticed the paleness of her face, the blue veins under her skin and the fact that her shoulders seemed even smaller than before. Setting the bag and shell on the table, he carefully gathered Tullia up from her seat. He walked a few paces to the bed and gently arranged her, removing her shoes and tucking a blanket over her.

He stared at her for a moment, her blissfully unaware face soft with sleep, before he sat on the edge of the bed. Fatigue was a constant companion to him, though it was something he could easily ignore. Though sleep was no longer a temptation, for nothing awaited him in the lands of his dreams.

He sighed soundlessly, his weariness heavier than normal, and studied Tullia.

It appeared to Sabin that she was always in constant motion, her face changing many times throughout the day. To see her face still and soft, showed just how young she was. Unlined, kissed with various beauty markings, and softer cheeks, highlighted her youth in a way that made Sabin feel a little aged. Her breath hitched a bit, before sighing out past parted lips.

He gently brushed away the strands of hair that draped over her face, his gloves preventing any type of sensation, but the warmth managed to saturate the fabric. He smoothed his thumb over her cheek once, then withdrew. Without her boisterous personality he noticed the dark circles under her eyes and the abnormal paleness to her face. Her eyes fluttered restlessly behind her lids, her lips seemed to quiver every now and then. She frowned slightly, her brows furrowing and her lips trembling.

Sabin widened his eyes, he had forgotten that mere hours ago, she had been through a living hell. She did well during the day, never hinting at the prior abuse…. But sleep had a way of summoning demons to torment the mind and distort rest into a place of misery.

Poor girl.

His gaze drifted away from Tullia as he thought about last night and all the events that led up to this very moment. He wasn't sure how long the little escapade to find a dragon would last, it could be a few days or months, but after he would need to help Tullia find a way to provide a comfortable living for herself. He pondered over possible careers… then he shook his head, it was useless to think of that when he didn't even know what she wanted to do. He would need to ask her first, then he'd help her. Of course, that would all have to be after the witch. His weariness increased tenfold with the thought.

Sabin went to get off the bed, he had a few things to take care of before being sucked into the selfish witch's plans… suddenly Tullia jerked right up and stiffened. Her eyes flew open, went wide and she stared straight ahead unblinkingly and completely frozen.

Sabin's head snapped towards her at her sudden movement. His eyes scanned the room, alert.

"Tullia?" He called to her softly, she didn't respond to him. Her body was rigid and unnaturally still. Sabin tried calling her a few more times, but Tullia remained unchanged. Gently he patted her face, no reaction. He turned her head so he could see her face and felt a shock of surprise shoot through him. Her dove gray eyes were clouded and sightless. Fine blue veins stood stark and webbed by her eyes. "Tullia?"

He stared at her, memories of soothsayers and fortune tellers swarmed his mind. They all had her face.

Her mouth opened and a language both silken and chiming came out rapidly. Sabin had never heard a language like that before, it was not something native to this realm. Tullia then jerked violently, slumping forward onto the bed, panting harshly. Sabin sat there, unsure how to proceed. He picked up her limp upper body, rearranging her to lay back down, her face a pale, damp mess. He brushed a stray hair from her face and tapped his fingers against his thigh, thinking.

Lost magic.

The witch had blathered something regarding to the fact that it took a heavy toll on humans. He watched Tullia for a few moments more, she tossed and turned, mumbling nonsense and breathing hard.

Sabin then stood up abruptly. He needed to hurry.

* * *

They pulled up to a guard gate in an area where only the extremely wealthy resided. Sabin didn't like the air; it was soaked in privilege and money. The guard was a scowling man with pale skin and ice blue eyes. He glared at them before calling to see if they were allowed in. Of course, they were, though even with permission the guard didn't let up on his glare towards them, even when Tullia waved happily.

"If he were anymore personable, I'd have invited him for the trip." Tullia commented, yawning at the end.

Sabin had awoken her as soon as he was done packing. Her face was lined with exhaustion and the dark circles more intense under her eyes than when she went to sleep. But she had smiled as if nothing was amiss.

He wondered what the lost magic made her see to make her so restless and he also wondered if the witch could weave a sleep spell on Tullia… if that would stop the lost magic's interference with her sleep. He tapped his fingers on his steering wheel.

"He's always unfriendly." He commented absently, driving down the narrow road.

"Well, at least he's consistent." She murmured.

Sabin rolled up to another set of gates, these ones intricately designed and gold with an eternal sparkle coating to ensure they glimmered even in the dark. Three armed guards were standing stiffly in front of the gate. Sabin rolled down his window.

The guards eyed Tullia, then stared at Sabin, before nodding at them. The golden gate opened silently, allowing Sabin to pass through.

"That was some serious eye contact going on." Tullia murmured, looking back as the gate swung shut behind them.

"He was scanning us."

"Like, checking us out?" She asked, looking over at him. "How flattering."

His lips twitched. "No. He was using magic to scan us."

He glanced over to see her head swiveling left and right, looking at the scenery. "Huh, double security?" Tullia asked.

"They trust no one." Neither did he.

The drive to the witch's main house was about a mile from the second golden gate. Dense forestry flanked the narrow road, a stark difference to the desert scenery from mere moments ago. In the dying light of day, the weak sun rays gently brushed the imposing tree's leaves, illuminating them in a golden glow.

"Wow, it doesn't feel like we are in a desert anymore. It almost feels like we're back east with all these trees…" Her eyes roamed over the imposing trees; her expression slightly shadowed.

"Indeed."

A few minutes of silence passed before they managed to break out of the dense foliage. The sight of a grand, oversized, and gaudy mansion greeted them. The entire structure was a bright marble white, with tall windows, dark green accents and flamboyant, curved accented designs. There were two flights of stairs separated by a giant Blackthorn tree, full of tiny white flowers. The witches must have frozen the tree in its blooming state, Sabin thought for the millionth time, for the tree does not bloom at the end of summer. The driveway was a gigantic circle with whimsical patterns in a deep blue color all over and a high gloss shine to it.

Sabin parked his truck close to the left-hand staircase and killed the ignition. He looked over to Tullia, to find her staring up at the house, her face momentarily dark before shuttering as she sighed. "I am under-moneyed and too real-world grown for this place. I can feel it."

Sabin's lips twitched. "Wait until the inside."

"It's probably too big, too fancy, and way too shiny." She pushed her hair behind her shoulder, her smoky gray eyes meeting his briefly, a smile on her pretty face.

She wasn't wrong.

Seconds later they were both standing in front of stain painted glass doors of what Sabin always thought of as hemlock design and knocked firmly twice. He wanted to smash the glass.

Tullia fidgeted with her dark hair and fixed her clothes. Sabin mentally prepared for their trickery. Witches were unpredictable. Whether they'd be welcoming towards them or not would be questionable.

The doors gently opened with a soft click, silently inviting them in.

"Stay close." Sabin murmured to Tullia and strode through the door.

Into the nest of vipers, they went willingly.

Chapter Nine

He stood looking down at the town that was currently in the process of burning down below him. He scowled. Did he not just save this village mere moments ago? The wind ruffled his hair, scattering black strands across a face that was praised, worshiped and feared by all. Impatiently he brushed the strands away and pinched the bridge of his nose before sighing. Humans were troublesome. Raising his arms up high, he sent a prayer before summoning the magic within him.

Summoning magic was an act that was simultaneously unpleasant and euphoric. The magic burned his flesh when called and seemed to destroy and rebuild him instantaneously. He was caught between pleasure and pain in a middle ground that held nothing but ice-cold clarity. Willing the magic to obey him, he manipulated the water consistency of the clouds to become heavy with rain. The first fat drop of rain opened the flood gates as a heavy shower soaked the once burning village.

He was not going come back a third time. He refused. If this village could not support itself against the world's inflictions, then it needed to be culled. Sniffing, he turned on his heel and began his trek back to his domicile. He commanded the rain to exclude him and wherever he walked, the rain did not *fall.*

"Saved the same village from devastation once again huh, Jiang Li?" An accented voice commented. Jiang Li cut an annoyed look at the seemingly innocent looking man-child skipping alongside him. He was annoyed that his rain did not touch him either.

"You're a long way from home, Ryujin. Isn't your mother worried?"

The boy flashed him sharp fangs. "Insolence. You're addressing a sea god, where is the respect you show for royalty? Do they not teach that in your lands?"

Ryujin was the sea god in his region across the sea and liked to brag about it constantly. He would often go into local towns and spread outrageous rumors about his feats, his power, and his form. Of course, the superstitious mortals took the claims serious and began to show their worship of him through their architecture and create even more outlandish stories and paintings of him.

Ryujin was nothing more than the man-child dragon of his tiny land that mistakes him as a sea god. Stupid mortals.

Jiang Li shot the younger dragon a side look. Ryujin not only looked young enough to still be considered a boy, with a soft, round face, too big eyes, smaller mouth and hair that was always messy around his face, he acted like a child without a stitch of shame.

Disgraceful.

Sea god... Jiang Li internally rolled his eyes. If Ryujin was a sea god, then Jiang Li was a turtle.

"Go home little sea god and play with your tide jewels." He picked his way

carefully through the rough terrain. It was no wonder humans carried out tasks clumsily, their two feet and body proportions were awkward at best. "It's past your bedtime and the tides will soon be high."

Ryujin laughed, completely unaffected by Jiang Li's blistering tone. "You're pleased that I am visiting a lonely dragon, such as yourself."

Jiang Li almost laughed and punched the foreign annoyance in the face. "Lonely? Hardly, more accurately, I voluntarily go into seclusion, not only for my benefit but also for the protection of others."

Ryujin raised his black eyebrows; he was now hopping belong side him. "Protection?"

"Indeed." Jiang Li said solemnly. "I have little self-control when individuals who lack basic etiquette approach me or hinder my progress. I find they are abhorrently abundant. Therefore, to avoid the cause of several funerals, I stay away."

Ryujin laughed, then his icy blue eyes became sharp and knowing. "You're fond of the village, you're fond of humans in general, even though they're pitiful beyond redemption." Ryujin's eyes flashed with contempt. "When another disaster hit, particularly in the case of this little village, you came running to their aid. All because of a single gift from a wretched child."

Heat rose along Jiang Li's spine; he forced his shoulders to stay relax and gently breathed in the rain drenched air to retain his internal peace. Though his hands clenched tight behind his sleeves. "The village has both lucks on their side. I merely happen to be the yin in their yang situations."

Ryujin hummed, his blue eyes sparkling. "Ruǎn xīncháng lóng."

Jiang Li became instantly exasperated with the conversation, the other dragon's barbs, and the uneven terrain beneath his feet. He once more drew the magic within him to shed his human form and release his natural appearance. He felt relief as his body grew, his skin hardened and rippled with a collection of blue scales. He felt his claws elongate and sink into the earth's freshness as he stretched up to relieve the ache that accompanied being in mortal form. Mortal shells were too tiny. He then shook his head, white hair swished around him before settling back away from his face.

Usually, he always liked to transform near a body of water, so that he could admire himself in his natural elegant form. However, he was thoroughly exhausted today and didn't want to trek to the nearest body of water, and he already knew he was beautiful. It was just nice to visually see his beauty. Just as he was about to take to the sky, something hard slammed into his side and sent Jiang Li smashing into the thick foliage. Snarling in outrage, he shot up from the earth, dirt and rocks sprinkling down, and hovered over his crash site, eyes wide and glowing as his muzzle pulled back to reveal crowded, uneven razor-sharp fangs. His claws were extended and poised for attack-

There was a guffawing sound to the left of him. Jiang Li snapped his head around to the sound and the snarl of rage deepened on his face. Ryujin was also in dragon form, grinning a big toothy grin.

Obnoxious creature, Jiang Li thought with a scowl as he shook his head.

Ryujin was the color of fire and soot, the deep black scales shadowing the dark red. Ryujin had the same long body as Jiang Li, though his red hair was spiky and lined his jaw and upper lip, whereas Jiang Li had an honorable thin mustache and flowing mane.

"Play with me." Ryujin commanded, his tail swishing excitedly, like an animal. A young animal.

Jiang Li sniffed in distaste. "You three-toed commoner, do not assume importance over me and try to issue commands."

Ryujin rolled his red silted eyes. "You and toes."

Jiang Li was offended. "I'll have you know, having five toes means higher status and a better grip. Like such." He darted towards Ryujin and gripped his tail. Jiang Li heaved, dug into the other dragon's tail and began to spin him around while ascending higher into the sky.

Ryujin gave a roaring scream, complimenting the heavy rain and dark, thundering sky. Jiang Li forced the air around him to assisting in creating a faster acceleration to his spin.

"Faster!" Ryujin cried out happily, to which Jiang Li decided to comply. He felt a smile tug at his lips.

Then Jiang Li... let go. Ryujin's gleeful screams disturbed the air as he shot through the sky like a piercing arrow.

Jiang Li chortled as he watched Ryujin's form become smaller and smaller, then blurred and finally disappearing entirely over a few mountains. He shook his head, roared out in victory and preened in the sky under the heavy curtain of rain he had summoned. He spun in three circles before curving up and darting south in the location of his precious home. Ryujin must have flown at least to the far mountains in the east...

Which a village sat directly at the base of.

Jiang Li's thoughts were silent as he rode the air currents home...

His nose twitched and his scales became ruffled.

Wáng bā dàn!

He jerked his big body sharply to the east, and tucked his limbs closer into him, for speed. He urged the magic to generate more wind to assist his body in flight. Nature can destroy villages, even other mortals can destroy villages, but Jiang Li was not going to have a human village destroyed by a dragon on his conscious. He'd never be at peace.

That Ryujin... such a bad egg.

* * *

Tullia didn't like the mansion. There was always a certain coldness and superficial air in sparkly mansions. This one was no exception. The entrance inside was gleaming unnaturally and perfect... perfectly cold and impersonal. There were fancy vases on equally fancy tables with supposed 'modern' flower arrangements in them. The floor was tiled in a fancy mosaic design, mimicking the gaudy trimmings and boarders.

Tullia suppressed a sigh, this brought back unpleasant memories of her childhood. Being cooped up in a big mansion, not being allowed to touch anything, being alone and bored.

Was it really a shocker she went a little (a lot) bonkers?

Suddenly, a woman with jade eyes, coffee rich skin, and short, sleek black hair appeared before them. Tullia jerked in surprise by her sudden appearance, but Sabin didn't even flinch. The woman's face, while pretty, was set in a firm frown, as if she was severely displeased by their presence. She wore a smart business suit and skyscraper heels. She nodded to them. "Follow me."

She then turned sharply on her heel and proceeded swiftly down the tunneling hallway. Tullia and Sabin followed her, making several turns, walking though long hallways, and even climbing up two staircases before the woman finally stopped in front of an unremarkable white door.

"The Grand High will be with you in a moment." She motioned for them to enter, nodded once at them and walked away, before fading completely.

Tullia stared after the woman, feeling oddly manhandled…. At least emotionally and spooked. "Spooky." Tullia looked up at Sabin, she felt her eyes were too wide. "I feel like I'm supposed to know what's up."

Sabin winked at her, his eyes becoming sunshine eyes. "It's merely theatrics. Come." He opened the door and strode in. Tullia toddled in after him and gaped in wonder. The room was spacious, with high ceilings and a funky looking chandelier of glass and seashells. The floors were an ash gray wood, and the windows went from floor to ceiling overlooking a thick mini forest and beyond that to the Vegas patchwork landscape of desert, homes and city.

The view comforted her; she was still in Vegas.

"Come sit." Sabin invited as he sprawled out on a couch that looked more like an experimental piece of art. Then Sabin's entire being imitated a statue as he let his head fall back and close his brilliant gold eyes.

He must be tired. He hasn't slept at all today, or last night. Tullia wandered closer to the imposing windows and stared at the scenery, thinking about everything and nothing at once. She was very tired; she'd been riding her adrenaline for the entire day. It seemed she had a never-ending day of shocks, discoveries, excitements, and stress. Her unintentional power nap back at Sabin's was anything but restful.

It made sense, since life liked to mess with her, that she'd have a vision of war and blood and shit while trying to sleep after the most traumatic moment in her life. She glanced at Sabin, he hadn't moved a single inch from when he sat down.

Her day had started with the intention of death, but it was the biggest win of her life. She felt herself smile out at the window, she may be ready to drop with exhaustion, but that didn't affect her excitement one iota. Questions popped in and out of her mind as time ticked, she stared, unseeingly out the oversized window.

How would they find the hidden city? It's a hidden city for a reason.

What dragon would they be sent to find? There are so many dragons, Tullia mostly had visions of Japanese and Chinese dragons, but what if there are other type of dragons?

How long was thing going to take? Days? Years?

Would the dragon know how to remove the lost magic?

Would it hurt? Tullia frowned at the thought. She didn't like pain.

Would they have time to sight-see when in the Philippines? She totally wanted too.

"Good, you're not late." Tullia turned around abruptly, startled at the suddenness of the Grand High's voice.

The Grand High looked lovely as she did haughty. She wore a pair of well-worn jeans, black boots that were strapped with dozens of belts and a low heel, and a white blouse with cut out sleeves and a plunging neckline. Her hair was no longer in tiny, long braids. Instead, she had a short afro with honey colored spiral curls.

She fluffed her hair as she stared at them, then frowned severely.

"What is this? Did I not tell you to pack? Did I have to provide you with a list?" She shook her head, and let out a long, exasperated groan. "I swear. No. If you're going to be seen with me, we've gotta fix your appearance. I won't tolerate you looking like trash next to me."

Tullia looked down at her ripped jeans (that didn't start out as ripped) and her too faded to see Coca-Cola shirt with SpongeBob flip-flops (she splurged on those bad boys). Sabin was wearing the same ninja-not-ninja gear.

Sabin didn't even twitch, he merely stared at the Grand High, almost defiantly.

She snorted at him, "As if anything would help you." Her onyx eyes latched onto Tullia, "However, I see potential under all that…" She waved her hand and her pretty face creased, but she didn't finish.

"Let the girl be." Sabin rumbled.

"Shut up. I'll do what I want." Her smile became a honey dipped blade. "I'm gonna fix you up."

Tullia was too tired and strangely too wired to really care. Though, she did make it a point to give the Grand High a tired, 'I don't care' face while hugging herself.

The Grand High smiled too widely before clicking her nails together, a small puff of blue smoke spurted from her fingers. "I'm taking that as consent. I'm going to do an overhaul on you!" She pointed a finger at

Sabin. "You, meathead, sit and stay. Good boy."

Sabin didn't move an inch from his sprawled-out position on the couch. He just continued to look at her with stone cold topaz eyes.

The Queen of the witches seemed somewhat satisfied with his reaction and clicked her nails together again, smirking. The room seemed to waver, then melt, Tullia stiffened as her vision darkened before a shot of blinding light startled here into squeezing her eyes shut and recoiling slightly. When she opened them, she was in an entirely different environment.

The room was cluttered, small, and homey. The walls were a faded white with many kinds of framed items from exotic butterflies to dried flowers. There was one big window that needed some TLC in terms of cleaning and a fat window seal that displayed jars with various liquids, a cage with a skeleton bird, various candles, and a giant bubbling flask of lavender liquid. By the window was an oversized dark brown leather couch and books were piled around the couch, on the couch and scattered in seemingly every corner of the floor.

In the middle of the room was a black, spiral staircase that led up to… a second floor?

"Come on now, we've got to get you decent, and we don't have much time." The Grand High floated up the staircase, disappearing up to the second floor. Tullia blinked, confused but nonetheless excited as she trekked up the stairs that wobbled way too much for reassurance.

She wasn't thin, but did the stairs need to be that dramatic with their shakes as she climbed up them?

On the second floor, it looked like a witch queen resided there. Darkly furnished and moneyed the room was positively gorgeous. Tullia's eyes wandered over the room and noticed that there wasn't any wall exposed for it was covered with pictures, paintings, tapestries, and relic looking items.

"I like all of your wall decor." Tullia commented, trying to hide the fact that the short stairway stole nearly every oxygen molecule from her lungs.

Seriously, it was disgusting how out of shape she was, she thought with self-detriment.

The Grand High looked at her from over a perfect shoulder. She gave her a very faint smile. "Yes, thank you." She threw a heaping pile of clothes onto her rumpled silky bed and then patted the chair that sat in front of a huge vanity. "Sit. I'll fix your hair and that pasty complexion to start with."

Tullia obeyed and sat. She began running her fingers through her hair with her unnaturally long fingers. At first Tullia was stiff, she didn't receive a lot of physical contact, but as the Grand High's fingers continued to play with her hair, the sensation was too good not to relax into. "Your hair is nice. But I think I have a style that'll really make you look your best."

Tullia nodded absently, melting under her touch, she didn't have an interest in her hair. "Sure, whatever you want." She really never had any money to spend on the luxury of getting her hair done. She barely had enough for food and gas. And to cut it herself?

No.

"When's the last time you've gotten a haircut? Your ends are disgusting."

Rude once again, but the flavor on her palate was bubbles and colors. So, Tullia's going to assume that the queen did not say it as a barb.

Tullia shrugged in answer. She didn't know.

"Hmm"

The Grand High went silent behind her for a few seconds, still playing with her hair then, spun Tullia around abruptly. Tullia inhaled quickly, as the Grand High caged her in by placing her too long fingers on each side of the arm rest. She lowered her face and placed it real close to Tullia's. There was a hint of acidic fizz, like a carbonated lemonade, as the Grand High grinned.

And it was at that moment, that Tullia saw the Grand High had no pores. Tullia had never felt the intense jealousy as she had when she witnessed the perfection of the Grand High's skin.

"This is my gift to you, petal. Make sure you properly appreciate it." Tullia was utterly dazzled by the Grand High's face. Gorgeous patterns of the creamy white designs and the rich dark brown color mingling pleasantly together on a very beautiful face…and a face that was so close to Tullia's not stunning face was too much for her brain to comprehend.

Was she even real? Did she have a glamour on too?

Tullia could only nod when it seemed that the Grand High was waiting for her answer. The Grand High's smile was sharp, almost frightening, as she withdrew. She held up her hands and they began to emit a smoke blue.

The Grand High's obsidian eyes flashed and the sensation of all her body hair being plucked out forcefully occurred… simultaneously.

The air from her lungs expelled harshly as her throat closed up and her entire body stiffened with misery. Tullia's eyes watered as a thin whine left her frozen lips as she hunched into herself. A hot throb overtook her entire body, overwhelming her executive mental functioning into short circuiting.

"Anything worthwhile involves some pain."" The Grand High chirped, she clapped her hands.

Tullia half heard her words as she pressed one of her hands to her face and the other between her legs. That was possibly the second most unpleasant, violating sensations she had ever experienced thus far in her life.

She heard the Grand High cackle as sweet bubbles danced on her palette. "Woman up girl. Pain is beauty." She gripped Tullia's shoulders and pushed back against the chair, forcing her to sit up straight. The edge of the lingered pain reduced somewhat, but now her whole body throbbed dully.

The Grand High grinned cheekily. "Hair." She ran her fingers through Tullia's long black hair again. Her hair began to waft with blue smoke. "So, I'm thinking soft mullet."

Her hair rose and then about six inches detached themselves and fluttered down around Tullia. She blinked seeing bangs and a gradual decent of her hair towards the back of her head.

Tullia tilted her head to the side, then shook her head to fluff the hair.

"Nah." She said after a few minutes of observation, not really impressed with the cut. She twisted her neck to look up at the Grand High. "Can you make my hair into a mohawk and color it like the rainbow?" She asked eagerly.

The Grand High raised her eyebrow but clicked her nails together. Tullia looked back at herself in the mirror… then burst out laughing.

"It looks so bad!" She cried through her laughter, hunching over with the force of her mirth.

A small chuckle. "You do look terrible."

"Okay, okay, what about a bowl cut?"

Another tapping of the nails and Tullia's hair was a perfect bowl cut.

"Oh my gosh, I looked like a rejected Beatles member." Tullia held up the short black strands. Then she gasped as a brilliant thought hit her, she looked up at the Grand High again with a wide smile. "Can you transform my hair into one of those popular styles that the pretty Korean boys wear?"

The Grand High snapped her fingers and a puff of blue smoke darted out towards Tullia. When she turned her head back towards the mirror her hair was quaffed, and the bangs were side swept in a popular Korean hair style. Tullia giggled then did a few finger hearts in the mirror.

"You make a very ugly Korean boy." The Grand High commented, as sweetness and bubbles filled Tullia's palette.

"Too true." Tullia sighed and leaned back in her chair. She did one last finger heart and this time winked.

"Now, let's get serious." The Grand High shook her head, and tried a few hair styles on Tullia, ranging from French bobs to undercuts. It was a blast to see so many different styles on her, but they eventually settled on a shaggy long bob in her natural hair color. Tullia liked her hair as it swished about her face, making everything a bit more dramatic and anime-like every time she moved her head.

"I love it!" Tullia exclaimed, toggling her head back and forth, enjoying the cool strands of her hair gently brushing her face and neck. She also adored the lightness of her hair. She didn't realize her hair was that heavy until majority of it was gone.

"Good." The Grand High commented, fluffing Tullia's hair messily.

"Thank you, Ms. Grand High." Tullia said as she looked up at her and smiled.

The gorgeous witch grinned back at her. "You may call me Cliona." She folded her arms. "The Grand High title is stuffy and only necessary when in court or when I'm threatening someone." She patted Tullia's head, as if she were a favored pet.

"Now," She clapped her hands together. "Hairs on point, body hair in check. Now for the really fun part, the clothes." She motioned for Tullia to rise, to which she obeyed.

"Hmm." Cliona stared at Tullia. "What's your favorite type of clothes?"

"A hoodie." She answered immediately. They were warm, soft and roomy. And when things got too intense, you can throw up the hood and hide.

Cliona made a noncommittal sound and clicked her nails together.

A cool sensation rushed over Tullia, she looked down to see a long sleeved, baggy mesh top in the color of a warm sand, jeans, and slick looking sneakers.

"Look in the mirror and…" The Grand High pulled the shoulder sleeve down to expose one shoulder. "There."

She looked at herself in the full-length mirror and thought for the first time in her life, she actually looked fashionable and adulty.

She twisted, looking at herself at all angles. She then looked at Cliona, who stood there, looking haughty and smug. "You're like a fashion angel!" Tullia marveled.

A high, tinkling laugh, "I am!" She agreed her smile softer on the edges and less perfect in its authenticity. "It has a hood too, so you can hide if you want."

Her eyes widened. "Can you read minds?" She pressed her hands to the sides of her head.

The Grand High raised her eyebrow. "What are you doing?"

Tullia pursed her lips. "This might prevent you from reading my mind."

She coughed, then shook her head, her fluffy golden afro wiggling from the movement. "No. You just seemed like the type to hide in hoodies—"

Oh. Tullia slowly withdrew her hands from her head.

"—and , yeah, sometimes I read minds." She said as she crossed her legs in the air and a tart frothy taste pricked its way along her tongue. Tullia put her hands right back up to her head and narrowed her eyes at Cliona. She knew it. A low, sultry chuckle. "Alright now petal, we are done here."

A sharp click, then once again, the room distorted, elongating and melting, before darkness began to restrict her vision and consumed it entirely. A streak of bright light and instant vision of a new surrounding disoriented Tullia. She blinked rapidly, trying to re-center herself and catch up on the new sensory information that began to flood her.

"Welcome back." Sabin rumbled. Tullia slowly turned to look at him, he was in the exact same position as before.

"I see you're comfy." She commented, unintentionally sarcastic and accusatory. Feeling still slightly raw from having all her body hair simultaneously ripped out of her forever and feeling as if Sabin didn't have the right to look so comfortable.

Petty, maybe, but what could she do, she was a petty bitch.

Sabin's gold orbs gleamed as the corners of his eyes crinkled slightly. Bubbles danced on her palette. "There's no need to expend energy when one does not have to." His gilded eyes became sunshine. "Your hair looks lovely by the way."

She shook her head, her hair fluttering all about her face, with a smile, feeling awkward under the compliment, but happy. Before she could answer, or thank him in a wonderfully inept way, the Grand High scoffed.

"Of course, she has nice hair." Cliona said haughtily, before taking a seat across from Sabin. She fluffed her blond hair as she waved to Tullia. "I helped revive it. Now, sit down, petal. We need to go over a few things before we get this show on the road."

Tullia sat next to Sabin, who physically moved to make some room for her.

"Alright listen and listen well, 'cause I am not repeating myself." The Grand High began. She crossed her legs over and clasped her knee with both hands. "We're going to a town called Gandara in the Philippines. There is a clan of witches who we have a good relationship with that is willing to assist us in the receiving end of the transportation on such short notice."

The Grand High clicked her nails together twice and a map of the Philippines appeared. There was an area that was circled in red.

"Biringan City is suspected to be located between that towns of Gandara, Tarangnan, and Pagsanhan." She sighed, leaning back. "My research specialists were able to confirm the suspected location of the city, but there's definitely something; whether it be a magic deregulater or a strong ass cloaking spell, that is blocking my magic from pinpointing Biringan's exact location." Cliona gorgeously sculpted face looked irritated. "Either way, no one can get an exact location."

"We will be backpacking between the three towns to find the hidden city then?" Sabin said.

The Grand High seemed to sigh with her entire body. "In a nutshell." She glared at nothing. "I should punish the goblin for this, are you aware of the humidity that the Philippines have? My poor hair…" She petted her golden curls lovingly.

Tullia tugged at her shorter locks nervously looking at the map. The red outline was awfully big.

"That part of the plan is irritating but easy enough." She looked at the two of them, "Once we manage to enter the city, for I have no doubts in my skill in finding that in which tries to hide, we will need an informative shifter. So, we're gonna need some OG shifters to talk to. The young crowd won't know shit."

"A senior shifter home visit then?" Tullia asked, smoothing her hands over her soft jeans. How were her jeans soft?

The Grand High threw her head back and laughed a chiming, bright sound. "Now that's a definite! After I place a disrupter in the city, so that I can always pinpoint the city's location, we'll be hittin' up an old folk's home."

"Shifters don't age." Sabin's baritone voice filled the air. "No old folks home."

"Shut up meathead, there's bound to be some sort of old people congregation somewhere and we will find it." Cliona tone was sharp and whip like.

Sabin shifted a bit forward, his first movement since he sat. "Perhaps a more diplomatic approach may work better to our favor."

The Grand High curled her glossy lips up in distaste, "There is something fundamentally wrong when a barbarian of a man wants to take the diplomatic approach." She stuck her tongue out and put a finger in her mouth, mocking gagging. "Boring. You sound like the Elders."

Sabin shook his head, completely unconcerned with the promise of violence in Cliona's voice. His second movement.

The Grand High raised her eyebrow delicately. "Then what's your plan? Do enlighten me."

"Simple. Talk to the local authority figures in Biringan."

"Boo." Cliona gave him two thumbs down. "Boring. What makes you think that they'll even give us the time of day?"

"Undoubtedly, someone will want to talk to us." He folded his arms across a broad chest. "Since we've managed to get into a hidden city."

"They could try and execute us on site too." The Grand High shot out. "That's why we should take the more aggressive approach. We will get results faster."

"At a price."

Tullia swallowed nervously, she fiddled with her hands on her lap as she listened to them bicker. Over the years, she had a few visions on shapeshifters. They were fantastical, changing into anything they desired in the blink of an eye. From what she has gathered in bits and pieces is that there was a royal family of Biringan. The person in charge was a woman with an ageless face and ancient eyes.

Tullia believed her name to be Caroline, or so she went by outside of Biringan City. She debated saying anything, after all who was she…

But, since this whole thing was kinda about her little quirk or whatnot…

"Um," Tullia hesitated, her small sound caused Sabin and Cliona to look at her. She felt the weight of their eyes on her and tried not to wilt too much. "I think there's a royal family in Biringan." She forced herself to sit still and not shrink back. She inserted herself into the conversation, she needed to be firm.

Cliona arched a perfectly sculpted brow. "Oh? And how do you know that?"

Tullia inhaled deeply. "I…I may have seen something like that, kinda, you know, with the… lost…. stuff."

Cliona's face brightened. "You have visions? Of Biringan City? Of shifters?"

"Of… a lot of things." Tullia added in nervously, she was uncomfortable talking about her visions, no one ever responded well to them.

The Grand High clapped her hands in delight. "Marvelous. We'll demand an immediate audience with the queen then."

Sabin said. "*Request* an audience."

Cliona waved him way. "Shut up, that's what I said."

Vinegar and bitterness clashed along her palette along with a sweet bubbly sensation.

"Maybe, we should have a plan B. Just in case." Tullia suggested, swallowing the thick flavor in her mouth.

After a few more ideas, disapprovals, insults (mostly from the Grand High towards Sabin), they all settled on plan A being trying to meet the Queen of Biringan and plan B finding a scribe or professor that was an expert on dragons in Biringan City. Cliona assured flawless communication between them and the residence of Biringan, for she had mastered the spell of communication in forty-seven languages, in the human realm and other realms too.

She was truly a model queen.

It wasn't a very good plan B or even a plan A, they were far too simple and lack a lot of important details. However, they all considered the plan a sort of improvising type method. Basically, they bullshitted everything as they went. It didn't scream competent in the least bit, but then again, they only had less than two hours to come up with it. So, it was pretty advanced for that kind of time frame.

Maybe. It was Tullia's first time, so she didn't have another example.

Cliona tilted her head, as if she was thinking about something…. Or listening to someone. Tullia raised her hands to the sides of her head.

Don't read my mind...

"We have a bit more time on our hands until the teleporter is ready. From there we'll have a car ready for us and begin the triangle journey between the three towns."

Tullia perked up; a shot of excitement filled her veins. She was nervous about the entire trip, it was all happening so quick, it felt as if her poor brain had not caught up with the current situation. Which made total sense due to the lack of time to process all the world-shattering occurrences of the day and her intense sleep deprivation. She looked at the Grand High, lowering her hands from her head. She wanted more information about the stuff that made her 'crazy'. It had been a thought annoying her since this morning.

"Grand- I mean, Cliona, could you please tell me a little more about what lost magic is?"

Cliona's fathomless eyes stared at her for a moment, the inky eyes unreadable and distant. "Lost magic is an enigma. I can't really tell you much about it." She rolled her shoulders, as if she were restless. "However, what I can tell you is it doesn't have any particular trait, other than it amplifies commoners magic by a thousand-fold." She gave Tullia a contemplative look. "Though, it has not been studied extensively, because it's nearly impossible to find and harvest and sustain. So, I am limited in knowing what the magic can and cannot do." She tapped her long, long fingers against her thigh, "I do know that it is rumored to be an original form of magic, before Gods and Goddesses existed in this realm."

Tullia scooted forward in her seat; her attention solely focused on the floating woman. Magic before the Gods?

"But, who was before gods and goddesses?" Weren't they, supposedly, *first?*

The Grand High raised both hands in the air and whooped, startling Tullia. "Finally! That forsaken magic origins theories and ideologies class comes in handy!" She reclined like a Hollywood movie star, propping her head in her hand and crossing her feet at the ankles. "Get comfortable, petal. I'm going to sum up two semesters worth of information on the origins of magic in less than an hour."

Cliona snapped her abnormally fingers and puffs of multicolored smoke filled the air.

"Alright, let's get some terminology correct. First of all, it's not a *who* was before Gods and Goddesses, but *what* was before and *what* is still here." She wiggled her fingers playfully. At least, Tullia thinks it was supposed to be playful. It came across more ominous as the smoke swirled around her. "There are several theories by the big wigs and small wigs," Cliona continued, she pulled a golden curl from her afro and wound it around her slender finger, "but there are only really two theories that have been supported by archaeological findings and clout."

The smoke twisted to a number one and the words 'Awakening Earth Theory'.

"The first theory, called Awakening Earth Theory, was discover by some old dude in the eighteen... no seventeen..." Cliona frowned, tapped her nails together thoughtfully before shrugging. "I suppose it's irrelevant, the who's and when's. Basically, the theory goes like this," the colorful smoke wafted into tiny little humans looking into a bright hole in the ground. "There was an ancient race of freshly evolved homo-sapiens that managed to tap into the doormat magic of the earth, through rituals and a lot of digging." The smoke transformed into little stick figures worshiping the letter T. "Trial and error led them to ascend beyond the constraints of humanity and thus begin their life as experimental magical beings. They awakened more magic from the land, transformed other homo-sapiens, gained greater usage of magic, became supreme beings, blah,blah, blah." Cliona made her hand talk dismissively. "And, naturally, this theory applies to all the other realms too." Cliona flicked her fingers out in a flippant motion, the smoke disperse the little figures. "The findings at Göbekli Tepe really bolsters this theory."

The Grand High looked at Tullia with her inky eyes. "Have you heard of Göbekli Tepe, petal?"

Tullia shook her head.

She grinned widely, showing all of her white teeth, and flicked her fingers out, commanding the smoke to swirl into shapes. "It's considered the Turkish Stonehenge and one of the earliest temple findings in the world. There are T-shaped pillars, organized wall structures, and evidence of people not actually living at the temple site, but the site was *clearly* used for something. Rituals and stuff." The smoke showed more letter Ts and stick figures around them with little swirls.

"A specialized team of witches, called the National Organization of the Dedication of Ancient Magic Study, or NODAMS," She seemed to roll her eyes and waved her hand in a circle. "I know, dumb name, but most national organizations have… fatuous acronyms." She shrugged. "It's an unspoken requirement." She waved her hand again frivolously, and the smoke moved. "Anyways, they excavated the site and found a high concentration of used magic in the pillars and in the area in which plaster was used. Further analysis of the site revealed the stone walls were magic touched, the plaster was assisted with high level magic use and the T-shaped pillars were just *drenched* in magic. Magic, magic and magic. What does this mean?" Cliona clapped her hands, startling Tullia, "it suggests that Göbekli Tepe is the first site, *the site*, in which humans awakened the magic."

Tullia felt Sabin shift next to her, seemingly bored, but he didn't express it. His woodsy, clean scent tickled her nose and seduced her to inhale more. It also made her concerned, did she smell good? She did put deodorant on, but was it enough? Maybe she should have showered…

The Grand High snapped her fingers, regaining Tullia's attention, and a bottle of water, a coffee pot, creamers, sugar, honey and mini, powder sugared beignets floated in front of Tullia.

"Drink up petal. I've a got a whole lot more to sum up to you." She spun lazily in the air, as a cup of coffee floated next to her. She sighed as she came full circle to an upright position. "One would think that with as far as technology has come with its advancements and the fermentation and precision shaping of magic throughout the decades that teleportation would be instantaneous."

No, Tullia did not think that at all. The fact that there was an actual teleporter fueled by magic and aided by technology was enough to nearly send Tullia in a state of coma-like shock. She'd never even seen things like that in her visions. She took the bottle of water, downed half of its contents and then made herself a mocha caramel latte with three different types of creamers and one scope of sugar. Sabin had snagged the giant plate of mini beignets and threw three at his masked covered mouth…. And all three passed through the mask and disappeared. Tullia gasped, pausing mid stir.

"Oh my Sabin, your mask just ate your food." She stated, wide eyed and astonished.

A short, wild bark of laughter erupted from Sabin. His gold eyes crinkling in the corners. "Special fabric." He said, as if that explained anything at all.

"Special fabric that I engineered." Cliona clarified, before she took a sip of her coffee, looking regal and smug. "It's tricky to integrate any type of spelling into fabric, but to make one permanent and weatherproof and machine washable?" She threw one hand in the air. "However, I did it and I nailed it and that's why I wear the crown."

Amazing.

Sabin held out a little pastry to Tullia, to which she took with delight.

Never refuse a pastry. That was a law Tullia created and abides by with dedication. You'd have to be a monster to refuse. Or on a diet. Which she was neither. Though the latter was probably in her future if she kept not refusing pastries.

Cliona glared at Sabin. "Those were not for you."
    Sabin simply stared right back at the Grand High and popped another three beignets into his mask that disappeared to his mouth. She huffed, clearly miffed, but seemed to let the supposed offense go. It was always

nice when Tullia ate sweets, most emotions, unless wickedly strong, could be smothered. She took another little beignet. The smoke suddenly morphed into the number two and the words 'Essence Development Theory' with a bunch of fancy swirls around the words.

Tullia crossed her legs underneath her and took a sip her coffee.

She paused, the warm liquid sitting in her mouth.

She had forgot, she didn't like coffee at all. Tullia has, stupidly, thought the Grand High was serving some sort of magical tasting coffee.

It wasn't.

It was just ordinary coffee, which was lackluster to her per usual.

"The second major theory, the one I vibe with, is that there is a supposed…." Cliona paused, seeming to collect her words, "'spirt' of magic. Not an individual person, not a collection of people or creatures, just pure, untouched concentrated magic that assumes its own identity. It's considered more than an animal, more than a creature, more than any other being…" She paused, and the liquid in Tullia's mouth was beginning to cause her tongue to tingle unpleasantly and activate her saliva excessively. Shit, she was going to have to swallow.

"Kind of like the concept of nirvana, but with a distinct personality." She snapped her fingers once more and the coffee cup floated to her lips, she took a sip without moving, "The theory goes that this essence, for it is assumed that there is only one, developed during the evolution of the worlds. As each race developed, the magic took bits and parts of the developing creatures, the changing environments and digested them, thus evolving itself and leaving pieces of itself in every realm. Which is why magic is applicable in every realm." Cliona wiggled her fingers in front of her thoughtfully. Tullia's jaw hurt from holding the now saliva saturated liquid and forced herself to swallow. The bitterness and thick artificial sweetness slid from her tongue down her throat.

She shuddered, disgusting. Ew.

Cliona looked down at her long fingers. "However, while magic is everywhere, it's anything but submissive nor is it particularly kind when you work with it." She flexed her fingers. "There is always a price to be paid when you gain control of more magic."

The slightly salty and savory, sweet taste invaded her mouth as the Grand High looked down at her hands. She was thoughtful and slightly sad. Tullia wondered what she was thinking, if she was being merely reflective or if there were any regrets in her ponderings on magic. Tullia looked down at her now warm coffee in her cup. The warm brown liquid gently rippled as she stared down at it as if it contained universe.

What would she be expected to sacrifice to rid herself of the magic?

The wayward thought made her blink. Tullia had never taken the time to assess the risks to the trip they were making. She assumed the benefits would outweigh any potential negatives that could occur. However, was her decision too hasty? The day had been... chaotic in both the best and the worst way. She couldn't process her situation any further than the surface level. If she tried her head began to throb.

Her nerves began to bunch along her spine. Was she overzealous in the thought of not having to deal with the visions any longer? Tullia didn't even ask the potential risks involved. Then again, no one really knew the risks... or the dragon did, but the dragon had to be found first. She began to gnaw at the flesh inside her left cheek with worry.

Did the dragon even know? What if he didn't? What would they do then? Could she even be free of the so called 'lost magic'? What would she do after? She had been conditioned her whole life to create an environment for herself that would accommodate her sporadic visions… she formed habits and built a little life for herself. How would she be able to move forward?

Her head began to throb with the severity of the questions battering for her attention.

Like a pansy, Tullia wanted to call the whole plan off. She wanted to go home to her crusty motel room, beg for her job back and only dream of a better life. Her tongue tingled with the words of rejection, her body was poised in readiness, to run away…

Sabin took her coffee cup out of her grip-less hands, startling Tullia out of darker ponderings. She blinked and watched as he downed her entire cup of lukewarm coffee before handing it back to Tullia without a single sound. She gaped at him, confused and a little relieved that the coffee wouldn't go to waste. Cliona laughed, boisterous and happy, a stark difference from her contemplative mood from mere moments ago. "Careful petal, this barbarian takes from others if you don't eat it quickly." Her perfectly curved face shining with an amused light.

Sabin didn't react to Cliona's words, but he tilted his head toward Tullia and gave a sly wink. Warmth coursed through her, making her tighten her grip on her cup. Tullia tucked both her lips in between her teeth to keep from smiling. Sabin seemed to be in her corner.

"Your coffee tastes bad." He said blandly to Cliona. "Must be cheap".

And the thought of someone… of Sabin in particular, with his imposing frame, not-ninja-but-ninja mask and his kindness toward her, being in her corner was enough of a comfort to allow her nerves to settle into the back seat of her mind. There were still no answers to her questions… yet. But, she wasn't all alone anymore, for the moment, and that in itself was the most treasured piece of knowledge. For she had always been alone.

"Your tastes buds only appreciate the taste of dirt, what the hell do you know of good coffee?" The Grand High snapped back, while looking down her nose at him.

There was a gentle knock at the door that stole the rooms attention. After a few seconds it opened and the same woman that showed them to the room now stood in the doorway.

"Grand High, the teleporter is ready when you are."

Cliona flicked her hands at the woman dramatically with an excited hiss. She looked at Sabin, gave him a dirty look, and then looked at Tullia. Her mosaic face was a fine blend of haughtiness and excitement. "Hope you're ready for a first-class experience, indigents."

Chapter Ten

The teleporter room was…. An utter disappointment.

It was a shocking disappointment because Tullia didn't know what to expect exactly, but the fact that the teleporter looked like a regular, upper-class living room didn't even cross her mind as one of the possible scenes. There were plush chairs, a giant chandelier, paintings that were probably iconic but Tullia thought were ugly, a Turkish rug, a complex orchid arrangement, fancy tables, a bookshelf, and a giant flat screen TV.

Utterly mundane and utterly disheartening.

"I'm shook." Tullia announced, unable to fully comprehend that the elegant room was a teleporter.

"First class teleporter." Cliona cooed, looking at the room with approval. "It takes big D magical energy to fuel this beauty. Which I got and then some." She laughed, fluffing her blond afro with that usual confident sass.

Tullia stood in the center of the room, her hands on her hips, dissatisfied on a basic level. She supposed she was secretly expecting something mechanical and 'teleporter obvious' looking. Internally sighing, Tullia thought back to all the sci-fi novels and movies she had seen and felt cheated by reality.

She had been bamboozled by the fantasy.

Sabin's tall, tall form looked around, seemed to judge the room within half a second and made a B-line to the sofa.

"Chandelier's ugly." He commented in his smooth, deep voice.

"You would think so, you uncultured meathead." Cliona snapped, though it lacked any real malice emotion. In fact, the emotion that covered her tongue was similar to a sweet and sour flavor. Tullia wandered around the room, looking at everything as Cliona ordered her witches about.

There was just a bunch of useless decor.

"I'm still shook." Tullia said again, looking at where Sabin lounged. His eyes crinkled at the corners slightly.

"Better get stable then." He advised seriously.

She gave a short laugh and made her way over to Sabin. She bounced a little as her butt made contact with the cushion. She approved of the buoyancy of the couch.

Cliona shut the door and looked at both Sabin and Tullia.

She clawed her hand in their direction and then flicked her fingers out. Tullia instantly felt a cooling sensation in her throat, tongue, and her ears began popping lightly.

Tullia jerked her head, shaking it a little at the unexpected sensation as she rubbed her throat.

"I've graced you with the temporary implantation of the language of the Philippines, all eight major dialects." She then gave a snarky grin to Sabin. "Well, at least I have to Tullia. I guess being magic resistant does not work in your favor today, huh Berserker?" Her tone dropped to a high pitched, phony sympathetic rhythm. She even pushed her bottom lip out and made her hand wipe away fake tears.

Sabin, once again, showed no reaction to the Grand High's jab. "I've got Tullia to translate for me, so I'm good." His tone was a bit frosty, though not mean.

Cliona scowled and jerked her chin up at him haughtily. She sniffed, turning her pretty face forward then gracefully stalked up to the delicately wrought love seat and sat like a queen at a coronation. Her eyes were glowing blue. She gripped the armrests and grinned widely at Tullia.

"Sit tight, petal." She said ominously, causing a kernel of worry to unfurl within Tullia's chest. Tullia opened her mouth to question what exactly *that* meant…

A disembodied voice began to speak in a monotone drawl, disrupting Tullia's intention. "Signal connected on Gandara part, preparing for transfer. We will be waiting upon your command for re-teleportation at any time. Transporting one male, two females in 3…. 2….1… Blessed journey, Grand High."

There was a sudden intense concentrated amount of pressure placed upon Tullia's entire body, holding her immobile against the couch. She was pushed back against the couch with a strength that Tullia began to fear that she may become part of the couch. Hot and cold flashes alternated in torturing her as her entire body went numb before becoming a live wire. She was being squeezed from all sides with the unseen pressure, air refused to go in or leave her body, therefore she didn't breathe or make a single sound as an unseen force toyed with her. Her lungs burned, her body became an entire, single throb and her world spun.

Hours, minutes, years later the sensations stopped abruptly and the air lightened. Tullia gasped in a lung full of air, still glued to the cushion, and repeated these deep inhalations until she no longer felt oxygen deprived. The Grand High, completely unaffected, rose elegantly, fluffing her hair.

"And we have arrived." She announced breezily and strode to the door. It opened and a crowd of people greeted her respectfully. The Grand High flashed a dazzling smile and began speaking in an effortless flow of Tagalog.

Still trying to recover, Tullia pressed a hand to her chest, offended that she experienced such suffocating pressure and still disappointed.

"Why was this entire experience anticlimactic?" Tullia muttered sourly, looking up at Sabin.

"'Tis life." He commented dryly, stretching his neck.

"You don't help with anything." She snapped, hugely irritated that she had no comrade to share her discontent with the teleportation experience.

Sabin shook his head as he lumbered to his feet, unaffected, towering, and silent.

Damn him.

Tullia felt as if she were peeling herself from the couch cushion as she slowly rose to her feet. She glanced back at the couch and felt a twinge of embarrassment. There was a deep imprint of her entire backside and buttocks on the couch. She examined the imprint of her butt, then patted her derriere and gave it a squeeze.

Was her butt always that big?

She gave her butt one more squeeze and, with a pleased nod, turned around. She came to an abrupt halt to find Sabin was watching her with his gold eyes. Instantly, she felt judged, and her face heated slightly. Tullia narrowed her eyes and crossed her arms under her chest defensively. "I see the judgment in your eyes and you better un-judge me right now."

Sabin didn't say anything, he merely shook his head again, this time in denial of judging her, but she freakin' heard his silent laughter and tasted the sweet bubbles on her tongue. She gave him the I'm-watching-you hand motion with a glare, before striding past his burly form. This time his laughter was not silent, but low and wild.

Exiting the disappointing teleporter room, Tullia's eyes greedily took in the new, foreign environment.

It was so beautiful.

The walls were bamboo, tightly pressed together within a dark wooden frame. The floor mimicked the walls, with seemingly smaller bamboo pieces and what looked like grass mats in some areas on the floor. The entire area was bathed in bright sunlight from an unobstructed balcony and tall plants sat prettily in corners and along some walls. While furniture was spare, limited to only a few chairs from what she could see, the space was open and airy and bright.

Tullia looked over to Cliona and saw her surrounded by dozens of people, who were speaking rapidly, seeming awestruck and excited by her presences. The Grand High stood taller and nearly outlandish in the quaint home with the petite witches clamoring around her. The Grand High did not smile, but she listened and responded in kind to their questions.

Tullia tilted her head, listening to the other witches speak nearly on top of one another. Understanding their words, understanding their inflections. She was fascinated. She understood them and the way in which their words flowed, their tone and their inflections were almost lyrical and familiar. The best part of the conversations was that nothing was lost in translation. There were no awkward or incorrect sentence structures, vocabulary was not compromised, the words flowed smoothly into her ears, and she understood everything they said to perfection.

She felt as if she had transcended mentally and metaphysically. She wondered, briefly, if this is what bilingual individuals heard and experienced on the daily. She also wondered if they felt secretly superior to monolingual individuals because she certainly did in this moment right now.

Cliona caught Tullia's eye and waved her over. Everyone around her went silent and simultaneously turned to stare at Tullia. Instantly, she felt awkward and way too bulky as she maneuvered her way through the throng of people to the center of the crowd. The Grand High gripped Tullia, yanking her smoothly by the shoulders and pulled her right in front. Dozens of eyes latched on to Tullia, assessing her.

Tullia's eyes darted from one pair of bright eyes to the next, panicking as sweat began to bubble up from her pores, until she landed on the bright golden eyes of Sabin, standing in the back with his arms crossed, watching her. He winked and her nerves became a little less frayed. They were only frizzed now.

"This," She gave Tullia a small shake, "is a human that holds the lost magic which we mentioned earlier." Tension stiffened her spine. She felt like she was on display.

Whispers and assessing looks commenced. Tart and fizzy and slightly bitter flavors coated her tongue. Stress crept through her chest and began to wind tighter with each tick of the clock. The Grand High summoned a wilted tulip and repeated the revitalization spell with Tullia, creating hundreds of tulips, to which all the witches gathered up and gaped over.

Shock was prominent as was the emotion of excitement that fizzled constantly over her taste buds.

Cliona allowed them to chatter amongst themselves for a moment, before regaining their attention by clearing her throat and speaking in their lyrical language. "We plan to extract the lost magic from her. However, we need a dragon for that task."

More murmurs and uncertain looks rippled throughout the crowd.

"I've already spoken to Pacifico; however, I want to ask everyone here to make certain no leaves were unturned. Therefore, does anyone know of a dragon I can talk to or where a dragon can be found?"

Silence. The slightly sourness of nerves fizzed along her tongue.

"Figured." Cliona muttered under her breath in English, she then asked another question in Tagalog. "Does anyone know where Biringan City is specifically located?"

Silence once more. A strong pungent flavor that was one of weariness overtook her palate. Her chest tightened.

It seemed, to Tullia at least, that the local witches did not like or trust Biringan City.

Cliona sighed, she released Tullia and crossed her arms. "I see."

A pretty Filipino woman with dark brown hair pulled away from her delicate face stepped forward, she glanced at Tullia briefly, before looking up at the Grand High. "Your highness, our clan leader apologizes profusely that he is absent for your arrival." She gave a shallow bow, then smiled. "We are grateful for your arrival, my name is Lyra, I am second in command of the Pearl of the Orient clan." Her voice was soft, melodic, but her tone as well as her words were rigidly formal. "We've been informed about the situation, and we apologize for offering so little information besides general facts on both a dragon's location and Biringan City."

The Grand High seemed to measure Lyra in the span of a few seconds, before giving her a small smile. "Nonsense, your clan has been most gracious with me, and I appreciate your hard work and the effort you have shown me in such little time."

Lyra beamed; bubbles danced along Tullia's tongue. "Of course, it's always an honor to be useful to the Grand High in any way possible." Lyra then clasped her hands together and tiny flecks of glitter puffed out. "If you may follow me outside, I have the vehicle you requested as well as the GPS system and equipment ready for your inspection."

Cliona nodded and followed Lyra as she began to lead her out, talking to her about other preparations they managed to accomplish. Before Tullia could think to move, the dense crowd of witches shadowed behind

Cliona, excitedly chatting to themselves about lost magic and the Grand High in their town.

Tullia waited until she was the last person in the room, then sighed in relief when the crowd left and the nearly unbearable tension in her chest lightened. She slowly trailed behind the mass of people through the house.

It is never a pleasant experience to be put on display in front of a crowd. She didn't like it.

"I suppose they don't know where a dragon or Biringan City is?" Sabin asked next to her, making her jump slightly in fright.

She turned reflectively and smacked his upper arm. "Stop being sneaky."

Sabin didn't react to her, but his eyes were luminous. "Can you give the gist of the meeting?"

Tullia sighed again. "Cliona proved that I had lost magic, Lyra is second in command of the Pearl of the Orient Clan and she is leading us to a car that we're gonna travel in, along with other provisions."

Sabin nodded once. "Alright. That's mostly what I gathered."

Tullia snorted. "Sure, you did."

An impression of a smile soothed her ruffled emotions and allowed her spine to soften slightly.

She stepped out of the deceivingly lavish inside of a rather simple bahay kubo and took in her surroundings once more. It was lushly green and damp. Palm trees intermingled with dark green trees and big, fluffy looking trees that were drenched in white looking cherry blossoms greeted her happily.

"Hey, I thought cherry blossom trees were only in Japan." Tullia pointed to the big white, fluffy trees.

A slender, round-faced Filipino man turned around from the bottom step, and looked up at her with a serious face. "Those are Balai-lamok. Though, a few call them the Philippine's cherry blossom trees. Their fruit is very good for women who have bad monthly flow." He looked at her with sparkling brown eyes and acidic bubbles flooded her palate. "You got bad flow? Would you like some?"

Tullia shook her head quickly. No thank you, she was fine.

He laughed and winked at her. "You can eat them even if you don't."

"I think I'm good for now, thank you." Tullia said slowly in Tagalog, testing out words that were foreign but eerily comfortable falling off her tongue.

He smiled, opened his mouth as if to say more, but the crowd in front of him had begun to chatter loudly.

A large hand pressed against her lower back. "Let's go." Sabin's low voice sounded in her ear and seemed to tickle it. He guided her through the throng of witches, they parted easily enough for them. Sabin, she supposed looking at him objectively, was intimidating with his ninja-not ninja gear and stature.

She heard Lyra's voice talking to the Grand High up ahead. "Here in Gandara, in the Eastern Visayas, we get front row seats to the Pan-Philippine Highway that cuts right through this cute village." She gave a slightly dramatic arm gesture towards the view in front. The Grand High surveyed the land wordlessly.

The Pan-Philippine Highway looked equivalent to a country road down a small neighborhood. There was only one lane for both directions that looked rather worn down and faded.

Along the highway, there sat various bahay kubo, some western styled homes, rusted stylized gates and shops that seemed to have been haphazardly made, but stubbornly sat through the years and refused to crumble. There were seemingly discarded piles of rubble and handmade detached looking porches with various advertising signs pocketing the free spaces between houses. There were also various cars, buses, and building material sitting ostensibly abandoned alongside the highway. Among it all, a sparse layer of liter sprinkled along with giant patches of mud and cheeky grass sprigs all amalgamated on the side of the highway. For a highway it was lazy, with only a few bikes toting side carts, a few motorbikes here and there, and that one random van chugging leisurely along. There was precarious telephone wired poles that tangled about in the treetops. Despite the houses and the telephone wires, everywhere Tullia looked there was intense greenery that both delighted and panicked her. She inhaled deeply through her nose, there was an acute earthly flavor to the air intermingled with the succulence of rain and the undeniable scent of human inhabitance.

A sassy chicken strutted in front of Tullia, causing her to stop. The chicken was clucking as it pecked the ground, strutted off and then pecked again. Tullia watched the chicken progress down the side of the highway, unaffected by the people or the vehicles that came far too close to the little bird.

What a bad-ass chicken.

When Tullia and Sabin finally made it to the Grand High, she said. "This is charming. I live in a desert so to see so much greenery surrounding me is certainly a refreshing experience." She eyed a small looking shop that was offering drinks and what looked like chips. "Are there any good food stops you would recommend?" Cliona asked.

"Of course, there are good food places to eat at in Dumalo-ong and in other towns too." Lyra led them to rusty looking shed, to where she motioned for it to be opened. A few witches ran to the door and hauled the giant door back with soft grunts. The door screeched and the squealing metal sent a sharp shiver down Tullia's spine.

Inside was an old jeep looking vehicle.

Lyra clapped her hands together daintily, glitter puffed out, then she smiled. "This is a 1974 Toyota Land Cruiser FJ40. It was mainly for military use, though isn't it too cute for that?" Lyra gave a cheeky grin, and Tullia decided she liked her. "It sits four people, if two are tiny." She eyed them. "Or three *big* people."

The Grand High eyed the car, but nodded. "This is excellent. Thank you." Lyra nodded twice quickly, she handed the keys to the Grand High, who in turn tossed them to Sabin. "I have a banquet being prepared for your dinner to show my appreciation for your understanding and hard work. There will also be a ton of alcohol. Enjoy it to the fullest."

Lyra beamed, though she tried to refuse. "We couldn't possibly accept such a thing."

The Grand High waved her words away. "I know you're only refusing as a formality, but please." She grinned wickedly at Lyra, who seemed to shuffle back a few steps from Cliona. "I insist."

Lyra nodded vigorously, ostensibly spooked. Tullia couldn't even blame her; the Grand High was intense as she was beautifully scary.

Cliona turned to Tullia and Sabin. "In." She ordered, then turned back to Lyra. "Now where are those good food places?"

As Lyra informed the Grand High where to eat, Tullia climbed in and looked around inside the jeep look-alike. It was spacious and plain; it almost had an unfinished feel to it but otherwise rugged and sturdy.

Excitement bubbled in her veins as she sat in the passenger's side. She felt like an explorer… or maybe a more accurate description was baggage that ate. However, she's not one to let labels stop her from enjoying a good time.

Sabin took the driver's side and shut the door. He started up the car and fiddled with the chair settings until he was satisfied. Tullia looked around in her seat then met Sabin's eyes.

"I am freaking out." She announced, a big grin on her face.

Sabin shook his head. "It'll be an interesting time."

The Grand High suddenly appeared in the jeep's back seat, making Tullia jerk in surprise. Damn it, she needed to get use to these two just popping up. "Alright, I got all the major shops from Lyra. We're going to one first before we begin this expedition. Drive now, Sabin." She crossed her legs and leaned back, looking every inch the Queen.

Sabin glanced at her through the review mirror, though he didn't comment on her haughty demand. Instead, he merely started the car and carefully began pulling forward.

The witches waved at the car, some jumping up and down, others shouting encouragements. Cliona waved regally at them.

Tullia saw Lyra give a double peace sign, to which she smiled at as Sabin drove onto the highway. Tullia waved back, even though she knew all the waves were for the Grand High. She then faced forward and wiggled her feet in excitement.

* * *

The Grand High ordered Sabin about in the car to a weathered looking open style bakery. Cliona snapped her fingers and she was standing outside the jeep. She fluffed her hair and strode up to the ladies working and greeted them with a rather regal greeting. She had a glamour on to cover her long fingers and glowing eyes. However, her skin was still a beautiful collage of black and white. Tullia watched as Cliona practically bought the entire bakery, the poor ladies where practically sprinting back and forth to keep up with her order. After about twenty minutes the Grand High crawled back into the car with four giant bags of fresh baked goods.

"Alright, now we may begin the search." Cliona fiddle with a compact device, before a mechanical voice started spouting out directions. "Obey this device." Cliona ordered Sabin after the voice ceased speaking.

Sabin wordlessly obeyed. Though he tasted of prickly irritation and a mild heat dashed across her tongue.

"Petal, look here." Cliona cooed, and a few pastry items began to float up. "Alright. I got some salted egg and pork *Siopao* with spicy sauce, *Ensaymada, Pan de coco, Binangkal, Hopiang ube, Hopiang hapon, monay, puto seko*, chocolate bread and cream puffs with spun sugar." She grinned widely at Tullia, wiggling her shoulders with excitement. "Which one do you want to try first?"

Tullia picked the *Ensaymada*. The first bite was confusing, but the second bite confirmed it was indeed delicious. But then again, it was a sweet, buttery bread with cheese on top. She finished the palm sized treat within seconds and Cliona allowed her to sample all the baked goods. She openly announced to Sabin though, "Barbarians don't eat pastries, so none for you."

Sabin shot back, "I thought you only liked to eat the bones of little witches."

"When I'm dieting, I do. They're low in carbs and fat."

Tullia giggled, and secretly shared half of every treat with Sabin when the Grand High wasn't looking. She found it was ten thousand times more enjoyable to taste Sabin's reactions than actually tasting them herself.

He adored the chocolate bread and the salted egg *Siopao*, sweet fizz coated her mouth when he tasted them. She found that he disliked the *puto seko*. Even without tasting his emotions, which was of distaste (slightly sour and pickled) his reaction of slightly stiffening, slow chewing and eye squinting was enough of a telltale sign to know he wasn't fond of it. All the other items he tasted, he neither liked nor hated. Besides the food, it was highly amusing to listen to the quips between a relatively quiet mercenary and an arrogant queen.

During the quiet lulls of their travel, the scenery was endlessly green with small surprises here and there. Tullia swore she saw a pair of glowing eyes at one point in the darkest pocket of the forestry. However, she forced herself to believe she made it up and that it was nothing.

For peace of mind.

The snacks provided by Cliona were bomb. Though different from the flavor combinations she was used to, the sweet with the salty and sweet with sour immediately made their way into Tullia's favored tastes.

Just under an hour later, they reach the outskirts of Tarangnan. Cliona became bossy once more and ordered Sabin around to various shops for food and a few souvenir places. Sabin rarely said a word to her domineering orders, though he did add a few sarcastic quips from time to time, to which Cliona threatened him violently. Approximately another hour later they were in Pagsanhan. Sabin drove on the main roads, hidden roads, back roads, side roads and every road in between while Cliona scanned the area. She said she was seeking a magical signature, or any type of abnormal magical flux.

They continued this pattern for about two days. Cliona and Sabin took turns driving and sleeping. Well, Cliona winked out to sleep… somewhere. Tullia thought it was her own bed back in Las Vegas, Sabin simply slouched down in the car with his arms folded and leaned against the window. They forbid Tullia from driving when she almost caused a multi-collision accident due to a lizard on the road.

In her defense, the lizard was the size of a baby deer and she's never driven in the Philippians before. So, excuse her and the accident didn't even happen thanks to Sabin grabbing the wheel and jerking it to the left to stay in the lane and Cliona freezing the space around them momentarily, so no one saw or reacted.

By the dwindling end of the second day, the novelty of being in a lushly green environment wore off. End of the third day, nerves were pinched for everyone and the cute jeep shrunk three times on the inside. Afternoon of the fourth day, Tullia wanted to jump out the window and take on the fate of roadkill. Also, the Grand High's 'instant showers' were violating and unpleasant and Tullia wanted a real shower.

"Something's not right." Cliona announced after an hour of driving back to Gandara for the *fourth* time that day. "We're getting nowhere on these roads. *Nowhere.*"

Tullia turned to look at her, Cliona was frowning, her hair was all tucked away underneath a bright yellow hair wrap, except for her edges in which were delicately styled. Naturally, she looked stunning as usual, however her thoughtful demeanor as she looked out the window seemed to capitalize on the rich tones of her two skin colors. She tapped a long finger against her iced coffee as her eyes blazed blue suddenly.

Cliona snapped her head towards Sabin. "Pull over. I want to confirm something."

"What do we say?" Sabin taunted, he had been more growly and sharp with Cliona's orders.

"Now or I shove my ice cubes in your ears." The lack of heat in her words made it funnier than threatening. Sabin found a spot on the side of the road and pulled over. Cliona got out with a snap of her fingers. One moment in, the next she was out. Tullia and Sabin climbed out the old fashion way by opening the doors.

Pushing her annoying hair behind her ears, Tullia watched as Cliona inhaled deeply. "I didn't bother checking the Pearl of the Orient's work on tracking unnatural magical residues. However, perhaps I should have personally seen to it for a more specific area location of Biringan City."

"Unnatural magical residues? What is that?" Tullia asked, strands of her hair tickled her cheek.

Cliona looked at Tullia with glowing pure blue eyes, she felt as though someone rubbed a pickle on her tongue. For a moment, Tullia didn't think the Grand High was going to bother explaining it to her, but then she sighed. "Anytime anyone or thing uses magic, traces are left, no matter how minuscule the magic amount used, you can always find traces. Pearl of the Orient clan assured me they tracked the residue of the magic used to conceal Biringan City, and that it was splattered all across the area between Tarangnan, Pagsanhan, and Gandara." She cracked her neck. "However, there must be more concentrated areas. *There must*. Because I'm not about our current situation."

She glanced at Sabin and Tullia. "Now, do not speak. I need complete silence." She closed her eyes and opened her hands, palms down and in front of her.

Stillness overtook the space in which they existed, canceling out infinitesimal noises and halting all and every sound wave. Cliona did not move an inch, she mimicked that of a statue of a beloved goddess, tall, regal, curved in a feminine way and striking with more than just physical beauty. The combination of her two skin tones glimmered under the sun, demanding the sunlight to touch and give worship.

Tullia was reminded once again that Cliona was extremely beautiful, and she was a potato.

Suddenly, Cliona's eyes opened wide. A thick stream of blue smoke slammed into the earth and seemed to delve deep into the hard surface. "I'll tear that cloak from the city. How dare it hide from me." She bared her teeth in a maniac smile, her eyes glazed and unfocused. "I'll expose them all to the world as punishment… Flay them all alive with the stares of everyone…"

Tullia swallowed thickly as a rotten and pungent taste assaulted her.

Insanity.

Wind whipped around them, swirling restlessly, disturbing the earth beneath their feet. Tullia saw a centipede thrash violently above the ground as the air tossed it around. She hugged herself and felt her body's warmth slowly leave her limbs. The air become strained and icy. Tullia could see her breath puff out from her.

"Come off of it, witch." Sabin coldly order, his tone a vicious type of command with a quality of someone who was lethal.

Tullia snapped her head towards Sabin and blinked. He was openly glaring at Cliona, his golden eyes oddly bright and his demeanor on edge. He looked dangerous, she thought with some surprise. She had never considered him anything other than sweet and gentle. He was always so kind with her. However, he tasted of a peppery restiveness and the strong pungent taste of viciousness.

Cliona unnaturally snapped her head to the side to stare at Sabin. She wiggled her fingers and a streak of blue darted towards him. Tullia yelled, lurched forward to interfere, however, before she could do anything the smoke harmlessly smashed against Sabin's pecs and instantly dissolved.

Heat coated her tongue instantaneously.

"Regain yourself witch." Sabin snarled lowly and cocked his head at her. "Or I'll end you here."

Cliona's eyes flared a brighter blue, her entire body seemed to vibrate with rage, the heat upon Tullia's tongue almost brought tears to her eyes. However, Cliona's eyes flickered back and forth from black to blue and back. She inhaled deeply through her teeth, making a sharp hissing sound. The blue smoke ceased to fall from her hands, and earthly noises slowly resumed once more. Cliona flexed her hands, her breathing ragged.

A few minutes passed, no one said anything as the Grand High continued her labored breathing.

"All there now?" Sabin's voice was deadpan and edged with cruelty.

Cliona cracked her neck. Her obsidian eyes glared daggers at Sabin. "Only you, Berserker, with your annoying maleness, could make my insanity hide away." She patted her head, gently fussing over her head wrap's design. "You're lucky your magic proof. I'd have made your heart explode."

Sabin gave a halfhearted shrug, his body stiff. "You're welcome." Though the words were said flippantly, Tullia tasted the darkness, the acidic taste, in her mouth and the heat from anger. She looked at Sabin, seeing him stare at the jungle before them. His eyes swirled and darkened to an amber honey color.

At that moment, he wasn't the Sabin she had gotten to know over the course of a few days; the Sabin that didn't speak, was quietly kind, and secretly liked sweets. Instead, a tortured stranger stood within Sabin's frame.

She didn't know him. At all. She only knew what he showed her. The thought brought a sharp pang to her chest. She thought they were closer... she thought....

She paused, self-reflecting. She thought a lot of things that were a bit unreasonable.

Tullia went to reach her hand towards him, to offer comfort, but he seemed so cold, so isolated, so untouchable that she hesitated.

"If we proceed the way we have been, we won't come close." Tullia looked towards Cliona, she was pointing to the jungle. "I sense… something *unusual* to say the least within that area." She turned towards them. "We have to head off road. I suspect we will have more luck than staying on main roads."

Sabin glanced at the jungle, his arms folded across his chest. "Very well."

"Finally, the meat-head isn't being a prissy." Cliona smirked, her hand on her hips.

"You finally had a good idea." Sabin replied, there was an undercoat of ice in his words.

Tullia looked out at the thickly layered trees. Their vibrancy and their lushness seemed to give off a sense of freedom, but with an edge of unpredictability. Like eating a whole gallon of ice cream as your first meal.

Cliona clapped her hands. "Alright, it's decided. We off road. Simple. Back to the car-"

Sabin shook his head. "Off-roading would be impossible, the forestry is too dense to allow this vehicle to move about in. We will need to continue our search on foot."

Cliona made a disgusted sound. "If that is our only option…. I suppose. I have some treats saved." She then smiled widely at Sabin. "You'll have to lead us in the ways of a barbarian, okay Sabin?"

"Try to keep up witch." Sabin responded and thawed a little.

Sabin looked at Tullia then. His eyes still darkly enigmatic locking onto her. The flavors on her tongue were all smothered by the heat.

"Good thing I packed a tent." He gave an impression of a smile shone in the way his eyes crinkled, but his eyes did not become sunshine, they were too dark to glow as she had once seen them.

It wasn't genuine.

* * *

Tullia liked nature. It was beautiful, it was important, it was a part of the world, it housed animals, it provided food… Everything came from nature, nature was the beginning and it will be the end. However, there is a huge difference between respecting and admiring nature from a distance, and to actually be in nature.

Being *in* nature, being directly *involved* with nature sucked ass.

The trees were intimidating in their stature, towering unforgiving over them, caging them in and blocking the vast sky above them; the insects were too abundant and far too brave (flying, jumping and crawling out right at Tullia); bushes grew where they wanted with absolutely no care; dirt was far too dirty and the composition was questionable in certain areas; the weather was sticky hot, and nature didn't give a damn about you or your situation.

Tullia huffed as she stepped over an uprooted root that was furry with green splotches and happened to be a bridge for a trial of skittering ants. The worse part about being in nature and it sucking so bad, is that Tullia had only been in it for about a few hours.

They had many, many, many more hours to go. And the thought made her want to cry.

She glanced at Sabin; his lumbering form moved with ease. Obviously, his too big feet would just crush anything that tried to oppose him from stepping and his body could probably bust through a brick wall with no damages. So, it seemed nature was no challenge to him. He also had the unfair advantage of having long legs. Tullia continued to stare at Sabin and had the most asinine idea to jump on him, so he could carry her through the-jungle-forest-nature intense journey that they were on like she was a backpack. However, it was hot. Oven hot. Wet oven hot. It was gross and to cling to someone would be awful.

She narrowed her eyes on his broad back. Okay, so it would require a lot of work for her to hold onto, but it wouldn't be that bad.

Tullia wanted to throw a fit and be done. So, she had catatonic episodes once in a while. So, she tasted everyone's emotions around her. So, she couldn't hold onto a proper job and live normally due to her labeled insanity which was actually 'lost magic' freaking her mental state up. Was being utterly miserable in a jungle worth it?

Was it?

Their beginning trek through the wilderness wasn't so taxing. It was mostly flatter terrain with trees and rocks, no biggie. The first hour Tullia was grateful to be mobile instead of stationary. The jeep had felt like a cage on wheels and was suffocating. There were fresh sights everywhere and a vividness that left her in awe as she ambled through. As the hours began to drag on Tullia's not conditioned body began to flag. She had a cramp, an ache, a quiver and numbness in various places all over her body. Plus, bugs were too abundant, and they were really freakin' big.

Eventually, Tullia ceased to feel her body entirely. She was operating on autopilot. The greenery began to blur around her, nothing was distinguishable. The bugs no longer began to create a paranoia for her. The uprooted tree roots were still an annoying feature, that made her trip continuously, but she felt bullied by nature into accepting that.

Sabin had mothered her all along the way. He made her drink water continuously, fed her, urged her to keep up, asked her if she wanted to stop for a break (to which Tullia always responded in a negative fashion due to her still intact and stupid pride) and kept a slow (not slow enough) pace.

She had stripped her sweater off ages ago, the Grand High had provided her with a tank top…. But it didn't help much.

It was hot as hell.

Tullia tilted her head back, sweat had dampened her hair and slicked her neck. She saw pockets of fading sunlight between the outreaching tree branches. A slight breeze caressed her face. The warmth of the forest sunk into her skin, through her muscles, and did not stop until her soul became warm from the sweltering heat….

…wrapping around his entire being, praising his deity like power. The sun kissed his skin in adoration. His skin rippled with a dozen different colors. He felt like a god walking through the jungle, mimicking the creatures he saw, morphing his entire being to his will, his desire.

He was a God. A physical God.

"Alab." Her voice called him, he turned to see Carolina standing tall and lovely midst the riot of greens. "Stop shifting so rapidly. You know that's not good for you." She was beautifully annoying.

"And why should I? I can be anything, anyone. Why choose one, when I can choose all?" Alab saw her face crease with disapproval.

"You tempt misfortune to visit you." Her voice, quiet and pleasant, sounded grating upon Alab's nerves. He had no need to heed Carolina who stuck to one measly form for majority of her time and called it her 'original' shape.

She disregarded her power, insisting upon a singular form. What she failed to understand is that they had no true form. They were amorphous.

To go against their nature by merely residing in one form was blasphemous to their nature.

"I seduce power due to my profound understanding on our nature, dear sister." He announced, puffing out his chest with pride. He was the best shifter, everyone in their clan believed this as a fact. He was the top shifter in physical activities, he mastered his abilities first, mentally he was incomparable, he could outwit a strategist and his power continued to grow substantially as the days passed.

Carolina shook her head at him. Her dark brown, nearly black hair swished like a waterfall behind her. The sunlight seemed to caress her dark brown skin, as if petting her. "Our gifts are not to be used like such, Alab. You know better."

Alab didn't believe in the supposed teachings on choosing a singular form to identify with enable to stay grounded with humanity. He didn't believe in living hidden from the humans, building a city for shifters to reside in peace within, and building up their community numbers with mere humans. He didn't like the limitation placed upon them in regard to their shifting. Carolina was merely mimicking their late fathers' teachings like a puppet. What she failed to understand was that times did not remain in a singular state of being, it changed as did nature, as did the lowly humans. Alab believed it was time that the humans experience a change and understand that they did not occupy the top stop in the food chain. Rather, they held no real power in this world.

His skin rippled from a dark gold skin to a pale brown then to completely colorless.

"Alab." Carolina snapped. "You're going to get stuck one day. Then what will you do?"

He turned to face her fully, annoyed, elated and feeling a sense of superiority towards his tradition laden sister. He spread his arms wide and elongated his face. "I am invincible, Carolina! Look at me!" He focused internally, forcing his shifts to increase in speed, alteration and diversity. "Look at me!"

Carolina's soft face seemed to tighten with anger. "Father did always say, it is hard to wake someone up who is pretending to be asleep." She clicked her tongue at him, folding her arms at him like their father always did.

The favored child, listening like a well-trained pony to jump for its master.

Anger rose within him. She believed herself self-righteous... she saw him as a mere pest that needed training. She saw him as below her. It was a false notion she carried. He was not to be tamed and brought to bow before the feet of those who were beneath him. Carolina was beneath him. His late father was beneath him. His entire race should be kneeling before him.

Pain splintered in his mind, causing him to flinch. This offended him deeply. He glowered at Carolina, feeling his anger morphed into a deeper emotion... a darker emotion. He began to look down on Carolina as his body stretched upward, elongating.

"Behold the power you ignore, sister." He laughed as a malicious thought slithered into his mind.

He wanted Carolina to cower before him. To make her quiver with fear at his mastery. To make her realize just how wrong she was. Alab elongated himself, shrunk his now ash gray skin close to his chunky bones, emaciating his form. Alab knew her fears. He decided to combine a few of them. He enlarged his teeth, mimicked a horse's skull for his head, clawed his hands, hoofed his feet and grew a long tail. He cocked his head and stared at Carolina.

"Witness this sister. See my power. I can create creatures that do not exist." He laughed at her tiny form below. "Now do you see? LOOK AT ME!" He screamed at her.

The forest around them silenced. He felt the creatures hiding, felt their fear of him, of his dominance... of his power. He waited for Carolina to mimic the simple creatures of the forest. Her face was pinched tight with fear, her big brown eyes seemed to acquire a sheen of moisture, though no tears fell. Her complexion was ash white and a fine tremor over took her rather diminutive frame.

Carolina did not scream though; she did not flinch away from his purposefully grotesque form. Instead, she slowly straightened her spine. "I see that you are corruption. You have corrupted yourself through your pigheaded thinking and egotism." She narrowed her eyes at him. "You allow our gifts to consume you and define you. You are a fool."

His head pounded with pain and grew foggy as his limbs began to span. He was angry. She made his rage burn hotter within him. He shook his head, dispelling the discomfort of holding an unnatural shift. He would hold this monstrous form, to prove his godliness.

"I am a God." He hissed. "I should be worshiped. I should be praised. I should not fear the thoughts of the lower life. The predator does not concern himself with the options of the prey."

"A man who talks too much, accomplishes little. That is all you have ever done, Alab. Talk and expect everyone to bow to you for the gift we have been given." Her condemning voice was an acid lick up his spine.

He sneered at her, fighting back the growing pain in his chest and head. *"You and your self-righteous proverbs."* He leaned in towards her, taking immense satisfaction in her slight recoil, in the further paling of her proud face. *"Try this one: New king, new character."*

He opened his mouth unnaturally wide, his elongated tongue rolling out as he roared with all his might in her face. Carolina did not move, even as she shuddered under the force of his scream. He then laughed, pushing her down into the dirt, just to see the proud, self-righteous face morph into a twisted, fearful expression. He stepped forward, and she scuttled back.

He felt his chest swell with satisfaction in seeing her finally acting upon her fear of him.

She was finally reduced to a pitiful state.

Finally.

He opened his mouth, to mock her...

Pain struck inside his chest and spiraled outward uncontrollably, clawing at his nerves, seizing them violently. He choked on his laugh and then screamed as a horrid burning sensation consumed his chest. He began to claw at his chest, backing away, stumbling on his awkwardly positioned hooves. He heard Carolina's panicked shout, he didn't understand it, the pain overrode all senses.

Blearily he tried to shift into a human, a plain human. He felt a fluttering, the feeling he usually got, euphoric, intoxicating sense of power, but it dissipated as suddenly as he had willed it to come. His limbs spasming as pain rush back *in to consume him.*

Panic ensued. He began to stiffen with effort as he tried to summon the shift again.

A flicker, then gone once more.

Ice encased him, freezing his limbs, numbing his claws and shooting icy pain all over his scalp. Alab screamed again, his hoarse voice clawing up at the sky for salvation from the agony. He swung his head back and forth, before fuzzily focusing on a tree, then running towards it. The force in which he connected with the tree was enough to render a deep fissure in the trunk that traveled up high on the bark.

The pain rolled through his body as he hit the earth with a jarring thud. His eyes watered as the anguish increased acutely throughout his frame. Alab stared at the sky, blue with a dotting of clouds. The serenity they offered only mocked him in his current miserable state.

His vision was suddenly filled with Carolina's hated face. "Alab! Are you alright?" Her concern, her fake concern, fanned the dying embers of his almost forgotten rage. "Shift to something else." She had the audacity to order him.

He really hated her. He hated her. He hated her.

*He lashed out, slapping Carolina's hand away, leaving an angry welt across her hand. "Do not offer your help to me, **putanginang aso.**"*

Carolina frowned, withdrawing her hand. "Alab, please, let me help you. You must be in pain."

He laughed as he began to stagger to his hooved... hooved... hooves. A deadness began to creep outward from his chest, smothering the torment in its path. "I feel nothing." He shook his head, looking down at his clawed hands. He willed the shift in only his hands... a flutter... a pinch... then numbness.

His entire body felt stiff, awkward and weak.

What had he done?

"Alab?" Her damned voice called out to him. Alab shifted his gaze from his claws to Carolina's deceptively pretty face. Her eyes, her judging eyes, scraped along his already bleeding nerves.

*"**Hayop ka.**" She said softly, a mere breath. "I'll help you, please brother, let me help you."*

*He bared his teeth, "**Malilintikan ka sa akin.** I'd rather remain as I am than ever receive your help." He lifted his heavy head high, managed to muster up as much pride as he could. The deadness now encased his entire frame. He felt no pain... he felt nothing. "Do not concern yourself with me, sister." He sneered the word. "I shall carry on my own way." He turned away from his sister and headed into the forest. His mind racing with a thousand possibilities, a thousand panics, a thousand rages.*

"Alab. Alab!" He heard her cry behind him, he ignored her. "I'll be waiting for you brother. When you need my help, when you need me, I will help you. Please, I will help you."

He snorted. He would never come to her. Never. Her generous heart was not as pure as she had fooled others to believe.

He managed to find a spot, hidden away from the main paths, and began to heal himself.

A flicker.... days... weeks... years... decades... Alab remained unchanged. His original form was that of a demonic thing. After many years, he could transform once more for a limited time, but ultimately, he had been reduced from a god to a cursed creature.

His rage never dulled. His anger was as poisonous as the snakes that slithered all about in the jungle. And all his anger was towards Carolina. She cornered him, she tested him, and he had disfigured himself, had ruined himself because of her. Carolina and her self-righteous disposition had caused Alab to become reckless. She had caused his deformity... his pain... his suffering.

He sat at the banks edge, looking at his now reluctant true form. Monstrous. He titled his head, thinking. His gnarled face twisted into a vile version of a smirk. When he gathered enough strength, when she gathered enough to lose...

Only then will he seek her, and he'd destroy her and everything she held dear. Just as she had effortlessly destroyed his beloved ambiguity and shackling him to a horrific form.

"While there is life, there is hope." He tapped the water, enjoying the disturbance the ripples created. "I'll borrow that favored phrase for now... then return it to her in kind."

Images of blood-soaked clothes, screams and fire flitted by... before...

Tullia blinked in shock as her vision was covered by black covered pecs attached to Sabin, who was carrying her princess style in the same jungle. She looked up to see a black cloth covered jaw of Sabin, who was walking through the jungle (effortlessly) while still carrying her.

Sabin was carrying her.

She looked up even further to note the sun was sleepy in the sky, painting pastel pinks, blushed oranges, and shy yellows all over.

"Um," Tullia didn't know how to start a conversation while being carried - it was a first-time for her - so she started with the basics. "So, I might have had a vision."

Sabin looked down at her, his eyes crinkled in the corners and the sunshine appeared. "Appears so. We didn't know when you'd be back, so I made the executive decision to carry you."

Nodding, while trying not to be as stiff as a board, but also not be dead weight in Sabin's arms she replied. "I see, thank you for that decision and not leaving me to become another bug crawly toy." She wiggled her feet. "I'm awake, so I can walk."

"I suppose you could." He was silent for a heartbeat, then, "However, you are providing me an excellent arm, chest and back work out." He flexed his arms, lifting her higher, before lowering her. He repeated the action a few more times.

She balked at his words, then frowned. "If you want something to lift, find a log. Put me down." Tullia did not appreciate being used as a weight.

Sabin gently set her down, only completely letting her go when she had solid footing on the soft the earth.

"Try to stay coherent, alright sweetness?" He teased, winking one of his honey bright eyes at her.

She scowled. "I see you're getting talkative. That's great." She muttered, though she refrained from saying what she actually wanted to say so she could recover some of her dignity.

"What did you see, petal? Shifters? A dragon? An answer on how to transfer lost magic?" Cliona popped up in front of her hear, floating with bare feet. Tullia noted that her toes were painted a dark blue and glittered in the splotchy sunlight.

"I saw..." Tullia began but stopped abruptly. She was confused on where to start with the vision since it overlapped with what she was doing, which was walking in the forest, and explain exactly what she saw. She didn't even know what she saw. "Shifters? I guess. I'm not really sure. They were having an argument."

"Hmm," The Grand High made a thoughtful sound, "But no mention of dragons? Or anything useful to us?"

Tullia shook her head sorrowfully. The Grand High shrugged. "Well, it was a long shot, but a player has to shoot." She spun lazily around. "Let's keep moving."

A slight breeze ruffled the leaves, creating a soft chime to gently accompany their crunching footsteps over the earth. A few strands of her hair dislodged and tickled her face. Carefully brushing them away, Tullia's eyes flittered over the landscape that looked so awfully familiar. Cold hands of foreboding massaged her shoulders as they continued through the thick forestry.

And the feeling of malice eyes tracking their every move kept the hair raised on the back of her neck and her spine stiff.

Chapter Eleven

Sabin was setting up the tent as Tullia sat on a flat rock that she had found with her toe after stubbing it to the point of nearly causing it to recede a few inches into her foot. She sat on the rock to punish it for nearly destroying her toe. Her body was a giant throb of pain and regret. They had trekked a few hours after nightfall, Cliona providing a bright orb of light to allow them to see and Tullia thought she was going to cry… then die from exhaustion. Finally, Sabin found a relatively clear spot to set up camp about thirty minutes ago, to which Tullia has been punishing the rock, not giving a flying rat's tail if something crawled on her because at this point, she'd have no energy for a freak out.

She'd probably just try to cry and then the exertion would send her over the edge and cause her to pass out.

Cliona had looked around their camp sight, snorted then tapped her fingers together twice before disappearing in a puff of blue smoke. She has been absence ever since. Tullia lounged like a deflated volleyball, watching Sabin skillfully set about their camping area, making a cute little fire pit and all. She was becoming less and less numb and more in pain with each resting second.

At the current moment, the score was mother nature one and Tullia negative twelve. This was why nature sucked, it made her use her body in ways that she shouldn't just to stay alive.

The Grand High suddenly popped up right next to her, scaring Tullia, though her reaction was dead mimicking the rest of her body. Tullia merely looked at her blandly even though her heart skidded a bit in her chest. Cliona smiled, gorgeous and model perfect, and held out a bowl of what looked like a very hearty pasta with veggies. Tullia looked up, Cliona looked refreshed and perfectly manicured with her silk robe and a pretty floral silk cap covering her head. Her dewy collage black and white skin glowed with supreme health and beauty. Tullia on the other hand felt like unwashed underwear of a fat guy who worked out for the first time in years at a Zumba class.

"Here, this pasta has all the essential vitamins, proteins, and veggies you need for recovery." She held out the bowl to her and Tullia eagerly reached out for the bowl, but Cliona pulled it away at the last minute.

That bitch.

"Oh, but before that." Cliona reached over and flicked Tullia's forehead… twice. A blast of blessed relief calmed the aches of her body as an icy sensation engulfed her being from head to toe. She squeaked a bit when the icy waves hit her delicate regions, but she felt reborn and revitalized and, blessedly, clean. The thick layer of sweat, grim, and emotional turmoil was wiped away with the Grand High's sweet magic as if Tullia just came out of the shower. A violating and involved shower with an ice block, but still a shower.

It was such an underappreciated feeling, but Tullia was now fully aware that the purification of one's body was not only a physical sensation, it was an emotional, mental and an all-encompassing state of being. Even if it was done with nearly inhumanely cold ice.

Tullia smiled up at Cliona, even as she rubbed her stinging forehead and shivered. "Thank you."

The Grand High gave a rather sharp smile. "I am ever generous to my charges." She then handed the food to Tullia and even allowed her to take it this time.

"Where is your tent gonna be?" Tullia asked, taking a huge bite of the pasta dish. An explosion of complex flavors both subtle and bold dashed across her palate, caressing each taste bud personally. Tullia wanted to melt into a puddle of elated pleasure that had just been overdosed in an obscene about of serotonin and dopamine. It was heavenly and beyond any type of pasta flavor she had ever experienced.

Tullia instantly decided it was magic pasta and she would eat it all.

Cliona snorted a laugh, "Me? Sleep in a jungle? Oh no, no, no, I don't do-" She waved her hand around in a frivolous manner, "outdoorsy stuff. Hiking is about it. No, I sleep elsewhere."

Tullia looked at the Grand High, after shoveling in another forkful of pasta into her mouth. She chewed just enough to ask, "You gonna teleport back to Vegas?"

Cliona had teleported away a few times during their torturous trek, though they were for bathroom breaks and snack breaks that she had shared with Tullia when she came back. Cliona gave a dramatic sigh and rested her delicately blended face on her slender palm. "Unfortunately, personal teleportation doesn't work that way. I can only teleport myself, at max, fifty miles away from where I am currently located. Which is why even I had to use a teleportation machine to get to the Philippines." She pressed her face more into her palm as she looked at Tullia. "Wanna sleep on the floor in my room tonight, petal?"

Tullia felt extremely flattered in a weird, slightly offended way that the Grand High would offer her an invitation to sleep indoors. However, if Tullia left with Cliona, then Sabin would be all alone in dark, creepy forest. Her heart gave a tiny, tiny squeeze at the thought of Sabin staying all alone in a dense, dark and creepy beyond description jungle like forest for an entire night without anyone to, at the very least, offer a distraction from the darkness.

Also, to be honest, sleeping on the floor wasn't exactly a temptation when compared to sleeping in a tent. Sabin had two axes to chop up any bugs that dared to invade her personal space, Cliona was more likely to slap Tullia if she woke her up and ask her to slay a bug. "I think I'll rough it for tonight. Camping is something I haven't done before." At least, not without being in a car in a brightly lit parking lot, though she's pretty sure that didn't count as camping. Tullia considered it as such though.

The Grand High gave her a disbelieving look, but shrugged her shoulders. "Suit yourself. I'll refresh you in the morning, so, at the very least, you don't look like baked road kill."

Tullia giggled, too tired to be offended, and continued to shovel the magic pasta into her mouth. Roughly twenty minutes later Sabin had not only the tent ready, but also had a small fire and managed to cook a whole can of beans and make a peanut butter sandwich for himself.

Quite the little camper he was.

It was the most peculiar sight to watch Sabin eat. He'd hold the food up to his mask covered mouth then the closer the food got to the mask the food would begin to fade. When the food made actual contact with his mask, it disappeared completely from his hand. So, it looked like he was pretending to eat like he was playing with a toddler.

As he ate Cliona announced, "We're gonna have to repeat this… *experience* shall we say, a few more times until we manage to get into the stupid city."

Tullia sighed with her entire soul. Nature was going to kill her.

"However, cause I'm bomb, I'm in the process of currently fine tuning a blend of magic to try and overwhelm Biringan's shield." Cliona crossed her long bare legs; she was reclining in the air similar to how one would sprawl on a couch. "Once it's, at the very least weakened, we can get a more solid location." She fussed over her cap, lightly smoothing it down.

Sabin nodded at the Grand High's words as he finished one can of beans. She eyed him, then turned to Tullia. "Last chance, petal, he just ate an entire can of baked beans… you sure you wanna share that small space with him?"

Tullia giggled, taking the last bite of her pasta, savoring the utter perfection that it was.

"*Quite dangerous, indeed.*" The raspy, deep voice wasn't loud, but it sounded as if a gun exploded by her ear with the unexpectedness. Sound ceased and the air frosted over. Warmth become a concept that was foreign.

Sabin, once lounging beside her rock, was a whirlwind of blurs before Tullia comprehended that he now stood behind her, facing the dark with his axes drawn at the ready. They seemed to glint hungrily in the flickering fire light. She forced herself to swallow the now soured pasta in her mouth and scrambled up to her feet. Her entire body was stiff and shaky as she frantically scanned the night drenched shrubbery.

"A demon." Sabin muttered, he flexed his hands on his weapons, his bright gold eyes fixated up… up…

She then saw it.

The creature stared at them. It appeared to be crouched on a rather thick branch of a tree, however its knees superseded passed its head and instead of human feet, the creature had large hooves. It's abnormally long arms, paper thin with ash gray skin lightly layered over bones, spread wide on the branch nearly two feet apart from where its skinny body sat hunched. Its face was a rotted horse skull with sunken sockets for eyes and a back of black matted mane.

It seemed to grin, baring its blunted, oversized teeth at them. "Welcome to my forest travelers. What brings you here in this hour?"

Sabin didn't reply, he shifted his body, obstructing Tullia's view and hiding her entirely behind him. However, she did not appreciate his effort and disregarded it as she leaned around his bulk to see the creature. Her curiosity outweighing her horror.

The creature was still as night in a graveyard, edged with energy was oozed toxicity. It was waiting.

"Who the hell are you?" The Grand High's voice was vivacious in its tone and too loud in the deafening quiet.

"Who are you?" It returned, mocking. It is hollowed eyes flickering.

He laughed as he began to stagger to his hooved… hooved… hooves.

Tullia looked over to see the Grand High standing tall, long and queenly with her hands on her hips and her chin cocked up. "Oh no, no, no. I ask the questions. You sneaked up on us when we were mindin' our business." Even in a silk cap, her beauty and dominance did not flicker.

She is so my hero. Tullia thought on a sigh.

The creature tilted its head painfully far to the left, then mimicking the motion on the other side. "You became my business when you entered my territory." There was a growl tinting the words as an oily decaying taste rippled violently over her taste buds. Tullia held her throat, to calm herself as she fought the vile flavor of cruel intentions.

...elongated himself, shrunk his now ash gray skin close to his chunky bones, emaciating his form.

Tullia furrowed her brows as flickers of visions occurred. The creature was horrifying to look at for long periods of time. But a niggling feeling of familiarity forced her eyes on it...

He spread his arms wide and elongated his face. "I am invincible, Carolina! Look at me!"

The creature cricked its jaw, a long, gray tongue lolled out before slithering back into the crevasse of his decomposing head.

"Alab. Are you alright?"

Alab.

Alab.

Alab.

Tullia felt her breath catch as her heart stopped, then pounded double time in her chest with the intention of breaking a rib. Memories of her most recent vision assaulted her mercilessly. This creature was the creature that Alab had turned into to scare Carolina… it was his form in which he was permanently stuck in. Tullia's eyes watered in pain as she stared at Alab in morbid fascination.

He was even more hideous than her vision had portrayed him as. It looked as though he had begun to rot on the outside.

"Calm down, ugly. No need to get hostile. We're peaceful little campers, just seeking Biringan City." The Grand High's reply was flippant, nearly teasing, but blue smoke wafted from her body and her hands were poised at the ready. She was floating a few inches above the ground, but instead of reclining she was 'standing' up right with her toes pointed down, her back tensed and her face set in cold lines.

The creature gnashed its teeth, the papery skin near its mouth seemed to tear slightly as it grinned. "Biringan City." The creature hissed the name as one would a curse. "A witch…." Its deadened eyes roamed over Sabin. "A cursed corpse of a man." When the icy lifeless eyes landed on Tullia her blood seemed to frost over in her veins. "And a less than average human." Its head tilted in an unnatural angle. "What an unfortunate trio."

There was a sour flavor that blossomed across her tongue, chasing away the oily evil. However, what he said was concerning. Less than average? Was that a new description for being certified in insanity? Did she look insane? Or was he just saying she looked stupid? She'd have to ask Sabin later… if she remembered.

The creature shifted suddenly as if to get a better look at all of them and her bladder trembled with fright.

No one responded to the creature's words, though it didn't seem to expect a response.

"Why do you seek Biringan?" Its voice was nails on ice and it spoke in a very old dialect. It was hard to understand, though its slower nearly clumsy speech made it somewhat possible.

"So many questions." Cliona muttered. "Who are *you*?" She demanded, ignoring the creature's question entirely.

"Me?" The creature drew back, still grinning that horrid and twisted smile. "I am Tikbalang." It seemed to relish in its title and expect them to understand what his title meant. "Now, answer me witch, why do you seek Biringan City?"

Tullia bit her lip and laced her fingers together nervously. The Tikbalang was a nightmarish and grotesque creature, the longer she looked, the queasier her stomach got. She noticed a long-matted tale eerily swaying from where the Tikbalang sat.

The Grand High seemed to examine the creature, sizing it up with her onyx eyes. "Why not?" Cliona replied with a shrug and a hard look on her face.

The Tikbalang went completely still, losing its grotesque grin. "Cheeky witch." It said ever so softly, slightly distorted. It gave a slow blink. Then grin widely again. "Seems the time now. I know where Biringan lies. I can show you where. *Tonight.*"

An acidic cayenne flavor scraped her poor little taste buds. Icy beads formed on her forehead, as she swallowed against the thick flavor consuming her palate. It was lying, and acrimonious. Tullia clutched Sabin's back, as a foreboding chill traced down her spine unpleasantly, causing her body to tremble.

Whatever it said was just lies dripping poison and ruin.

"Oh really? How convenient." Cliona's voice was deadpan.

The Tikbalang laughed coldly, hoarsely. "Ah, you do not believe?" He clicked his tongue softly. "You see me, yet you doubt?"

"Seeing isn't everything." Cliona said casually, she flexed her hands in preparation.

The Tikbalang seemed to grin sardonically. "It appears there is some intelligence." Suddenly it stood up tall on the branch. It was skinny, knobby and twisted looking. The Tikbalang jumped down from its branch, landing with a soft thud upon the ground. It straightened jerkily and regarded them with its hollowed eyes. It seemed to curl and uncurl it's claws slowly, methodically. "Can I not convince you to come with me then?" It asked bluntly.

Tullia pressed herself tighter against Sabin's back, taking little comfort in his heat against the icy pain and soured bitterness that the Tikbalang tasted of.

"Leave us alone." Cliona commanded, her face hard and as beautiful as a diamond. "We will find Biringan by ourselves."

The Tikbalang grinned hideously and erratically shrugged its bony shoulders. "I do so enjoy watching fools wander about in my forest." He gave a derisive wiggle of his fingers, "Good luck, idiots. Have fun failing. I'll be watching." His grin darkened on his skeleton horse face, he pointed at them. "Remember, all forests have snakes." He chuckled darkly. "I'll be waiting for you." He stood tall and knobby before them. His eyes seemed to latch onto Tullia's specifically, the coldness in those depths, the cruelly inhuman look in them shot a dart of glacial fear deep within her heart, causing it to stutter and loose its rhythm.

The Tikbalang waved sarcastically, looking ever so demonic before fading out, then disappearing entirely back into the dense forestry and it was as if he never was.

The silence reigned for a few minutes after the demon vanished before the soft sounds of the night life in nature came alive once more. The frosted air thawed and became muggy with humidity; however, Tullia still retained the chill in her bones and the taste of blood and heat lingered.

"Annoying ass piece of trash." Cliona rumbled, she patted her head, making sure her wrap was secure. Her motions hard and angry. "I'm going to need some chamomile tea now. I am in battle mode and no asses were whooped." She seemed to give a whole-body shrug before turning towards Tullia and Sabin. "I've had enough of this." She swirled her unnaturally long pointer fingers around towards the sky. "I'll see you both in the morning." She snapped her fingers, with extra sass and puffed out, leaving behind a thin blue smoke stream.

Sabin seemed to shake himself, then tucked his axes back into his holders on his back. "I didn't think a demon would be inhabiting this area. Such luck never comes in fruitful ventures, only hazardous ones." Sabin turned to her, his gold eyes alight with a fire that would consume a person and leave nothing of them behind. "Come Tullia, let us rest now. It won't be back, at least tonight."

Rest he says, as if a something monumental didn't happen to rattle her mindset and set her nerves on a razor-sharp edge. Rest was the last thing on Tullia's mind, hiding under a blanket and maybe a long, long, long prayer. Rest was an unfamiliar word to her right now. Her mind kept playing loops of the vision she had of Alab and Carolina… and of tonight.

She felt as if her mind was wired on adrenaline and cocaine.

An icy finger traced down her spine. A foreboding prick, like the tip of a knife, made loops on her poor nerves. Words, ideas, theories, and questions became lodged in her throat from years of suppressing what she saw… what she thought. She forced her throat to swallow, ignoring the pain as her unspoken words settled heavy in her chest and nodded to Sabin.

The thick taste settled into her throat, blocking her words.

* * *

Tullia was stiff and silent. Her face was drawn, as if she were tucking herself away. Sabin was concerned as he guided her to the rock she seemed to favor and sat her in front of the small crackling fire he had made for cooking.

"Warm yourself a bit." He instructed, not liking the lack of warmth to her skin despite the night air being balmy and humid. She looked through him, her gray eyes glossy and far darker than usual on a pale face. Sabin tried to feed her, hoping she'd regain her cheerful disposition, but she wouldn't eat and she held her quiet, disturbing Sabin. A few minutes went by, Sabin tried to engage her in conversation, but her responses were short and halfhearted and lacking the warmth she always had when she spoke.

Sabin sighed, he leaned back against a tree truck, enjoying the rough texture against his back. He thought a moment, he remembered the stacks of books littering about her room and the way her eyes glimmered with bright excitement at the thought of hearing a story from Sabin.

A bedtime story… to chase the bad event away and give sweet dreams instead of nightmares.

He peered at her through half lidded eyes. Her eyes were glued to the flames, the shadows made the softness turn haggard and sharp. "You wanna hear a story, sweetness?" He saw her jerk in surprise, then her big doe eyes fastened on him in blank shock.

She wiggled her feet, before she pulled them up to hug her knees. "Sure." Her tone was shy, but her soft voice hinted at excitement.

He had a feeling he chose the right path to entice her.

"When I first became a mercenary, I was given an assignment to fetch a bird called La Tanrrilla. It lived near riverbanks between what is now Guatemala and northern Brazil." Sabin shifted. "Apparently, there is a legend associated with the bird. If you kill it, then bury the corpse just until the flesh rots, then dig up the right leg only and peer through its hollowed bone towards the person of your desire, you can win their love." He felt his lips twist up. "Of course, after you look at the person you desired, the person who does the peering needs to seclude themselves for twelve hours. No one can see you and you cannot see anyone in that time or it won't work. That's how the…spell of sorts works. If done right, then the person will win the affection and love of their desired person."

When he had first been told of the legend, he thought the whole thing exasperating and absurd. It seemed more of a fool's lazy way for love, rather than working hard on wooing their heart's desire.

Tullia turned her body to face towards him. She was interested, as he thought she might be.

"I stalked the bird, in that forsaken place, they're quite elusive." It was a nightmare trying to find the piece of poultry in the rain forest when no one helped due to the language barrier and the fact Sabin looked like a cause of death. Which, he was to many. "I finally managed to kill one after nearly a fortnight."

Tullia was now leaning forward, her entire attention was on Sabin, and her eyes, once shadowed and burdened, now shimmering with blooming light. The urge to smile, tugged at his lips.

"What did the bird look like?"

Ah, finally, she asked a question.

Sabin thought for a moment. "A duck-turkey hybrid with red eyes." He gave an uncertain shrug. "Very ugly."

Tullia giggled. It brightened the space around their camp.

"I had to chase the ugly duck-turkey into the river, where I finally caught it." Luckily, the animals of the rain forest did not impede on his hunt. They most likely could sense the death that shadowed his steps and poison that perfumed the air around him. "When I snapped the creature's neck, there was a loud…" he hesitated, "A creature came barreling out from the shrubbery. It was a massive creature." Sabin was startled to see the monstrosity looming so tall.

"What creature?" Tullia asked, she had shifted to sit crossed-legged on her rock.

"It had one bloodshot eye on top, where a human face would usually be and a gaping mouth on its stomach area, scaly skin, sharp claws and it's feet were backwards." He shook his head. "But, more than it's monstrous appearance, what was more horrendous was its stench." Sabin had been everywhere, battlefield, under a mound of corpses, soaked in blood, in trenches with excrement, but that creature's smell nearly brought tears to his eyes. It smelled worse than any other stench he had experienced. And that was merely from a distance, up close, Sabin had the urge for the first time in his life to pass out.

Tullia smiled. "A stinky one-eyed beast? So, what happened next? Did you die with the ugly bird?" A curl to her lips teased a smile to his lips.

"Not quite. The beast was screeching at me from the shore line, it's one eye glaring at me, as it clawed the air. It clearly wanted to impose harm on me. However, it wouldn't come in the water."

He shrugged, stopping in the middle of his tale and waited for the undoubted inquiry that would follow. Sabin had managed to pick up on certain key elements that his long since deceased uncle incorporated when he told a story, and that was to pause and simply wait. His uncle was the best storyteller in his entire clan. People would not move, not dare utter a sound or breathe when his uncle sat to weave a tale or to recount an adventure.

It often led to a riot after the story, all the Viking men, women, and children sitting still for so long, it because dangerous.

Besides, Tullia seemed to like to ask him many questions. He watched Tullia fidget, clearly eager to hear the rest. A few minutes went by before Tullia heaved out a rough sigh of irritation. "Well? Obviously, you escaped. How? I need the middle and the ending stuff! Don't leave me hanging, man!" She slapped her thighs with impatience, her pretty face scrunched up with irritation.

Sabin's lips curled in amusement under his mask, then continued as she demanded. "The beast paced by the riverbank and continued to scream at me as I stood in the river." Sabin shook his head at the memories. Here this fearsome creature was afraid of a little riverbed of water. At least, that was how it appeared to Sabin. "I stayed in the water for a bit, but the damned beast began to lodge boulders and dead tree trunks at me."

Nearly took off his head a few times, it's aim was precise.

"I was forced onto the shore, since the river was deep and the creatures are not kind." Sabin had seen the alligators and the snakes that lurked in the murky water. He did not wish to fight the beasts in their element. "Once I got on the shore, it then charged at me."

Tullia covered her mouth. "Oh no."

Sabin nodded. "It smelled awful up close. I managed to dodge its attack and ran into the jungle, hoping to lose it in the dense forestry."

He didn't want to needlessly kill the creature. He was done with that sort of business. However, if the creature continued to hunt him, it would lose its life that was what Sabin had thought. Sabin was not prey.

"Well? Did you lose it?" Tullia was bouncing by her leg anxiously.

Sabin shook his head. "No, I made it worse for myself. That beast clearly knew its territory and struck me with a hand sized rock to the shoulder. That jarred me enough to slow me down and then, even with its feet turned the wrong way, it was upon me."

Sabin instinctively rolled his right shoulder as a phantom throb of pain in remembrance occurred. The damned beast nearly tore his arm off with the force of the throw.

Tullia was now biting her lower lip; she had inched forward on her rock and was now enraptured with Sabin. Her big gray eyes gleamed with curiosity, amazement, and impatience. Sabin regarded her, he liked the way in which the fire light and shadows danced across her face, enriching her skin tone, and making her look alluring. Her skin turned a warmer cream color, and her eyes took on the trait of a starlight glow. It was a much better look than her previous colorless and creased complexion.

Sabin's rage fluttered as his chest seemed to become restricted, he inhaled deeply, trying to ease the tension and continued his tale. "The creature, which I learned a bit later from the locals was called a mapinguary, got me in a headlock and began to spin me around frantically, yelling all the while and pounding my back."

The damned creature nearly broke his back and made him go deaf.

"It threw me around a bit, against trees, some rocks and I think a rock wall at one point." Sabin thought back at that moment, it was as if he were a child's toy and the child was throwing a tantrum.

Tullia shook her head. "How are you still living and not disabled?"

A curse that revives him each and every time. He was forced to whole and functioning.

Sabin felt a satirical smile twist his lips. "Luck I suppose." He flexed his hands, his biceps tensing. "I had enough and finally managed to get it to let me go, by stabbing it in the tongue as it yelled. Its breath was the main cause of the wretched smell." Sabin flared his nostrils, the remembrance of the smell caused sharp tingles to occur in his nose. "Once it dropped me, yelling even louder than before, I turned to leave, but unfortunately, another mapinguary appeared out of nowhere."

"There were more than one?" She gave him a disbelieving look.

Sabin shook his head. "There was a small community of mapinguary in that particular region of the rain forest. I was unfortunate enough to be dragged into their village, tied up against a tree, my ugly duck-turkey bird was confiscated, and I was yelled at for seemingly hours."

Dozens of the one eyed vermins came awkwardly strutting out, all at once from various places, like roaches. They all looked at Sabin, looked at the bird carcass, looked at the stabbed mapinguary, who was bawling, loudly, looked back at Sabin, then back at the bird carcass, then they all began to yell simultaneously while flapping their arms. It was as if they were having a debate over him and the ugly bird thing he had killed.

"Why where they yelling at you?" She asked, resting her head on her knees.

"The damned bird." The words came out harsher than he intended, but Tullia threw her head back and laughed. Though the night had descended hours before, it felt as though the sun was rising already. Sabin glanced up at the night sky, swathed with stars and a crescent moon.

"Okay, okay, what happened next?" She asked, her voice thick with humor.

"I was trapped against the tree longer than I would have liked; the annoying creatures wouldn't stop yelling." Sabin shook his head. "I don't know how they aren't already discovered by humans, they're so damn loud."

Tullia's giggle tugged at his lips.

"I've never experienced that type of torture before," and he had plenty done to him, "My head wanted to implode and my brain wanted to leak out of my ears."

Tullia made a face of sympathetic pain twisted with humor.

Sabin still remembered the unnatural decibel they whined at and the continuous roaring and screeching. His rage had nearly consumed him, it was a miracle that those creatures didn't become massacred.

The one thought that managed to remain while the noise threatened to liquefy his brain was that, somehow, someway, he was going to make them pay for this. Not by blood, no, not by his rage either, but he would do something so bloody annoying to them, they'd never want to yell another single vowel sound again.

"I made a solemn vow to myself; I would see the creatures suffer dearly for their torment and hindrance." It had been the only thought he had as the minutes stretched by.

She crossed her legs underneath her, she looked highly amused as fire light fluttered over her features. "And did you manage to execute your revenge?"

"I did." Sabin felt the warmth of righteous self-satisfaction spread across his chest, taking away the tightness briefly. "It was apparent that one yelling session was not going to put an end to the... *debate*. They kept at it through the night and until dawn before their volume finally, blessedly, quieted and they dropped down to sleep where they were."

Simple creatures, he had thought with a red hazy fog over himself.

"Once I was convinced, they were deep in their sleep, I managed to loosen the rope around me just enough to escape." He had dislocated both shoulders and dislodged a few joints in order to slide out of the vine rope that was haphazardly tied around him. It had taken a few good jerks to put everything right in his body and the pain was a sharp burning sensation, but the pain felt like tickles compared to the continuous ringing in his ears caused by the damned creatures.

Tullia raised her eyebrow, a mischievous smile on her face. "So, what was the revenge?"

He felt a warmth of satisfaction in his gut. "I connected all of their backwards feet together with each other with the twine I had." He had purposely used one of the most complicated knot designs.

"Would that have held them together though?" She asked, unsure.

"It was heavy duty twine. Good stuff."

She laughed, shaking her head.

"I was fortunate enough to come across a little herd of sleeping howler monkeys roughly a few feet away from where the mapinguary were sleeping. I roused them, then lead the monkey's right to them. Screeching and all."

He admits, he was a bit childish and… theatrical with his revenge. He couldn't blame his rage for his actions, it had been dormant even through the entire mapinguary's trial. Perhaps because the damned creatures were so loud, he couldn't feel his rage.

Tullia's face was wickedly delighted. "Naturally, they all awoke."

He nodded. "They did."

"And with their feet tied together, I'm sure they were an absolute mess." She had her fingers laced across her knees.

"Indeed." Sabin couldn't help but chuckle at the remembered images those giant eyed, scaly stomach mouth creatures, falling all over each other, giving out short screams in panic; becoming frantic when they realized they were all stuck together.

"The creatures made the mistake of swatting at a howler monkey." The monkeys took deep offense, and then began to attack and ignore Sabin. "I gathered the ugly bird and left the scene of the howler monkeys now attacking those damned creatures."

Sabin had watched long enough to feel satisfaction of the chaotic scene, but he made sure to catch the eye of the first mapinguary who had caught him. Sabin could identify him due to the blood stain around his mouth area. When its giant eye met Sabin's eyes, he had held up the bird carcass toward the creature, relishing the way the mapinguary's eye widened, as if shocked, then narrow with rage. It tried to scream, but the howler monkeys did great honor to their name, their howls allowed for no other noise to even stand a chance at being heard.

Tullia clapped her hands, rocking back slightly with delight. "I feel a little bit bad for the mapinguary. Do you think they got out of the knots? Or do you think they are still connected like a King Rat situation?"

Sabin shrugged. "Who knows?" He held no affection towards the beasts.

Tullia shook her head. "Such indifference." A smile played around her lips. The fire was crackling accompanying the soft night sounds. "Was your client happy with the ugly bird?"

Sabin felt his rage growl, he choked it back and down. "The useless, rich brat had moved on from his affections and preferred science. He had no need for the bird anymore."

Tullia raised her eyebrow. "He certainly did a three-sixty on you."

Sabin shrugged. "That's the way of a spoiled child." The *ergi* tried to weasel his way out of paying too. He had undergone torture from mapinguary's screams for nearly an entire day for an ugly bird. That boy was not going to receive his services for free.

Sabin saw Tullia swallow, then rubbed the tip of her pink tongue along the seam of her upper lip. "Did the rich man do something to make you angry? Besides moving on from the bird bone love spell thingy."

Sabin tapped one finger against his arm. He did not have any tells for anyone to guess what he was thinking or feeling. "He didn't want to pay my fee." Sabin slowly, watching Tullia. Her silver eyes were hooded by the shadows of the firelight. "However, I made him see reason." The *ergi* had the nerve to hire two rogues to try and coerce him into agreeing to leave without pay. Sabin barely managed to keep his rage leashed so not to slaughter them, but blood was spilled. When the rich boy's goons where incapacitated he became horrendously fake and jolly as he quickly gathered the money owed to Sabin with his sweaty hands and spitting out flowery phrases of praises.

She seemed to flex her jaw, swallowing. "Oh, you had to get rough with him then, huh?"

Sabin was shocked. He knew he hadn't moved a muscle and Tullia was human, she couldn't read minds. But she could be exceptionally good at guessing. "I did and I got paid."

Tullia's laugh was contagious as she threw her head back and allowed for the darkened forest around them to absorb the sweet sound.

Sabin enjoyed her humor for a few minutes before nodding. "Moral of my tale, don't tie me to a tree and yell at me. I'll get you back."

Silver orbs shimming with humor clashed with his dull eyes. "And don't try to skip the bill, or else you'll get rough."

Sabin felt his lips tilt up. "Right."

The sounds of night settled deeply, and the air became sluggish. "It's late, go rest now Tullia, we've to be up early. I want to try and leave before the witch comes back." Sabin said. It would start their day brighter if they managed to begin without the annoying witch.

The soft, warmth of Tullia's face went tight and pale, her smile was brittle at best. "Yeah. Okay. Just let me go to the bathroom first."

She stood up, shaky, and stumbled towards the fire. Sabin darted forward, catching her arms gently and tugging her to safety. Her slight weight crashed into his chest. He moved his hand from her arm to her shoulder, holding her to him. Her shoulders trembled lightly, and she was still chilled. He thought that a tale of one of his lighter missions was enough to relax her before bed and perhaps give her mind something to think on. However, she was clearly spooked still by the interaction with the demon.

"Sweetness, what's the matter?" He gave her shoulder a soft squeeze; her bones sharp under his palms. He could see her face, but her gray eyes skittered across his face, never pausing in their movements. He had seen this reaction from prey caught in his traps.

"I'm fine, I guess my legs were shaky from all the hiking today." She gripped his wrist with cold hands.

He didn't take his eyes from her face. "You're not a very good liar."

"No, but I'm a fantastic bullshitter. I'm just not on my A-game tonight." There was a sharpness to her tone that made him want to pinch her cheek, but the underlying unsteadiness made him squeeze her shoulder again.

"Don't try and charm your way out of answering my question, sweetness. What's the matter?"

She gave a huff. "So nosy. It's nothing…" She trailed off, seemingly in conflict with herself.

"It's something." He said bluntly, watching her face tighten and her dusk kissed eyes stared at Sabin for nearly moments on end, before she sighed loudly. "Fine, you big bully." She shrugged off his hand and paced back a few steps.

Sabin felt… offense. His rage snared the emotion, amplifying it a bit before he choked it back.

"I… know…" She whispered haltingly, her hands came together in front of her stomach. "Who the tikbalang is." She bit down on her lower lip. "His name is… was Alab and he had a sister named Carolina. And he got stuck in that form…." She paused, her voice shrinking. "He thought he was a god with his shapeshifting powers, so he tried to overpower his sister… Carolina, he tried to scare her. But he ended up becoming stuck instead."

"You saw this? In a vision?"

She nodded, swallowing. "It was a recent one too. When I… blanked out this afternoon and you had to carry me." Her face tinted a delicate pink.

So, this was the reason of her discomfort.

Sabin folded his arms and leaned back. "I see. So, the tikbalang is a shapeshifter."

Tullia hugged herself, a shiver going through her slender frame. "No, he used to be a shapeshifter, I don't think he can manage shifts anymore. At least, not like he used to." Another shiver. "I also got the strong impression that he's still angry… still wants revenge on Carolina, his sister. He believes she's the cause of his… well, of his current super scary state."

Sabin hummed. "A lesser man would shift blame away from himself." He thought for a minute. "And his sister is a shifter?"

Tullia nodded.

"You think she's in Biringan City?"

She gave a slow blink. "Yes? She's a shifter as well, and… I think so? I think she's…" She stopped talking, her swallowed, then shook her head. "I'm not sure."

Sabin folded his arms; she was suppressing something. However, Sabin was not the type to pry. "He's a shifter, and Biringan is a city for shifters, so why isn't he in the city then?"

Tullia's shoulders came up and down in a harsh motion. "I don't think he knows where Biringan City is. I think he's rogue."

Sabin didn't understand the language of the creature, but he felt a thinly veiled hostility from it loud and clear. He had ignored the conversation and focused on the creature's body language and tone inflection.

Sabin looked at the sky. The moon, bright and full, was high above their heads. It had gotten so late. "Right. Our theory thus far is that the demon was once a shifter named…" He looked at Tullia.

"Alab." Tullia supplied.

"Alab. He got stuck in that… form and blames his sister."

"Carolina." Tullia input again.

"Who may be in Biringan City."

Tullia coughed, then seemed to physically lurch. "I think she's super important there."

Sabin raised an eyebrow, watching Tullia physically jerk about as words seem to fling from her mouth without her consent. "She's maybe a queen or royalty or something, and I think she has a grandson named Chito. I had a vision, a while ago, and I saw them talking about true form, which totally fit from what Carolina was telling Alab and well…" She drifted off; her dove gray eyes wide, shocked, her arms slipped from her body and hung by her sides.

Sabin watched her for a moment, confused by her reaction, then slowly shook his head. "I see. You saw all these through your visions caused by the lost magic." He glanced back at where the demon had sat, grinning and beckoning. "I'm not sure if that'll be of any help to us, but any knowledge at this point is welcomed."

Tullia nodded silently. The nighttime sounds loud and nearly grating in their shared contemplative silence.

Sabin let out a deep breath. "We will need to be more alert from here on out. I'll inform the witch of your visions when the sun greets us. She may be able to add more to the picture." The witch had intelligence far beyond what she displayed. She was a creature as intelligent as she was deadly.

"You believe me?" Tullia voice was incredibly small, her face was a mixture of disbelief and frail hope.

"Yes." Sabin said simply, surely. He didn't see any reason not to believe her. She had not proved herself to be untrustworthy. She proved that she was trying her best with what she was given in life and Sabin had a soft spot for those who toiled away unfairly in life. Though she hadn't spoken much on her visions, he did not sense false intentions from her words.

Her eyes took on a dewy shine. She blinked rapidly, looking away. Sabin felt an odd urge to give… give…

Sabin cleared his throat. "It's late now. If you have any other visions regarding the demon or the hidden city, let me know right away."

She looked back at him then, her smoke drenched eyes wide and reflective. She had eyes that could consume a soul. "You trust… what I see?"

Sabin's lips twitched. "Do you trust what you see?"

Tullia blinked, surprised, then looked contemplative. "I do." She said slowly, wringing her hands together tightly. "I do trust my visions. I think they're accurate."

Sabin gave a nod. "Good. Then I'll trust you."

Her smile was wide, wobbly and raw. "Thank you, Sabin."

He looked at Tullia, seeing her slim shoulder and her small hands, taking in her petite height and the softness of her frame. His eyes lingered on her smooth face, big silver eyes and curved lips. She was a delicate looking woman, baring such a burden. He reached out and gently squeezed her shoulders for comfort.

"Anytime, sweetness." He gave her a wink, before dropping his hand. "Don't fret. Alab," At her nod he continued, "will not be back tonight and it is late. You need to go to sleep now. You had a very hard day and you did good enough in it."

Tullia slowly nodded, her eyes half masked, fighting the siren call of sleep. She blinked heavily then yawned. Sabin offered his hand to her, she looked up at him, accepting his hand. Even through his glove he could perceive the sweet heat she radiated. She suddenly paused, gripping his hand tightly. "Wait a minute. What do you mean by 'you had a very hard day' and 'you did good enough in it'?" She gave him a rather feisty look. "For someone who has never ventured in the area of physical expenditures, I think I did more than 'good enough'. I owned that dirt floor while I walked all over it, okay?"

She had an interesting way of speaking, but Sabin could discern the message fine enough. "Indeed." He pacified, feeling mirth gather in his chest.

Her silver dusted eyes narrowed. "Now you're just patronizing me."

Sabin's chest lightened as the mirth climbed into his throat. He fought the urge to laugh. "Not at all."

She held her glare for approximately four more seconds before huffing. "You're lucky I'm tired or you'd get more sass."

Sabin bit his tongue to keep from laughing out loud. She reminded him of a fussy kitten. Very adorable, very harmless and very cheeky. He guided her to the four-person tent and watched from the opening as she situated herself into a sleeping bag. Once she was settled in, Sabin gripped the outside zipper to shut her in it.

"Aren't you gonna sleep too?" She asked, her tone had softened considerably, and her words slightly slurred together.

"In a bit. Rest now."

Sabin zipped up the tent entrance and wandered over to his little fire. He sat there waiting until the soft sounds of her breathing deepened and slowed to a rhythm held in deepest depths of slumber. He checked in on her, her form was still, save for the slow rise and fall of her breathing. Assured she was a slave to sleep, Sabin took off his gloves and mask. Rubbing his jaw, Sabin savored the night air against his skin.

It appeared with the damn demon lurking around in the woods with vile intentions Sabin wouldn't be getting any sleep on the expedition.

He wouldn't allow for a frozen shifter demon to ambush him.

It wasn't his first time going without sleep and it most likely wouldn't be his last. He wouldn't die from it, he'd already tried. Though he managed to wise up from the first attempt and learned a few tricks to make the experience of lack of sleep… bearable.

Cracking his neck, Sabin fisted his hands and slammed them deep into the ground. The soft soil easily accepted his fists, while the firm underground put up a stanch resistance, though it failed to keep him out in the end. He gritted his teeth against the pain of the impact, he waited. Within mere moments the throbbing pain in his hands and forearms were gone, in its place the familiar coolness of the curse magic raising from the bowls of the earth greeted him.

The frigid tendrils caressed his hands, healing them, before slithering upward, searching for what it needed to mend. As soon as the magic reached his nose, Sabin inhaled deeply. The magic became excited and quickly dispersed all throughout his body. His fatigue melted away rapidly, leaving him invigorated and oddly hyper. Grunting, he yanked his hands free from the earth and shook off the clinging bits of dirt. Sneezing, Sabin made his way to his bag, plucking out a bottle of water, and rinsed his hands, then applied a liberal amount of hand sanitizer afterwards.

Rolling his shoulders, Sabin stripped his shirt and head wrap, but put his gloves back on his hands. Then he dropped to the ground and began to expel some of the extra energy that the curse magic had provided him. He performed various exercises that had once tortured him, now provided a comfort in their actions. He worked out silently, mindlessly, all throughout the night until his muscles quivered and sweat coated his skin. Finishing, Sabin rose from the ground, damp with sweat and fulfilled. He looked up at the sky, a pearly gray color began leaking upward into the star stubbed blackness of night.

A balmy breezed caressed his sweat moistened body. Controlling his breathing, Sabin poured a warm bottle of water over him. He shook his head, pushing the too long strands of hair out of his face. When was the last time he shaved his head?

Six years ago?

Ten?

Sabin never cared to remember.

He allowed himself to complete a few more exercises as the sky continued to lighten, teasing pinks, oranges and baby blues to emerge from hiding, chasing the darkness from the sky. Soft, sleepy sounds began to evolve slowly from nature, silencing the lingering nocturnal sounds. A few hours later, Sabin sat and drying off under the weak sun rays as he greeted the dawn. He heard Tullia's soft sigh and the gentle rustle of fabrics.

Such a hushed sound brought him comfort and a warmth to his cursed soul. Even though she was asleep, she was there, and knowing that he wasn't the only one…

He watched the sun yawn upwards in the sky slowly.

It was a beautiful morning.

* * *

~Four days later~

Yeah, she was over this. They tromped all over the stupid forestry-jungle place and what did they find? Nothing, except big ass bugs, nasty ass bugs and bugs.

She was not built to be in nature for more than one day. Even one day pushed her to her limits. The first night she slept, she woke up unable to move any part of her body. And now, going on four days with the same hiking and nature happenings? She was going die, and on her tomb stone it would say: 'The Legally Insane Girl Expired from Lingering in Nature Too Long'.

Nights were the worse. Nightmares and evils seemed to be awake and active within the shadows of the forest. Tullia's anxiety was at an all-time high with the fear that the tikbalang would pop up and eat them, like the clown did to the little kids in It. Every horror novel she had ever read she sincerely regretted it in the dark of night in a random Philippine Forest. She felt eyes tracking her every movement, like a physical sensation. She felt stalked, like a small, sitting rat.

Though Sabin did try to put her at ease, telling her funny adventures he had been on, once the laughter faded Tullia would taste the remembrance of the hostility and menace that the tikbalang gave off. She looked up, the cage like canopy of leaves and branches that gave a claustrophobic feel as bright blue pockets of the sky mocked one with a sense of lost freedom. Tullia faced forward, her eyes wandering over the scenery without seeing anything specific.

This sucks.

Her eyes eventually came to rest on Sabin's broad backside that was in front of her. She would trace his shoulder blades with her eyes and recall the strength in his arms when he held her those few times.

Then she'd undoubtedly begin to think of the first night they shared in the jungle, and she would get all sappy over it. She couldn't help it, it was the first time anyone had listened to her, and not only accepted what she said but believed her words. He didn't take her words as the ramblings of leaking insanity. The warmth created by Sabin accepting her visions, of trusting her and not brushing her off as delusional… it heartened her in a way that brought her peace and a small smidgen or fortitude. It meant everything to her. Though she doubted he understood the importance of his seemingly simple and quick acceptance.

Tullia's foot suddenly felt weighed down, breaking her from her sweet reminiscing. She looked away from Sabin's backside, looking down to see a thick bodied snake leisurely slithering over her foot. It took a moment to process the scene before her.

There was a big snake slithering across her shoe.

It stopped moving.

Its scaly head swiveled up and the snake's bright gold slit eyes seemed to glare at her. As if her foot had offended him by being underneath him.

There was big snake on her shoe and was staring at her now.

There was a snake. It was on her foot.

Its tongue flicked out.

Tullia let out a horrified shriek and yanked her foot out from underneath the snake. A hoarse hiss followed by a rather large snake head rising up higher from the thick foliage occurred right after her shriek of terror. It's slit eyes narrowed on Tullia and it bared its fangs.

Screeching again, Tullia stumbled back and tripped on a freaking root. She hit the ground with her butt, which jarred her entire body but her eyes never left the reptile. It seemed to believe she was now an easy target (which she was) and slithered forward, before quickly darting towards Tullia. Its mouth opened wide and fangs glistening with poison.

She stopped breathing…

Sabin's burly ax came slamming down on top of the snake's head, executing it mercilessly. The snake's head rolled and came to rest in the center of Tullia's splayed legs. The mouth still wide and poised for attack. A single drop of lethal poison from the right fang slowly sagged then dropped the ground.

Tullia couldn't breathe correctly. Her lungs were trying to hug each other within her chest as she stared at the snake's head. Sabin made a muffled clicking noise with his mouth and withdrew his blade. It made a sharp, wet ting as it dislodged from the snake's body and the soft earth.

"You alright?" Sabin bent down and grabbed her hand, pulling her up effortlessly and with Tullia doing nothing to help him as she tried to curl away from the dead snake on the ground.

"Oh yeah, totally great. I'm wide awake now." She grumbled, pressing close to Sabin as he led her away from the attack site. "I'm really having a great time. The great outdoors is the best. Being in nature is just so freakin' magical. You know, 'hashtag blessed.'" Her sarcasm was slightly on the hysterical side and her tone was drenched in dismay, to which Sabin gave a small chuckle. It was low, barely audible, but his rumbling mountain mirth could not be muffled.

"It's not easy, just take your time and watch your feet. The terrain is pretty rough, even for me." He gave her hand a gentle squeeze before releasing her. "There's a lot of critters hiding in the foliage. So be careful."

Tullia gave him her malicious glare that came from the depth of her exhausted soul. "I hate you. I hate you so much." She gave his meaty arm a slap. "Go trip and scrape your knees."

Sabin was silent for a moment, then a wild laugh, straight from the deepest parts of the jungle and the highest tops of mountains, the sound was deep, encompassing, and bright. It was the type of laugh that was the center of all and any party, it was the sound of vital life. Sabin's wild laugh overtook the entire space, brightening the world for a few short seconds. Bubbles of the sweetest taste filled her mouth. He stopped just as it began, but Tullia felt entranced.

"You are a funny one." His gold eyes were bright and feral. A riot of bubbles both spicy and sweet swarmed her mouth.

She snapped out of the wonder that his laugh incited and gave him a rude gesture, to which his eyes crinkled and brightened like sunshine.

"Commoners! Hurry up! We've got more forsaken jungle floor to cover. I am not about to spend years to find this damned city. Let's move it!" Cliona's voice rang loudly among the trees.

Sabin glanced in the Grand High's direction. "It seems the witch is impatient."

"I'm a *Queen witch*, you ignorant piece of trash. Address me as such." Cliona's voice was sharp, and venom filled. She was too far away for Tullia to taste what she was feeling, but by the tart bubbles from Sabin, she most likely would be feeling a type of annoyed amusement.

Tullia felt a giggle in her throat. Her chest that was once tight was now light and she felt a little better after the whole snake attack. She began walking behind Sabin, eyeing the ground suspiciously for anything that was creepy or that crawled. The ground was scattered with wood pieces, leaves both fresh and decayed, roots that rebelled against the earth, and the perky weeds in-between everything. Tullia carefully trekked along, gingerly picking her way through the tangled mess of the jungle floor.

She began thinking, for the millionth time that day alone, about how much she liked the indoors and urban environments much better when a blast of wind whipped her face roughly. Tullia recoiled, squeezing her eyes shut tightly, to try and preserve their moisture. The blast disappeared as fast as it came. Huffing, Tullia looked up to make a comment to Sabin…

She blinked and came to a dead stop. Tullia slowly turned in a circle, her eyes roaming, her brain not accepting what was before her. Her eyes fastened to the impossible scene before her.

In front of her was the entrance to a city gleaming under the high sun. The buildings stretched up impossibly tall towards the sky, gleaming under the sun, and belittling everyone with their stature. New York City, San Francisco, Tokyo…. every city Tullia could think of paled in comparison to the sheer presence and sparkle of the entrance of this unknown city. And she wasn't even inside. She was standing at the entrance, decorated with tall pillars that had delicate lines, interweaving in swirling patterns among various other textures. It looked three dimensional and resembled, to Tullia, the floor of the jungle in which she was trekking in. Besides the pillars, there was no wall or any dividers from the jungle scenery to the urban city's environment. It was just the pillars, and honestly, it made a statement.

Breathless from the sheer force of the city's presence, Tullia turned to Sabin, words of amazement on the tip of her tongue…

Her words shriveled. Right, he wasn't with her. She spun in a slow circle again just to confirm that she was indeed all by her lonesome.

Trees.

More trees.

A funny looking bush.

And more trees.

She was indeed alone.

All alone in a jungle forest at the entrance of a hidden city that has a bunch of shifters. Biringan City…this must be it! Panic threatened to hold her immobile, but the excitement and thrill of seeing something hidden was a delicious temptation that muted the full effect of fear that tried to surface within her.

She looked behind her once more, only dense, dark forestry greeted her. Cliona and Sabin would find the entrance eventually and if not, maybe Tullia could manage to finally be useful, and get someone from Biringan City to help her.

Hopefully.

Swallowing thickly, Tullia squared her shoulder and inhaled the humid air, coughed a bit as her lungs protested at the too deep, too moist air, and walked into the city's entrance.

Alone.

Chapter Twelve

Syra stopped and listened. The air was still and musty with tinges of stale rainwater. No signs of a living creature in the cold, brick stacked house. It was by chance that she wandered upon it. It was in the middle of Hollowed Forest, covered by thick, dead shrubbery. Syra scanned the dungeon-like room with a narrow gaze.

It was dingy, smelly, dusty, dark and dirty. However, it was secluded, close to a freshwater stream, hidden, and quite spacious.

A perfect workshop and hideout for an escapee and an outcast.

She supposed she could knock a hole into some of the walls and add some windows. And she knew how to create and power a ward that would protect her from intruders. Syra bit her lip to contain a smile, this clearly abandoned hut, and the area around it was now all hers.

She claimed it. She could finally live as she wanted. She could finally be free.

A tiny scuffling sound caused Syra to stiffen and turn towards the sound with her short sword drawn. In the far-right corner, there was a pile of dead leaves.

It quivered a little.

A critter? Perhaps dinner?

Syra raised an eyebrow and crouched slightly, approaching the corner, poised for attack. The pile quivered again, dislodging the leaves a little to show dingy pink... feathers?

Syra frowned, she was right in front of the pile now. Carefully, slowly, she brushed the leaves away with the tip of her sword to reveal a tiny... baby alkonost? Weakly, it turned its head, a thin, dirty human baby face framed with puffed feathers looked at her. Its eyes were bright pink, blood shot, and teary. The body was a small, somewhat disformed body of an owl.

Syra gasped in surprise, then felt her heart scrunch at the way the little baby tried to cry, but instead a small, strained squeak emerged. It struggled to shuffle away but ended up only being able to cower back in fear. Sheathing her sword, Syra knelt, peering closer to the baby.

"Oh my. You poor puffy looking thing." Syra slowly scooped the baby alkonost up, gently arranging the little thing in her arms, despite its weak resistance. The baby squeaked but fell silent as it looked up at her. A fine tremble overtook the tiny baby's form and the bright pink eyes blinked rapidly. It was filthy, malnourished, frightened and clearly traumatized.

Syra smiled, pulling out a handkerchief from her pocket and tucking it around the tiny alkonost's body. She cooed to the baby, swaying back and forth. "Poor baby bird."

The tremble went away after a few minutes of cooing softly. The frightened look soon transformed into a look of weariness, though the stiffness never left its tiny frame.

Syra didn't mind nor did she feel hurt. She didn't mind the distrust. She distrusted everyone she met and this baby was obviously thrown away, so naturally it would be weary of her intention.

Syra didn't even know her own intentions. All she knew was it was a baby, and she was not the type of person to inflict cruelty on a baby.

"Pretty baby, you're so dirty. I bet you're hungry too. Do you want some food? Now, what do baby alkonosts eat?" Syra walked to the front door, where sunlight tried to crawl in the encrypted home. The alkonost shrank back into her arms fearfully as Syra stepped fully out into the light. It gave a puffing squeak of panic as the baby squeezed its eyes shut and huddled closer to Syra.

Syra gently placed her hand over the baby's eyes to lessen the brightness. She gave a soft whistle, and a miniature pony (whom she affectionately named Bulky) came trotting into view and right up to Syra. It snorted, which made the baby alkonost squeak out a hoarse cry.

"There, there." She comforted, petting Bulky's velvet nose as she gently bounced the baby. "He won't hurt you one bit." With a final pat, Syra walked around, rummaged through the giant saddle pack that Bulky carried and produced blackberries, jerky and an apple. Syra sat down under a giant, bushy tree and began experimenting which foods the baby alkonost could eat. It ate all the berries greedily, nibbled on the meat somewhat, and refused the apple entirely. Syra tossed the apple to Bulky, who snatched it right out of the air with a loud, happy crunch.

She looked down at the baby and felt her heart swell. The alkonost was drowsy, it seemed to cuddle close to Syra's chest. She leaned down, to get a closer look at the baby, but drew back sharply.

A rank stench wafted from the tiny thing.

"Sorry, puffy. You need a bath more than you need sleep." Syra awkwardly stood, trying not to disturb the tiny baby and marched to the creek that was about thirty paces away. She dipped her handkerchief into the water, then began to wipe the baby down. It fussed, squeaking continuously in discomfort.

Syra soothed. "Hush, hush little one. I know it's cold, but it's almost done." Turns out the alkonost was a girl and she was indeed disformed. One of her tiny legs looks to have been broken and never reset. So, it healed at an awkward angle where the clawed foot turned inward. It would pose a problem when the baby began to walk and hunt.

Five minutes later and wrapped in a fresh handkerchief, the baby alkonost was no longer dingy. Instead, her feathers were a soft baby pink, pale yellow and white that were more puffy than feathery.

Syra smoothed the fuzzy pink halo around the baby's face. Bright pink eyes watched her, though they were less weary and shinier.

"What shall I name you then?" She asked, rubbing the baby's head once more, enjoying the downy feel. She stared at the baby alkonost and the baby stared right back.

Pink.

She was so pink.

A pink cutie.

Syra smiled suddenly, "Rozovy." She declared, tapping the baby's nose lightly. "You shall be my baby Rozovy."

Rozovy cooed softly. She puffed her feathers slightly, as if approving of the name.

Syra smiled. Her heart lightened and for the first time in her existence, she felt happy. "You and I, my Rozovy, we shall begin again. We no longer need to live a life alone and hurt."

She walked back to the abandoned shack, with a precious baby in her arms. Rozovy cooed softly, snuggling deeper into her arms and just like that, Syra fell in love.

* * *

It was such a divergence to walk into a modern industrial city from a mini, uninhabited jungle. And Biringan was not just any old city. It was a gorgeous, sprawling city on the inside. Tall, shiny buildings that seemed to glow under the natural light. There wasn't a piece of liter anywhere, the air was piercingly fresh, every advertisement looked brand new, no signs were broken or missing a light bulb, or dirty, the freakin' sidewalks looked freshly paved and had that freshly cleaned sparkle look to them.

Not even four steps into the city, stress consumed Tullia and compelled her to dart into a small enclave that appeared at first to be an alleyway, but was too shallow to accomplish that title, between two towering buildings. She peaked out onto the street and observed the happenings for a few moments.

The city went against everything she knew about cities. The biggest contrast was that it was so clean. She was utterly dazzled. She gripped the corner of the wall harder, looking at the stores. It seemed she was in a shopping district of sorts. There were a lot of shops advertising food, drinks and other goods… she blinked in surprise. There was a Gucci boutique. She examined the other stores within her line of sight; Apple, Fendi, Urban Outfitters, and a Sephora…

Amazing.

The street was also extremely busy. Various people, of various races, from very fair skin to the deepest dark skin, were shopping. The only commonality that the people shared was that they were all extremely beautiful. Too beautiful. Filters and airbrushed beautiful.

She sighed, looked down at herself then sighed again, only this time with her entire body. Tullia looked and smelled like she's been trekking in a jungle for the past few days. Which she has, but it was the point that she *looked* like it that sucked the most.

She touched the tip of her tongue to her upper lip, contemplating her next move. Most likely, the hidden city probably didn't have a visitor center, so that course of action was null and void.

She currently had two problems. First, Sabin and Cliona where not with her. She was all alone in the hidden city (which nearly scared the pee right out of her) and didn't know the consequences of being in the hidden city.

What would happen if they found out she was an outsider? The prospect raised the hairs on the back of her neck. Would they confine her? Throw her out? Forcibly make her a citizen? Sell her off in an auction? Kill her?

Tullia shrank back from the masses of gorgeous people, unsure, unwilling, and flat out scared to chance their reaction to her.

Her second problem was she was becoming... correction, she *was* freaking out. There were too many things that could go wrong. She still had spontaneous visions, she was all alone in a foreign country (though, bonus she could communicate and understand the language), she was hungry, she wanted the Okinawa milk tea with boba that was being advertised by the cafe across the street, and she didn't know how to proceed solo with the plan…

She felt useless and not adult enough for this type of undertaking. She needed a real adult to be with her right now and hold her hand.

Suppressing the urge to cry, because tears never solved anything and made her face look even more unsightly than it probably already was, Tullia inhaled deeply. She breathed out slowly and repeated the process until she was a shaky semblance of a calm lake… during a thunderstorm with hail.

So, faking it hardcore, but at least it distracted herself enough to allow rational thoughts to flow forth. Tullia looked out on the street again and tried to think back on the visions she had on shapeshifters. It was hard to remember; the shifter visions were less pronounced than other visions she had like the elf visions or the Naga visions.

She supposed because shifter visions were more 'modern human like' and not fantastical and mythical. They resided in a city that looked like a human city… they looked like humans….

Tullia felt the skin on her face stretch tautly with the force of her concentration.

Maybe…. It was… with the thing… and that one person…*Damn it, remember, remember, remember and the reward is the Okinawa milk tea with boba… remember…*

Her vision wavered slightly and became less vibrant as the colors around her drained away. Her heart stopped, then throbbed painfully fast in her chest as dread seeped into her bones.

Was she having a vision? *Not here! Come on!* She stiffened and slammed her body back against the wall. Pain vibrated throughout her body, but her peripheral began to blacken and spread. She slid down the wall, breathing harshly. Tucking herself tightly into the corner, Tullia helplessly watched as her vision continued to become restricted by the darkness before going black entirely.

* * *

Sabin violently chopped a branch away, stomping on it as he passed by and stalked through the thick vegetation.

Cliona was silent for once.

Good. He wasn't in the mood for her chattering. His raged dug its claws into his chest and began to tear at him, as if it were trying to break free. He wanted to kill… anything… everything. His control was razor thin and frail.

Tullia had disappeared without a trace. One moment she was trailing a bit behind him and when he looked over his shoulder to check on her, she wasn't there.

Gone. She was gone.

As if she was never behind him. They had searched the area for her, but Cliona claimed that Tullia was far away, the witch could weakly sense her own magical signature that she had placed on Tullia, but that meant she was quite a distance from them.

Sabin glared at the dense forestry accusingly. His hands fisted and his jaw clenched tight. He should have had her walking in front of him so he could've kept an eye on her. He wanted to bash his head against a tree repeatedly as punishment for his lack of attention. They've tramped around the jungle for four days now, his guard slacked due to the inactivity, and he became indolent.

He knew better than that, therefore it was his fault they were separated. He was a poor excuse of a guardian.

"She must have tripped into Biringan City when we weren't looking." Cliona commented, her eyes took on an iridescent sheen as she tried locating Tullia. "I bet my fortune that it's a cloaking spell on the city, which is why it feels as though Tullia is underwater."

"And?" He asked, slashing another innocent branch in front of him.

"I know she's east from we are, but that's about it." She paused, seeming to contemplate something, "We searched the entire area… why did we not get sucked into the city?" Another long stretch of silence as they stomped through the now thinning jungle. Then the witch snapped her fingers and made an annoying sound that caused Sabin's rage to jump violently. "I think I may have cracked the case! It's an idea, but I think…the entrance to Biringan city *moves*." She held out her hands with those unnaturally long fingers to him. "Which is why people 'trip' into it and why Tullia was able to get in, but we weren't. There's no exact location, because it's not *in* an exact location. It constantly roams around in this," She waved her hands around, "*place*. Tullia probably hit the roaming entrance at the right time." She smacked her forehead. "I don't know why that possibility was never brought up. But then again, a roaming entrance is rare."

Sabin squeezed his ax handles, loosened them, then squeezed them again. He felt restless and on edge. He was her self-appointed designated guardian and he had failed her already. Worse yet, when he thinks about her all alone in a hidden city, not knowing how the people will treat her, not knowing how she's feeling, and imagining her gripped by a vision, vulnerable to anything… anyone…

His rage roared and a deep pounding occurred in his head.

His peace was now nonexistence and his beastly rage was growing by the moment. He was unaware how much Tullia impacted him… until she was gone. Cliona's eyes flickered from a bright glowing blue to a deep black. She eyed Sabin wearily as he struggled to focus his mind off his rage and onto a solution.

If the entrance moves, then they too should move.

"How do we track it?" He growled, slashing a branch that jetted awkwardly away from the trunk. It offended him by existing in that position.

"The only thing we can do is catch up to it and trip in it ourselves." Cliona looked at Sabin. "That's all we can do at this point."

Sabin felt the rage ever present sharpen and shift painfully inside of him. He rolled his stiff neck. No relief was given.

How dare they take her from him… How dare they insult him… how dare they make him fail… How dare the entrance move…He'll make them pay… everyone…

Inhaling deeply, he tried to picture the lake, the glass surface reflecting the pastel colors of dawn, the sleepy dew of morning glow… The image blurred then darkened.

It pissed him off.

Sabin clenched his teeth, annoyance feeding into his rage. He looked around, desperate for inspiration that would quell his rage from infecting his mind.

The slenderness of the trees, their towering height, the noiseless shift of the leaves in the gentle breeze….

It all pissed him off.

Inhaling the damp air, Sabin tried to think again, beginning to slowly panic, of something soothing…. His mind went blank. The lake scenery had never failed him. It had always soothed him. It was his best memory of his human life…He didn't *have* a backup. He never *needed* a backup. Anxiety twisted sharply inside of him, causing his heartbeats to pick up and further stimulate the rage to burn hotter within his veins.

His breathing turning ragged as his vision began to tint red and narrow dangerously.

Kill, kill, kill, kill, kill, kill…

Sabin began to taste the heavy iron flavor over his tongue, the slicked feel of it on his skin… he heard the cries, the screams, the deaths….

He felt his lips peel back from his teeth.

Everything was an annoyance. Kill, kill, kill, kill, kill….

"Tullia's now heading northwest." Cliona's voice scraped upon his nerve endings, he cut her a jagged look. He blinked heavily as the rage began to seep into his blood.

She pissed him off.

The witch didn't flinch, but he saw. He saw through her facade to the trembling uncertainty and the thin thread of fear that began to weave around her.

Good. She should be afraid of him. She often forgot that she was at a disadvantage against him.

"Don't get crazy on me now, Berserker. We need to find Tullia to get into Biringan city. Remember Tullia? Short? Black hair? Too pale for her own good? Remember?"

Tullia.

He blinked slowly. An image of Tullia grabbing her butt as she stared down at a couch flashed in front of eyes. His lips twitched. Her face had been shocked, then haughtily smug, all while she maintained a grip on her own butt.

Humor trickled into his heated rage, cooling it slightly. Another memory of her with the siren's shell, smugly telling him her plan…

Male strippers?

His humor increased, allowing his rage to dull and his vision to clear. He snapped his head from right to left, cracking his neck, relieving a bit of the tension.

"Right." He rasped, "Northwest?" His voice was pitched lower, grating metal on gravel. He needed action, standing still allowed the rage to swirl restlessly inside with no outlet.

"Yes." Cliona answered instantly. "She's now going *northeast*. This entrance is a grade-A jerk. The direction changes every twenty… fifteen seconds."

Sabin turned his blades in his hands, he watched the light glint off the stained metal. "Looks like we need to be quick then." He tucked his blades away and rolled his shoulders. His entire being focused on a single goal.

Hunt down the entrance.

If the entrance was found, then Tullia would be found.

Simple.

Cliona bared her teeth. "Fine. A minute." She spread her arms wide, threw her head back and exhaled thick blue fog. It sat above her for a moment, then morphed into thin spears and darted in various directions.

Cliona looked at Sabin, her face, a strange kind of beautiful, was filled with concentration. Her head snapped to the right and bared her teeth again in a sinister grin. "I got a better lock on the entrance. It's northeast from here, going approximately 90 miles per hour. Probability of turning 96%. Direction unknown." She raised her eyebrow at Sabin, "Can your bulky ass run fast?"

Sabin didn't answer, he simply began running northeast. The witch darted ahead of him, flying through the air and weaving her body through the small openings of the trees without disturbing a single leaf. Sabin's method consisted of him merely barreling through, recklessly, uncaring. Accepting the lashes, the pain with relish.

It felt good. He felt refreshed. He felt focus.

Even though his rage was still boiling in his veins, at least he was moving.

***

Tullia saw Chito. The prince of Biringan City as a teenager. His hair was shaved, his face was more feminine, and he had a rather bulky build. She had seen him multiple times throughout the years. He was interesting and very angst. But, thanks to all the visions, she knew just a few things about him like he was a prince and he liked to change his appearance a lot.

He was also transparent and discolored right now.

Weird.

Usually, her visions were in HD. Tullia watched Chito window shop leisurely.

An itch tickled her nose, she scratched her nose absentmindedly. She looked down at her nails. Crap. They were filled with dirt and she had just touched her face. She was going to break out in a million pimples...

Tullia blink down at her hand. She could see her hand. Hers!

She looked down at her body, shocked that she could also see her body. Her super sweaty, dirt crusted body. She snapped her head back up to see Chito, a faded version, looking at a shop that sold hair accessories. He passed right through a woman with a shock of red hair. Tullia scrambled up to her feet, unsure and slightly giddy. She *never* saw herself in visions. She *never* could move or think independently from her visions. Usually, she was only a witness. Seeing, hearing, sometimes feeling, but nothing like this. Tullia swallowed thickly, staring at the memory-like transparency that was Chito.

It appeared he was done looking at the store. He stalked along the sidewalk, walking *through* people, past the coffee shop and turned right, disappearing from her line of sight.

Tullia blinked, then in a split-second decision, ran after Chito. He was a member of the royal household. He was her way in to meet with the Queen or whoever was in charge. Sprinting past beautiful people, who stared after her which was horrible, but luckily the feeling was fleeting.

Huffing, Tullia turned right and saw Chito up ahead, still in a sulking strut. If she followed the vision Chito, he'd lead her right to the palace eventually. He had to go there some time; she knew he lived there. She just hoped it was sooner rather than later. Vision Chito walked the alleyways that had clean, almost sparkling garbage cans lined up neatly and held no graffiti on their shiny walls. He walked in a park that had an abundance of exotic flowers. He lingered especially long in an open art gallery within the park. There were statues, paintings and sculptures in various styles from surrealism to abstract to contemporary. They were all so lovely, Tullia almost got caught up in examining them herself that she nearly lost sight of transparent Chito.

He wandered between buildings again, window shopped again, and lounged on nearly every bench he saw.

Come on, Tullia thought on a wheeze as she fast walked to keep up with his long strides. Her sigh of relief transformed midway into a groan when he sat on a bench for all but three seconds then up and left.

This kid had way too much energy.

Suddenly, transparent Chito stopped dead in his tracks and hunched in on himself. Tullia frown, watching as transparent Chito shrank and became frighteningly thin. The once closely cropped hair grew thick and brown all the way to his now slender shoulders. He looked in the window, posed a little, did a small twirl then seemed to bounce off once more.

Tullia sagged; she had a sinking feeling she was going to be led around for miles on end by this hyperactive kid.

Groaning, Tullia broke out into a slow jog to keep up with Chito. She seriously needed more cardio; it was pathetic how out of shape she was.

* * *

"Right there! Right freaking there! Five hundred yards right in front of us! *Haul ass*!" Cliona's voice was screeching with victory. Sabin hunched closer to the ground to gather more speed. Sweat dripped down his face, soaking his face covering and stinging his eyes as well as his fresh cuts. After five hours of chasing Biringan City's entrance, they were finally close enough to enter it. It had changed direction on them multiple times, fluctuated in speed and, on a couple of occasions, relocated entirely.

"Hurry, hurry!" Cliona hissed; she flattened her limbs closer to her body.

Sabin gritted his teeth as the hot sting of pain from overworked muscles began to intensify. His stomach felt as though it were about to rip. His lungs were trembling, his mouth was flooded with the coppery taste of blood and the humidity of the jungle seemed to cook him alive.

It didn't matter. Minor inconveniences. Pain was always a source of inspiration to him; it propelled him to go even faster.

"Faster!"

Faster.

Faster.

Faster...

A strong, welcomed blast of air engulfed him. Something black flickered in his peripheral. Sabin blinked, not slowing his speed, and slammed into a stone pillar a second after he saw it. He felt his head split and warm blood oozed down over his face. His vision blackened, and his ears rang loudly. His neck wrenched back painfully, he felt his shoulder dislocate, his lower back strained and his knees nearly shattered with the force in which they hit the concrete ground. Pain consumed him entirely...

Maddened him. Defined him in that moment. He savored the throbbing agony, allowing himself to be carried by it to a numb state of being.

He faintly heard Cliona's cackles behind him, he didn't understand what she was saying, but it didn't matter. She was insane too.

Sabin closed his eyes and waited. Whether it be in a hidden city or a different realm, it would always happen when his blood was drawn. It started from where his body was connected with the earth. A cool, damp touch slid up his shins, encased his knees and then wrapped around his entire body seamlessly. His curse began to heal him. He felt the blood, that was gushing from his head, trickle, then stop. He felt the tightness of his skin on his forehead mend together. His neck realigned, his back muscles were restored, and his knees were no longer numb. All the scraps and every bruise were healed, though the scars… the hideous markings were still there.

They always were.

Sabin inhaled deeply, the cool, dampness went inside, fixing his thirst, his exhaustion… though it didn't touch his rage. It never did. When he exhaled, he was whole, and the cursed magic dissipated into the air, leaving him ice cold and strangely detached.

"That's always so damn creepy and unnatural." Cliona commented, staring at Sabin as if he were a freak. He was, but then again so was she in her own genteel way. He rolled his shoulders and stripped off his face mask and shirt. They were soaked with blood and sweat; he wasn't willing to aggravate his rage any further by suffering any discomfort.

"Water." He commanded of the witch. Waiting.

"Sure thing." A sugary tone. A huge waterfall dowsed him completely and suddenly. Sabin coughed, but said nothing as the frosty water soothed his overheated flesh. He rubbed the water over his exposed skin, getting rid of the sweat and blood meticulously.

He heard Cliona clear her throat, and when Sabin looked at her, she raised her eyebrow haughtily and folded her arms. "You don't order a queen around, Berserker."

"The fact you constantly call yourself a queen, diminishes the title." Sabin retorted.

She scoffed. "No. It reminds simple minded-commoners who I am, how I am to be treated, and not to try me." She gave him a pointed look, then a disgusted look. "You need a haircut."

Sabin shook his head, dislodging some of the water from his hair. He sighed, then gathered up his ragged locks and twisted them back into a knot at the nape of his neck as he had many times from his past.

He had forgotten about his hair entirely. He didn't realize it had grown quite so long. He took his torn, bloody shirt, found a clean part and wiped himself as best her could. He then balled the shirt and his ruined mask and tossed it at Cliona.

She hissed in disgust and the material caught on fire and burned to ashes before ever reaching her.

"Filthy heathen!" She screeched, shooting a line of fire at him. The warmth dried his damp skin and his soaked hair, though the flames did not burn him.

When the flames ceased, he smirked at the witch's enraged face. "Much appreciated, *oh generous Queen.*"

She shook with rage and swore heavily and creatively at him. Ignoring her, he took the vape out from his pant pocket, inhaled deeply and exhaled. A cloud of white smoke puffed away from his mouth as the taste of jeweled espresso lingered along his palette. Sabin then carefully tucked it back into his pocket.

There. He *looked* normal. Not ruined. Not hideous. Not monstrous.

He glanced at Cliona. She had on a glamour as well, though it only took care of the unnatural features. Her skin remained a melange of white and black and she was still abnormally striking. She looked over at Sabin, her now deep brown eyes glittering with annoyance under the sun.

"Let's hurry and find Tullia. You piss me off and I want food. ASAP." She strode ahead of him. Sabin didn't respond, he rolled his shoulders and walked through the entrance of the hidden city.

* * *

He darted through the trees. Silently shadowing the witch and the corpse man as they raced to the portal's location.

He supposed they were useful for something after all. He had been trying to gain access into Biringan City for a few years, though the ward put on the roaming portal only allowed for humans, human descent, and shifters to enter. Nothing else. So, the witch would be able to enter as would the oversized heathen.

However, Alab was not of human descent, he was once a shifter, and now after many tortured years, he was no longer a shifter, but something other. So, the portal rejected him, it merely passed over him. From then on, he had tried to piggy back with humans that had aimlessly wandered in his forest. Unfortunately, he never managed the timing quite right. But now, these idiots gallivanting the forest would be his way in. Though he had to time it *just* right, for once.

Jumping slightly from branch to branch above the two, Alab kept close.

"Right there! Right freaking there! Five hundred yards right in front of us!" The witch screeched, he saw her dart forward, flying deftly through the thick shrubbery.

Alab dropped to the ground, shrunk his body down painfully small and increased his speed. He was five paces behind the big, tactless idiot. In the past, Alab had always trailed behind humans from a few feet…

He eyed the burly man, assessing him; his gold eyes were flat and cold. His entire being was focused on smashing through the vegetation. He wouldn't be aware of something to the side of him, now, would he?

Alab hunkered lower towards the ground, summoning his weak shifting abilities to shrink his disfigured form even more. Swathed in camouflage, Alab went as close as he dared to the big man, now about two paces behind.

Faster…

Faster…

Faster!

The tang of familiar magic accompanied by a strong gust of air transported Alab to the entrance of Biringan City. Those damned pillars burned his eyes as they greeted him silently.

Finally.

Lowering his still shrunk body, Alab turned sharply, avoiding the two idiots and as well as smashing into anything as he ran right into the city. He gradually slowed his pace, running alongside a tall wall before coming to a dead stop.

Shaking off his shift, Alab felt a grin stretch his mouth.

Finally, he had made it inside Biringan's defenses. Alab inhaled deeply, feeling the air expand his lungs, before breathing out.

Seems like his sister was indeed accomplished, had even built a small oasis for their people.

He flexed his claws, before jamming them into the solid wall. The stone wall now had five, large holes in it. He dragged his claws through the stone, enjoying the pain, enjoying the destruction, savoring the moment, the impending devastation he would deliver to all the unknowing citizens of Biringan. It was soon to be under a new ruler, a powerful ruler, a brave ruler. Not a spineless one that hid their kind. He'd amass his people into an unstoppable army against the haughty humans.

As he should have done before Carolina tricked him into weakening his power.

However, first step was to thoroughly humiliate and destroy his sister, Biringan's *beloved* queen, Carolina.

He ripped his claws out of the stone wall, and laughed.

* * *

Tullia wanted to strangle transparent Chito. She had never witnessed a more indecisive person in her entire life! He had changed his appearance a total of seventeen times.

Seventeen!

In the span of five hours as he gallivanted all over the city. He never went into any shops, never stopped to buy anything, only looked, and then moved on. Which sucked, because Tullia was now slowly decaying from lack of water and food and exhaustion. Sabin was carrying all the supplies, including her wallet, in his forever man purse thing, so Tullia had nothing. Not that she was one hundred percent sure that she could use her visa here, but she'd at least try.

Chito, now with warm brown skin, long gold hair and a curvy body, slowed his walking pace to a slow shuffle. His face, now with bold features, darkened thunderously as he paused about thirty feet away from a gleaming white building that had delicate designs all over it, a loudly stylized roof and, even in the dying light of the day, it nearly blinded Tullia with its regal magnificence.

"Wow." Tullia murmured, mesmerized by the building.

"Chito!" A high pitch voice called out. Tullia looked to see a teenage girl waving from a window, her appearance was the same as Chito's, memory-like faded and slightly out of focus. "You're in trouble! Lola is waiting for you in your room!" Her voice was pitched in a taunting range that only a sibling could manifest.

Chito scoffed and marched forward towards the building before fading away completely. Tullia blinked, surprised, then looked at the white building contemplatively.

The sun sat low and heavy in the sky, painting in pastels with its fatigue.

Obviously, this was where she was supposed to go, so go she will. Hesitantly, Tullia began to walk toward the entrance of the big, shiny white building.

A prickling sensation rose the hair all up along her arm. She rubbed her arms, slightly chilled even though the air was clement. A few minutes later she came to a heavily flowered entry way. The doors were frosted glass and trimmed in gold.

Picking up her pace slight, Tullia was a few feet away from the entrance when rough hands seized her. Tullia let out a panicked squeal, as her feet left the ground and her head snapped back from the force of the grab.

Tullia looked up to see two tall, intimidating men. They were dressed in business casual clothes and looked like CIA agents on their day off with dark shades and close-cropped hair. Tullia shrank back, frightened under the sudden, unexpected assault.

Her heart pounding away in her chest, not enjoying the real-life thrill of being seized.

Swallowing against the tartness of suspicion that they both tasted of, Tullia forced a bright smile. It wasn't the first time she wandered where she wasn't supposed to.

"Hi! I'm sorry, but I'm looking for the Queen of Biringan? It's extremely important business. Is she in here?"

"I've never seen you before." One guard with sharp eyes narrowed at her. "Where did you come from? Who is your spouse?"

Spouse?

"Good question." Tullia wiggled her feet nervously, her mind spinning with possible stories. "I can explain it all, do you mind putting me down."

"Who is your spouse?" The other guard had a hard face and was glaring hard at Tullia.

They didn't taste of hostility, though they *were* extremely suspicious of her. She could taste the tartness douse her palette.

"I'm not married. I came in from the jungle. I was trying to find Biringan City."

One of the guards raised an eyebrow. "You came from beyond Biringan's boundaries? You're new to the city?"

Tullia hesitated, this seemed like a critical distinction to them. "Yes."

Both guards exchanged both knowing and exasperated looks. The tartness morphed into one of muted flavors.

"That makes more sense. Then you are going to need to register."

Tullia tilted her head, confused. "Register?"

The guard with the icy eyes smiled, his demeanor softened. "Yes, all new personal must register right away into Biringan's citizen registry. We run a tight system here, everyone is accounted for so that this city remains unburdened from the outside world's plagues."

Both guards set her down gently. Tullia turned to face them, she rubbed her arms, they didn't hurt, it was more to get the feeling of their hard hands off her skin. "Plagues? Like diseases?"

The guard with the pretty red hair shook his head. "Social problems, like homelessness, hunger, unemployment, and so on." He waved his hands, "We do not have those types of issues here in Biringan, and we all work hard to keep it that way."

"That is amazing!" Tullia exclaimed, Biringan sounded too perfect to be real, then again it was believed not to be real... but it is real because she's standing in the city talking to people who live in the city. So, it was real. She just confirmed it.

Trippy.

"But, I'm just a visitor, so to register would be unnecessary. Maybe a check in?"

The guards gave each other an indescribable look. The muted emotion became starchy tasting. When they looked at her again, their faces were stern. "There are no visitors in Biringan, only residences."

Tullia furrowed her eyebrows; she folded her hands protectively in front of her. "I don't understand."

The red-haired guard sighed. "You cannot leave. There's a saying in Biringan, everyone is welcome, no one can leave. We need fresh blood to keep our city in bloom."

She blinked in shock as dread crept up her spine slowly. "And for those that don't fit in Biringan City?"

The guard with sharp eyes tilted his head. "Such as those who do not comply with Biringan's rules? They are sent away. Mostly underground."

Uh-oh. What the hell does that mean? Something told Tullia she didn't really want to know the answer to her question.

Ice frosted her lungs, making it hard to breath and to act natural.

"Oh, I see." She forced a smile, squeezing herself to keep the shakes under control. "Got it, I'll go find that registrations office then, thank you!" As she turned to leave, a hand seized her arm once more. Tullia stiffened; she didn't like people touching her. She especially didn't like when people thought she could be man-handled. She tilted her head up and felt the frown on her face.

"It's nearly dark, I'll escort you and get you settled." It was the guard with the icy eyes. He tasted serious, like how steamed vegetables tasted serious. However, even though she did not feel threatened by him, she did not sense he had bad intentions, but she couldn't register as a citizen! She was going to leave after talking to the Queen about dragons. Simple.

She wasn't about to become a permanent residence in a hidden city. And she had a feeling that this serious-tasting guard would make sure she filled in everything correctly before leaving her alone.

"I can find it myself if you just give me directions." She smiled, trying to wretch her arm from the guard's hold. His grip was firm. "You're on duty, I'd hate if you got in trouble because you left your post."

He eyed her again. Was there something on her face? Why did he keep eyeing her as though she was a dirty kitten? "You're new here, you will not be able to find it, especially when it is dark." He looked to the man with red hair. "You'll be fine here without me?"

The red head smirked. "It'll be tough, but I think I can manage."

The man with cold eyes nodded. "Come." His grip tightened slightly, and he began to practically drag her away.

Damn it. Not good. The redhead waved. Tullia waved weakly back with a strained smile.

She went along with the CIA look alike guard for a few paces before tapping his hand. "I can walk on my own."

He looked down at her, seemed to analyze her ability to do that, then nodded, releasing her. They walked a for a few minutes, the daylight dimming further and further with each step they took. Tullia's panic began to grow the further away they got from the royal building.

Tullia bit her cuticle nervously, tasting the coppery flavor that characterized blood.

Just what in the hell does she do now? Her freestyle adventure went awry and now she was being escorted by a guard to get registered as a citizen in a hidden city in which now she can never leave. Might as well have been a police officer bringing her to jail.

Her vision flickered, distorting, before fading and then going partial color, like a 1920's film. Tullia blinked, her eyes darted to the guard beside her, he was a bit distorted, but he was still there besides her. A little boy with big green eyes and dark brown skin was darting towards them. Tullia jerked out of the boy's way, even though he passed seamlessly through the guard. She turned around to watch the boy stop about twenty paces in the middle of the path. He looked both ways to his left and right, as well as behind him before dropping down to his knees. He seemed to fumble a little with… something on the ground, before lifting up.

Tullia blinked as the boy lifted part of the ground up and then slide under it, disappearing without a trace.

"Is something wrong?" The guard's blunt hand on her shoulder caused her to flinch. She needed the guard to leave her for just a few minutes. She side-eyed his hand on her shoulder and a flicker of a light illuminated within her.

What was the one thing that most men shudder at the thought of?

A hysterical, inconsolable woman in tears.

Brilliant.

She looked up at the man's ice-colored eyes and willed herself to become an A-list actress. She summoned the saddest stories she had ever read. She felt her eyes widen and her lips tilt down as her lower lip trembled. She sniffed a little and her voice came out fluttery and weak. "I-I think I dropped my ring back at the entrance when you guys grabbed me and frightened me." She looked back at the path from which they came, biting her lower lip as the threaded her fingers together. "My mother gave me that ring, before she died."

Tullia looked back at the guard; she made her face go into a sad puppy dog mask. The guard looked highly uncomfortable. He cleared his throat, shifting away from her slightly. "I'll just radio Mio to keep an eye out for it. No one comes this way but few that have access. What does the ring look like?" He pulled out his radio from his hip.

He's not flustered enough. Tullia inhaled deeply.

"*No!*" Tullia suddenly screamed; the guard's face shrank back with fright. "We have to go *back*! I have to find that *ring*! *Now!*" She grabbed his shirt, clutching it between her fists. She pressed up close to him, invading his space, though it was a bit ridiculous since he was so much taller than her. His hands were frozen by his ears. "Please, *please*… it's the only thing I have to remember her and now that I'm going to live here and all of my mom's stuff will be… it will be…"

Tullia begged tears to surface. Her citizenship depended on her tear production. She clenched her fists tighter, and forcefully thought of never eating a single carb for the rest of her life. Her eyes suddenly began to fill at that carb-less, most saddest thought.

She felt her face crumple, and the guard looked utterly horrified. Tullia honestly believed that the stress and the emotional toll of the pass five days is what allowed the swift rise in tears.

It wasn't her best week; it was quite hard.

Tullia suddenly broke down, tears dripping from her eyes, and she purposely set her sob volume to extra loud for a dramatic effect. Her body crumpled and her chest felt tight. She shoved the guard away and buried her face within her hands. Her salty tears stinging some of the small cuts on her palms.

The guard made a panicked choking noise. "Hey, hey don't cry." He awkwardly patted her back. "It will be found. You're overreacting."

Tullia whipped her up, the guard shrank back under her wild, red rimmed glare. "*Overreacting?*" She whispered; she shoved a finger into his solid chest. "You try losing your most valuable possession that your most treasured person gave to you!" Her voice rose with each syllable. "You don't understand!" Her voice cracked, quickly she covered her face and, forcing a louder sob. She dropped to her knees, drama-like. Her knees began to throb due to the impact, but Tullia ignored it.

"I—I'm sorry." He stammered, the taste of panic, raw and fishy nearly broke her character. "I—I'll go help Mio look for the ring! J-just calm yourself. I'll be back within five minutes. I'll have the ring." Tullia tilted her head up slightly to peek at the fidgety guard. He edged away from her, looking back towards the area in which they came from.

She hid her smile. "Thank you, thank you." She continued to sob loudly, sniffing as she wiped her eyes. "Okay, I'll wait right here. Please, please hurry and find my ring."

The guard nodded quickly, looking like a cartoon character with the way his head bobbed quickly, before bolting back the way they came. If he were a cartoon character, there would have been a long trail of smoke that followed him with how fast he ran.

Tullia stayed on the ground for a couple minutes. Mostly to give herself a moment to actually calm down and to pat herself on the back for a Grammy worthy performance. Her eyes felt hot, and her nose was clogged with snot, but she freakin' did it! She rubbed her eyes free of tears, and coughed a bit to clear her throat. Inhaling deeply, she did box breathing for four breaths. Standing up, Tullia brushed the dirt from her knees. She ran over to where she last saw the vision-boy disappear under. Squatting down, Tullia inspected the ground. It appeared to be… completely normal.

Great.

Since everything that was happening was super out of the norm, could she get a rewind on her live action vision? She waited, thinking that maybe the universe would answer her…

A few seconds passed in the still evening and Tullia huffed.

Okay, so apparently that was too unrealistic. Dropping to her knees, she dug her fingers into the ground, feeling around in the firmly packed dirt for a handle or a latch or something…

Her fingers slipped into a small enclave. Pausing, Tullia curled her fingers in the ditch, she jerked, but it wouldn't budge. Rolling her shoulders, she readied her muscles for an intense weightlifting session and pulled up with her entire body's might. The door gave way easily, throwing Tullia off balance.

Letting out a small yelp as Tullia's body tilted forward due to the momentum and fell forward into a pitch-black hole. Hitting a dirt floor with a jarring thud, Tullia coughed violently as her vision swam a little and the dirt door slammed shut above her, encasing her in a musty smelling darkness within the unknown.

Chapter Thirteen

There were two aspects to the tiny crawl space that was very intimidating. First, it was extremely small and the fear of being stuck and dying in this tunnel was a very real possibility. And Tullia was not skinny by any definition. She liked carbs a bit too much and cake was just too awesome to say no too. The second aspect is that it only went in one direction. She had started (fell) at the beginning of this tunnel, now she had no choice but to see where it took her. Bonus factor of the tunnel is that she heard a lot of scurrying, a lot of insect-like hissing, and she may have felt a few of those critters around her, but her mind refused that logical deduction and kept insisting she was merely brushing against roots.

Taking shallow breaths, she began to crawl forward.

Time was nonexistent in the dark space of the tunnel. Tullia felt as though she was crawling to a different continent. Her hands begin to take on a dull throb, her back throbbed, her knees were destroyed, and her shoulders were debating whether or not to just detach themselves from her torso.

To distract herself, questions circulated in her mind and she tried to theorize answers to the said circulating questions.

Why was this tunnel here? *For children to sneak in the royal, shiny building and get free food...?*

Did the guards know about it? *That would suck. But she was confident that he would get stuck instantly even if he did know about the secret. There was nothing he could do. Unless he shrank himself. Can shifters do that? Crap. They so can...Were they even shifters?*

Tullia began to crawl a little faster.

What if the guard is waiting on the other side of this tunnel? *That would suck.*

Who uses it? *Mice, bugs and small sized people.*

Who built it? *Someone with an intention.*

Where does it go? *Ideally, the royal shiny building. A not ideal possibility, to the ocean or large body of water.*

Her stomach whined loud enough that she was worried someone above ground would hear it. Side-note, she was really hungry.

How was the creation of this tunnel carried out? *With sticks, three dogs, a pack of bacon, and water. Definitely.*

How long is this tunnel? *Too long.*

A few dark years later, Tullia's forehead smacked into a solid wall of dirt. Sneezing, due to inhaling some of the loose dirt particles that sprinkled down, Tullia began to grope carefully the walls and ceiling, searching for a latch.

Her fingers slid into a crevice and she shuddered a little as her mind flashed with horrible, horrible possibilities. Gingerly, this time, Tullia pushed up slowly, moist dirt fell on her as the lid silently opened. Stretching her upper body to peek out from the tunnel, Tullia's eyes roamed the area deliberately. It wouldn't do to get caught right now. There were a bunch of bushes and some really pretty flowers, plush and lush looking trees, a little swing set and quaint tables with pots on them. Other than that, she saw no signs of people that would arrest with her. Carefully, slowly Tullia crawled out of her hole, continuously looking around for any guards. No one was in the little garden that was nearly over run with flowers and delicate looking trees that seemed wide awake in the dying daylight.

How pretty.

Still looking around some more, Tullia saw a pair of French doors that were magically outlined in thick, green, bushy vines. Without another thought she headed towards those doors, brushing her hands against the flowers.

Please be unlocked, please be unlocked, please be unlocked....

Tullia tentatively tested the handle, utterly relieved when it turned easily.

Thank heavens for small miracles.

Looking down at her hands she softly groaned, they were covered in dirt and seemed aged in an unflattering way. Slipping through the door and quietly shutting it behind her, Tullia ignored the fact that her hands were filthy and pressed them to her heart. Underneath her palm, her heart was pounding erratically like a five-year-old on a new drum set.

This was a lot of excitement for Tullia, more than she had experienced (even sneaking in Vegas shows didn't compare to this kind of thrill) and right now she wasn't sure how to proceed or how to properly breath.

Giving herself a moment to figure out her breathing situation (it wouldn't do to pass out right now), Tullia inspected where she was. The interior was a stark difference from the exterior. Instead of a modern, coldness to the design, there were warm colors, personalized in the pictures and knickknacks that decorated the walls. From the French doors she was caught between three hallways, all of them held pictures on the walls and furniture that seemed comfy rather than fashionable. It reminded her of what a grandmother's home would look like. It exuded tenderness, comfort, and love.

Tullia inhaled a spicy, warm scent as she eyed all three directions. Then did what any logical person would do.

"Eenie, meenie, miney, mo…" Her finger landed on the middle hallway.

Decided.

Tullia began to cautiously travel down her chosen hall, looking at the pictures on the wall. A lot of them where portraits of children in black and white, though there were a few in color and less formal. Tullia couldn't help the smile when she spied a picture of a girl holding a giant fish with a disgusted look on her face and a handsome man in the background laughing at her. She traveled down a few different halls, turning in a few directions, and passing through rooms that were clearly for celebrations or gatherings. Tullia tried random doors that would appear nearly at random in a wall. However, they proved to be useless, majority of them were either locked or storage rooms for cleaning supplies.

And weirdly, she ran into no one. Not a soul.

Well, this was beginning to suck, her stomach agreed with her. Loudly.

Tullia wandered around as darkness settled outside. As she wandered, she managed to find an elevator and stopped to stare at it for a bit.

Wow, snazzy.

Internally shrugging, she got on the elevator to the seventh floor, because she liked the number seven. As the elevator hummed, pulling her up at a leisurely pace, Tullia thought back to the visions she has had about Chito and about Biringan. She has had a few visions on shapeshifters, but not specifically of the Queen of Biringan. Recently, she had seen Chito mostly, which leads Tullia to believe that maybe Chito is the King of Biringan?

That seemed wrong somehow. Chito didn't radiate the aura of someone who ruled a city. He seemed more… squishy than anything else.

Tullia leaned against the elevator wall, watching the number flick to three. A yawn escaped her mouth just as the elevator doors opened. Strolling out casually, because she needed to talk to someone at this point, Tullia wandered more halls before coming to a floor-to-ceiling window that encompassed the city's nighttime glory.

It looked like it had in her vision.

Her breath left her lungs as she drank in the sight. It was a vast landscape of buildings beginning to glow, sleepily twinkling in the dusk of evening. The black buildings were strong against the sky with their brilliance, seeming to tease the darkness. Tullia looked up to the tops of the glowing buildings, strings of lights were connected between the buildings, creating an interloping network of illuminations that mimicked a spiderweb design. Instead of the people of Biringan walking under stars, they walked under millions of tiny lights.

Tullia pressed her hands against the glass, marveling at the sheer luminosity of it all. After a few more moments of admiring, she pulled away and, to her horror, the once flawless glass now had two perfect, dirty hand prints. She stared at it for a few moments, then rubbed over the print a little, trying to erase it. She should have known that dirty hands trying to clean was never going to help any situation. It only made it worse. Now instead of perfect hand prints, it looked like a three-year old's finger paint project gone wrong with dirt. Tullia sucked in both her lips, staring at her mess then sighed.

She didn't have time to be an adult about this particular situation. So, Tullia quickly left the scene of the crime, jogging down the hall.

Sorry to whoever has to clean it! I'm so sorry!

After putting enough distance between her and the now marred windows, Tullia resumed her leisurely exploration. A tiny part of her felt bad for entering the royal family's home, uninvited, and wandering all about. However, a bigger part of her was too curious and way too desperate to consider manners.

Turning yet another corner, expecting another uninteresting hallway, Tullia felt herself jerk in shock then freeze. Her eyes popped open wide and her mouth dropped.

It was Chito. The very same Chito from her vision… it was Chito from when she saw him talking to his grandmother.

Seeing him in person was equivalent to seeing a celebrity. She knew who they were, but they had no idea who she was. Tullia stood frozen, staring at Chito as he tapped away on a fancy looking phone, looking slightly deadened.

He was very beautiful in a subtle way. He had androgynous features, big eyes, sharp jaw, high cheek bones, and a strong chin. His skin was a cinnamon brown and his hair was a sleek curtain of rich dark brown that framed his slender upper body. He wore a white peasant blouse with a pair of baggy, ripped and faded mom jeans with a pair of well-worn brown, stylized boots.

Tullia bit her bottom lip and thought how best to approach him as he sluggishly made his way to her. She didn't know if he could help her, but she had an inkling that his grandmother, Carolina, was related to the royal family in some way. If she could get Chito to introduce her to Carolina, then maybe Carolina can introduce her to the Queen of Biringan.

Closing her eyes tightly, expelling the air from her lungs, she straightened her shoulders. Opening her eyes, she focused in on Chito and just went for it.

It was do or die baby.

"Chito!" She called, fast walking towards him, waving slightly frantically. She smelled a slightly sour and musty smell coming from her underarms that was utterly nauseating. Tullia pressed her arms tightly down.

She needed to be showered twice.

Chito looked up, seemed to process that she was a stranger then blinked. His face was surprised at first, however it shifted to suspicion edged with mild panic. She could taste the riot of confusion and slight fear dash across her tongue, a sweet and sour fishy taste.

Acting fast before he could say anything, Tullia rushed towards him and beamed. She clasped her hands together and tried to make herself non-threatening.

"Hi, don't freak out." She began, to which Chito raised his eyebrow at. "My name's Tullia, I came into the city through the portal thing, *finally*. I've spent like five days in that godforsaken jungle searching for the portal to get into Biringan City, which is why I look a little wrecked at the moment." She took a step away from him, just so he'd have a higher probability in avoiding her stank. "I'm looking for the queen, I don't know if you know her... but I think your grandma, Carolina, might." Tullia's lungs nearly collapsed due to lack of oxygen. Gasping in air to catch her breath, she quickly rushed on before Chito could say anything or scream. "You see, I have lost magic within me, which has been royally messing up my life. So, we," She waved her hands in tight circles, "as in my group that is currently M.I.A., need to find a dragon. The goblin from the pawn shop said that a shifter from the Mabuhay clan would know where a dragon is. Which, the Mabuhay clan is in Biringan." She took a deep breath, replacing all the air in her lungs. "So, long story short, here I am. Do you know where a dragon is?" She smiled. Still breathing embarrassingly loud.

A moment of silence stretched uncomfortably long.

Chito shook his head slowly as his soft brown eyes widened. He looked both bemused and fascinated. He still tasted of confusion though.

Tullia huffed. "Well shit." That sucked a little. "Okay, do you know if I could talk to the Queen of Biringan or your grandma, Carolina, that would literally be the biggest charity you could do in the world right now."

Chito shook his head again. "How are you here?" He asked this in English.

Tullia stared at him, confused. Did she accidentally speak in English to him? She could have sworn she was speaking in Tagalog. Did the spell that Cliona put on her wear off?

"Sorry." She tried again in Tagalog. She felt her mouth and tongue take on a different rhythm. "My name is Tullia, I came through the portal—"

Chito waved his hand to stop her. "No, I understood what you said, I just don't understand how you got inside this place. No one is supposed to be here, but family. And you are not family."

"Well…" Tullia dragged out the word, thinking of an acceptable response that would not get her thrown in a deep, dark prison. She pressed her hands against her stomach, it began to make it known verbally that it required substance.

Chito was staring at her, his eyes becoming more and more cold.

"I had a… vision. A little boy pulled up a section of the ground that led up to the entrance to this building," She motioned a square shape with her pointer fingers, "which then he disappeared under. Turns out it was a one-way tunnel, which was freaky, and then I ended up in a garden and then I ended up here." She twined her fingers together. "I still need to see the queen, though."

Chito opened his mouth, but a muffled whale noise had him pausing. Tullia felt her face flush with embarrassment.

Chito eyed her stomach and she tried to suck it in and cover it with her hands. She gave a weak laugh. "My stomach isn't usually so rude in conversations."

A sudden taste of sweetness and bubbles filled her mouth as Chito let out a gentle chuckle. "Are you a shifter?"

Tullia shook her head.

"I see. I don't know what to think. You're strange to say the least." He shook his head. "Well, my lolas will have my head if I allow anyone in their home to go hungry, invited or not." He began to walk past her, waving at her to follow him. "Come on, let's clean you up a little." He eyed her dirty appearance, his melted chocolate eyes met hers. "Then I'll get you something to eat so that stomach of yours can stay silent long enough for you to explain your situation to me. Slowly. You speak too fast."

If Tullia didn't know for a fact, she smelled worse than rotten sewage waste in the middle of a desert summer afternoon, she'd hug him.

She'd hug him hard and maybe cry.

"Really?" She said as an elated feeling overcame her.

"Hurry." He merely replied.

She smiled, agreed to his brilliant plan, and followed Chito deeper into the royal building.

Things were actually taking a turn for the best!

* * *

The sky had tucked the sun away for slumber. Though in Biringan City the nighttime was not only wildly active, it was accompanied by an abundance of stringed lights that glittered overhead like tiny suns.

Once they had entered Biringan, the witch had staggered and faltered after ten minutes of searching for Tullia.

"I need to recharge." She had growled, using her legs to walk instead of floating. She staggered to a darkened enclave where the artificial light's tendrils did not reach. There were always places such as these in all cities, and creatures like Cliona and him would always crawl to them. "Chasing that portal and tracking the muffled signature drained me entirely."

Sabin had followed her unstable form and leaned against the wall. He gave her a flat look, exhaling roughly, he gnashed his teeth to keep his rage down. Sabin did not want to stop, he wanted to hunt for her, he wanted to continue… but he needed the witch's magic nose. "It's because you used all your magic to fly instead of using your legs." His tone was an octave above a snarl, his rage seeping through.

The witch whipped her head around to glare at him with her eerie eyes. She stomped her foot. *"No it wasn't!* You're stupid and know nothing." She put up her hand to him, palm facing out and whipped her head to the side. "I'm going to recharge, don't bug me, berserker."

"Be quick about it." He ordered. They have only scratched the surface of Biringan, the sun had already retired for the day and the throngs of people made it seem as though the entire population of Biringan was out under the little lights. And most importantly, they still have not recovered Tullia yet.

Anxiety crawled up his spine at the thought, poking his rage.

"Oh?" The witch grounded out between clenched teeth. "If I wasn't drained, I'd make something solid land on top of you. Like a sewer lid. Or a toilet. Or five toilets. Or a filled porta-potty." She folded her hands, interlacing her fingers as she spread her legs apart hip-distance. She glared at him with her demonic eyes on a uniquely beautiful face. "All I need is twenty minutes. I'll be at full strength to gather our little missing flower. Until then, be a good boy and sit tight." She closed her eyes then sighed. Her entire body became encased in a light layer of pale blue smoke as she rose up off the ground three inches. She exhaled, stilled, then remained floating.

Sabin watched the witch for a moment, then shook his head. Such eerie creatures' witches were. Everything she did it all seemed like an unnecessary theatrical hassle. He rubbed his jaw in agitation, waiting for the ludicrous witch to finish. He contemplated leaving to continue the hunt by himself, but Cliona's magical nose would be faster than his tracking. Then the witch would never shut her gob about it. Besides, Sabin turned his head to look at the busy street. There were several individuals wearing what looked like uniforms. Already, Sabin spotted more than a handful. It appeared Biringan's security was abundant.

It made sense, after all how do you keep a hidden city hidden? Crowd control and reinforcement. Or so Sabin was hypothesizing. He didn't know if Tullia had avoided detection or if she were in custody currently. However, Sabin had confidence that wherever she was, she was crafty enough to keep herself from getting hurt at the very least.

He stood still in the shadows, watching the people with hooded eyes, searching through the faces for a glimpse of Tullia, hoping she'd be in the crowds.

She wasn't.

The enclave they hid in was ignored by all, making them nonexistent. He rolled his neck and felt the restless energy fuel his rage. He glanced over to where the witch still floated, mumbling incoherently as she recharged. He looked back to the crowds, gritting his teeth as his rage dug its claws into his gut.

This was going to be a strenuous night for his patience.

* * *

Too bright. The lights would be the first thing destroyed. Light was not supposed to exist in the night.

Alab explored inside of Biringan, cloaking his form in invisibility, a trick he managed to perfect over the years, though the pain never dulled when he did it. He took in the environment that would soon be his to control with a sharp eye. The buildings were tall, the streets were spacious and clean, the lights were gaudy, and the shifters…

…were *repulsive*.

Many of them had *humans* on their arms as lovers or friends. They chatted happily with *humans*, shared food with *humans*, mingled freely with *humans*… Alab shook his head, sneering at the disgusting sight before him. Humans were similar to dogs; at most they were meant to be pets to shifters. Humans were meant to be *beneath* shifters; they were meant to *serve* shifters, they were not meant to walk beside shifters, and they were certainly not meant to breed with shifters.

He felt himself grimacing at a small human woman with short brown hair and a softer than average frame holding a human shifter abomination, look up happily at a shifter in male form with no hair and a husky frame. Alab watched as the couple, a human man and a shifter in female form, interacted intimately for a few minutes. He then shifted his attention to a group of shifters with one human male, laughing together, playfully pushing each other. He looked at two women, both human, giggling while sipping some type of fancy drink, eyeing a lone shifter in male form.

Alab continued to observe the citizens of Biringan City, walking through the thongs of people, both human and shifters, for a few hours.

He nearly vomited.

He came to the conclusion after witnessing a nauseating proposal of a shifter in male form to a plain human woman, that the city was contaminated beyond salvation. The shifters were allowing this pollution to remain and even spread into the shifter line of genetics. Humans had no place in a shifter city unless they were to be pets or slaves.

It seemed he'd need to rebuild the city from ground up, both physically and genetically.

The offensive lights would have to be renovated second. First, the humans needed to be purged immediately. Alab looked around the unaware crowd, feeling more convicted with each human he spotted mucking up an almost perfect shifter city, then grinned when two human teenage girls pranced by, ignorant of their surroundings and chatting at high speeds.

He'd start there.

* * *

Tullia was on cloud nine.

Her hands were clean, firstly and she was eating what Chito called his lola's famous spicy beef over garlic rice with a fried egg and a side of roasted vegetables. Tullia pointed to her bowl of food with her chopsticks. "Is it possible to get this recipe? I don't think I can live without this anymore."

Chito gave a small smile, his eyes shining with a smugness. "My lola doesn't share recipes outside the family."

"I am utterly destroyed." She looked down at her bowl, took a bite, chewed slowly, then looked back at Chito. "You wanna marry me then?" Her mouth shamelessly full.

Chito's eyes widened, then he smiled sharply. "How bold." He flipped his long black hair over one shoulder, he rested his cheek on the palm of his hand. His gorgeous eyes eyed her without a single interest. "I'm afraid you're not my type."

Tullia twisted her upper body to face him as she placed one hand on her chest while she took another bite of the spicy beef. It literally melted in her mouth. "How dare you." She said between chews. "You didn't even give me a chance, I could pop rock your socks off."

He looked confused but by the bubbles popping all along her tongue, he was at least entertained. "Not a chance, *syota.*"

Tullia put the back of her wrist against her forehead. "This is the saddest day of my life, I simply cannot live without this food!" She mock wailed, taking another bite while keeping the dramatic pose. She looked at him from the corner of her eyes. "You got a brother? Or a young single uncle?"

Chito coughed then a laughed bubbled from his mouth as his eyes nearly closed with humor. He lightly smacked her arm. "You're shameless!" He shook his head, sending his long silky waves rolling. "I'm sure my lola will be willing to make this for you again. If you praise her enough."

Tullia pointed her chopsticks at him. "That will be no hardship to carry out. This food is worship material. This is the type of food that is worthy to found a new religion on."

He shook his head. "You're silly." His brown eyes turned sharp, and he eyed her with curiosity. Bubbles mixed with a sour and sweet taste. "Now tell me how you got in Biringan."

Tullia took a long sip of her iced black tea flavored with hibiscus flowers.

So delicious.

"I think, we need to back up a little bit further." Tullia set down her glass and looked at Chito seriously. "Just so everything can make sense."

Tullia explained first that she had lost magic and how she was diagnosed officially by the Grand High. She told him of the visions that had plagued her life since she could remember of different races in different realms. She told him how she saw different time periods, different historic events from wars, to weddings, to mundane happens that were significant in their own way either through alliances, personal relationships, or friendships.

She even told him about her visions about him and his kind.

Chito's eyes widened at that part. "Get out."

Tullia nodded. "Seriously. Like when you were a teenager and had a hard time sticking to one form or how your grandmother refused to let you go and explore the world because you didn't stick to one form regularly."

Chito's jaw dropped in astonishment; a slightly sour taste tickled her tongue.

Tullia continued in a rush, to assure him. "Nothing weird, don't worry." She fluttered her hands about, because that's just what you do when you want to reassure someone. "I didn't see your entire life, just select bits and pieces. Which is why it's amazing to actually meet you in person. You're like a celebrity to me."

His face reddened at her words.

"It's surreal and makes me feel as though, I don't know, fate?" She shrugged, unsure how to describe the nearly dizzying feeling of rightness she felt as she continued to talk to him.

She then decided to explain how she met the Grand High and Sabin. Tullia summed up briefly the happenings in between with the vampires and her having mini freak out sessions here and there. She finally told him of their plan, their trek through the Philippine jungle with the goal of finding and talking to the queen of shifters. They needed to see if she knew where a dragon was so that they could find the dragon and, hopefully, he will know how to expel or transfer the lost magic from her body so that she could live a peaceful, not medically insane, life.

She could go get a degree…

Hell, maybe she'd write a book at this rate.

Chito listened to her with rapt attention, rarely asking questions, and sipping on his tea slowly.

When she was all finished, they had drunk three glasses of tea and, in the middle of her tale, Chito had brought out what he called kutsintas that once again, his domestic goddess of a lola made. Which was a brown sugar rice cake with coconut shavings on top.

So delicious.

Chito shook his head, pushing away his empty plate and tucking his hair behind both ears. "That was better than a K-Drama marathon."

Tullia felt full and slightly out of breath. She can't remember the last time she talked so much to another person. She smiled over at Chito. "Glad I could entertain you." She tapped the empty glass with her nails, hugely nervous and a whole lot more than simply sweaty. She looked at him. "Do you believe me?"

He looked at her, his brown eyes gleaming, and smiled gently. "The fact that you're here to tell me the tale, yes I do." He stood up, lightly dusting off his flowy shirt. "And I want to help you."

"Really?" Tullia felt hope tighten and lighten her chest at the same time. "You really believe me?"

Chito gave a soft laugh. "The fact that you made it into Biringan City and into the Mabuhay Main building without getting caught, tells me that you're both desperate and serious. Besides, I am a generous person." He gave a little smirk as he pointed to himself. "I just happen to be my lola's favorite grandchild, so if I advocate for you, I'm sure she'd be willing to help your cause. It's such a simple request after all and lola would love to talk about her past travels."

Stank or not, Tullia jumped off her chair, nearly tripping in the process, and body slammed Chito with a bear hug. She squeezed him tightly. "Thank you. Thank you. Thank you! I freaking love you." She nearly sobbed, squeezing his slender frame with all her might.

Chito hugged her back softly. "You might want to let go of this one-sided love for me."

Tullia grinned up at him and was about to respond when there was an echoing slam and a shout filled the kitchen air, startling them. Chito and Tullia jumped apart as a guard stood by the doorway. His face was drawn with stress and pale. He tasted of sour fish and pungent nerves. "Chito! There you are!" He glanced at Tullia. "You can flirt with your girlfriend another time. Biringan is under attack, we need to get you to a secure location." He darted forward and gripped both Chito and Tullia's wrists, his hands were clammy and rough, then proceeded to drag them both out and down the hall at a vigorous pace.

Tullia's legs began to cramp.

"Attack? Biringan? Attack?" Chito's voice was pitched higher, and the strong flavor of sour fear flooded her mouth. "What do you mean?" Chito easily kept up with the long-legged strides of the guard. His long black hair hypnotically swishing around his lean frame.

Tullia tried to muffle her pants of exertion.

The guard's grimly lined face unnerved Tullia and caused her heart to stutter in its rhythm. "There is a tikbalang in Biringan City."

Chito gasped in horror and Tullia gave the guard a wide-eyed look. "A tikbalang? They aren't supposed to get through the portal, Mary made sure of that. How on earth did one manage to sneak in?"

The guard shook his head, his dark eyes focused forward. "Who knows? Now's not the time to ponder it. What matters is that it is in and we need it gone." He kicked open a door with his foot and dragged them up a flight of stairs. Tullia almost whimpered, why the hell did they need to climb stairs?

"There are two strangers fighting it right now, a man with axes and a witch."

Sabin and Cliona are in Biringan? They're fighting the tikbalang? Tullia's stomach tightened painfully. The food that was sitting in there churned nauseously due to the stress that abruptly surged through her system.

"Why do we need to get to safety then if people are fighting it?" Chito didn't appear to be straining himself in the least bit as he spoke and ran simultaneously. You'd think by his tone that he was taking a leisurely walk instead of being dragged at an unreasonable pace. Tullia needed to get in shape, this was just awful being winded all the time.

But on another note, as the guard forced them at a grueling pace up too many flights of stairs, they did not respect people with shorter legs and a mildly active lifestyle.

The guard made a sudden right turn, jerking Tullia's arm, creating a slight throb. The guard gave Chito a quick assessing side look. "The tikbalang is… violent. It attacked our citizens in the district, there are a few dead already." His voice faltered, sadness, a salty flavor, washed her pallet. "We've managed to clear everyone we could find away from the demon, but it wants the queen to come out."

The guard seemed to grit his teeth; heat brushed against her tongue. Chito made a distressed sound. "We aren't taking any chances with anyone from the royal family. This building is on lock down as is the east side of the city where most of the citizens reside."

He increased his pace, to which Tullia was now sprinting besides him so that her arm did not get torn off.

"Where's lola? What about the twins? Where's my mother? Papa?" Chito's voice quivered slightly and became shrill with each name.

"Be calm, Chito. They are safe and secure. Your mother took majority of the house to the theater to see that movie with that one actor…um…with the long hair?"

"Thor?" Chito provided, incredulously.

The guard nodded and did a clicking sound with his mouth. "That one. Except it's a triple feature. Thor one, two and three."

Tullia huffed, sweat begin to pop out from her pores, but managed a clear. "Aren't those old films? They should be out of the theaters by now."

"Yeah," The guard's tone was enervated. "However, Lady Darna enjoys… the lead male actor immensely. So, she has the theater keep those movies on hand for her use and frequents them regularly."

Chito made a scoffing sigh, he leaned back to give Tullia a deadpan look. "My mom has the biggest crush on the actor, she likes to see him on a big screen instead of at home. She even had my dad shift into him for Halloween, just so she could say that was her husband and hang on him."

Tullia could understand the want to do that, wheezing slightly, she said "Well, he is really good looking."

"His shoulders are ideal." Chito agreed, he used one of his hands to fan himself.

If Tullia had air to spare, she would have laughed.

"And his biceps?" Tullia added with a grin.

"I like his personality. He's sweet and funny." Chito and Tullia looked at the guard, surprised by his input. The guard didn't look at them, instead he shrugged causally. "It's understandable why Lady Darna holds immense admiration of the actor."

Tullia and Chito shared a glance between each other before breathlessly giggling.

The guard then increased their pace *again* as he led them through more halls, turned in more directions and even took them up three more flights of stairs.

Just how big was this damned palace?

Finally, he came to a dead stop at a dark blue door with tiny white specs on it. Tullia tried not to wither and breath too loudly as she squinted to look at the door through her darkening vision. The door was entirely dark blue with flecks of white, yellow and light blue. It screamed indie and looked like a night sky. The guard threw the door open without fanfare and managed to non-offensively fling them both into the room that looked like a galaxy hipster had a rave in it then got into their feels.

Tullia, still trying to regulate her breathing, took in the room. The walls were amazing. They were the once popular and highly trendy galaxy dark blue, pink, and white designs. Diamond star studded silks hung in from the ceiling in draping folds, creating an encompassing effect. Tullia was overwhelmed for a few moments, until the guard's harsh voice broke her from her wonderment.

"Stay here. I'll come and get you when it is safe to come out."

"Wait," Chito frowned, a deep groove appeared between his eyebrows. "Why can't I go to the rest of my family? Why am I being quarantined in my room?" Chito asked in a rapid fire way to the guard.

"I don't have time to answer your questions. Just stay here." The guard's tone became laced with frost and impatience.

Sour fear and the zesty heat of anger covered her palette thickly. Tullia watched as Chito folded his arms, and glare at the guard in extreme displeasure. "I am part of the royal family; you'll do well to remember that Vedasto." His tone was upper crust and arrogant.

The guard didn't seem phased, in fact humor crept into his stern face. "Your aunt is my wife, kiddo. I saw you born and wiped your butt. We *are* family."

Chito seemed to deflate, his eyes became dewy and his lower lip jutted out. He seemed so very young and so very innocent.

The guard's strict face softened slightly. "Everyone is safe and unharmed, I promise you. You were the last one to be accounted for. To relocate you with the rest of your family in the east side of the city is far too big of a risk. I need you to stay here, in your room, just in case so that your family can know your safe and so that we can protect you."

Chito swallowed thickly; Tullia watched as he pulled himself together. "Why do I have to stay in my room?"

"If an emergency happens and the Mabuhay Main building is breached by the tikbalang, not only is your room deep within the building, but we know specifically where you are, and we can get you out more efficiently than if you were to wander around."

Chito stood in silence for a few short seconds before sighing, his body sagging on the exhale. "I understand. We'll stay here." He seemed to withdraw into himself, the sassy boy from mere moments ago was gone and, in his place, a little mouse was present.

Vedasto smiled, which transformed his face into something that was surprisingly bright and subtly handsome. He nodded to both of them then shut the door. Chito turned to Tullia, opened his mouth to speak, but Vedasto opened the door again. His head poked through and he had a mischievous grin on his face as he looked at Chito, then at Tullia, then back to Chito. "Good job. She's pretty, though a bit dirty. Don't create a baby while alone, not yet at least."

Chito's face darkened several shades, his hands fisted by his sides, tartness and a coconut flavor bloomed over her tongue as he stomped his foot in embarrassment. "IT'S NOT LIKE THAT *STUPID*!" He shouted. The guard merely sniggered and shut the door again.

Chito's body frame was stiff, and his left eye twitched slightly. He eyed the door hard, probably waiting for it to reopen. When a full minute went by and the door remained shut, Chito turned to Tullia, a stiff smile on his face even though his shoulders sagged again. "Well, looks like we're stuck here for a bit."

Tullia blinked at Chito.

Oh no, she couldn't just sit in a room while Alab, A.K.A. the tikbalang attacked Sabin and the Grand High. She'd be labeled the worse member in their group and truly claim the title of useless baggage if she didn't do something.

She didn't want to be the deadbeat in the group.

Tullia shook her head slowly. "Sorry, I've got to get to where the tikbalang is."

Chito stared at her. "Are you stupid? Why on earth would you want to go where the tikbalang is?" Sassy Chito made a comeback.

It's not necessarily that Tullia *wanted* to go to where the tikbalang was, but more of a sense that she *needed* to go to where Sabin was. And Cliona. "I can't just stay here. My friends are out doing a showdown with the tikbalang. The man with the axes," she did a chopping motion with her hands, "that's Sabin. The beautiful witch," she flickered her fingers out dramatically like the Grand High always does, "that's Cliona."

Chito's eyes lightened with understanding, but he still shook his head in denial. "Even if you go there, what are you going to do?"

Good question.

Tullia shrugged. "Be a cheerleader? I don't know what I can do to help, but maybe I'll get inspiration once I'm there. I can be a distraction or something along those lines." She walked to the door, half expecting the door to be lock, but she was able to pull it open.

Chito must really be a good boy. She turned to look at said good boy.

His face became openly worried, he twisted his hands together nervously and depuffed in personality. "I don't think you should go. You're human right? No offense, but humans are useless in these types of situations. They're only liabilities." He seemed to quake under her sharp look. Shrugging, he tugged on a strand of his dark hair. "You know, mystical…. Magical beings and that sort of stuff."

Tullia huffed. "First, anything followed after 'no offense' is offensive." She held up two fingers. "Secondly, humans are cool, and they are adaptable. Not all of them, some are annoying, and most are stupid, but a few are cool and can keep up with things. Now," she faced him fully. "What floor are we on? And what floor is the garden located?"

She was bound to be lost with all the twists of the stupid maze of a house had.

Chito rolled his eyes and shook his head again at her. "You're gonna get lost, I can already tell you have a terrible sense of direction. I'll lead you to the garden." He straightened a little. "I'll also help you to the district. I am the prince after all."

Sassy Chito seemed to have something to prove to Tullia and the city.

* * *

Sabin watched as the demon roared, smashing windows and street carts. Screams filled the streets as people ran away from the violent creature in panicked masses, scattering like mice in the light.

Cliona stood beside him, fully recharged, staring at the scene dispassionately with her arms folded. "It's that thing from the forest." A pause as a particularly high crescendo of screams arose. "So, what are we gonna do about it?"

"Should we even interfere?" Sabin countered. He was already on a razor thin thread with his rage, any more excitement may ignite his berserker. He watched the tikbalang grip a girl with long black hair, yanking her back cruelly. The girl was crying, cowering in the demon's grip. Sabin clenched his teeth, vibrations of memories caused an itch in his hand and a tint of red to his vision.

A ram suddenly crashed into the demon's side. The demon didn't budge from where it stood, but it dropped the girl and snarled in rage, turning its attention to the animal. The ram charged again, distracting the tikbalang as a woman in a black uniform darted forward, grabbed the girl and dragged her away.

"What are you talking about? Opportunity is greeting us! If we help, it'll work in our favor. Defeating the tikbalang, saving Biringan City from the demon?" Cliona grinned up at him with a maniac smile and did a sweeping gesture under her chin. "The Queen will obviously want to thank us personally."

Sabin raised an eyebrow. "They could possibly accuse us of bringing the demon in the city and choose to persecute us instead."

She shrugged, "So?" She wiggled her fingers, little sparks danced between her fingers. "No one incarcerates a queen. Besides, we simply need a chance in front of her. This little stunt will ensure that."

Sabin exhaled harshly, he looked back at the demon with the skeleton horse face and soulless eyes. It was now ripping up a light pole up from the ground and using it to smash more windows bashing the shifters in black uniforms that began to attack him in swarms. The beast was strong, it would be a thrill to kill.

Sabin flexed his jaw, his rage writhing within. "We still have not found Tullia." The tikbalang managed to smash the light pole into one shifter's head, sending them flying across the street.

Cliona gave a groan. "She's a big girl. She has survived on her own without a big, dumb babysitter for years." She pointed at Sabin not so subtly. "Surely she can survive for another twenty minutes while we spank this demon down."

The tikbalang had now discarded the light pole in favor of physically gripping the guards and throwing them haphazardly into each other, laughing gleefully when they hit the sides of buildings or landed in trees.

Sabin felt himself grimace as his rage jumped up, ready to be unleashed, to be used against anything… against everything. Shoving his rage down, he silently reached behind him and withdrew *snubba* and *slatra*, the itch in his palms, burning. "Let's make this quick."

Cliona laughed roguishly. "A berserker, irritated over the fact that he has to fight?" She clicked her tongue in disapproval. "Well, I'm always in the mood for a good brawl." Her body began to emit a royal blue smoke color, she rotated her wrist, and flexed her body similar to that of an alley cat. "A berserker like you should jump at the chance to partake in a bloody fight."

He once did. Now he hated the part of himself that became excited for blood to stain his blades again. Sabin rolled his shoulders then began to walk out of the darkened enclave that they had squatted in. He squeezed his ax handles, comforted by their strength, comforted in their familiarity… haunted by the weight of their history.

His rage danced gleefully within him, expanding…

Sabin propelled it away from his mind, pushing it down within him again, before pulling his right arm back and snapping it forward, throwing *snubba* at the demon's chest.

A direct hit. A wet crunch. A scream of pain. Of rage. The skeletal horse face swung in his direction, its hollowed eyes seemed to glow with death and blood.

Sabin's answering look was just as feral. He felt his lips peel back in a ghoulish smirk.

Bloody confrontation and death were the elements he was raised in and it was where he felt at home.

He would enjoy the fight and all the blood that spilled.

* * *

Tullia felt at once comforted and nervous as all hell.

She managed to pump Chito up enough through their little trek through the maze-like halls to come with her and play hero. Though he was reluctant and frightened and occasionally sassy, he had deemed her a walking corpse if she were to go by herself.

Which she felt was a bit of an exaggeration, she was crafty, but then again she was not willing to push lady luck.

Currently, she followed Chito at a fast paced jog, once again wishing her cardio wasn't so pathetic. They had secretly left the Mabuhay Main building the same way in which Tullia had sneaked in, through the hidden garden tunnel. It was still just as small and horrible as she remembered it, though it was a bit nicer with someone else crawling through the space to share her pain.

"How did this tunnel come to be anyway?" Tullia asked, trying to distract herself when she felt more than dirt brush against her hands and bare legs.

"I made it when I was fifteen. I needed an escape route and something to do during the holidays." His answer was nonchalant but there was a strong note of pride in it.

"How cool, so how did you make it? Did you turn into something?"

"I switched between a woodchuck and a badger. They dig pretty big tunnels, and their claws can't be beat."

"How cool." Tullia repeated in a murmur, her eyes finally adjusted to the dense darkness of the tunnel. If Tullia knew Chito on a more personal level, she would have made a pass at his butt since it was literally right in front of her. However, they weren't that close… yet.

She had just formed a new side quest, and that was to become friends with Chito.

Quicker than the first time, the tunnel crawl was over within seemingly seconds and then they were up above ground and running *again*. Tullia followed Chito through a park and down a few alleyways that still looked super sparkly clean, past bushes and trees… everything became blurred after a while and Tullia could only focus on her lungs not collapsing and Chito's long, swishing hair. Eventually, just before Tullia's lungs were about to burst, Chito grabbed her arm and roughly dragged her down behind a short stone wall with decorative bushes.

Tullia managed a gasp. "What?" But Chito held his finger up to his lips. She heard loud stomping footsteps and loud voices and her thudding heart.

"Did you get everyone?" A female voice demanded.

"Yes. The northside of the city where the demon is wrecking, is evacuated. The only two left in that area are the witch and the man with the axes." A male voice responded.

Tullia jerked slightly at the guard's words.

"They are not citizens of Biringan City, I don't know where they came from…" A harsh breath of air, "but it doesn't matter. They're trying to stop the damned creature and that's all I need to know right now. Luttia, is the eastside secure?"

"Barriers are put in place by Mary and the majority of the armed force is there, on guard and waiting for the queen's orders." Another female voice responded.

"I suppose I'll have to be satisfied with that for now. Myran," There was a hitch in the woman's voice, "has instructed us to retreat to the eastside as well and await further orders." There was heavy frustration in the woman's voice at being put on standby.

"Myran said the queen directly told him to not interfere." Again, the tone was funny, a mixture of sorrow, rage and defeat, "The queen said she would handle the tikbalang personally." The male voice was strained with distress.

"I don't like that." A sharp statement.

A harsh sigh. "She is our queen and I'll follow her orders above all else."

"So would Myran. But this order must be killing him slowly."

A brief moment of tense, unhappy silence, then a tentative question. "How many dead?"

"Eight. Humans." The male voice was heated.

"Monster. Attacking our most defenseless citizens." This was said through clenched teeth.

Silence occurred once more, and the heavy salted flavor of sadness was painful to swallow.

There was a soft sniff before a female voice barked. "Let's move out!" Heavy footsteps resumed, faded then disappeared altogether.

Tullia looked at Chito, whose face had gone pale and his emotion tasted of sour fear and salt.

When his almond eyes met hers, he seemed even more panicked. "The queen is going to fight the demon." His tone was quiet, disbelieving. "Do you know how old she is?"

As he continued to stare at Tullia, without really seeing her, she saw the panic continue to build rapidly within him. She tasted the salty, sweet, and chaotic spice flavor that accompanied the emotion. Acting without thought, Tullia cupped Chito's face.

"Calm down." She put force into her voice, willing his panic to dissipate. "You're not going to help your queen by panicking. Calm. Down."

She watched his teddy bear eyes shake with stress before deepening into a rich mocha color. His breathing evened out and the tenseness of his jaw relaxed bit by bit.

Tullia kept a hold of his face, "Good. Keep it together man. There's a whole lot at stake here."

He gave a small, jerky nod, Tullia released his face then stood up. She wiped her brow, disgusted with the excessive dampness, and put her hands on her hips. "Where do we go from here?"

Chito slowly stood up from where he was crouched, his legs were shaky, but they held him up. He glanced around the area and sighed. "We need to pick up the pace." His sharp brown eyes sliced to her, "No offense, but you're slow. If we go at your speed then we'll get there when the fight is over."

Tullia gave him a dirty look. "Dude, again, 'no offense'," she air quoted 'no offense', "it's offensive. I know I'm slow, but have you been listening to me? Did you conveniently forget that I was out in the jungle for a few days?" Tullia ran her hand against her head, and quickly wiped the oily sweat off her hand.

She so needed a shower, three days ago.

Chito merely shook his long hair behind his shoulders. He gave Tullia a rather shaky, and slightly snarky, but beautiful smile. "It's all in good fun. Though it's still true."

Good fun her aching lungs, ribs, legs, feet, back and chest. Tullia just tried to glare her best at him, though she had the feeling it was more of a deadened sweaty look than an irritated look. But she did give him a look.

Chito inhaled slowly, looking into the distance, and looking somewhat cool. "It'll be faster for us if I go pony then you ride my back."

Why did he not offer this sooner? If this was thought of sooner, then she wouldn't have suffered the unnecessary exertion and they would have arrived there sooner.

The hell. Her quivering legs felt cheated and abused.

Then his words fully processed in her sluggish brain. Tullia then put her hands on her hips and looked at Chito's form. "You're going to 'go pony.'" She clarified, saying the phrase slowly.

Chito pulled a sarcastic, defensive look on his pretty face, "Yeah? I like the Power Rangers comics and their catchphrase. I believe it applies to me because I can morph into anything. So, it makes sense."

His logic made sense, and Tullia found it adorable that he'd reference his shifting like that. However, … "Isn't there one that says 'it's morphin' time'? Shouldn't you say that instead? Wouldn't that be even more accurate?" Tullia asked, Chito frowned. She saw him thinking, then his brown eyes narrowed on her.

"Tullia, that sounds lame and childish." His tone implied a 'duh', as if she should have known this before ever suggesting it. Tullia chose not to respond, she didn't want to burst Chito's bubble that his phrase 'go pony' wasn't exactly not lame and not childish either.

Chito sighed, he took off his flowy shirt and pants. Tullia looked away quickly, feeling heat rise to her face and feeling slightly embarrassed.

"I'm going to change now." He said. Tullia's curiosity turned her eyes back to peek at Chito, he raised his arms high into the air. On his exhale, he shifted his form. His transformation was amazing to see in person and nearly unbelievable, almost as if her brain didn't accept the occurrence. His form seemed to grow, and his current look melted away, blurring, before reshaping into a completely new arrangement. His new appearance was that of a mini pony that was a silky brown color with a black tail and mane. He bent his elegant neck to pick up his neatly folded clothes in his mouth. He shook his head, then motioned for her to 'get on' stomping his hooves.

"Why didn't you just do this before all that running?" Tullia muttered as she slowly approached Pony Chito. She gripped his mane gently, then looked him in the eyes. "I'm sorry in advance if I pull your hair too hard. And if I'm heavy. And if I don't smell great." Then she tightened her grip and jumped, hopped and straddled Pony Chito in one attempt.

Tullia resisted the urge to do a happy wiggle, in respect towards Chito. She gripped his hair tightly and clenched her thighs tight around his flanks. She didn't know how to ride a pony, but she was pretty sure the main idea was to not fall off.

Pony Chito gave a snort then a soft whinny, lightly shaking his head before clomping through the streets at a pace that had Tullia clinging for dear life. He purposely went fast, she thought as the scenery went by in a blur.

Yet, she'd take the terror of riding bare back on a shifter pony over running any day.

* * *

Sabin ducked under the claw that aimed for his head and swung his axes in return at the creature's emaciated thighs.

It dodged.

The gush of red, the scream of pain did not occur.

His rage screamed at the disappointment. His brain churned with intensity. Sabin rolled, avoiding the heavy stomp of the decayed hoof, it made a deep indent in the concrete. The creature growled, its hollowed eyes glaring at Sabin.

Sabin looked at the demon. It was a bony thing, seemingly decayed and frail, but the creature was crafty and stronger than it appeared to be. He couldn't land a single blow to it, he couldn't even manage a scratch, which incited and intrigued his rage. Sabin shot a look to the witch, she was picking up cars, streetlights, and anything near her and launching them at the demon. She was also casting many spells; he could tell by the way her lips moved and her eyes remained a solid blue color.

But the demon was unaffected and even seemed to be enjoying itself.

"This is saddening, I expected a challenge." The horse's voice cackled out into the balmy air. The sound was like a corpse speaking for the first time after being buried for years.

The witch gave a shriek of rage, her glowing eyes alight with insanity. She raised her arms up in an erratic manner, her lips moving and teeth clicking together. The ground shook underneath them and pieces of the street began to rise in the air. She then rotated her hands to face her palms towards the demon, and the shards of the street rotated toward it as well. When she closed her hands the street pieces flew at a blurring speed towards their threat. Sabin leapt out of the way, to avoid being hit and rolled a few times.

Thick clouds of dust bloomed in the air where the demon once stood.

Suddenly a car came soaring from the dust and directly towards the witch. Her eyes widened in shock, but Sabin ran swiftly and launched *snubba* at the car. *Snubba's* impact against the car derailed its path and pinned it instead against a bricked wall. It wouldn't do for the witch to meet her end just yet.

"Convenient weapons, corpse." The demon sauntered out from the now thinning clouds of dirt.

"Fucker." The Grand High snarled, her hands opening and closing.

It grinned.

The demon was tall, as tall as a Jotun, though less meaty and spindlier. Though its skin was nothing like he had ever experienced. His axes seemed useless against it, as if he wielded feathers instead of the solidified blood of the Gods and steel.

Skin the creature... make a coat... make a shirt... wear it for all to see, to know, to fear.

He shook his head, dispelling the thoughts. He didn't need to do that anymore. He couldn't die and felt no pain, so what was the point of armor?

Trophy... trophy... tradition...

Sabin gnashed down on his teeth. There was no trophy to be won here and his clan's traditions died when he discovered the lies. Sabin eyed the demon; its attention was focused on the witch. It had begun to lob objects at her, from cars, to benches. He eyed the creature's neck and the back of its horned skull. Sabin ran to collect *snubba*, and face the demon again.

Everything had a weakness; everything had a chink. He would find this creature's weak point and he would end it.

First, he had to get closer to the beast, then he would need to test his blade on every surface of its skin until he smelled blood. His rage screamed with glee as blood-soaked thoughts saturated his mind. He spun his blades in his hands, grinning.

Chapter Fourteen

Insane they said. Idiotic, they said. Impossible they said. He was wasting his time trying to discover the start of the beginning. It was a fool's hope.

But here he stood at the center of all. At the beginning of everything. The sun was high in the sky and the white trees shone under the rays, glimmering, and swaying in the gentle breeze.

He could feel it. It was different from other sites he had visited. He felt it, pulsating in the air strongly, throbbing in the earth underneath his hooves. His heart was pounding in the exhilaration. He swallowed, resisting the urge to stamp his hooves and cry out in joy. It swirled in the air, thinking itself invisible, but he saw it, he felt it. It brushed against his exposed skin sending the sharp spikes down his spine...

"Cicero?" The crude voice scattered his joy and brought him back to his present self. He turned to see his disciples watching him eagerly with wide eyes. His little lambs, he held their minds and souls in his hands. He could imagine their breath being suspended, waiting to hear words drip from his lips like the Gods Nectar.

"This place has great potential." He announced. He would reserve his emotion until he was certain this area was everything he felt it was.

His followers chattered amongst themselves with giddiness at his proclamation.

"Then we must test it." Another of his disciples said and there was a murmuring of agreements around him. The blood thickened in the air.

"Indeed." Cicero looked at the space, elation soaring in his heart. "We need to test this site's ability." A smile bloomed over his face, "Let us go searching."

A murmuring of anticipation, the rise of an ambrosia sensation, and the intoxicating giddiness of what's to come.

* * *

Pony Chito came to a hard stop that jolted Tullia and made her already bruised shoulder throb again. She stayed frozen on Chito for a few seconds before she was able to convince her limbs to loosen and then release her death grip from him. She, more or less, fell to the ground on her knees in a heap of boneless human jelly.

Chito shifted back to his human form, shook his head much like a dog would, then got dressed once more. When he was completely clothed he looked down at Tullia. He smoothed his dark hair back. "Your grip was a bit tight on my hair. I may have lost a few strands."

She waved up at him dismissively, still trying to recover. "I apologized in advance, you can't come back at me." She exhaled, feeling so much better by not being on a shifter horse. "But, I'm sorry again if you get premature balding because of that."

Chito chuckled and gave her a smile.

A scream yanked their attention towards the vicious sound.

Tullia saw the Grand High stretched her arms out, the blue smoke became so thick around her, her figure was barely discernible. "Let's see what's inside your ugly horse face." Tullia squinted and saw two glowing blue eyes and straight white teeth. The smoke swirled into a tornado for mere seconds, before clearing. She saw Cliona clearly then, and she looked terrifyingly insane. Her eyes were pure blue, and blue veins seemed to pulse all over her face. She curled two fingers down to make a handgun sign. She then put her hands in front of her. "Bang, bang!" She jerked her hands up and two giant smoke balls shot out of her fingers. The smoke darted straight into the tikbalang with little fanfare. When the smoke hit, he gave a short roar of pain, trying to swat it away. Tullia watched as blue smoke began to curl around him, encasing the creature's knobby form entirely in a thick layer of smoke. Cliona tilted her head up and let out a groaning sigh, her head drooped further back and her body shuddered.

As her head twitched spasmodically, her hands tensed in front of her. "Such a nasty thing." Cliona's head snapped forward, her face twisted with a wicked grin, she ran the tip of her tongue across her upper lip. "Let's break him slowly."

"We make it bleed." Sabin growled, his voice was gritty and raw, as he ran at Alab with both of his massive axes gripped in his hands, though it didn't seem to hinder Sabin in the least bit. The tikbalang saw Sabin, screeching, it raised his claw to swipe at him. However, Sabin lurched at the last moment, avoiding the claw swipe and dolphin diving forward between the creature legs. He slashed the back of the Alab's skinny knees, dashing away when he screamed and swiped his nasty claw again.

Alab suddenly began to cough, his scrawny chest jerked, and his claws jerked up to his face, burying themselves into his skeleton face. Another scream of pain and rage coated the air.

Tullia looked at Chito, who was now crouched down next to her with wide horrified eyes.

He slowly turned to her, face pale."Those are your companions?"

Tullia nodded, feeling like a cool kid and having a whole lot of pride because they looked bad-ass. Chito looked back at the fight, she noticed his eyes were full of admiration and they were following Sabin's movement devotedly. A slight blade tip brushed against her spine and irritation bloomed briefly across her mind. She shook her head, utterly confused by the feeling.

Focus.

"Alright, here we are. Now what can we do?" She asked, forcing her eyes away from the fight and on to the scenery. Everything was in shambles. It looked more like a dystopian city than the once pristine city she had first seen. The sidewalks were cracked and littered with debris; shop windows were shattered; lamp posts were sticking out randomly from walls; the streets were torn up in a haphazard manner; and the lights that twinkle magically above, were out in patches and some were flickering eerily.

"The poor city." She murmured.

"How could this have happened?" Tullia looked at Chito. His face was leached of color and his eyes took in Alab with utter dismay. "The city…" His voice was thick with sorrow. A salty flavor coated her tongue, drying Tullia's mouth out.

"What can we do?" Tullia repeated, thinking over scenarios where everyone lived.

Chito gave her a startled and offended look, the rims of his eyes dewy. "It's a stupid idea in the first place to be here when neither of us can fight. Not like them." He pointed at Sabin and Cliona. "So, the answer is we do nothing, we watch and prepare for the trauma this whole thing is going to cause."

Tullia gave him a sour look, ignoring the sour taste of fear that coated her mouth from Chito.

Alab wrenched his hands out of his face and gripped a metal chair, hauling it at the Grand High with a heavy launch. She narrowly avoided it spinning to the side with a wide grin. The tikbalang span around, grabbing another metal chair and Tullia saw that the back of his knees where Sabin had sliced were undamaged.

Tullia grimly eyed the tikbalang's reptilian skin. Apparently, it was as tough as it looked, almost like armor.

"We need something that can pierce the tikbalang's skin." Tullia absently commented. "If Sabin's axes didn't do anything, what else could?"

Chito gave a groaning sigh, looking back at the fight with a slight glare and bit his lip. "Fire?" He suggested softly. Tullia raised an eyebrow at him. He shrugged, "Fire may work. Water may be a universal solvent, but fire is a universal destroyer."

"I like this thought process." She looked around her, eyeing the store names. They were all restaurants or clothing stores, no hardware stores in sight. And no flamethrower stores either.

How inconvenient.

"I doubt any of these places sell flamethrowers huh?" Tullia said glumly.

"We don't need that, that's too much drama." Chito scoffed, "We just need a little spark and a flammable liquid." He pressed himself tightly against the little wall of the planter they sat behind, his chest was rising and falling fast. He peeked at the fight. His eyes traced the scene, then his eyes followed Sabin's bulky form.

Another brush of random irritation.

"So then, wine?" Tullia's tone was a bit forced.

Chito shook his head, still watching the fight. "No, wine doesn't have a high volume of alcohol."

Tullia cocked her head to the side. "Vodka?"

Again, Chito shook his head, "No. For this to work, we need a suicidal alcohol. We need eighty percent or higher in alcohol concentration."

Tullia's jaw dropped. "That's a thing? Might as well be drinking rubbing alcohol then."

Chito nodded in agreement. "Well that type of liquor is usually used as a base for infusion drinks. It shouldn't be used as a shot liquid."

Tullia put her hand on his chest. "I'm still in shock that people actually consume that percentage." And she thought the Prosecco she had once was strong.

"How innocent of you." Chito cooed softly, a slight smile on his own kind of beautiful face.

Tullia gave him a dirty look, this boy looked like he was fresh out of high school and he had the audacity to act more experienced than her? She sniffed, then decided to be the somewhat bigger person and stayed on topic. "Do you think one of the restaurants might have what we're looking for?"

"Duh." Chito grinned, "I don't know where you came from, but in Biringan we shifters know how to take and handle our alcohol."

Tullia gave him an eye roll at his obvious bragging. "Alright, awesome for you. Now let's go." She glanced at the rumble taking place literally feet away from them and noticed that Sabin was now on the tikbalang's back and trying to choke it with the steely part of his ax across its throat. There still was no blood from Alab. Tullia lifted herself up into a crouch, preparing to run….

"Whoa, whoa, wait," Chito restrained her gently with a hand on her arm, "You're gonna actually go?"

Tullia furrowed her eyebrows, did he think she came all this way to watch? "Yeah, that was the entire plan."

Chito's eyes seemed to shimmer and Tullia's tongue was swarmed with a smoky fish taste, which Tullia began to deduce was the taste of worry and anxiety.

Chito turned his head to stare at the tikbalang. His eyes then trailed over the destruction he caused from the streets to the buildings. He looked back at her, his eyes were darker, determined. "I… I think it'll be faster if I… go by myself."

Tullia felt her eyebrows meet her hair line with surprise. "Excuse me? If this is another one of those 'no offense' statements, I will punch you."

"Hey, that is a capital offense here to threaten a member of the royal family." Again that smug, I'm-super-important-and-you-can't-do-anything-to-me-cause-you'll-totally-get-in-trouble tone. Like a rotten six year old toward their older sibling.

Man, that totally chaffed her.

Her face must have shown her irritation, for Chito gave a half smile and a small amount of bubbles tickled her tongue. "I have to see something." He seemed to shrug, a little depreciating. "Call it a self-test. Let me go and at least see if there is alcohol to be found, if there is then I'll come back."

"Or you can just grab it when you see it." Tullia offered, like don't come back empty handed, it's better to be efficient in this scenario.

Chito rolled his eyes. "Ever heard of a scout? That's what I'll be."

"Or," Tullia suggested, "You could be the retriever and the scout." She held up two fingers, "Two for one deal."

Chito's face was not amused as a vinegary flavor infiltrated her mouth. "I look, I find, I report, I no grab." He made an X shape with his two pointer fingers.

Tullia narrowed her eyes at him. "What is that? That wastes time. Just go-go a different animal that can grab it."

Chito drew back, his right hand poised over his chest and his face crumpled with offense. "I'll have you know, that scouting is depicted as a very important and highly dangerous job."

Tullia frowned at him, eyeing Chito with a stank eye. Where was he getting his ideas? Did he think this was a casual situation to play out a novel scene? This was real life. She had a feeling that Chito didn't get out much. By the set of his mouth and the stiffness of his body, he was going to do it and he was going to put up a huge fuss if he did not.

She gave a quiet groaning sigh and ended up waving him away. "Fine, fine. I'll wait right here for you, go-go scout master." She folded her arms tightly under her chest. "Be safe okay?"

Chito nodded, then shrank down and melted once more, but this time he was swallowed up by his clothes. A little lump writhed and squirmed in Chito's clothes. Then a tiny rat head popped up. His nose twitched and he looked up at Tullia with wide black eyes.

Tullia felt her lips twitch with humor. "I see you chose to go-go rat, huh?"

Rat Chito seemed to squeak violently at her, swishing his tail with aggravation, before darting away, disappearing instantly within the chaos of the rubble.

Tullia sat back, she really hoped he just grabbed the stuff they needed. Cause she couldn't shrink down and go-go rodent.

* * *

Carolina stared in utter horror. That mishap creature that used to be her brother.

He was more grotesque than she remembered, as if he started decaying slowly. She stood on top of the shortest building in her Biringan, watching the creature behave in a mindlessly violent way as it was attacked by the witch and the ax-wielding man. He was making a mess of her beautiful city. Buildings were smashed, roads were destroyed, and some of her lights were out. Her precious lights…

"Your highness." Carolina looked behind her to see her head guard, Myran, breathing heavily, face strained and eyes nearly wild with grief. "As ordered, all the force is focused on keeping civilians safe. We have quarantined them all in the east quadrant. All but the ones the tikbalang managed to get to." His tone was steady, but she could see his bleeding heart in his face.

Pain caused her heart to stutter. To lose even one of her precious citizens in her city in such a vicious, unwarranted way… a quiet rage brewed strongly within her, accompanied by bitter sorrow. She should not have allowed Alab to run wild for so long. She should have ended him when the first rumored tikbalang made an appearance. But she didn't, she still held the hope that he would find himself.

Now that hope, she realized, was foolish. All the while he had festered in isolation and rage, turning savage and violent. Her heart throbbed, then hardened. She would avenge the innocence that were slaughtered cruelly tonight, by butchering their killer. She looked towards Alab, watching him swing wildly, roaring loudly, and examined him existing in his disgusting state of hate.

Carolina heard Myran's suppressed emotion behind her. She could feel his pain and she did not fault him for his struggle with his emotions. She was asking him to not fight, not to go and personally avenge his love. Instead, she was asking him to stand on guard.

"Mary has put in place a barrier and all of the city's guards are standing at the ready in defense." His voice was hoarse from suppressing his grief.

She closed her eyes, her heart wept as she swallowed back the pain of knowing… knowing that every death was her fault.

"Good." Carolina opened her eyes, her resolve steely. She studied the way in which the witch was shooting blue smoke at her brother as the burly man ran towards him, slashing him repeatedly. No blood fell from him. "No one moves from their posts until I give word to do so."

She looked back at Myran, his jaw was clenched and his tan skin three shades paler. "Your highness, I beg you. Let us help. Let *me* help."

Carolina shook her head, she took off her dark blue sweater, a present from her Lyra, and passed it to Myran. "No. No more shall die by his hand. This is something I should have done long ago, when the stories of tikbalang arose."

She had caught wind of an ugly, grotesque skeleton horse faced demon stalking the jungles, leading travelers astray and being nasty to humans. She chose to ignore the rumors and stay safe in her city. She chose to ignore the traveler's death. Even recruiting a witch to add protection to her city… to herself. She was no better than Alab, no less guilty.

Now, her brother, no, the tikbalang was here in her city. Destroying her city and hurting her people.

And she knew why.

She caught Myran's face between her hands. A fine tremble shook his form. "I will defeat it. Your duty is now to protect your children. To protect everyone's children."

Myran was a strong boy, but as strong as he was his sorrow forced tears from his eyes. His face was stone cold, but his grief was palatable. She leaned in and pressed her lips to his forehead, wishing to take his pain, knowing she never could.

When she withdrew, Myran's eyes held a deep, quiet sadness that he would carry for years to come.

Inhaling deeply, Carolina nodded to Myran. "I will kill him, and we will have a proper mourning."

She saw him clench her sweater in his hands as his sad light brown eyes pleaded with her to reconsider. She gave him a faint smile as she ignored the plea, then summoned her gift to consume her, melting her form away as she walked off the edge of the roof and leapt towards Alab.

* * *

Tullia watched the violence all alone, feeling small, feeling useless, and feeling unsafe. She tried to fold herself as small as she could. Chito was taking forever and a year. She came up with multiple scenarios that might help. However, she was worried that if she ran in the middle of the fray with rocks to throw, that Alab would throw stuff back and then Sabin would try and help her, stretching himself thin and getting hurt. She didn't know if Cliona would help her right away… she might help solely because she was the lost magic's vessel. But then again, kind of understanding the Grand High's thought process, as long as Tullia wasn't dead, then it probably wouldn't matter what state she was in.

So, the most helpful option for everyone was the one where she was forced to sit and wait until stupid Chito came back. She was subjected to endure her state of complete uselessness and the fact that she was indeed powerless in this type of situation.

Again.

Chito was right, this wasn't very smart.

Swallowing against the acid in her throat from stress, Tullia pressed herself tighter to the stone wall, wishing that Chito would hurry up so she wouldn't be so alone and inept. She closed her eyes against the fighting. It wasn't entertaining and it wasn't exciting.

Go-go something fast and hurry Chito...

"What are you doing here, dear? Are you alright?" This smooth voice, speaking in the dips of Tagalog, asked her gently.

Tullia gave an involuntary gasp of fright, her eyes flying open wide and snapped her head up to witness a beautiful woman with light brown eyes, light brown skin, and a delicately crafted face with timeless eyes. Those age-soaked eyes look at her in concern, her black hair fluttering around her face. Tullia's eyes widened even further, drying out her eyes, as her mouth became slack with amazement. It was Carolina in the flesh.

She was even more beautiful in person than the vision had portrayed her to be.

"Carolina." Tullia breathed.

Her lush lips curving up slightly in a soft smile, stunning Tullia further. "How bold. And you are?"

"T-Tullia." She stuttered clumsily. Tullia didn't know how to converse with such a beautiful person. The Grand High made it easy, since she had a boisterous personality and ran her position like a CEO Mafia.

But Carolina was different, she was a matriarch and there were very specific rules involving things and it required a different skill set that Tullia did not have.

Carolina gently patted her head; the touch was soft and warm, dispelling the panic that had woven a light fog around Tullia's brain.

"There, there, Tullia. Seems like you've managed to evade the round up. I'm afraid it's too dangerous to move you now, it'll be safer if you simply stay put. Alright dear?" Her tone was still gentle, almost loving, but firm.

She made a move to stand, but, panicked, Tullia grabbed her hand, stopping her. When their eyes met, Tullia felt a rush of apprehension. "That's Alab. He's here to kill you."

Carolina's eyes widened. "How do you know of Alab?"

Tullia stared at Carolina, at a loss for words. Carolina's face came closer to Tullia's, searching for the answer to her question with narrowed eyes. She swallowed past her nerves, past her fear and forced her words out.

"I saw it." Tullia said, her voice sounded odd. Sounded breathless and soft and prophetic.

Carolina's face alighted with understanding as her long-lashed eyes evaluated her. "You have the gift of sight then?" She inquired, Tullia shook her head.

"No, I can't see the future, only what has already happened."

"Ah," Carolina gave her a curious look as she tilted her head. "So, then you possess a type of back sight?"

What a cool name that Tullia hadn't even considered. Then again, she didn't think any of this was actually real.

"Yeah, that's pretty accurate."

Carolina again smiled softly. An ear-splitting roar snapped their attention to see the tikbalang wildly swinging his skinny limbs around, trying to dislodge Sabin from his back. Sabin was hammering one of his axes in the tikbalang's back as he gripped the demon in a tight choke hold with the other ax again.

He was so strong...

"My brother has a debt to settle with me, this I was already aware of." Tullia looked back to Carolina as she spoke. The side profile of her face was timeless with its stark intensity and sorrowfulness. "I don't wish any more innocence to be harmed in his insane path to get to me." She stood up, looking regal and like the ultimate old school image of a queen. "So, I will go to him."

Wait.

She seemed about to say something else, but rapid squeaking interrupted her. Carolina tilted her head, frowning in confusion, before a small black rat came scurrying out of the debris with jerky movements.

The rat squeaked happily, before it grew and shapeshifted into Chito. A butt naked Chito, who was grinning the prettiest smile.

Tullia's eyes didn't know where to look and a heavy awkwardness settled firmly into place.

Where does she look? Her eyes itched, nearly tearing, to look in the most inappropriate, yet obvious place.

Do not look. Do not look. Do not be that weirdo.

"*Chito!*" Carolina looked utterly horrified when Chito shapeshifted back. His face went from triumphant to pale in a mere breath span.

"Lola?" His voice was as small as his little rat squeaks he did mere moments ago.

Carolina's face was stiff, and her beautiful light brown eyes lit with a type of rage that was the most terrifying. Her rage coated Tullia's tongue in chili and heat as did Chito's sour fear.

"Why are you here?" Her tone was deceptively gentle.

Tullia saw Chito shrink into himself, looking so very young and swallowing hard. "I-I…" He swallowed again, Tullia could see the sweat rivulets begin to drip down his forehead. "I sneaked out. To help."

The heat in Tullia's mouth intensified.

She saw Carolina inhale sharply and deeply, as if to quell her fury. "*Help?* You were going to *help?*"

Chito didn't answer, he merely stared at his lola with frightened doe-like eyes.

Carolina spoke through her teeth. "You are in so much trouble when this is over." She snapped her fingers and shoved her finger in his direction.

"Don't move an inch from this spot, or I'll kill you and take away your hot water privileges." Tullia's eyes widened and her mouth formed an O. It appears lola doesn't play when she's mad. Chito didn't say a word, though he nodded vigorously which was probably the wisest course of action. She pushed her long hair behind her shoulder, still glaring at Chito. "You'd assume the grandchild of the queen would be more intelligent than to pull something as stupid as this."

Tullia's eyes widened, she whipped her head around to stare at Carolina, then she looked at Chito, and finally she looked back at Carolina.

A click echoed in her mind as everything came together. Carolina is the queen of Biringan City, the grandmother of Chito, and the sister to Alab, who wants revenge on her for his current form.

The completion of the whole picture was satisfying.

Carolina then looked to the fight, her eyes becoming shards of ice. A steamed vegetable taste accompanied with minty coldness filled her mouth, which felt so good after the painful heat of the queen's rage.

"This must end." The queen was staring at Alab with resolution. "I must end it." She straightened, her unbound hair creating a beautiful, silky background to her strong form. She inhaled deeply, then her stature grew, ripping her clothes in the process as she sprouted dark and silver hair over her body, her face elongated and flattened out. Tullia watched, awestruck to see her third shift so up close and personal and the queen shapeshifter at that.

The queen had morphed into a silver-back gorilla. She shook her newly transformed body, flexing her hands and rotating her head. There was a sudden scream of something unnatural. Tullia snapped her head back to look at the tikbalang, who had managed to sink his claws into Sabin's side, his face a nasty snarl, as he flung Sabin off his back as if he were nothing more than a rag doll.

Tullia let out an involuntary shriek of horror as she witnessed Sabin's brawny body cascade through the air as limp as a soggy piece of bacon, before crashing onto the ground, rolling on the jagged street before stopping. He was completely still.

Terror flooded every nerve ending she had, sending painful shocks throughout her body, as heavy tones of dread speared through her heart. Scrambling to her feet she rushed over to Sabin's limp form, tripping on some of the debris (stupid debris) as she hastily ran head long to him, ignoring Chito's faint yell at her to stop. Her eyes were glued to Sabin's big still form.

Please don't be dead. Don't go away. Don't leave...

* * *

He glared at the bothersome man's now silent form. Snorting in satisfaction, he turned his head to the nasty witch.

One insect down, one more to go. They were pesky, but they'd yet to do any damage to himself.

Alab gripped a long, tall pole, ripping it free from the ground and spun two times before hurling it at the annoyance that was the witch. She managed to dodge it gracefully with her floating form, but it wasn't his intention to hit her with it. Just distract her as he closes the distance between them. When she faced forward once more, Alab had the pleasure to see her pure blue eyes widen a fraction with shock before he rammed his claws into her midsection.

The choke from her mouth and the smell of blood was an addicting provocation that fueled him into spinning the witch's stiff body a few times around, digging his claws deeper into her, before releasing her. He allowed himself to savor the sight as her bulky body smashed into a stone bench, cracking it with the force of impact. He watched a small cloud of dust rise from the disturbance, but the witch's form was still.

He flexed his claws, enjoying the wetness of her blood. He brought his hands up and went to lick them…

A heavy weight landed on his back, nearly driving him to the ground. Giant fists began bashing his head, rattling his brain with pain. Screeching in rage Alab reached back, sunk his claws into the thing on his back and flung it off. He saw a… gorilla sail through the air, then morphed into the shape of an eagle. He eyed the eagle as it shrieked, circling around to face him before morphing again into a giant gray elephant midair. Alab dove out of the way of the heavy grounding smash of the massive elephant. He turned around at the sound of heavy stomping of the elephant that charged at him. Alab braced himself, leaning forward and readying his hands, sinking his hooves into the ground.

They collided violently; the contact vibrated throughout his frame painfully. Alab gritted his teeth as he managed to grip the shifter's tusks. The beast pushed harder into him, causing his hooves to sink further into the concrete as he was forcibly pushed back. Alab met the eyes of the elephant and instant recognition flashed through him. Those damned eyes she insisted on having in every form.

An upsurge occurred with him, as boiling rage doused his entire being.

"*Sister*. Long time no see." He pulled her head to the side sharply, twisting it hard to the left.

Suddenly, the tusk he held firmly in his grasp melted away and a strong fist smashed underneath his jaw. His vision went dark temporarily, but he was jarred to consciousness when he hit the side of a building, his bones cracking, his body on fire at the impact, as he fell to the ground mercilessly. Glass rained down around him, creating a deadly sound. He tilted his head to see Carolina transform into her 'original' form.

She looked the same as he had remembered. Long black hair flowed freely behind her, her lithe body stood taller than most women and her face was just as poetic as a flower in bloom.

Disgusting.

She stared at Alab with cold brown eyes that looked down at him. She had always looked down on him. Nothing had changed about this self righteous suck up.

"How dare you come into *my* city and hurt *my* people, Alab." Her voice was above a growl. Not feminine in the least bit.

Alab slowly got to his hooves, shaking off the dizzying effect her punch did to him and the glass that stuck to his skin. Once he stood tall, he gave her a wide, wide grin. "Sister. So good to see you."

Her face remained unchanging. Alab sighed dramatically. "No words for your dear brother who you haven't seen in centuries?"

"Of course, I do." She bared her teeth back at him. "Get out."

Alab chuckled. "So cold." He tilted his head at her. "Carolina, I was merely helping you. Your city is polluted with urchins. *Humans...*" He tensed his claws, "are disgusting creatures. I was merely assisting in the extermination of such pests. You may give me your thanks now."

He received immense satisfaction in the rage color that filled her cheeks and the way her eyes darkened with a dense sadness. Yes, she knew of the loss and this loss he had dealt her would linger, would torment her. He had destroyed her pretty little city, her safe place and killed those in which she viewed as hers.

She would be haunted. At least, until he killed her that is.

She remained cold and unmoving; determination written all over that face. Nails raked down his spine as his molten rage re-awakened within him. She was the bane of his life. She caused his deformity, she caused his suffering, she was at fault for everything these past miserable centuries. Her and her self entitled, self-righteous attitude that had destroyed his life.

He would destroy her life in turn.

"You truly are a monster. This is the only chance I will give you. Leave and you may keep your life. Stay and I'll show you the strength of the Queen of Biringan." Her voice cracked out like a whip, strong and sharp.

She wanted him to leave?

Alab began to laugh, a mere breathy chuckle at first that escalated into a hysteria that sent spit flying from his deformed face and his frame to hunch over with mirth. "You seem to have gotten funnier, *Queen.*" He shook his head, his bones creaked. "Look at me sister." He spread his arms wide, he opened his mouth widely. He watched her flinch. "What life? I have no life that is worth keeping. I am merely a *tikbalang*, a demon that leads human travelers to their demise." He pointed at her. "It's all thanks to you, you *deformed* me, you *ruined* me, you *caused* this!" His voice rose with each accusation. By the end he was roaring at her. "The deaths I have caused lay upon your head!"

Cower. Cry. Crumple under the weight of his words.

Carolina didn't flinch again, didn't hunch, didn't even blink at his accusations, instead she slowly shook her head, her eyes clear and hard. "You ruined yourself. And you know it. Nothing destroys iron but its own corrosion. You chose to ignore the truth and that was your downfall. You chose to kill, I had no hand in that."

I'll make you cower before I rip you apart limb from limb.

"Ah, high and mighty as always." Alab snapped his teeth together before he bared them at her. "I'm going to slay you now, sister. I shall drag your corpse all through this city before I burn it to ashes. And the death of all your precious shifters and humans will be marked on your soul."

Carolina raised her head high, looking like a queen. "You are welcome to try… *brother.*"

A soon to be dead queen looked down upon him.

Alab did not wait for another invitation, he charged at her. He watched closely as Carolina's form melted away underneath brown fur. He collided with a brown bear. She roared in his face, her fangs large and deadly. Alab returned the sentiment and smashed his horned skull into her head.

She chuffed, shaking her head, swiping a heavy paw at him, but she was unstable on her feet. Alab didn't waste any time; he tackled her to the ground, sinking his blunt teeth into her meaty shoulder, feeling pleasure in the gush of warm blood that filled his mouth. Her flesh trembled under his jaw before vaporizing away. His jaw clicked shut. Growling he looked down to see two small beady eyes glaring at him from the head of a tiny black mamba. She hissed, baring her puny fangs.

Alab snorted, reaching up to crush his sister's pathetic form. However, when he went to snatch her, she was gone. He felt the cool scales of her miniature form slithering up his neck. He jabbed his neck, pulling away his hand. Empty.

He felt her on his jaw.

Slap.

Nothing.

Suddenly her infinitesimal snake head appeared before his eyes, fangs out. He didn't see her move, but he suddenly felt the bloom of heat rush from his neck to the rest of his body. Growling, he swatted at her and ended up knocking his head with his own claw. He felt the sharp sting of multiple bites all over his neck and shoulders. His vision began to blur before doubling. His knees gave out, slamming into the ground, jarring his body into a violent set of shakes that caused a hot, slicing pain to pound throughout his entire body.

His breath quickened, his throat convulsed, and wracking coughs overtook him. His head became heavy and hung limply as drool began to drip in thick globs from his mouth. He gagged, coughing before throwing up, hacking deep, wracking coughs in between, spraying vomit everywhere.

Venom...

As his stomach continuously heaved and his body churned on itself, his mind seemed to snap, and a flood of darkness consumed his thoughts.

She would not win. She would not beat him. SHE WAS GOING TO DIE BY HIS HANDS! HE WOULD WATCH THE LIFE LEAK FROM HER EYES!

He forced his shift, forced his crippled limbs to shrink, to elongate. He inhaled deeply, opening his shifted eyes from the perspective of a black mamba. She sat coiled a few feet away from him, watching him. He hissed at her, grinning, feeling triumphant as the venom fizzled out within his newly shifted body. A black mamba cannot be affected by its own venom.

Carolina shifted, her hair hung in her face, but he could see her sneer on her mouth. "Father did say weeds are hard to kill." She hunched, rippling slightly as she grew into a creature that no longer roamed the earth, but was large and had a mouth crowded with machete sized teeth.

Carolina's giant yellow eyes pinned him with a glow of fortitude.

Alab jerkily shifted back into his frozen form and began to laugh as he dodged the snapping mouth of Carolina's dinosaur beast. Darting between her legs, he leapt onto her protruded back. He grabbed the fin like protrusion, he thrummed his claws against it.

"A dinosaur… how *desperate*." He gave a hard wrench and an extremely satisfying snap occurred under his claws. A deafening roar of pain caused the buildings around them to tremble. Alab's ears ruptured and he felt the blood trickle down his ear. But he continued to laugh, even though the world was silent around him, he laughed as hot blood—Carolina's blood—squirted out and soaked his entire front.

He would bleed her dry.

* * *

Tullia skid a little under the rubble as she reached Sabin's still form. She knelt beside him, hovering her hands above his battered body, unsure where it was okay to touch and where it was not. Sabin had his mask was off, but a glamour was still in place with the plain faced man from before. Though his face was bloodied and bruised making it less plain and more battle roughened. His eyes were closed, and his breathing labored. Tullia looked over his body, seeing his ninja gear torn and soaked through with what looked like an excessive amount of blood made her heart speed up in fear for him. Especially a nasty slice on his ribs. She could see *bone* and it oozed red blood rapidly.

Get pressure on that....

Scrunching up the torn material from Sabin's ninja suit, Tullia used one hand to apply pressure on the worse of his wounds. She pushed into him, cringing at pain that she had never experienced, but knew it had to hurt like a bitch. She looked from the wound to his face and swallowed down the anxiety that seemed to want to choke her. Sabin's glamoured face was so still, though his color looked good, which was disconcerting. It looked as though he was sleeping with blood all over him. Was the color all due to the glamour? Was there bruises on his face and the glamour hid that?

At that precise moment, she decided she hated the glamour.

Sabin said his face held disfigurements, but it was silly to keep hiding them right? I mean, they knew each other for almost a week, people see each other's faces all the time.

Gently, Tullia touched his cheek. The texture was rough and raised.

Tullia slowly dragged her fingers over his face softly, documenting mentally that she did not encounter a single smooth part of Sabin's face. She touched his forehead, there was a massive cut there, his cheeks, his mouth, his chin, his eyes… and when her fingers brushed his nose, which was *not* were the glamour nose was but further to the side, it twitched then suddenly Sabin inhaled and let out a startling sneeze.

Tullia jerked her hand away guiltily from his face and watched as Sabin blinked heavily, letting out a slight grunt of pain when he tried to move. She pressed harder on his wound as she leaned forward. "Don't move. You may or may not be bleeding out and I may or may not be saving your life."

Sabin's bright gold eyes latched on to Tullia's, there was a slight glaze to his tawny depths, but the warmth they exuded towards her made Tullia's heart skip. "There you are." He smiled, his eyes turning into rays of sunshine, warming her soul. "You alright?" His gold eyes traveled over her, inspecting her person.

She began to feel shy and aware that she looked and smelled like an uncleaned dumpster with maggots and a family of diseased rats mating in filth. Shaking off the feeling and addressing the obvious. "I'm fine but let's focus on you. You're really hurt." Tullia looked down at where her hand was on him, her hands had blood all over them. "How bad does this hurt?"

Sabin sighed. "I'll be fine." He closed his gold eyes again and inhaled deeply. Tullia rose with the expansion of breath. His body seemed to vibrate and give off a golden sheen before turning ice cold. Tullia felt her eyes widened as she saw the deep gash on his forehead begin to sow back up, leaving dried blood behind. Her hand began to vibrate intensely, as if she got electrocuted. She jerked her hand away in reflex, flexing the sensation away. Looking down at the wound on his ribs she saw perfect skin poke through the dried blood. She looked at Sabin's face, his glamour was in place, but it seemed to become fuzzy, like an unfocused picture.

When he opened his eyes, he was back in focus. The gold eyes looking at her didn't see her, they were clouded like death and seemingly unseeing before warming up and returning to normal after a few slow blinks.

Questions swirled within her mind. She tried to filter out the most important, the most confusing… However, her first question was, "How… how was I able to see some of your wounds through the glamour? Does it not hide wounds?"

Sabin grunted, sitting up slowly, jerkily. "Means it's wearing off." Once he was sitting up, he looked over her head, watching the fight. She studied him as he flexed his jaw.

She felt a cold distance between them growing. It was as if they just met, that awkward tenseness between strangers. She felt Sabin tucking himself away behind the icy wall that he seemed to carefully construct over the past few days through his stories and his reason for never sleeping. Tullia had finally caught on when she noticed his sleeping bag was never even touched and when she'd wake up in the middle of the night from some sort of nightmare, to see him doing some sort of grueling exercise in front of the fire. He always faced away from the tent and was always swathed by the darkness.

A sharp stab. She felt she was practically stripped bare to him, practically transparent, yet she didn't even know his last name or where he was from. Hell, she didn't even know what his actual face looked like. Swallowing against the coward within her, against the urge to withdraw to stave off potential pain, Tullia forced herself over that ominous wall he built.

She'd been taking risks all day; she wasn't about to stop that trend now.

"How did you heal yourself, Sabin?" She wanted a strong voice, a confident voice to come out. However, in reality, her voice was normal, if not on the softer side that suggested uncertainty and accusation.

When Sabin told her a little part of his past, of being a mercenary he tasted of sour regret and a deep sadness with a burning rage that had Tullia retreating from questioning him further out of respect. However, it was clear that Sabin was more than a mercenary. More than a human.

Perhaps she didn't have the right to ask him yet, they were new friends… but there was this measured distance between them that often made Tullia feel insecure with their friendship. It was as if Sabin was keeping her at a distance. It felt as if he wasn't allowing her to be close to him, even though she stood right beside him. And damn it, she liked him, and she wanted to be his friend, so he was going to get over the whole 'distance' thing and deal with her being his friend.

Sabin's gold eyes looked back at her face, studying it for a moment with a slight coldness. She tasted a hint of… *something*, but Sabin wasn't particularly feeling anything or if he was, he was hiding it. "Now's not the time for questions, sweetness."

He stood up, offering his rough hand out for her. She looked up at Sabin's solid form.

"Will you tell me later then?" She pushed.

An acidic taste scurried across her tongue along with a salty flavor. He didn't say anything for a long moment and Tullia felt her heart sink within her chest. She tilted her head and raised an eyebrow. Did he not trust her? Why did he behave as though he'd always be there for her, but he didn't expect or even want her to be there for him?

She narrowed her eyes at him, almost daring him to say no.

Then Sabin's mouth gave a faint smile. "Alright then. Later I will tell you."

The softness of his tone and the faint salty, vinegary flavor made her curious about why he felt nervous. She gave him a serious nod, relieved, and gripped his hand.

They were going to be BFFs once Tullia helped him get over whatever his insecurity was. Once Tullia was up off the floor, Sabin brushed himself off and retrieved his axes that had fallen a few feet away from him when he smacked the ground. A loud roar made Tullia give an involuntary scream of pure terror and jump. Snapping her head in the direction of the violent noise, she saw a dinosaur with a hanging, bloody back fin.

The tikbalang was laughing hysterically, its eyes were glowing with insanity and he dug his claws into the meat on the back of the dinosaur and began to dig.

Tullia winced at not only the volume of the second roar, but the pain it exuded. She looked around, trying to find the Grand High, but she was nowhere to be seen.

Tullia furrowed her eyebrows. "Where's Cliona?"

Sabin rolled his shoulders. "Taking a nap on a bench."

Tullia looked up to Sabin, confused. "What?"

Sabin shook his head. "Looks like the demon went up on her."

Tullia felt the horror display itself on her face. Sabin saw it and chuckled.

Chuckled.

"What is with that reaction? Is she okay? Is she dead? How can you laugh like that!" Tullia's voice was shrill at the end.

Sabin put his hand on her head. Tullia glared at the condescending action.

"Be calm, sweetness. Of all the years of knowing the witch, there is one thing I am certain on. She recovers quickly, and once she does, she's hellbent on revenge."

Tullia whacked his hand off her head with a hard smack and looked back towards the fight between the demon and the shifter queen. Carolina was rapidly shifting between animals to fight Alab, though every animal she shifted into bore a large wound that gushed thick globs of dark red blood on the ground. Alab was beginning to dominate the fight, landing more blows and slashes, causing the queen to stagger badly.

"The poor queen…" Tullia murmured, wincing as Alab wretched Carolina's bear head back cruelly.

"I've never fought a creature where my axes won't cut through its flesh." Sabin seemed a bit miffed by that, his eyes narrowed and heavily shadowed. "My axes never fail to cut. Anything. Even stone."

Tullia was jolted by his words in the remembrance of her and Chito's plan. She turned to Sabin suddenly, gripping his arms tightly. He looked at her, startled. "We came up with an idea." She said excitedly. "And we think it might work."

Sabin raised an eyebrow. "We?"

"Oh, Chito and I." She turned around, searching for Chito. She found him crouched in the same spot she had left. Tullia took a moment to study Chito. He was completely nude, yet he wasn't exposed. Tullia squinted and noticed that Chito, even though he was naked his delicate parts were not exposed. It's as though they didn't exist, it was just a continuation of smooth skin, like a doll. Feeling like a pervert for staring with such intensity, Tullia averted her eyes and simply decided it may be something that would never be explained to her. And she was okay with that.

Tullia looked back at Sabin with a strained half-smile. "The plan was to light him on fire."

Sabin seemed to process that for a split second, his smile was devious and fanatical. "I'm on board with that plan."

Tullia felt her lips stretch wider. "We need alcohol and a strong electrical current. Or, you know, fire would be awesome too."

Sabin rubbed his jaw, leaving a black streak across his sharp chin. "If we get the witch up from her nap, we could possibly have a source of fire." He stared at the tikbalang thoughtfully. "Alcohol would be an excellent base to ensure he actually lights up."

Tullia patted Sabin's meaty forearm rapidly. "I'll get the alcohol then, Chito will come with me. He knows where it is."

Sabin looked at Chito again, evaluating him, and then looked at the tikbalang, before looking back at Tullia. "You sure?" She knew what he was seeing, but she was impressed that his face didn't even twitch in surprise at Chito's state.

A human cry of pain cashed through the air. Tullia whipped her head around to see the queen of Biringan pinned to the ground under the claws of the tikbalang. Her entire body was a mess of torn skin, seeping with blood, and choked in dirt. However, it was clear that while she may be down, she was far from being out. Tullia saw the white of her teeth in a grimace of rage as she morphed into a small snake. She slithered up Alab's rail thin arm rapidly, then her body began to grow into that of an anaconda. She wrapped herself around his arm a begin to entangle him.

Tullia looked back at Sabin, her eyes panicked. "Hundred percent. We got this, so go help the Queen!"

Sabin raised an eyebrow, he jerked his head in the direction where the fight was occurring, "That's the queen of this city?" At Tullia's nod, Sabin made a thoughtful sound. He seemed to come to an instant decision and nodded. "I'll wake the witch." His face became stern when he looked back at Tullia, "Be fast about getting the alcohol and be safe. Don't get hurt." He then crouched slightly and sprinted to the other side of the battlefield, looking more like a ninja blur than a buff dude running.

Probably for the best though, she didn't have to admire that scene if it were in slow motion. Tullia looked back to where nude but not exposed Chito sat, watching the fight with horror stiffening his features.

She ran back to him, once more tripping on the debris, nearly killing herself in the short jaunt to which the shivering shifter sat miserably. Upon reaching him, she crouched down beside him, making sure to avoid any eye contact with weird places, and shook his arm wildly when he didn't acknowledge her the instance she was beside him. "Come on! Plan's still on! We've got to get the alcohol like stat!"

He seemed completely frozen; his teary eyes glued to the heated battle. He shook his head minutely. "No. I'm not moving. My lola said so." His tone was monotone, his lips barely moved to produce his stupid words.

Tullia ran her tongue over her upper lip, her palette numb, meaning Chito was in shock. She gave him an evaluating look, frowning at him all the while. "By the way, why didn't you tell me your lola was the queen?"

Chito blinked, he turned his head to look at Tullia with slightly glassy eyes. "I thought you knew. Didn't you have a vision?"

Tullia gave him an exasperated look. "I didn't see *that.*"

Chito shrugged, clearly unconcerned, he turned back to watch the fight.

Tullia glared at him, she shook his arm once more. "Chito, you have to show me where you found the alcohol. We have to hurry!"

Chito shook his head again. "She said not to move." He glanced at her; his honey drenched brown eyes seemed to hold a flicker of a spark. A faint whisper of vinegary irritation hit her palate. "Hot water privileges are at stake."

Tullia felt herself becoming beyond irate. "*Hot. Water.*" Tullia repeated slowly. "You're going to sit and watch your lola get beat by a demon because you're scared of losing your hot water privileges?" She gripped Chito by the ear and pulled. Hard.

Chito yelped but stilled his head when Tullia twisted her hand a little more. "What if the tikbalang kills her? Huh? What happens to your hot water privileges then? What happens if the tikbalang destroys the city? What about your hot water then?"

Tullia's blunt words caused Chito's eyes to widen with surprise then rim with tears. "My lola… can't… be beaten by a tikbalang. She's the strongest shifter in the city. She's my lola." His voice was small and weak with childlike simplicity. "She'll beat him."

Tullia huffed a half laugh and gave a small shake of her head, she released his ear. "Is she the strongest shifter against those outside the city? Chito—" Tullia stared at him, wondering how someone could be so naive and so unsure and so… clueless. "Chito, look. Look at your lola." She pointed to where the queen of Biringan was. She was bleeding, limping and still fighting but it was clear who had the upper hand. "She's hurt, Chito. She's *losing*. Do you not see that?"

His grandmother gasped in ragged breaths, bleeding from multiple wounds as she stood battered and faltering in front of a knobby-limbed creature that seemed untouched. Chito's big brown eyes glimmered with horror and frail incredulity as he finally *saw* his lola. He seemed riveted on the huge gash on her side that still bled freely.

Tears that sat poised in on the rim of eyes, began to drip down his cheeks. "Lola's… hurt." His voice cracked, he looked back at Tullia, lost and wounded. His entire world fractured. "She could die, Tullia… my lola could actually die."

Tullia's heart pinched at Chito's distraught face and the bitter and salty taste of his fear and sorrow. She gently cupped his face. "Chito," she said very gently, staving off his growing panic, "I need you to decide what you're going to do. Right now. And I need you to know that whatever decision you make will be your defining point for who you are and what happens to your lola."

"What?" He breathed the word, his eyes wet and wide.

It clicked.

Tullia gave a raspy laugh. "I know what your lola was talking about when she told you to know who you are before going out into the world." Tullia's heart was pounding in her throat, fear, conviction, and stress making her tone hard. "It doesn't matter what you look like, she was looking for more from you than just physical consistency. She was looking for character confidence." She wiped away his tears, leaning her forehead against his. "Who is Chito? Is Chito someone who does not move when someone tells him too? Is Chito someone everyone can count on? Does Chito have the strength to do what is right when everyone is telling him it's wrong? Does Chito go against the grain or swim in the same direction with the salmon?"

She released him, standing up. "Only you can decide who you ultimately are." Tullia shook her head. "You can't listen to what one person or even a million people say you should be, you can't deem their words as your law. You decide who you want to be, you decide what is best for you, you decide what you want to do. You decide, Chito." Tullia paused, thinking about how she came to be in her current situation. How she decided so many things about herself based upon others, based upon diagnosis, based upon others' preconceived notions of her. She took their ideas about how she should be and how she was to heart. She shook herself free of those thoughts. Now was not the time for self-reflection.

"In the end, it is up to us to decide who we want to be and only we can change who we are. Everyone has that ability, and it is the fears of the world and the words of others that make us unsure of who we are." Tullia felt as though the words were more of a reminiscence of her own character acceptance. How she stopped trying to be someone she wasn't, by leaving everything she knew and searching for a place she could just simply… be.

She embraced herself, her diagnosed insanity, her love of books, her ability to taste emotions… and despite everything she had and everyone that was against her… she was trying to make the best of who she was. She was kinda rockin' the certified insanity label.

She studied Chito's damp, pale face. She held out her hand towards him. "So, what are you going to do right now Chito?"

Chito looked at her hand, his eyes slightly red and still damp, contemplating. "That… was a really cheesy line you fed me at the end." He finally said, looking up at Tullia with a half-smile and less dead eyes.

Tullia clicked her tongue, instantly offended. "It was not cheesy! It was serious and intense! And really? Out of everything I said, you capitalize on that?" She withdrew her hand, and put both on her hips, glaring at him.

He shook his head, his silky locks caressing his shoulders delicately with the movements. "I'd bathe in frozen water my entire life if it saved my lola."

Tullia gave him a hard smile and offered her hand to him again, he gripped her hand with a steely strength under the soft palm. His eyes held quiet determination within their dark depths. "I know where to go. Keep up with me, okay?"

She gave his hand a hard squeeze in affirmation.

"Owe, let go!" He yanked his hand away from her grip and gave her a guarded look. "What were you trying to do? Crush my entire palm with your burly man hand?" He glared at her innocent hand.

Tullia drew back slightly, super offended. "Well, excuse me for not moisturizing properly while I survived in a jungle environment, trying to find this hidden city while you sit pretty up in your swanky building."

Chito shook out his hand. "That is no excuse. You have to treasure yourself more, Tullia."

Tullia stared in disbelief at Chito. Then gave him a tight smile. "I'll keep that in mind." Her tone was snarky. He was beginning to have a bad personality.

He sighed. "I have a great coconut hand cream that'll repair those craggy hands." He held up his hand to her. "But later, right now we've gotta hurry."

He turned and began to speedily pick his way across the debris littered street. Tullia noticed that Chito had no butt crack. He really turned his body into a doll. Tullia gritted her teeth in annoyance and looked down at her hands.

They were normal hands that were admittedly a little dry.

"Hurry up!" Chito yelled. Tullia flexed her hands before following behind the delicate, pansy-hand prince of Biringan.

* * *

He darted towards where the witch laid sprawled out, staying low so as to draw no attention to himself. Though the demon and the shifter were completely consumed with fighting each other, Sabin figured an earthquake wouldn't stop them.

However, to be cautious was never a bad idea.

Sabin glanced back frequently, scanning the streets and keeping part of his attention on Tullia. His eyes followed her every movement until she ducked into a building behind the naked shifter male. He didn't like that, but Sabin didn't deem the boy as a threat to Tullia's well being. However, he'd break every bone in that shifter's body if he did anything to her. He'd do it slowly too.

Once he no longer could keep tabs on Tullia and the shifter boy, Sabin turned to observe the witch. Her body was sprawled out in an unnatural position on the stone bench. He could see her chest rising and falling with breath, which was a good sign. There was a deep wound on her stomach that was wet with fresh blood. The left side of her face was bruised badly, and there was a nasty gash on her forehead, seeping blood that began to dye the fabric of the gold head wrap she wore with a complex twist knot.

It appeared the haughty witch was smacked down like a flea by the demon. She was going to be extremely angry once he woke her up. He tugged at his bag strap to shift it in front of him, then he flipped open the flap and rummaged around in it for a few seconds. He pulled out a bottle of warm water. Unscrewing the cap, he took a long drink, replenishing himself, then when half the bottle was empty, he dumped the rest on Cliona's unconscious face.

Her eyes flew open as her face snarled up in rage, teeth bared and eyes wild. Her hands darted up and a concentrated shot of blue smoke shot from her hands. It would've hurt, if he wasn't magic resistant. However, since he was, the blue smoke harmlessly dispersed once it encountered his chest.

"Have a nice nap?" Sabin blew some of the lingering blue smoke away from his face as he screwed on his water cap.

Cliona looked around, slightly dazed but by her glowing eyes and clenched teeth she was undoubtedly seething. Sabin silently watched as she took in her state of being. He watched silently as she documented each cut, each bruise. Her fury grew and the lack of ration in her eyes diminished. She cocked her head to one side spasmodically, then jerked it to the other side.

"I'm going to mount his skull in my front yard." She murmured dreamily, as she ran her hands over her wounds, her hand was glowing brightly, and a faint sizzling sound could be heard. "Then I'm going to use his bones as a wind chime for my pet cemetery." When she removed her hand, the wound was gone. She went over her entire body, and when she found the deep gnash on her head she seemed to go still. She traced the wound with her bony fingers.

"My hair." She pressed her hand firmly to her head, held her hand there for a moment and when she removed it there wasn't a trace of any damage that had been done to her. Or any sign of hair loss.

She ran her tongue over her top teeth, watching the fight proceed hungrily. Her nails clicked together methodically, sparking as she did so. "I want to kill him even more now. I want his horns… I'll make a headdress with them." She uttered softly, sharply articulating each word.

Sabin crushed the water bottle in his hand and tucked it back in his bag. "How's a barbeque sound to you?"

She cut a sharp side look, her head tilting up and to the side strangely. "As long as that tikbalang is on the menu and I'm grilling him… I'm a happy girl."

Sabin smirked, his rage hissing. He did appreciate the witch's bloodthirsty mentality and lack of sanity in certain situations. "Then I'll leave the cooking to you."

Cliona bared her teeth at him eagerly, glaring at him from the sides of her eyes. "Didn't I just say I'm cookin'?" She looked back at the fight. "I cannot allow him to continue to exist."

Sabin nodded. "Standby then. Tullia's getting the fuel to douse him." At her confused look, he added, "We're gonna set him on fire."

She cracked her neck, flexing her fingers in anticipation. "Good, petals here. But why wait? Let's try and char him up now." Her entire forearm became consumed with bright blue flames. The witch fully faced Sabin, her eyes feverish in their black depths. "He looks crusty enough to catch some flames."

Sabin slid his eyes to where the demon was. He was practically mauling the shifter, the queen of the city as Tullia declared her to be.

"Imma burn his horns off. Then shove both up his—"

"This does it, witch." Sabin interrupted. "Stop talking and do it." At this point, if no one interfered the queen would be killed.

Cliona clawed her hands and laughed loudly, madly before craning her arms back behind her head.

"Fire, fire, fire, fire, fire, fire, fire, fire," She chanted rapidly as a bright flame on her arms grew and grew larger with each word. The mass of conflagrations swirled restlessly within the cradle of the witch's mismatched arms until she whipped them forward at a blurring speed, hurling the ball of fire at the demon.

Her screeching howls of insanity, incited his own rage to scream along with her.

Chapter Fifteen

Everything was in partial ruin. Tullia entered what looked like a bar that had a massive brawl and was now under renovation. Picking her way carefully through the shattered glass and wood pieces, Tullia made her way over to the bar top that was, thankfully, still intact with an impressive display of alcohol.

Chito was three steps ahead of her, nimbly picking his way through the wreckage like a ballerina. He jumped up on the bar top effortlessly and began to scan the contents, sucking in his cheek in concentration. Tullia climbed on top of the bar far more clumsily and slowly.

"Wine… okay wine… oh, good wine… cheap wine…" Chito was muttering to himself, the chinking of bottles echoed gloomily in the demolished space. Tullia stared at the wine displayed above the bar, then looked down behind the bar. There were crates of opened bottles and a few bottom shelves filled with sparkling bottles. Jumping off the bar top, Tullia dedicated her attention to going through all the bottles on the bottom.

It was a surreal moment, the clanking and the chimes of the glass bottles being shuffled around filled the entire wrecked room, while muffled animal screams and violence infiltrated through the cracks and holes, bringing in an inauspicious tension to the air. Long seconds dragged by no one said anything, focused on their task.

Vodka… only 50%.

Rum…only 40%.

Whiskey… only 46%.

Gin… only 49%.

She went through all the bottom shelf alcohol and huffed, ceasing her search and sat crouched in front of the hard liquor. None of them went over fifty percent in alcohol concentration. Resting her arms across her knees, Tullia felt her body sag, she looked to the left, taking in the taps, pipes and an unlabeled jug of clear liquid…

Tullia's eyes widened, she quickly shuffled to the jug. It was un-labeled, and the bottle looked well used. Shaking the big bottle, Tullia unscrewed the cap and put her nose to the mouth of the jug. She jerked her head back and blew out a rough breath through her stinging nose.

She'd know that scent anywhere, it was a lingering stench that occupied hospitals and doctors' offices.

Rubbing alcohol, she thought with a sinister little voice in her head, then twisted her body to face Chit's direction. "Chito! I found rubbing alcohol!"

"Sweet." Chito hopped off the bar top. He shook his head. "They have a good selection of wines in stock. Did you manage to catch the name of this restaurant? I'll have to come back here when they fix up the place." Tullia looked up at Chito as he pranced over to her. He examined the jug she found and took a sniff test as well.

"I *think* it may be what we need, but it also could be lower in alcohol percentage than some of these." He motioned at the hard liquor section that Tullia had searched.

A loud, vibrating bang caused the floors to tremble and the walls to quiver all around them. The wine bottles rattled pugnaciously together above them, vibrating right to the edge of the ledge, though, thankfully, they did not fall.

Yet.

"Looks like we either grab this or a bottle over there." She flung out her arm to the bottles of hard alcohol. "Though none of them go above fifty percent."

Chito gnawed at his lower lip, eyeing the bottles then studying the jug. Another piercing scream permeated the air, Chito winced.

"I guess we take a chance." He grabbed the jug and hauled it up easily.

"I'm surprised you can manage that with your delicate hands." Tullia quibbled, pulling herself up to her feet.

Chito shot her a sarcastic look and clicked his tongue at her. "You know, when someone's not trying to crush my hand under brute strength with their chapped burly man hands, they're actually quite capable."

Tullia huffed, admitting defeat for the moment and waved Chito's sassiness away. "I don't have man-hands. You're wasting time. Hurry."

Chito's giggle followed behind her, exasperating her further.

Upon making it out of the building, Tullia's eyes widened to see the Grand High, looking eerily depraved, launching fireballs at the tikbalang. They hit him directly, extinguishing as soon as they came in contact with the Alab. Though Tullia didn't think that the fire was useless. The fire seemed to claw char marks into the tikbalang's flesh, causing him to roar with temporary agony.

"It appears that I failed to snuff out your life, witch." He cracked his long, bony neck, opening his mouth so his tongue slithered out as he released a deep growl. "I'll fix that." He gripped the struggling lioness by the neck and slammed her down, face first into the ground. The crunch was audible, and the lioness went limp. Chito let out a strangled whimper, Tullia clenched her fists and swallowed hard.

The tikbalang rose up, stretching his emaciated form, his right claw dragged the limp lioness up. He snapped his teeth at Cliona, seeming to grin as cracks appeared by his jaw. He tossed the queen of Biringan to the side. She hit a metal trash can and slumped on the ground. Her form quivered then melted into her human shape. Her hair was matted, crusted with dirt and blood, and her sun-loved skin was bruised, pale and bloodied.

"Lola…" Chito choked, squeezing the jug hard to his chest.

"Come to me then, witch." The tikbalang sneered, flexing his claws at her. "Let me peel that pretty face off."

"An ugly beast does not order a queen." Cliona put her hands together, she inhaled deeply, as blue smoke violently whirled around her. Tullia gripped Chito's arm as the Grand High opened her palms and a thick stream of bright blue fire blasted out and directly smashed into the demon's surprised face.

A profane scream seemed to vibrate the air and crack it, so shards of sound splinted out painfully all around.

"Burn bitch! Burn! Burn!" The Grand High shrieked with insane glee, laughing hysterically as the fire she produced created sinister shadowing to her face. Her fire engulfed Alab's form completely, intertwining with intense turbulence, swirling higher and higher into the air. Cliona gave one final rage drenched screech before she dropped to the ground on her feet. The fire ceased to pour from her hands and Tullia saw her hand hang limply from her side as she sagged slightly, panting. However, once she stopped feeding her fire tornado it shrank until the flames existed no more. Once the flames were gone, the tikbalang still stood, but he was charred completely on the outside.

There was a pause in the air, a deep silence filled with potential energy. Suddenly Alab gave a jerk, cracking the crispy layer of charred skin that flaked and fluttered to the ground in a fine, deceptively soft looking powder.

The tikbalang shook his entire body, similar to a deranged beast with his uncoordinated and awkward movements. His resounding growl chilled the blood in Tullia's veins, she felt Chito press himself against her backside. Fire doused her tongue.

"That it?" Alab's tongue flicked out and swiped around his jaw, licking away the black from around his bony mouth. The Grand High looked enraged, her lips were pulled back from her teeth. "How disappointing." He darted towards here in a blur, his gangling form swift and precise. He appeared in front of Cliona, his right claw raised, ready to slice her, but Sabin's burly form slammed into him at the last second.

Tullia felt jolted out of her terror stiffened state at that scene. Heart trembling with fear she whirled around on Chito, gripping his shoulders she pulled him close to her face. "You have to pour it over him, like five minutes ago!"

Chito had a fine tremble to his form. "How am I supposed to pour it over him? He's ten feet tall!"

"Really? He seemed more like nine and a half feet to me." Chito shot her a dark look. Tullia held up her hands, making peace fingers. "Go-go bird or big bird or something."

"Do you think a bird's claw has enough dexterity and fine motor movements as a human hand to tilt and pour accurately?"

Tullia stared at Chito. Waiting for either the punch line or the answer.

Chito jerked his head forward, eyes wide, waiting. "Well?"

"I don't know! It sounded sarcastic and rhetorical! Do they?" Tullia shouted.

Chito rolled his eyes, the brat, then put one hand on his hip. "No. They don't."

"Okay, fine… they go-go turn into something with dexterity to pour that has wings or is over ten feet tall." She thought for a moment. "Go-go giant flying squirrel."

Chito held one hand towards her, palm out, his face twisted into disgust and offense. "I'm feeling attacked with you abusing my catch phrase."

Tullia clicked her tongue, mimicking his pose. "Not your catch phrase, babe, you stole it from a kids show."

Chito opened his mouth, but a shrieking sound, accompanied by a loud crash and a demonic laugh interrupted him and his sass, stealing all the color from his face.

Tullia whipped her head to look at how the fight was progressing this time.

Sabin was trying to snap one of the tikbalang's arm as Cliona seemed to be crushing the demon in place with a thick amount of blue smoke. Alab was shrieking, violently jerking underneath the swath of blue smoke and Sabin.

Tullia turned to Chito. "Can't you shift into something like that?" She motioned towards the mess of a creature.

"Lola always forbid hybrid shifts." He uttered, his tilted eyes were wide and slightly damp. He glanced towards the still form of his lola, and his bottom lip trembled.

Ah. Tullia understood why. She looked back at the fight, in the span of three breaths it had morphed to where Alab was now standing and aiming his giant fists towards Sabin, trying to hit him. Though Sabin proved to be utterly unpredictable, going left, then up then right, then left then ducking...

He looked like a buff spaz.

"But... I can do it."

Tullia snapped her head back towards Chito. He wasn't watching the fight, he was still looking at Carolina's still form. She saw his eyes fill full of tears, though none fell and his jaw was clenched tight. "I've never been good at listening to my lola when she told me not to do something. So, I've practiced a bit."

He gave her a wobbly smile, then inhaled deeply, seeming to cleanse himself of doubt and insecurity. His eyes were sharp when he looked back at Tullia. He set the bottle down and shifted without fanfare into a massive hawk with golden red feathers and a razor-sharp black beak. Chito puffed his feathers then hopped closer to Tullia.

"Okay, I'll get everyone away from the tikbalang, you pick the right moment to dowse him." She put her face closer to hawk Chito. "Don't mess up. We only got one shot at this." Hawk Chito blinked and tilted his head in a bird-like way before thrusting his beak forward and pecking her forehead.

Tullia gave an involuntary gasp at the sting and put her hand to her forehead. "The hell!"

Hawk Chito puffed his feathers, then hopped over and on top of the jug. He spread his beautiful wings and began to flap. Without much theatrics, Chito managed to lift the jug off the ground, clasped in both his claws. He gave a puffed screech before ascending higher in the air.

Tullia ripped her eyes away from Chito's slightly gawky form and focused her attention towards the brawl.

Inhaling roughly, then coughing a little due to all the debris in the air, Tullia ran to the Grand High. "Cliona!" Tullia shouted a few feet away. Her head tilted in Tullia's direction, but the Grand High's attention didn't waver from shooting blue fire balls at the tikbalang. Tullia tripped over to her, her heart thudding in her chest. "Cliona! I have the fuel! Chito's going to pour it over the tikbalang so he'll stay on fire."

Cliona looked over at Tullia, her eyes crackled with power, and she tasted of insanity.

Her head dropped to one side, "'bout time." She murmured, ceasing her fire she rubbed her hands together grinning. "Let's base this bitch then."

Cliona lowered her hands towards each other, tensing her fingers. Small, playful flames danced between her fingers bouncing off her palms. Cliona flexed her fingers and the flames began to increase in their buoyancy and speed. Her shoulders hunched and her head tilted back a bit. Tullia looked up and watched hawk Chito in the sky, staggering a little bit with the giant jug in his claws. Squinting in the light smudged darkness she saw Chito's claws quiver before melting slower than she had seen him do before. Two child size hands were in place of the hawk's claws.

That's freaky. Tullia covered her mouth, holding her breath in case her breathing disturbed the delicate balance that was occurring right now.

Suddenly, Chito's form jerked, then began to jerkily descend. Tullia jerked, her eyes widening as she helplessly watched Chito's baby hands shaking violently while his wings feebly flapped in the air, barely keeping him up. Chito gave a screech of what sounded like a pain fueled anger and managed to rip off the cap and messily tilt the jug down to pour the liquid out. The liquid splattered all over the tikbalang and Sabin in slow motion. Globs of alcohol dripped and seeped from their bodies. Sabin was straddled on Alab's shoulders, trying to rip off the demon's horns by standing on his skull and heaving. Both became startled when they suddenly became drenched, but Sabin recovered quicker, and he stomped viciously on Alab's head before launching himself off.

The jug that Chito held hit the tikbalang in the head, making a hollow sound, before bouncing off harmlessly. Alab bared his teeth, glancing above, but he lunged at Sabin, snapping his oversized blunted teeth at him, his sunken eyes bloodied and enraged.

"He's based now." Cliona's eyes went entirely blue and sparked with little white streaks of light, like lightening shots.

"Wait!" Tullia lurched at her, grabbing onto the Grand High's upper arm to stop her fire. A small pinch occurred in her throat as the fire fighting between her fingers grew insanely violent. The Grand High's hands shook with stress as fire began leaking out of her hands and dripping flames onto the ground. She laughed wildly and Tullia jerked her hand back in horror, screaming, "No!" just as Cliona flung her hands out widely, unleashed her violently tumbling fire. The flames appeared to claw through the air eagerly, gaining speed towards Alab and Sabin who were wrestling on the ground.

Cliona's shrieking laugh, the terror, the suspense at watching the flames reach out greedily… Upon first touch the flames seemed to shrink slightly away before exploding in a giant cloud of blue, engulfing both Sabin and the tikbalang.

Tullia heart ceased to beat within her chest as a wall of roaring fire came alive and cackled into the night.

"No," Her lips were numb, and her limbs were heavy as tears began to gather in her eyes. Sabin was in the thick wall of fire, burning with Alab.

"He's just fine, breath now petal, before you pass out." The Grand High's voice was brusque and rattled her enough to blink in confusion. She looked up at Cliona, wide eyed and teary. The Grand High was smirking at something. Tullia turned her head, and saw Sabin, completely soot covered, just a few feet away from the roaring fire. The relief was a nearly painful shot through her limbs, causing her whole body to tremble and the tears that sat on the cusp of falling .

Thank the good lord. How in the world did he…?

Ice scraped her spine at the anguished scream that rented the air. Alab's screech was different from his other screams of rage. This one was stripped raw; it bruised the air and held a bloody edge of human torment. Tullia tasted his pain, that sharp sting of million venom-soaked needles jabbing her palate. She gagged, pressing her hands to mouth, watching with horror as the silhouette of the tikbalang, mangled and misshaped within the flames distort, then melt… crumpling… dripping…

All the while his screams of pain reverberated the air excruciatingly.

… it was hot… it was so hot… he was melting away… he was going to die…

Strong arms turned her body away from the horror as her face was pushed into a solid, ash covered shoulder. "Shh." Sabin murmured; his arm was wrapped tight around her waist and his big hand cupped the back of her head to keep her from looking at the awfulness. He smelled of sweat, steel, and burnt earth, but he was so warm and his warmth seeped slowly into her cold, cold body. "Don't witness this."

Tullia stiffly clutched at him, breathing hard, and at that moment she realized that she was shaking so hard, she was going to fall apart. She tried to swallow, tried to breath past the horrid burning rot that she tasted, but those small tasks proved to be impossible. She pressed her face harder against Sabin's shoulder, focusing on the pain in her face and the almost painful tightness round her waist rather than the slow pain of Alab's death.

The scream died away slowly, the sound of a crackling fire in its wake seemed cruel and horrible. Eventually, the fire stopped producing its deceptively gentle sounds and silence blanketed the air.

Tullia's palate was numb… it felt burnt and dead.

Sabin loosened his grip on her, slowly he released her and Tullia mimicked him, even though she didn't want to let go quite yet. He was so comforting, like a teddy bear. Except he was even better, because he had two giant axes. She frowned at the thoughts, uneasy at the dependency thinking, Tullia drew away from Sabin's warmth.

Once she was completely on her own, she took in a shaky breath trying to steady herself from the image and auditory hell that would revisit her at night. A shiver radiated out from her chest and traveled through her body. Her hand felt warmth, startled she looked down to see Sabin's rugged hand grasping one of her own. Looking up at him, his eyes conveyed strength as he gently squeezed the hand he held. Tullia gave him a very wobbly smile, trying with every ounce of her being not to cry.

A very witchy laugh was a blessed distraction. "Look at that." Tullia looked over to see the Grand High smirking, she was clearly enjoying the scene of what was left of the tikbalang. "Damn, I'm amazing." She looked over at Tullia. "Thanks for the booster shot, petal."

Tullia felt the ice sweep through her once more. That's right, she helped in killing the tikbalang, she gave the Grand High more power behind her fire. It was odd, even though the tikbalang was evil and twisted, the knowledge that she purposefully helped to end another creature's life was… hard.

Sabin's rough hand gave a gentle squeeze, but this time it did nothing to quell the solidifying knowledge that Tullia directly helped in killing someone.

He was bad... he killed a lot of other people...

Tullia slid her eyes to the charred mass of what used to be a living breathing being. Her emotions were a mess, and her mind couldn't process a single thing, except for the fact that she assisted in his brutal extermination.

"Lola?" Chito's broken, small voice interrupted her out of her emotional conflict. She turned her head to see Chito kneeling by his lola's still body and gently pulled her upper body to rest on his lap. He was sniffing a lot, but no tears fell. Tullia jogged over to where he knelt, tasting his acute fear through the extreme sour on her palate. He patted her cheek softly, but the queen didn't wake to consciousness. He looked up helplessly at Tullia with his big eyes and lower lip that trembled uncontrollably. "Why isn't she waking? How… how do we wake her up?"

Chito's cinnamon skin was smeared with a bit of blood and dirt.

The Grand High strode over to the two, examining the queen of Biringan as one would to a piece of puzzling art. She made a thoughtful sound, clicking her nails together twice. "Hey, petal, let's see if we can raise the dead with your juice." She grinned widely over at Tullia, her teeth glossy and perfect on her bloodied and bruised face.

"She's not dead!" Chito snarled, his face twisting into something violent. "She's breathing."

Cliona rolled her eyes in exasperation. "Relax, I'm going to help your grandmama out, baby face." Cliona held a hand out to Tullia and then held the other hand up to face the queen. Thin tendrils of blue shot out and wrapped around Carolina and Tullia. When the thin threads touched Tullia's wrist, she felt a pinch in her throat before a rush of adrenaline surged through her.

The Grand High grunted, biting her plump lower lip. "What…a… *delicious*…. punch…" She slurred; her eyes flashed pure neon blue for a split second. Tullia saw the once thin threads become thick and overtake Carolina's motionless form.

Chito looked nervously at Cliona, hugging his lola tighter, but he didn't utter a word of his distrust. Seconds passed by and the azure smoke ceased. Tullia shuddered at the suddenness in which the draw of power stopped and dropped within her. She felt Sabin's rough hand touch her head briefly and her shoulder, as if to steady her.

"Lola?" A thin breath.

A sudden crack, then a loud coughing fit roused the queen of Biringan. Blood and mucus ran down her mouth as she continued her gagging coughs. Chito hovered anxiously over her, gathering up her hair and patting her back.

"Lola, breathe, breathe." Chito chanted, the smoky taste of concern coating her tongue.

Another harsh breath, then a sneeze before the queen's confusion clouded eyes focused and sharpened. Carolina's slender body tensed with sudden awareness, she looked around and then at Chito with alarm. "The tikbalang?"

"Not to worry, your highness. The tikbalang is dead. Burnt to a crisp." The Grand High studied the queen of Biringan, her magnificent cream and coffee face completely expressionless.

Carolina's eyes snapped to Cliona's, and they stared at each other, evaluating each other, sizing each other up silently. "You killed the tikbalang then?"

"Yes." The Grand High motioned with her long mosaic fingers towards the pile of charred flesh a few feet away from where they all stood. "Would you like to see what remains of it?"

Carolina glanced at the pile; her face tightened and her lips compressed into a thin line. There was a slight hint of salt, but when she looked back at Cliona her eyes were iced. Nodding, the queen of Biringan stood with supreme grace, waving away Chito's offered assistance. She was stained with blood, bruised, completely nude with missing genitalia like her grandson, and disheveled hair, but her posture dared anyone to refute her status as a queen.

Carolina let out a melodic bird call. She glanced at Sabin and Tullia but dismissed their presence in favor of Alab's remains. She dusted herself off lightly, though Tullia thought it was mostly the nerves that made her fidget in that manner.

"My guards will be coming to help," She paused, "dispose of the body." The queen of Biringan suddenly strode over to the burnt remains of the tikbalang, her back stiff. Everyone followed behind her silently.

She seemed to be analyzing the charred mass of what was left of her brother. Though her face didn't change in expression her emotions were a riot of grief, anger, relief, guilt and pain. It was a wild flavor combination that went from salty, bitter, spicy, to a flat line earthy taste.

Tullia quietly cleared her throat and tried to swallow the stale flavors.

Her sigh was heavy. "A life wasted wallowing in anger, has wreaked havoc on so many lives."

Sabin gave a slight jerk at the queen's words. Tullia looked up at him, curious about his reaction. His glamour was on tight, showing a neutral expression on a plain face. However, Tullia caught the faintest taste of a very deep and salty flavor.

A muffled hissing groan weakly filtered through the air. Everyone stilled, listening. Another weak groan before it dissolved into a thin scream. Horror, dry and gritty against her tongue, coated her mouth in excess due to everyone's emotions being in sync.

Except for the Grand High, she was just irritated. "It just won't die." She growled as she glared down at the still living tikbalang.

Tullia hesitantly looked down. It was hard to distinguish Alab in the darkness, however, subtle movement gave her eyes direction in where to look. It was a horrible and disgusting state in which Alab was put in. His horse shaped skull was blackened and had cracks of deep red sores that oozed with thin, sluggish blood. His body, already emaciated, seemed further shrunken, twisted, and crisped with pockets of peeling black skin.

Tullia reared back, when the hallowed eyes, empty swung to her briefly.

Carolina looked down at her brother, Tullia tasted her sorrow, salty and dry, but she also tasted the heat of her resolve and her anger.

"I hope you find peace in the afterlife, brother." Carolina's tone was soft, nearly tender, though her expression as she looked down at Alab was cold, except for the tears that rimmed her pretty brown eyes.

He managed to crane his spiny neck up and glared up at her, his charred face twisted into a cracked grimace of a laughing corpse. "I curse misery upon your house, Carolina." He then spat at her with all the strength that remained in his brittle body. The spittle sprayed disgustingly all over the queen's face and neck, but Carolina didn't bat an eye. Cliona scoffed, she slammed her heeled boot down on Alab's crisped forearm, snapping it off and crumbling it to dust under her boot. He roared in pain, his teeth a stark white against scorched skin.

Carolina wiped her face delicately with her hands then looked at Sabin. "If you could."

Sabin nodded once, then reached behind him for one of his axes. Tullia clasped her hands together as a mass of fear knotted in her throat. She shuffled back a bit, as nausea churned her stomach sharply. Her shoulders bumped into something warm and solid. She looked up to see Chito's sharp jaw clenched, there was a fine tremor in his body. He looked down at her, and when their eyes met a feeling of comradery sparked between them. Chito and Tullia were the only green ones in this situation, and it felt as though they were going to crack under the intensity and the weight of the situation. Tullia turned and sidestepped around Chito until she stood next to him. Tullia gripped his hand and the fierce, nearly painful squeeze of his hand comforted her.

"Can't do it yourself? Pathetic as usual." Alab's raspy voice mocked, his body was twitching, trying to move but his limbs were cauterized into a paralyzed state.

Sabin held one of his black axes. His blade caught the faint light in the darkness and gleamed red for a split second.

Carolina stared at the blade, her face pensive, then looked back down at Alab. "Goodbye, Alab." Her tone was labored and resolved.

Raging insanity flooded the tikbalang's sunken eyes. He screamed curses drenched with mania, his voice rang out through the empty city, a tortured, ugly sound. Chito suddenly pressed close to her, his body shaking violently. Tullia reached out and wrapped one arm around his waist hugging him close. Chito let go of her hand and wrapped his arms around her, sharing his quivering warmth.

Sabin glanced at Tullia. He mouthed, "Shut your eyes."

She obeyed, then peeked. Sabin swung one of his massive blades up high above his head, then swung down in a blurred motion. A sharp whistling sound cut the air slicing through the deafening roars. A meaty, flaky crunch noise wafted in the air and a dull thud seemed to linger far longer than any violent sound should. Tullia saw a fluttering blackened bit in the air. A heavy silence descended then, blanketing out minute noises.

Tullia didn't look down at Alab's severed head. She didn't want to see it, she didn't have the nerve to see it. Instead, she closed her eyes again, protecting herself, squeezing Chito and pressing her face into his shoulder.

Shuffling sounds occurred. More crispy sounds. Soft sounds... rustled sounds....

A warm hand tapped her back, Tullia slowly lifted and turned her head to see Sabin's topaz eyes looking at her kindly. "Everything is over."

She simply stared at Sabin for a moment, confused. He tapped her shoulder again, his eyes looking at Chito's arms around her. Slowly, Tullia let go of Chito and came to stand on her own.

"How are you fairing?" Sabin's low rumble chased away the cold that seemed to bury itself into her bones. Tullia managed to smile a little at him.

Before she could answer, a loud, hawking bird screech drew everyone's attention to the sky. A flock of ten large birds of prey swooped down and shifted midair, landing with a unified thud. Chito let go of Tullia completely and stepped a half step back.

"Your highness!" They called, rushing around her and poised to attack. Their eyes glinted daggers at them, their faces pulled back in snarls. Hostility and distrust, spiced pickles, soured her palette.

"Calm." She held her hands up. "Everything is resolved now." Carolina said as one guard draped a jacket around her shoulders, the jacket attempted to swallow the queen's slender frame. A guard also came over to Chito, eyeing Tullia wearily, as he wrapped him up in an oversized jacket as well.

"Your highness, we need to get you to Mary immediately." A male guard didn't dare touch the queen, but his hands hovered with uncertainty in the air, like Chito's did. Tullia understood the reason, Carolina looked rough, there was a lot of blood, a ton of dirt, and discolored places on her pretty brown skin that promised to bruise spectacularly.

The queen waved away their concerns with nonchalance. "I'm fine. Just dirty. We have more pressing concerns than my appearance right now." Her eyes, bright and ancient, looked at the now dead remains of what used to be the tikbalang and her brother.

A silence overtook the space, a mourning type of silence from the queen. Tullia turned her eyes to her hands, laced them together and squeezed them tight, watching her finger tips turn red.

"Your highness?" A guard asked after a long moment. Tullia looked up at the queen. Her face was smudged with dried blood and black streaks of dirt. Her eyes, gorgeously shaped and divinely colored of honey drenched chocolate, held a sheen of deep sorrow.

"He…" She paused, swallowing thickly. Her face became hard. "The tikbalang will not receive a *lamay*. It was a monster, only intending to hurt and destroy. Instead, it will be broken down further by fire immediately and his ashes will be scattered out in my personal garden. I pray that my beloved plants will soothe his soul's rage."

The guards nodded. Carolina inhaled and seemed to perk up very slightly in posture like a flower under the sun. She sighed, and it was more than a release of air.

"Prepare a *lamay* for all the loved ones lost on this day. Everyone is to gather at the royal building with food and games and music and tales of their lost loved ones." She snapped her fingers, blood dripped from her elbow. "Gather the bodies, have them prepared accordingly." The queen looked at a guard with a too pale face and hollowed eyes, her entire frame softened and her voice gentled. "Myran, get everyone to gather flowers. I want all the city's flowers to be present for this *lamay*."

He bowed his head and rasped. "Yes, my queen."

She stared at him for a moment more, before closing her eyes wearily. "Summon Mary and Lyra… I'll need to cleanse myself." Carolina, even though dripping blood and musing in a way that told the violent tale of her confrontation with the tikbalang, she stood tall and regal.

Tullia watched the queen approach them imperially. The guards twittering anxiously, watching her approach them with hawk-like eyes. Tullia felt nervous as she took in the ever-present beauty of queen Carolina. Albeit it wasn't so much her beauty but her aura that was intimidating with the intensity it exhumed. She stood before Tullia, taller than her by five inches, but Carolina might as well have been six foot seven. Swallowing thickly, Tullia offered a bow to the queen. Sabin bowed as well and even the Grand High offered a bow of her head.

Carolina smiled slightly.

"You three helped save my city," She paused, looking at each of them, "and my life from the tikbalang." She placed a hand over her heart. "For that, I am in your debt." There was another short pause. "Tell me your names."

"Your highness, my name is Cliona. I am the Grand High of the Black Blood Coven in North America. These are my companions. Sabin and Tullia." She motioned elegantly to the both of them with unnaturally long fingers. "We have come to Biringan City in the hopes someone in your city can answer a simple question for us."

Carolina raised her eyebrow. "It must be an important question for you all to travel so far." She regarded them with narrowed eyes. "Well, we shall discuss your question at a later date. I must attend to my people and begin the healing process for my city. That is my priority, you understand?"

The Grand High bowed her head again. "Of course, please allow us to assist you in any way you see fit, your highness."

Carolina gave a small, but genuine smile. "Mahalia, please escort my three guests to the Mabuhay building. They need to clean up before they pick flowers for the *lamay*. Also, inform Lyra we will be needing enough food to last three days for the entire city." Carolina glanced at Chito. "You go with them as well, Chito."

A lushly formed woman in a guard uniform bowed in understanding, Mahalia turned to them then. Her head was shaved, and her skin was the color of tropical sand lovingly caressed by the sunshine. She did not smile and her eyes were sharp jade green. "Please, this way."

Cliona, Sabin and Tullia began to follow the pretty guard through the destruction. Chito followed too closely behind Tullia, his emotions were dull under the coat of his shock, whereas Sabin and Cliona were only exhausted.

Tullia's eyes seemed to be tugged in the direction where the tikbalang's body lay and she had no strength to resist. His body appeared to be melted into the street asphalt, the head was a few inches away from its body at an unnatural angle and its hollowed eyes, once bright and hostile, were now empty pits of nothing.

A shiver went down Tullia's spine as she ripped her eyes away from the corpse. An eerie tickle teased her shuttered mind, that seemed to whisper a presage of more like this to come.

Chapter Sixteen

They had been escorted to their room by stiff faced guards and instructed quietly where to meet. Tullia had showered, washing herself twice, feeling like a film of death was clinging to her skin no matter how hard she scrubbed. She tried not to remember the specifics, but once she decided she didn't want a detailed visualization, her brain capitalized on it. Her mind replayed everything that had occurred, detailing the particularly horrendous scenes. Highlighting the blood. Freeze-framing on the charred body.

Her brain was such an asshole to her sometimes.

After giving up on scrubbing the death on her, mechanically she dressed herself in the white dress laid out for her and combed her hair. The wet strands tickled her damp neck, she flipped her head upside down, then tussled her hair. When she looked at herself in the mirror, she saw the semblance of a little girl with the poofy white dress and her black hair slicked straight and glossy from the water. She looked very gross. Rolling her eyes, she shrugged and left. On her venture down the hall, she managed to run into Chito. They didn't exchange words; they didn't need to though. He jerked his head in a wordless motion, then continued to walk on. Tullia followed behind him, and she was led outside to a night garden that was in full bloom.

Colorful flowers blossomed and juicy looking fruits glistened under the night sky.

Chito began to gather a bushel of white flowers, plucking each flower up delicately with his smooth hands. Tullia followed suit. There were a few other people picking bouquets of flowers, some were crying silently, and others were stone-faced.

Everyone was silent, no one spoke as the preparation for the *lamay* was being done. It took an entire night and a whole day until it was finally prepared and ready.

Now there was a gathering of the people, grouped into a giant room where the flowers covered every available surface, food was abundant, and the color white brightened the room. The decor was a polar opposite of the emotions saturating the room.

Tullia sat wearing the same white dress that made her look twelve, holding a full glass of very fruity, watery wine, and stared at the people that Alab managed to kill in his craze.

They all wore beautiful clothes and looked angelic, as if they were merely sleeping rather than dead. There were three men, two teenage girls and five young women. They were all surrounded by a mountain of flowers, stuffed animals and candles as people touched their feet, their hands, and their faces. A woman was weeping silently staring at the two teenage girls, a man had placed his hand over one of the dead woman's hands and rested his forehead on their bound hands, silent tears dripping from his eyes. Tullia swallowed against the thick knot in her throat and tried to clear the curdled taste of everyone's grief from her palate. She was fighting back her own tears as she watched mothers' breakdown, husbands' quake silently, fathers silently cry, and everyone seeming to fold in on themselves with sadness.

There was one man, the guard that stood by the queen with the too pale face, sitting in front of a casket that held a small woman with dark brown hair and richly dark skin. He held two children on his lap, who had passed out from crying hysterically, rocking them slowly, as he stared at the woman. No one disturbed him, but they also didn't give him space. Everyone seemed to press against one another and silently give comfort by simply being next to them, silently offering food and drinks, gently placing hands on shoulders or heads.

Tullia's heart wrenched with pain. She rubbed her chest.

"Hello, my dear." The soft voice startled her and blessedly eased her urge to cry. Tullia's head snapped up to see Carolina standing next to her, seeming drained and exhausted but still working that regal glow in a simple satin white gown with a delicate black rectangle over her left breast.

"Your highness." Tullia went to stand, but was halted by a gentle touch of the queen's hand on her head.

"Sit." Carolina sat next to her, folding her legs and leaning back against the chair. She didn't say anything, simply watched her people mourn, as Tullia had. The queen then held out her hand to Tullia. She took the queen's slender hand in both of her hands and pressed the back of the queen's hand to Tullia's forehead. She had seen Chito do this, she knew it was respectful, hopefully it was the right course of action.

If not, it would get very, very awkward.

"I'm sorry for the pain and the distress that has befallen your beautiful city." Tullia said softly. She looked up at the queen, pulling Carolina's hand away from her forehead.

The queen looked at Tullia and smiled forlornly. "No one is to blame but Alab for the loss of these precious lives today. So do not apologize." She gave Tullia's hand a tender squeeze. "Life is a wheel, my dear. Sometimes you're up, sometimes you're down. Unfortunately, we all met under ill-fated circumstances." The queen sighed, her eyes tinted red and dewy. "Although pain and sorrow are never easy to accept, one must learn to deal with them."

Tullia nodded in agreement. Then silence enveloped them as they sat, holding hands and watching the mourning procession continue with hushed voices, various savory scents and soft weeping.

"Tell me your name again." Carolina raised her hand up with two fingers pointed up, and a woman came over quickly and passed her two cups filled to the top with a light red liquid. The queen passed Tullia one cup as she took the other for herself.

Tullia took the drink, she already had a drink, but when a queen gives you a drink you do not decline. Besides, two drinks are better than one.

"My name is Tullia." She took a long sip of the fruity wine. The flavor was growing on her the more her pallet became accustomed to the sharp flavor. Her chest felt lighter and lighter with every sip and the emotions of the room, dulled on her palate.

"Tullia…" The queen mulled over, took a long drink, nearly finishing the entire glass. Then she sucked both of her lips in, as if to savor the taste, before exhaling. "It seems as though fate has brought you here and has put you in my city, Tullia"

Carolina leaned back on her chair and looked out at the mass of mourning people again. Tullia saw her jaw tighten, then she looked back at Tullia, her eyes slightly gloomy and shiny. "I would not have been able to defeat Alab without your help. I fear…" She paused, her face expressionless and if it weren't for the soured, spicy and salty taste that coated Tullia's tongue she'd have never guessed Carolina was struggling with sorrow, anger and fear. Tullia took another drink. "I fear I would've died, and my people and my city would've been destroyed by him." Her voice did not falter, not even the slightest quiver in her soft voice.

Tullia gave a small, depreciating smile. "I didn't do much. Sabin and Cliona were the ones doing all the work."

Carolina shook her head, wagging her finger at her. "You are the reason they came to my city in the first place. Do not take your role of influence so lightly." She looked at Tullia from the side of her eyes. "On another note, it appears that you've managed to inspire my grandson into… dangerous inclinations." A warning note in her voice.

Tullia averted her eyes and sipped on her drink as sweat began to gather on her brow. That didn't sound like a compliment, it sounded very much like a rebuke.

A soft chuckle. "As a grandmother, I fear those… tendencies will lead to him being hurt." Tullia looked back at the queen and she had slouched ever so slightly in her chair, her drink was completely empty. She held her hand up again and motioned for the girl. The queen was handed another drink. "Looking at it from a stranger's point of view, this is a very important and healthy development for him as a shifter and as a person."

Carolina then suddenly faced Tullia with her entire body. Her perfectly ageless face, still lined with sorrow, had soft hints of humor. "Do not teach Chito crooked habits though. Like your sneakiness."

At Tullia's confused look, the queen raised her eyebrow. "I heard that you managed to sneak past the guards into the Mabuhay's main building, which no one, except for the royal family, is allowed to venture into." Her look was one of inquisitiveness, slight reproach, and amusement.

Tullia shrank back a little and made an 'O' with her mouth. She worried with the spindly neck of her wine glass. "In my defense, I didn't' know." At the queen's unconvinced look, Tullia continued weakly. "I needed to speak with you and I was also trying to get away from being a permanent citizen of Biringan. So, I had to escape from the guards and I thought a more… subtle approach was better?" She phrased it as a question with high level uncertainty.

The queen tilted her head slightly. "I do not understand. Permanent citizen?"

"The whole, everyone is welcomed, but no one leaves once you enter Biringan." Tullia did very appropriate air quotes.

Carolina suddenly giggled, her small hand came up to cover her mouth. "Oh dear, that saying is," Another giggle, "It's similar to…" She waved her hand, thinking, "an idiom. Not to be taken literally, but symbolically." She smiled. "In Biringan, my citizens know that they always have a home to return to if they leave. If they decide to never come back, then that is alright, but Biringan will always have a place waiting for them. I believe that is what the saying represents. It is not a forceful cage to keep you chained here."

Tullia didn't think the guard understood that the saying was only an idiom, he seemed to believe that was the law and he enforced it.

"Usually humans who come here don't want to leave because their family life was bad, or they had nowhere to go, or they simply fell in love with my city. Whatever the reason, they usually end up putting roots down in Biringan." The queen gave her a sly look. "Would you like a citizenship in Biringan my dear? I can grant it right now."

Tullia shook her head. "Your offer is too generous, but I have a home I want to get back to once this adventure is over."

More like, she wanted to choose where her home was to be once this adventure was over.

The queen shrugged flippantly, finishing her second cup of wine. "If you ever change your mind, Biringan's doors are always open to you." She patted her hand in a motherly way, bringing tears to Tullia's eyes.

For someone who was never genuinely offered a home, never given the beautiful gift of knowing she had a warm place to return to, Carolina's offer was a beautiful healing kiss on her shy soul.

She gave a wobbly smile to the queen. "Your offer means the world to me."

Carolina stared at Tullia for a moment, before leaning over and gently pressing a kiss to her forehead. A few tears slid from Tullia's eyes.

She took Tullia's full glass of wine and drank half of the glass, lightly smacking her lips. "Now, my dear, tell me how you have come to my Biringan and why you need to speak with me."

Tullia sat up straighter and inhaled deeply. This was her chance and one step closer to ridding herself of the lost magic. Tullia decided to start at the beginning.

* * *

Sabin sat in a corner, away from the mourning people. His heart ached for them, he knew the losses of those who were kin, and knew their pain. Though the acuteness of the loss would dim, it would not disappear entirely no matter how long one lived. He would know, his heart still clenches at times.

Sabin was sometimes taken aback by the melancholy that would come over him when a small occurrence triggered a memory of his mother, his father, his people… He forcefully shook his head to dispel the memories before they could solidify into images. His most hated emotion was sadness, his rage became too great to contain.

Sabin distracted himself from his thoughts by scanning the room. He saw Tullia talking with the queen of Biringan. She was quite animated, using her small hands freely as her face flowed with continuously revolving expressions. Sabin watched her for a moment, entertained and amused. He found he liked to study her, she always seemed to be lively and interesting, a pretty distraction. She was such a compact thing with her shiny black hair swishing with her head movements and her big gray eyes glimmering with a happy light. Small she was, but he often forgot her stature due to the brightness of her smile she often wore on her lips. He had never met a full-grown woman with such an innocently quick smile.

It was something that he found refreshing. There weren't many creatures that smiled simply because they found joy in being alive, it was usually calculated or sly or a deaden smiled with no meaning.

He forced his eyes away from Tullia's rosy face and continued his scan of the room. He spotted the witch across the room talking with a rail thin woman that had poofy brown hair and a scattering of freckles all over her face. It looked like they were in the heat of a cold war discussion, and everyone gave them a wide berth. Except a rather burly man that stood next to the poofy haired woman, glaring openly. Sabin moved on; the witch could handle herself. He instead began looking at the citizens of Biringan, who were eating slowly, mourning and playing small games with an absence of laughter and joy. Sabin sipped the rice wine offered to him slowly, not particularly enjoying the flavor, but drinking it anyway for the comfort of a familiar action and the slight burn of alcohol.

He looked down at the reflective liquid in his cup. He didn't drink wine; he preferred the hard liquors that allowed for numbness after a time. He thought they were ingenious creations; they tasted of poison and saturated the body quickly into an unfeeling state.

He dared not touch any drinks of old. Such as mead, ale or beer, they were drinks he despised for the wealth of memories they conjured in their amber depths.

A memory flittered at the edges of his mind.

Sabin was hunched over his fourth glass, trying to ignore the bustling tavern tables behind him. He wanted quiet, but quiet wasn't available and this tavern was the only place that sold liquor to his liking. All the bottles tasted as the air smelled outside. Stale, strong, and seemingly designed to kill you if you consumed too much.

Luckily, the bar owner knew him and the regular patrons, all locals, knew not to disturb him. He had established that he could and would crush anyone who interrupted him during his numbing session. He was feared, but this was a fact that had never changed for Sabin.

Which is why no one sat at the bar top on his days in. It was his spot from dusk to dawn. Sabin nursed his drink at the bar top, struggling to quell his rage that prickled over the rowdiness, over the people, over the night air, over the stains on the counter top. However, though fickle, Sabin was winning, drowning out the urge to scream and the rage through the dark amber liquid. The sour flavor eased the fury into a deadened state. Hopefully, by his twentieth drink he could sleep without a riot of nightmarish memories.

When he first discovered the amber poison, he had downed an entire bottle, hoping to kill himself. Instead he found a dark sleep that allowed for no dreams to enter his mind. He slept like a corpse after and found a new sleeping medication.

He downed the rest of his drink, clenching his teeth through the nearly painful burn it provided. He swallowed thickly, inhaled sharply then motioned the bar wench for another. She scurried about, a big and ruddy girl, pretty but with her nervous disposition she was off-putting. Her brow was dripping with sweat as she placed another glass in front of him. Her hand shook, but she did not spill any.

Tis the way it always was. Tis the way it will always stay.

A loud slam and stomping boots silenced the tavern's patrons momentarily with surprise. A man, tall, darkly dressed with a flushed complexion and a patchy jaw strode in. The man had a face that seemed to sneer at everyone as he swaggered in the tavern. Sabin took a sip of his new drink, unconcerned with the puffed-out man. The silence held in the bar and deepened as the stool on Sabin's right scraped along the wooden floor from being roughly pulled out. Sabin didn't bother to look at the man, he only waited, his dulling rage flickering with excitement.

"Wench! Get me some gin!" The man spoke too loudly in such a silence. Sabin gritted his jaw as his rage fluttered in his stomach. Sabin wanted to punch him, he flexed his fingers.

The bartender looked at the man wearily then said, "I shall fetch it for ya sir."

"Step on it." The man snapped loudly, huffing and puffing in his seat next to Sabin. Annoyance flared sharply, tightening his chest and stomach in preparation for action. Sabin felt the eyes of the too loud man on him, felt his evaluation, felt his breath. His rage stretched, scratching him.

"Ya rough lookin' thing-a-mabob, ain't cha?" He drawled sloppily. Seemingly already intoxicated and plenty stupid.

Sabin slid his eyes to the man, indolently evaluating him. He was big and brash, but that's all there was to him. Sabin could see under the heavy brow that the man's eyes were still young and soft, not completely hardened by life and its treacheries. Though his intelligence was lower than that of a rock, Sabin had enough life experience to be able to pick out dim witted people. They usually made it easy, like this bum.

The man became impatient when Sabin didn't answer him right away, he fidgeted then frowned severely at him. Sabin felt humor tug at the darker side of him. This boy was far too cocky, his seemingly good health was in danger.

"Here you are, sir." The bartender placed a small glass in front of the burly man. The liquid in the glass gave off a strong smell and was clear like fresh spring water.

The man gave Sabin a pointed glare before turning his attention to the bartender. He grabbed the glass and slugged the drink down in one go. Sabin watched as the burly man seemed to silently convulse in his seat. His already flushed face darkened into an unnatural shade of red before tingeing purple. His hands gripped the bar top and his large frame stiffened. Sabin was mildly impressed that the boy managed to remain silent through the careless way in which he consumed the strong drink. Sabin couldn't contain his chuckle when the boy finally breathed in, clearing his throat roughly to cover up his breathy coughs. The man snapped his blue eyes to Sabin, glowering at him.

"You got something to say, ya corny-faced lobcock? Eh?" The man's tone was almost shrill and there was a sluggish quality to his words. Sabin raised his eyebrow in amusement, keeping his face tilted down to obscure most of it.

Sabin didn't say anything, rather he took another sip of his drink.

"Ignorin' me now?" The boy reached out and slapped Sabin's glass from his hand. A gasp sounded as the glass tumbled from Sabin's grasp and shattered spectacularly to the floor. Sabin slowly looked down at his destroyed glass, the amber liquid of his whiskey seeping out into the wood, escaping him.

"See what happenin' when ya ignore your superior be talkin' to ya?" The thick guttural English accent grated upon Sabin's last stretched nerve. He slowly turned to face the idiot boy that had awakened his almost quelled rage.

The cocky look on the boy's face melted away as Sabin's faced him fully. His face covering was off so that he could drink, thus his ruined face was on full display under the dim lights of the tavern. The boy leaned back slightly, looking horrified by Sabin's disfigurement.

Tis the way it always was. Tis the way it will always stay.

Sabin smiled, baring his teeth causing the boy's eyes to widen amusingly wide. Sabin hooked his foot on the bottom of the boy's stool and dragged him closer. He purposely put his face very close to the boy's.

"Name?" Sabin murmured softly, staring at the flickering blue eyes on the pretender.

The boy swallowed nervously but shoved his thick chest out and lifted his chin in feigned confidence. "Oliver 'The Wall' Crocker." His tone was prideful and expecting, as if he expected Sabin to recognize the importance of his title.

He didn't, Sabin had never heard of this Oliver boy. He leaned in closer to Oliver, eyeing him intensely, allowing him to see the beast that prowled restlessly within him.

"Listen well, Oliver. You're going to pick up my tab and I'm going to overlook this insult. And you, get to keep your limbs intact." It was a generous offer from Sabin.

Oliver quivered, but it appeared he had more guts than brains. "I've never seen ya mug runnin' around. Who are you to tell me what to do when ya insulted me!"

Sabin cracked his neck, trying to alleviate the tension. "I don't run in small circles, boy. You wouldn't see me on the street, if you did, you'd be dead already."

Oliver forced out a laugh, his spit sprayed wetly on Sabin's face.

His rage lurched, Sabin choked it back. If he gave in to kill this boy, he wouldn't stop until the tavern floorboards were soaked with blood.

"W-what you ramble 'bout man?" He stood up clumsily, towering over Sabin. "I'm bigger than ya." Oliver's tone was too loud again. The boy's face was set in hard lines. His stubbly jaw clenched tight. "I've survived these rough streets for all me life, I can take on an ugly lout like yourself. Easy."

Sabin leaned back on his stool, contemplating.

This boy was going to get himself killed with his cocky way of thinking and talking.

Sabin's rage screamed, and Sabin gave in, grinning widely, Oliver the Stupid flinched, and Sabin enjoyed that. "So you say?" Sabin tensed his muscles, ready to strike.

"C-can you gentlemen take this outside?" The bartender quivered as he asked the question, Sabin did need to look at him to know he was pale, sweaty and trembling.

Oliver sneered at him, Sabin merely raised an eyebrow. He waited to see what the boy would do. Oliver jerked his head towards the door. Sabin slowly stood up from his seat, forcing the boy to step back from him. The stupid boy was right about one thing though; Oliver was taller than Sabin, but he wasn't bigger. However, to believe his size was everything in a fight was a fatal mistake. Sabin grabbed his new drink that the bartender had supplied him at one point and finished it in one toss.

Oliver pressed his soft gut into Sabin's stomach and the putrid sourness of his breath hit his nose.

Snap.

Sabin then struck out, slamming his meaty fist into the boy's face, feeling the bone crunch underneath his heavy fist, relishing in the hot blood that sprayed out, feeling giddy at the high squeal of pain.

Sabin didn't give Oliver a chance to recover. He grabbed the back of his neck, and in the boy's dazed confusion he followed Sabin's guiding hand... right into the bar top. He may have slammed the boy's head a little too hard he noticed as spiderweb cracks occurred where the impact was made. Oliver went limp and fell to the floor with a dull thud.

"My drinks are on him. Make sure he pays it. Or I'll come back for him." Sabin growled at the bartender. He snatched up his face covering, kicked the *boy's unconscious body out of his way, and then strode out of the bar. His rage was laughing.*

The cold night air eagerly met him, scratching his face with their stinging icy edges. He walked briskly down the filth covered cobbled street, allowing the night air to torment his ruined face. The sour smelling streets did nothing for him, his rage wasn't satisfied, it wanted more blood to be spilled. Those few drops were not enough to satisfy him, he wanted to bathe in the iron smelling life force until it went cold. He saw movement from the corner of his eye, before a group of street urchins scurried over to him, their cheap knives gleaming weakly under the moonlight.

Sabin laughed loudly as his rage exploded out. Sabin grabbed one skinny boy by his collar, elated by the way in which the kid's face ashen and—

"Sabin?" Tullia's soft voice broke his unimportant memory of a darker, uncaring time in Sabin's life. He looked up to see Tullia in a simple white dress that was childishly simple. "I spoke with the queen." Tullia announced as she stood in front of him, looking proud. "I told her everything and she sympathized with our plight." Tullia sat down next to Sabin, brushing her shoulder against his upper arm. "She asked for us to wait until the end of the wake, then she promised she would speak to all three of us about where we can possibly find a dragon."

Sabin nodded. "Good."

She seemed to vibrate a little, then huff. "I think you mean, 'that's seriously amazing Tullia, I don't know how you did it? Are you like magical or something?!'" Her voice dipped into a heavy west coast accent from the states.

Sabin nodded again. "Totally."

Tullia's giggle was sudden and unrefined, with a few small snorts intermixed and it was the best laugh he had heard, for it was genuine.

They sat in silence for a few heartbeats. He could feel her soft warmth beside him and her gentle presence easing his mind from his haunting memories. He looked down at Tullia, she was swallowing frequently and fiddling with her hands.

"Are you alright? Does your throat hurt?" Sabin leaned down a bit, trying to get a better look at her face. Her dove gray eyes met his and there was a guardedness, but her smile was bright even though it was dimmed by sadness.

"It's—" She bit the side of her lip, then continued, "…just that…" She paused again, her eyes shifted away, "everything tastes bitter and salty, but I'm alright."

Tastes?

Sabin looked at the food, he could see some of the dishes being salty, but the majority of the food was either sweet or savory. Perhaps due to the stress her tastes were distorted?

Sabin had experienced that once; his mead had tasted of dirt for a week straight after a particularly savage massacre. The eldest of that village had been a mere sixteen summers. Sabin slammed the thought back, and inhaled deeply. That order had been the first where he began to question his Gods' intentions… but he realized it far too late.

"Hey, Sabin, do you think we could go talk in private?" Her light voice fractured his spiraling thoughts, drawing his attention to her. She looked up at Sabin through long eyelashes.

Her face flashes across his mind, her wide gray eyes looking at him with confusion and anxiety. He looked away from her, hoping for a person, the witch, even a demon to appear and distract her. He didn't answer her right way, but Tullia didn't rush him. No, she was a quiet pressuring presence that sat so still next to him that without the soft sweet gale scent and her heat, he'd have thought he was sitting alone.

His gut tightened as his mind instantly flooded with millions of denials, of excuses, of rejections. It was natural she was curious; he was unnatural and Tullia supposed him to be a mortal.

As minutes dragged by, Sabin's honor, what he had left of it, would not allow him to negate his promise to her. He'd make his tragic bloodied tale harmless enough. He slowly turned to face her and met big gray eyes that shimmered with expectation on a cream face that was pinched tight with nerves. He felt a slight twist in his chest, shoving away the feeling and internally sighing, Sabin stood up from his seat. He snagged a bottle of rice wine from the table next to them and a bottle of what looked like rum, and two slender necked glasses. He looked back at Tullia and motioned to the table. "Bring some snacks, sweetness. This will take time."

Though dread uncurled in his gut, making his body cold, her reassured smile on a reddened face warmed his chest. She gave him a mock salute and quickly darted away. He watched as she gathered a bowl of fruit, a few sweet rolls, and a disproportionate number of cookies piled messily on a single plate. Once complete, they both left the mourning hall quickly. Sabin had managed to catch a glimpse of Cliona, glamour-less yet still flashy in a skin hugging white dress, now chatting with the Queen of Biringan. They both had a throng of admirers clamoring around them as well.

Sabin walked besides Tullia with the agenda of finding a hidden spot to talk. He had become good at discovering places where the dark lingers, and the light avoids.

They walked down the darkened hall for a few minutes, their footsteps the only sound to be heard. Patches of moonlight offering the dimmest illumination was their only source of light. However, this darkness was one of simple quiet. There was nothing alive in this blackness, it was unsullied and peaceful.

Tullia suddenly jogged past him suddenly, managing to spin around even though her small arms were full of treats. She grinned prettily at him. "I know of a place where we can sit and have a picnic. It also has a secret tunnel, but that's for another time." She fluttered back around, leading him confidently through the hall. Her white dress was a beckon in the dark as it fluttered innocently and sweetly.

Sabin was charmed by her, as usual, and followed without another word. After a series of twists and turns they ended up in front of a pair of French doors. Tullia dramatically threw them open and strode out into the night. Sabin ducked through the doors to find himself standing in a night garden in full bloom. The air was a cool caress across his skin, even as the balmy heat lingered tenaciously, the fresh air seemed to ease the tension he didn't notice was knotting his shoulders. He never did care to be confined indoors with a bunch of strangers.

Tullia had wandered over to a bench swing that contained a bright yellow cushion. She sat on it gingerly as she carefully set the tray down. Then waved Sabin over, kicking off her shoes and tucking her pale feet under her. He obeyed her silent command, settling himself on the swing slowly. They situated themselves in silence, Tullia began to split up the food as Sabin poured the wine first. He handed a half-filled cup to Tullia and filled his cup to the brim.

He'd need the other bottle later. He was going to need it to calm his agitated nerves that rattled his rage while his tale had been told. Dredging up old memories was never pleasant. The memories she wanted him to share were not happy from beginning to end. He drank deeply from his cup, the flavor of sweetness and then the acidic aftertaste of the alcohol warmed his throat. He inhaled the balmy night air until his lungs were so full that they threatened to burst.

"Alright then." He looked at her, she hadn't sipped her wine and her tiny self was curled up and twitching a bit.

"Okay, so, um." She swallowed, "I just thought that in order to be best friends, we need to know a bit of each other's backstories. But it's not fair if only one back story is revealed. And to be honest, out of the two of us it's a no-brainer to know which one will have a way cooler history, so I'm going to go first." Her babbles were fast, and she fiddled a lot with her glass.

Best friends?

Sabin blinked in surprise; he felt a little disoriented. He had thought that he was to tell his tale, not hear hers.

She inhaled deeply, and Sabin decided to simply allow himself to be pulled in by her charisma. If he wanted him to know her, then he would be honored. "As a little girl, besides random visions of random things, I also am able to… to well…" She swayed her head, looking up, then shrugged, "I'm able to taste the emotions of others."

Sabin raised an eyebrow. "Taste them?"

She nodded. "Yup. For example, when someone is sad, I taste a ton of salt. When someone is… tired, or weary, it's bitter like Brussels sprouts."

She scrunched up her face and stuck her tongue out in disgust.

Sabin examined her. He supposed the lost magic that she possessed could distort her mortality. Tasting emotions seemed harmless enough. "You taste emotions?"

Tullia nodded.

"Have you tasted all of them?"

She thought for a moment, taking a sip. "I've tasted enough I guess."

Sabin chuckled.

"Don't laugh," She tried to frown, but her lips kept tilting up. "This did not come with an instruction manual where I could look up what I'm tasting. I used context clues and pieced everything together." She shook her head, her black hair whispering around her face. "You are the first person I have ever told."

He bowed his head towards her. "I am honored." Sabin was curious. "What do the other emotions taste like?"

She gave a sigh. "Sadness is salty, when someone is depressed it's an intense seaweed flavor. When someone is super irritated, it's like a lot of black pepper was sprinkled into my mouth. Usually, when there are a lot of positive emotions, like someone being amused or happy, it's bubbly and sweet, like soda. Anger tastes like chili paste was painted on my tongue. It's so hot and absolutely the worst!" She fanned her face with her hand.

"Do you taste them all the time?" He asked.

She nodded. "It's super annoying. I'll be eating a grilled cheese sandwich and when someone is thinking her boyfriend is cheating on her, boom! All I taste is tartness and my grilled cheese. I can't enjoy food, unless it's super sweet or there is no one around. It's tragic really."

Sabin couldn't imagine that, tasting something that was a mere emotion instead of solid food.

"Okay, that is my big bad secret that only you know." She tittered nervously.

"Thank you." Sabin said. He knew she was trying to get a fair exchange of information about each other.

Tullia looked at him and gave him a small grin. "Ready for the background details?"

Then she told him.

Tullia told him she grew up in a lavishly affluent area with a mother, father, older sister and older brother. All of whom wished she would disappear, hence why her excessive stays at various mental hospitals from ages five to seventeen. She told him of some of her visions; a handful of her antics that she tried to replicate from the visions; and the overbearing consequences she received. She said she left her home after her eighteenth summer and traveled the land. Her goal was to find somewhere to exist without being labeled mentally insane. She then told him about a few of her jobs she had done, and Sabin was amused with some of her silly tales.

She was a very risible lass and seemed to get into far more mischief than was good for her. Sabin thought she seemed to gloss over much of her past and use humor as a deflection of sorts, but he wasn't one to judge when he planned to do the same with his. Except, without any humor, it was a tool Sabin was not equipped with.

After finishing her tale with how she got hired at the motel as a live-in maid, which involved a stick of gum, a homeless woman, and a stale muffin, she trailed off. Then she gave him a big smile that was nearly as strong as the sun's rays at noon. Her big gray eyes were watching him expectantly.

Sabin picked up a giant strawberry from the platter and ate it, in five small bites. Tullia was patient, nibbling on some cookies while staring at him in expectation.

Sabin let out a gust of air. "It's a long, long story… and I'm afraid I have to start from the beginning."

He had been running a few different scenarios on their far too short trip to the garden on how to tell her the least amount about him and his curse; and what he did in the time in-between. He managed a rough outline that gave basic facts without delving into details. That should be enough for Tullia to understand and still accept Sabin's presence. It struck him, in a cruel, dark way, that he didn't want this tiny woman with her velvet snowy face and big eyes to think of him as… *evil*. Twisted was an acceptable conclusion she could come to, but not evil. He was a far cry from the wild berserker he used to be. He had gotten soft, too mellow, more so now.

It was unavoidable, she wanted them to bond, and she was in his care so it was only natural. Perhaps helping her, helping her find a cure, would cure a part of him. He hoped at least.

She blinked those glittery dove eyes.

Right. He'd gloss over the bloody bits of his past, which was the majority, and focus on key points. Childhood was up first in his timeline.

"I grew up in a small clan on an island that is now called Iceland. My clan and I constantly roamed the land and went out to the sea, to find those to pillage. We hunted, we ate, we praised, we feared, we celebrated. It was very simple and a very barbaric time." Sabin's gaze fixated on a little lone pink flower in the midst of a mass of light blue flowers. It happily bloomed in the mass, not knowing any different. Not knowing it was different.

"So, you were a child. Hard to imagine." Her voice was teasing, making him want to smile.

"I was." He said solemnly, "And I was raised as a warrior since birth. My father was a Viking, my mother—" Sabin's lips curled up in a smile, "was what she referred to as a hearth warrior. They groomed me to be the clan's berserker, I had to prove myself to the clan that I was the most violent, the most bloodthirsty, and the most dangerous at an early age."

And he was. No one defeated him from age six to age twenty-eight. It wasn't until twenty-nine, that he finally tasted the pain of being slayed and the waves of death slowly submerged him into darkness. That was his first and last meeting with defeat as a Viking. Tullia shifted, sprawling her body a bit more over the swing, causing Sabin's body to shift slightly to give her more room. He was slightly amused at the way they seemed to synchronize with each other's movements. The night air was comfortable and exotic to Sabin, though his childhood had been dead to him for centuries, he still reminisced about the harsh winds and frost in the air during the nights.

One could not sit casually outside for long stretches of time.

"After a while, my father deemed me worthy enough to go on a Viking raid with him on my tenth summer."

His thoughts hesitated to remember that raid. He had slayed his first man on that raid, had changed from a posing warrior to an instant life taker within a span of hours. Sabin had stabbed the man in the chest, he had drunkenly rushed at Sabin with a candlestick. He had never forgotten the man's face, craggy and dirty, laying in a pool of blood as his once heated blue eyes drained of life. Sabin also hadn't forgotten his fear from that day. It was the cold, heart gripping fear that drove him into a blind frenzy of slashing anything, anyone that moved near him. Screaming with a soul filled fright as he unseeingly swung his too big weapon haphazardly.

Once the raid had stopped; his father had congratulated him on his bravery by giving him a walloping slap on the back and a rough ruffle on his head. All the grown-up men had cheered his name, prophesying him to be a great man and destined for Valhalla. Sabin had sneaked away later that night as his father and crew were celebrating their successful pillage by going over the stolen goods and drowning themselves in liquor. He ran back to the body of the old man, still laying on the ground, but now the body was cold and stiff. Sabin had shed tears over the man, over what he did, knowing it was shameful but unable to control the reaction.

Sabin made a vow to never cry again, and he still upheld it to this day.

"It was… a life altering experience." Sabin murmured, staring at the red liquid in his half empty glass.

"What happened?" The soft question that fell from her lips would go unanswered.

"In my clan," He began instead, "I would not be recognized as a man and I would not be allowed to enter Valhalla if I did not excel at the art of warfare." Sabin took another long sip of his drink, he looked over at Tullia. She sat curled up like a kitten, nibbling on her sweets as her quiet silver eyes watched him with vivid interest. "I believed that I could not change anything in my life, everything was predetermined. Therefore, everything I did was in the name of my Gods to gain their favor in granting me an afterlife as an honored warrior."

That was all he thought of in those times.

Sabin's father encouraged him to kill anyone and everyone on pillages, which was a great honor to be a part of. They were their enemy, they scoffed at their gods, and they hoarded goods. Sabin had idolized his father almost as much as he worshiped the gods. Of course, he wanted to please him, and he did make his father proud.

He made his gods proud too as he fed the earth the blood of innocence, supplying the god's insanity. He truly had become a rabid, diseased bear…

A small cookie was suddenly in his line of sight. "Eat."

Sabin blinked, but obeyed without much thought. Taking the little cookie from her, he popped it in his mouth and mechanically chewed, not really tasting a thing…

Sabin unexpectedly coughed as heat crawled down his throat from his fire coated tongue. He felt disoriented, ripped out of his clawing darkness within his remembrances and shoved into a softer space where flowers bloomed at night and a nymph sat, laughing at him. He looked at Tullia, almost betrayed by the fact that she handed him a contradictory cookie.

Her smile was deceivingly innocent. "It's a chocolate chili cookie. Yummy?"

Sabin downed the rest of his weak wine, clearing his throat he stated firmly. "I do not favor spicy foods."

Tullia's face seemed to pinch with suppressed humor. "Vikey no like spicy?"

Sabin blinked at her, bewildered by her entire being momentarily, which apparently was enough of a reaction to incite a giggling fit from Tullia. Sabin watched as her face turned an interesting shade of red as she soundlessly laughed with intervals of harsh gasps. She hunched over enough that Sabin became concerned that her treats were going to spill from the plate.

Sabin waited, giving Tullia time to recover and trying to figure out why she was laughing so hard. Though her good humor was infectious, it managed to brighten his darkened state of mind.

"I'm sorry." She breathed, wiping her eyes and placing a hand on her chest. She looked at Sabin. "Your face… the whole thing…" She waved her hands around, giggling again.

After another small bout of laughter, Tullia managed to control herself. "I'm sorry, please continue." Her eyes danced with both satisfaction, relief, and amusement; a look Sabin didn't think was possible while hearing his tale.

Sabin raised his eyebrow at her inquisitively, but felt his lips curl. His brooding mood was broken due to her silly laughing fit. He poured himself another glass of wine, took a sip, this time savoring the fruity taste.

"To shorten a long-winded tale, I adhered to the code of the bear, I slew without remorse, pillaged for the greater good of the clan, and after a few years of livin' alone in the woods, I was deemed worthy of the title berserker."

He could remember that day as if it merely happened an hour ago. In his clan, there was a tradition that those who completed their first raid and planned to become a berserker, was to live alone in the woods. They needed to prove themselves able to survive and thrive in nature. He had just eaten three rabbits in his shallow cave that he had carved by hand out of the side of a cliff. His father had found him, dirty, wild and half mad, and escorted him roughly to where only the revered warriors trained. Ten men, rugged, hard and imposing stood waiting for him in their war paint and fresh blood on their weapons.

The clan's berserker was dead, he was laid in front of the warriors, wrapped in his bear pelt and his face leached of all color except for the smattering of blood and his face paint.

"You lived all alone in the woods at ten?" Tullia's voice was tinged with shock.

He nodded absently, still seeing the ferocious face of the clans once celebrated warrior. Even dead he wore the snarl of an animal on his lips, his brow was creased heavily, the set of his hands clawed. He resembled the likes of a diseased animal more than a human. And that was to be his fate.

"Aye. I had to develop bear-like instincts, so that I may become a bear to bring honor to my clan. I had to be fierce, fearless and ferocious when I fought, all to be worthy of the title, berserker." He often wondered if he too looked like that berserker when he died. More animal than man, his face disfigured in a nasty snarl.

He felt like an animal more so than a man near the end of his human life.

Tullia tucked her legs underneath her as she brushed a silky strand away from her soft face. "Is that the highest rank you can go, being a berserker that is?"

Sabin felt a grim twist of his lips occur, he swirled the liquid in his cup, contemplating whether or not to pour some of the other drink. "No, it was not. However, no greater title existed to my father than berserker." He felt a grim smile curl his lips. "He often said, 'when one had it, one was invincible.'"

Tullia was quiet for a breath. "You obviously got it." She stated.

Sabin gave a halfhearted shrug. "Yes. I fulfilled my father's hopes." He looked back at the small pink flower swarmed by the blue flowers, he found, mysteriously, he wanted to destroy the blue flowers to allow the pink one some space. "He did groom me well for the title." He muttered darkly in a thin breath.

Mercilessly, nearly cruelly his father had drilled him with violence and wildness. However, in-between bouts of brutality his father would give him gruff affection, feeding his starved soul and completely erasing the earlier savagery done.

Making it all worth it.

Until he discovered the reality of his gods and his clan.

Sabin saw her tilt her head to the side slightly and shove a cookie into her mouth, chewing quickly.

He cleared his throat, wrestling his emotions down. Tullia must have tasted some horrid flavors and he couldn't help but feel guilty knowing there was not going to be anything pleasant from here on out. "My clan had a ritual passage for becoming a berserker." He gave her a side look. "I had to slay a bear and fashion a trophy that I could wear from its skin."

Tullia leaned forward a bit, her sweet gale scent warmed and iced him simultaneously. "What color was the bear?"

He blinked, it was not a question he ever considered anyone asking him. "It was a fierce black bear."

The biggest, meanest one he had found. It had several scars all along its hide and grotesquely giant teeth. Sabin had followed the giant beast for a while, noticing that the bear would act oddly. Act insane and attack trees or viciously claw its face. Sabin thought the bear's pelt would be fitting on him, hopefully the bear's essence of savagery and insanity would imprint into him on the battlefield.

It did.

Tullia nodded. "Good call, a black bear pelt on you would have really brought out your eyes." She studied him again, before nodding with conviction.

Sabin stared at this girl, her doe like eyes seemingly guileless on a face with softer angles and a delicate mouth that often smiled. He was powerless to stop laughter exploding out of him. He hunched over slightly as he laughed. She was more concerned about the color of the bear matching his eyes than his methods or even the fact that he did slay a bear just to wear its skin on him.

Such an odd girl.

"Ah," He sighed, leaning his elbow on his knee to prop his face up as his other hand gripped his drink. He looked at Tullia and felt his grin stretch a bit wider over his face. "Aren't your priorities interesting?"

She gave a very delighted smile that turned her face from puerile prettiness to a ripe beauty. He shook his head; she was indeed effortlessly charming.

"Right, well I got the title berserker and fought many, many, many battles for my clan." They had given him sacred drinks and foods before a fight, making him crazed and powerful… and cruel when violent. "And after a few years, I was finally slain, by a man who fought in the name of Christianity and his one true god."

The memories of his warfare days were saturated with age, but Sabin's mind preserved the viciousness of his actions. Of the intentionally cruel behaviors he performed on enemy soldiers. Of twisting and pulling off the arms of wounded soldiers, beating them to death with their own limbs, ripping open jaws, scalping soldiers then stuffing their mouths with their sliced skin to suffocate them…

His rage was coated in insanity that had caused Sabin's soul to be drenched in blood, to be scarred beyond redemption, to become a hideous blemish of humanity.

Sabin couldn't remember the man's face who ran him through with a sword for the seventh time, but his mind at that moment, for the first time since he became a berserker, was clear and coherent. It was the first time since he became the berserker that he wasn't untouchable or immortal. Sabin flickered a glance at Tullia and felt another smile tug at his lips.

Her hands were covering her mouth and a look of horror was painted across her pretty face.

"I didn't feel a thing." He reassured her. Which was partly true. He didn't feel the pain of being stabbed seven times, but he felt his life draining from him as he slowly went cold, and the world slowly went dark around him. The last sight he had was of dirty snow, stained with blood and a pair of boots still occupied by dismembered feet. "Don't fret. The past is something that should not be mourned, rather, it should only be observed."

Her face didn't ease from its frozen horror look, but she lowered her hands away from her mouth. "How?"

Sabin reached over to gently pinch her cheek. "A sword."

She shook her head. Sabin purposely ruffled her hair to become messy, taking delight in the way she gave a huffing hiss, smacking his hand away and delicately fixing her hair.

"You trash troll." She muttered, glaring at him with dewy eyes as she tried to smooth down her now fluffed hair.

He chuckled. "Afterwards, when I passed, I woke up in *Valhalla*. I was chosen by a Valkyr and brought before Odin." Even though he was now disillusioned, his exuberance, his awe and his reverence upon first awakening in *Valhalla* was a feeling Sabin would never forget. "It was incredible." The hall was grand, glittering in gold as weapons and shields made up the ceiling. The floor gleamed so brightly; Sabin could barely stand to look directly at it.

"*Valhalla?*" Tullia's eyes glittered with interest. "Where is that?"

Sabin shook his head. "It's a place only in Asgard. Though, I doubt it exists anymore. *Valhalla* means 'hall of the slain', and only those who die honorably on the battlefield receive the honor to enter. The rest, go to Hel."

"Well damn." She propped her face on her hand. "What did *Valhalla* look like? Was it like the movie?"

Sabin raised his eyebrow. "Movie?" He couldn't hide the disgust in his voice. "*Valhalla*… was unlike anything I've ever seen before. It was not something man could fathom. It is not something one could recreate. The hall was… massive, tall like the stretch from the ground to the sky, and wide, like a forest cleared of trees. It was lined with gold and gleamed brighter than a midday sun. Weapons hung from the ceiling, and they too were bright gold and encrusted with precious stones."

Sabin had remembered panicking momentarily, thinking he had survived and had been dragged into the enemy territory for torture. There was no honor in dying by torture and he had instantly become enraged that they had dared keep him from dying on the battlefield. He was still armed, his axes still blood stained, and began screaming, roaring like an animal searching for something to butcher… to kill…

Then *she* appeared before him.

"I was soon escorted by a *Valkyr* to the All Father's throne room." Sabin swallowed as acid came up in his throat at the memory. He quickly stole a mango from Tullia's horde of food. Sinking his teeth into it, he made himself feel satisfaction at his hard bite into the soft, sweet fruit.

"A Valkyr?" Tullia's tone was interest. "Aren't they like angel-warrior women?"

"No." Sabin said instantly and took a second bite into his mango harder than necessary; the sweet taste was welcomed as he reminisced over his first encounter with a Valkyr... with *Hildr*.

Sabin would never forget that creature either for as long as he lived. She went against everything he had been told a Valkyr would look like and behave like. She did not reflect the fables of man, a fact she took the utmost pride in.

Her hair was a deep red that was riotous with various jewels and braids around her strong, pale face. Her eyes, the color of iced sapphire jewels, seemed to glow ferociously surrounded by thick, black war paint that dripped down her face. She wore a sleek black headdress that came to a sharp point in between her eyes plated with multiple gold runes of strength, death and blood; delicate black wings curved up five inches from her helmet and more wings draped down to her sharp jaw. She wore a simple white dress that pooled around her feet in excess. It was stained with blood at the hem. Her dress was strapped with multiple black leather bands across her bodice, and shiny, blood covered daggers tucked neatly in the straps. Black feathered sleeves encased her shoulders and hung from her arms to the floor in a black, shimmering fall.

She was at once glorious to behold and bloodcurdling to witness.

"No, Valkyr are no angels. They are the choosers of the slain. They pick up the souls of the worthy warriors killed in battle and take them to the All Father so that they may fight alongside him." Though what Odin had his warriors fight was reprehensible.

"I met Odin," Sabin said, his voice thick with suppression, "one of the gods I had worshiped my entire life." He had dropped to the floor upon meeting him. Stunned, in awe, and humbled. "He made me an einherjar, it was an honor, and I fought alongside other worthy einherjars," Battles more vicious than he had ever witnessed while living, "and I feasted for years." He drank mead, ate as much meat as he could stomach and fought for Odin. He never wavered when Odin pointed his finger at the enemy. "I lived by the phrase; any enemy of my god is condemned to die."

Anyone Odin was against, Sabin obeyed as did his fellow einherjars. Why did he need to question his god that provided a warriors' paradise for him? That praised him? That rewarded him? That made the hell he went through while living all worthwhile?

"What happened then?" Tullia asked, her tone pitched low, she must have sensed the foreboding. She must have tasted the death and blood of his emotions, the rot that his regret and their betrayal caused him to feel.

Sabin sighed, he reached over and grabbed the bottle of gin, yanking off the top with his teeth. He spat out the top crudely and took a hefty sip, pleased by the burn and the heavy pine flavor.

Remembrances were taxing on him.

"I wanna sip." Tullia demanded, leaning forward to take the bottle. Sabin pulled the liquor away.

"No, no, sweetness. It's too strong for you." The burn lingering in his throat.

Tullia's kitten fierce glare was very adorable. "Don't tell me what's too strong for me. I'll be the judge, not you."

He shook his head, but handed it to her, watching and waiting. One good thing Valhalla did was teach him to never deny a woman what she wanted, she'd end up pulling out her weapon and trying to behead you if you did. Tullia put her lips to the mouth of the bottle and took a mouth full- she then jerked the bottle away and twisted her head to the side and spat the gin out onto the dirt.

"Oh my gosh-" She gagged, coughing too. Blindly, she fumbled for the treats and managed to grab an apple, biting into the flesh multiple times to fill her mouth with the sweet flesh. She had one hand pressed at the base of her slender neck and the other holding the half-eaten apple. She was chewing furiously, her cheeks puffed full with apple, as she stared out into the garden with a nose scrunched in disgust.

Sabin chuckled. He warned her.

"I just disrespected the queen's night garden." She mumbled after a few moments and one entirely eaten apple later, looking down to where she spat with repugnance and regret.

"And the gin." Sabin added.

She waved her hand at him in dismissal. "That offended my mouth." Sabin shook his head, suppressing the urge to laugh as Tullia glared at him. "Continue please." She ordered, reaching for a cookie this time.

All humor died within Sabin, he tilted the bottle from side to side, looking at the liquid sloshing within.

"I was… disillusioned. Fed lies by my gods and made into a feral dog that when told to jump, I leapt as high as I could without thought." Shame always accompanied him when his past was recalled. How could he have been so blind? How could he not have seen the erosion of the gods? How did he not notice his fellow einherjars going missing? How did he not see the rot of insanity? "My ignorance maintained my blissful life and cost so many others theirs."

To think that his slaughtering, his indiscriminate killing, was once his source of pride and honor to him, dissolved into a depraved and ignominious burden he now forever carried on his soul.

"What did your gods do?" Tullia asked, her body tense, her face pale and her lips pressed so tight together they became bloodless. She was swallowing frequently, what did she taste? How did his heavy, burdensome, guilt laden emotions transfer onto her tongue?

She must have such an awful taste in her mouth. A rotting taste flowing with fresh blood.

"Do you know, what makes a god strong?" Sabin murmured, then answered in the same breath. "His devotees. How much they are worshiped; how much they are given from humans is what generates the gods power." He exhaled. "Valhalla was beautiful; however, it began to slowly decay." Sabin had noticed there was less mead, less meat and the once gleaming halls, dulled to a scuffed brass. "And my brethren, my fellow einherjars began to disappear… slowly. I didn't notice at first." The table became lighter and lighter with bodies, the food rotted, the mead soured. "I was led to believe my violent actions were for something greater. Something that Odin had vowed to us, to me and—"

Sabin cut himself off abruptly, as the memories of his last few days in his mock warrior's paradise overwhelmed him. He had felt betrayed. He became aware of his surroundings and began to take notice of how his heaven looked tarnished and cheap. Of how his few remaining brethren looked lifeless. Of how his revered gods began to panic before him, thinking him less than an animal, *treating* him less than an animal and gnawing their fingers to the bones in paranoia.

"What?" Tullia's silk smooth voice broke him from his reprieve

Tears trapped within his chest began to suffocate his heart and strain against his ribs. He did not deserve to cry; he was a monster made by his environment and by others. However, the most painful part of his past was that he allowed himself to be made a senseless beast that killed when his masters snapped their fingers. He allowed himself to be thought for, to be directed and committed sins that haunt him to this day. He had been like this from his first conscious moments of his life. He had allowed others to guide him through their notions, their ideals and then adopted them as his own without question. He did not deserve to cry, not after all the slaughters he has done to the young and the old and everyone in-between. He doesn't have the right to mourn his past, not when he has taken lives for reasons that were cowardly as they were evil.

Sabin truly did not deserve to live. However, it would be a mercy at times to die, but his curse ensured his penitence, ensured a personalized hell. He'd rather be whipped daily for centuries on end, than have his memories lurking within him, ready to strike, ready to wither his heart and cause his soul to throb with unreleased grief. He swallowed thickly, his chest contracting tighter. "We were fed false promises. I was committing wrongs towards innocent people for my entire life, made to believe it was the right thing for myself to do."

Tullia's soft hand slid over his garment covered wrist. A gentle comfort, one he did not feel, he did not deserve but would cling to nevertheless.

"What finally ended my lingering loyalty was that I discovered that my gods could indeed die." A revolutionary concept to him, he thought them untouchable. He thought that since so much was different from man's stories of the gods, that surely the concept of death was false as well. "I discovered that they were losing their powers, weakening due to the spread of Christianity." They sought to revive their importance in the world, by sending us, his einherjars, to slaughter the peaceful farmers, destroy peasant homes, ransack poor villages; slander their beloved god in vile ways. Sabin gave a huffing, humorless grunt, reining back his anger that stirred, his guilt that consumed and wrung his heart raw.

He shook his head, his neck tight. Odin's plan fell through, their attacks only made the poor victims more god fearing, rather than reviving their belief in his gods. They thought his attacks were their fault for not worshiping enough. Well, enough of them thought that way. A lot believed otherwise, believing the correct notion of sabotage. His mood suddenly dived, turning black with the memories that came after his gods realizing that their slaughtering was all for naught. "My gods became rabid *creatures*. The gods in which I had believed flawless were reduced to sniveling, greedy cowards riddled with the faults of man." His inhaled deeply, clenching his teeth, gnashing them violently to quell his rage that surged. He wished to slaughter his gods, but while weak and withering, they were still more powerful than him.

"And…" He heard her hesitate, and he did not look at her. His eyes found the little lone pink flower in the midst of a hoard of blue flowers. Those damn suffocating blue flowers. "And when you realized that your gods were not well?" A pause, "you left?"

"Not at first." Shamefully he tried to justify their orders. Tried to justify his actions. Tried to justify everything. However, it came to a point where his justifications were no longer applicable to his gods. "Eventually I did, though."

He remembered the exact moment he had defied Odin's command.

"No."

A heavy silence. No one moved, everyone's hateful eyes were on him, the Valkyr had drawn their weapons. The remaining gods stared at him in stunned silence.

Odin's one eye iced over. "What did you say, boy?"

Sabin stiffened, his heart thundering in his chest as if he were on the battlefield with ice giants. No more. He was through being the pet of an insane god. He lost his admiration and respect for Odin, for all the creatures in Asgard. They were worse than cowards. "I will no longer obey your command." He spat in front of the All Father.

Odin's eye gleamed with a feverish rage. His face creased heavily; his rotted teeth bared. "You think to defy me? You think to abandon Asgard? Leave your Gods?" He rose, his still strong body seemed to vibrate, his power suffocated the room. "After all I've given you, do you think you can leave?" He snapped his fingers. "Just leave on a whim, boy?"

"You are unfit to be a god." Sabin declared with every ounce of certainty in his entire being. "I do not acknowledge you as one anymore."

Odin seemed to pause, his face still, then smiled pleasantly, his cold face wrinkling. Then Sabin dropped to his knees as a pain unlike any other he had known consumed him entirely. As if he were being torn open and cooked.

Sabin should have been more subtle about it. He should have never confronted Odin head on. He knew he was a cruel god on his benevolent days, he just thought he'd be less cruel with a direct approach. That was the Viking way, but Sabin was wrong. So very wrong. He should have mimicked Loki, but he never comes away scot-free either.

"And when I did, Odin punished me. He said that my soul's sin would be wrought upon my physical body, and I would be immune to death for an eternity." He drained the remaining liquid from the gin bottle, relishing in the burning that mercilessly lit his throat on fire. "He engraved my skin with scars." Odin had pinned him down, after making him suffer through fire, and slowly carved ruins of death, warnings, and curses upon every inch of his flesh and mangled his face to rival that of a draugr.

"I was to suffer in isolation, no longer part of my brethren on earth and disowned by all gods in Asgard. I was also to bare the physical shame for an eternity." He remembered Hildr had laughed hysterically when Odin proclaimed his sentence, watching with her taciturn blue eyes as he writhed in agony on gilded floors. He had never known that there was a type of pain that was so acute it paralyzed one into silence, trapping the person in a frozen state of consuming pain.

The pain had cleansed him, had humbled him, and had killed the Sabin who was once in awe of his gods and eager to please them.

The only mercy Odin gave Sabin was blacked blood blades, made out of his fellow deceased einherjar blood. They were bigger axes than he was used to, but he once had many, many einherjar brothers. He had named the blades in a broken state, snubba, to curse, and slatra, to butcher. Those were his only companions throughout his years, and he swore to use his cursed blades at his own discretion and not under orders.

He gently placed the empty gin bottle aside. "I was awakened, for the first time in my life that day, and I forsook Odin and Asgard." He forsook his entire existence.

That day he was ruined and tossed from Asgard, Sabin had disowned his heritage and his clan's name. He had come to terms with the fact that his people were a fanatic group that sowed seeds of chaos and death. They were people that thrived off blood, off violence and off of the belief that their way of life brought them to a higher level than everyone else. And their fervent worship of Odin that they had bred him in, had damned him.

"I was banished from Asgard and lived as an immortal among mortals and that's where I am still." Sabin turned and looked at Tullia, her face pale and tears dripped down from her dove gray eyes.

Sabin started, then smiled behind his mask, he reached over and wiped her cheeks gently, not able to feel the texture of her cheek or the wetness of her tears due to his gloves. And for a moment, he wished he could feel this woman's warmth and the tears she graciously cried for him. No one did, she was the first. "Don't cry, sweetness. It all happened so long ago." He said softly.

"But it still happened." She murmured throatily. "To you." She cupped his hands that were paused on her cheeks and pressed them firmly to his face. He could almost feel the softness. She shut her eyes; fat droplets of her tears dripped from her long lashes.

Sabin didn't say anything, simply continued to hold her face. It was the most intimate moment, filled with tenderness and sadness, and after a long minute, she sniffed, releasing him and he withdrew. She then rubbed her eyes far too roughly before looking at Sabin.

"Thank you."

Sabin raised an eyebrow. "For making you sad?" He shrugged, "Such a strange one you are."

Tullia's pink lips twitched before she shook her head. "No." She reached out and gripped his hands, squeezing them tightly. "For telling me. For going through all of that horror just so that I could know you better. Thank you."

Sabin studied her small white hands that gripped his gloved covered one. He then looked down at her tear rimmed eyes and pale face framed by a thick mass of midnight black hair. Gently, he gave her hands a small squeeze back.

Someone knew a fraction of who he truly was, and a faint idea of what he did. And she thanked him for telling her. After centuries of keeping his tale to himself, of his true past locked away to rot within him. His chest lightened by a fraction and his heart quivered. Though it was slightly terrifying, a small kernel of warm balm spread over part of his soul.

She didn't hate him from his story. That was… good.

She sniffed. "Kay, we're best friends now. You can't cancel this subscription, it's forever. It's done, so yeah."

Sabin turned his palm up to hold her small hand firmly in his. He wasn't ready to relinquish her offered warmth.

"I suppose that's alright." He responded, the night becoming even more beautiful.

A gentle silence enveloped them as they sat beneath the moonlight in a blooming garden. Sabin's eyes were once more drawn to the lone pink flower again.

The tiny pink flower still stood out even though it was crowded by all the blue ones, a small breeze ruffled the mass, shifting their positions to reveal an even smaller pink flower huddling tightly underneath the other big pink flower.

So, it wasn't alone in the blue riot.

Sabin dragged his eyes to his hand that held a softer hand, then looked up at the moon and closed his eyes.

So, the little flower wasn't alone.

Good.

Chapter Seventeen

Three days after the *lamay* Carolina had sent them a formal summons to appear before her at nine am sharp to the throne room. Casual attire was permitted, manners were required. Tullia had freaked out a bit, she hadn't met a sane queen in a formal setting before and asked Cliona for a nice dress. She couldn't wear the white mourning dress, it would be disrespectful, distasteful, and just no.

The Grand High first put her in a dress so tiny, with green sequins and black tassels, it didn't cover her butt fully. After twenty minutes of pleading, Cliona had her wear a white dress with sunflowers all over it that went past her knees.

She felt super girly. It was weird, but she didn't hate it and when she walked the dress swished around her legs which was a fun sensation.

Currently, Tullia, Sabin and Cliona were standing in the throne room, waiting for the queen of shifters. They were in front of a throne that had delicately wrought iron designs of masks and flowers in bright colors all around the backrest. There was a thick wooden base, glossy and simply carved with a cream cushion for the seat.

"Now *that* is a throne." The Grand High murmured, lounging in the air while tugging on her hair. She went back to the tiny braids; except this time, they were a dark honey gold and glittered throughout like sunlight. She also wore a dress made of a riot of purples, oranges, and reds that draped around her form in adoring wisps.

"Try not to waste all your magic energy on floating." Sabin murmured back, causing Cliona to sneer at him.

"Stuff it, you bulky meat bucket." The Grand High snapped back, whipping her hair over her shoulder, neatly smacking Sabin in the face. He didn't react, merely gave Cliona a side glance of disinterest. He tasted of amusement and annoyance as did the Grand High. Tullia giggled, went to say something but the door to their right opened with little fanfare and the Queen of Biringan glided in with a small entourage of five guards and Chito.

The queen was decked out in a gown that hugged her upper body then loosely outlined her bottom half. The gown, a dazzling mixture of earth browns and soft yellows, cinched at the waist and had puffy, layered shoulders. She wore a heavily beaded belt that made gentle hollowed clicking sounds. She strode up to the throne, her guards spread out around the room and Chito stationed himself to her left. When she faced them fully, Tullia saw the queen's hair slicked back with an elaborate golden crown of flowers, leaves, and a ring-shaped halo. Her crown stopped to hover right above her ears.

Around her neck hung a necklace strung with small brown beads that draped down past her chest. Sitting upon the throne, the Queen of Biringan regarded them with cool eyes. She looked beautiful and powerful. However, Tullia found her eyes drifting to Chito and quickly away with an urge to smile. He looked so interesting, dressed in black slacks and a form fitting white blouse that ruffle at the neck and the wrists. His long hair was slicked back into a ponytail over his left shoulder that was held together with a golden flower clip. He looked more like a pirate than a prince of a hidden city.

He gave Tullia a small smile, Tullia waved back subtly.

"Let us get the formal speech out of the way." The queen gave a slight smile before positioning her head to a regal tilt. "Due to your brave assistance in the execution of the tikbalang, I have agreed to honor your request." Tullia was startled to hear perfect English flow from Carolina's mouth. She had become accustomed to the nearly lyrical Tagalog that to hear her native language gave her mind a start. The queen's smooth brown face glowed with beauty that only intensified when she smiled. "Strange as your request may be, nonetheless it is within my power to do so. I have indeed met a dragon, *eons ago*." She waved her hand in insouciance. "We spoke briefly, and never even became acquaintances, but when I got lost on my way to Mount Wudang, he kindly guided me through the right path." She paused, "That is, after blathering continuously about his title, his feats, his popularity, and the honor I had received by simply seeing him." She rolled her eyes in a very unqueenly manner. "I believe he went by the name…" She paused, snapping her fingers. "Jiang… Li? I believe. He proclaimed himself to be the only 'great river dragon.'"

Tullia felt a jolt go through her. The name caused a few chimes to sound within her head and a sharp eyed, beautiful face flashed in front of her. She inhaled deeply, forcing herself into a stillness when a jittering sense of excitement bubbled within her.

She'd seen him. Jiang Li the dragon. She didn't know when, but she had seen him through one of her visions.

The Queen of Biringan tasted exasperation. "He was…conceited and arrogant…" She paused slightly, "And *very ancient*. But, he was kind enough to help me on the right path to my destination, so he wasn't an entirely evil entity."

"How did you know he was ancient?" Tullia asked, curious.

The queen's lips curled ever so slightly, she tasted of something… unfathomable. "An ancient being gives off an aura that will dominate any space they choose to occupy and when you look them in the eye—" She leaned forward, the tiny hollow clunking sound brushed the air, "you see the weight of age. His eyes were dark as they were heavy with the passage of time."

Tullia looked into Carolina's eyes, a stunning honeyed brown that seemed steady, unwavering and aged like the finest brandy.

"What region did you meet him at, your highness?" Sabin's rumbly voice tickled Tullia's spine. She had been hyper aware of him ever since he shared his past with her. It was both a beautiful and unfamiliar concoction of warring emotions within her. It made her want to hug him and cry simultaneously.

She'd get over it eventually.

Carolina's age-deepened eyes glanced away from Tullia, she leaned back and looked up thoughtfully. "Hm, the regions might have changed since I was last there. I believe his main residence was near the hometown of that famous poet…" She frowned, "Ah, what was his name…" She looked at Chito and waved her hand, "He's the poet you chose as your history project, with the poem about the man on a spirit journey."

"'Li Soa'?" Chito responded."By Qu Yuan?"

The queen snapped her fingers. "Yes, Qu Yuan! Jiang Li was located roughly near Qu Yuan's hometown." She folded her hands delicately in her lap. "I remember that tidbit because the dragon was long winded in his praises for Qu Yuan. Apparently, the poet was his favorite mortal."

There was a pause of silence, then the Grand High's sultry voice filled the room. "You, incidentally, managed to run into a dragon while lost in ancient China?" Cliona asked slowly, her face carefully blank.

The queen looked amused. "Yes, luck is my right-hand lady. Always has been."

Cliona tilted her head forward in acknowledgment, Carolina continued. "However, I have confidence that wherever I was lost was in Jiang Li's territory. He treated me coldly, I think he thought I was some sort of invader. He knew I was other instantly, but he didn't know what other, that I am certain. He became less hostile when I explained that I was a lost traveler."

"Do you remember any defining landmarks when you met the dragon?" Sabin probed a bit more. "Or a specific direction?"

Carolina tapped her nails against the curled arm rest, staring at the ceiling in thought. "One landmark that stuck with me were some hanging coffins right above a whirlpool and the river never was out of my sight." The queen shrugged. "That is all I know about a dragon though… Oh!" She clapped her hands suddenly, sitting up straighter. "I also met another dragon in Japan roughly fifty years ago." She waved her hand dismissively. "Give or take a few decades. He was quite flashy, and bold with his bright red hair and spiky clothing. He went by the name Ryujin, and he was very knowledgeable in which street food vendors served the best foods. However, I'm afraid that is all the information I have for you on him. He was gone too fast before I could speak more than a sentence to him."

"There is another dragon, in Japan you say?" The Grand High cupped her face, her fingers framing her face.

"Yes, I met him in Osaka." She nodded, folding her hands daintily in her lap.

Cliona tapped her fingers together thoughtfully. "Mm," Her thoughtful sound penetrated the air, "Aren't shifters supposed to know where other shifters reside?"

The Queen's face became a condescending sneer. "Child, dragons and shifters are not the same species. Think of shifters like dogs, loyal and pack orientated, and dragons like snakes, aloof and sneaky. Simply because I am a shifter does not mean I have the exact location of a dragon. Do you have the exact location of every cult leader?"

Cliona's face was neutral, but there was slight offense, a pungent flavor that splashed across Tullia's tongue.

There was a silence, an absorption and quick mending of facades.

"Very well," The Grand High said briskly, "So, there is a dragon in China, somewhere, and one in Osaka, Japan." She tilted her head, staring at the Queen of Biringan with pondering eyes. The queen stared right back, unruffled by Cliona's strong gaze. Carolina even gave a small smile. Tullia tasted respect at Biringan's queen, also slight frustration.

"Well, their location could have changed since I went. If you are going to hunt down a dragon for information, I would try to find Jiang Li first. He is older. He may be snotty, but he would undoubtedly know the next step for you to take for your cause." Carolina shrugged, her poofy shoulders stiffly following the motion. "Though he'd be the most difficult to deal with."

"Aren't all people with power a pain to deal with?" The Grand High gave a soft laugh, a self-mocking laugh, though Tullia had to swallow against the slightly acidic taste. "We thank you for your time, your highness." She said respectfully and bowed her head, before smiling a sharp grin. "Your information was most valuable."

The queen's small smile broadened. "Is that all you wish to ask me?"

A split second of silence before Tullia asked enthusiastically, "Can I have the recipe for your spicy beef please?"

The queen blinked, before her head tilted back, and a tinkling laugh filled the room. She shook her head, clapping her hands together. "Ah, such boldness is refreshing." Her Tagalog sounded more like a song from her lips.

Tullia smiled, enjoying the sweet taste of good humor. "I had to try."

Carolina's smile gentled, a sweet, fizzy emotion swathed her mouth.

"Feel free to linger in the city for as long as you like." The queen then rose and smiled at everyone. "Lunch will be served at three." She casted a sly look to Tullia. "You can ask me again for the recipe."

* * *

"Kind of anticlimactic, the whole meeting. I mean, she accidentally ran into two different dragons in China and Japan? How does that even happen?" The Grand High blew a raspberry. "Incidental meetings or whatever, at least we have some direction in which to go and a backup plan if necessary. So, it wasn't a total waste of time or energy to come here." The Grand High was floating, her silver sandals teasing the floor with how close they were yet how they remained out of reach. They all stood outside the throne room; a low hum of excitement coursed through Tullia. She wanted to do a cartwheel down the hall.

"So…" She began, "we have to go to China now?" Tullia asked, pricks of excitement raced up her spine.

"No," Cliona shook her head, golden braids softly swishing around a gorgeous black and white face, popping her excited bubbles. "We need to go back to Vegas. China is a big country and I'm not about to dive into that mess without a specific location on this dragon. I'm not roughing it again." She flicked her head in a way that announced her status as part of the upper class. "That's too insane."

"Not that you actually roughed anything." Sabin rumbled from beside Tullia, sounding similar to a disgruntled sibling. The Grand High flipped him off. "I do agree that we need to narrow down our focus and take a moment to regroup in Vegas." Sabin continued, not reacting to the vulgar action.

"Would you look at that, meat-head is actually saying something intelligent for once." Cliona's sharp barb seemed to roll over Sabin without a single scratch. His golden eyes cut a look to the Grand High.

"Try not to tire yourself out with all the floating you've been doing."

Cliona sniffed, flipping Sabin off again. "I'm going to go away from you." She looked at Tullia and wiggled her fingers. "We leave tomorrow at nine. But, I'll see you, petal, at three for lunch." She glared at Sabin. "Go trip and fall out a window, you grunt."

She clicked her nails together and winked out, leaving only a very faint blue tint of smoke behind. Tullia and Sabin were alone together for the first time since the first day of the wake, which was four days ago.

She peaked up at him, feeling stupidly shy. Sabin wasn't looking at her, he was looking out the window that poured bright sunshine into the hallway. He tasted of nothing, which was an odd sensation for Tullia, someone always felt something. Even boredom had a flavor. It was cardboard. Disinterested was flat soda. And tranquil was cucumbers.

"So, what are your plans until chow time?" She asked him, admiring his dark profile. Even though he was being bathed in bright, loving sunlight, he remained shadowed. He was a pocket of dusk that the sun seemed to never touch, not because it didn't want to but because it simply couldn't.

Sabin's bright gilded eyes shifted to focus on her, causing Tullia to quiver with expectation.

That was probably my new BFF-itis.

She got the impression of a smile. "I'm going to take a nap before we eat."

Tullia blinked at the unexpected answer. "Huh. So, berserkers take naps?"

Another smile impression, though this time it was a sarcastic one. "Not usually, but diplomatic interactions take a heavy toll on Vikings. We require rest after non-physically violent events." His tone was deadpan, Tullia almost burst out laughing. She managed to refrain by the thinnest of breaths. "Also," Sabin continued, his tone was dry, "when you get older, you realize that sleep is not an enemy."

Tullia raised an eyebrow at him, "Wow. You managed to sound not only extremely old, but also kind of lame, Sabin." She shook her head in mock disappointment, placing a hand over her heart in mourning of his not dead coolness.

Sabin tilted his head to the side. "I apologize for your clouded judgment." He reached out and patted her shoulder very gently. "I'll see you at three for lunch."

Sabin then lumbered off, his big form nearly consuming the slightly narrowed hallway. The sunlight avoided his broad shoulders as he passed by the windows, longingly reaching towards him, before pulling back sharply. She felt a warmth blossom in her shoulder as she shook her head, amused despite the lack of humor in his gate. Tullia turned to go to her own room.

Truth be told, exhaustion weighed heavily upon her. The trek, the whole being lost episode, the fighting, the mourning, the listening, the talking, the relief, the food, the new plan…. It was all so taxing for a girl who's only real adventure was leaving her parents' home at eighteen and going to McDonalds at three am for some fries even though she had already brushed her teeth.

Her limbs felt heavy, and her upper body had a hard time staying upright and her feet throbbed. However, despite her physical fatigue, her mind was active with thoughts. Jumping from idea to idea, never settling on a particular thought and spasmodically flashing with faces and places that she had seen time and time again. A feeling, a soulful feeling rose within her at the rightness, at the almost preordained direction that they seemed to be going in.

She paused in the hallway, her excitement surging through her, dulling the fatigue momentarily to allow her to let out a soft squeal of excitement while curling into herself. After jumping up and down exactly twice before stopping because too much cardio was happening, she continued down the hallway as if nothing odd occurred.

Her lips twitched.

They were going to be dragon hunters next! She giggled, reaching out she dragged her fingers across the wall. The cool smooth texture caused her fingertips to easily glide—

—over the smooth stone surface of one of the many jutting stones dotting the hidden landscape. It was beautiful for a giant gaping hole in the mountain. It was easily seen from the sky, but not from the ground. Which is perfect, no human could fly, and he doubted they'd scale the mountain to marvel at a hole. They were rather limited creatures, in intelligence and physical abilities.

If he hadn't flown so high and traveled so far due to his deep offense, Jiang Li wouldn't have known of this interesting crater's existence. He looked around, pleased with the depth in which the hole had managed, there was plenty of room for him to fly around if he pleased. Lots of room for him to comfortably sprawl out if he so desired. There were even little bushes in the crater, small and spindly trying to hide from the intense daylight that poured in. Some little bushes even managed to grow on the side of the craggy walls. Thick grassy spots wildly speckled crevasses and stood stiffly in patches on the rather littered floor. The thick grass hosted small weedy flowers whose thin stems seemed to bend slightly with the weight of the fat petals. A thin fog hung in the air, creating a frosty moisture. The ground was firm beneath his human feet.

Though open and simple in its limited landscape of rocks and weeds, Jiang Li was impressed that he had managed to find the little spot vacant. Caves were often popular with pests and shrines were not his style. Jiang Li examined the droopy flower with delight. Even if this area was taken, he'd have killed them easily. What he wanted, he received. He was the Great River Dragon, he wanted for nothing for he received all.

Walking along the perimeter of the hole, Jiang Li studied the environment critically, noticing the dips and dives in the floor. He supposed in order to refine the landscape he could fix the defects with some mud, though tedious he supposed he could exert the effort if it were to be his. As he walked to the center of the crater, he heard low rumbling. Jiang Li paused in his motion, listening. A low rumble again accompanied by the ground underneath his human feet quivered. He frowned, noticing the thin spider webbed cracks that began to rapidly spread. He lifted one foot up, leaning down closer to inspect the cracks. Were there a horde of pests' underneath?

The ground suddenly crumbled in and Jiang Li was then falling with giant pieces of once rock flooring. A roar of rage left him, how dare the ground abandon its duty in supporting him! He flung out his arms, claws extended to grip the rocky sides to stop his rapid descent, but his claws met only air. Snarling, Jiang Li braced himself for impact, his feet hitting the ground mere moments later with a loud thud and a cloud of dust blooming upward.

The force of the drop, the unexpectedness and the hardness of the ground jarred Jiang Li, his legs protested but he dismissed their nonsense. He was the Great River Dragon; he did not feel discomfort or pain unless he willed it.

Brushing his hair out of his face, Jiang Li surveyed his new environment. It was dark, the landscape was rocky and rough. He looked up, squinting against the sun that crawled in through the hole. Pieces of the ground from above were concaving in and falling down to the second layer.

Jiang Li moved deeper by a few steps into the space, to avoid the falling debris and it was surprisingly warm... and smelled rather unpleasant. Wrinkling his nose, Jiang Li ignored the smell, humans often smelled worse, and they were oftentimes unpleasant for his eyes to view as well.

He took in the entire landscape with a quick sweep of his eyes. It was filled with rumble, dirt, dust and rocks. He tucked his hands in his robes, then nodded.

Rocks were not the worst landscape. Boring, but not the worst. The upper-level landscape was better, but this may prove to be an acceptable area as well.

It wasn't his ideal dwelling area, but it was remote enough to where humans could not wander and deep enough to provide sufficient shelter. With a little work, he could make it a dwelling for a Great River Dragon. Nothing good mud and a few plants can't fix.

He looked up and through the hole. Thoughts crept in. Unpleasant thoughts. He didn't want anyone else to know about his new home, because no one would be welcomed in his domicile. Neither human nor creature. As far as everyone knew, he died or was merely a myth. As it was, the crater was not hidden, it was on display from above.

He shuddered to think of that stupid Japanese dragon discovering his abode. He'd never leave him alone and likely live with him.

And humans...Humans disappointed him and his presence seemed to be disregarded entirely. The new generation lost his protection when they lost respect for him, believing a mere human could ever possibly be a descendant of a dragon.

Jiang Li snorted, growling at the human's daring audacity to even conquer the notion that they could possibly be cut from the same cloth as he was.

Degenerates.

He inhaled deeply, calming his swell of anger, then coughed as the faint, but strong smell of rot and gas choked him. He cursed that pompous Yellow Emperor and his family and his descendants and his subjects and his cattle and his grass and his crops and his rocks and his dirt.

The truth is that everyone worshiped that Yellow Emperor who was supposedly immortalized into a dragon. Which was false, a human could not become a dragon. It was a ridiculous notion. It was an offensive notion that was popularized and held with reverence and understood as a fact among humans.

This was why he would shun humans entirely. If humans didn't taste abominable, he would have devoured the royal family in an instant. As it was, they were far too crunchy and unsatisfying to munch on.

Shaking off the unpleasant thoughts, he dipped into the magic within him, feeling the painful euphoria rush up to greet his command eagerly.

Humans didn't have magic. They could not be descendants of great dragons, such as him. They were lowly creatures, designed as insects and given half a wit.

He raised both of his arms and felt himself grow as he shed his puny human form. His limbs flourished, his body stretched, and his soul sighed with the sharp joy at being uninhibited. Being confined to a tiny human appearance for multiple hours was suffocating. Stretching out briefly, he rose within the air and flew to the opening of the giant crater bursting into the sky, ridding himself of the smell and embracing the icy winds that caressed his scales. He circled his crater, eyeing the opening critically. He liked the way mountains came up high around the depression, like a defense, like a barrier.

First, he had to fill his crater. He was a Great River Dragon, and there was no water anywhere. It was a defect that was unacceptable and needed immediate rectification. Jiang Li drew upon his magic, painful pleasure trickled through his veins, boiling them. He forced his magic to take upon the permanent form of water, wrestling with the intangible into a tangible form. He reared his head back, then, feeling the gurgling rush come up his throat, he opened his mouth as pure water blasted out. He applied the water over the opening, spreading it and forcing it to hold itself steady, creating a thin layer right at the top of the opening. He nurtured the water until it began thickening and growing to *cover the entire hole. Jiang Li flew higher up in the sky, to evaluate his work. He frowned; his layer of water was completely transparent.*

There was no privacy at all and quite visible to everything. Even a human could see through it. If a human managed to stumble its clumsy, flatfooted way up the mountain.

Huffing, Jiang Li inhaled deeply through his nose and forced his magic to rapidly build within him. He gathered magic tightly to him, so tightly it was just shy of the point of agony before releasing it through his mouth in the form of a thick blast of water. He concentrated his water blast in the center and caused a ripple to occur in the thin sheet of liquid, though it did not break through. A violent tremor occurred. The water bubbled up and clawed its way outward. His water grew, greedily seeking more space and bullying the earth into submission creating taller mountains around his perfect water.

The sky became sleepily painted in pastels before seeping into a deep black. He continued to feed his water, watching it grow deeper, grow wider, and grow more dominating over the area. This was why water ruled supreme, land was weak to water and powerless to halt water's progression. Once the sky lightened and light rays of the morning sun hit Jiang Li, he finally stopped. His limbs quivered as he stretched his jaw, until a relieving crack occurred, he swiveled up and ascended higher into the air to survey his work. His tail swished with pleasure as icy winds petted him with reverence at a job well done. What was once a giant gaping hole in the mountain, surrounded by bare rocks was now a large body of water that was flanked by gentle mountains and spare greenery. His water sparkled under the daylight's rays, looking clear and unfathomable and the most attractive feature of the whole mountains.

Which was only natural since he was a craftsman.

Yawning, Jiang Li spun once in the air, before diving straight in the center of the water, reveling in the cold that slicked his scales. He burst through the opening to his new treasure lair, surely with two spaces he'd have enough room for all of his glorious items. Small water droplets fell from his scales onto his earth floor, and he delighted in it. The light that tried to penetrate his water's density took on patchy, distorted effect, deepening the interior of the crater and casting a softer, subdued glow.

He looked up at his water skylight and, for extra measure, he placed a tinted layer of water over the opening, so anything inspecting the bottom of his glorious lake would only see earth, but he'd see them.

Yawning widely again, Jiang Li stretched his body out before laying down and curling up under a particularly strong ray of sunlight that was basking a flat rock. Which would be his favorite spot. He eyed the little flower tucked tightly against it and a thin patch of grass with delight.

He'd move all his treasures later; they would be safe for the time being.

*Right now, his extensive use of magic had fatigued him. He strode to the flat rock, made himself comfortable by stomping in a circle then rested his head on his claws, his nose was close to the little weedy flower. It smelled fragrant. He had much to do from restorations to relocating his beloved trinkets... **but I just need five minutes,** he thought as darkness gradually overtook his vision.*

He'd never be bothered again. He'd never need to feel anything destructive again.

A hardwood floor suddenly filled her vision. Tullia was on one knee, hunched over in a pose of one of those sniper green army men toys that came in a giant bucket. She shifted slightly, her body stiff and very sore. A sudden sharp pain that twisted her muscle in an unnatural way caused Tullia to gasp. A charley horse occurred in her right calf and she may have pulled her back out. Pressing her lips together to prevent a shout of profanity she laid down on the hard, cold floor. She rolled onto her back and gripped her seizing calf with both hands, gritting her teeth to ward off crying out. She didn't know how long she was in the vision, it felt extremely brief, but apparently it was long enough to cause her calf to seize up.

The hardwood floor was murder on her back and the hot throbbing pain seemed to dominate her entire body. A few minutes later, the cramp loosened up enough to only be a dull throb instead of sharp twisted one. Tullia got to her feet shakily, rubbing her back, huffing a little as she roughly smoothed out her sunflower dress, her body now sore and stiff.

Slightly limping and not so slightly stomping down the hall, she made her way to her room with none of her previous excitement. It was always nice to be reminded of why she was on this fantastical adventure. Cause the lost magic was really screwing up her life in a not so positive way and giving her freakin' muscle cramps.

Continuing to her room her fatigue doubled as the last tendrils of excitement died a hard death within her. Turning down the hallway where her room was, Tullia saw Chito leaning against the wall next to her door. She smiled at him, putting an effort into not looking like she wanted to hack up a side wall with an ax.

"What's up, go-go boy?" She greeted him with a cheeky grin.

"Just checking the doorknob, making sure it's not crushed by your burly man-hands." Chito's reply was far too sassy for what she just went through.

Tullia let out an exaggerated, annoyed huff. "As you can see it's not, because I have normal hands that are generally found on females."

Chito made a show of inspecting the perfectly round, glossy brass doorknob. "Looks a little dented."

Tullia glared. "Seriously, I'm going to kick you down a flight of stairs."

"Might have better results if you used your burly hands to push me instead." Chito's smile was blade sharp. "They're stronger."

Tullia clapped her hands together and looked towards the ceiling. "If I wasn't a guest in your home I'd probably insult your mother. And deck you."

Chito laughed as he pushed off the wall, his puffy pirate shirt seemed to exaggerate the bounce of his movement. "Actually, besides the doorknob, I was just wondering… what are you going to do when… you leave… Biringan?" The tone of his voice was casual, but a strong taste of longing, dry and slightly salty, coated her mouth.

Tullia eyed Chito with slight heat, then exhaled her irritation out. "Well," She said, super conscious of how she gripped the doorknob and turned it, opening the door to her borrowed room. "We've discussed it a bit, but our first order of business is we have to go back to Las Vegas, to the Grand High's headquarters." Tullia began to tick off the tasks to be done once home via her fingers. "We need to research where Qu Yuan's home is," One finger, "then the surrounding areas of his hometown," second finger, "what major river is by his hometown," three fingers, "and then possible locations of where the dragon could be outside of one and two." She waved Chito in her room, untying her hair that was put in a painfully tight, but pretty, ponytail. She ran her fingers through her hair, feeling immediate relief from the sharp tension. Though her hair was now crinkled in an odd fashion.

Oh well, comfort over style.

"Well, you might want to look in Zigui County, China first. Qu Yuan's original hometown sank a while ago. So, it got relocated to Zigui County." Tullia turned to raise her eyebrow at Chito, who then gave a small, sassy one shoulder shrug. "When I like something, I wanna know about all of it."

Tullia laughed, placing her hair tie on the dresser. "Zigui County, huh?" She turned and sat on the edge of her bed. Her body wanted to melt into the softness of the mattress. "I'll tell the Grand High and then she can have her underlings do some research." Tullia knew for a fact Cliona would not do the research personally, she'd probably get a full body massage and a spa treatment.

Maybe she'd take Tullia, maybe Tullia would just invite herself and use puppy dog eyes.

Chito giggled, he looked around her room before sitting on the small bamboo bench.

"You should also bring a gift to the dragon, when you find him that is. Dragons are vain, at least according to you know, mythological tales." Chito patted his knees excitedly. "Perhaps, since he likes Qu Yuan, you should bring him a book of ancient Chinese poems. Or, a small decorative dragon boat. Did you know that there is a festival to commemorate Qu Yuan? You see—"

Tullia listened to Chito chatter about Qu Yuan and potential gifts that would earn favor with the dragon. Chito's adorable chattering caused his pretty face to light up and his entire demeanor became jittery. After a while, Chito's cute chattering died down, but his obvious excitement and almost tangible yearning caused an idea to pop into Tullia's head.

"You should come with us." Tullia said spontaneously into the brief silence, she had sprawled out on the bed, her face towards Chito. Her upper body's muscles went on strike after thirty seconds of sitting on the bed, so laying down was the only option.

Chito's gorgeous eyes widened and he leaned back in surprise. "Me?" He put a hand on his chest, as if utterly surprised.

Tullia gave a slow blink, his astonishment was bubbly and tart. "Yeah, you'd probably soften the dragon up better than we ever could with your common interest in Qu Yuan's poems."

Chito's eyes were still wide, he didn't blink at all as he stared at her. Tullia continued, a little unnerved by his whole no blinking thin., "Plus, you'll get to explore the world, or at least parts of the world. Basically, wherever we need to go to get rid of this lost magic within me, you'd go too." She shrugged her shoulders against the mattress she was laying on, trying to be nonchalant. "It'll be fun. You know. Maybe. A little."

"I—I can't leave Biringan." There was a slight panic in his tone. He stood up abruptly, the bench scraping across the wooden floor in his hast.

Tullia looked up at Chito. "Why not? I thought you wanted to travel?"

He emitted a delicate snort. "Why? Why?" He delicately pressed his fingers on his temples, looking down at the floor. "I am the prince of Biringan City." He gave the floor a serious look. "The city just went through a traumatic event, the royal family, which also includes me, needs to be present to help rebuild the city and the safety for our people." His tone became higher and his speech picked up. "Not to mention the royal family needs to rebuild the people's confidence; this event took a major foundation away from everyone, no one feels safe and that falls on our shoulders." He stiffened, and he tapped his shoulders. "That burden falls upon the royal family's shoulders. No citizen should feel unsafe in

Biringan." His breathing was slightly ragged when he finished and Tullia slightly regretted asking him.

He still did not look at Tullia. His eyes were trained on the glossy floor, as if the floor threatened to eat his feet and he was vehemently arguing why the floor shouldn't.

She felt as though she caused him undue stress. He was putting off his dream for the good of his city. She should respect that.

Aiming for a lighthearted air, Tullia smiled. "I'm sorry, Chito. I was ignorant about your duties and insensitive with my offer. You have a very important role in the city, and of course, you need to stay here to help. I get that."

A bitter, salty flavor coated her tongue, chased by heat then a sour tartness. She swallowed against the conflicting flavors and furrowed her brows in confusion. She didn't understand what he was feeling. But she knew that he was upset to say the least.

Chito inhaled deeply, finally looking up at her and then smiled. It was forced and looked awful on his otherwise uniquely beautiful face. "No, I got overly excited." He strode towards the door, his gate was stiff and awkward. "You look tired, get some rest." He opened the door swiftly and left, closing it softly behind him.

Tullia stared at the door for a moment and sighed.

The door reopened suddenly, startling Tullia. Chito popped his head back in. "Just a reminder, lunch is at three and don't squeeze the door handles too hard. I can feel your finger imprints in it." He ducked out before Tullia could respond.

Tullia glared at the door, then dragged her right hand up to look at her plain, regular sized and definitely more on the feminine side hand. She opened and closed her hand before huffing in irritation.

The mattress was really soft.

Stupid go-go boy making fun of her hands. She'd get him. After a nap. A nap that she wouldn't tell Sabin about, because Tullia still viewed naps as the enemy.

* * *

Chito was on autopilot.

He managed to make his way to his room, change his clothes into something comfy, turn on vibe music, and lay on his bed all without a conscious thought. He stared up at his puffed ceiling that mimicked the night sky. Biringan was so bright, the stars stayed hidden, so he had no real stars to look at, only fake ones. He sighed, folding his hands over his solar plexus; inhaling deeply he began to practice mindful meditation.

Inhaling, he tensed all his muscles, winding them tight.

Exhaling, he slowly allowed the tension to leak from his body.

Repeat. Repeat. Repeat.

His thoughts drifted over everything that had transpired over the last four days. First, a demon managed to get in and make history in Biringan. Then a crazy, dirty white girl sneaked into the Mabuhay building and dragged him into the fight with the tikbalang. After he totally helped kick ass, they held a wake for the people that were killed in the attack. Chito's heart throbbed painfully, causing him to flinch. The guilt he experienced on his soul when he found out who had died and the relief he felt when it wasn't any of his family members almost made him feel sick.

His mind seemed to circulate between being dragged to where the tikbalang was and him purposefully defying his lola's command and not staying put. He even defied one of her laws which she didn't know about (and she will never know about because he wouldn't ever tell her) and did a hybrid shift.

He was a bird with human hands.

A big bird, with human hands.

He remembered the feeling he had when he was ascending into the air. His heart was racing, his blood seemed to pound through his veins and a piece of his soul fluttered free before it settled firmly within him. He was terrified in that moment, the warning his lola had given him echoed loudly as he struggled up in the air with the heavy jug.

Unnatural concoctions leave the mind in a state of ruin and the body a horrid mess of devastation. Don't try to make something that is not so in the world.

Though anxiety was battering his senses at the time his heart had never pulsed so fast nor had he ever been more aware of every single cell within his body. He was acutely sensitive to each sensation from the slight breeze to the dim lights to his own sweat glands working overtime.

He had never felt that before. He had never been more connected to himself than he was in that single moment.

Chito thought back to what Tullia said during the heat of battle, when he had faltered with fear and confusion.

Who is Chito?

It was really a stupid question, naturally he knew it. He was Chito, the prince of Biringan.

Who is Chito?

He shifted his eyes to look at his map that was plastered on one side of his wall. He had put up that map when he was fifteen, multiple pins sticking out from where he wanted to go in the future. He had promised himself he was going to travel the world as soon as he could.

A twinge. He frowned. Tullia had invited him to join her traveling party, but he had panicked, and he said… he said… no.

He turned down the opportunity to go explore the world.

He had told her that as the prince of Biringan, he couldn't leave because the city was in the midst of a tragedy, which was a partial lie. He could technically leave the city, if he wanted to. He was the lowest ranking prince in the Mabuhay clan, he didn't hold a prestigious position, nor did he really do much in terms of being a critical figurehead for the people of Biringan. He merely had a title and the recognition as a royal family member. Nothing else.

His lola, she was a critical figurehead, even his mother and father. Chito was… not.

He sat up abruptly, his bare feet hung off the bed, his mind becoming shy at the thought of leaving.

He wanted to leave, the world was a tantalizing promise that held secrets and wonders best left to witness personally… individually… fear suddenly crept into his mind heavily laced with doubt.

You've never left home; how will you survive?

You'll be eaten alive within seconds upon stepping out of Biringan….

Travel the world when you're too scared to travel in some parts of your own home at night?

Lola won't be there, mom won't be there, you'll be truly all alone and then you'll die.

HAHAHA.

He physically shrunk away from the negative thoughts. He focused on his feet that hung a few inches from the floor.

In the end, it is up to us to decide who we want to be and only we can change who we are. Tullia's voice broke through the thick fog of depression that began to settle around him.

You decide who you want to be, you decide what is best for you, you decide what you want to do.

He nodded slowly at the words, the negativity thinning. He *wanted* to travel. He *wanted* to explore. He *wanted* to go on an adventure.

It felt that he was born to do that.

You decide, Chito.

He wanted to be a risk taker. An adventurer. Be an Indiana Jones minus the actual archaeology stuff, because he found that part sort of boring. And a lot less danger in his travels too. And he wasn't going to wear a hat or carry a whip.

Chito snorted at the lame thought, Tullia's lame lines might have rubbed off on him. She'd be leaving soon, with the witch and the really tall and really buff man. His heart sank at the thought, before his mind began to churn.

When they left, the city would go under renovation. Knowing his grandmother, she'd use it as an opportunity to completely revamp the city, to keep people busy and not grieving. And Chito would-

He would…

Still be in Biringan wanting to leave.

Lola probably would give him a task, such as overseeing some new construction. Or maybe she'd have him assist in planting more flowers in the city. Both tasks could easily be given to someone else, he wasn't truly needed. Again, he wasn't critical in the city.

He…

Everyone has that ability.

Chito stood up slowly from his bed, his gaze still focused on his feet, his heart in his throat, his mind in suspense.

So, what are you going to do right now Chito?

He…was going to go. A surge of rightness settled his racing mind and steadied his heart.

He was going to go with Tullia and the buff guy and the floating witch. A smile curled his lips. He was going to help them find the dragon and then he was going to help them talk to the dragon and then he was going to travel with them to somewhere new; to many new places.

His heart began to race again, this time with anticipation, causing his blood to dance within his veins, urging him into action. Chito's happy mind focused on a single thought.

Find his lola and tell her his plan and hopefully she was in a good mood to give her blessing.

His body flung into motion, he raced from his room and sprinted to his lola's chambers. Memories of growing up seemed to gently float by…

Of him running down the same hallways at various ages, laughing, crying, singing, stressed, late, dancing, going to hide, going to the night garden, going to the kitchen.

Chito frowned slightly, he ran down the halls a lot. He skidded slightly as he made a sharp right turn. His lola's room was at the end of a hall with two giant pale oak doors. Chito didn't slow his pace as he approached, instead he sped up.

"Lola!" Chito called, barreling through her bedroom doors. They slammed open and bounced off the walls behind him piercingly. Chito paid very little attention to them, panting in exhilarated exertion. "Lola! I have to talk to you!"

A heavy, sharp sigh. "You better not have damaged my doors or walls." Chito turned to see his grandmother, freshly cleaned and wrapped in a fluffy robe with her arms crossed. Her wet hair slicked back from a young face that hid the weight of age beneath the smooth surface. She raised a black eyebrow. "Did I not teach you manners?" She threw her hands up in the air. "Apparently no one has manners in this family, no one knows how to knock. This room is not a common area for all to come and go as they please."

"Lola," Chito finally caught his breath from the sprint, "I'm sorry."

She hummed slightly. "What was so important you nearly broke my doors off?"

Under his lola's heavy eyes, he froze, feeling two inches small. He swallowed, nervous in front of the one person whose approval meant everything to him.

You decide who you want to be, you decide what is best for you, you decide what you want to do.

Squaring his shoulders, he faced his lola with as much confidence as he could muster. He had decided, and he was going to do it.

Not even his lola would stop him. He decided he was going to go, so he was going to go.

He was also going to throw up after he was done, his stomach was heavy with knots at his intentional defiance.

"Lola, I have something I need to tell you."

* * *

The sunlight was cleansing as it was blinding. It was sticky hot outside, Tullia's sweat glands were over dramatic for the first five minutes in nature and now she was a slicked creature of discomfort and disgust. Sabin, Cliona and Tullia had just passed through the main gate entrance to Biringan City, they needed to leave the roaming portal in order for the Grand High to signal the Pearl of the Orient clan to come and pick them all up. However, they'd have to hike a bit, which really, really, *really* sucked. Apparently, Mary, the witch living in Biringan refused to assist Cliona in anything travel related, claiming it would put the citizens at risk to create a soft opening.

Cliona held her hands up. "Hold up, I need to do something real fast."

Tullia watched as the Grand High closed her night spread eyes and began to emit a thick fog of blue smoke. She turned upside down and held her hand out to the earth. A concentrated blast of blue neon smoke shot into the ground. To Tullia, Cliona seemed to be feeding the earth beneath her with the thick fog. A few minutes passed, the heat baking Tullia a little more before she finally asked. "What is she doing?"

Sabin was watching her with jaded, gold eyes. "I believe she's doing her magical signature or whatnot on Biringan."

Tullia pursed her lips before tilting her head to look at the Grand High. Even upside down and her legs crossed in the air, she was picturesque.

A few more minutes floated by, Tullia turned to Sabin. "Hey, Sabin, look at my hands." She stuck out her hands to him, palms down. "What do you think of my hands?"

Sabin's honey deep eyes studied her outstretched hands for a few seconds, before he looked back at her. "They look like hands."

Tullia narrowed her eyes. "Just hands?"

Sabin shrugged. "They look like hands." He repeated.

Tullia wiggled her fingers. "Yeah, but what kind of hands?"

Tullia got the distinct impression of confusion from Sabin. "Average hands?"

She jerked her hands to her sides, irritated. So, it wasn't obvious that her hands looked like girl hands? That's literally all he needed to say to take away the low key annoyance of Chito's jabs.

"Okay." She said, "Do I have burly looking hands?" She decided to be blunt with his dense berserker brain.

Sabin paused, and there was a bubbly sensation along her tongue. "Burly hands?"

"Yeah. Burly man hands. Are they?" Tullia waited. Sabin shook his head, amused, then he fell silent.

She stomped her foot in frustration. "Sabin! The hell, don't leave me waiting!"

Sabin blink in surprise. "What?"

Tullia threw her hands up in the air – the nerve — before holding out her hands towards him again. "My hands! Are they burly man hands? Or are they normal girl hands? Answer!"

Sabin suddenly burst into laughter. It was a deep rolling laugh, that rumbled wildness and energized the space around them. It even had

Tullia's heart thumping a bit faster.

He should laugh way more, she thought.

"Well?" She prompted sharply once he was done with his little sense of humor and her heart stopped tripping in her chest from the utter freedom of the sound.

Sabin shook his head. "Your hands fit you." He took one and rubbed his gloved thumb over her knuckles twice.

Tullia inhaled at his unexpected touch, but glared fiercely at him. "That doesn't answer a damn thing. I need to know this in layman's terms."

Before Sabin could answer Cliona exclaimed, "Done!" Tullia looked over to see Cliona flip right side up, dusting her hands and smiling a perfect happy smile.

"'Bout time." Sabin grumbled, dropping Tullia's hand.

Tullia eyed him evilly, he never answered her. The jerk. If he thought he could get out of answering her, he had another thing coming. This was not over and she could get quite annoying if she really wanted too.

Cliona waved him away. "Now, I can come back here whenever I need or want to." Her gorgeous smile was tinted with a mischievous gleam.

"Naturally, you are all welcomed back." Everyone snapped their heads to see Carolina and Chito standing at the grand decorative entrance of Biringan. The queen was looking at Cliona with an eloquent look, while Chito was smiling happily at them with a palatable excitement in his stance.

"Your highness," The Grand High greeted formally, her eyes cool and fathomless.

"I've come to see you all off." She said softly, then her expression turned aristocratic. "And to ask a favor."

Chito beamed and gushed out. "I'm coming with you guys to go find the dragon!"

Cliona drew back and raised her eyebrow. "Say what now?"

Carolina looked at Chito and then Tullia, her smile was strained but there was a firmness in the curve, an acceptance in her face. "Yes. My grandchild will be in your care, please look out for him."

Sabin looked at Chito, he didn't say anything, but she could taste his disapproval, smokey and tart. "This venture does not guarantee safety. We cannot promise you a safe voyage, prince."

Chito's exuberance dimmed a little, but he squared his shoulders. "I can handle this trek, I helped you take down the tikbalang."

Sabin cocked his head to the right and then shook his head. "Every battle there is a pairing of sorrow. And many battles do not end in victory. Did you forget the lives lost in Biringan from the tikbalang?"

Chito looked stricken by Sabin's words, as if he didn't consider that fact.

Sabin's eyes narrowed. "I'm against this. He's far too green."

Chito's dark eyes held a sharp glint. "Though I have never set foot out of Biringan City I am well educated, and I can shapeshift into anything." He held his pretty, manicured hands up. "I'm an asset to your team."

Tullia fought a smile while Sabin shook his head, the Grand High merely looked disinterested in the whole situation. As if she wouldn't even consider Chito's presence.

"Mmm," She made a distracted sound, looking over the lushness of the jungle. "I don't believe his presence will be a hindrance. However," she turned and gave a sinister grin at Chito, "travel expenses and food are not provided. Neither is your safety. Can you deal, prince?"

Carolina stepped forward, her queenly aura powerful and dominant. "Naturally, as the prince of Biringan City he has funds to allow him comfort on your exposition with enough to share." She gave Cliona a very direct look, "And to maintain good standing with Biringan and the *entire*," a heavy emphasis, "shifter community, which stretches far and wide, an extension of protection to my precious grandchild would not go unnoticed."

Cliona tasted of vinegar, a small dash of heat and a velvety decadence of a begrudging respect. She gave a shallow head nod in understanding. Carolina smiled demurely at odds with her enormous energy. "As one queen to another, I thank you in advance for looking out for Chito. In return, as a sign of good faith, I will permit your magical signature on my land within the portal." She tilted her head slightly to the side, her eyes were steely blades, almost daring the Grand High to disregard her words.

The Grand High eyed Carolina with a new-found perception, then sighed. "Of course, your highness." Cliona seemed to straighten in her floating position as she latched her dark abyss eyes onto Chito. He seemed to quiver, wanting to wilt under her penetrating gaze. However, he managed to keep eye contact with her. Cliona grinned savagely, "Make sure you keep up, okay Cheeto puff?"

Sabin shook his head again, clearly, he wasn't too fond of the new group member, but he reached out to pat Chito on the back. Chito seemed to lurch forward under the force of Sabin's too rough pat.

"Don't falter." He said simply in a gravelly voice.

Chito blushed hard, sneaking quick glances at Sabin and Cliona. Tullia bumped her hip against his and smiled. "Welcome to the traveling gang."

Chito smiled widely, excitement bubbling from his eyes. "Thanks. I'll be useful."

Tullia became infected with his excitement and found herself grinning widely. Chito slung a bag over his shoulder, "Now, how is the rest of my stuff going to be transported?"

It took her a moment, then Tullia blinked. "What?"

Chito gave her an innocently confused face. "Yes, the rest of my luggage." He then motioned by the entrance of Biringan to three whole sets of luggage in an array of colors. "I can't live in a bag for who knows how long." Tullia mouthed an 'oh' as she took in the quantity of what Chito thought he was going to bring. She shot a glance to Sabin, his mask covered face didn't reveal anything, but she tasted his exasperation, a flat taste with pepper, that gushed over her palate.

"I don't think that's gonna work." Tullia murmured, looking back at Chito.

He drew back, affronted, "Everything I packed was only strictly necessary. I can't live without anything I packed." His face, beautiful and smooth, was dead serious.

Tullia raised an eyebrow, she seriously doubted he packed only necessities.

"Chito," Carolina's soothing voice called out. "I did warn you that you brought too much excess."

"*Lola!*" Chito whined. "I need all of them—"

"No." Sabin interjected with a hard voice. "What you have in that bag." He pointed to Chito's shoulder bag that was strapped across his chest, "will be good enough."

A look of pure horror flashed across Chito's face. "How am I supposed to maintain basic hygiene if I don't have at least soap, shampoo, lotion, a manicure kit, lip balm, and at least seven different outfits with matching shoes?"

Sabin crossed his arms. "You only need one set of clothes."

Chito's face creased harder with aghast. "One outfit? One? That is *not* possible…" He shoved his hand in his long, long hair, holding onto his head.

The Grand High looked highly amused. "Gotta take what you can carry, baby."

Chito weakly glared at the ground in front of Cliona, then glanced at Tullia with deep suspicion. "Where's your backpack?"

Tullia pointed at Sabin. "We share a bag."

Chito put his hands together in hope, and looked at Sabin with big, brown eyes. "Then… can't you share with me too? Just a little."

Sabin didn't seem phased by the cute begging. "That will not all fit in my bag."

Chito slumped, looking childlike in his depression at Sabin's answer. "But… then what should I do?" He looked back up at Sabin with wide, pure eyes.

Tullia watched Sabin, utterly amused, as he subtly softened under the honest reaction of Chito's confused disappointment. He slid his eyes to look at Tullia, she gave a small shrug and a pity smile.

The ball was in his court, and she was not about to steal it.

He gave out a rough, small sigh, unfolding his big arms to hold up one glove covered hand. "I can fit *five items* and *five items* only, in my bag, for you. You must carry the rest."

Chito's entire face beamed. "Can you fit twelve?"

"Five." Sabin's tone brooked no arguments, but Chito seemed a bit happier, nonetheless.

The Grand High reclined in the air, crossing her jean covered legs. "A hippie now joins the group." She shook her head, eyeing his multicolored baggy pants and his billowy peasant shirt.

The comment seemed to go over Chito's head. "Ms. Grand High, please help me decide!" He skipped forward and boldly grabbed Cliona's hand and began to pull her along, much to her offended shock. "I'll show you what I packed and the outfit combinations. Help me decide, I know you'll be honest." The Grand High allowed herself to be pulled towards the luggage, but she seemed unsure how to react. Her head snapped back and forth between Carolina and Chito's on hers.

Tullia saw her eye twitch and tasted the vinegary irritation.

"Sabin! Get over here too! We need your stupid man's purse!" Cliona yelled, glaring daggers at him with her pure black eyes.

Sighing, Sabin strolled over leisurely to them, he looked at Tullia and rolled his golden eyes, causing her to giggle.

When she went to follow. "Tullia. A word." Carolina beckoned her over instead. Once over, the queen grabbed both her hands. "You have inspired my stubborn grandson beyond what I've tried to encourage. With you by his side he will flourish into the person that he was always meant to be." She moved her hands to cup Tullia's face gently. Her hands were soft and warm. "Please, teach my Chito how to be himself."

Tullia felt the pressure behind the weight of her request, but smiled at the queen nonetheless. "I'll do my best, your majesty."

Carolina's answering smile was radiantly gorgeous, she pressed her forehead to Tullia's. *"Ignat ka."*

"Salamat po." Tullia said in return, absorbing the warmth from the Queen of Biringan's touch, allowing it to settle softly in her soul.

Chapter Eighteen

"Alright now," Cliona stood in front of a hoard of tittering witches. Her hands were on her hips and her feet, encased in heels of ridiculous height, were actually touching the floor. She meant business. "Jiang Li." She said slowly, "A river dragon in China. Supposedly, he should be located in or near Zigui County, but he could be between Mount Wudang and a big ass river near there." She surveyed the crowd, they looked upon her with a trance like devotion. The silence in the room as everyone waited for her command was layered with suspense. The Grand High flicked her long silky black hair behind her shoulder. "I want a specific location of this dragon's whereabouts. I want a list of possible locations he may be in and I do not want an area over three football fields, understood?"

A sea of unison nods. The Grand High's elongated fingers waved them all away, "You all have three hours. Get it all done. Don't dilly dally."

As soon as she finished speaking the witches scurried about, rushing off to complete her orders. They left with such a frantic focus that one banged into the door frame face first, fell, popped back up on her feet and darted out the door with a bounce. It was almost as if she were a cartoon character.

Tullia sat on a couch that was set up in the Grand High's counsel room, which was like a modern-day throne room. It was a spacious area with a high ceiling, multiple chandeliers, a long white gold table, plush gold chairs and sleek, modern decor. There was no throne, but a very expensive looking executive chair sat at the head of the table.

Tullia was happy to be back in familiar territory with only a twenty percent chance of getting lost. They made it back to Vegas and, despite being three am, the Grand High was greeted with enthusiasm by dozens upon dozens of clamoring witches.

Before getting to Vegas, Chito, Sabin and herself had to hike their way to the main road. Cliona had teleported out to wait for them in the (disappointing) teleporter. That hiking journey to the highway took a few hours, then they had to wait until one of the Pearl of the Orient clan witches found them idling on the side of the road under a sun that seemed far too generous with its sunshine.

Now, though exhausted and smelly, Tullia felt giddy as she ate a bag of hot Cheetos that she snagged without a single stitch of shame from a small desk table when no one was looking. It was fun watching everything take place while she munched. Sabin stood against the wall and Chito was sitting next to her, fidgeting with excitement. His head swiveled back and forth, up and down, and side to side. He looked like a featherless owl with the way he took in everything with wide, glowing eyes.

Though she couldn't exactly judge him, she did that the first time too.

Cliona turned to face them once the modern-day throne room was empty, looking beautiful with her two-colored skin types melding together hypnotically underneath the unnatural lights. "They will have the information in 3 hours. So, in the meantime do what you want. Stay, leave, sleep, whatever. I'm going to play queenly catch up. Make sure no revolts or a coup d'etat are in process." She snapped her fingers and a tube of lip gloss appeared. Cliona applied the gloss and seemed to eye Tullia. Smacking her full lips that now were gleaming with sparkles, she flicked her fingers towards Tullia.

Tullia gasped, nearly choking on a hot Cheeto that was in her mouth, as ice engulfed her body and a springtime scent of fresh soap with a hint of lavender surrounded her. It was momentary, yet it was the most uncomfortable sensation that caused the mere seconds to become suspended for an unholy amount of time. Once over, Tullia felt as if she had done the whole nine yards in the hygiene department.

She stared wide eyed at the Grand High who flicked her long raven hair over her shoulder. "You were filthy, petal. You're welcome." She gave a haughty single wave before winking out, a thin trail of smoke was left in her wake.

Tullia let out a ragged puff of air but relaxed more into the couch. Now that dried sweat wasn't a thin crusty layer over her and her clothes were no longer slightly damp from her excessive perspiration, she could enjoy her snack that much more.

Sabin pushed off the wall as soon as the Grand High was gone. "I have errands which I must attend to." He looked at both Chito and Tullia. "Do you wish to come or—"

Chito vaulted off the couch, he was beside Sabin within a mere second, interrupting him before he finished. "I'll come! I want to see Las Vegas!"

Tullia giggled at Sabin's slightly wide-eyed look, she popped another spicy Cheeto into her mouth, before rising from the couch. "I'll come too. I think I need to do some laundry."

Sabin nodded, the strong flavor of relief coated her pallet with its cooling, almost cucumber taste. She repressed another giggle, it seemed he didn't want to be alone with Chito's nearly explosive excitement.

They left the Grand High's mansion, with Chito blatantly marveling at the cold and fancy decor inside the Grand High's home. When they made it into Sabin's truck, Chito shoved his upper body between Sabin and Tullia from the backseat. His hair rushed forward to frame his beautiful and androgynous face.

His smile was wide and innocent. "Where are we going?" His voice was pitched higher with anticipation and Tullia could feel the vibration of barely leashed exhilaration.

It was a sweet, bubbly riot from Chito's emotions that overtook Tullia's mouth, like a little swarm of sweet bees without stingers.

Tullia looked at Sabin, expectant.

Sabin glanced at both her and Chito once, before starting his truck. "Laundromat."

Chito gasped, then made a sound of wonder. "Like in the American sitcom where that group of people who live above the coffee shop in New York went? That type of laundromat?"

Tullia shot Chito a look. "Are you referring to the sitcom *Friends*?"

Chito gave her a wide-eyed look. "Yes. They have that kind of thing in Las Vegas? I thought that was a big city thing. Vegas is not a big city. Is it?"

Tullia shook her head. "Laundromats are… a thing everywhere. Not just big cities."

"Huh," Chito's big brown eyes were glued to the outside scenery as Sabin began to drive them away. "Why are there trees here? Wouldn't they catch on fire with the dry heat of the desert?"

Tullia propped her face against her palm to stare at Chito without getting a kink in her neck. "I think your ideas about a desert city are a bit off."

Chito frowned, though he didn't remove his eyes from the outside scenery. "How so?"

"Well, first off, trees can grow in the desert. There are desert trees. And other trees manage to survive with some assistance. Grass even grows here, and it doesn't catch on fire. I mean, a desert isn't hell personified."

When Chito looked at Tullia, his eyes were so wide, they began to bug out. "You have grass here?"

Tullia smiled and shook her head. "You may want to pay attention to what you see, Chito."

Sabin shook his head, though his mood was slightly amused, according to the taste of subtle saccharine that now filled her mouth.

Chito nodded, then he bombarded them with endless questions.

Correction.

He bombarded *Tullia* with endless questions. Sabin didn't utter a word, the freakin' jerk. He just sat in his seat, in silence and drove. Tullia answered as best she could, though Chito's questions were equivalent to the credit run at the end of movies. She didn't know when it was going to end, and it was too much to process all that info.

Eventually, Tullia began to answer his more outrageous questions with embellishments and creative alternatives, strictly for her amusement.

Does the mob still run the casinos? *Yup. And they enforce taco Tuesdays at the casinos too. No one dares to order anything but tacos on Tuesday. Remember that, if we go on the Strip.*

Are there houses for the residents only on the Strip? *No, but we get an entire casino hotel to ourselves. Tourists can't get in, it's for residents of Las Vegas only. You have to be a resident for at least a year though.*

What do the kids do while their parents work? Is there a school at the casinos? *Actually, what happens is that every child is assigned to a mentor, they are then groomed to fulfill a position in the casino based upon a poker face test given to all children at the ages of seven, thirteen and seventeen. If they pass the poker test, they are allowed to choose which occupation they wish to study. If they fail, then their options are more limited.*

Sabin was highly amused and Tullia felt slightly bad for the fibs, but it was all in good fun. Plus, she'd tell Chito the truth… later. Maybe. If she remembered. An hour later Chito was standing in a twenty-four hour laundromat, looking around the place with dark eyes and an open mouth. The laundromat seemed to have a grease tint to the interior and the yellow and green theme was very…classic she supposed. If you didn't look closely or didn't look at all, the laundromat was nice enough.

"I feel… so connected to the western sitcom right now." His tone was breathy and utterly delighted, his flawless English tilted slightly in a pretty accent.

Tullia laughed.

Sabin had dug around in his forever man purse thing and discreetly pulled out another bag.

Tullia clapped in mock amazement, Sabin gave a fancy hand wave and a slight bow of his head. He put the bag in front of her.

"Yours."

Tullia held up the bag, it was a bit puffy with crumpled clothes that gave off a not so good funk. "I don't remember wearing this much."

"You did." Sabin said deadpan as he pulled out another bag, way smaller than hers and placed it in front of him.

She narrowed her eyes at him. In his bag there were only black items. He literally wore one color. In fact, he wore one type of outfit.

Or was it…. Just *one* outfit? She eyed him, he was in his glamour, so she couldn't see what he was actually wearing but he was wearing clothes…

Right?

Tullia decided to leave that mystery alone, some things did not need to be discovered. She turned to Chito and saw him blatantly staring at a woman who took off her shirt and threw it in the washing machine, leaving her only in jeans and a see-through pink bra. The old man and reception boy stared intensely at her too.

"Don't stare." She muttered and gently shoulder bumped him, but with the way he jolted you'd have thought Tullia took a two by four and gave him a good whack.

"I'm not!" Chito's tone was defensive, his face reddened slightly. "It's just… this entire place… is different from what I thought it would be." He side eyed an elderly man who had a bunch of women's clothing he was putting into one machine. Then he seemed to focus on the shiny appearance of the stainless-steel washing machines.

"It's just… not what I expected." His tone went dull.

Tullia giggled over the flat, coconut flavor in her mouth. He was clearly feeling out of place and disappointed in his surroundings.

"Not very similar to the sitcoms." Sabin murmured; his plain glamoured face smiled blandly then he tossed one of Tullia's dirty shirts towards her.

Tullia stared at Sabin's hidden appearance for a moment. His face was plain, forgettable and nondescript. It was weird looking at Sabin like that. She found she preferred his ninja mask over the glamour. She had a hunch that his face looked nothing like his glamour either, and she felt that was character defamation in a way.

Sabin had this quiet, intense presence, to diminish it with this lackluster look was… gross.

She forced her eyes back to her black bag. She had clothes to wash. "I swear I did not wear this much. I better not find anything of yours in my pile, especially tighty whities." Tullia mock huffed.

Sabin gave her an uncaring side look. But a brief hint of carbonation on her tongue made her want to smile. They began sorting their clothes. Tullia learned the hard way that you are forced to care when doing laundry if you want your clothes to not be ruined.

Sabin was faster than her, his clothes consisted of black and a darker black with some variations of black. He ended up dumping a medium sized wad of clothing into a single machine, dumping a precise amount of soap and then shoving a few coins to get the machine tumbling and rattling about in a concerning way.

"So…do you guys always do your laundry here?" Chito asked, he watched them with slight boredom, leaning against one of the machines.

"Yup." Sabin looked around the laundromat, probably scanning for danger.

"I used the one at the motel I lived at." Tullia untangled her bra from one of her shirts. "This laundromat is much nicer than the one I was using though."

Chito made a thoughtful sound, his attention drifting away, probably thinking he should have stayed in Biringan or maybe back to the shirtless woman. Tullia focused on her task, then picked two machines that would more or less clean her stuff. All the while she kept stealing glances at Sabin, who lounged like a really big bear next to her.

Does he really only have one outfit? Is he actually wearing clothes right now or is he butt naked?

It seemed unlikely, impossible even. She saw a few articles of clothes in his bundle.

He must have at least a few shirts. Does he own any other color clothing besides black? Was even his underwear black? Tullia almost snorted out loud. Questions about Sabin's choice of clothing kept circulating her mind until her withheld curiosity exasperated her.

"Hey, Sabin, weird question, but do you have multiple ninja outfits? Or just one?" Tullia asked, and bit off the question about what color his underwear was.

There were lines, even between newly formed BFF's, that just didn't need to be crossed to invite awkwardness into the party.

Sabin raised an eyebrow. "I have a few. I mostly use the glamour, so there is no need for variation in my attire."

Tullia evaluated him for a moment. "So, essentially, you could go naked and no one would know?" She threw her dark clothes in one machine, then her lights into another one.

"I would know." His tone was slightly scandalized. Tullia laughed as Sabin passed her a few dollars in quarters. "And it would make me uncomfortable. Clothes are for *my* comfort."

Chito giggled.

Tullia opened her mouth to give some sort of semi-clever reply about being an undercover nudist, before her limbs seized by her sides. Her breath slowed, and her heart rate dropped to a slow, thudding pulse as her vision of the shiny washing machine dimmed, tilted then disappeared entirely as night swathed waters surrounded her and screams of the dying deafened her.

* * *

Sabin felt Tullia stiffen and become unnaturally still beside him. He slid his eyes to her, her face was too pale, nearly translucent and made the veins that branched on her temples and forehead starkly visible. Her dove gray eyes were blank and wide.

"Tullia? Are you alright?" Chito shuffled closer, leaning down to peer at Tullia's iced face.

Sabin saw her form begin to tremble, her jaw clenched, her fists become bloodless, and her small frame seemed to shrink within itself.

Without a word, Sabin gently pried open Tullia's hand to get the coins he had given her. Her hand held no warmth and there were perfect indents of each coin in her palm. Slamming the coins in the machines, ignoring the groaning creak they made from his excessive force, he wrapped one arm around Tullia's shoulders. Mashing her cold form to his side, he tried to absorb her iciness that seemed to ooze from her tiny form. He casually, gently maneuvered her body, stiff and mimicking that of a plastic doll, as he strode to the flimsy chairs lining the dingy, cloudy windows. He sat down; the chair squeaked loudly in protest, dragging Tullia across his lap so that she could lean against him. He forced her head to rest against his shoulder, to hide her face from the nosy eyes. He rubbed her neck, trying to ease the unforgiving rigidity and tried to wrap as much of himself around as he could to stave off the icy chill that radiated from her skin. Chito had followed him, gingerly sitting on a rather unstable chair, staring at Tullia with concern.

"What's wrong with her?" He asked hesitantly, glancing up at Sabin with anxiety. His hands laced together, turning white and his dark eyes troubled.

"Lost magic." He stated simply, if Tullia didn't tell him, it wasn't Sabin's place to inform the young prince.

Chito made an O with his mouth. "So, is this her having a vision of the past? Of someone else's past?"

She told him then. A twitch within him poked at his drowsy rage as Sabin gave a hard nod in confirmation. Tullia's soft frame jerked to the side, nearly sending her to the floor. Sabin caught her, then wrapped an arm around her waist tightly, pinning her plush form to his body, repressing a shudder at the wintry tendrils that seeped from her into him. He rubbed her arm and back briskly, hoping to warm her.

Chito was studying Tullia's drawn, pale face with a pitying look. "Does it happen randomly? No matter the time or place…" He pushed a heavy lock of black hair behind his shoulder, a pretty and delicate motion, "Poor thing."

Irritation flickered against his mind, he was agitated by the way she was being spectated and pitied. Sabin placed one of his hands over her face, hiding it away from Chito's naive probing, pushing her face into his neck.

"She'll be alright." His tone was rough, sharp and just shy of a bite that would have made it unkind. Chito still shrank back slightly from the abrupt edge to his tone. Sabin clenched his teeth, forcing back his groggy rage that sleepily stretched out within him.

Tullia shivered violently.

The laundromat was warm, more on the stifling side, but with Tullia in his arm, he felt as though he was holding a block of ice.

Sabin tilted his head back, looking up at the ceiling. Chito was silent by his side, probably wishing he had stayed back at the witch's home instead of sitting in a two-star laundromat. Sabin inspected the stained and thinly cracked ceiling, he didn't know how long Tullia would be out, but once their clothes were done, he'd have Chito hold her so she doesn't freeze. He squeezed her tighter against him, willing his heat into her and willing her vision to be swift and easy.

* * *

It was so cold; her scales were stiff and her blood felt sluggish in her veins.

She looked up, afraid a knotted and nauseated sensation took residence in her chest. The waves were vicious, slamming into the jagged mountain side, clawing at the sand, seemingly determined to gain further purchase. A disgusting creature thrashed in their sea, tainting it, causing fear and terror of the water.

Bodies... partial bodies... pieces of bodies littered the sand. Bodies that once were whole, laughed and lived, now laid discarded like a child's broken toy. She resided on the shore, whole on the outside but broken on the inside, as the wave tried to reach her.

"This vile creature is undefeatable." She turned her head to look at him. His face, rough and stern, was drawn down tight. His eyes bleak and his lips curled in an agony that this was their end, that the beast was not to be defeated and they were destined to lose.

"We've lost countless." His eyes, glazed with pain stared beyond her, at the creature that rose high and horrid against the dark sky. It bellowed, trembling the ground, taunting the survivors to try again and share the same fate as the floating corpses. A sleet of ocean water sprayed down from the monster's enormous body.

Its dreadful face swiveled, a massive jaw with crowded, jagged teeth were bared in a vile grin.

She looked back at her love. He was fierce and stern and secretly funny when he was away from worshiping eyes. She had adored him upon first sight and had only managed to fall deeper into him as the year's passed by. She touched his face, his dark forest eyes, glowing and sharp latched onto her.

"I love you." She said simply, knowing he was a male who appreciated short, direct messages. "And I will still love you in the next life as well. You will find me this time, right?" She smiled, forcing her tears deep down within her chest. She would not cry. His eyes widened with an expression she'd seen only once, and that was when she informed him he was to be a father.

Except, there was no humor in this situation.

"You will not." He seized her arms, his grip unforgiving, his tone harsh and his face, dark and intense, was etched with dawning panic. "You will not."

"Nirah," She said softly, "The Jomungandr will destroy our people if we do not do something now. I have to set up a boundary, so that the creature is at least contained." She peered into his jewel eyes. "This will not be permanent, but we need time to find a solution to exterminate the beast. We do not have one now, but I believe you will find one."

His grip tightened and it was painful on her arms, but Pandra did not utter a word of protest. She was going to hurt her male, hurt him by leaving him to lead their people alone and leave him with their young daughter to be motherless.

"You cannot not." He searched her face, his face tightened, she knew he saw her resolute and knew she was the only one who could possibly have a chance at containing the beast.

"Another priestess can do it. Not you." He growled, dragging her to him, black scales slick with water but warm with life. He was such a strong male, he would survive without her, but he would be alone and that hurt her heart. But

her wishes and reality did not harmonize.

"I am the strongest priestess of our clan. The monster is approaching our territory and will kill everyone." She gently pushed back to look into his eyes. "I am but one, that can save many."

He snarled his rage at her, baring his sharp teeth. "You are **my** one, the one that matters the most."

She smiled, her chest tight and her eyes stinging, this hardened male...she did love him so much.

"Nirah," She said softly, "What would a King and a Commander do? Sacrifice one to save many or allow everyone to die?"

His snarl deepened, his arms flexed, and his tail snaked up to intertwine with hers, before pinning her tail to the sand. The monster screamed, rattling the earth they stood on. They paid it no mind. Their eyes did not veer from each other.

"We either all die and allow the Jomungandr to win, or I put up a boundary and buy us time." Pandra's tone was soft, she was pleading with her Nirah's commanding side. He would know that what she said was logical, his head would, his heart would protest.

His eyes blazed with angry understanding and tormented grief. "I am King," His tone was bitter, "I am sending my Queen to die for the survival of our clan"

"You don't send me anywhere; I'll decide where I go." She gave him a mock flat look, her chest still so tight with sorrow.

Nirah was startled into a small grin, his pain and rage momentarily banished *under the memory she managed to summon.*

"You have not changed since I first met you. Still unruly, reckless, and beautiful." He released her arms, the rush of blood back into them tingled but Pandra didn't feel it, she was concentrating on Nirah's claws that gently cupped her face. "You are my heart."

"You must be happy—" She began.

Nirah nipped her nose hard, stopping her words. "I will bear life without you for our clan and for our daughter. That is all I will do. Do not tell me otherwise."

Pandra swallowed thickly. "Alright." She said softly. Selfishly, she loved his words. She rubbed her face against his, savoring the slide of his scales against hers. She withdrew and looked at her male once more before turning towards the vicious waves. Their tails slid against each other before contact was gone.

"You better wait for me." His tone was a grating sound, raw and painful, she turned to look at him, he had not moved, but his claws were fisted and blood dripped from them. "I will find you and you better be ready for me. I'm going to punish you for this."

"I look forward to it, my love." She smiled, looking at her strong and brave Nirah for a moment, "Tell Chava every day that I love her."

"Our daughter will always know of her mother's love, she already does now."

Pandra smiled, feeling the tears swell, and blew him a kiss, a kiss he caught with his bloodied right claw and placed over his chest. A motion he had always made for her, saying he would not allow her affections to be freely floating in the air, he would claim them all.

She felt her throat tighten and turned away from him, if she didn't go now, everyone would die. The brutal waves slammed into the sand and screamed their beckoning call to her. She inhaled deeply and dove into the water without another thought. Ice encased her body, stealing her warmth and breath. Gritting her teeth, she forced her limbs to move, cutting through the death thickened water. The current was trying to drag her back to the shore, rejecting her from its bloody depths, but she'd be damned if that happened.

No one and nothing told her what to do.

Her arms became numb and her tail was sluggish with fatigue. The water seemed to darken further. Pandra tried not to look too closely at the things floating in the water.

A movement she caught from the corner of her eye, though she may as well not have seen it. A thick tail barred with jagged spikes struck her in the side. Pandra spun in the water, her side on fire. She gritted her teeth and forced her body to dive down then up.

She looked sharply to the right and felt utterly sick. There were coils and coils of scales, all moving. She felt her eyes widen with horror at the sheer magnitude of the monster. She swam faster, her chest pounding and her entire body one giant throb. She looked up from under the water, the sky was dark, drearily so, but there was enough light to be seen. Pandra darted up, her tail working double time to propel her up and her chest a mass of pulsating nerves.

She felt as if something was going to eat her whole.

As soon as she broke the surface she screamed. "Jomungandr!" Her voice shrill and ragged, not from exertion, but pure terror. "Face me!"

The water stilled. The air was still. Time stopped. Then a single ripple.

Pandra's hard panting hurt with each exhale as she waited. Hoping that the monster would humor her, so she could begin.

The water rippled again, almost gently to reveal two, beady, dead red eyes surrounded by dark blue scales.

She felt her heart stop momentarily as she stared at the creature of horrors, before it restarted with a vengeance. Then the Jomungandr rose from the water, just enough for its massive head to surface entirely.

Pandra began to quiver, she was petrified to the point she wanted to cry. It was the ugliest feeling. The giant snake hissed down at her, its mouth a mess of jagged, layered teeth. Rot blackening in between some teeth and other teeth held a variety of yellows. The slicked blue scales seemed to glint like drawn blades. Its tongue slithered out, fat and forked, tasting the death clotted air. The monster's tiny red clouded eyes pinned Pandra in place.

You called, priestess?

It's low, amused hissing voice slunk into her mind, unwanted and forced, making her recoil with disgust. Pandra stared, immobile, at the giant snake monster as dread began to saturate her limbs and mind, scattering her bravery to pieces.

It was too big...

They should have just run...

They should have abandoned their home, started a new life...

They were all going to die...

Yes, you should have. But you are foolish. Now all are destined to

die.

That damn snake. Pandra lifted a trembling hand and slapped herself hard across her face. The pain cleared her fear fogged mind and her eyes were finally able to narrow at the creature. How dare this disgusting monstrosity mimic their beautiful form. She savored the blood that covered the inside of her mouth.

Such a cheap trick, she thought with disgust, baring her teeth.

The snake seemed to sway, as if unbothered by her words.

Pandra placed her hands together, sucked in air with heavy moisture and began her chant. Her hands glowed, her body became colder as magic was called. Her songs were to incite the magic; her request was to create a barrier, her offer...her life force. The Jomungandr stared at her for a moment, amusement was an easy read in its demented red eyes.

You think your weak magic can stop me, priestess? I was made from the Gods.

"You are but their creation, do not think yourself the same." She hissed, salty water dripped down her face as her heart thudded as her request was ignored.

Oh, but I am more. Much more. *A wet, strangled chuckle that was everything horror.*

She gritted her teeth, this monster's voice inside her head was vile and saturated her mind with gore.

"You are but a thing that should have never been!" She yelled. "You are an abomination!"

The monster seemed to jerk; a thick, bubbling sound erupted from its hideous mouth. It took Pandra a moment to recognize what the creature was doing, but it was...laughing. Laughing at her and her words and her people.

Rage, unholy rage tinted her vision and then drenched her mind, destroying any lingering fear within. Pandra forced herself to block the creature from her mind, her eyes fastened on its fogged beady little eyes.

She started screaming her chants at the dark sky and over the sounds of crashing waves.

The ugly snake stopped its nasty sound.

Enough.

She felt the heat of the answer then, the numbing cold that seemed to shoot through her entire being. She smiled widely. Her request was granted.

The Jomungandr opened its mouth wide and dove towards her.

A jagged blade of pain ruptured within her, she felt as though her entire being was being unraveled from the inside. Pandra locked her jaw tight, she would not scream out her agony. Let her Nirah think she did not feel anything. She felt her request answered and now as payment, her life was being sucked out from her body.

Magic demands a price. It is never free.

The Jormungandr's snarled mouth smashed into an unseen wall, it reared back and darted forward again, only to smash its ugly face again. It growled, its eyes blazed with fury and insanity, then it seemed to pause, as if tasting the magic she called with its long tongue. It looked at her then, and began to laugh again, seeming to find her silent pain, her dying humorous.

Priestess, enjoy your death.

A dark glint in the monster's gigantic, faded eyes.

You'll be accompanied by your clan in a little while. Until then, sweet nightmares, priestess.

A dark chuckle, before a white-hot intensity stole over her eyes. Her last thought was of Nirah, the day Chava hatched all those years ago. His big body cradling their tiny girl, his face, so savage, was soft as he peered down, inspecting his child with a tenderness that no one in the clan would have believed. Chava's tiny claws reached up, Nirah put his face down for their daughter to touch him.

I will miss them so terribly.

* * *

Tullia's supple body gave a hard jerk and seemed to suspend to the point Sabin feared she snapped her spine, but then she deflated within seconds. Her body sagged completely into his, a plush cheek pressed against his collarbone and her hot breath, ragged and puffed, heated the base of his throat through the thick fabric. Sabin took his hand away from her face, he realized he had been hiding her face from Chito the entire time. He peered down at her.

Tullia's was flush with a cherry red color, there was a faint outline of his hand on her face and a fine sheen of sweat made her face glisten and look swallow. She blinked heavily, rolling her head slightly as if she was trying to rouse herself. Her dove gray eyes skidded, roaming continuously without seeing anything.

"Tullia?" Chito scooted forward on his seat, hovering but not quite touching her. His smooth face was pinched tight with concern.

She blinked heavily, her head lolling slightly to face Chito. She didn't say anything, her smoky eyes were haggard and moist. Sabin watched as her face seemed to slowly lose composure, crumbling little by little, before she buried her face into Sabin's neck and clutched at his shoulders with her slim arms.

Sabin felt her wracking sobs, though she didn't make a single sound. Briefly, he wondered why she did not release her cries.

"Tullia?" Chito asked again, he seemed confused and helpless. Sabin was in the same boat, but he didn't want other people to catch on to their situation.

Sabin stood with Tullia cradled in his arms. "Chito," he saw the boy flinch slightly at his tone. "Come with me."

He didn't wait to see if he listened, he would. Sabin left the laundromat and strode quickly to his truck. The light chill in the air stung his eyes, but he ignored the weather. The weather was nothing but a nuisance at times. He unlocked his truck and opened the door. He set her down in the passenger seat, he felt her grip tighten on his neck before weakening, allowing him to pull away. Sabin tried to look at her face, but she kept her head bowed and her hair concealed her entirely.

"Chito, sit with Tullia. I must finish with the clothes." Sabin was about to shut the door, when Tullia's dull gray eyes met his, freezing him place.

He had seen that look. He had worn that look. It was a look of hardship and fresh loss.

"It's always hard when someone dies. It's very, very hard. It hurt so much." Her voice was hoarse and wet. He frowned, his eyes slid to Chito, he was staring at Tullia with anxious eyes.

"Give her comfort. I will be swift." Gently, Sabin shut the door and raced back into the laundromat. He ignored the startled looks from people when he all but charged into the place. He roughly switched out his clothes into the dryer. He was a bit gentler with Tullia's clothes, trying not to see what he was grabbing to preserve her modesty. Once the clothes were out and switched into the dryer, he placed the dryer at the hottest setting for the shortest time. Once set he eyed everyone in the shop, an old man, a tattooed woman and an old couple that was bickering loudly were all absorbed in their own worlds.

Good.

Sabin calmly rushed out the front doors again and made a beeline for his truck. He saw Tullia, still hunched in the passenger seat and Chito patting her back. His mouth was moving, but his words seemed to have no effect on Tullia.

Sabin waved at Chito to unlock his truck, to which the boy did and Sabin opened Tullia's door again.

He leaned in and studied her. She was hunched, her dark hair still hanging over her face. But Sabin saw the glistening dampness through her strands of her hair and the droplets that lingered on her chin.

Sabin reached forward and brushed his gloved hand along her jaw, wiping away the tears. No one said anything, the sound of traffic and city noise filled the air. Sabin looked around the parking lot, it was relatively empty except for a few shuffling patrons of the nearby bar and the gas station.

Long, long minutes passed by.

Tullia then sniffed. "Do you have a napkin?" Her voice was thick with sorrow.

Sabin opened his glove compartment and ruffled through a few miscellaneous items before pulling out a crumpled napkin.

"Here, sweetness." She took the napkin he handed her and blew her nose. Then she sighed. Her face was pale, ruddy and wet. She looked aged and haggard by five years, turning her fresh innocence into a harder, sharpened edge.

"Do you want to talk about it?" Chito asked gently.

"Hell no." She murmured, roughly rubbing her eyes with the heels of her hands. "I need some meds. I got a headache."

"Alright, sweetness. Sit here for a bit more. I have to get our clothes out of the dryer."

"I'll help." She said dully, but Sabin placed a hand on her shoulder to keep her in place.

"Stay." His tone came out harder than he intended too. Tullia's blood shot eyes drilled into him.

"Mm, okay." She looked exhausted, her usual sass was missing from her, and Sabin found he didn't like its absence.

"I'll be quick." He promised again. And he kept his word. He nearly sprinted back into the laundromat, heading straight to the dryer. There was an old man staring at the dryer spinning, but Sabin didn't have it in him to be cordial.

"Move." He growled. The old man frowned at him, his small eyes behind thick spectacles glowered. Sabin returned the man's glare with one of his own.

The old man grumbled about the younger generation having no respect for the elderly. Sabin snorted, he was raised without respect and managed to cultivate some in the centuries he had lived sometime after his disfiguration. Though not much. Would the man tremble if he knew that Sabin was well older than his great, great grandfather?

He looked at the elderly man, he was aggressively talking to another washing machine, poking its glass surface with a snarled face.

No, he wouldn't, Sabin thought.

Ripping open the dryer door, Sabin took out partly dry clothes and shoved them in a wadded bundle into his bag. A light pink color caught his eyes, for it was such a soft color amid his dark clothes. Sabin touched the tiny bow on the pink fabric lightly, then jerked his hand away. He stuffed the rest of the clothes in his bag, feeling hotter than usual and slung his bag over his shoulder.

Striding out of the laundromat for the final time, Sabin saw Tullia's forehead pressed against the window of his truck. Even from a short distance, her face was glittery with sweat. He slid into the driver's seat, throwing his bag in the back next to Chito and starting his truck, he heard Tullia's ragged breathing. He glanced over at her, her lips were pallid and were pressed together tightly.

Silence consumed his truck while he backed up and began to drive away. Silence had always been a faithful companion to Sabin, however, he found he didn't care for its company in this situation. He glanced at Tullia, no change. Then glanced at Chito, he was looking at her with a worried expression, but Sabin could tell he was at a loss on how to handle the situation. Which was unfortunate. Because Sabin was poorly equipped to deal with anything delicate, he had hoped Chito would be more capable.

So, Sabin said the only thing that always came to his mind. "Are you hungry? Do you want something to eat?"

There was a pause, he could feel Chito's eyes staring at him and sensed his disapproval. However, Tullia sniffed a bit, then nodded.

"Yeah. Can we get some tea too?"

He'd get her anything she wanted as long as she didn't cry anymore. He liked it when her steel eyes were dry and smiling, not wet and red rimmed.

"Of course, sweetness."

✶ ✶ ✶

His truck smelled of over saturated grease and meat. Sabin had gotten her a fried chicken meal that she had given a small smile to and dug in without much prompting. Then he bought her a caramel milk tea with boba from a specialized tea shop. It was what the lady behind the counter had recommended when he said he needed a sweet drink.

It felt immensely satisfying to watch Tullia eat what he had given her.

After the quiet sounds of food consumption, and Chito's verbal delight in the food, a low thrum of tension permeated the greasy air. Sabin glanced at Chito, but he seemed absorbed in his drink, he was staring at the boba balls at the bottom of his cup with a frown.

"The boba back home was never this soft or chewy." His frown deepened.

Sabin internally sighed, his rage quivering, but dormant for the moment. He looked at Tullia, her face was still drawn and withered looking. She was composed and quiet, but she was internalizing whatever scene she was forced to witness.

Sabin knew nothing good came of suppression.

"You are hurting yourself with your silence." Sabin said softly, watching her.

A sharp side look, turning her soft dove gray eyes into glinting blades. "Oh."

"You do not need to speak," Sabin shifted, he didn't need her odd gift of tasting people's emotions to know what she was feeling. He could feel her irritation and her defensiveness. "But you need release of sorts."

"Release?" She snorted.

"Yes, perhaps exercise of some sort." He suggested.

"After I just ate a bucket of grease and a pure sugar drink?" A spark, that sass that amused him, flashed in her eyes.

Sabin shrugged, suppressing a smile. She may have been put through an ordeal, but she was far from being broken.

Good.

"Sabin has a point." Chito interjected softly, "You don't have to keep it in Tullia. It's not healthy for you."

A beat of silence. "You say that to me after I just ate a bucket of grease and a pure sugar drink?"

Chito gave a short giggle. "You know what I meant." He touched her shoulder very gently, "You're not alone."

The air that had warmed slightly became silent as Tullia fiddled with her half full tea.

"I guess I'm not." She said quietly after a moment. Then inhaled deeply and exhaled harshly. "And I guess I should…" She paused. When she spoke again, she didn't look at them. "I… have seen a thousand deaths. I felt them. I have witnessed a thousand sorrows. A thousand griefs. A thousand…" She swallowed with effort, "You'd think I'd be conditioned to them by now. That I'd be numb to them, unfeeling. Like… like a corpse." Her voice faltered. Chito put his hand on her shoulder, Sabin saw him squeeze. Tullia sniffed and swallowed thickly. "But I am not. I see their final moments; I feel their final emotions and… I hear their final thoughts…" Fresh tears escaped her eyes as she looked up at Sabin. Grey, bloodshot and sad eyes stared at him. "It kills me every time."

"You saw someone die?" Chito ventured softly.

She let out a bit of a ragged, dry laugh, her eyes dropping from Sabin's. And he missed her eyes on him. She looked very fragile at that moment, with her small frame folded smaller with grief. "If only." She wiped a tear away from her cheek. "Death never seems to be simple and it's always so very sad."

With that breathy, layered statement, Sabin understood what she had been subjected too. Flashes of his friends, his clan and family dying in various ways. By disease, by blade, by fire… They all felt different, but they were all burdensome with the grief they caused upon him. He often wished he had died to spare himself the shredding torment on his soul.

"That's true," Chito said softly, "Do you want to tell us what happened? It may make you feel better?"

Tullia took a giant sip of her drink, chewed the boba vigorously for a few moments, before swallowing on a sigh. She shook her head.

"No, I'm done talking about it." She said finally. Chito opened his mouth, but before words could be utter, Tullia shook her head again, this time vehemently, holding her hand up. Her black strands whipped around her face. "I don't want to talk about it. I can't… I'm… tired of all the sadness."

Sabin instinctively reached out and patted her hand that was squeezed a bit too tight around her cup, denting it in a bit. He could feel the slight tremble in her fingers through his thick gloves. He could understand her mentality of not speaking upon the sadness. Sadness is a burden that weighed upon the soul. Sometimes to push it away is the only salvation for the pain.

"Alright, sweetness. You did good." He said, his voice sounded gruff and short, but he didn't have the skill of the silk smooth tongue.

Her eyes, dewy with unshed tears, looked up at him, a sheen of appreciation was projected from her as well as darkened streaks of sorrow. Her gaze always made him feel a fine blend of disconcerting and enlivened.

Sabin winked, then slid his eyes to his clock, the hands indicated they have been out for far too long. He sighed internally. It appeared they were going to be late.

The witch was going to be particularly bothersome in her irritation towards their tardiness.

Chapter Nineteen

"Well hello there." Cliona glowered at them all as they passed through the threshold, and vinegar doused Tullia's tongue instantly. Chito pressed close to Tullia, one of his slender hands clutched her upper arm tightly with stress. When they arrived at the Grand High's home, a very nervous and jerky maid quickly ushered them in. Then she proceeded to rush them through the house with sharp motions and frustrated grunts as she scurried in front of them.

Sabin's pace did not falter from steady strides. Tullia skipped by his side, feeling the caffeine racing through her veins. Chito seemed very torn between the maid's near frantic walk and Sabin's easy gate, so he settled with an awkward side shifting waltz.

Once they reached the modern throne room, as Tullia dubbed it, they came face to face with a very incensed Grand High. She was lightly smoking blue as she floated in the air, her arms folded.

Tullia swallowed thickly, the milk tea she had now became a sour after taste in her now dry mouth. "Do you know what time it is?" She didn't wait for a response, she moved on. "I said three hours. Not five hours."

Her tone went glacier cold.

The Grand High wore a tracksuit that emphasized the fact that she was gorgeously sculpted, with her hair pulled back into an unforgivably tight ponytail that went down to her lower back in thick black waves. Her face, a delicate collage of snow kissed white and rich as the velvet night skin, was creased with displeasure. Her glossed lips were set in a deep frown.

Sabin didn't react, he tasted of exasperation as he strode in arrogantly, unfazed by her anger, silently maneuvering his way to the sofa. He sat down, still ignoring the Grand High and sprawled his massive body out on the couch. "We are, as you always say witch, fashionably late." Sabin's gold eyes took on an edge as he stared at her in an almost challenging way.

The blue smoke that the Grand High emitted started to become thicker as she glowered at Sabin. He gazed back at her coldly with his mostly masked face, the tension in the air began a hard crescendo. Tullia was tense still by the door, she was waiting for the flames to appear on Sabin's ninja mask due to the heat in Cliona's inky eyes. However, as fast as the anger soared, it dropped swiftly back down when the Grand High merely let out a long, pained groan. "If you weren't magic resistant, I would turn you into a candle then burn you down…slowly."

"Hmm," Sabin propped his big, booted feet on the coffee table, folding his hands across his abdomen. A classic masculine position. "I thought you didn't fancy me?"

Tullia sunk her teeth into her bottom lip to keep from laughing out loud, the aggravation in Cliona's emotion was salty and flat in depth. Tullia began to enter the room slowly, with Chito shuffling along right next to her, still clutching at her arm. Cliona turned her midnight drenched eyes to the ceiling, ignoring Sabin's quip, then she turned her face to Tullia.

"Hurry and sit down." Her tone was sharp but not vicious, more irritated than anything else. Tullia quickly scurried to Sabin's side, sitting down on the soft sofa and dragging Chito down with her.

Safe and sitting.

The Grand High eyed everyone for a moment, before flicking her fingers out, the lights dimmed and blue smoke crept in the room from the ceiling corners.

"My witches have succeeded in locating three possible areas in which the dragon could be." She snapped her fingers as she reclined regally in the air.

"Turns out a lot has changed since the shapeshifter queen went to China. The three gorge dams submerged Qu Yangs original hometown, so it was moved to Yichang, which is in Hubei, China." She snapped again and a map appeared with an outline section of where the new hometown was. "Wudang Mountain is roughly four hours away from the Yangzi river, which is the river right next to Yichang." A red X appeared over a mountain range with the name Wudang and the Yangtze river was labeled.

Tullia was already confused though.

"Now, listen carefully for this will all connect, and I am not repeating myself, cause I'm not about this lecture life." Cliona flexed her fingers. "The Wudang Mountain contains Taoist temples and monasteries that are associated with the god Xuawu, which is a black turtle and snake god."

He liked the way mountains came up high around the depression, like a defense, like a barrier.

A symbol of a black turtle entwined with a black snake was placed above the Wudang mountain.

"Here is what my brilliant anthropologist and archaeologist witches hypothesize. Jiang Li is a river dragon; the Yangtze river is the largest river in Asia. The Wudang mountain range is not only occupied by a group that worships Xuawu, to which a dragon would not disrespect a god by encroaching on his territory. Plus, the mountain range is pretty far away from the river. Therefore, Jiang Li's location would be limited to the river side. And!" Cliona took a deep breath. "Where would a dragon who's into himself like to be? Obviously, the largest river in Asia. The Yangtze."

Tullia didn't understand what the Grand High was talking about. She sneaked looks sideways at Sabin and Chito. Both had focused eyes and expressions (she couldn't completely tell with Sabin's face, being all covered and whatnot, but he looked collected and super worldly, nodding every now and then, so she assumed he knew what was going on).

Well, she was the idiot of the group and she had confirmation.

The water bubbled up and clawed its way outward. His water grew, greedily seeking more space and bullying the earth into submission creating taller mountains around his water.

Tullia shook her head lightly to dispel the lingering remnants of the vision. This one was a persistent thing, and she didn't understand why. However, she did not want another vision, not after the last one.

"So!" The Grand High clapped her long hands together. "What does this mean? It means that there is a high chance that the dragon, since he's a river dragon, will be located close to the Yangtze river. Also, since he's a supposed fanboy of Qu Yuan, we will have better luck if we try to find Zigui's original location. Which what is Zigui?" Cliona didn't wait for anyone to answer. "It's Qu Yuan's original hometown that was submerged. Which is actually upstream to the new city." The Grand High was pointing and motioning with her fingers in upward motions. "Again, the waters from the reservoir submerged it completely, which actually occurred quite recently." There was a red arrow that pointed westward from Yichang. "There's a high probability that the dragon will be within fifty miles west of Yichang."

There were even little bushes in the crater, small and spindly trying to hide from the intense sunshine that poured in. Some little bushes even managed to grow on the side of the craggy walls.

Tullia stared at the floating map, the Grand High's voice fading away. From what Tullia managed to piece together, with an extreme amount of effort, the logic was solid, everything she said made sense. A tugging sensation within her mind rejected the Grand High's seemingly tight logic and kept flashing to dragon made mountains and lake, with a hidden underwater sinkhole and dragon in it. The hidden crater could very well be in the Yangtze's river…Tullia didn't know for sure.

Tullia flexed her jaw, the tingling sensation of words wanting to be spoken, but fear choked her holding them back. She didn't want to sound stupid or worse, she didn't want to sound too confident and then she was wrong. Clearly the Grand High's team researched the little facts they had to go on thoroughly, and they came to very sound, logical conclusions, whereas Tullia had a vision that may or may not be the actual location of the dragon. She didn't even know where the hole was. Besides it was covered with water, so what did that make it…a lake?

She bit her lip as doubt began to saturate her mind. Just because there were a few instances where her visions were correct, it doesn't mean they were always accurate. Besides how long ago was the crater cover-up done? Was he even still there? Probably not.

"There's also a chance that the dragon moved." Sabin input, his deep voice vibrating through her ear, echoing her fears. "Just because he does not age, does not mean he remains in the same location." His tone was light enough, but Tullia could taste a bitter flavor that was faint, but very much present. She glanced at Sabin curiously, was he thinking about himself, who did not age? From some of his stories he shared with her on that one night after the wake, he had never stayed in a place longer than two years. Was he always changing too? Or was he forced to change and become transient due to this situation? "He may be hiding in a cave, miles away from a river."

Her entire being agreed with his words, except it wasn't a cave. More of an underwater hideout with a magic seal.

Cliona wagged her finger at him, "Listen, meathead, the Queen of Biringan said he was a fanboy of this dead poet. You don't just freak out over anyone to anyone. That's a dedicated level." She clicked her tongue. "Besides, it's our best bet to start there. The Yangtze river is huge, lot of surface area to choose from."

"There are also other rivers in China to consider." He countered; his tone was level with a blatant edge of stubbornness.

Cliona gave a hissing sigh. "Then where would you start? Huh? A small, dinky ass river or a big one?"

Tullia had the impression that Sabin bared his teeth under his mask. But before he could say anything, most likely a smart-ass comment, Chito spoke.

"Either way," He said quickly, trying to diffuse the once again rising tension, "since Jiang Li is, supposedly, a conceited river dragon it would make sense to look near the biggest river in China first, then consider other rivers if he can't be found." Chito's voice tilted prettily as he spoke English.

He was turning out to be such a pretty person.

Humans disappointed him and his presence seemed to be disregarded. Therefore, he would disregard humans entirely.

Tullia chewed on her lower lip, thinking, trying to push away the doubtful clouds that fogged her mind. Everyone's voices faded again and her senses blurred as she focused intensely on what was bugging her.

Everything said…was wrong.

Dead wrong. She'd bet her right hand on that.

She slid her eyes from the diagram to her hands. Her normal, not burly, girl hands. Again, logically, everything the Grand High was saying made complete sense. She raised her eyes to look at Chito as Sabin and Cliona argued on the dragon's location. His focus was intense on the arguing, his bright brown eyes darting between the two of them. Tullia looked back at the map. Her eyes seemed to want to ignore the river entirely.

He wasn't there.

He wasn't anywhere near the river. He…left the river. That felt right. He wasn't by the river.

He would disregard humans entirely.

A river dragon who forsook the river…what did that make him?

A rogue river dragon? Just a normal dragon?

Sabin's short sigh drew her attention back to what was being discussed. The Grand High snapped her fingers, the floating diagram disappeared, and the lights turned back on.

"Very well." Sabin's voice was flat, but Tullia tasted the slightly musty taste of someone being sulky.

"Damn right it's all well." Cliona flicked her hair over her shoulder with intense arrogance.

He's not there.

"Now, before I was so rudely questioned, besides an exact location along the riverside, there is one more slight problem." Cliona let out a giant sigh, looking up at the ceiling momentarily. "Unfortunately, the closest clan of witches is located in Shanghai." She flicked her finger out and the map appeared again, only this time with Shanghai circled in red. "Which is way too far away to consider asking them for aid. So, we must fly to Shanghai and travel from there by car then by foot. Bottom line, it's gonna take a hot minute."

It would take weeks at the very least to get there and to begin the search for a dragon that wasn't there.

He's not there.

Tullia pressed her lips together tightly, while forcing her stiff throat muscle to swallow. Fear kept her quiet, because what if she was wrong?

"We need to book flights then." Sabin stated. The Grand High blinked at him, then started laughing, she bent over slightly as she convulsed with genuine laughter that sprinkled that air with tinkling chimes.

Tullia giggled, the bubbliness on her tongue from Cliona's deep humor tickled her.

He's not there.

Laughter within her died swiftly.

"Berserker," The Grand High sighed, wiping her eyes in a dramatic fashion. "I don't fly commercial; I don't even fly first class. I'm above all that. We're going to take *my* plane."

Sabin shrugged his big shoulders, clearly uncaring.

Cliona began going into the details of the travel plans, where they would stop first and where they would begin their search. It appeared that her little witch underlings prepped travel plans too.

Which was smart.

He's not there. He's so not there.

Tullia flexed her jaw, becoming anxious as the thought began to loop within her mind in a repetitive manner.

He's not there. You're wasting time, he's not there. He's here.

The image of the beautiful lake surrounded by mountains came into her mind, bright and slightly disorienting.

He's there.

"So, since it is getting colder, make sure you pack something warm. Cheeto Puff, you got warm clothes?"

He's not there.

"I have a shawl." Chito said brightly. She squeezed her hands together.

He's not there.

"Uh-huh." The Grand High's tone was disinterested and slightly skeptical.

He's not there.

"You're from the tropics, so I'm going to have my people pack you something. I don't want to hear you whining and I don't want to waste any magical energy to craft you something."

He's not there. He's not there.

Cliona focused her big eyes onto Tullia. The inky depths seemed to swirl.

He's not there. He's not there. He's not there. He's not there.

"Petal, I'm dressing you." She turned to Sabin, then turned her nose up at him.

He's not there. He's not there. He's not there. He's not there. He's not there. He's—

"Not there." Tullia blurted out. She slapped her hands over her mouth, shocked by the fact that she spoke without her permission. How dare Tullia speak without her permission.

Cliona furrowed her eyebrows, her intensity focused once again on Tullia. "You're not getting out of it. I pick your outfits. You can't dress."

Annoyance was tart along her tongue. Tullia nodded swiftly, happy to be misheard, panicked that she may slip up again.

She felt eyes on her. She turned to see Sabin looking at her with his bright tawny gaze.

Don't look at me. He's not there. But I don't know for sure.

"What's on your mind Tullia?" Sabin's deep voice, night drenched and velvet, soothed her frazzled nerves somewhat. Tullia shifted in the plush chair, painfully aware that the eyes of everyone in the room watched her, and waited for her to speak further.

He's not there.

Well, Tullia was never one to truly fight off a losing battle. Here goes nothing. *I'm insane anyways, at least legally, so she could whip that out as an excuse if things got weird.* Tullia inhaled.

"Jiang Li, he's not by the river. I—" She paused, swallowing the knot of fear clogging her throat, "I saw him create his lair from a hole in the ground… Well, it was more like a crater and then he made a lake or something over it. And I think that's where he is and it's not by the river. It was on a mountain. Maybe." She twisted her hands in her lap, nervous. She wasn't used to speaking about what she saw in her visions. It was crazy talk…to normal people.

Chito bounced closer to Tullia on the couch so that his thigh pressed against hers. A faint smell of vanilla and mangoes wafted from him. "You saw a vision? *Another* one?"

Tullia blinked at his excited reaction, then squirmed a bit, anxious with all the eyes still on her. She gave a short nod. "Yes. I saw the dragon." She tried not to recoil from the stares. They weren't mean stares, they weren't even stares that said she was crazy like she was used to getting.

After all, they all proved it; she wasn't crazy. She was just forcefully influenced. She straightened her spine.

"He's not near a river, but in a lake." Her voice made an effort not to sound weak, but it didn't sound confident, it was similar to a timid mouse squeak.

"A lake?" The Grand High said slowly, she tilted her head, regarding Tullia. "A great river dragon up and ditched the biggest and baddest river in Asia to be a *lake* dragon instead?" Cliona folded her arms, clearly, she was not impressed. "I'm not convinced, petal."

Tullia swallowed the dry and sour taste of the Grand High's skepticism, but Tullia wasn't crazy anymore. They did prove it. And she could actually be useful, she could actually help with the lost magic's side effects.

"No." Tullia inhaled deeply and faked a steady, firm voice. "He's not there. He had a falling out with the human race, or so the vision I had suggested. He abandoned his river and occupied a lake that he created to hide a giant hole in a mountain top."

She waved her hands about in the air as she spoke, thinking about how to articulate what she saw so that they could understand.

The Grand High's face was wrinkled with confusion, and Chito looked bemused.

Tullia wilted a little, then chewed her lip. "It was this hole in the mountain originally. And it was deep and rocky…"

"A crater." Sabin supplied; his tawny eyes were warm. This helped her to unshrink herself a little.

She had one person at least that was listening to her seriously.

The Grand High still didn't look convinced. "Petal, how sure are you that it was the dragon we need?"

"Don't we simply need *a* dragon?" Sabin countered before Tullia could speak. "Why must we hunt for this specific one when Tullia has provided us with a more specific location to a dragon?"

"Shut up Sabin, you're dumb." The Grand High flicked a silent explicit at him with her middle finger.

Tullia pressed her lips together to stop from laughing, with her nerves strung so tight she may end up crying like a lunatic.

The Grand High's face was considering, and a cold draft entered the room. "If you had the answer the entire time on the location of a dragon why didn't you speak up?" She then cut Tullia a hard look. "Girl, I did not need that type of travel if it's unnecessary."

Tullia felt a chill go down her spine. The Grand High was angry, the heat on her tongue was proof enough. She quickly held up her hands in defense. "I didn't know of his location until literally after everything had happened in Biringan. I only saw it recently."

"How recent?" The Grand High's consonants were pounced harshly.

Tullia shrank back a bit. "R-right before we left Biringan City?" Sabin shifted in his seat, moving closer to Tullia. Chito took her right hand in his, squeezing it a bit.

The Grand High didn't say anything for a very long minute, almost making Tullia pee from how hard her bladder was trembling. The heat on her tongue dimmed then faded completely. Cliona groaned loudly. "If only you had seen that a few days earlier, then there wouldn't have been a need to go there and talk to the Queen and get sweaty and gross from the humidity." There was an intensely salty flavor in Tullia's mouth, making her desperate for some water.

Swallowing thickly against the desire for water, Tullia managed, "Well, on the bright side, you put your magic inside the hidden city, so it's no longer hidden from you." Tullia raised an eyebrow at Cliona's beautiful and irritated form. "I'd say it was a win." The ending was said weakly as was Tullia's smile.

She rolled her eyes, but the salt flavor lessened as she crossed her arms. Tullia watched her tap her unnaturally long fingers against her forearm, thinking. "So, a giant crater that's covered by a big body of water in China, right?"

A small pinch and a strong feeling of rightness, Tullia nodded eagerly. "Yes."

He was there.

A harsh sigh. "Let me summon my witches again for re-analysis."

* * *

Tullia didn't know how the Grand High's witches did it, but they presented her with two possible locations based on geography and recent monster sightings in China.

"Many humans can see the other creatures," One of the Grand High's witches told Tullia briskly as she was fiddling nervously with her papers. Her eyes never left Cliona as she spoke with the other witch. "But the majority cannot. Which is why these sightings usually don't become national news. More, location specific news I suppose."

Tullia found that utterly fascinating. When she asked why some humans could see things but others could not, the witch shrugged, jittery like a rabbit on speed.

"There are a few theories, mostly it has to do with the sensitivity of the human and the location, for some locations are magic drenched, and of course, the willingness of personal beliefs. If they don't want to see it, they won't. Or if they don't want to believe in it, then they won't see anything either. However," The witch turned her cat narrowed green eyes to stare at Tullia gravely, "Just because you don't want to see something, it doesn't mean it is not there."

After her somber words, the witch quickly scuttled away as the Grand High motioned her hither before Tullia could ask her any more questions.

The two locations in China where Jiang Li, the ex-river dragon, could possibly be were either Heaven's Lake or Qinghai Lake.

The first and most plausible location, to Tullia at least, where the dragon may be living was Heaven's Lake located on the border of China and

North Korea. It was a cratered lake in the Baekdu mountains and looked utterly gorgeous from all the pictures shown on the slide show. The fact that the water was cratered, surrounded by mini mountains, as Tullia thought of them as, matched what she saw through Jiang Li's eyes. Though he didn't bother to admire his handy work for long, he was more focused on the water aspect of the lake. According to the witches, there had been a few sightings of creatures swimming in the water, but none of the pictures were very convincing in terms of the quality or the sighting credibility.

Plus, another negative about Heaven's Lake was that it is a tourist destination. This fact had Sabin frowning, at least that was Tullia's impression from the crease between his eyes.

"If he dislikes humans, this place is far too busy with them."

"I know he did. But I think it was a very, very, very long time ago." Tullia murmured.

The second option was Qinghai Lake, which was the largest lake in China. Apparently, many people have sighted a dragon in the lake, with an army troop giving a description of a dragon with a snake like head and black scaled body. Tullia dismissed the lake in her head immediately. Jiang Li was an array of blues and whites. There wasn't a single dark spot on the dragon. Plus, where was the crater and the mountains?

After Cliona dismissed her little followers with a nod and a wave of her hand, a brief pondering silence encased the room.

"So," Cliona said, "You see the two lakes, which one?" She looked to Tullia for this answer, and Tullia found Sabin and Chito's eyes on her as well.

The spotlight was intense, but Tullia tried not to wilt. "I think…Heaven's

Lake would be our best bet."

Fake the confidence, fake the confidence….

"Why?" Sabin asked, his tone wasn't distrustful, nor did he taste of any malice flavors of distrust, just curiosity.

However, the question still dinged her fragile confidence of sanity.

"Um," Tullia rolled her shoulders, trying to loosen the tightness, "I saw Jiang Li create his body of water, the water pushed the earth around it up to make the mountains surrounding the water bigger," She made a cratering gesture with her hands, "creating bigger mountain peaks." She looked at Sabin briefly then flickered her eyes away quickly. She didn't want to look too closely. "I also think that the description of the other dragon in the Qinghai Lake is wrong, Jiang Li is a blue river dragon, not black."

Chito seemed to digest this, he played with his long hair between slender fingers, then said, "What if there are other lakes, unknown lakes in China with no rumored sightings of a creature in it and that is where he is." He surveyed the room, looking at everyone, "That is a possibility."

Tullia thought about it, and decided he was so right. Just because there were monster sightings doesn't mean anything. Jiang Li could've never left his little crater once he entered it for hundreds of years, thus no sightings. He could have even moved somewhere else. He could have been stealthy in leaving his crater too. He was a mythical creature; he could be mythically sneaky. He could have reclaimed humans and moved back to the Yangtze river. Tullia looked at the Grand High. "Perhaps, we should have more information on crater lakes in China? Just in case Heaven's Lake isn't the one? Maybe your original plan is better. I mean, the dragon could have moved. I—I don't know the exact time frame or anything."

The Grand High tapped her fingers together rhythmically. "Petal, you're being wishy-washy. And that'll take forever and a decade to pinpoint all of China's crater lakes." She ran her tongue over her upper lip.

Sabin crossed his arms over his chest. "We need to see what Tullia is seeing. Do you think you can draw it?" He was addressing Tullia.

She opened her mouth to respond that artistry skipped over every bone in her body. But the exalted sound the Grand High made had Tullia looking over at her instead. Cliona stared at Sabin, her face surprised and thoughtful. "Well, look at that. Mr. Meathead actually had a good thought." She turned her beautiful face towards Tullia and smiled radiantly. Tullia's eyes burned under all her beauty. "Tell me petal, do you know what the lake looks like from your vision? Can you recall details from what you saw?"

Tullia nodded slowly. She had the image in her mind, as if she had personally been there to witness it. It was a very blue lake with mini mountains encircling it protectively.

"Alright then." A silvery glint shown in the Grand High's fathomless eyes. She held out her hands, palms up and beckoned Tullia over with her long fingers. "Come here." Her voice was soft, seductive.

Tullia found herself standing without a single hesitation. She was a queen and Tullia did believe in manners.

"Witch." Sabin grabbed Tullia's arm, his gloved covered hand was warm, and the fabric was rough on her bare skin. "What are you going to do?"

Cliona bared her teeth at Sabin. "Sink my nails into her face and tear out her eyes so I can look into them."

Tullia blinked, the Grand High was lying, the sooty flavor all in her mouth confirmed it for Tullia. But still, the imagery was scary, for the Grand High would do it if she felt like it, of that Tullia was very, very certain.

When Sabin simply waited for her truthful answer in distrustful silence, the Grand High gave a hissing sigh.

"I'm merely doing a projection spell, meathead. What she thinks about will be displayed to all of us to see." Her words were said slowly, like she was talking to someone of low intelligence and her tone was frosted. "Like you suggested. *Stu-pid.*"

Tullia's eyes widened in horror. Whatever she thought of, everyone could *see*? What if she thought of something stupid? Or inappropriate? Or what if she didn't think of the right thing? Or what if she suddenly remembered the most embarrassing thing that had happened to her? Like tripping on air then falling on her face in a McDonalds and dumping her entire drink all over her, which then put her grandma bra (that she found on clearance at Walmart) painfully outlined due to her wet shirt, in the middle of a lunch rush.

She bit her bottom lip, suddenly hugely nervous.

"We all need to see what she's seeing. Stabbing around in the dark isn't going to help anyone and time is of the essence. We don't have centuries to crack this case, Tullia will be long dead by then." She heckled at Sabin. He didn't so much as flinch at her icy rage, though apparently Chito could feel some intense draft, and slid as far away as he could get from Sabin on the couch.

"Your mind holds rot in it and I don't trust you." Sabin said simply.

"I'm invested in this girl." She haughtily whipped her hair behind her shoulders. She managed to look down at him even though he was hulking in his height. "I'm not stupid, I do not harm my investments. I'd sooner do you harm, Berserker."

A very small tang of humor. "You could certainly try, witch. You wouldn't manage any damage." His deep voice seemed to vibrate up Tullia's spine. "After all, you can only wield *magic*."

"You mock me as if it's a mundane task." Cliona's lips curled back over straight and perfect teeth. "I can wield it to throw things at your big ass head."

Sabin shrugged, not disagreeing with her. They were like siblings, Tullia thought with some amusement. Their relationship was an intensified sibling rivalry that involved fire, blades, and savagery.

How nice.

Cliona turned her hotly irritated eyes at Tullia. "Come here." It was sharper than last time, but not unkind. The beautiful woman was not to be disobeyed, Tullia went forward again, Sabin's hand slid from her arm, releasing her, and she missed the solidness of it. It was reassuring and friendly, something she had never had before.

The Grand High held out her long fingered hands towards Tullia. She saw the blue smoke waft up from her fingertips. Tullia held her hands up and over the Grand High's, not touching. The blue smoke didn't touch Tullia, it almost seemed hesitant to touch her directly.

The Grand High closed her eyes, her mouth opened slightly, and her brows furrowed with concentration. Tullia thought hard over the vision that she had, about the crater lake, the little crumbly rocks, the way the dragon filled the hole up with water…

Her bladder twinged, she kinda had to pee. The milk tea had processed through her and now her bladder was full and ready to be emptied.

Tullia ripped her mind away from the fact that she had to pee back to the dragon. She focused on Jiang Li falling through the floor to the second layer… then smelling sulfur…

Tullia yawned then, her jaw cracked with the force and her eyes watered. The Grand High's eyebrows rose and fell, seeming in deep concentration. Tullia felt her brows furrowing too, trying hard to keep her mind from wandering.

Jiang Li… the blue water inside the crater… the other things…. Merrows… Naga…

Tullia frowned, thinking over all of the mythical creatures that she had seen. It dawned on her that she has never seen a unicorn in any of her visions….

Does that mean they don't exist!?

That would be very, very saddening. Unicorns were awesome, at least, the way humans interpreted them. Except there was that one horror movie about a unicorn…

The Grand High suddenly wrapped her long fingers around Tullia's hands, clutching them tight. She gasped and Tullia felt the world tilt violently then explode in a flurry of colors and images.

Her vision of Jiang Li consumed her, but this time it was in HD quality. It was as if she were actually standing in the crater and feeling the slight breeze that tiptoed through the air on a rather icy day. She felt like she was part of the scene instead of just seeing the event. Faintly, she heard a flurry of words, but she didn't understand them, and it seemed so very far away. Besides, she was in a crater right now. Tullia saw the sunlight pour in, touching every craggy wall and the smell of dry earth, a touch of sulfur and a frost ladened scent that thickened the air magically. Her view seemed to flicker, pause, then push forward *fast*. Tullia gritted her teeth as the speed in which the environment around her swirled. Then, once her vision of Jiang Li was finished, it rolled into another scene of the Japanese dragon, in all his playfulness and grandness. He was stomping through some field, then her breath escaped her when the Japanese dragon dove and crashed into the ocean, where a lightless palace sat amid the deepest recesses of the ocean. Fish with jagged teeth and bulging eyes scuttled amongst the coral.

There was a mass of Merrows, floating in a tight circle with their sleek fins and sharp looking claws. Tullia squinted at the group, just what are they doing, when she was flung up and out of the inky water and onto the sand. The sun was bright, painfully so, and the air swirled with the sounds of hisses and crushed sand. The Naga's were slithering about in the sand, their armor clanked and glistened dangerously. Before Tullia could fully process the scene the ground, once yellow sand, darkened and became muddy as fat raindrop pelted the ground punishingly. Thin rivulets of red bled in the rain. A heavy sob could be heard underneath the screaming downpour and an icy frost slid up her arms.

No. No. No. No. She couldn't shut her eyes.

Tullia felt her internal scream as the view slowly inched up. More red, blue black fingernails...

NO. NO. NO. NO. NO. NO!

Hard hands gripped her shoulders and yanked her against a very solid chest. The scene melted away in a fogged blur of red, blue and black. Tullia exhaled sharply, her muscles lost all the starch they had and became unstable jelly. She felt dizzy, blinking rapidly to try and regain her vision. She had never had that many visions at once, it felt as if someone had fast-forwarded them like a movie. It was a horrid sensation. Her legs wobbled then gave out entirely. Before she smashed her knees on the floor, Sabin scooped her up and pressed her tight against him. His warmth was delicious and Tullia realized just how cold she was and how deep the chill seemed to seep within her. She wrapped her arms around Sabin's ninja clad shoulders and buried her face into his ninja covered neck.

That was just awful. She felt as if she had been physically dragged through an icy bone yard with zombies and ghouls and spiders. She squeezed Sabin tighter, fighting the sudden rise of emotions, fighting viciously against the tears that climbed her throat and began to rim her eyes with moisture.

She would not cry dammit. She cried way too much today and it was super embarrassing to cry in front of people. She could cry later, when she was alone and when it was dark.

"It seems," Cliona gasped on a particularly reedy laugh, "Petal has certainly seen…a lot." Tullia peaked at the Grand High. She shook her head, her silky hair splaying back and forth wildly in her ponytail. Her pure black eyes held an insane gleam. "It reaffirms why I am going the distance for this." Her smile was twisted and mean, she clicked her nails together and a huge image of what the dragon, Jiang Li, had created floated into the air like a hologram.

"This is what the dragon looks like." She studied it closely, then clicked her nails again. "And this is what he made." She rotated the image a bit. "We will compare a few cratered lakes and see which one is the closest in resemblance then rank them down from there."

Cliona looked at Sabin, her twisted smile turning into a snarling baring of her teeth. "Judging me? Of course, it had to be done. Look at the results." She tilted her head to the image that was plucked from Tullia's vision. "We can't just go off of her description. Look at how accurate this is compared to what she was saying."

Tullia trembled a little, her heart still racing and her mind still churning with disorientation. She wished she could see the image the Grand High was using if her eyes would frickin' focus.

"You trespassed far further than welcomed, hag." Sabin's tone was… *demonic*. Dark, bleeding with rage and doused with fire. Tullia was still numb, she couldn't really taste his exact emotions. She got traces of rot, insanity, heavy spice, rage, and a salty… gagging flavor….

"Well," The Grand High seemed to drawl, Tullia caught wisps of blue smoke, "It got us results did it not? You act as if I skinned her. The lost magic may have taken me deeper than I needed, but what's done is done." One of her shoulders came up in an indifferent shrug. "Besides, knowledge is power."

Tullia swore she could hear Sabin's teeth grind under the pressure of his clenched jaw. She could see the stiffness in his neck, so much that a tendon was sticking out through the fabric. "You violated her."

Tullia's eyes finally were able to focus, she saw Cliona curled up, like a python readying for a strike. "*Violate?* Hardly." She said through her teeth. "It's her mind that I was all but dragged through."

"So, you didn't know how to stop it then?"

Silence. The Grand High's face went arctic.

"You knew," Sabin growled, "yet, you continued. You could have broken her."

The Grand High snorted, waving her hand at his words. "You treat her as if she's spun of glass, she's got a bit more substance than that."

"She is human, and you seem to forget that." Sabin's tone was condescending. "It is not a mystery why all your other…investments broke."

Cliona ran her tongue over her top teeth. Her dark eyes impossible to read. "What do you know of my investments?"

Sabin's arms flexed around Tullia. It briefly flickered in her mind that when Sabin was around, she had never felt more protected and more female than she did in this moment. The tension rose to a nearly shattering level, breaking her from her wayward thought. She wanted to tell them both to drop the whole thing, but if Sabin could get the Grand High to not do what she did, fast forward all of her visions at mach speed, then that would make Tullia's life less nauseating.

"You try to groom successors, since natural magic is dwindling in your children. Yet, you keep breaking all the ones with potential." Sabin's voice was frost coated steel.

Cliona snapped her teeth at him. "You think you know everything." A flash of white in her midnight eyes, a touch of pungent insanity. "Fine. I'll make sure to put on kiddy gloves when dealing with Tullia. Now do me a favor, shut up for the rest of the day. Or I will summon all the butter knives in the world to be embedded into your skin. Repeatedly.

And endlessly."

Sabin didn't say anything, but he didn't need to. Though Tullia didn't think that the epic threat that the Grand High had growled out scared Sabin, there was no sour tasting fear on her palate, but instead they seemed to come to a mutual agreement. Then tension eased, though it did not dissipate entirely. She felt Sabin shift, then he began to walk. She heard and felt Sabin sit down, probably back on the couch by the soft squeaked sounds. Though he now sat, he did not release Tullia, rather he gently re-positioned her on him.

She inhaled, then winced as a sharp, hot pain drilled deep into her head on her left side. Then a steady throb began to pulsate from the pain and the light seemed to drive sharp daggers into her brain through her eyes. She buried her head into the crook of Sabin's broad shoulder and neck. Though he lacked any sort of softness, the extreme firmness was comforting and the clean, woodsy smell was soothing. And the fact that Sabin was a person, rather than a pillow giving comfort made her chest tighten.

It was turning out to be a very long day, she thought as Sabin's steady heart rate thrummed rhythmically under her ear from his neck. Her thoughts melted into the darkness that reached up within her.

And for the first time since she could remember, she did not dream as she slept.

* * *

Tullia's soft breath warmed the fabric covering the side of his neck. Her body became a solid weight in his arms as the stiffness left her entirely. Her softness pressed against him firmly and her warmth began to permeate through his clothes. She was a tiny furnace.

The witch had called in her cult minions, then barked out rough commands to them. Sabin could feel her hostility, her excitement, but he chose to ignore it and focus on the softness that was Tullia in his arms. The fact that she had fallen asleep on Sabin, without hesitation, gave him a complex feeling between exasperation that she was far too trusting and satisfaction that she trusted him. His rage had been a vivid beast within him as he spoke with the insane witch. He almost wanted her to summon those knives, he wanted her blood to stain his hands and wanted to laugh as horror bloomed across her face when she realized what he truly was. The witch fancied herself powerful. She was. Not against him though. After all, how can you kill someone who cannot die? Who is fueled further into madness by pain?

It is the same as trying to harm the air.

He was held back by a sheer thread. The fact that Tullia was in his arms and she was not untouchable by death kept his rage internal. It screamed and tore his insides, but it was contained.

Chito fiddled nervously on the couch next to Sabin, he had a phone and was swiftly tapping away at the screen. Sabin hated phones. Though they were better than birds, he still hated them. He briefly wondered if the boy harbored regrets about leaving his plush royal life and joining a less than stable crew. However, the thought was insubstantial and faded quickly. Sabin's attention became focused on Tullia again. He made note of the way she fit in his arms, the way her curves molded into him and the way her scent, ripe sweet gale, began to fill his lungs, intoxicating him. He was in a sensory heaven and hell of sorts, gently petting his ever-present rage into a comatose state while aggravating it simultaneously.

"S-Sabin?" Chito's timid voice ruptured Sabin's infusion of Tullia's essence and poked at the rage within him. Sabin cut a look down at the boy. He rubbed Tullia's back with one hand, trying to calm himself. Her small, vulnerable spine under his hand highlighted how fragile she was. And the girl was sleeping on him.

Would she be calm if she knew just how blood soaked he was? Would she cower if he described how he killed them all? How his cursed axes ate the blood greedily? Would she shudder at who he killed? At the reasons why he killed?

His rage wavered under Sabin's calm action and Tullia's supple weight on him. His heart mimicked her slow heartbeats and his rage receded enough for him to answer the prince calmly.

"Yes?"

The prince shifted, uneasily. "Um, is…" Sabin saw the prince cut a swift look towards where the witch prattled about. Her hands waved wildly and her hair nearly stood up. His voice dropped to a soft whisper, "is the Grand High…evil?"

Sabin heard her snort, but did not address him, it would appear she left that to Sabin.

He felt himself sigh internally, if only she was evil. Rarely are creatures ever wholly evil or wholly good. He'd have easily removed her if she was doing more harm than good, but she was doing a lot of good by exterminating vampire vermin and keeping an iron clad fist over her coven from running wild. With that being said…

"Not entirely. She's almost gone though." He murmured, his eyes glancing at the witch. She was still wiggling her fingers rapidly, but walking away with her groupies flouncing around her. "And she knows it. She has too much pride and a facade to upkeep in front of her cult though."

"She's almost gone?" The prince's confusion and the tilt of his head reminded him of a small pup. He felt a small twitch tug at the corners of his mouth.

"She's insane." He put it bluntly. "But she has just enough sanity to keep the insanity in line." He paused, "Barely." He finished.

Chito was quiet for a moment, Sabin could feel him digesting what he was told. Then when he spoke his voice was very, very low. "She's dangerous."

To those who weren't magic immune, he supposed she was lethal. "Indeed."

The prince paused again, longer this time. "She's not truly an ally to us then."

Sabin shrugged, but kept quiet. The witch was in this little escapade for her own selfish reasons. She wanted Tullia's lost magic, Tullia wanted it gone. The witch had the connections to make the seemingly impossible, possible. Chito was merely along for the ride. Everyone had their reasons, none of them were selfless.

"Then what about you?" Chito turned his entire body to face Sabin. He glanced at the prince, disinterested.

At his non answer, Chito said, on a slight huff, shaking his head in a way that Sabin had come to associate with the privileged. "Well? Are you an ally? Are you Tullia's lover? Is that why you protect her?"

Sabin stiffened with surprise. His arm tightened around Tullia to the point she made a soft protest. Sabin forced himself to loosen his arms, but he still felt the sharp unexpected astonishment that was laced throughout his body.

Lover?

Chito seemed to blink in surprise. "Well, yes. I thought Tullia was your lover."

He pressed his lips firmly together and forced himself to relax each and every muscle by sheer will. He didn't know he had spoken out loud and he was flustered by the assumption that he was Tullia's *lover*…it was inconceivable. He instinctively looked down at Tullia's face. Her eyes were closed, her dark lashes stark against her pale face. She had very little color in her cheeks and her lips were the palest shade of pink. She had a very small beauty mark about her left brow…

He was stunned to realize that Tullia was very pretty. She was adorable when she was awake, bouncing and animated, like a small creature. He liked her upbeat energy. But asleep he could see the fine details of her features. The slight tilt of her eyes, the deep indent above her lip, the very faint, delicate blue veins on her eyelids, and the soft arch to her eyebrows.

He knew Tullia was female, but he now saw that she was a *woman*. He swallowed, his hands becoming awkward and his body becoming hyper aware of her body over his.

"You're filth of the earth. Anything you touch will be stained by your sins."

Blood droplets began to drip onto her pale skin from his face, staining it. Her check bled and her nose began to drip red…

He ripped his eyes away from her face, his rage roared back to life, bigger than before. His heart thundered in his chest; his mouth became dry; his breathing became ragged. Sabin had forgot. He had forgotten that he was. He exhaled slowly and looked down at Tullia, her face was clean and spotless.

Good.

She wasn't *his*, he was protecting an innocent from the vicious insanity of the witch. There was nothing more, nothing less. The fact that Tullia was agreeable and pleasant to interact with made Sabin lower his guard. His razor-sharp panic subsided at the coolness of his logic, though his rage did not cool.

The rage swirled in him, like a caged beast looking for an opening to attack and consumed.

He closed his eyes briefly, the lake of his youth, smooth, gray and sleepy filled his vision. His rage fluttered, seemingly hissed, unperturbed by the scene. He tried to force the serene over him through the image, but, naturally, one cannot force serenity.

His thoughts swiftly, nearly panicked, went to Tullia. On how her nose wrinkled with delight when she first took a sip of her tea today. Or the way she looked at him, curious about if he wore anything other than his mercenary attire. Which he didn't. Her gray eyes seemed to glitter whenever she spoke of pleasant things and all things she spoke of seemed to be pleasant.

His rage quivered, then yielded, settling down within him for a blessed moment.

Guilt flooded him when he opened his eyes, using Tullia as a method to calm himself down from his rage seemed to tarnish her in his mind. Almost as if he were making her to be some sort of cheap whore.

"Sabin?" Chito might as well have screamed his name, his heart jumped in his throat and his muscles seized in surprise. His rage flexed but stayed subdued within him.

"No." Sabin answered too fast and too hard. "I am but a contracted mercenary." Chito flinched at his tone.

He was forgetting himself. And he was reminded today, through a question that led to a thought not yet formed. He was just a mercenary. A bloodied, sullied, cursed mercenary trying to atone for the unforgivable sins he committed.

He would live his days out alone, until time itself stops.

He glanced down at Tullia's sleeping face. Sabin looked back up, seeing nothing.

He would not acknowledge anything. For it didn't matter. In the end, he would always be alone.

He was cursed to be.

Chapter Twenty

"This creature... is but a mere... human woman?" The sneer and anger in Akio's voice was a vivid sound in the quiet night. A sound that made the woman, whose back was towards them, hunched and trembling, become still. She did not turn around.

Feathers rustled; claws scraped along their weapons in readiness. But no one moved.

Hiroto eyed the female wearily. She was not a Tengu, that much was blatantly obvious. She did not have any feathers adorning her upper back and arms, she was wingless and had light hair. No Tengu was ever born with light hair, it was always a flawless black.

The creature seemed to wait for them. Her disturbingly bare skin, featherless, fur-less, was speckled with dirt, marred with scars and stained red in certain areas.

Hiroto held his claw up to his kin, to still their rustling impatience.

"Creature." Hiroto barked, his claw on the hilt of his sword. "You have *committed grievous crimes against our kind. We will not forgive your vicious attacks."*

They would face the creature head on, it was their way. The men behind Hiroto were the very best warriors of his clan. They were fearless, skilled and deadly. They had all but demanded to come along with Hiroto once the creature was discovered. They wanted its blood to bathe their blades.

The creature seemed to shudder at his words before it jerkily rose from its crouched position. It turned, facing them. Hiroto suppressed his disgust and his horror. It was female. She was barely clothed, save for pieces of scraps hanging low on her slender hips and two filthy sashes hanging across her chest.

Her face was savage. Her deadened blue eyes were slit like snakes and her teeth, jagged and sharp bared. Her lower jaw was discolored, and the skin seemed to be stretched too tight over her entire face, making her look gaunt. Her complexion was colorless, save for the blackened areas all around her eyes and mouth. Her light hair was limp, long and lifeless all around her nearly emaciated form.

She may have once been a less hideous woman, but now this woman was nothing more than a dirty beast.

She sagged her neck to the side, studying them with the intelligence of a predator. Her face scrunched in hostility.

For a shameful moment, Hiroto was frozen with fear. The female was... completely other, *one he had not encountered before. Scolding himself for his fear, he puffed out his feathers on his arms, back and chest, to make himself look bigger. Then glared at the creature.*

"You're the creature responsible for killing four of our younglings in our peaceful village and maiming our women."

His announcement was punctuated with low growls from his men behind him. To hurt the young and the innocent was an act that was shameful.

"I didn't kill them." Its voice was...beautiful and it startled him. Clear, crisp and light with a tilting accent that spoke of lands Hiroto could only imagine. The creature swayed in the still night, her eyes glinted with malice. "I ate them alive."

Hiroto stiffened and his men squawked with a searing rage and disgust. Their anger seemed to amuse her, he could see it by the way her fingers twitched and her vicious eyes glowed with mirth.

One of his men spat. "You have no honor to do such a thing."

"Coward!" Another one yelled.

Her mirth fell away from her face instantly, her eyes narrowed.

"Coward?" She swayed up, lengthening her body, flexing her clawed hands in a feline manner. "My prey are the children; they are what I hunt. And I am successful." A very cold grin full of sharp teeth glinted under the moon.

One of his soldiers stepped forward, as if to charge her, but Hiroto held a hand up to stop him.

"Why?" He was curious like a cat, a fault his mother had often scolded him for when he got into trouble due to his inquisitiveness. However, he had been taught by his master that the more one knew about his enemy, the greater the chance for success. So, he felt as though his curiosity was useful.

Hiroto had no information on the creature. Therefore, he needed to know more.

She slunk down again, snake-like and coiled. "Well," Her deadened blue eyes shifted, then shot right back to them, hungry and ferocious. "It's a long story. But now they taste good."

Acid filled his mouth.

"Disgusting beast." A raged filled tone, "I shall slaughter you and feed your corpse to the fire." Akio snarled, his sword was fully drawn, and he was advancing on the creature rapidly.

"Akio," Hiroto snapped, but he didn't listen. He was too enraged, his feathers puffed and his strides purposeful. Hiroto clenched his jaw, he should not have allowed him to come, he was too emotionally involved in this creature's killings.

The creature watched him approach, not moving. When Akio reached her, towering over the skinny creature's form, his sword held high and proud, she looked up at him. Then smiled serenely.

A blur, then a small, wet sound occurred before Akio's big body jerked harshly once, twice...then became still. Moments later he crumpled forward in a lifeless heap by her dirty feet.

The creature's mouth was a brilliant red, her jaw worked as she chewed furiously. Hiroto jerked, stunned by the scene. His strongest warrior was now lying dead by the feet of a tiny, foreign, dirty creature. Slayed in a matter of moments without being given a good battle. His throat was torn out and there was a gaping hole in his chest...through his armor.

His eyes snapped up from his now dead friend to the female. She stared at him, ice chips for eyes and a slight curve of her thin lips. She mocked him. Hiroto let out a roar of rage, drawing his sword.

He pointed his sword at the creature that was eating a part of his best soldier and dear friend.

"Your blood will feed my blade." He growled, the bloodlust of battle rising within him. He needed to see her blood drip from his sword.

She didn't say anything, only watched with unblinking eyes. Hiroto whipped his sword down and charged at the creature with another roar. His men followed suit, adding in their own war screams.

The creature smiled, chunks of pink flesh in between her teeth peeked out. She darted at them, her mouth opened in a silent snarl and her eyes bloodshot, pale claws extended.

The creature was fast. Hiroto could barely see her attacks. One moment she was in front of him, the next her claws were sunk into his ribs. Her face was disgustingly close to his for a mere second, before she was gone.

Hiroto gasped at the feeling of being stabbed and stumbled, his knees hitting the hard dirt with a jarring force. The creature flitted between him and his soldiers. He couldn't see her attack, but she'd stay still for a mere second. Watching the faces of those she attacked with a radiate smile. Hiroto gritted teeth, ignoring the white-hot pain in his side, as he struggled to his feet. He stood still, studying her flitted movements, his heart bleeding as he watched his beloved men fall to the ground, still and bloody. When one his men choked, his face ashen as the creature dug into his neck, Hiroto summoned every ounce of his determination and forced his agonized body to sprint. He saw her scrawny figure, saw her smile, raised her sword and swung it down.

A thud.

Hiroto's eyes focused, his sword was sticking out of the creature's chest, his sword had cut through the tough bone of her shoulder and sunk deep into the upper part of her chest.

A fatal move. Relief began to trickle into Hiroto painfilled body, this nightmare was now over...

The creature turned her head at him and snarled. With one hand she yanked the sword free from her body and used it to drag him closer to her. She flung his soldier away, and picked Hiroto up, as if he had the slight weight of a small child and not a full grown Tengu. As if he didn't tower a foot and a half above her.

"You hurt me." Her smooth voice said simply, woodenly, before she threw him. Hiroto let out a short-jagged scream as he flew through the air and landed painfully on the hard earth, skidding against the dewy grass. Coughing, Hiroto struggled to move, a lightning bolt of pain tore through him, stealing what little breath he had and seizing his limbs. He felt the blood rise up and seep out of his side wound. The bruising pain of his encounter with the hard earth stunned his muscles and locked his bones in place.

He floundered and made it halfway up, before a solid weight of the creature slammed into him, pinning him down. Hiroto was breathing hard, trying to quell his fear as the creature flexed her body above him. She peered down at him, her blue eyes flickering.

"Interesting." She tilted her head, studying him. "I've seen a lot of creatures, but not your kind. You don't look human at all. You have beaks like birds and feathers too." She stared at him, before pressing her fingers into his side, digging deeper at his wound. He grunted; his jaw clenched so tight he feared his beak would crack. He would not show the creature anymore weakness. She gave him a horrid smile, "And you are delicious. You taste like poultry."

"Creature..." Hiroto grunted but she shook her head fast. A bit of blood flicked off her mouth and onto his face.

"Lamia," She crooned in a voice that was almost beautiful. "Address me by my

name, bird." Her voice tilted in strange places making it hard to understand her.

Hiroto's anger rushed to his throat, but he choked it back. Anger would kill him. He needed to live, so he could plot her demise. Fear, pain, and the hot bite of wrath throbbed in synchrony with his wound that the creature's disgusting fingers continued to play with. "What do you want?"

She paused; her dead eyes blinked once, twice. It's as if she had never before been asked the question. Then her ice blue eyes seemed to darken and tarnish. "What I want I cannot have." A low whisper.

A weakness, he thought, his hope peeking out from the ruins within him.

"There must be something we can offer, so you leave our children alone."

"Children..." A very sad look crossed Lamia's face, Hiroto started but the look was gone in an instant. Her face was once more gauntly evil. Hiroto's feathers prickled with foreboding. "You want me to leave your precious children alone?" A sneer, "Then bring me men, beautiful men. And I'll eat them instead." She grinned; a glob of blood clotted by the corner of her mouth. "Don't worry, they'll enjoy it...somewhat." She looked up to the sky, then pointed up with a blackened finger.

"Every quarter moon," She looked down at him, her eyes glowed, "One man, here." She then sunk low to peer into his face. He could see the blood lust in the dark cerulean abyss, smell the stale blood on her rancid breath. He could also see the fine lines all over her face. It looked as though she was cracking. "I'll be waiting and if I don't get one..." She then threw her head back, her long locks flying as she shrieked out a laugh, rough and ugly. She never finished her sentence, but the creature didn't need to. He already knew what she would do. She seemed to flicker slightly, before crawling off of him, and sauntering away into the thick forest. She did not look back at him, she didn't need to.

Hiroto watched her disappear into their once beloved forest, now ruined with her rot. He laid on the grass, his mind racing, his heart thudding and his eyes leaking with tears. Long moments passed before he forced himself to stagger to his feet, his back throbbing and his side on fire from where she had sunk her filthy nails in.

Hiroto looked up, the moon was shining in the clear black sky, uncaring about the blood that soaked into their earth. Tears continued to fall from his eyes as he gazed at his fallen men, men that he had fought numerous battles with, only to be slain by a tiny, dirty, female. He turned away from them, pain in his heart and anger in his stomach.

Thirty days until a quarter moon.

He limped towards the village. He'd be damned if he gave her anymore of his children or his men. And if he couldn't, she'd have him, and his people would flee.

* * *

Sabin was jet lagged, but alert and highly amused. He couldn't help his amusement. The witch was grimacing, her arms were crossed, and a malice glare was darkening her glamour concealed brown eyes. She was clearly upset, and Sabin found it funny to see her pouting like a child. They had managed to fly to an airport in Xinjiang in the witch's private jet. It was a flight that lasted nearly thirty-five hours long and Sabin was glad the witch was covered in wealth and willing to spend unconditionally. He'd have surely gone mad if he was made to sit with other humans in a too small area, thousands of feet in the air. Though he would not thank the witch, her mouth knew no modesty nor humility and lavished enough praises upon herself that Sabin felt he did not need to add anymore hot air to her ego.

The witch also managed to arrange a private drive from the airport to Changbai National Park. Sabin had to drag a nearly unconscious Chito and a groggy Tullia from the plane and into the car. However, once they arrived at the park, that is where Sabin's amusement began. There were shuttle buses that were to transport tourists to the station that sat at the bottom of the Changbai mountain.

Though the witch tried earnestly to get a private ride up to the mountains, she was met with stanch resistance, to which Cliona frightened them with colorful threats that many of the workers did not understand. She would have been more excessive in her intimidation, however, she was on magic probation.

"I want to turn everyone into a Bobo the Clown doll and have children beat on them." She muttered darkly under her breath, crossing her legs jerkily with displeasure.

The witch wasn't allowed to use any excessive magic in Fukang. A notion that at first made her laugh with the arrogance of the powerful and conceited. But when her little sycophants explained the importance of low magic use, Sabin had the pleasure of watching the arrogance melt into angry disbelief, then resentful understanding.

If the witch were to use her normal amount of magic, which to Sabin was excessive, her magic would thread out into the air, disturbing the dormant magic that the dragon had weaved over his domain in Heaven's Lake. If he is alerted to the fact that another magical being was in his territory, a magical being that possesses a *substantial* amount of magic, he may become hostile and attack their group first before giving them a chance.

Thus, put them in their current situation: On a shuttle bus with twenty other humans and a too enthusiastic tour guide chattering in a twisting Chinese dialect. Sabin didn't understand what the guide was saying, even though it was supposedly an English tour, but Sabin didn't particularly mind, the man had a pleasant enough voice. The air had the beginnings of a deep frost as they continued up the mountain, though still warmed by the weak sun. It reminded him of his ignorant youth, of the time right before autumn lost its hold and gave way into winter. Though the smell of cheap gas and sweat ruined any other memories from surfacing, Sabin leaned back somewhat content in his plastic seats. He had to take two since they were made unreasonably small. However, despite the small space next to him, Tullia had crammed herself beside him, her whole right side pressed against his left side.

She was equivalent to encased fire; with the warmth she rendered and gave off. Her attire made him fight a smile every time he looked upon her. Once she was aware that it was going to be cold on top of the mountain next to the lake, she insisted on dressing extremely warm. She was wearing three jackets and a giant puffer jacket in a bright pink color, making her look like, as she said, "A pink marshmallow character from a rejected anime series". Sabin had shaken his head at her, he didn't understand what she meant, and he wasn't sure he'd ever understand even if she explained it to him. She looked well padded, if not overly so, but the hat with the two white pom poms and the thick white scarf were a bit excessive. However, Tullia had insisted vehemently.

"I do not like the cold." She had staunchly repeated as she continued to layer herself. "I grew up in the cold. Hated it. We had drafts coming in from every corner of the house. I avoided the majority of the states that snow occurred in, which was practically everything on the east and north. And my visions which include any temperatures beneath sixty-five degrees ended in death, frostbite, and misery. So, I am anti-cold weather all the way."

Sabin still found her layers to be a bit uncalled for, even with her reasoning. However, she seemed to be content snuggled tightly in her coatings, sitting besides him quietly, rocking against him as the bus ambled up along the road. He looked down, two fuzzy pom poms that jiggled on her hat gave him the oddest urge to flick one. He squelched it and looked towards the lush scenery.

"It's pretty." Tullia's low voice murmured out, she tilted her head up to him as he looked down, "but it's still too cold." Her gray eyes sparkled as a sun streak dashed across her face. Her cheeks had turned a bright pink as did the tip of her nose. Making her look more cherubic and guileless.

"It's only thirty-nine degrees." He told her solemnly.

At her look of pure disgust, Sabin couldn't help but chuckle. She was such an amusing girl.

"I want to buy myself an island, then I want to live on that island for two reasons. One—" She held up a pink glove covered finger, "because honestly the majority of people suck. And two, it doesn't get cold on an island."

Sabin nodded; the cold did not bother him. He was born during a blizzard and was raised where frost fell heavy upon the land. Living on an island would be torturous for Sabin, too much heat ignited his rage. Though, living on an island to avoid people was understandable, Tullia's logic was stable. People, for the most part, were ignorant, selfish creatures. They bothered him more than the heat.

"I'm sure you enjoy the biting cold, huh?" Sabin looked down again to see Tullia's big gray eyes staring up at him. There was a strand of her midnight hair that had stuck out of her hat and curled down to her temple.

"I do not mind the cold." He agreed.

Her dark brows tilted down. "Well yeah, it'd be weird if you didn't since you're a Viking and all." She muttered, trying to fold her arms and giving up quickly when the layers she wore would not yield to the motion.

Sabin smiled. He then looked back out to the sunshine drenched scene.

Viking. He has not been one for centuries.

* * *

"Ugh. Stairs." Cliona groaned and even stomped her foot in displeasure.

There was a white stone staircase flanked by a wooden railing. The terrain beside the stairs was rocky with thick patches of weeds peeking out from between the rumble. The hills right beside them were lush with greenery and in the distance shades of green covering land could be seen with trees huddling together in various spots.

It was so green in an unfamiliar way that was awe inspiring.

"This is really awesome." Tullia said, she couldn't seem to absorb the opulence of the foliage in full, it was all so…

So…

So, different yet familiar in a subtle way.

Chito stood beside Tullia, he was also layered like she was in a puffer jacket, except his was a light blue. "It's green, like my country, but it's so different. Even the air smells different."

Tullia looked over to see the Grand High glaring at the steps as if they had personally offended her. She was disguised in a glamour, but her skin was still a delicate blend of silky melanin and cream. Her now dark brown eyes scanned the surroundings, she spotted two men carrying a traditional Chinese carrying device, which looked super awesome, and smiled.

She waved them over. They hesitated a bit but pranced over to Cliona, wide eyed and jaws loose enough for them to dangle.

Cliona knew she was beautiful, and she knew of her impact on the two men. She gave them a blinding smile, then spoke rapid, perfect mandarin Chinese. The men nodded, stunned, but they tasted of nervousness, a pickle flavor, apprehension, a bitter coating over her tongue, and lust, a decadent and rich taste. They lowered their little wheel-less red seat so she could get on. Tullia saw blue smoke waft out from the Grand High's fingers and dart at both men's arms, curling around their biceps and forearms loosely before sinking in. They lifted the Grand High up with ease, which seemed to shock both men, though their faces were perfectly smooth.

"See you." She wiggled her fingers and crossed her long legs. The two men began to climb the steps nimbly and swiftly.

Chito gaped at the whole scene, then heaved a sigh. "Was that the only one?"

Tullia looked at the prince, with narrowed eyes. "Even if it wasn't, you're walking with us."

He groaned in dismay. Sabin, silent and indifferent throughout the whole scene, started up the steps. "Come." And that was all he said.

Tullia flounced to his side, exerting a ton of effort due to his legs being a million miles longer than hers and him being a million times more in shape than her too. And she was pretty weighed down by all her warm layers.

To which she refused to give up.

"I am royalty too. I should get the same treatment." Chito was huffing, but he didn't taste of anger, more like irritation as he stomped up the stairs. His long black hair was tied back in an intricate braid that swished like a cat's tail behind him, as he bounced up each step with a passive face. Tullia had watched him braid his hair before they left, but she still didn't understand how he did it. His fingers went way too fast for her to comprehend the pattern.

Tullia tilted her face up, the sun was strong, just like in Vegas, except the air was different, tinted with an exotic breeze that brushed against her face. And it was too damn cold for her taste, but it was still refreshing.

"You know," She began, her breath slightly winded from the twenty steps they cleared. "The sky is the same, everywhere you go. It's always following you." She reached her hand up, her pink gloved hand clashed with the bright blue cloudless sky. "It's surprisingly comforting." She squinted against the heavy rays of the sunshine.

She loved sunshine.

"I do not think the sky is the same." Sabin murmured. "The sky is different under every piece of land."

Tullia turned her eyes to Sabin. His gold eyes were fastened forward, he didn't look at the sky.

"So, we see a different sky in a different country?"

Sabin glanced up, looking thoughtful but there was a hard glint in his eyes, a cynical hardness. "Yes. The sky is but a patchwork of the dominant emotion reflected. Just like the earth beneath our feet varies, so does the sky."

Tullia thought about this for a moment…

"So, when war happens…"

"The sky bleeds." A dead tone, a rotted flavor.

"Then why isn't it always red?" She challenged him.

A small side look. "War doesn't last forever, sweetness."

Tullia digested what Sabin said, rolling the idea over in her mind. "Yeah, I'm not a fan of your theory." Tullia said, her brain rejected his far too abstract notion and it did not connect with her. "I think, different land composition or not, the sky is always the same." She looked at him this time. "How you interpret its presence is different. Also, I'm pretty sure there is a science thing on my thought to prove you wrong." She snapped her finger at him, just to seal the deal on her deduction. Though with her gloved covered hands no sound was emitted.

Still it was the action that mattered.

He shrugged. "I do not care what science has found. I've lived long enough to see that often it's proven wrong within a few years with something else."

"Wow. Someone's a cynical pot of cold loving wonder." Tullia huffed. How many freakin' stairs did they climb? Her quads were burning.

Sabin raised his hand and flicked one of her pom poms. Tullia swatted his arm. "Don't touch my pom poms, you pessimist."

A subtle bubbly flavor, amusement, kissed her pallet and that made Tullia happy.

The rest of the climb was done in silence, though it was the kind of silence that held familiarity and comfort as the soft sounds of nature buzzed around them. But Tullia felt as though she had died twice on the journey and was reborn only once. The stairs sucked smelly ass, the air was too thin and cold, there were too many steps and her stupid pride kept her from accepting Sabin's offer to carry her.

She was dumb. What was pride anyways? It sure wasn't worth her now shaky legs and damp shirt with her excessive sweat and lungs that couldn't handle deep breaths anymore. Oh, and a muffled body odor smell coming from her armpits due to excess perspiration and exertion.

She was just so gross sometimes.

When they reached the top, Tullia was underwhelmed and slightly angry. There was clattering of people filming and taking pictures with their phones, and cameras of the blue, blue lake and perfectly shaped mountains. However, Tullia found herself glaring at the scene. This was not worth the torture of the stairs.

"It's beautiful." Chito marveled, he was perfectly fine, not winded in the least bit. His cheeks were a bit darker but other than that he looked beautiful and fresh.

He sucked.

"Yeah, yeah. It's not like it's exactly the same as the internet picture." Tullia grumbled, stuffing her out of shape-self back into her puffer jacket.

She actually had to remove her layers, that's how much effort the stairs demanded of her.

Chito looked at her, then smirked. "You should try walking upside down on your hands. I think your man hands would support you better with less effort."

Tullia stared at Chito as she took off her two pairs of gloves. She then flipped him off with both of her hands. After about a solid five seconds, she put back on her gloves, mostly because her fingers were freezing, as Chito snorted with amusement.

"'Bout time." The Grand High stood with her arms folded, she was eyeing the people with disinterest. "There's only so much a simple view can do for me." She looked over at them and clicked her tongue, her dark eyes flashing. "While you guys were taking a nice, easy stroll up to the lake, I found a place that can get us closer to the water. Come on." She sauntered away, her long figure sashaying in a provocative way. Many eyes were drawn to her form rather than the scenery.

Tullia grumbled, she didn't want to walk anymore. "Please tell me there are no more stairs?"

Chito slung an arm around her shoulders and dragged her forward. "Come on, man hands, don't be a baby."

"I'll be what I want, go-go boy." She snapped but wrapped her arm around his puffer jacket waist. She didn't have friends, much less skin privileges with anyone, so to be shown affection in such a casual way made her entire body warm.

It was something she didn't really know that she was deprived of until she had a little taste of it.

She felt Sabin quietly stalk behind them, amused and content. She supposed an ex-Viking would find comfort in the nearly, inhumanly cold outdoors. The Grand High led them down a wooden slatted path. Tullia noticed that there were no tourists on this path, and it was flanked by big rocks, loose rocks, and dirt. About five minutes later, they came to the end of the path with a wooden fence and a sign that probably said "Dead End Stupid, look and leave" in Chinese.

"There is a fence." Chito announced. It stood as a silent barrier that really held no power but offered a symbol of authority placing a boundary from the path to the gradual but steep slope of nature down directly to the lake.

"We have been defeated by a wooden fence." Tullia declared, stiffly placing her hands on her hips. Her puffer jacket was warm but limited her movement. However, she had no regrets. It was toasty and awesome, but a little damp due to her over perspiration from the stair workout. "What do we do?"

A small beat of silence. "Are you guys morons? We step over the fence and carry on." The Grand High's voice was sharp and haughty.

Queen mentality. No boundaries held her hostage from what she wanted to do.

"But, people could come down this path. Plus, there is security monitoring the area." Chito looked behind them. "I'm pretty sure an official is going to scold us at any moment, our goal is to keep a low profile."

Cliona snorted. "It is painful just how straight laced you are, Cheeto Puff." Cliona demonstrated climbing over the fence and made a showy motion of being on the other side of the fence.

Tullia applauded the Grand High's actions, they were extremely graceful.

She gave Tullia a side look, she tasted of confusion and a bit of good humor, but said, "Now come on."

Sabin was the first to climb over, his giant girth and long legs made stepping over the fence seem like he was stepping over a rope on the ground.

Chito was a bundle of nerves, but his excitement was tangible and fizzy against her tongue. His long legs did not seem to have a problem scaling the fence, even though he was only slightly taller than herself. Yet, when it was Tullia's turn, the hip high fence turned out to be an enemy. She struggled to lift her well insulated leg up high enough to clear the top of the stupid barricade, but her heel kept smacking the top.

A deep chuckle, hinting at a waterfall of laughter, Sabin picked Tullia up like a little kid by putting his hands underneath her armpits. Usually, she'd object and be quite offended, for her armpits were a major tickle zone. However, due to her layered thickness, she barely felt him. He gently set her down right in front of him. She looked up, ready to thank him, but a loud shout startled her. She quickly turned, nearly tumbling to the ground in her effort. Thankfully, Sabin grabbed her upper arms and pulled her close to him. Tullia was already aware that he was a solid man, but it was always a shock to her, *girly* senses, to feel just how strong he was. Even through the layers she had on.

It was awesome.

Another harsh sound had Tullia looking up. A slender, older Chinese man was vigorously shaking his head, "No." He motioned for them to come forward, back behind the wooden fence. Tullia stiffened and tried to shy away from the man's obvious authority, but Sabin's broad form didn't have any yield to it and well…she was stuck as the front man.

"Not safe. Go back." The older man snapped out, waving his hands more vigorously. "Hiking trail, other way."

The Grand High folded her arms as the man came to stand right in front of her, the wooden fence the only thing between them. She easily towered over him, but then again, the Grand High towered over most people.

"Uh-uh. I'm not here to hike and I go where I want." He scowled up at her, she bared her teeth down at him. "Turn around and forget." She blew a thin cloud of blue smoke in his face, and the man's face scrunched up in horror and offense, before smoothing out. He blinked, looked around, nodding, then turned around and simply walked away.

"And that's how you fix that." Cliona twirled one of her melted chocolate curls. "I did not suffer a bus ride and being out in nature, only to be denied by a patrolling human and a stupid fence. Nope."

Chito giggled into his hands, Tullia smiled and stepped forward so she was no longer plastered to Sabin's awesome torso and he took a step back to give her some room. The Grand High waved her hand in the air, a very thin blue fog enveloped them.

"I should have done this before, but I thought the horde of Neanderthals looking at water would have kept the patrollers busy. We won't be seen anymore." She glanced at Sabin, her lush lips twisted. "Except you. You're *magic proof.*"

Sabin didn't even blink his pretty gold eyes to her jab.

"Miss Grand High, you can't use magic this close to—" Chito began but Cliona held up her beautifully manicured hand to him.

"Eh. Zip it. What I used isn't noticeable. It wouldn't even hit the dragon's radar as a disturbance. Now come on." The Grand High trudged down the steep slope with a smooth gate, as if there wasn't a ton of tiny rocks and loose dirt.

Tullia looked down at the steep slope, then shook her head. She was sure to die if she even attempted to walk down. Some things didn't need to be tested to find the answer to, because the answer was obvious.

"Um." Tullia bit her upper lip and patted the sides of her legs nervously. "I am not equipped to climb down. I think I'll die if I attempt too." She looked at Chito, who was in the middle of morphing' into a –

Sabin's strong arm swiped her legs from underneath her. Tullia gave a shrill little squeal as she tumbled backwards, but she never hit the ground. Sabin's other arm had scooped her up beneath her shoulders and he was now holding her up high and tight in his arms.

Tullia, stiff and breathless, wheezed. "You jerk."

A chuckle that was lush as it was deep. "I apologize in advance for this." Then Sabin took four large running strides down the slope, then leaped.

Fucking. Leaped.

Tullia almost released her entire bladder and passed out.

* * *

"Well, it's still beautiful, even up close. But it's still just water." The Grand High announced, almost as if she was granting the land her approval for its beauty.

Tullia was sitting on the ground, it was cold, and hard and there were a few sharp little rocks trying to leave an imprint on her booty, but Tullia could care less. Sabin nearly forced her soul to leave her body when he literally jumped down the steep, rocky, unstable slope, without a stitch of hesitation, and then proceeded to slide down with his feet.

"I hate you." Tullia had gasped out when he came to a nimble running stop right on the lake bed. He gently set her down and Tullia, unfortunately, had to hold onto him a moment longer so she didn't faceplant in the earth. Once she got her balance somewhat stable, she showered Sabin with a rainfall of slaps from both her hands wherever she could reach him.

Sabin took her blows without much physical effect; he even had the gall to poke one of her pom poms. "I appreciate your thank you pats, sweetness." His tone was pure enjoyment and the bubbly sweet flavor over her tongue made her more irritated at the hulking, ninja, Viking man.

"*I hate you.*" She repeated with a final slap, her energy drained completely, she just didn't have the heart to keep slapping him for her own benefit. She sank to the earth and there she remained. His stupid, very warm chuckle soothed her as it did irritate her.

"So, the crater thing is in the center of this lake then?" Cliona glanced over her shoulder to look down at Tullia.

She nodded woodenly, looking at the sparkling water that winked under the sun happily. The chill in the air was uncomfortable but refreshing in a way that Tullia did not want to experience ever again. She was sure that if she wasn't so damn tired and didn't have her wits scared out of her, the whole nature scene would have been even more beautiful. But as it was her eyes watered under the intensity of the sun rays and her vision was blurred and the light wind, which was filled with tiny ice shards, stung her cheeks. And she was hungry. So, the scene was majorly dimmed in her eyes.

"Yeah." She confirmed, when the Grand High continued to look at her. Tullia's voice was similar to the undead. Cold and stiff.

Cliona nodded. "Tired?"

Tullia gave a shrug, irritated and wanting a bed or to just lay on the ground and something warm to drink. And some pasta. And some chips. And a cupcake. Maybe a dozen strawberry cupcakes. And that tea Sabin got her. She really liked that tea.

"I got you, girl." She snapped her fingers and a blast of arctic air slid underneath her clothes and was particularly cruel to her feminine parts.

Tullia shrieked and jumped up from the ground. She stumbled, but Sabin caught her easily with one arm. Tullia clutched at him, her heart thudding wildly in her chest as the cold receded as quickly as it had come.

She felt so violated.

"There you go, petal. I freshened you up. Bonus is it'll be less of a shock to go into the water." Tullia's wide eyes looked at the Grand High. Cliona wiggled her fingers and had a smirk on her pretty face. "Takes only the tiniest pinch of magic."

She wished she were magic resistant; Sabin didn't have to suffer the Grand High's 'help'.

"Do it to Chito." She demanded, squeezing Sabin's arm tightly. Sabin shook his head, but she felt and tasted his smile, a sweet caress of amusement over her tongue. She was still irritated at him, but it was fading quickly.

The Grand High glanced at a zoned out Chito, his handsome face was expressionless as he surveyed the landscape. He managed to get down just fine without anyone's help. She was too busy seeing her life pass before her eyes to really pay attention to what he morphed into. Though he probably transformed into a bird or something.

The Grand High flicked her fingers at Chito. His cry of surprise and little dance of discomfort made Tullia feel a little better. It might have been super petty, but in this particular moment she didn't care. Someone had to suffer with her, and unfortunately, Chito was the one.

"Alright. We are all awake and ready." The Grand High clapped her hands, then looked at the water. She stared at the pool of clear blue for a moment before announcing. "I'm not getting wet."

"We packed aqua suits in Sabin's bag." Chito began, "Your assistants—"

"Worshipers." The Grand High corrected snootily.

"Ah yes, well they provided a measurement of the exact center of the lake. We need to swim out—"

Tullia completely missed the coordinates that Chito spouted, partly because usually when it came to numbers that wasn't about money, she wasn't a very good study. However, the second part was there was an intense heat on her tongue from anger, then an alien icy cold that made her mouth feel numb. Tullia turned to the Grand High. Her face was void of any emotion.

"You know what," Cliona said in a clipped manner, interrupting Chito once more. "I am not about this." She clapped her hands and blue, smokey tendrils flew haphazardly from her fingertips. Her feet left the ground as she began to float once more. She clicked her nails together and her clothes morphed into a stunning gray halter top, tight dark jeans, wickedly high spiked heels and glittering accessories all over. She patted her head, which was now wrapped in a bright orange silky head wrap.

Tullia clapped for her, it seemed appropriate, the Grand High was glamorous.

"Ms. Grand High," Chito said urgently, his face pinched in a panic. "You can't use magic! Your advisors clearly stated that—" He began, but Cliona cut him off.

"Cheeto Puff, do you know why they are called advisors and I am called a queen?" She didn't allow him to answer, instead she answered her own question, "Because they advise, but I decide. And right now, I decide that the faster we get in there the faster this gets resolved. Magic is our fast way in. Besides," She gave a roguish smile, "the dragon's what, a few thousand years old? He'll probably be slow on the uptake to a magic surge like mine. He might even confuse it with earthly magic that's lock in the now dead volcano."

She inhaled deeply, ignoring Chito completely who still tried to forewarn against magic use and cupped her mouth with her hands and blew. A giant blue bubble formed from her hands and encompassed her entire floating body. Then the bubble kept growing until it was about the size of a handicapped bathroom stall.

When the Grand High stopped blowing, she motioned for Tullia. "Come now petal, you too Cheeto Puff. I'm going to need those coordinates that you were spouting before. I missed them because I was ignoring you."

Chito stood where he was, unsure and miffed. Tullia felt a hand at her back, giving her a gentle nudge. She looked up at Sabin's plain, expressionless glamoured face, which she was beginning to dislike, he nodded to her to go to the Grand High.

"Go on now."

She was still slightly peeved at him and wanted to smack him some more, but she wanted to meet the dragon more than she wanted to pummel Sabin's beefy biceps.

Tullia walked up to the bubble then stopped right in front of it. If she walked into it would it pop?

"Just walk in, it won't pop." Cliona was highly entertained at Tullia's clearly confused look.

Inhaling deeply, Tullia walked into the bubble…and then she was inside the bubble. There was no resistance, no bubble-like texture, nothing cartoony occurred, like she thought there was going to be. She felt her shoulders sag. Everything was a let down today. The dragon better make up for the crappy day she was having. And his cave thing better be warm, she felt like a stale popsicle in the freezer even with all of her layers.

Chito scurried over and inserted himself in the bubble, he hesitated like Tullia did too, but he didn't seem put out by the lack of texture to the bubble. Cliona then clicked her nails together and the bubble rose a few inches off the ground. Tullia stiffened and Chito seemed to shrink a bit into himself.

"Sorry caveman, you're magically intolerant. I can't help you." Cliona's tone was saccharine sweet. She blinked her big, night sky eyes at him innocently.

Sabin didn't react, his face didn't even twitch. Instead he rolled his shoulders, as if preparing, "Not that you would if I wasn't."

She laughed crazily, insanity creeping in the high notes of her voice. "Too true. Too true. See ya down there." Cliona bared her teeth in a wide grin at Sabin. "The water's freezing by the way." Then the bubble floated out over the water.

"Alright, Cheeto Puff, coordinates." The Grand High lounged back in the air.

Chito's throat worked for a moment, before he seemed to summon strength within him to calmly say the coordinates.

The bubble turned and floated faster above the lake water. After about a few minutes, the bubble stopped, then dropped....

.... Straight into the lake. Tullia gave a short scream and grabbed onto Chito's hand, he clutched her back as the bubble hit the top of the water. The Grand High laughed at them. They watched the water slosh up, up, up... and then over them completely. Then the bubble descended into the water.

Tullia had the urge to hold her breath but quelled it with effort. She also had the urge to pant but quelled that with even more effort. She looked around for a distraction. There were a few feet of speckled blue water then there was…blackness. Her stomach gave a twist with anxiety. Her eyes tried to look away, but everywhere she looked it was the same scene. Blackness, blackness…A tiny little fish wiggled by lazily. Tullia looked at Chito, to see if he saw the cute fishy swimming by, but his eyes were shut tight and his hand was clammy on hers, though he did not loosen his grip.

Well, he wouldn't be helpful in distracting her anyways. Instead she began to examine the bubble barrier. There was a blue tint to all the magic that the Grand High used, which was cool, it made Tullia feel safer in the fact that there was a barrier between air and not air.

She wondered if the Grand High liked the color blue.

"Do you like the color blue, Cliona?" Tullia asked as they sank further into the lake. It was mostly to distract herself from the oppressive blackness that loomed mere feet away. It was surreal, but the surreal was beginning to become reality to Tullia.

Which was surreal.

She gave Tullia a side glance. "I don't mind the color. Though my favorite is gold."

"Gold?"

Cliona grinned, perfect white teeth gleamed. "My skin was made to be adorned and dusted in every shade of gold, from rose gold to dark gold.

All gold was made to worship me."

While gold would be stunning on her cream and melanin lush skin, the Grand High was a beautiful woman, so Tullia believed that she would look good in anything. Tullia sucked in her lips, Cliona seemed willing to talk without any sleight of hands, she chanced another question.

"Why is your magic blue then? Do you get to pick the color? Why is it not a gold color?"

"My magic is blue?" Cliona sounded surprised, she gave a light laugh. "I do not see my magic, no one should be able to *see* actual magic, it is only supposed to be felt." She looked at Tullia, her inky eyes glowing. "How odd." A pause, "Well, I look good in all shades of blue too."

Tullia's eyes widened, did she just uncover another superpower that she didn't even know about? She looked at the blue bubble, does that mean the Grand High couldn't see the bubble barrier? Could Chito? She looked at him again and pressed her lips together to keep a giggle at bay. His eyes were still screwed tightly shut though this time he was mouthing a prayer… or wait…

Tullia focused on his mouth, then her giggle escaped. He was singing Sunshine by Aerosmith. She knew that song, she was slightly surprised Chito knew it.

Just when she was about to disrupt Chito by asking if he knew any other Aerosmith songs, the Grand High exclaimed a victorious cheer. The bubble jerked and came to a sudden stop.

"Here we are. The bottom. Not too bad of a trip down." There was loose sandy dirt, disturbed by the bubble, creating a small cloud of brown that swirled up. The Grand High surveyed the mud with a critical eye. It was surprisingly cold at the bottom of the lake. Tullia had assumed that the Grand High would heat the little magical bubble, but apparently, she didn't want to. Maybe she was only heating up her side of the bubble. Tullia was tempted to go over and stand really close to the Grand High, but her self-preservation held her back.

No matter how sane the Grand High acted at times, Tullia knew for a fact she wasn't entirely functioning with a full set of cards. She hid many blades in her deck.

"Hmm," She stomped her foot on the ground, solid. She then held up one long finger and pointed towards the ground. Her finger glowed blue just slightly as she slowly dragged it in the air. A few minutes dragged by. Chito let go of Tullia's hand, his cheeks pink as he wiped his hand on his jacket. Then more minutes ticked away in utter silence. Tullia looked around, trying to see where Sabin was, but the bottom of the lake was murky with distorted sunlight. She did manage to see a bunch of little and big fish wriggle by, but they weren't too interesting.

"Ms. Grand High, can we help with something?" Chito's voice was soft and slightly hesitant.

"Hmm, you can help by being quiet. I'm trying to scan the lake floor bed for a magical concentration. Once I find it, I will break it and then we are in." Her tone wasn't unkind, but it certainly wasn't friendly.

Tullia watched as Chito flushed and folded his arms. Tullia looked up, they were deep in the water that the sun looked so far away and so dim.

"The hell," Cliona growled, the taste of vinegar strong on Tullia's tongue from the Grand High's irritation. "It's a big ass opening and we are in the center of this stupid lake. I should be picking up *something*. But no. I got nothing."

Tullia inspected the ground beneath them. "Maybe it's more of a thing that you have to push on to find. Like a secret button."

The Grand High snorted. "Okay." The sarcasm was tangy but didn't bother Tullia in the least bit. She was beginning to become accustomed to her sass.

"The barrier to the opening is probably extremely old, so you might not be able to detect it as magic anymore. It's probably melded in with the natural earth." Chito was examining the lake floor bed with a scrunched-up face.

"It's always nice to know that there is a useful brain under all that pretty hair." The Grand High dropped her hand and huffed. "Alright. If I can't pinpoint where the opening is…"

She held her hands up in a clawed like fashion by her shoulders, they began to smoke a thick blue fog. "Then I suppose I gotta blow up the entire bottom." Her face twisted with maniacal glee as she raised her hands above her head. She truly looked like a witch at that moment.

"Ms. Grand High! Please don't!" Chito's high panicked voice rang out in the bubble. Tullia watched as Cliona's black eyes turned to look at him sharply.

"What?" Her voice was a growl, bordering on a hiss.

Chito flinched, clasping his hands together nervously, he stuttered on, "If-if you blow up the ground it w-would only serve to anger the dragon. This is his territory, and we must show some decorum and respect."

There was a severe pause, one filled with tension and hostility.

"Ugh, political relationships are a pain in my ass." She dropped her hands. "If we can't blow up the ground, then what? Find a soft point in the magic? That will take eons."

"Hypothetically, there should be a weakened point in the magic near or in the center of the lake, which is why we had to go to the center." Chito's tone was neutral, and Tullia knew why. This information had already been said by the Grand High's groupies.

"And we're at the center." She said, her tone was deadpan.

He nodded, nervous, "We need to press firmly onto the ground, as Tullia suggested, until we find an unnatural give."

"Unnatural?" The Grand High said incredulously, she made a disapproving clicking sound then. "I am not getting my hands dirty."

"It's not a problem," Tullia hunkered down to her knees, the dirt at the bottom of the lake wasn't disturbed by her movement. Was it because of the bubble barrier? "So, if my hand sinks through and I feel…what? Air? Space? Then we found it?" She looked at Chito, he nodded in confirmation, squatting down next to her.

"Okay! Time to make some mud pies!" Tullia then began pressing her hands down and around in the mud. There was a slight resistance from the bubble barrier, but after a few good pushes, she was able to feel the cold, soft and gritty mud at the bottom of the lake.

"That meat head would've been helpful. He's immune to magic, so he could probably just pop right through it." Cliona muttered. "Always here when you don't need him, absent when he might be useful for once."

Tullia patted around, her hand only encountering firm, unyielding earth.

Thin clouds of fine dirt swirled up from her hands. Chito and Tullia patted around in the dirt for the next few minutes. She felt like she regressed to a toddler and was having an underwater play date with Chito.

But it wasn't all bad, she was being useful and gave her enough warmth to endure her hands becoming slightly numb from the cold.

"Oh look, there is that slow poke." Cliona sighed, Tullia looked up to see Sabin's big form swimming, quite fast, towards their bubble. It didn't appear he was wearing a mask or a diving suit, just his regular ninja gear. She waved at him with one mud covered hand.

"It should be here; we are at the exact coordinates based upon the size of the lake." Chito murmured, he was frowning, and a tiny line appeared in between his eyebrows. "We should feel…something."

Tullia patted the ground again with both hands, more clouds of dirt swirled up and around them, mucking the water clarity. Just what exactly were they supposed to feel? Would it be like a hole? Or would her hand just start to sink in? Or would she touch the dragon's back? Or…

The ground seemed to quiver under her fingers, she paused in her exploration, then she felt the quivering rippled outward. The perceived hardness of the lake floor dipped and her hand went down and through, disappearing completely. A damp, cool space is what she could feel from her hand that she could no longer see, she wiggled it around happily.

She began to smile; she turned her head to tell them what she found but her hand was suddenly grabbed on the other side by something cold and scaly. Her eyes widened in horror, but before she could scream, she was yanked down with extreme force. She smashed down against the lake floor, feeling the slight resistance of the earth, then feeling her body being consumed by the dirt floor.

She could faintly hear Chito's panicked yell and the Grand Highs curses, but Tullia was quickly consumed by the earth as the pressure on her wrist increased. The thing that had grabbed her released her instantly when she was on the other side of the earth. She found she was now free falling in utter darkness. Tullia's breath caught, her lungs seized and the most horrific feeling of her stomach smashing into her chest and her heart clogging her throat occurred. Her eyes were glued to a seemingly endless abyss as gravity clawed at her...

Tears sprung in her eyes as she fell, not knowing when she was going to meet the ground and die, but knowing she was going to and soon.

She was going to die.

Her mind held that thought and everything else dimmed. It was the most horrid repeat of that one single thought, that her life was over once she smashed to bits onto the hard ground that probably had sharp rocks and become ground meat. She inhaled raggedly, and she finally screamed with all the terror that swelled painfully inside her.

Chapter Twenty-One

Hard, wet arms snatched her in the air, and she was spun so that she saw the ceiling of water instead of the dark abyss.

"Hold on." Sabin's hot breath growled in her ear and Tullia stiffened all over. He spun with her pressed tight against him in the air once more before he launched her up further in the air.

Tullia's throat loosen enough for her to let out another shrill scream.

"Hush now petal." The Grand High's voice was cruelly amused. "I got you." Tullia found herself squeezing her eyes shut and flung them open to see Cliona surveying the area with her inky black eyes. Tullia was floating and she hated that she was floating. Her heart was trembling in her chest and all the blood in her body was shriveled with fright.

"P-please can we go down to the ground. Please?" Tullia's tone was tight, high and mousy sounding.

"Mm, in good time." The Grand High said distractedly as she gently descended in the air. Tullia tried to find composure as they slowly approached the ground, but her heart remained lodged in her throat only until her two feet made contact with solid ground.

Her knees were jelly, and supporting her weight was a seemingly impossible task for her poor legs. Luckily she remained upright by some miracle. Inhaling deeply, the moist and dank air choking her slightly, she managed to convince her heart to go back into her chest and her stomach to move out of her chest.

When all her organs were in the right place, Tullia looked around for Sabin.

He must be some sort of nut job and acrobatic specialist, because it was a long, long way down from the top and for him to land...

Her eyes spotted a massive form laying utterly still and looking unnaturally broken among crumbled pieces of rocks.

Tullia's heart was torn, then bled painfully. *"Sabin!"* She cried.

"Oh, I know." The Grand High's voice was scathing. "So dramatic. I would have caught her Sabin. There was no need for you to head dive and take a stupid fall like that." The Grand High's voice was chiding with undertones of sarcasm.

Tullia lurched forward, stumbling a bit as she sprinted to Sabin's still, wrecked form. The scene was way too familiar and her heart seemed to writhe within her at the sight. A pool of bright red blood was underneath his head and where his mouth was, the fabric was wet and darkened. He wore no glamour this time, or maybe it wore off. Either way, he was severely hurt. Quickly, Tullia dropped to her knees, smashing them in the rumble of rock sprinkled around him. She felt no pain as she stared at him. Her hands fluttered uselessly above his head as an unintelligible sound of panic emerged from her lips. His eyes were closed, and he didn't appear to be breathing. She put her hand directly under where his nose was, there was no air to be felt.

Definitely not breathing.

"Stop panicking, the bastard can't die." The Grand High's tone was casual and Tullia was upset at her nonchalance. It was like hot knives being shoved in her spine. Just because he couldn't die doesn't mean anything. He could still feel pain, still hurt and he was still a living being.

She shot a glare over her shoulder, but Cliona wasn't looking at her, she was still inspecting the interior of the once-volcano-turns lake. Chito jogged to her side, his pretty brown skin pale and his eyes were wide and wet.

Tullia forced herself to swallow. "He's fine." She managed in a half strangled half falsetto voice.

He said he couldn't die, but that drop…

She looked up; the ceiling of water loomed high above their heads.

"He just needs a…moment. This happened in Biringan, and he was fine." Her words were fast spoken and shrill but Chito just nodded and knelt next to her, watching and waiting. She loved him for his acceptance and his patience in that moment.

Eternity passed by, withering her nerves, and straining her patience. Then doubt crept its nasty self in her mind.

What is going on, it was different last time, last time he was still breathing. This time there's no breathing and a ton of blood is still leaking out of him.

You killed him, he saved you and then he died because your dumb ass fell through the magic floor. Technically, she was pulled, but overall, it was still her fault because she was a useless liability.

She bit her lower lip hard as she continued to wait, hoping for no physical pain, for Sabin to stop playing dead.

The pool of blood became larger around his head.

Tears rose swiftly and violently in her eyes, sitting heavy on her tear ducts.

A soft golden haze slowly began to illuminate Sabin's form, glowing the brightest around his head and underneath him. Chito gasped in shock, as the golden glow continued for a few moments and a clean taste of mint filled her mouth briefly, before Sabin grunted and opened his eyes.

His eyes frightened her. They were the eyes of the dead, white and clouded. However, after three blinks Sabin's beautiful tawny colored orbs returned.

Tullia sighed in relief, then choked on stale tears in her throat. Sabin sat up slowly, Tullia hoovered and gently touched the back of his mask-covered neck. When she pulled her fingers away, the color red stained them vibrantly.

"That was some fall." Sabin remarked causally, looking up. Chito shook his head, silent and in disbelief at him.

Tullia was flabbergasted at first by his insouciance, then she suddenly became hugely upset. She smacked his beefy arm very, very gently, glaring furiously at him. "Thank you for the save but stop scaring me like that!" Her voice was still too high from the stress. "You died and that was so horrible. So, no more moves like that. I don't care what's going on. Stampede, volcano explosion, gigolo attack," She motioned an 'X' motion with her arms, "But no. No more."

Sabin's tawny eyes twinkled, clear and *alive*. "No promises." She lightly slapped him again on the shoulder, she wanted to smack him again, but she was so emotionally wrung out that she just sighed heavily instead. Her poor heart was going to age rapidly if he kept doing this. Sabin got to his feet, helping Tullia and Chito up on his way.

Stupid man. Freaking her out and all that. She was officially over the trip. Between the cold, the free falling, and the whole Sabin dying but not really, it was all not cool, and she wanted to leave.

"Oh," Cliona's voice sounded like a purr, "looky looky. Hey there pretty boy." The Grand High cooed seductively. They all turned to look and standing in the mist of the dim light was an extraordinarily beautiful man.

Jiang Li.

The dragon was breathtakingly gorgeous. More so in person than her visions had portrayed him as. Tall, slender with moon pale skin and hair so black it looked blue under the peaking sunlight in the otherwise dim underwater cave. His face was stern, no lines dared interfere with the flawlessness of his face. He had thin lips, tilted eyes the color of night darkened water and a severe jaw line that resembled a blade's edge.

His beauty distracted Tullia so much that she almost failed to notice the lack of taste and his exhuming coldness.

The dragon tilted his head very slightly, he said a short sentence in lyrical Chinese, his posture was relaxed, though his face remained unyielding and unwelcoming.

"He literally just called us vermin that are going to make it in his stew for an afternoon snack." Chito whispered, the dragon seemed to narrow his eyes as they roamed the group critically. Chito moved closer to Sabin and Tullia, hiding behind their backs.

Cliona raised a haughty eyebrow at him. "A few things need to be addressed, dragon. First and foremost, I am the whole. Meal." She ran her unnaturally long fingers down the sides of her generously curved hips. "You'd be so damn full from me you wouldn't want to eat for the rest of your *life*." She held up two unnaturally long fingers. "Secondly, no one eats me without my permission, and baby boy, though pretty, you don't flip my switch."

The dragon seemed to sigh with his entire body. "I see. You are not just vermin, you are lowly *urchins*. This will be more exasperating than usual."

"He. Did. Not." The Grand High glared, then turned to address Tullia. "Is he blind, deaf and dumb?" She motioned at herself again.

Tullia shrugged, then addressed the dragon directly. "You are Jiang Li, the great river dragon, correct?"

Jiang Li's face did not change in expression. "Do not say my name so casually, human. It disgusts me greatly." His tone was biting.

He tasted of the cold, but nothing else. It was like Tullia had a bunch of ice cubes in her mouth. She swallowed, unsure how to continue. "We've been looking for you—"

"We traveled to this cold ass place and down to the bottom of a cold ass lake to see your cold ass." Cliona interjected, repositioning her head wrap while glaring at the dragon.

Again, the dragon didn't react, he merely stared at Tullia with his dark cold eyes, waiting.

She swallowed down her thick nerves, and inhaled, urging for bravery in her tone. "We need your help." Tullia surmised with a weak smile.

Another slight tilt to his head. "How unfortunate. I am not assisting anyone today." He said instantly. Finally, Tullia tasted his faint disgust towards them, and a white-hot rage. It was sharp, tangy and nauseated her most violently.

Clearing her throat, trying to talk over the flavor that began to slowly grow stronger and dominate her mouth. "If you could just tell us—"

"*Leave.*" He snapped, his pupils glowing a pale, pale white blue and elongating to mimic that of a reptile. Hot spice suddenly consumed her mouth and scorched her tongue.

She began to cough. "But—" Tullia went to say more, but the heat overwhelmed her, causing her to begin to hack violently. Her eyes dripped steadily with tears, she hunched her shoulders as painful throbs radiated in her mouth.

Sabin's big hand cupped the back of her neck, he tilted her head and dropped four mints into her mouth. The icy peppermint flavor caused her mouth to tingle but at least there wasn't an inferno inside her mouth anymore, but she still would like water. Sabin patted her back as she continued to cough slightly. Giving him a grateful look.

Cliona clicked her tongue. "This arrogant oversized lizard won't listen to a commoner, petal. I got this."

The Grand High hovered right above the ground and stared Jiang Li down with an intensity that could melt steel. Tullia blinked rapidly, trying to clear away the tears that trickled from her eyes.

"I will ask you politely once more." Jiang Li's voice held a hint of a growl. "Leave. Or I will eat you."

The Grand High scoffed. "I order you to shut the hell up and listen to what we have to say."

Tullia wanted to slam her head against the stone wall. They were not going to get anywhere with the dragon at this rate. She heard Sabin give a tired sigh and saw Chito cover his mouth with horror.

The dragon stared at Cliona, his face smooth, his emotions no longer burning her mouth, then he began to laugh. His laugh was light as air and powerful as a waterfall. It was entrancing.

Jiang Li shook his head, his silky black hair swishing over his shoulder, a hard smile on his face. "I will acknowledge your…boldness, witch." His eyes traced over Cliona's impressive appearance with a calculating gaze. "I can see that you've given much for your magic. Tell me, how great is your strength?"

She raised her eyebrow haughtily, "I could make you my personal cabana boy for six months without reinforcements. Easy."

He made a thoughtful sound. "Just six? More pitiful than I thought."

Tullia was about to interject, for the hostility in the air rose to a treacherous degree, but the Grand High got in the dragon's face and began to smoke blue. Jiang Li didn't flinch, he merely observed her almost lazily with his predator eyes.

"Listen here, lizard boy, unlike you, who was imbued with magic upon creation, the rest we *pay*. There is a price that magic demands. It takes a piece of sanity, morality..." She spread her arms wide, "physical appearance. What I look like is what I have sacrificed in order to gain more magic. Acknowledge it and respect it, you overgrown lizard or I'll *make* you respect me by showing you just how much you can suffer at my hands."

The dragon stared at Cliona with ominous eyes, before he gave her a small, ruthless smile. "Well met witch. I acknowledge your power and the sacrifice."

The Grand High jerked her head high, her nose elevated in the air. "Damn straight you will. Sacrifice or not, I am, and always will be, effing fabulous with anything on this glorious creation of a human body." She motioned towards her body without an ounce of modesty.

The dragon looked highly amused. "I see you lack humility along with your sanity."

Cliona jerked her chin up even higher and even more haughtily than before. "A queen does not need to humble herself for no one. Especially when she's this queen." She pointed to herself and stuck out her tongue to the dragon.

"Distasteful." He scorned, folding his hands together in front of him. His silky looking robes swished gently around his slender arms. Tullia could taste the savory flavor of humor from Jiang Li and the vinegary puckering sensation of irritation from Cliona.

"I still refuse to assist you." His tone was steely.

Cliona huffed. "You haven't even heard why we need your help."

The dragon shrugged, a delicate motion, uncaring. "Does not make a difference as to why you need me, the crux of the matter is that you do need me, and I do not like you."

Cliona clicked her tongue, "I thought Chinese dragons were supposed to be generous and piteous."

He shot her a sharp-eyed look. "I am viewed as a god to my people, why do I need to be even more generous with you when I have already graced you with my presence and spared your lives?"

Cliona scoffed. "And you say I lack humility. Someone's ego is over inflated."

The dragon cut her a jagged, black look. "I have more magic than you, witch. I can defeat you as easily as the witches I have conquered in the past."

Cliona smirked, her eyes flickering. "You've been asleep a long-time gramps. A few things have changed, like witches no longer being used as dragon fodder." She began to smoke blue again and her eyes glowed with an unholy light.

The dragon sniffed in distaste. "Always quick to violence, arrogant beyond reason…seems 'things' as you've stated have not changed too drastically with you *disposable* witches."

The Grand High seemed to quake with anger, little white static sparks occurred around her as the blue smoke thickened. She inhaled deeply before spinning around to face Chito, still smoking blue. "We've gotta find another dragon. I don't like this one. He's got one too many river rocks shoved up his ass."

"Crude." The dragon hissed.

"Your highness, perhaps…" Chito began quietly but was cut off by Cliona.

"No. I'm done with that oversized handbag. We're leaving. We can discuss our next course of action as we leave this old piece of leather to his ego and his dank sinkhole." Cliona floated back over to where they all stood, still emanating thick blue smoke and still royally pissed off by the spicy pickle taste in Tullia's mouth.

Tullia thought for a moment, staring at Jiang Li's unforgivable form. She had seen him a few times in her visions, he was a tad playful when coerced to be and egotistical to the extreme, but Jiang Li was also very kind. Though he would not admit, nor did he want that feature highlighted.

He saved villages, provided rain to the crops when there was a dry spell…

However, what was complicated with Jiang Li, is that he needed to be won over before his subtle kindness would take effect. Perhaps, she could lure him in through his curiosity.

Hopefully he was curious enough to take the bait.

"I have lost magic within me." Tullia declared, her voice raspy from the damage Jiang Li's anger did to it. However, despite her dry voice, the fact that she had something so rare should at least interest him into talking with them. He wouldn't be able to resist the lure of the mystery that lost magic offers.

Hopefully. She is assuming a lot, but at this point there was nothing more to lose.

Everyone looked at her and the dragon seemed to pause, the agitated air around him stilled. He eyed Tullia as if she were a mouse that had begun to lecture him on cheese lattes.

"A human containing lost magic?" He sniffed in distaste. "Impossible. That magic is far too rare and far powerful for a mere human to handle. It would drive you mad."

"Well, technically I mean, I totally am." She smiled. "I'm talking to you, aren't I?"

Jiang Li sniffed again. "You certainly are… *questionable* intellectually to continue to address me in a familiar manner. I could easily dismember you."

Tullia suppressed her smile, she tasted the faint, very faint, tickling sensation across her tongue. Curiosity. He was beginning to become at least a *little* curious. "You could, but if you did what would be the honor in that? I'm clearly no match for you, it would not be a fair or even an interesting fight."

Jiang Li eyed Tullia with a new-found gaze, he seemed irritated with her but also begrudgingly amused too.

She took it.

His silence was enough for Tullia to escalate matters. "Wanna see it?"

"The lost magic?" He confirmed, at Tullia's nod the dragon seemed to heave a giant, tired sigh. "Very well, human. Show me, quickly now."

"Your highness," She turned to Cliona. "Can you do the revitalization spell again, please with the tulips?"

The Grand High jerked her chin up in silent agreement. She clicked her nails together and a single withered tulip appeared. Tullia reached out to touch the flower just as Cliona extended her magic toward her in the form of a wispy strand of blue smoke.

An explosion of healthy, perfect, in bloom tulips littered the ground within seconds, bouncing with health as they hit the earth.

The dragon stared at the mountain of tulips on his cave floor with cold blue eyes. His face was expressionless and cold. He tasted of nothing but ice. He said nothing either for a long moment, everyone seemed to be holding their breath, in suspense to what the dragon would say.

"Is this all you went by?" He said slowly, he clicked his tongue with disapproval, then his eyes flared. "Allow me to...*confirm.*"

Cold, slimy fear slithered up Tullia's spine as he looked at her. There was a malice taste to Jiang Li's emotions now, like steel and blood.

He flung his hand out and a jagged white bolt darted at her. Tullia gasped in fright, her entire body recoiling with a sense of danger at the vicious jolt of magic headed straight towards her. Before she was hit, Sabin's broad back suddenly consumed her vision in a mere blink, blocking the bolt of white. Sabin's back flexed, his muscles seeming to go taught before he exhaled harshly and growled low in his throat with a bleeding rage.

"Well." Jiang Li's voice was amused. "That was dramatic of you."

"You thought to strike her with enough force to kill a horse." Sabin's entire frame seemed to subtly pulsate. A deep flavor, both ironed and heated doused her palate.

Sabin's anger…no, his *fury* was something she had not experienced. It made her entire mouth numb.

"You stand." The dragon's tone was flat and chilled, completely indifferent.

"You meant to kill her." Sabin's gravelly voice was now rougher.

"Hardly kill. She wouldn't have died from that." Jiang Li scoffed coldly.

Tullia gripped Sabin's arm, she found a slight tremble to her hands. Swallowing thickly, she peaked around his bulky form.

The dragon looked at her disinterested. "And why have you come here with this…lost magic?"

He seemed to be merely humoring them now. He merely wanted them gone. His curiosity withered sharply; exasperation was the only emotion he had now.

"I want it gone." Tullia stated bluntly out of a rage numbed mouth. Her voice sounded younger than she was, it sounded like a lost child.

The dragon blinked slowly. He tilted his head to the side, confused, "And?"

And? *And?*

"Do…do you know how to get rid of it?" Tullia asked with a lame wave of her hands, Sabin still stood mostly in front of her, and she wasn't about to ask him to move. She felt safe the way he shielded her and the way his gold eyes never left the dragon's slender form.

Jiang Li tilted his head to the other side, looking more feline than dragon, his glorious black hair falling from his shoulder. "I wonder."

Tullia waited, the dragon merely continued to eye her with obvious distaste, saying nothing more.

"Can you tell us how to…at the very least, transfer it please?" Tullia finally asked, trying to keep face. Trying not to shout at him. Trying not to become angry herself. She didn't get angry often, she noticed that nothing ever good comes of her anger. In fact, it always makes everything one hundred times worse.

He looked bored now. "You speak oddly." He folded his arms in front of him. "What will you give me in return if I share my knowledge?"

Tullia suppressed a sigh, she looked back at Chito, who pulled a subtle 'he's a serious jerkface'. Tullia widened her eyes and nodded in agreement. He fumbled slightly with his bag but pulled out the small dragon boat replica and a book of ancient poems from a collection of old dead dudes, that had Chito freaking' out about, when they received it from Cliona's witches. They had given them the two items before they left for China. They said it would be an appropriate offering to an ancient dragon.

He handed them to her and gave a very exaggerated nod towards the dragon. Tullia's shoulders slumped slightly as she timidly walked out from behind Sabin, much to his dislike. But he didn't stop her as she walked closer to the dragon. Her nerves were causing all of the sweat glands that she possessed to begin to secrete at once. Which seriously sucked because she had like seventeen layers on. The dragon was much more beautiful up close and much more inhuman looking. His eyes tracked her movements, as a predator would its prey. She held out the two gifts they got him, a subtle tremor to her hands.

"We've brought you a dragon boat replica, in your honor, and, since you are fond of the poet Qu Yuan, this is a book of similar styled poems. Please accept them in return for your knowledge of lost magic."

The dragon stared at her gifts for a moment. He then took them from her hands, making sure to not touch her in the slightest. He looked at the two items before tossing them onto the ground ferociously in a single violent manner. The dragon boat shattered, the sound vicious in the enclosure, and the book became dented and scuffed as it slid a bit across the ground. Tullia gasped in shock and snapped her eyes to Jiang Li, his eyes were in slits and glowing. His rage filled her mouth with painful heat. Tullia stiffened and took a step back, her fear rising swiftly as she choked on the heat in her mouth.

"Do you think that those cheap human-made trinkets will earn my favor?" Jiang Li sneered, his face losing its human aspects and becoming more reptilian. "Insulting."

A sharp sound of metal in the air rang out before Tullia was jerked back and shoved behind Sabin's burly form once more. Chito's warm, thin arms encased her shoulders, and Tullia sunk into a friendly hug, grateful for their comfort. Chito hugged her tight, she heard the frantic fluttering of his heart against her cheek.

"Old leather skin's cranky 'cause he got woken up from his nap." Cliona snapped her fingers, blue smoke wafting from her curvy form in anticipation. "I thought old dudes liked to flaunt their knowledge to the younger crowd?"

Jiang Li hissed. "You come into my domain, loud and disrespectful, demanding compliance from me." His skin receded as glimmering scales overtook his exposed arms and all over his face. "Offering me petty, useless trinkets. *Insulting.*"

Tullia coughed, his anger was intense, but under all the heat there was an acute bite of intense salt. She didn't know why he was sad, but even though he was rude, nasty and downright scary, they didn't exactly come into his domain respectfully, nor did they politely ask him for a favor. If someone sneaked into her home and went on and on about needing her help, she'd be a bit miffed too. Not as upset as Jiang Li, but she supposed she wouldn't offer them any refreshments at the very least.

Coughing into her sleeve, Tullia broke away from Chito's embrace, hard to do when the danger and bloodlust rose to an unholy degree in the room, but she did it. Tullia stood next to Sabin, he held out a thick arm, blocking her from going any further and her heart, pounding unforgiving in her chest, tightened at the gesture he made.

She was always surprised by the sweet feeling that came along with someone who actually cared whether she got hurt.

She didn't have any intention of going beyond Sabin, instead she stayed where she was and said. "We apologize, Jiang Li. We were thoughtless and not respectful towards you or your home. Please forgive us." She bowed her head to him. "We really need your help. Please."

Silence reigned for an endlessly moment in the antagonistic air, before a rough growl shattered it all. "Leave. This is the last time I will be asking."

Tullia looked up, Jiang Li was back to his complete human form, but he was glaring at her. His entire demeanor was stiff with resentment.

She nodded, disappointed. "We will leave." Tullia waved to the Grand

High, who looked both angry and lethal, still wafting with blue smoke. She sneered at the dragon and came to float next to Sabin. Though like Sabin, she didn't take her eyes off the dragon.

"Tullia, there is still the dragon in Japan." Chito murmured, Tullia looked back at Chito, he stood awfully close to Sabin's back, but he looked at her, "Lola made the Japanese dragon she met, *Ryujin,* out to be a bit more…social." Tullia nodded in agreement.

She looked back at Jiang Li, his eyebrows were furrowed with confusion. "Who spoke, are there not only three of you urchins?"

Cliona raised an eyebrow; Tullia could tell she didn't care for being called an 'urchin'. The Grand High snapped her fingers, and Chito appeared right in front of Tullia.

"Our last team member, you wouldn't let us introduce 'cause you're an asshole." She said flatly. Chito stiffened and seemed to shrink into himself under the dragon's piercing gaze.

The dragon's dark sapphire eyes latched onto Chito with a strange intensity. They widened as his pupils narrowed into tiny slits, his irises flashed white. He inhaled deeply through his nose and when he exhaled a thick white fog came out of his mouth.

He pointed at Chito, to which the shapeshifter stiffened further in utter panic, he backed up hastily next to Tullia and grabbed her arm tightly with both of his. "You, with the long black hair. Your name." He demanded, his face flashing with scales.

Terrifying was merely a word, until you felt terror and Tullia felt that terror now the way in which the dragon's gaze became…obsessive.

Chito blinked, he looked down at Tullia with wide, dumbstruck eyes, then looked back at the dragon. "M-me?" He stuttered, confused and panicked.

"Yes. You. Your name." Jiang Li's gaze never wavered from Chito's trembling form.

"Ch-Chito."

The dragon processed that. "Just Chito?"

Chito seemed to hesitate, then cleared his throat. "My n-name is Chito Balagtas."

The dragon nodded, thoughtful. "Chito Balagtas. I approve of your name."

"Thank you?" Chito seemed uncomfortable and terribly bewildered. He shuffled closer to Tullia, pressing firmly into her side, which forced her to press tighter against Sabin's battle-ready side.

She was not mad at this situation; the cave was cold, even with her many layers, and they were warm. Plus, they both had a nice muscly feel to them. She found she was particularly fond of the feeling of a firm man chest and a firm man side.

"Chito, you are permitted to stay." He glanced disinterested in the rest of them. "The rest of you may leave. Now."

Tullia blinked, Chito froze entirely behind her, his hand spasming on her arm.

At the lack of motion or reaction from anyone, Jiang Li became impatient, and seemed compelled to pronounce, "Chito is mine now." He folded his arms and Tullia tasted savory satisfaction and sweet delight. "Your essence is complementary to my own. Therefore, you shall be my consort and accompany me in my daily routines for the rest of your natural life."

Wow, that was some proposal.

Chito pressed harder into Tullia, his grip on her arm also tightened just shy of the point of pain. *"Yours?"* His voice broke, panic laced through his words.

Snap, Tullia thought, every girl's dream is happening to Chito right this moment. A hot guy claiming his person. Too bad it was super *not* hot or romantic in the least bit. In fact, it was high key terrifying and beyond creepy. Even though Jiang Li is gorgeous, he was a massive jerk.

Well, looks like that only works in books.

Cliona started laughing. *"You are mine now."* She mimicked in-between giggles. "Such a time capsule."

The dragon ignored Cliona, though he did cut her a jaded side look. "Yes, Chito," He repeated patiently, "you are now mine. Rest assured, I will pamper you, you will need for nothing for the rest of your life. Now, come here."

Chito stared at him in a complete state of shock. "I-I respectfully decline." His tone was thin and reedy.

The dragon tilted his head slightly as if he didn't understand. "This is not a matter of acceptance on your part. I have decided. This union is inevitable, therefore resign yourself. I will treat you the best out of all my treasures."

Tullia looked up at Chito, his left eye seemed to twitch, and he continued to apply pressure to Tullia's side, to which pressed her closer to Sabin's big body. And he did not move in the least bit. She didn't say anything, instead she wrapped one arm around Chito's quivering waist in comfort and continued to enjoy the warmth from two bodies in the dank ass cave.

This reassurance seemed to steady Chito a bit. "With all due respect, I refuse." He said again, this time with some starch in his voice.

Jiang Li paused. His entire body seemed to go still, as if in disbelief. His head tilted further to the side in contemplation. "Nonsense." The dragon finally moved, he strode towards Chito, his movements similar to a waterfall caressing a rocked face wall. Chito dragged Tullia back with him and Sabin stepped in front, halting Jiang Li's progress instantly.

Though the dragon was not interested in Sabin, he seemed to devour Chito with his eyes. After a few heartbeats of an interesting kind of silence, one that had the Grand High raising her eyebrow and exchanging an interested look with Tullia. She wiggled her long fingers and the word SPICY was spelled out with the blue smoke then vanished within seconds.

The dragon finally looked at Sabin, his ice blue eyes glaring.

"Move." The dragon commanded Sabin.

"Step back." Sabin retorted, his voice harsh and low, such as that of gravel being smashed under a heavy tire.

Jiang Li regarded him momentarily, his frosty eyes assessing Sabin's lethal axes, before begrudgingly conceding to the order, though he returned his ardent attention back to Chito.

He appeared to inspect Chito, from what he could see of him, Chito was mostly hiding behind Tullia, but he was taller than her. He tapped his lips in a query. "You are male?" He seemed unsure, he was staring at Chito's face then surveying Chito's chest and lower half, which made Chito blush brightly, as if scandalized, and tuck his body more behind Tullia. "You look female. Are you some sort of creature that is not gender specific? Like a frog?"

Chito seemed to become so irritated and frazzled that he forgot to be afraid. "I am Prince Chito of the Mabuhay Clan." He all but snarled out, his brown eyes flashing with pride. "And yes, I am a man."

"Mabuhay?"

Chito raised his head high. "Yes. We are a renowned shapeshifter clan."

"Ah, so *you* are a shapeshifter then." Jiang Li smiled, and he was so devastatingly beautiful it hurt to directly look at him. "I was worried for a moment." Tullia felt Chito's heartbeat speed up at the sight.

Her heartbeat was also throbbing pretty hard too from that sucker punch of a smile.

"Jiang Li, we really do need your help…" Chito began, his body relaxed slightly against Tullia, the tension in the air dropped a bit to a breathable level.

Jiang Li didn't seem to hear him, instead he spoke over Chito. "Good, good. Since you're a shapeshifter there is nothing to worry about. You can simply change your gender. Same face but different body."

Shock rippled from Chito and the cave became utterly still for a heartbeat.

Oh snap, he just said that. Tullia thought with disbelief. Jiang Li might as well have started stripping and speaking German, for Tullia wasn't sure what in the hell was going on.

A searing fury and a blistering kind of indignation came in sharp waves from Chito. Tullia's mouth was going to be burnt at this rate and she'd never taste a single thing ever again.

Irritation, a pickle-like flavor, slinked in the mix and stroked her now burnt tongue.

"I won't." Chito growled, with enough sass to kill as he turned his nose up at the gorgeous dragon. "This is my true form." The quiet rage in Chito's voice, though spoken softly, blistered the ears with its concentrated intensity. "And I have no need to change myself to suit *you*."

Jiang Li's delicately handsome face was openly confused. "Nonsense, you are but a shifter. You are as ambiguous as the wind." Those cold blue eyes latched onto Chito. "You have no true form."

The hurt that her friend felt was a sour, puckering flavor across her tongue but the heat of his anger chased away the hurt and made Tullia's eyes water. She squeezed Chito's waist, mostly so he'd stop being so damn angry, but also for support. Jiang Li didn't understand that his words caused a devastating effect for Chito, he merely stood there looking expectant, haughty, and proud. And he did all that while standing very much alone.

He is indeed a time capsule. Stuck in a mind frame where everything is stagnant, and nothing is ever new.

"I wish to leave now." Chito's voice was steady, but his emotions were strung tightly together. She didn't know how he kept his composure, he held himself nearly flawlessly even though it was a tidal wave of emotion that he was keeping at bay behind that pretty, composed face.

The dragon raised one eyebrow and snorted. "Leave? You are turning down a great honor to be my consort?" Tullia tasted a faint raw fishy flavor, a panicking flavor.

Chito's answer was him turning his face away from Jiang Li in rejection. The dragon looked befuddled, as if no one has ever told him no before. His blue eyes slid to Sabin who was still poised ready to attack in front of him.

"Exactly my thoughts." The Grand High raised her arms.

"I'll give you a location you must go to find out more on how to get rid of your lost magic." Jiang Li said quickly, folding his arms in front of him neatly. He was striving for unperturbed serenity. Cliona paused, looking at the dragon with a raised eyebrow, waiting. "But in exchange for my help, I get to keep the shifter."

The temperature took a dive, going from icy to arctic in a split second. Tullia snapped her head to look over at the Grand High and shivered at her look. She was sparkling again and looked horrifically other worldly.

"How dare you." She murmured. "I will never *sell* another living being," She hissed out, "for *anything*. You could offer eternal life, endless magic, even lost magic to me on a gold platter and I would sooner slit your throat and watch you choke on your own blood."

She flicked her fingers towards the dragon and to Tullia. She felt a pinch at the back of her throat as Jiang Li's face morphed from haughty arrogance to baffled disbelief then to pompous indignation.

"Release me, *witch*." Jiang Li's eyes turned a pale, pale blue.

"Oh," The Grand High's voice was pitched higher in a mocking tone, "is my pitiful, expendable self, outperforming a dragon in the magic department?" Tullia saw Cliona stroll up to the apparently frozen in place dragon on her own two feet. She looked up at him, which was shocking to Tullia. The Grand High was always so tall and bigger than life it seemed. She looked down on others, no one looked down at her. But the dragon was actually a whole two heads taller than her. Maybe she just seemed that way because she was always floating a few feet above the ground.

"Dearest me." She sang softly in a classic 1950's American voice while giving a razor-sharp smile. "How about this, why don't you," She pressed a sharp nail into his chest, "tell us how to transfer the lost magic from one person to another and I'll unfreeze your scaly ass in forty-eight hours instead of seventy-two."
   Jiang Li curled his lips in a snarl. "Not until my condition is met."

The Grand High's malice smile slipped from her face. "Are you deaf?" Cliona hissed, flicking her finger up to touch right underneath his jaw. A bead of blood swelled. "I won't sell anyone."

The dragon snorted. "This is hardly that sort of transaction. You require my help, I desire your shapeshifter. It's a fair trade."

"You are seriously outdated for this world now." Cliona said, slapping the dragon across the face. The sharp sound echoed throughout the cave, though Jiang Li's head did not move. "You should stay in your little underground cave and fester away quietly."

Jiang Li merely raised his eyebrow. "Was that supposed to hurt?"

"No," She chirped, "I know you have a thick scaly ass. It was to insult you."

"That's enough." Sabin's strong voice penetrated the vibrating friction, Cliona glanced over her shoulder to Sabin. Her eyes glowing with hostility and borderline insanity as she stared at him. Her eyes seemed to scream, *'you did not just tell me what to do'*.

"He's not willing to help us and his price is far too high. Let's go." Sabin had secured both of his axes on his back. "Just get them to the surface, witch. We are wasting time."

Jiang Li made an irritated sound, a cross between a growl and a hiss. Sabin pushed them towards Cliona. Tullia gave one final look at Jiang Li, who looked detached with his flawless face unlined, but he tasted of disbelief, an earthy flavor, surprise, anger…and sadness.

"Go back to sleep, cranky pants." Cliona clicked her nails and giggled then Tullia's vision tilted and slowly blackened. Jiang Li's beautiful but lonely form faded gradually within the black.

When she blinked again ice air smooched her eyeballs, bringing tears to the surface and pain. She shuddered then blinked rapidly as she looked back at the lake. It was glistening calmly under the weakening sun. Poor Sabin actually had to swim up and out of the lake manually.

"That dragon pissed me off." Cliona said, stomping on the soil and huffing. "I should have turned him into something, like a punching bag or a slug and then poured salt on him."

"You put a spell on him in there so he couldn't move right?" Tullia asked, she fumbled with her jacket, then managed to zip it up to her neck once more. She adjusted her scarf, all while keeping an eye on the lake.

Watching for Sabin.

"A simple freeze spell." She said dismissively. "It would have never worked if he wasn't so distracted by Chito's sexiness over there," Chito made a choked sound, "and I did tap ya for some of that extra lost juice. However, even with that, I don't think it'll last for as long as I want it. Maybe a few hours at most." Tullia turned to look at Cliona, she saw her inhale the crisp air then began to float again. She tugged on her orange head wrap. "Let's get a move on. We need to get out of this little tourist spot and on the jet. We're going to Japan."

"We have to wait for Sabin." Tullia stated. She was not leaving without him. He was her BFF, and BFF's don't ghost each other.

The Grand High pulled a face. "No, we don't. Come on."

"Well, I want to wait for him." Tullia said; she wasn't going to leave Sabin behind. Even though she was one hundred percent confident that he could totally catch up to them in no time at all. She was still going to wait for him.

Cliona groaned, she spun upside down. "That meathead could out travel all of us. He's a part time mountain man, complete with no manners and slower speech. We do not need to wait."

Tullia looked around the area, found a decent sized rock and began to dust it off. She then sat down. She stiffened as the chill on the rock traveled through her butt to the rest of her body.

Ugh, the cold sucked.

Chito bounced over to Tullia and pushed his way onto her rock. She would have said something about needing personal space, but it was cold and sitting on the rock made her colder, so any type of body heat was welcomed at this point.

Tullia watched the lake, looking for ripples to announce Sabin's arrival. She heard the Grand High groan. "I swear, I want to just teleport you right to my jet."

"If you do I'll somehow figure out how to mess up all of your spells." Tullia threatened, turning her head to frown at Cliona. She was not sure that she could actually do that, but she could see the Grand High's magic, and usually it reacted when she touched it. So, she'd basically molest Cliona's magic every chance she got.

And that would make her a bit creepy, but she'd do it to make a point.

The Grand High raised her eyebrow, and snorted as she looked away. "Okay then, I'll see you two. You take too long; you find your own damn plane." She turned her head up regally, then clicked her nails. Tullia saw thin blue smoke cloud around the Grand High's form, before dissipating quickly.

She frowned, clicked her nails again, but this time Tullia didn't see any smoke. Huffing, she began to float back up the craggy, loose stoned slope. She seemed to lag a bit before dropping suddenly to her feet.

A deep silence occurred. The Grand High seemed to vibrate with fury, Tullia's palate was on fire with her anger.

It was a shock that she could still taste the heat after all the abuse in the hidden cave of a crusty dragon.

"Damn it." She kicked a stone with her high heels. "I'm drained because of that stupid handbag." She looked out at the lake with her pure obsidian eyes that were exhausted and annoyed.

"Are you alright?" Chito's tone was concerned.

Cliona sighed, her shoulders slouching. "I'm out of magic. Seems like the lost magic doesn't play nice with my magic. It sucked my magic reserves dry. Damn. It must be when I used it to overcome that dragon's magic strength." She suddenly stomped her foot. "Damn dragon. It's all his fault. He better stay frozen for a few years then!" She huffed, looked around, then stomped over to a flat rock and sat down with sass, crossing her long legs and folding her arms. "That meathead better hurry up. I only got so much warmth left." She crossed her arms and began to silently pout.

If the day hadn't sucked so much, Tullia would have had a hard time not laughing, but as it was she was miserable and drained of any and all emotions. Tullia looked back out towards the lake as did Chito.

The lake was a smooth gray sleet as the sun moved downward in the sky.

Sabin did need to seriously haul ass though. It was cold.

Chapter Twenty-Two

Jiang Li couldn't move. That vexatious witch had frozen his limbs, immobilizing them for gods know how long. While irritated by the petty trick, Jiang Li was confident that he would be mobile in a few minutes. A mere witch, queen or not, could never have enough magic to hold a dragon for long.

Dragon's were imbued with magic, witches collected magic through different means.

However, he would have to go after them upon the principle of their offensiveness towards him. Not only did they dare freeze him in his human guise, they took the shifter away.

They took away the shifter that had a similar smell and aura as his friend once had. His beloved dead friend. Jiang Li would recognize the scent and the aura anywhere. He had memorized it, soft and sharp with a simmering edge, and a shy light. And he had thought he would never feel it again...

But the shifter...

The shifter had it.

It had taken him a bit to understand why he was so on edge with that trashy little group, but when the shifter spoke…his aura rushed over Jiang Li and he knew of peace once more.

Even if the shifter were a human man, he'd have bargained to covet him. But since it was a shifter…Now it was possible…What Jiang Li could never accept, what he could never feel…he could allow himself to feel now. His heart raced with the idea that he could fully allow himself to feel more than what he had in the past.

But those accursed creatures took him away from Jiang Li. That in of itself was unforgivable.

A scraping sound, interrupting his ponderings. Jiang Li hissed at the burly man that they left behind. He was currently scaling the side of the rugged wall with two black axes. Jiang Li watched him with furrowed brows.

This man was an enigma. He certainly wasn't human, that much was obvious, but he wasn't a natural creature. He seemed to be the most lethal of the group, his energy vibrated with barely leashed violence, yet he acted docile.

"Your…acquaintances left you on your own. Are you not mad?" Jiang Li asked, the man was making quick work of his wall climbing.

"Couldn't be helped." A stoic answer. A useless answer. A boring answer.

"You also died." Jiang Li remarked. His eyes trekked over the man's progress. He had remembered hearing the man's heart cease its rhythm of life, his breathing no longer continuing and the smell of strong iron scenting the air. After a few moments of the girl with short black hair panicking over his corpse, Jiang Li had felt…old world power. The kind that has been absent for centuries subtly arises deep, deep from the earth and into the man.

Reviving him.

Jiang Li didn't know how the magic managed to resurrect a corpse with life. Not even a dragon could give life back to that of the dead. The magic placed upon the man was profane as it was powerful.

The man didn't answer, Jiang Li tried to tilt his head. His neck was still frozen. Damned witch. He'd break each of her abnormally long fingers.

"You are not human." He stated bluntly.

A particularly violent strike at the wall from the man's ax, but nothing other than that for a reaction.

"You have the stench of the gods of old." Jiang Li mused. "Yet, you are clearly not a god. Then, what are you?"

The brawny man twisted to look at him. His face was covered completely by black fabric save for his eyes, his vicious eyes. Jiang Li felt a sudden need to be in his natural form while facing off with this…unnatural abomination.

The man's eyes glowed gold with a leashed inhuman cruelty. Jiang Li didn't dare look away from that terrible gaze, he felt a twinge of ice shoot up his spine and stiffened his entire body. A few breaths passed as Jiang Li stared at the monster in human guise.

The man then coiled, as if to spring, but he did not launch himself at

Jiang Li, instead he propelled himself upward and through his barrier, disappearing right up into the lake water above.

Jiang Li's breath he hadn't realized he'd been holding escaped him in a soft rush. Then a deep quiet surrounded him. The absence of sound usually soothed him, it was his favorite noise. However, with his limbs frozen and the light dimming from above the quiet only served to inflate his anger higher.

They all would pay dearly for their insult.

* * *

He looked at the human man standing next to him.

The man was thin, almost painfully thin, and his hair was hidden beneath a strange flat hat that tied beneath his chin and his cheeks held youth in their roundness. The features on his face were arranged pleasantly, he often compared the peasant's face to that of dragons and royals and found his peasant's face was in perfect harmony. Jiang Li was walking with the man as he gathered his ripe vegetables from a pitiful garden.

Jiang Li had wandered upon him in his usual walking route he always took after he had slept. He was offended to be blocked by a shabby little hut and a pathetic garden. He was contemplating knocking the wretch down, but a man of slender proportions came ambling up the hill.

He had been overly polite and humble, which soothed Jiang Li's offense. He decided to allow the hut to remain. The man invited him in and offered him tea in a wooden cup.

Jiang Li accepted, simply because he was curious. The peasant was bold to offer him tea. The green tea was strong and hot, it warmed his belly in a comfortable way. The man chattered for an agreeable amount of time, his voice low and soft, his face clam and bright. His aura exuded a peace that Jiang Li only felt when surrounded by nature in solitary.

The sun in the sky tucked itself away, and Jiang Li was surprised to find that he had enjoyed himself with a peasant human. So much so that time had escaped him.

He had excused himself from the peasant's home deep within the night.

The peasant man had expressed his concern for his well being by traveling at night. Jiang Li was amused. Nothing was more fearsome than him, and nothing was a threat to him. He left, continuing his walk, enjoying the moon rays.

The sun rose and lounged in the sky, before dipping low behind the mountains again, revealing the creeping chill of autumn. Jiang Li walked his usual path again, and once more he came across the shabby hut of the peasant man. Jiang Li's eyes roamed the surrounding area, he saw the man ambling about, his back was bent as he carried a giant basket, brimming nearly full with vegetables.

"Ah," The man exclaimed softly, and bowed to Jiang Li, his smile rivaled the sun. Jiang Li inquired about his health, interested when the man pulled out oddly shaped rocks and twisted sticks.

The man beamed up at him, his soft voice chattering about his humble art he plans to create. "It is my hobby." His tone was drenched in stars and sunshine.

Jiang Li again spent hours at the man's hut, listening and giving advice. He watched the man create his little art piece, happy and clumsy. Jiang Li was amused at how bad it was, and how comfortable he felt, drinking a very weak rice wine. He ate ugly little pancakes, and a warm silence engulfed the air around them.

When the sun rose, Jiang Li left.

And so the pattern had been established with them.

He had learned that his peasant was an honest man, though reclusive and timid, he was bright and held a profound knowledge of nature's temperament. Jiang Li enjoyed discussing various topics with him, for a human hermit, he was better company than most distinguished dragons.

However, the more time he spent with the peasant, the more he began to notice uncomfortable details. Frivolous details.

How the man's eyes would crescent when smiling and fine little lines would fan out from the corners. How his peasant's thin fingers would flex when he was describing something in detail. How his nose would wrinkle ever so slightly when he ate or drank something that was good. How his eyes, at first appearing black, were streaked through with dark browns and warm amber colors.

He didn't understand why he was noticing small nuances about the man, but he brushed them aside.

As the days passed Jiang Li noticed new lines that crept onto the man's face; noticed the gradual sagging of his body; noticed the whitening of his hair; and noticed the slowness of the man's movements. Though his mind and soft voice never wavered.

Were humans so quick to age?

Jiang Li made a passing remark about the man's aged appearance, and the man smiled.

"I have aged because I am a human man." He said, a bright smile, happy though withered. "For which I thank the gods fervently for every day. To live forever, would burden my heart. I am far too weak to endure time in that manner."

His comment slithered in Jiang Li's heart and pricked him. "You are but a mere mortal." Jiang Li said harshly, wounded, and angry by the man's words. Confused by the man's words. To be immortal was the goal of humanity, was it not? "A simple flicker of flame before extinguished. That is all you will ever be."

The man laughed, it sounded hoarse and brittle. It was not as energetic as it once was mere days ago. "But I flickered still." His eyes were set deep within a heavily lined face. "And I would like to think my flicker was bright enough to be useful to someone."

Jiang Li's chest tightened. He did not visit the man for a few days, his chest was behaving in a strange way whenever he was near his peasant man. He found it discomforting and pleasant.

The leaves withered and fell from the trees as the night grew long and the winds blew colder.

Jiang Li made his regular walk, walking slowly and thinking deeply about a multitude of ideas that he would like the peasant man's input on.

He made it to the hut, sitting darkly in the heavy snow. Jiang Li frowned. The roof was covered with holes and the flimsy door was askew. Striding forward Jiang Li pushed open the door and paused.

The small room was dark, covered in snow and debris. It had not been lived in for some time. Did that man move?

He looked towards the valley, there would be a town there. The man often spoke of the town's people, saying they were kind and generous. Jiang Li headed in that direction. The sun was high in the sky by the time he made it down to the little valley. The village was small and impoverished. Greedy eyes attached their gaze to him, and the town seemed to become still as they all watched him. He surveyed the little buildings, noting the shabby little huts and stalls.

It seems that his peasant's hut was actually less shabby than the town.

He spied a vendor stall, selling fruit and strode up to it, the eyes following. The vendor looked pale and nervous, his fruits were half rotten and began to release an odor to signal insects. "The hut up top of the hill." He said, tilting his head toward the direction of the hut. "Where is the man that lived there?"

The vendor stared at Jiang Li, beads of sweat appeared on his forehead. "Hermit Chang?"

His name was Chang? It dawned on Jiang Li that he did not even know his peasant's name. An emotion he had never before experienced twisted his stomach unpleasantly.

"Yes." He bit out harsher than he intended.

The rotten fruit vendor seemed to glance to his right and left, his eyes skittered. "That old hermit died a few years back."

Jiang Li froze. His peasant had...died? It had only been a few days since he last visited him and while old, he certainly seemed to have a few years left in him.

"How?" Jiang Li demanded; his throat constricting and his eyes began to burn.

The vendor gave a tittering chuckle. "He outlived his generation. He died because his life came to an end."

Jiang Li strove for composure, he wanted to shake the puny human for more information.

End of his life...

"Where is he buried?" He said through his teeth. "I wish to pay my respects." His words were sharp and exact.

The vendor blinked, confused. "I do not know where he was put. I think he was buried in his home."

A pause. Surely, he misheard. Surely his peasant's kind would not dishonor him in such a foul way. "Repeat to me what you said."

The rotten fruit vendor paled, his eyes skidding from one side to the other,."H-he was buried in his hut."

A violent rage descended upon Jiang Li. These dirty little villagers dishonored his peasant by burying him in the earth floor of his home, then leaving it neglected?

His rage must have been visible, for the vendor skittered back a few paces and began to babble. "He was a hermit of the mountain. He had no family or friends in this village and only came down once or twice a month for grains and such. We thought it would be best to keep him where he was comfortable for his resting place." He raised his hands up.

The justification did not soothe his anger. But his anger cooled quickly when his peasant's face flashed in his mind. He was a calm man; Jiang Li knew he would have smiled and not caused a scene.

"I see." He said stiffly, his throat tight and his heart became irregular in beats as his chest seemed to gain a heavy burden.

Jiang Li turned and strode away, the villages of the shabby town staring at him as he left. Jiang Li forced himself to walk to his peasants' home. He forced himself to think over the time he spent with his peasant human.

A rush of unknown emotion overcame him, powerful enough to cause his entire frame to shudder and come to an abrupt halt. Wetness dribbled down his face. Offended, he touched right underneath his eye, when he pulled his hand away his fingers were stained with water. He stared at his fingers, he looked towards the sky, bright blue with no clouds.

Then the water came from him.

He never knew his peasant's name. His peasant never said his name, and Jiang Li never asked.

He looked down at his feet as he continued to walk, the wetness not dissipating from his face as he finally made it to his peasant's hunt. The wetness did not ease even when he cleaned up his peasant's hut, making it into a humble shrine. He stood still, staring at the little shrine as he leaked water. A memory dislodged and filled his vision. It was of him and his old mentor, who was now hidden away and sleeping for a few centuries.

"We do not hold the same constraints as humans do with time." His eyes were void of emotions as he looked out on the lake. "We do not keep time the same. Days to us are years to them. Be sure to remember this, when interacting with humans."

Jiang Li had forgotten. He had been too ignorant, and he had let his uncaring attitude about time take away his friend.

He told his peasant that he had enjoyed their moments together greatly, then left. His heart hurt deeply, and a weight began to form within it.

He did not return to his peasant's shrine ever again.

* * *

Tullia was reclined in the most comfortable jet chair. It was plush, soft and fluffy and Tullia was melting like butter near an active volcano. Chito lounged next to her, his (beautiful) feet propped up on a lush footrest and a tray of garlic shrimp on his lap.

Life was warm and awesome at the moment.

She had taken the hottest shower she could handle, which was divine and enlightening for she didn't think that jets had showers and was wrapped up in comfy soft yoga pants and a pink sweatshirt.

Honestly, Tullia was trying to absorb this moment into her very soul. This was luxury at its finest and she would never experience anything similar to this status again, so she was going to milk it for what it was worth. Which it was probably worth a lot.

Tullia waved the personal flight attendant over and politely asked for another extra sweet strawberry mocha shake with extra coconut whip cream. Her plan was to indulge in everything, then probably gain a ton of weight as a consequence, but she was hopeful that the Grand High could just make the extra weight go away, just like she did with all of Tullia's body hair.

She wasn't going to acknowledge that she was literally banking on that hopeful idea that may or may not be accurate.

The flight attendant came back with a sweet smile and the best drink ever. Tullia thanked her and took a healthy sip, ignoring the concept of calories and basking in utter, blissful ignorance.

After Sabin made it out of Heaven's Lake, not even shivering from the icy water, they all quickly made their way back to Cliona's private jet. The Grand High was very low on magic, she couldn't even summon enough to teleport *herself* back to her jet. So, she was forced to trek back manually and the entire time she had a deep scowl on her beautiful face. Their squad looked weary, cold, and moody as hell. No one dared to stop them, but everyone stared.

That whole trek took a few hours, which felt longer due to Cliona's whining and the cold, but finally they were en route to Japan, to the head witch family that housed the Kitsues. There they would ask for their help in hunting down Ryujin.

"We probably should have just gone to Japan in the first place." Cliona had muttered when they boarded her private jet, kicking off her heels as soon as they entered. She snapped out orders to her attendants to get the jet off the ground and the showers ready.

They jumped to it at once, bustling around like little rabbits with coyotes after them. Chito, Tullia and Sabin had been escorted to their own bathrooms.

Just how big was this jet?

Once in her private bath, Tullia thoroughly washed her body, twice. She found she sweated in a place she didn't even know sweat could secrete.

Ew.

She probably took two hours to simply cleanse her entire being, then another hour testing every single face product that was stocked in the bathroom. The only thing that would have made her cleansing process heavenly was the absence of the vision she had of Jiang Li's past. It was sad and it was very lonely. She didn't know how long she was out of it, but the face mask that she put on her face was completely dry and her back hurt from the way she was bent over her toes. She was considering doing a pedicure, but now she was over the idea.

When she left, she smelled like a goddess walking in a flower field as sun rays beamed out of her face. Sabin had propped himself against a window and stretched his long legs out in front of him, looking like a ninja as always.

"You gonna sleep?" Tullia had asked, taking a seat across from him, nearly sighing with delight at the fact that she was now clean and sitting.

"No, I'm only resting my eyes." He murmured.

Tullia stared at Sabin, clad in clean ninja gear with a mask that showed only his eyes.

Eyes that were closed. He was very much sleeping.

Wasn't it uncomfortable to sleep with his mask on?

Tullia thought about telling him that he could take off his mask, but Chito appeared then, with a plate of food, a bright orange shawl over his shoulders, and his long black hair free. It was at that moment she became suddenly hugely hungry.

Tullia ate her weight in carbs, sugar, and fat. The Grand High had made one appearance before the sky darkened completely into the night.

"Imma cut right to the chase. Point blank, it sucks that Jiang Li was a crusty, dusty stank face." Cliona played with her hair, she had switched out her orange head wrap for a curtain of light brown hair that fell just past her collarbones. "So, right now we are flying straight to Japan. It'll be about an eight-hour flight, so settle in. I've already talked to Rihito, he is the most powerful kitsune-tsukai in Japan and he has agreed to assist us, in return for a favor." She sighed, her hands going to her hips and shaking her head. "It was unavoidable, but I agreed. He's in the middle of training his clan members, so, be on your guard. Their stupid fox familiars will try to play tricks, and maybe even possessions."

She shook her head again, though she was anything but annoyed. In fact, Tullia caught the flavor of sweet bubbles. The Grand High was excited. "But it shouldn't be too bad. Rihito is very hospitable, and his resources are vast." The Grand High's ink bled eyes held a wicked gleam to them. "I do love their games and it's always fun to get more than given as long as you know how to trick the tricksters." She winked at Tullia.

"Can you play their game for me then?" Tullia asked, ignoring the flash of anxiety at the thought of being possessed by a fox demon.

"I'm going to have to, petal. They'll try to get you if they get a whiff that you're important." Tullia saw Cliona eye Sabin. "I won't help you though. In fact, I might even help them get you."

Sabin opened one tawny eye. "If you want to make me an enemy in the house then I'll consider you one as well."

The Grand High grinned widely. "Challenge accepted." She looked back to Chito and Tullia. "Now, stay quiet. I need to recharge. If anyone wakes me up, I will eject them from the plane without a parachute." With that threat she sauntered out, her pink robe swishing around her thighs.

Her threat wasn't a true threat, since no one had any energy to make much noise, Tullia literally got the workout of her life and Sabin had held his 'resting eyes pose' for the past thirty minutes without moving an inch. And that was before the Grand High came in to do her announcement.

They had been flying for a few hours now, the sun was gone, and thin wisps of clouds were sprawled in the deep night sky.

Tullia was warm, sore and tired but sleep refused to come to her due to the faint salty flavor on her tongue. She turned to look at Chito. His face was serene and flawless. His brown skin was glowing with health, and he ate delicately, like a princess. Picking up pieces, one by one, and nibbling all while maintaining perfect manners.

Tullia paused, and flashes of her shoving her face full of food and inhaling sugary drinks like water filled her vision quite vividly.

She flexed her jaw as embarrassment tried to consume her.

Great, she demonstrated, quite thoroughly, that she was slovenly and gluttonous. She glanced back at Sabin, he was still and quiet, his brilliant gold eyes closed.

She didn't understand exactly why, but her embarrassment died a little inside when she saw that Sabin didn't see her eating like a pig.

She swallowed again the thick saltiness in her mouth. Thank the Lord.

Turning back to Chito she gently touched his arm. He took his attention away from the dark night sky to look at Tullia.

"Hey, are you doing okay?" She asked softly. He was sad. She tasted it, and taste does not lie. But Tullia didn't understand why he was sad.

Did the shrimp remind him of his Lola? Was he homesick? Did he feel sick? Did he want to stay longer at Heaven's Lake?

"I'm fine." He smiled, but it was the type of smile reserved for strangers, guarded, small and polite.

"I can't believe you just lied to me like that." Tullia propped her face up on her hand, drilling Chito with her eyes.

He furrowed his eyebrows, a tangy flavor of annoyance whispered over her tongue. "I'm not lying. I'm just tired."

Tullia clicked her tongue at him, which made Chito's annoyance become a touch bolder on her palette.

"I can taste your sadness stupid." Her voice dipped into a teasing tone. "Talk to me, bottled up emotions taste bad."

He raised an eyebrow. "Taste my sadness?"

Tullia decided to be brave, they were in it together and he already thought she was weird.

"So, along with random debilitating visions, I can taste what people are feeling. Happy tastes sweet, sad salty, angry spicy. Other emotions have different tastes too, like irritation, indifference, disgust..." She trailed off, thinking.

It got complicated sometimes, but she could always identify the flavor (sweet, sour, tangy, fruity), and would generally piece together the emotion associated with it.

Chito's face was smooth, but she tasted his surprise and his embarrassment, a sweet and sour combo. He cleared his throat primly. "I see. And what do I…taste like now?"

His cheeks heated, Tullia gave him a light smack. "Don't make this weirder than it already is." He chuckled.

"Your emotions taste like salt water right now. So, you must be sad or depressed about something."

His face crumpled a bit. "Was that why you were eating excessively?" His tone was concerned and so pure with innocence, it hurt. "Because I tasted bad?"

She felt her eye twitch, then flexed her jaw. No, she was simply a pig, but she would let him think that way to not look like a super glutton.

Sorry Chito, she thought as she gave him her best apologetic smile with a nod. Chito looked away, he fidgeted in his seat. Tullia waited, she didn't want to rush him or force him to tell her what was wrong. Usually, when people talked about what was bothering them, their emotions would intensify then lighten, as if by letting them out made them feel better, feel lighter.

A few minutes passed by in silence, before Tullia said. "Hey, you don't have to tell me. I didn't mean to be nosy. I was just concerned." She touched his wrist; his brown skin was warm under her fingertips. "You can talk to me, I'm a very good listener, but you don't have to, okay?"

Chito looked at her, his big brown eyes glossy. "No, thank you. I just…I just am bothered by what the stupid dragon said. That's all."

Tullia nodded. "He was a huge asshole."

Chito gave a half smile and nodded, looking down. "I suppose I've been sheltered. I'm just being overly sensitive. Growing up around shifters, gender is not really…given a lot of importance, you know? Gender becomes fluid for us. You are you, and you love who you love without change." His tone was heavy with sorrow, he looked back at Tullia. "I was just shocked at Jiang Li's assumption that I'd readily change for him and it got me thinking that…I guess there must be a lot of people that would think that way too. And it made me sad."

"I think the shifters' thought process is beautiful, I wish everyone thought that way." She said, then thought over his words. Chito had spent a lot of time changing his appearance, trying to find the one that he wanted as his original form. He had a hard time settling on one, so for someone to assume he could easily change himself to suit themselves would be very hurtful. And it would seriously piss her off if that happened to her.

"He was insensitive and arrogant." Tullia declared. "Just because you have the ability to change, does not mean he can dictate that change or change who you are."

A flare of heat and pepper spice ghosted over her tongue. "Yeah. And how can he just dismiss *my* preference? I don't want to be in a 'female' form, I like how I look."

"You're super cute." Tullia agreed.

"I *am* super cute. And I will like whoever I want. And I don't like that dragon." His agitation caused his tilting accent to become heavy and his hands jerked up and down with his emotion.

Tullia propped her face up with her hand. "You know Chito, you're gonna meet a lot of people like Jiang Li, who are narrow minded, mean, and small. However, you'll also meet some people who are accepting and wonderful. You can't let anyone drag you down."

Everyone tried to drag her down in her family, in the institution, in life, but not everyone was *bad*. She had met beautiful people in the most interesting scenarios. From the homeless woman who shared Prosecco with her, to a gas station old man who told her of his grandkids when she was recovering from an episode. Those souls, kind and nonjudgmental, made all the difference sometimes and brighten her day when she thought there was no light in her world. They also gave her hope in people.

"I suppose I have to learn to get over it." He sighed, leaning back against his fluffy seat.

"You can always rant to me. Or," Tullia sang, tapping her fingers together in a plotting way, "We get revenge on everyone of the 'naysayers'."

At the tilt of his head and the taste of confusion, she began to elaborate.

"Basically, we're going to shove it in everyone's face about how awesome we are. After we do our little thing, let's explore the world entirely and maybe…" She nudged his elbow gently with hers, "Maybe we can find you a lover after all this is over. One that fits your fancy."

Chito's smile was slow. "A lover?" He flipped his long black hair over his slim shoulder. "I mean, me being single for so long goes against the natural order of nature." He looked at Tullia, a wicked gleam in his dark brown depths. "We should find you one while we're at it too. It's, how do you Americans say it, kill two birds with a stone?"

Tullia laughed and her eyes darted to Sabin's sleeping form. Her heart seemed to trip a bit in her chest and her blood rushed to heat her face. She looked at her lap, feeling shy and perplexed.

Why on earth did she look at Sabin? Gosh, that's her best friend/savior/ninja man. The caffeine must be getting to her. She needed to calm down and just stop.

"Oh, but we need to make sure, for you, that we find someone with more manlier hands than yours." Chito's pretty smile turned impish. Tullia scoffed and wiggled her perfectly normal fingers at him.

"Listen here, go-go boy, I—" There was a heavy jerk that rocked the plane violently, and the oxygen masks above ejected out, smacking Tullia in the face.

"Ow." She mumbled, putting a hand up to her forehead. Another violent jerk sent Chito slamming into her and pushing her off the fluffy chair and right on to the not fluffy floor.

"*Ow.*" She cried out, the jet floor was hard, and her boobs got smashed against it. That did *not* feel good. Strong hands slid underneath her arm pits and heaved her up to her feet. She looked up, surprised, to see Sabin towering over her, his gold eyes solemn and beautiful, per usual.

"What the heck is going on?" She asked him as he gently set her down on her feet. He kept one of his hands on her shoulder, to stabilize her most likely.

He didn't look at her, his gold eyes were looking out the plan windows. "Don't know. I suppose we're under attack." She could see his strong jaw clench beneath the fabric of his face mask.

Tullia waited for him to elaborate, when he didn't, she let out an annoyed huff. "Sabin, this is new to me. I need a little bit more detail. Just in case you forgot, my daily life before all of this—" She waved her hands frantically in the air, "—consisted of reading a mountain of books, cleaning dirty motel rooms that needed to be bombed, and an occasional two am McDonalds run. Not exactly a thrilling life."

The plane lurched and she heard Chito give a yelping scream behind her. Tullia did not tumble to the ground, thanks to Sabin's firm hold on her shoulder. Sabin looked down at Tullia, a gleam in his tawny depths. "Really? Seems to me it could've been pretty adventurous. The perils of not knowing what would be found in the hotel rooms."

"Ugh," Tullia suddenly shivered, all the people who visited the hotel were disgusting. Who the hell pooped in all corners of the room? Who the hell forgets their prosthetic eye in the nightstand drawer? Who thinks it's a good idea to stuff the toilet with toilet paper then proceed to use it without flushing? And what kind of person brings and forgets an urn in their hotel room? "You just brought back past traumas. The bathrooms were the absolute worst."

Sabin chuckled. "Not surprising." A pause, the plane vibrated, and began to mimic a mini earthquake. That was not a normal thing to occur while in the air. Tullia gripped Sabin's wrist.

"I believe the dragon is attacking us." His eyes were staring out one of the small plane windows. All she saw was darkness in the night sky. She furrowed her eyebrows.

The dragon? "As in, the river dragon, Jiang Li?" She asked.

Sabin shrugged. "Unless you know of another one."

"I am not understanding where all this sass is coming from." Tullia muttered, she felt his smile, even though his mouth was covered. Chito let out a blood curdling scream.

Tullia jerked around in surprise. She saw Chito cowering against the seat, his eyes wide and glued to the little airplane window beside his seat. She followed his line of sight and felt her stomach drop and her mouth become dry.

A giant reptilian eye, blazing with fury in its frozen blue depths staring in. It blinked twice, looking up, down, side to side, then disappeared and the night sky was once again in view.

Tullia gaped out at the now empty window, then turned to Sabin. "That was terrifying."

Sabin shrugged again, his eyes passive. "I've seen worse."

Tullia ignored his offhand comment. They were thousands of feet up in the air, trapped in a flying metal machine, and an angry dragon was messing around with the plane. That was a very fantastical definition of terrifying and soon-to-be very dead people.

A low growl, unlike any other natural growl, rumbled outside like thunder and the plane then shuddered forcefully in distress.

Oh no. A chill slid up her spine as her stomach became weighted with boulders of soured fear.

"He's trying to take down the plane." She stated flatly and looked at Sabin.

"Perhaps." He responded just as flatly; his eyes went to the ceiling then back to the window. Her stomach then began to cramp and a thick layer of nervous sweat coated her palms. "Might want to sit down and buckle in, sweetness." He glanced down at her, his tawny eyes bright and her palate filled with tart bubbles. "Was that detailed enough for you?"

"Wow, you choose now to have a personality. You have the worst timing for unfunny jokes." She quipped disapprovingly, pushing off his hand from her shoulder and stomping over to her seat. She pushed Chito firmly back into his seat, then flung herself into hers. She inhaled deeply. "Today just sucks." Tullia gripped, as she quickly strapped on and tightened her buckle around her waist, then folded her arms angrily. "First, we go through the cold; then Sabin jumped off a cliff with me, which I swear I lost half my soul in that; then I fall into the stupid under lake cave thing; then Sabin dies and gives me a freaking heart attack; then the dragon turns out to be an asshole times ten; and now the plane is going to crash due to said asshole dragon and I'm so, so tired." She flexed her jaw as the food she inhaled earlier twisted in her stomach.

She was not going to throw up. She was keeping every single calorie inside her damn body.

Sabin gripped the back of his chair, one hand holding a bulky black ax as warning sirens began to scream in the plane and the little oxygen masks continued to dangle and bob viciously in front of her.

"The day was long." Sabin agreed calmly.

The plane jerked hard to the right. The oxygen mask smacked her head again, and her head began to throb. She rubbed her forehead, glaring at the mask. "Long? It was a freaking eternity that is still going!" She leaned her head back against the headrest, then turned to look at Chito.

He was staring at them, his big eyes bulging out on his face pale. Tullia noticed that his shrimp was scattered all over the floor. This was why you ate food quickly, to avoid being wasteful. However, they were under attack by a dragon while they were in a plane, so it was understandable, but no less wasteful. Tullia reached over him and fastened his buckle, tightening it extra tight. She didn't want Chito to go flying anywhere and die.

That would make her incredibly sad.

"There. Now you're buckled in and secure. Kind of." She smiled at him.

Then Chito seemed to break. "Why are you not freaking out!? A *dragon* is trying to take down the *plane*! We are thousands of feet up in the air and a *dragon* is going to make us crash *and we are all going to die!*" His voice cracked in several places and beads of sweat appeared on his forehead.

Tullia held up a hand to him, slightly offended that he thought she wasn't losing her mind. "Whoa there, go-go boy. First of all, you can shift into something with wings, okay? You will not die if you remember that fact. Me? I'm totally dead, like one hundred and ten percent dead-dead." She informed him gravely, her heart was thundering in her chest, and the acid taste of fear corroded her palette. "I am freaking out by the way. In this situation right now, this is how I freak out. I do not have a set freak out for all occasions. They come to me as the situations arise. And right now," She pointed to the ceiling with both of her pointer fingers, "—it's a seemingly calm facade due to the impossibility of the situation. I mean," She gave a strained laugh, "what airfare practices emergency protocols for dragon attacks?" Her voice raised in volume and the serene tone began to chip away. "There are none! Just in case you're wondering. *There. Are. None.*"

Suddenly, a door slammed open, causing Tullia and Chito to jump with fright. Cliona stalked out, smoking blue in a pair of red silk pajamas that covered mile long legs and a curved figure with bare feet poking out at the bottom.

Tullia looked down at her bare feet and thought the Grand High had the cutest feet in the world. Her toes were sprinkled with white and one entire toe was white amongst the spread of sultry onyx skin.

The Grand High looked like artwork that came alive. She was so beautiful and alluring. Her usual ink-colored eyes were a winter blue. She clicked her tongue in fury, her head covered by a silk black bonnet made her look adorable. She lightly pressed her abnormally long fingers gently on her forehead. "This flying handbag is trying to break *my* custom, eighty-four-million-dollar private jet?" The Grand High's teeth were bared as she looked out of one of the small windows. "Uh-uh. He's about to provide me with an entirely new leather wardrobe." She clicked her nails and thick blue smoke poured from her entire body in strings.

Tullia watched as blue smoke covered every area of the plane, before sinking in. She watched as the Grand High rolled her neck slowly. A thin little wisp, no thicker than a thread piece, darted toward Tullia. It wrapped around her wrist, hoovering above it for a moment before sinking into her skin. A pinch occurred in the back of her throat and the Grand High's body flexed tautly.

She inhaled through her teeth, grinning. "That power rush is delicious." Her icy eyes glanced at them. "I hope everyone is strapped in. There may be some turbulence and possible aerobatics." Then Tullia's body and head were pushed back hard into her seat from the force of the pressure as the Grand High lifted her hands up and the plane took a direct ninety degree turn down.

For the second time that day, the breath was forcibly expelled from her lungs and Tullia felt her soul leave her body.

* * *

Jiang Li looked at the flying creation. He had circled around the contraption multiple times, not touching it, but it still baffled him. It was obviously human made. Nothing natural was quite so…*unnatural.* What was confusing him, is that he could smell and sense the shifter and that crass witch's magic, but he could not see them. They were in the flying creation.

He tapped the flying thing lightly with his claw, it swayed and there was a little dent from his nail, but other than that nothing happened. The contraption continued on flying. He waited a moment to see if they could come out and properly receive him, but nothing happened. He tapped it again.

It swayed again, then nothing.

Jiang Li furrowed his eyebrows. The thing made such a loud continuous sound and smelled atrocious. It was insulting both his ears and his nostrils. He circled it again, it seemed the front held humans. They were making strange faces at him, and one's eyes rolled back and fell promptly asleep on the floor.

Slovenly creatures.

Jiang Li flew up and around the thing, examining the object critically. It had flat wings on the side of a pea-pod body. It was loud in the sky, thundering about, and smelled rancid. If these things were occupying the air, no wonder why Jiang Li nearly choked when he took to the sky.

Revolting.

676

He spotted a small, soft glow of light coming from only one side of the machine. He peered in the tiny hole and was surprised to see the shifter, the girl and the old magic man standing amongst the furry seats. The shifter met his eye and seemed to become startled, his eyes widening and mouth opening wide. Even with the ridiculous face, the shifter was quite pretty for a man.

Jiang Li pulled back to examine the flying construction once more. He wanted in, but it was clear that the thing would not support let alone fit him. He tapped it again after a moment of thought.

Was this really a human creation? It seemed too complex for a mere mortal to ever conceptualize and produce. It must just be magic made. The machine seemed to quiver, then suddenly dive down. Jiang Li huffed in surprise then quickly followed. The machine picked up speed as it headed straight towards the ground.

Was it going to crash? Would it kill his shifter?

Jiang Li became anxious; he didn't like that he didn't know what the machine was doing. He also didn't like that he didn't know what the machine was.

It appeared he had hidden himself away far too long, and humanity seemed to move along with time just fine without him.

An uncomfortable feeling filled his chest. He dismissed the feeling and reached out to grab the contraption. The thing made a sharp right and flew up. Jiang Li scrambled up to follow, it was quite fast and nimble for its girth. It cut through the sky like a blade and was as haphazard as a bee in the wind. However, he was the great river dragon, he was better than the flying human made contraption. He would always be better. He managed to keep pace just fine. After a few minutes Jiang Li's blood began to race, and giddiness stole over him. He had not played in a while, the wind, frigid and sharp, felt good against his scales. The sky felt good to be in again, freeing him. He circled the flying machine, playfully tapping it with his tail. He laughed when he saw it spin wildly, before steadying.

He initially came to punish the arrogance of the witch and take his shifter back. However, he could postpone his lesson in manners to play for a bit. He felt his tail wiggle with delight as the contraption zipped up and away higher in the sky.

It had been so long since he'd been out. He would savor the moment.

* * *

The Grand High was floating, her toes barely touching the ground, her hands clawed, her teeth bared, and her gorgeous two-toned face creased with rage.

"I can't shoot him if I am controlling the damn plane." Her head turned to Sabin. "Why don't you do something, berserker, instead of lounging about. You got a gun?"

"No." He said his tone was hard and calm, but Tullia knew he was nauseous as all hell.

The plane tricks were dizzying and made Tullia want to vomit. Her vision was slurring and everything around her was blurred. The only reason Tullia had not thrown up yet, is simply because her brain couldn't process the action with all the freaking knots of stress delaying communications in her body.

A small blessing.

"Then start throwing stuff at him! Put those muscles to work, you stupid man." She snarled. "I don't know why I need to do everything."

Irritation prickled Tullia's palate and she nearly heaved at the flavor combined with the nausea she had going on. "If I open the door while *you're* controlling the plane it'll suck us all out into the air. It'll only create more problems, not solve any, witch." Sabin's voice was clear, sharp, and edged with a density that Tullia could not quite discern. But she knew it was one of violence.

A hiss. "We can't shake the damn beast. I thought he'd have crashed into a mountain by now."

Sabin's big hand dented the head seat of the chair he was gripping, like it was a flimsy soda can. "Land the plane then, bring him to the ground so we can face him. I tire of this sickening ride."

Grand High glared at him, "Oh, you think you could drive this plane better?" She snapped.

"Didn't say that." Sabin retorted calmly, the plane gave a hard jerk to the right, before resuming somewhat steadily.

"Sounded like it." She turned her nose up at him in offense.

A heavy thud then occurred, the plane jerked harshly down, then bobbed up sharply before coming to an abrupt halt. The air inside the plane was thick with sweat and tension. A groaning high-pitched keening began, then steadily increased in volume.

The Grand High looked up and frowned.

A loud pop, then a crunching sound and metal began screaming all around them. Tullia flinched down in her seat, turning around to peek and see parts of the ceiling and floor begin to dent inward in specific places and wrinkle in others.

Everyone watched in stunned, helpless alarm as giant, sharp white teeth began to sink through the ceiling and the floor, beveling the metal.

"This Leatherface is trying…to eat…*my jet.*" Cliona's voice was astonished and filled with horror.

Sabin heaved his ax up then slammed it down on one of the dragon's sharp teeth. Tullia saw the ax vibrate and a very small scuff form on the dragon's tooth.

"He's got some formidable teeth." Sabin's tone was aggrieved yet still calm. But he tasted of wildness, like grass and an energy drink. He raised his ax again.

A deafening roar instantly filled the air accompanied by a screeching howl, then a bunch of terrifying transformer sounds before half of the plane was ripped off. Air whooshed in and tried to pull them out. Tullia's ears throbbed with the screeches of the winds and tears filled her eyes, blinding her.

Chito gave a gasping scream of terror mixed with a panicked flurry of Tagalog words that Tullia no longer understood.

Tullia forced her eyes to open and squinted through the tears that generated from the wind. She saw Jiang Li's head pull back, his giant jaw releasing the scraps of metal that used to be the rear part of the plane. He turned and stared at them in all his glory. His head contained a shimmering collage of blue and white scales that glimmered in the moonlight. His massive teeth gleamed too as pieces of the plane continued to flit from his teeth down to the ground.

Was there a town below? Tullia sure hoped not or else they'd get squished, she thought distantly as the metal meat fell from the sky. The dragon growled, a giant black forked tongue slithering out to lick his now scuffed tooth.

The dragon was beautiful and terrifying. With his long, twisting body encased in glimmer blue scales and thick feet tipped with razor sharp claws flexed in the air. The dragon's head was adorned with two black horns that curled up straight above his head and was surrounded by a thick covering of soft white hair that swished around energetically in the hard wind. The dragon's massive head stared at them with glowing icy blue eyes. His nose had a giant white patch of scales right above two wide nostrils. The white hair that encased his lower jaw and flanked the side of his face, softly framed the dragon's unforgiving jaw line, alone with a thin mustache on his upper lip.

He was freaking scary as all hell.

Tullia saw Sabin lean back, holding his ax and the back of a chair, and used both feet to kick a seat at the dragon. The seat flipped up and smacked the dragon in between his eyes. Jiang Li reared back, seemingly shocked, before his eyes sharpened in offense and his eyebrows tilted down in anger.

Uh oh.

One of his claws rose, his mouth opening wider on a snarl…

The plane jerked forward just as the dragon claw swiped and missed them. Tullia saw Jiang Li's body twist in the sky, it was at that moment she comprehended just how massive he was. He darted up and out of sight. She swallowed, her heart tripping wildly in her chest. She faced forward, her legs quivering, and her mouth dry with dread.

Shit just got real.

Cliona was staring at the hanging metal scraps that swayed precariously in the harsh wind, her mouth pinched tight. Suddenly, a metallic taste filled Tullia's mouth and a heat that was so hot, it was numbing.

The Grand High's mouth moved, but Tullia couldn't hear due to the shrieking wind and scratching metal. She looked back at Sabin to see him holding himself firmly in place, with one ax embedded in the floor of the plane, and the other ax poised ready.

"He ripped my *favorite* plane in half!" Tullia whipped her head back to see the Grand High's face set in a nasty frown. "This cheap handbag…No more playing."

She snapped her fingers and the plane stopped moving in the air again. Then it fell.

Fell….

The force of gravity clawing at them made Tullia scream for all she was worth. She faintly heard Chito's scream, but between the screaming air, her ears being partially deaf, and her screams she didn't hear much else. She closed her eyes as she prayed with every atom in her body.

Dear Lord,

I'm sorry I haven't spoken to you in a while. If you could, please make my death a quick, painless one.

Amen.

Oh, and please make Chito's death painless too. And please make Sabin...not hurt?

Tullia peaked at Sabin to see him catching a bag that was thrown at him. He slugged the bag over in his broad shoulders, then dislodged himself from the plane and instantly he was sucked out of the half-chomped side of the plane.

Tullia gasped in horror filled awe. He was so cool with his mysterious ninja but not ninja facade, and so not in touch with common sense. She watched him, fall up in the sky then disappear entirely and within the thin clouds.

Tullia blinked and the next thing she knew she was floating probably several thousand feet up in the air. There was a thundering crash, followed by what sounded like a lot of nature being destroyed and animals screams of terror. Tullia stiffened, then looked around to see the first half of the plane rammed against a rising hillside and a bunch of puffy green trees dent, smashed, and torn out all around it.

It oddly looked like a discarded child's toy from all the way up here.

"This dragon will learn a very valuable lesson today." Tullia snapped her head up to see the Grand High, still secreting blue smoke, staring straight ahead. "And I'm not even going to charge him. Aren't. I. Generous." There was such a viciousness in her tone, it sent a shiver down Tullia's spine. She followed the gaze of the Grand High and saw the gleam of silver in the moonlight accompanied by a shimmering blue. The dragon then dove down, curling and twisting about in the direction of where the plane wreck was.

A loud roar rumbled over the dark hills, scattering the sleeping birds away in fear and some of the other mammals too.

"Let's get you two somewhere out of the way, so mama can work quickly." Tullia heard two taps of the Grand High's nails, then they descended quickly, not as fast as a drop, but certainly not at a comfortable speed. Tullia gritted her teeth as the awful sensation of gravity scraped up her body, tugging her organs out of place and causing all of her muscles to become tense. Chito gave a yelp and seemed to make baby animal noises of discomfort every now and again.

It comforted Tullia. And humored her too as her heart thundered in her chest and her breath became gasps.

"Now sit and stay." Cliona sat them abruptly on a middle branch that was thick, sturdy, and rough on her butt. "I'll come get you when I'm done." Tullia looked up at Cliona, still in her silk red pajamas and bare feet poking out. Then she was gone, a thin wisp of blue smoke was left in her place.

The night was tranquil, despite all the drama that happened earlier. The moon was full, the sky was clear, Chito was panting, trying to recover from the plane fright. All in all it was a nice night to be alive. A breeze caressed her bare feet and Tullia's body registered, that it was freaking cold, and she was only wearing one layer of clothes

She curled into herself, shivering. "Chito, can you go-go warm furry animal then let me cuddle you?"

"I am not in the mood to be cuddled." Chito's accent was thick, and his tone was hollow. He tasted of tart shock and raw terror.

Tullia pressed her lips together to keep from calling him selfish, because he could get warm at any time he wanted, and he won't share that gift with her even though he knows she is anti-cold. Okay, he may be traumatized by the whole plane and dragon incident, but Tullia didn't think that gave him the right to be a jerk, but she supposed she could be empathetic.

Slightly miffed and a whole lot cold, Tullia curled into herself to try and keep at the very least, her important internal organs warm. Tullia turned to look up at the sky to see a blur of….something dart across the sky. She frowned, scanning the sky with unblinking eyes.

All was still.

She bit her lip, knotting her hands against her stomach in worry. She had a feeling that the dragon was back in action in the sky, and that's where Sabin was.

Sabin most likely is entangled with the dragon, since he was the first one ejected off the plane, the Grand High would be right behind him, ready to tango…but were they alright? The dragon was huge, way bigger than the Tikbalang and definitely way older and stronger. Plus, Tullia and Chito weren't there to help take the dragon down either…

Because we're super crucial, she thought cynically. Tullia turned to look up at the sky. The stars were clustered in an adoring way all around the big pale globe. It was gorgeous and something a city never had and something pictures could never capture. The feeling of being so insignificant and so alive blended into one as she looked up to the sky in a foreign land.

There was a soft scuttling sound, then Tullia's hand tickled, she looked down ready to scratch the itch that dared to offend her hand, then froze. A mutant with beady black eyes, multiple legs that dwarfed its frame and a fat body with white and brown spots, crawled over her hand that was on her stomach, and then paused.

Freaking paused.

A rolling wave of pure repulsed terror, worse than the fall into the dragon's lair, and worse than the whole plane aerobatics, overtook Tullia's entire being. She flung her infected hand up sharply, flicking the giant bug off and let out a peal of sickened screams, while vigorously waving her now tainted hand.

"What! What!" Chito yelled, startled by her sudden outburst. Tullia cringed away from her hand that the ugly, big bug sat on and made a whimpering sound.

"Chito, I need a flamethrower to cleanse my hand!" She whined, trying to get as far away as she could from her limb.

"What?" Chito's tone was less sharp and more confused.

"A huge bug that looked like a science experiment went wrong, crawled on my hand and then sat on it!" She shuddered at the phantom flashes of the tickle, disgusted and wishing she had hand sanitizer.

Chito made a scoffing sound, gently pushing her shoulder that was pressed against him. "It's just a bug."

"Just a bug? Did you see the size of that fu—" She began, then something fluttered from the corner of her eye. She jerked her head towards the motions and another bug, with wings and huge pincers perched itself on her outstretched tainted hand. She felt her eye twitch as she screamed again and forcibly shoved herself back into Chito, flinging her hand wildly.

She'd have to cut off that hand now. It was beyond redemption and she didn't want to be attached to her.

Chito yelled a wordless cry and then they both began to tilt backwards as gravity clawed them down. The huge bug flew away from her hand gracefully as Tullia tumbled from the branch and began to fall towards the ground backwards.

She screamed, hating everything, then lost her breath as tiny leaves scratched her on her way down. She closed her eyes and tensed her entire body, waiting for a spine breaking greeting from the ground. A hard-hairy arm snaked around her waist and brought her to an abrupt stop. Tullia coughed as the hard arm was unforgiving against her soft stomach. Her poor stomach began to ache as her head spun dizzy from the sudden stop and her screams. She looked down at the arm that held her, it was thick, hairy and covered in black fur. She slowly looked up; a male gorilla's face stared down at her.

There was a deep silence between the two of them as they stared at one another.

"Chito?" Tullia asked softly, thinking back hard to any type of information she had on gorillas in China's wilderness. Were gorilla's native? Was this even a gorilla?

The ape seemed to huff, his brown eyes twinkling deep within the wrinkled black skin. He pulled her up, pressing her against a hairy chest and began to scale down the tree with nimble quick movements.

Tullia spied Chito's clothes on the gorilla's shoulders and relaxed slightly. The gorilla was indeed Chito.

Or it robbed Chito of his clothes. But the ape didn't smell like a wild ape, it smelled good, like soap and something floral, so it was a high probability that it was Chito.

Or a well-groomed ape.

When they made it to the ground, Gorilla Chito (hopefully) placed her away from him and began to shrink and morph in that unnatural way. Relief swamped Tullia, okay so it was Chito.

He then stood before her, and quickly got dressed. Tullia politely turned around so that he could have some privacy. Even though he transformed his boy bits into that of a barbie doll look-a-like, so there wasn't too much to see.

"Since we made it to the ground, thanks to your freak out, what do we do now?" Chito's voice sounded tired, and a prickly sensation poked her palate.

"Excuse me, we would've had to climb down eventually, and you darn well know it." Tullia looked up, the trees tried to conceal most of the night sky, creating a heavy shadow on the ground. "Well, we can either go to where Sabin and Cliona are fighting Jiang Li." Chito pulled a face that clearly said, 'that's dumb, what're we gonna do to help them', "Or, we go try and find the plane wreckage."

"Why would we try and find the plane wreckage?"

"Because Chito," She growled, "I want to see if I can find my shoes and my gloves, and winter gear cause I'm cold. In case you haven't noticed, it's below sixty degrees outside and I do not have warmth!"

Chito's face was blank for a moment, then bubbles popped along her tongue which pissed her off. He smiled, and Tullia was reminded that

Chito was a very pretty person. "It's more like it's sixty degrees outside." He looked down at her feet, she curled her toes from the attention, then slipped out of his cheetah print flats he was wearing. "Here wear my shoes, you're a city girl, so you'll probably destroy your feet if you were to walk barefoot in nature."

Tullia placed a hand on her heart, she felt emotional tears of gratitude fill her eyes. "You are so kind. Thank you for understanding my pain."

Tullia brushed off her feet as best as she could, then slipped into his shoes, happy that they were a bit bigger than her shoe size. The last thing she needed was for Chito to have smaller feet than her, he'd be merciless with that knowledge.

"I think we should go find the others, I don't know this area and I don't know what wildlife resides here." Chito looked at the dark forestry, his eyes sharp and searching.

Tullia nodded, "Sounds good. If they're anything like the insects, we are in serious trouble."

Chito looked up and seemed to trace something in the sky with his finger. "Alright, lets go that way." He pointed off in some direction. Tullia stared in the direction for a bit then shrugged.

"Lead the way." She said brightly. She didn't know what direction he pointed off too, but she was horrible at directions, so it'd be best if he took over that area of their little spontaneous hike.

They both began to stomp through the thick foliage in the dark, searching for a witch, a dragon and an ax wielding beef cake.

Chapter Twenty-Three

Sabin floated down from the sky, the parachute that the witch had thrown at him was functional. He did have his doubts, but it turns out there were no tricks from her. She was far too upset to torment Sabin. It was a nice reprieve. Turning hard to the right, Sabin swung towards a grassy area void of trees. He would land on the ground, where he was meant to be and no longer take residence in the air, and then find Tullia and the little shifter.

The witch probably put them in some tall tree, thinking it would be safe. His eyes scanned the trees, looking for predators that lurked in the tall grassy fields. He found a few, their eyes flashing and their teeth gleaming within the darkness and sighed.

The night was going to mimic the day he just had, long and seemingly endless.

He turned his attention upward, enjoying the calm descent down. The night air was a kiss of ice on his face. His mouth twitched at the thought of Tullia, she'd undoubtedly be cold with only one layer of clothing on. He'd find her soon enough and give her a jacket from his bag. The sky was clear and bright, the moon sat in the velvet sky, shining its glory down to the darkened earth.

While scenic, there was a coldness to the night, with its indifference to their situation, though Sabin always thought that the moon was apathetic to events. Inhaling the crisp air, Sabin exhaled harshly. He tilted his body slightly, angling it just so-

A blurred movement from the corner of his eye, Sabin snapped his head towards it and saw the gaping mouth of the dragon, his yawning abyss of a throat and the jagged teeth coated in saliva rushing towards him. He ripped the straps of the parachute from his chest and threw his arms up, sliding out the harness. The dragon rushed past him, the force of his wind sent him flying in another direction. Sabin heard the vicious jaw snap of the dragon above him and the shredding of fabric.

He spun in the air, his stomach tightening with preparation, his mind slewing with phantom pains as he tumbled rapidly down to the earth. This was not his first time being airborne without a parachute. He managed to stop spinning, thankfully, and saw a bushel of trees charging at him. Sabin flattened his body as much as he could and began to pick up more speed. His eyes were glued to the treetops that swayed and flickered in the light breeze.

He gritted his teeth, preparing for the pain his body would be subjected to.

The trees began to melt together and turn...orange?

Sabin slammed into gelatinous...sugar? Sabin's mouth was filled with the orange firmed goo and instant, offensive sweetness tortured his taste buds.

Sabin forced himself to swallow the too sweet substance and to remain calm. He couldn't move, though everything around him jiggled violently. Then it began to quiver and melt, dragging him down the earth, not gently but certainly not cruelly either. Sickly sweet remembrance of the orange stuff lingered in Sabin's mouth. He shook his head, then looked to his right to see the witch standing a few feet away from him. Sabin spat in her direction, trying to expel the sweetness.

His rage shuddered within him, disgusted and angry at the fact that the witch forced him through that.

"What was that shit?" His mouth moved before he could hold his tongue. Interacting too much with that woman was hell on his nerves.

The witch glanced at him, her eyes were a vivid blue and glowed faintly in the darkness. "It was jello, you uncultured swine."

Sabin swallowed again, the thickness and abusive sweetness still clouded his mouth.

"And it was orange because that is the best flavor." She added in, staring up at the sky. Her tone told him she thought he was an idiot. However, that was the tone she often used with him.

Sabin spat once more before he withdrew *snubba* and *slatra* from his back, rolling his shoulders in preparation for the upcoming confrontation.

"Now, just so we're clear," Sabin glanced at Cliona, her sharp face serious, "I saved your ass because I don't want to wait for you to regenerate. I want that overgrown lizard skinned tonight and I want this done quickly. My beauty rest was interrupted."

Mine too. Sabin thought with an irritation that vellicated his rage within.

To the witch he only nodded once.

"Tullia—" He began but she cut him off with a scoff.

"Your bae is fine. Up nice and high and sitting waiting for her big strong caveman to get her down." She looked at the sky again and bared her teeth in malice. "Faster he's dead. Faster we get the hell outta here."

Sabin turned towards the sky as well, he saw the curling and twisting form of the dragon against the night sky. A dragon that was aiming towards the two of them on the ground.

"Twenty minutes." Sabin said flatly. "I'll take the legs." He gripped *snubba* and *slatra* hard in his hands. He felt them pulse with excitement. Ready to feast.

Cliona clicked her nails together and began to float. She inhaled deeply and blew out a thick cloud of white smoke around them, concealing them from view.

Sabin felt his lips curl in excitement as the bloodlust burst forth.

* * *

Tullia stepped over a log, desperately ignoring the chittering sound of big ass insects and their movements that were far too close to her.

"Are we going the right way?" Chito asked, his tone edged with a temper.

Tullia thought about lying, then shrugged. "No idea."

Chito stopped dead in his tracks, his look was pure disbelief.

"What?" He asked sharply.

Tullia glared at him. "Dude, you literally stopped being the leader after you tripped on a rock, thus I took over the navigation. With that being said, I feel like we should go in this direction." She dramatically motioned in front of them.

"You feel, like, magically feel, or you feel like in a dumb intuition way?" A snarky question.

Tullia gave him a confused look. "Since when is intuition dumb?"

"Since you have it."

Tullia gasped, extremely offended, and Chito sighed. "Look, Tullia, we are out in a jungle, lost and practically defenseless."

"As I have suggested multiple times," Tullia raised her voice while looking up at the sky in utter exasperation, "You go-go elephant, I ride on your back, and we stomp through this bitch."

Chito pulled his long hair forward and folded his arms. His high arched eyebrows rose. "With you sitting on my back, I'll develop spinal cord issues. Also, I don't want you to ride me."

Tullia clicked her tongue. "Didn't need to phrase it that way. You're making it weird."

At the taste of Chito's confusion, Tullia knew her words went over his head and dramatically sighed. "Go-go giraffe and look over the trees then to see where we are."

Chito pursed his lips. "The biggest giraffe in the world would not be able to see over these trees."

"Oh my gosh, Chito!" Tullia groaned in a demonic chipmunk voice. "You're the only one with a superpower here, and you won't use it."

Chito rolled his eyes. "Let me transform into a bird and go look for them."

"You want to leave me, a plain Jane with no weapons nor superpowers, except crippling visions, alone in a foreign jungle at night?" She paused, watching his face. "Now I truly know how you feel about me."

Chito put his hand to his forehead. "Look, I'm not shifting into an animal in which you can ride on."

"Why!" Tullia stomped her foot. "You went go-go pony mode in Biringan." She argued.

"That was the first time I ever allowed someone to ride on my back and I felt so oppressed and was nearly crushed by your big butt." He pointed his finger at her butt accusingly.

"Wait, wait, wait." She held up her hands. "You think my butt is big?"

"It's huge." Chito snapped without any hesitation.

So, it must be true. She thought she was making it up, but no, she did have a big butt.

Tullia smiled. "You're the best, even though you're selfish, you know just what to say to make a girl feel better."

Chito's face twisted with utter confusion, the sweet and sour flavor didn't bother her, she was far too elated.

"You are so weird. Are all Americans like this?"

"Well, about that—" She began, but a roar that rumbled the earth and made the leaves quake on the trees overtook the air around them. In the silence that followed the roar, absolute stillness encased them and held the forest, as if all the living creatures were frozen in terror.

A few seconds passed in the unnatural state before the ecological sounds of nature continued. Tullia and Chito looked at each other.

Then Tullia snapped her fingers and pointed at Chito as she said, "Ha! I knew we were going the right way! Don't diss my intuition again, go-go boy!" She then laughed wildly.

Chito pulled a sour face, clearly mocking her, then they began to fast walk in the direction of the roar. Tullia ignored the acidic taste of fear that slid over her tongue and the fluttering of her heart.

* * *

Ten minutes later, after an awkward fast walk and lagging jog they both came upon a botched clearing with trees haphazardly chucked into other trees and giant craters of dirt.

A dragon, long and elegant stood with his two hind feet clenched into the earth and his front claws splayed out in the air. His serpent eyes seemed to glow as they scanned the area. The Grand High and Sabin were nowhere in sight. Jiang Li's scales hit every shade of blue known to man and shimmered enigmatically under the moonlight. They almost seemed to flutter, as if the scales were feathers being ruffled by the wind. A sharp tail, with a tufted patch of white hair swished agitated, slashing treetops down to size without any effort.

His big eyes, cold and sharp, roamed the area hungrily, looking for something…then they landed on Tullia and Chito, who, like idiots, step out in the open. His nostrils flared and his neck swung, turning a heavy looking head fully in their direction. White hair that defied gravity floated whimsically around his angled face.

Oh shit.

He saw them. Chito gripped Tullia's arm, his nails digging into her sweatshirt sleeve and right through into her skin. Tullia's heart seemed to stutter then kick into overdrive and pound into her chest. They both curled back under the weight of the dragon's gaze. The sensation of a predator's gaze was muted because the acid of fear flooded her palate and burned her tongue. The dragon reeled back, lifting himself higher in the air, then dove towards them, a malice glint in his eyes, his slightly nubby front limbs extended, his claws flexed-

"Alright, you sad sack of scales." Cliona landed right in front of Jiang Li. Her form looked small and delicate when compared to the dragon's hulking form. Her hands placed on her hips; her leg was outstretched in a classic dominant pose of a bad ass bitch. The dragon, who had reeled up at the Grand High's sudden appearance, bared his teeth slightly, his thin long mustache right below his nose swished with seeming irritation.

Her long, long fingers began to glow bright blue. "Imma skin you with my bare hands. After all, the color blue looks so damn good on me." Her tone twisted into something vile that crawled through hell and soiled Lucifer's throne.

Jiang Li roared, a sound that vibrated and made her ears bleed in pain and destruction. Tullia's vision blurred from the agony incurred due to inhumanly loud sound, but she saw the Grand High leap high from the ground, dodging the dragon's claws that had slammed down to where she once stood, and exploded a bomb of blue smoke around her. Jiang Li drew back, his mouth open in a terrifying snarl, displaying rows of jagged, gleaming teeth. Tullia heard the Grand High's screaming laugh as she dove at him within the fog, clawed hands extended, her face peeled back in a sneer.

A roar polluted the air with its violent vibrations, rattling Tullia's entire body. Hard hands gripped her shoulders and pulled her back. Her knees wobbled and her frame was mush, but she managed to stay upright.

She looked up sharply, getting a cramp in the process, to see Sabin, his gold eyes were fastened on the dragon. "Don't move from this spot." He commanded, his voice, a rough slide of metal on gravel. His eyes shifted to look down at her and Tullia nearly flinched back. There was a visible prowling of…something in his tawny depths. The thing in his eyes were made more intense by the fact his entire face was swathed in black cloth.

Tullia felt pinned, felt as if she was prey under his eyes as he continued to stare at her. A type of self-preservation took over her and she nodded, to which his eyes, molten and violent, slid away from her face and Tullia could inhale deeply once more. It was then, when his eyes were away, she noticed that Chito was next to her. She also noticed that Sabin held his shoulder as he held hers. Cupping the shoulder and curling his finger into the bicep.

A hot flash and a sharp sensation in her chest had her frowning. Her eyes fastened on where Sabin's hand was. She forced her eyes away, confused. She felt Sabin's big hand slide away from her shoulder, she glanced at Chito, relieved that he too no longer had Sabin's touch on him. Tullia scowled, shoving the feeling she refused to name down within her.

No.

"Good. This will take time." Tullia watched as Sabin gazed at the dragon's twisting form. His eyes suddenly flashed back to Tullia.

He reached behind him, his body flexing and Tullia forced her eyes to remain on his face and not his awesome, flexing biceps. He pulled his forever man-purse from his back and handed it to her.

"There is a jacket in there. Find it and get yourself warm." She saw the glint of warmth melding with the other organism in his eyes. "I know you're a baby to the cold."

She blinked in confusion. The cold that she had been immune to for the last twenty or so minutes seemed to infect her all at once. She shivered violently, clutching the man-purse to her chest, warmed (emotionally) that he remembered she hated the cold. Then again, she made it obvious, so he should, if anything, remember that one fact about her. He reached behind him again and unsheathed his black axes. Sabin twirled them in his hand, clearly comfortable and accustomed to their weight.

"Don't move." He repeated, looking at both of them with a stern warning, before jogging off towards the dragon being bitch-slapped around by the Grand High. Tullia did a double take at the scene to make sure her mind wasn't exaggerating and felt her lips curve. Cliona had the dragon bound and was using a tree that was coated in blue smoke to smack the dragon back and forth across the face.

Sabin sprinted up to the scene and made a beeline straight to the single claw that touched the ground. He swung his axes up over his head, then slammed both of them down in perfect coordination right into the dragon's foot.

Jiang Li bellowed in pain, hissing and snapped his giant head towards Sabin, but then a tree was shoved in his mouth. Tullia saw the dragon's abdomen quivering right before he spat a thick stream of water at Sabin, sending him flying, then Cliona. A blue bolt of what looked like lightning hit the side of the dragon's head as the Grand High cussed quite fervently as she dripped water. Her black bonnet was now flat and dripping with water.

"Should we help them? Tullia asked, but Chito was sitting on a rock, watching the fight vividly and shook his head.

"Sabin said to stay." His wide brown eyes glued to the fight. "And you're insane if you think we can offer any type of assistance."

Tullia frowned at him, but decided she was too cold to continue on in her current state. She began to dig around in Sabin's forever man purse, looking for that jacket he had foretold about. "What are you talking about? We can distract the dragon, then they can quickly knock him out and we can go on with our quest."

Chito pulled a face. "Distraction? Basically, like damsels in distress."

Tullia mimicked Chito's face of disgust and incredulity, as she pulled out one of Sabin's big black boots. Wrong thing. She shoved it back haphazardly. "Uh, no. *We* will distract. As in provide a useful skill that will assist our teammates."

"You just twisted the words. It's the same thing." Chito rolled his eyes. She yanked out a pair of Sabin's socks. Where the hell was all her stuff? She looked at the giant black socks (even his socks were black?) and mentally shrugged. She stepped out of Chito's cheetah print flats, dusted her feet as best she could and pulled up the sock right under her knees over her yoga pants.

Damn.

"How is it the same thing?" Tullia demanded hopping a little to get her other foot in the sock. A hissing growl vibrated the earth beneath her feet, making her balance that much more unstable. Tullia turned to see Sabin ducking under the dragon's swishing tail. His axes glinted under the pocket of moonlight through the dense trees above. Seems like the Grand High lost her hold on Jiang Li, he was now thrashing about almost wildly with his claws.

"Because we are practically useless! We are going to need rescuing when the dragon's attention is on us." Chito's tone suggested she was dumb. She turned to look back at him.

She gave him a really strong glare, as she handed him back his shoes. She then began to rummage through the bag for a jacket and her own shoes. Socks were well and good but the ground was still icy and sharp. "It's called a team effort. And every role is important."

He scoffed, clearly being a wet blanket in this situation. Tullia decided to ignore him and his negativity. She watched Scooby Doo, she knew the importance of everyone's role, even the distractions. After far too long fumbling through a bunch of random crap in Sabin's forever man purse, she managed to find flip flops in her size and her pink puffer jacket that smelled like sweaty ass, but she was still going to wear it cause her teeth started to fight each other.

Exhaling harshly, Tullia threw the purse against the rock that Chito sat on and turned back to face the fight. She began to assess the situation. The Grand High was now clutched in the dragon's grip, cursing him six ways to Sunday for daring to touch her in his scaly hands and Sabin was up on the dragon's mane. He was dangling and swiping at the dragon's claws that tried to swipe at him.

Tullia nodded, then clapped her hands once, thinking.

The situation was assessed, and it didn't seem to be in their favor. She swallowed; her throat becoming dry as she took in the whole girth of the dragon. Truly comprehending the size of him made her feel like a fruit fly newly hatched. She would never admit it, but Chito made a valid point, honestly, what were they going to do besides become live sacrifices?

Tullia pushed away negative thoughts and inhaled deeply. She strode up to the fight, her step measured and her breathing even. She felt a tingle in her spine and a pinch in the back of her throat. The dragon's blue eyes met hers, their depth a violent swirl of anger…and desperation.

"Jiang Li." She felt her throat loosen and her limbs relax. A surge of something unfathomable swelled and overflowed, causing her mouth to open of its own volition words dominated the space around them, seeming to consume the noise. "Stop."

The massive dragon reared back; she saw his serpent eyes narrow before he threw the Grand High at Tullia. Tullia, like a dumb-ass, opened her arms intending to catch the tall curvy witch, but the Grand High righted herself and simply stopped mid-air. The dragon shook his head violently and Sabin's ninja clad self-went flying into the trees. A crash was heard then the sound of leaves being viciously disturbed before the quiet regained its place in the night.

"Indeed. Enough of this foolishness," Jiang Li's voice, deep and distorted coming from the mouth of the dragon and was frosted with ice covered steel.

The shimmering blue dragon that was Jiang Li rose on his hind legs, showing his snow white under belly. His frame did a rolling shutter, sparks of white seemed to pop all along his frame as he then shrank dramatically and morphed in a blurred, indiscernible way. Mere seconds later the human version of Jiang Li. Complete with his smooth blue-black hair, a white robe and a blue belt sash.

Tullia tilted her head in query. Where'd his clothes come from?

"Nuh-uh. The loser can't call a truce." Cliona hissed, her otherworldly appearance, her black hair was wild around her fierce face, her silk bonnet gone, and her eyes sparking was intense. She floated right in front of Tullia, looking every bit powerful and cruel in her battle-ready posture.

Jiang Li stood, regal and unflinching against Cliona's rage fueled glory. "I did not call a truce. This play is tiresome. We have many things we must discuss."

"*Play?*" Cliona repeated, surprised and seething. Tullia tried to clear her throat quietly so the heat from her rage wouldn't choke her.

Her poor mouth would never be able to taste anything ever again at this rate.

"You destroying my plane, attacking us in the forest and getting my hair wet is your idea of playtime?" Her tone vibrated with her contempt. "I should just kill you right here and now for your offenses."

Jiang Li's face was expressionless, and the way the moonlight pockets caressed his face seemed to make it hard and callous. He shrugged ever so delicately. "You were playing in my skies, and I obliged you even though you were rude and barbaric in my home. However, that is a different matter altogether." His posture, already stiff and proper, tightened and seemed to exude an air of generous emperor. "I have reconsidered your offer. I will be accompanying your group throughout your travels."

The Grand High was dead silent for a moment. Tullia was shocked and she faintly heard Chito make a gagging, choking sound behind her. Then Cliona raised her head up high and looked down on the dragon as she sneered, hand on her hip. "You think we want you now?"

"You need me." Jiang Li stated arrogantly.

The Grand High threw her head back and laughed dramatically, cruelly and beautifully. "That was the best joke I heard all week!" She cupped her pretty face, and smiled meanly at the dragon. "Nuh-uh. No, we don't want your help anymore. Now, last chance for you to crawl out of my sight before your life ends here. Begone you flying satchel." She shooed at him with her long, long fingers, like he was a stray cat.

Jiang Li did not flinch, though there was a flare of anger at her blatant disrespect, Tullia could taste that much even though his face was perfect serenity, and her tongue was numb from all the anger.

"You are in no position to refuse my generosity." He said without a stitch of hesitation. His face was smooth, his emotions were somewhat smooth too, though they were a bit prickly with irritation.

"Why are you dumb?" Cliona sighed. "Too many years alone in a cave with only rocks to talk to sure did a number on you huh?" She clapped her hands together. "Let me dumb it down for you. We. Do. Not. Like. You." She gave an emphasizing clap with each word. "Go. Away."

Jiang Li stared at Cliona, clenching his jaw, he seemed to strain for a diplomatic tone. "You're being dense. I am the oldest dragon alive that is still awake. The Japanese dragons are much younger, they do not have the knowledge I have." He delicately placed his hand on his chest. "They know not the secrets of a world barely formed. You will waste your time."

Cliona sighed. "Only a man would boast about being the oldest. It is no accomplishment, everyone gets old. Even the dead age."

"But the dead don't speak." Jiang Li's face was downy looking and nearly white as freshly fallen snow.

The Grand High growled, smoking blue again, she raised her hand towards him. "Get lost lizard brain."

Jiang Li sneered at her in disdain, but just then Sabin strolled out of the forest, looking a little scuffed, but otherwise the beef cake was wholly intact. Jiang Li eyed Sabin's nearly casual stroll towards them. His heavy looking axes were still tightly gripped in his hands and glinted with violence under the hazy light of the moon.

He stood next to the Grand High, his back facing Tullia, rolling his shoulders in restlessness. He didn't utter a single sound, he merely stared at the dragon.

"I am joining your group." He announced again with egotism.

"The hell you are!" Cliona snapped, baring her teeth at him. Sabin glanced back at Tullia, his gold eyes were enigmas, then looked at the dragon, still not saying anything.

Tullia felt the insanely strong urge to intervene. Biting her lip, but throwing caution to the wind, she stuttered up next to Sabin, she looked at Jiang Li, allowing herself to really examine him.

While he looked like perfection and the embodiment of serene and unyielding, she noticed that his pinky fingers were rubbing together, and he blinked far more than necessary, and his lips twitched slightly every few seconds.

Tullia pressed her tongue to the roof of her mouth as she tasted the faintest flavor of over salted eggs, the taste she associated with anxiety, and felt a little bit of sympathy for Jiang Li. There was a little niggling feeling in the back of her mind, a feeling that she knew the reason he wanted in their group…

She tried to follow her thought…but it was like a record player's needle scratching to a sudden stop on a song. It just wasn't meant to be thought of right this second. But…

He was anxious, he wanted to be in their group. Though he was a jerk initially and still is high handed, if he could help them…then wouldn't it be a win for everyone?

"I think we should let him join." Tullia said. Jiang Li's eyes flashed to hers, the surprise he had shown was quickly concealed.

"Petal, let the adults talk, okay?" The Grand High's tone was chiding and condescending, but Tullia didn't take offense. Instead, she looked at the Grand High.

"He's right, he is the oldest dragon, he has the information that we need."

"Yeah, so he says, baby. He's also an asshole and a prick who destroyed my jet and I don't like him."

All points she made were valid.

"You don't like me." Sabin countered dryly, his deep voice complimentary to the rich night.

"Yes, because you're annoying and dumb. But you don't break my stuff." She put her hands on her hips. "Besides, he wanted to trade the information he had for Chito. If that doesn't say something about his character, I don't know what does."

Jiang Li's eyes seemed to wander over causally to where Chito sat, the look in his eyes was indiscernible, but intense. Tullia looked back at Chito, he was still on the rock, and he caught her eye and shook his head animatedly. He was against the dragon joining too.

She looked back at Jiang Li. She didn't think he was a bad person. He was merely stuffy, he just needed to be aired out. "He's outdated." Tullia said simply. "He just needs a few updates and he'll function better."

Cliona snorted. "A few? Petal, he needs an entire reset." Her obsidian eyes roamed over him with contempt. "No. I don't trust him."

Tullia looked up at Sabin. "What do you think?"

Sabin shrugged uncaring; this reaction finally seemed to break the faux tranquility over Jiang Li.

Jiang Li glared at Sabin. "You speak of me as though I weren't present." His teeth clicked and his accent, light, and tilting, became thicker. "You are being stubborn for no reason."

Sabin shifted. "What's your objective? You were dead set against us."

Jiang Li didn't say anything at first, but Tullia could taste the slight sour edge of discomfort.

"I have…reflected on my actions. I was hasty with my emotions. I am not familiar with the world as it is today. To have an entourage who understands the functions of the world would be beneficial for me, I could then observe and learn."

"That's a front if I ever did hear one." The Grand High said, yawning loudly.

Jiang Li huffed, the first sign of exasperation Tullia had seen from him. "I can provide you with many ideals of the origins of lost magic." The confidence in his tone could not be denied. "One being is a portal, guarded by a creature unseen." His words were clipped, angry and controlled. "No one that has passed through the portal and has made it back alive. Their corpses have been tossed back out. Mangled with twisted expressions."

A deep silence occurred between them all, the sounds of nature, gentle and uncaring of the atmosphere, became deafening in their normalcy.

Tullia sucked in both of her lips to keep from smiling. It hit her in the most inappropriate moment that this entire situation was funny. Here she was listening to a conversation that a dragon was having, about a portal with a witch, an immortal Viking and a shapeshifter. Life sure was hilarious at times, Tullia thought with a dark edge. A cricket chirped next to her, causing her to jump with disgust.

She hated bugs.

Jiang Li straightened further, looking regal but a bit placid. "It is… rumored…that it is…the first and last portal where lost magic came through to bind the worlds together. That portal would be the first place I would recommend trying." He paused, his slender shoulders rising and falling disjointedly. "Though, your odds of surviving are low and there is no knowledge of what is beyond that portal."

A shorter silence, before the Grand High clicked her nails together. "And where…is this mysterious portal?"

"I require my condition to be met first, before I divulge any more information." A shark-like answer.

"Nuh-uh." Cliona said in exasperation. "Yeah, you don't get conditions. You broke my jet. Do you know how much that customized jet cost?"

Jiang Li raised a slender eyebrow. "Jet? I do not care what it is nor the perception of it's worth to the lower class."

"Did you just call me a peasant?" Cliona hissed, she pointed at him. "The role of crusty, old wet blanket has been filled." She gave a very exaggerated glance at Sabin, to make it obvious about who she was talking about.

It made Tullia beam a little inside that she wasn't the wet blanket. Sorry Sabin, she thought, glancing at him.

Sabin seemed to ignore the witch, his focus was on the possible threat of the river dragon, his heavy looking axes, though dangling by his side, gleamed brightly every now and again in a deadly reminder of potential violence.

"Your hostility toward us is apparent, dragon." Sabin's voice was deep and smooth and sage like.

She saw Jiang Li's jaw clenched, but he remained silent. His eyes were fathomless and cold.

"And I don't trust your hostility." The flatness in Sabin's voice tasted similar to fish. "I don't trust your motives."

"My motives are nothing but pure, I assure you." His answer was quick. "I will swear to not bring harm to anyone in this group."

Sabin's silence was one of distrust. They just needed something to bind Jiang Li to his word. Perhaps…

"Why not make him sign a contract then? Since he's saying he doesn't want to bring us any harm." Tullia suggested.

Cliona's deep onyx eyes stare at her for a few moments, then she grinned widely. "I have a better idea." She faced Jiang Li. "If you want in our little posse, then you're going to need to do a blood pact with us."

Sabin stiffened and the dragon's calm facade broke entirely. He hissed out air and his perfectly smooth face twisted with something akin to horror and he physically took two steps back.

The Grand High smiled tranquilly, clearly elated. "No? Oh well, too bad."

Jiang Li's face was tight with anger and Tullia's tongue was ravaged by bubbly fire. "A blood pact is binding." He said gravely.

Cliona crossed her long legs and leaned back, reclining in the air. "Blood pacts work both ways. It would give us nice security about you and your shifty behaviors, and you'd get security as well."

Sabin rotated his axes in his hands, thinking. "And what exactly would be the conditions?"

The Grand High made a snarling sound. "No backstabbing, no double crossing, no justification for the first two and no physical violence between any of us."

Jiang Li's frame seemed to soften a bit. "Oh," The Grand High grinned, "And no kidnapping or withholding information. Bottom line, we all agree to operate as one unit, no independent soldiers here."

Sabin glared at the Grand High for a moment, Tullia could taste his smoky concern. She could taste the dragons near desperation and extreme reluctance, a bitter seaweed flavor, but his face was a mask of indifference.

"Tik tok dragon. Hurry the hell up." The Grand High sang, she began to spin slowly to an upside-down position. She looked particularly insane from the way her hair was spazzed out and the way her bare feet with her cute red painted toes splayed out tensely.

Jiang Li's dark ocean eyes glowered at them. *"Deal."* There was such a strong taste of contempt it was almost as if Tullia sucked on a particularly sour lemon.

"Awe, damn it." Cliona sighed but snapped her fingers and blue smoke puff out and around them.

Chito gave a sudden, surprised squeak as he was pulled from his rock and put right next to Tullia.

"Hands out." The Grand High purred, her fingers caressed the air. A vibrant wisp of smoke seemed to flow from her long, long fingers.

Weaving in and out and glinting ominously.

Sabin shifted heavily, he tucked both of his axes back behind his back and unsheathed a small flat razor blade.

Tullia stared at the blade, then her stomach felt heavy, and her palms began to leak sweat.

The Grand High had a flourish as she held her hand open. The glinting blue smoke suddenly snaked across her palm, then vanished. Blood, dark and red seeped up from the line on her palm. Her onyx eyes locked onto Tullia, her grin was tilted and too wide. "Want help petal?" The silver tipped smoke appeared between her fingers again and seemed to wave at her.

Tullia swallowed, her heart thundered in her chest with a creeping chill.

"No. I'll do it." Sabin barked, his voice, sharp and hard, made the Grand High blink slowly as she looked at him. She gave him a particularly vicious look, then turned her intensity towards the dragon.

"Come here, gecko brain. Let me help you cut through that thick skin." Her voice dipped oddly and seemed to slither out of her lips.

Jiang Li bared his teeth at her coldly.

Tullia's hand being gently grabbed snapped her attention away from the cold hostility between a witch and dragon, in favor of the giant mercenary ninja. His gloved hand was firm around hers, but very gentle. He smoothed her fingers away from her palm. She saw that her palm was creased with dirt and held patches of dry skin.

She looked up at Sabin, his gold eyes were clear and calm. The blade winked at her in the moonlight.

"My hand is super dirty." Tullia said, her voice higher pitched than normal. "You can't cut me."

Sabin's eyes twinkled with mirth. "I carry antibacterial hand sanitizer. I also disinfect the blade every time I use it."

Tullia's slight chills of fear, became tight little bundled nerves of anxiety. "Aren't you a good boy scout?" Her tone was thin and sharp.

An impression of a smile. "After going through a few plagues and pandemics, you learn to combat dirt."

A brief thought, how many plagues has he been through? However, the thought flitted away quickly when Sabin started cleaning the blade.

"But, what about after? Open wound plus the jungle plus no band aids equals losing my entire hand."

A chuckle. "I have a first aid kit." He nodded towards the discarded forever man purse that laid smugly next to the rock that Chito had sat on.

"I hate you." She huffed. "Why do I need to cut my hand?"

"Tis part of the blood oath. Blood is involved."

So. Freakin. Vague. Did she look like she participated in blood oaths regularly? Did he think that modern education goes over blood oaths, their history, significance, and safety measures for modern day blood oaths?

At her pale, panicked face Sabin let out a small chuckle. He dipped his hand into a little crease in his ninja shirt. He pulled out a bright yellow pouch and ripped open the top. He pulled out a wipe and a strong scent of lemon hit her nose as Sabin took her hand again and began to wipe away the dirt.

It struck her as oddly intimate the way Sabin held her hand, carefully holding her fingers, and his gentle, thorough wipes over her palm as he cleaned her hand. The warmth from his hand, even though it was gloved covered, still managed to permeate through to her hand.

When her palm gleamed pale and spotless in the dim light Sabin pressed the blade to her palm. Tullia's stomach tightened, and fear was a hot cold flash in her. He pressed down and swiped. A sting, like a paper cut, then a subtle burn. Tullia watched as her blood crept out from behind the flap of her skin to leak out onto her palm.

She followed Sabin's hand as he pulled away and watched as he cleaned the blade with another wipe. Then when the blade was clean, he took off one of his own gloves.

Tullia stared at his exposed hand with an intensity that was rude, but she couldn't help it. His hand was big, tan and laced with scarred abrasions and lesions of mangled skin that was ghostly in color and puckered. He drew the blade across his palm, his gold eyes staring at the blade rather than looking at his hand.

Sabin's eyes met hers and, in that moment, Tullia caught a glimpse of an ugly demon that Sabin hosted within him. As fast as it appeared it sunk deep into Sabin's eyes, hiding its hideous self away. His gold eyes slid away from Tullia's, her palate a salty, sour, bitter mess, as he looked at Chito.

"Need help?" His voice was thick and stony.

Tullia turned to look at Chito, he was shaking his head. His long black hair swished silkily around him. He lifted his right hand, it melted slowly then twisted into a bird's claw with razor-sharp looking talons. He cut his hand without much fanfare with his go-go talon hand.

"Good, we're all bleeding." The Grand High's demanding voice forced their attention towards her. "Now all hands out."

She stuck out her hand, palm up. Tullia mimicked her as did the others. The Grand High's black enriched eyes scanned them all, then blue smoke crept in around them from the trees. The air became weighted, and the chill in the air became biting.

The Grand High lifted her hands above her head, her long, long fingers flexed towards the sky.

"Witness, sincerity and solemnity. Tonight, we all bind our blood together in an oath that can only be broken by completion of our objective or death. A Queen, a shifter, a dragon, a cursed man, and a human woman." Cliona's voice was honeyed, dipped and soft. "We've come together, and we bind ourselves to each other for the purpose of our task to trust each other." Her hands lowered and she held her bloody palm out again. "We've presented our blood to the sky and the earth as proof of our devotion towards our goal."

The hairs on Tullia's neck rose. A living...*other* watched them.

"Conditions will be instated with each drop of our blood. If they are broken, then the offender dies." A wicked smile, then the night darkened around them. The tree's shuddered, rattling their leaves. "No betrayal between or amongst each other." A drop of Tullia's blood lifted from her palm. "No forgery or lies between or amongst each other." Another drop of her blood lifted. Tullia watched with wide eyes, fascinated and a whole lot freaked out. "No violence or harm between or amongst each other."

Tullia looked over at Chito and Sabin. Now there were three drops of blood floating right above everyone's hand.

"We bind each other with our blood to give each other security in our unit and the ability to put our faith in one another. Betray the blood oath, and you will die."

A breeze began to pick up and the insects stopped their small noises and the air thickened with power.

"Our witness to the oath is mother moon and her sky, betray our bond and they will see to it that you die." The Grand High's silky-smooth voice was a velvet kiss in the night, tinged with an icy undertone.

The moon sat in the sky, viewing them with an otherness that nearly frightened Tullia. She fluttered her eyes away quickly when she saw a grin on the pale surface of the moon. Tullia saw their blood droplets raise and come together, melding collectively into a fat droplet. A sharp sound vibrates the air as the blood droplet dropped to earth, sinking into the soil, and disappearing entirely from view.

A weight settled on Tullia, subtle but suffocating in its presence. The silence between them was significant, acknowledging and understanding. Nature seemed solemn around them, as if acknowledging the gravity of their situation.

They were now bonded together through their blood, until the end of this journey at least.

"Alright," Sabin said casually into the quiet, his voice complimenting the nighttime quiet instead of disturbing the stillness. He stuffed his mutilated hand quickly back into his glove. "Where is the portal?"

Chapter Twenty-Four

"Well, this is fun." Tullia smiled at her hands, which were back in her warm gloves. Where Sabin cut her throbbed a little, but it was a minor discomfort. They were in a transport plane that held clotted cream from the UK and assorted scones as cargo. The plane rumbled, jiggling the jars of the cream and the boxes, creating a clattering of sharp and jumbled noises.

Chito pressed in closer to Tullia for the thousandth time. If it weren't so damn cold, due to the plane not being insulated or whatever they do to keep the passenger commercial planes from feeling bloody cold, she'd have shoved him away. As it was, he was already pushing her into Sabin's lap. Not that *she'd* mind sitting fully on his lap, but it was rude and for some reason it was embarrassing for her to take the initiative.

Best friends or not, she was too grown for that action to be innocent.

On top of being smothered, she was being glared at by a beautiful blue-eyed serpent man and she had a huge idea why. Firstly, Chito gave Jiang Li a wide berth and stuck to Tullia like super glue. It got to the point where she had to demand private time for bathroom trips.

Jiang Li, while flawless and expressionless and nerve-stuttering beautiful, Tullia felt and tasted his hostility and anger towards her. She was certain it was because of Chito avoiding him like the plague and Jiang Li wanted to be closer to Chito. The feeling that she couldn't trace before hit her like a freight train when she boarded the little plane. He wanted in their group because of Jiang Li's peasant man, but Tullia wasn't one hundred percent sure.

Exhaustion seemed to become heavier and heavier as time dragged on and all Tullia wanted was to sleep in a bed and not be cold.

They were headed back to Las Vegas to the Grand High's mansion, or what Tullia has dubbed as 'central witchy intelligence'. Her underlings were magical when it came to fast, efficient research. She supposed that was only appropriate though.

She was surprised that they were flying in a plane, but then again, the Grand High seems to be an entire movement of a person. Turns out that her pilot and flight attendant had bailed out of the plane as soon as Cliona had taken over. Tullia was so jealous of that, they got to miss the aerobatics and the nausea. However, even though they left, they borrowed (stole) a new plane to come and pick the Grand High up.

How they found a plane in the middle of the dense forestry of China, was beyond her.

Hours dragged by, Tullia snoozed every now and then while Sabin and Jiang Li were having a statue contest, and Chito trying to morph into her side every few minutes.

She may be legally insane, but this was pushing her poor patience to the limit and making her actually *feel* insane.

"Attention passengers, we will be landing in twenty minutes." A voice came through the speakers above, crackly and distorted.

Jiang Li's eyes narrowed as he looked up, clearly looking for whoever said that. His confusion, a wild mix of tangy and salty, infiltrated her mouth.

"It's a speaker. It's something that amplifies and transports a voice to different…um areas. Depending on the speaker's location." Tullia explained.

Jiang Li didn't move a single muscle, but his eyes cut to her just to give an icy glare. Tullia internally sighed, not sure how to handle the unreasonable outward hostility.

Twenty minutes later the plane managed to land in the Grand High's backyard safely. Which was a feat since the plane was huge. It was noon, the sky was gray and rain fell from the fat clouds.

Really? Tullia thought, disgusted, rain in the desert right this minute? Thanks, mother nature.

If she were superstitious, she'd have taken this as a sign of a foreboding type of message. But she wasn't so it was just an annoyance.

Cliona's entourage was waiting for her in the rain, their eyes eager and their bodies poised ready, vibrating with excitement.

"Set up the meeting room. Stat. I want fresh coffee and good food out at the ready. I want breakfast, brunch, lunch, linner, and dinner, all set up. And don't skimp on the butter." Cliona's voice was sharp and fatigued, but she looked every inch of perfection with her hair wrapped up in a gold head wrap and a body-hugging brown jumpsuit paired with gold heels and hoops.

Even in the muggy weather she seemed to glow.

Iconic.

They were ushered inside, Tullia and Chito were given quick 'magic baths' which were, as always, violating but refreshing and way faster than traditional showers though not as satisfying.

A whirlwind of activity and a storm of witches later, Tullia, clean and with a fresh pair of underwear on, was sitting at a stainless-steel table with a spread of every type of food you could imagine in front of her. From lobster, to fluffy scrambled eggs, to ribs, potato salad to waffles, to chicken, to pork…

Tullia clenched her jaw tight to prevent any drool from coming out. Her stomach woke up and was ready to aggressively digest everything.

"Dig in everyone." Cliona announced, then looked at Jiang Li. "And you, leather ass," She pointed her fork at him, "you better start with the whole magic portal business while we eat."

Cliona clicked her nails and she had three plates loaded high with everything on it. She began to dig in without much fanfare, popping a whole boiled egg into her mouth and Tullia decided she would dig in too.

Tullia grabbed some eggs, a chocolate chip waffle, a thick slab of bacon and doused her plate with sticky, sweet syrup. Breakfast was the best meal after all, so it was only right to start with it.

She glanced over at Chito, he had more of a seafood medley on his plate, to which he was eating daintily from. Tullia then slid her eyes to Sabin's plate, and saw he had an obscene amount of meat and greens piled high on his plate. There was also a cinnamon roll hanging precariously from the edge, trying to hide behind the heap of sausage. Tullia almost 'awed', but she controlled herself. The precious image of Sabin's cute little cinnamon roll would brighten up her darker moments. He's so cute. Big Viking dude with all his meat, and his little cinnamon roll.

"You are as unrefined as ever, witch." She then fluttered her eyes over to the dragon. Jiang Li did not eat, he looked at the food with mild contempt, but focused his attention on relaying the information, while stealing obvious glances at Chito.

"There have been many curious beasts throughout time, scholars and the philosophical sorts, seeking answers to origins unknown." He looked at one of the witches standing by the Grand High's elbow. "Fetch me a cup of hot green tea."

The witch slid her eyes to Cliona, at her nod she scurried away.

Jiang Li's dark blue eyes watched her with a cold snobbishness then resumed speaking. "It is only natural to be curious and since many creatures' lives span indefinitely, ponderings are what keeps them alive and...active."

Tullia bit into her waffle and felt her taste buds melt in utter delight at how good it was. Denny's has nothing on good home cooking and this waffle was now the "waffle" she would judge every other waffle to.

"Many creatures with magic, have used theirs to try and document magic's origin. The wish to know its genealogy." Jiang Li tilted his head, a smooth wave of blue-black hair slid from his shoulder. Tullia shoved a whole bacon piece in her mouth, listening intently. "They would judge areas based upon the resurgence of magic that occurred each time they used their own magic."

The witch maid came back, holding a floral teacup and rose shaped tea pot. Jiang Li said nothing as the witch placed it before him softly, pouring hot tea into the delicate sup. He didn't even bat an eye at the excessively feminine design. Instead, he took a small sip from the teacup.

"Mediocre, but consumable. You are dismissed." Again, the witch looked at the Grand High for direction, she waved her away with a smirk on her face, staring at Jiang Li's expressionless face.

"You think to embarrass me, witch, with your pettiness."

"Oh, is the big dragon quaking because his masculinity is threatened by a teacup with some flowers on it?" She snorted, and crudely pointed a lobster tail at him. "Listen gecko breath, my house, my stuff. You don't like it, I don't care. Go without, then." She dipped her lobster tail in a red sauce and bit into the soft white flesh, looking savagely beautiful.

Jiang Li ignored her words, scoffing at her then taking another sip. Tullia didn't understand why the dragon was miffed, the teacup and pot were cute and complemented Jiang Li's ethereal beauty.

If anything, Cliona did right by him.

"It has been documented that there is a strong magical signature in a couple locations around the world. Such as Damascus, Athens, Faiyum, Varanasi, Jerusalem, and many others. These locations are steeped in magic, which is why they held their preservation for so long, despite human rubbish and interference."

Tullia took a sip of water and stuffed her mouth full of another bite of waffle.

"According to the records, a faun by the name of Cicero traveled around the land, trying to find the strongest area in which magic pooled. It is believed that the larger the 'pooled' magic is, the greater the chance of discovering magic's origins…or the secret to magic."

"What records do you go by?" The Grand High asked, her brows furrowed, and her pretty face scrunched. "I've never heard of these records nor this tale."

Jiang Li sipped his tea, he cut her a sharp side look. "This tale does not make it into a written form for any mere creature to have access to. This is a sacred tale that has been passed down through generations by many ancient races."

"Uh-huh. Cause that's the way to preserve something through time. Don't document it, write it down, or make it known." She shifted, her movements elegant and smooth. "And yet, here you are, spilling the beans so that you can get your kicks of the new world order." Cliona's voice was razor sharp, Tullia could taste the dark humor she emitted with the bacon. It actually went really well together. She quickly shoved another piece in her mouth.

"I do not know what beans you are referring to, I don't much care for them, but this tale is not secretive. Anyone who wishes to know it, need only ask. However, many creatures are choosy due to the sacred nature of the tale. Unfortunately, I am sharing the knowledge with lesser beings, instead of intellectuals, but some things are unavoidable."

Grand High clicked her tongue at him, and this time pointed a cob of corn at him that dripped in a spicy seafood sauce. "Don't you be looking down on us. You're the real piece of ignorant trash here, you troglodyte."

Jiang Li managed to look down his nose at her, and then continued on with his lesson as if the interaction never took place. "As the retelling goes, Cicero traveled throughout the continent and the neighboring continents. After several decades he managed to gain a cult following of various creatures and, in his last hours of life, stumbled upon the strongest and oldest magic marked area."

"How was the location determined to be the strongest?" Sabin asked, his voice rumbling like distant thunder forewarning the earth of a cleansing rain.

"It is said that faun had…abnormal abilities. I suspect the protagonist was a chimera or another type of beast of that caliber, however that is only my thoughts. In the tale, the faun managed to test the area of its magic with a simple spell of devotion. It was performed and cast over the closest town's people or clansmen. In many locations, a handful of people would become infatuated and devout in every word the faun uttered. He would then test the strength of the spell casted, by ordering the spellbound to slay themselves for him."

Tullia froze, her eyes flashed up to Jiang Li. His face was solemn and quiet. Tullia looked at the Grand High, her face was neutral as she leaned back in her chair.

"Mmm. I suppose…" She said slowly, "that would be…the best indicator to see how strong the magic hold is over someone." Her onyx eyes drilled into her glass of red wine. "To take away a living creature's free will is something that is not easily controlled, even with magic at play." Her voice was even, but a sour flavor infiltrated her palette. "To have them voluntarily end their life under magics influence is unheard of. Self-preservation and free will are more dominant than any magic of today."

Jiang Li nodded. "Which is why the faun ordered it. Many locations the faun tested, only a couple spellbound devotees would follow his directive and indeed kill themselves. The others either ended up becoming mentally broken or running away in fear then dying later on."

Tullia looked down at her plate that had a disproportionate amount of syrup to waffle ratio. The cold memory of the man's suicide in that motel ripped through her mind like a bulldozer. The taste of death on her tongue and the buildup and crescendo of emotion...it was awful, the turmoil...Tullia's stomach lurched at the loose notion of just what those poor creatures were forced to do.

She felt her heart begin to pound as fear slithered into her chest and her sweat glands went into hyper-drive as the memory of the man's suicide began to loop. She looked at her plate, the syrup tinting red and thickening, Tullia felt herself wanting to gag-

A warm, gloved covered hand wrapped around her suspended one and gave a light squeeze. Air filled her lungs at once, lifting the dawning horror and easing the tension in her gut. She followed the trail of the big hand on her hand, to the thick forearm, then over the sculpted bicep and straight to those gold eyes.

"Your hand is sticky." Sabin murmured, a twinkle in his sunshine eyes. It took a moment for her throat to become unknotted and allow words to escape.

"Screw off, I get involved with my food." Tullia whispered back hoarsely, but she couldn't help the small smile that tickled the corners of her mouth.

A gentle clank of a teacup being set down on a saucer, caused the tender moment to dissipate between them. Sabin removed his gloved hand from her and Tullia instantly missed it. "Also, when Cicero casted the devotion spell on the nearby creatures, only a handful or one or two would become afflicted. And not all the spellbound followed his order. This trend continued on for all the locations, until he encountered the forest of white."

"Oh, so suspenseful." The Grand High took a sip of her wine. "Can we get to the location already, you freakin' handbag?"

Jiang Li may as well have been carved from stone with his reactions towards the Grand High. He merely gave a cold glance to her. "In order to understand, one must have patience to endure."

Cliona clicked her tongue but took a bite of her corn.

"The forest of white was named for the abundance of white blossomed trees that dominated the area. Luck was on Cicero's side, for beyond the forest there was a modest community of hundred or so human nomads that had stopped for a temporary stay." Jiang Li poured himself another glass of tea from the rose shaped tea pot. His movements were light with a touch flourish, just enough to captivate you into wanting to watch him.

"On the night of a waning moon, magic's lowest point, he casted the devotion spell on the nomads. Instantly, in the dead of the night, all the humans from the clan, young and old, came running to him. They were the most fervent in their enthusiasm towards him. He was their god personified and they were his faithful worshipers." Jiang Li took a sip of his newly poured tea. Tullia shoved a piece of semi-cold waffle into her mouth. It was way too big, so syrup dribbled out the sides of her mouth.

It was right at that moment Jiang Li's dark blue eyes looked at her. His face didn't change from his emotionless blankness, but when his eyes flitted away Tullia sagged in her chair and wiped her mouth with her napkin. Of course, he had to look at her when she was being slightly sloppy.

Great. Just super.

"Cicero, wasted no time and ordered them all to kill themselves. And every human nomad, from the children to the women to the men, died with a smile on their face and their throats dripping blood."

An eerie shiver scraped up Tullia's spine at the imagery her mind produced…it *seemed*…familiar…but not. She shook her head, not willing to encourage any type of remembrance for something so macabre.

"The spell he casted was so strong, it spread onto Cicero's followers, who were jealous of the attention that the nomad's received and each killed themselves to prove their devotion to him and his cause. The once white budded trees, whose soil was now blood soaked, drank from the tainted earth, and their petals tarnished with the blood of the magic bound."

"So, it became a Judas tree?" Chito said, he was leaning his pretty face on finger laced bridged. The dragon's eyes seemed to linger longer on his face as he nodded slowly.

"They pose as Judas trees, but they are the witnesses of the manipulated suicide of the nomads and Cicero's cult followers. They bleed in remembrance during the season they all were murdered in."

Tullia noticed that Chito's plate was still full of food that was most likely cold.

How disrespectful, she thought with disdain and finished off her eggs, trying to ignore the unnerving atmosphere that Jiang Li created.

"Great, so everyone died." Cliona's tone seemed uninterested, but her jet-black eyes were rapt on Jiang Li. "The goat dude, what happened to him?

"Cicero lived." Jiang Li's voice was icicles in the arctic. "He became fanatic with elation. It is said that the backlash of magic tore his mind in two."

"A Dr. Jekyll and Mr. Hyde scenario." Tullia mused, so he became split.

Jiang Li glanced at her briefly. "I do not understand that reference. Cicero became insane."

"Ah," Tullia leaned back, embarrassment hot in her face and sour in her gut. "Nope. Wrong reference."

Damn it. Why did she open her mouth? Did she know anything about this shit?

Tullia grabbed a piece of peeled orange and stuffed it into her mouth. The slightly sour fruit, since it wasn't in season, did a good job of erasing her embarrassment and keeping her mouth full.

"Cicero's mind became empty except for one fixation and that was to discover magic's birthplace."

"Didn't he already find it with the origin?" Chito asked, he finally took a small bite of shrimp that had been sitting on his plate for far too long.

Jiang Li shook his head, his blue-black hair swishing like quiet water ripples. "No. He found where magic had entered the realm, which was its origin to the earth realm. Now he wanted to know where magic was birthed." A slight smile curled his lips, and even though the smile wasn't directed at Tullia, she felt her heart skip a beat. She saw Chito tilt his head, his long dark hair hiding most of his face. But Tullia tasted his sour and sweet embarrassment.

"In order for Cicero to do that, he took all the pooled magic into him and crafted a sustaining portal, manipulating it to follow the trail of magic and to go back to its beginning, to where it was birthed from."

Jiang Li took a sip of his tea, looking cool and collected while the room dripped with tension from his story.

"Cicero passed through the portal, never to be seen from again."

A small beat of silence then—

"Son of a bitch!" The Grand High threw her empty plate at the wall. Tullia jumped at the shattering sound. The witches scurried to clean up her mess.

"It is said that with the portal's creation, came the birth of a guardian whose sole purpose is to protect the portal. Many have tried to find it, none have been successful. This is where the story ends." Jiang Li concluded; he folded his arms neatly on his lap.

Sabin leaned back, as did Chito and Tullia merely looked down at her plate.

"Ugh, that story was vague as hell and patchy with its details." Cliona griped. She was frowning. She licked an empty lobster tail, then threw it down. "Alright, let's recap, shall we? A goat dude goes on a quest for the origin of magic, tests each spot that has supposed 'pooled magic' with a suicide spell on the people nearby. He gains followers, finds the origin of magic—"

"To this realm." Jiang Li interrupted calmly.

Cliona pursed her lips, then sighed. "He gains followers, finds the origin of magic *to this realm*," She stressed with a wide-eyed look at Jiang Li, "casts his spell, it works on everyone and then his followers get jealous and they end themselves. Trees turn pink, a portal was made, a guardian was birthed, goat dude goes MIA…then nothing."

Tullia giggled at the summary of the dragon's story. Jiang Li raised an eyebrow. "More or less."

"*Super.*" She said with false enthusiasm, then snapped her fingers and looked back at the five witches standing along the back wall. "Fact check everything you can. I want specific locations, Judas trees may be a star landmark, and somewhere with ancient nomad or civilization trademarks. I also want magic readings of the areas, the latest to date. Oh, also, check for any folklore on realm travel or hell portals…" She waved her hand in an airy gesture. "Something to that effect. Now go."

Five witches scurried out of the room, their face set in hard determined lines.

The Grand High sighed heavily. "Okay, well, great. For now we will wait to see what my minions find. Until then, I need to attend to important matters. You're free to roam. You go anywhere you're not supposed to, you'll be shocked with a low volt of electricity, and that's also how you'll know where you're not supposed to go." She then smiled brilliantly. "I placed a shock spell on all forbidden rooms."

She clicked her nails then disappeared entirely. Leaving her signature thin trail of blue smoke in her wake.

Multiple witches began to clear the table of food. Sabin came lumbering to his feet. "I'm going to rest."

Tullia bounced up. "Me too!" She was drowsy when they were eating, now that her stomach was more than full, her fatigue doubled, and the floor was looking attractive for her to sprawl out on and pass out.

Sabin nodded, then glanced at the dragon. "I assume you'll be fine?"

Jiang Li merely gave him a cold look of arrogance and a slight chin raise.

"Good." Sabin said easily, he began to make his way out of the room, Tullia got up and trailed behind him. Her gait was lethargic and mimicked a penguin. Man, she ate way too much, but regret was absent. Her right hand was suddenly captured by Chito as he tugged her to him. He pressed himself quite tightly against her, causing her to stumble a bit, but his arm wrapped around her waist and kept her steady.

Tullia didn't say anything, even though the hot spice of anger from Jiang Li scorched her palette. It was only till they were out of the dining room did Tullia slap Chito's shoulder.

"What is wrong with you? Am I a Velcro strap or something? Why are you suddenly all up on me like bees to flowers?" Tullia's tone was light, she didn't want to hurt Chito, but she needed him to realize that his actions were glaringly obvious and making Jiang Li more hostile towards Tullia.

Chito squeezed her hand and waist before letting go.

"What are you talking about?" His tone was innocently pure.

Tullia looked up at him and scowled.

He knew damn well what this was about. Exhaustion was sudden and thick in Tullia's mind, she didn't have the will power to argue with him. Instead, she exhaled loudly and followed Sabin, ignoring Chito. Sabin was making various turns and walking down long hallways with stuffy looking pictures on the wall. She didn't know where he was going, but she didn't care.

She would follow him anywhere at this point, her body checked into autopilot mode.

Sabin stopped at a door that looked like a million and two other doors that they passed. However, when he opened it, the room was threadbare save for bunk beds lining the walls and a giant window dead center of the room.

Looked like a military or boarding room sleeping quarters.

"Dibs on top!" Tullia said with a too loud voice and stumbled over to one of the beds. She made quick work of her shoes, kicking them off, and climbed to the top of the bunk with the efficiency of a six-year-old.

When her back hit the mattress, the tension melted away and her eyes slid closed automatically.

Crap, she had a bra on. She clumsily groped her chest, then relaxed again. It was a soft bra, so it wouldn't be too bad.

She heard sparse murmuring, but the sweet kiss of sleep dragged her under entirely.

* * *

He did it. He did it!

The rushing sound of chaos and chimes vibrated his skull. The portal seemed to pull him apart and squeeze him tight all at once. He saw nothing but a flurry of colors rushing by, dazzling him into in-coherency.

The whirlwind he was in lasted forever, but seemed to stop abruptly, disorienting him. And then he was met with utter darkness. A thick film-like sensation swathed him, like a thousand spider webs, covering his senses entirely.

He swallowed and tried to open his eyes wider, hoping to catch any light...but light was completely absent.

Blinking rapidly, he tried to comfort his eyes from the harsh stinging. Coming from a sunshine drenched field of white trees to the utter blackness assaulted his eyes and made them throb relentlessly.

He frowned, his vision was no clearer and the darkness was still absolute. Shaking his head, he cocked his head to the side, listening.

Silence. A deep silence that ate any sound.

Swallowing against the thick bile of budding fear, he hesitantly began to take small steps forward. The deafening silence did not abate, it smothered his sounds so that they were indiscernible even to him. His hooves made no sound. He could not hear his breath, his heart, his voice...he called out a few times. Or at least he thought he did, his voice was soundless, he couldn't hear it.

He stretched out his hands, seeking a wall, a tree...anything.

But there was nothing. He didn't see anything. He felt nothing. He heard nothing.

His mind raced, his heart thudded painfully in his chest. His tentative steps became faster, but still he heard no sound.

He was now running, phantoms of monsters conjured around him, jeering at him, snapping their fangs at his limbs, barely missing. He cried out, his voice mute. He was in a void, soundless, touchless, tasteless...

His mind bent, then seemed to shatter slowly as madness cruelly picked away at his sanity.

You think you are worthy?

He stilled, panting, swallowing and drenched with fear, he strained his ears to hear.

Your arrogance, your disregard of life...insulting...

He gripped his horns, as pain shot through his body, it felt as though hot pokers were shoving their way through his limbs haphazardly.

You think to use the knowledge for your own gain...

How foolish.

The hot pokers inside of him turned ice then began to...slither. He contorted, the pain so intense it stole everything from his breath to his thoughts. He existed in the pain and knew nothing beyond it.

You are not the one. You are only an insignificant fool.

Fragments of partial words penetrated the consuming pain. Then everything suddenly ceased.

He gasped, coughing as the oppressive silence began to crush him. It swirled around him, snake like, but foreign and cold...so cold. He was being tormented, by being sensory deprived and 'sensing' the dangers, but the anticipation stretched his nerves on edge and caused his heart to suffocate within his chest.

Darkness oppressed him, silence tortured him, the void fed on his degradation... and he lost his sanity slowly, knowingly, and painfully. He began grabbing himself, his horns pulling at them until they no longer sat proudly on his head. He clawed out his eyes, trying to clear the darkness from his vision.

He felt a laugh, but he was too busy tearing at his ears to dislodge the silence from them.

Then it all stopped. And he knew no more of what once was. Only nothing existed to him.

* * *

Tullia jolted up from her dead sleep. Her heart thudded, and the feeling of it was a blessing. Her loud gasps soothed her frayed senses. The white sheet covering her legs was a beautiful vision. She could hear. She could feel. She could see. Tullia stuffed her hands into her hair and inhaled slowly, trying to regulate her breathing.

She didn't dare close her eyes; she was too afraid of not seeing. She touched her face, she could feel the random bumps and the plushness to her cheeks.

Thank God.

"You alright, sweetness?" She snapped her head over to the right and

Sabin's masked cover face filled her vision. His eyes, tawny and alert, watched her with concern. She swallowed, unable to express how happy she was to be able to see his face, to be able to hear his words.

The vision she just experienced was the worst one yet. She had never been sensory deprived. And the intensity of a mind breaking under that the torture, made her realize that she was a whole lot more sane than she thought she was.

"Tullia?" She blinked at a deep voice saying her name and the touch of a big glove covered hand on her shoulder.

"Yeah, yeah, hi." She rasped, realizing her throat was tight and dry as all hell.

Sabin's eyes were vigilant, and they seemed to peer into her. She had the urge to curl up and hide. "Wanna tell me about it?"

Tullia took her hands out of her hair and wrapped her arms around herself. "No. Not, right now." She whispered.

He nodded, but he didn't move away.

Tullia began to shiver, her nerves alive and jumping as if the sensory was too much, but not enough. She coughed, then sniffed, hunching her shoulders higher towards her ears. Her breathing became too loud in her ears and her heart pounded too hard in her chest.

"What do you need?" Sabin's voice, soft and low, made her twitch.

Tullia squeezed herself, feeling the ice in her veins. A thought flittered, embarrassing her, but she glanced at Sabin and swallowed. The request was a shameful one to her, but her pride was long dead and self-preservation took priority. "Can you…can you, um, hold me please?" Her voice was a bare whisper, but it boomed in her ears, as if she screamed it.

Tullia did not need to ask Sabin twice, he scooped her up, easily from the top bunk, and held her tight against him. His warmth and the steady beat of his heart brought tears into her eyes. She pressed her face to his hard shoulder, enjoying the way the pain from her nose chased away her tears. She wrapped her arms around him and squeezed him, reassured that she could indeed feel him.

It was okay. She was not in that void, she had all of her senses. She shuddered and Sabin hugged her tight to him. Tullia noticed that the room was swathed in dim light, and Chito was sprawled out on a bottom bunk with one leg off the side and an arm thrown over his eyes.

Tullia adjusted her head and curled up into Sabin. His heat was intoxicating and his heartbeat at that moment was her favorite song.

Tullia wished that Sabin was there for all of her bad visions. She wished he were there to cuddle her when she was little. After she saw wars, carnage, deaths, and torture.

She may have been less broken, less scarred if he were there.

She smiled, enjoying his evergreen musk and his solidness. She didn't realize just how nice it was to be held together by someone when she was on the verge of breaking.

After all, she was the only one that had ever held herself together.

Chapter Twenty-Five

Tullia had a handful of regrets in life. Her top regret is not keeping in touch with Olivia from the mental ward, not taking that second piece of cake at her sisters' birthday party, not exacting a detailed revenge on her school bullies....

But at the top of her list was allowing Chito to braid her hair.

Chito was trying to braid the top section of Tullia's hair. And from the way he was yanking her hair as if she felt no pain and her strands of hair were super glued on her head, she would never, never, never repeat this mistake.

It hurt too much, she didn't even care what her stupid hair looked like at the end of the torture. She'd probably mess up her hair after a few minutes anyways.

"You have pretty good hair." Chito's surprised comment was a bit insulting.

"Geez thanks." Her sarcasm was weak under the tension in her voice. She closed her eyes, trying to block the pain and the lingering embarrassment from the early morning with Sabin.

He held her in his arms until the dim light became brighter and chased any lingering darkness away. Once it was bright and Chito started stirring with light snores and grunts, Tullia, coming fully to her senses, shyly made Sabin put her down. She quickly escaped to the bathroom; her palate covered with a smoky, soft, concerned flavor. She felt her cheeks burn with embarrassment and her heart race with utter panic.

She died a little under the weight of the embarrassment, writhing silently on the bathroom floor. After about five minutes of that action, she picked herself up and manually washed herself from head to toe. She also manually dried herself and realized just how nice it was not to have a violating magic bath.

When she stepped out, fresh and clean, Chito brushed by her, sticking his tongue out at her playfully before shutting the door in her face. Sabin was sitting on one of the beds in his ninja gear.

His gilded eyes looked at her when she came out and the impression of a smile was in his golden depths.

"Better?" His voice was a physical caress that Tullia was ultra-aware of.

"Yup, all better." She forced a small smile and moseyed on over to where he sat, confronting the stupid feeling. She broke down before on Sabin, and she bounced back. This time should not be any different, her embarrassment was an overreaction that made no sense. She was emotionally high from her abusive vision, that's all. "Thanks, for your help this morning."

Sabin nodded, his gold eyes vibrant in the early light rays.

"Did you have a vision?" He asked softly.

"I… I had a vision." She confirmed, flutters tickled her stomach and swarmed up to her chest. "I think…no." She cleared her throat, looking away from Sabin's intense eyes. "I know it was Cierico, from the story Jiang Li told."

Her visions, it seemed, stopped becoming random and instead chose to be more direct and in line with reality.

"What happened?" His voice was a rumble of rolling thunder and cleansing spring showers wrapped into one.

"He…was nowhere. It was just blackness. There were no senses. He couldn't hear himself or his steps, or his breathing or his screams…He couldn't feel anything if there was something…" She shook her head, knowing she was jumbling up everything, "He was completely deprived of all senses. He couldn't even feel pain." Tullia remembered him ripping off his ear, trying to bring his senses back, trying to scream, but everything was….gone. It was as if he ceased to exist but was still conscious. "His mind broke and it caused him to go insane. It was…terrifying." A small shiver rolled up her spine. A large hand landed on her back gently, and gave small, sweet pats.

The reassurance, it appeared, was never going to get old for her. It brought such a warm feeling in her chest that consumed her whole body, she wanted to hug Sabin for his simple kindness.

She held herself back.

"But, I did notice something in the sensory depraved darkness. There was a…" She huffed, thinking back, trying to look beyond the terror and remember. "There was a voice, but it wasn't a voice per-se. It was more like a feeling that Cierico experienced."

Sabin was a patient man as he waited for her to gather her words, she glanced at him, his eyes were still watching her, his big hand beginning to sear into her back.

Tullia found herself being shy under his honey drenched eyes. They simply were too sweet for her to handle. "W-what I mean to say it that there were disembodied words I suppose that basically told Cierico that he was not worthy and that he offended…" She waved her hands about, trying to think of the appropriate words. "…it? With the way in which he used magic to end lives."

She glanced up again, Sabin's eyes were focused on the hardwood floor boards. She tasted nothing from him, but he was most likely churning the words around in his head. He withdrew his hand from her back and folded his hands together in a pondering steeple

"Whatever that force may be, it seems to be searching for something in particular." Sabin murmured, pondering out loud.

Tullia pressed her lips together, to keep from giggling. The way in which he phrased it, made her want to respond in either a Chewy voice or in an R2-D2 response. However, Tullia was ninety-nine percent sure that her reference would go over Sabin's head, so she refrained.

Sabin made a soft musing sound, then shifted back. Tullia leaned back with him.

"I suppose, since Cicero was nowhere, you didn't manage a location?" His gold eyes slid to her, she shook her head.

"It was a void." She said with conviction.

He nodded in understanding then silence cottoned the space between them. It was soft, comfortable, and tangible.

Tullia went to say something, but Chito opened the bathroom door with a flourish that was both dramatic and unnecessary.

"I need to cleanse myself." Sabin stood up swiftly, his burly form more pronounced. Chito pranced out, looking beautiful with his long black hair loose and his one-piece tan jumpsuit giving him a slender cat vibe.

Chito preened past Sabin to sit next to Tullia as Sabin disappeared into the bathroom. A few seconds went by before Chito asked, "Want me to do your hair?"

* * *

Sabin showered, the cold water stinging his muscles. He kept his eyes trained away from any part of his exposed skin. The ice water was cleansing and quieted his rage that was far too close to the surface for his liking. He didn't like to sleep, and avoided it if he could. Even after all this time, his sleep was elusive and wrecked with never ending nightmares. He once thought of killing himself by depriving himself of sleep. It worked, but he merely regenerated as he always did.

Though with that tactic, he ended up in a coma for an entire week. He was taken to the morgue, under the assumption that he was already dead.

Miserable experience, it was as if he were trapped in his blood-soaked memories until his body had completely recovered, then upon his awakening, he found himself buried under a pile of partially rotted corpses which was utter misery.

So, he forced himself to sleep sometimes, though he could postpone the act for a few days with the help of the curse through the earth, but even that only assisted so much.

He managed to close his eyes for a few hours, but rest was now a myth to him. His mind wandered and his memories knocked continuously on the door of his consciousness. He never answered, but that never discouraged their actions.

He tried every ancient remedy for peaceful sleep from hemlock to dormouse fat on his feet to valerian root to beer. Nothing quelled his nightmares.

Except woven tales.

He had found stories calmed the busy thoughts in his mind, it gave him something to focus on rather than his memories. In the old times, he had often laid hidden near the bard's campfire, and memorized the storyteller's words. Then he would repeat them when he was alone and needed sleep. He also enjoyed the way that each time a bard told a tale, the details would change, from character's actions to monsters. It was different every time.

It amused him, though it made him frustrated at the same time. Every time the bard sang, he'd have to memorize a different detail. He had dozens of variations of the same stories. Bards became fewer and fewer as he traveled to different lands. Languages shifted, twisted and changed, leaving Sabin behind.

So, he forced himself to learn their tongue, distancing himself further from his native language and reconstructing himself as a different person. He took jobs for rich sultans, snobby noblemen and petty kings. He was treated as a dunce and paid pitifully. Sabin didn't mind though, he used them to learn their culture, their words…and to steal their transcripts. He saw that the rich hoarded books. And when he discovered that the leather-bound pages held stories of the bards, without the bards, Sabin had been determined to own them.

However, the rich had the tendency to laugh and scorned those they believed beneath them in their endeavors to learn. Sabin disagreed, but rather than arguing with the deaf ears and blinded eyes, he chose to simply do what he wanted through underhanded means. When he discovered that the symbols used were indistinguishable to him. He tried to spy on young nobles' lessons, but he proved to be far too big for spy work. He ended up having to threaten an educator with his particular vice of visiting the whore house after his lessons with the young masters, crying out his pupils' names.

He managed to learn to read and write in multiple languages. Once he was fluent enough in his comprehension, Sabin began *borrowing* books from his clients. At first, he borrowed children's novels, filling in the gaps of the forced tutor lessons. Then he began to advance to philosophical texts, religious texts, scientific texts…

He found them all enjoyable and at the very least he found them amusing with their ideology which was oftentimes vastly different from his. He memorized their symbols, recited them until his mind was filled with them, exhausted by them and muffled the knocking memories, allowing his mind to rest for a spell.

Sabin turned off the water, focusing on the white tiled wall that was beaded with water droplets. He quickly left the shower, roughly pulling the shower curtain away. He brusquely dried his body, and just as quickly dressed in clean clothes. His eyes staring at the white hand towel hanging crisply on the handle the entire time. Gold hair fell in tangled knots around his face botching his vision.

Annoying.

He rubbed his raised and jagged jaw, wishing hair would cease growing on his head and relocate to his face. However, Odin had seen to it that he would be bare faced for eternity. Taking away his masculine pride and dishonoring him on an intimate level. However, he had retained enough of his culture to maintain his hair. He ran a comb through his locks, disgusted at how long it had grown on him. He seemed to comb his hair for ages, then finally his hair was smooth and laid heavy against the middle of his back. Sabin looked around, searching for material to tie his hair back. He pulled out a knife from his pocket, eyeing the shower curtain. He cut a few thin strips at the bottom.

Clumsily, he braided the strips, unimpressed by the thinness and the flimsy material. After he braided the material a few times, he gathered his hair, hair that was beginning to become a mane, and wrestled it back into a controlled gather at the back of his head.

Sabin reached for his face cover and slipped it over his head. Tullia's scent, the soft sweet gale fragrance, was gone and now he only smelled fibrous cotton and cheap dye.

The remembrance of Tullia brought sensation of her soft body, her warmth and her velvety breath saturating his neck and sinking into his skin. He forced himself to wash and change clothes, but he mourned the loss of her essence.

He had been awake, lying in the bunk underneath Tullia, the memories locked in his mind were particularly insistent with their knocking. He had been in the middle of reciting The History of Tom Jones, when small choking sounds had begun to quietly take up space in the air.

Sabin had listened, had heard her breathing turn ragged and her fearful noises grow more panicked, like a small animal losing a chase with a predator. He had just sat up to check on her, when he felt her violent movement and her soft gasps of terror. Her face when he saw it was bone white and glossed with a sheen of panic. He's seen that look a few times, on the faces of people when he came in the name of his gods.

It was the most pleasant shock that Tullia had requested him to hold her. He with his blood-soaked hands and cursed soul, managed to give, for once, comfort to someone instead of instilling fear. He knew she only sought him out due to his proximity. However, Sabin would gratefully accept the gift of trust she handed him and protect it. It had been a long time since someone trusted him without any ill intentions.

His chest warmed and his rage, always prowling, was utterly still, as if it were absent within. Sabin had not been absent of his rage in centuries. He nearly buckled to the floor and wept with utter relief. It wasn't until the light strengthened in the room, and the sounds of sleep twisted into dawning alertness that their small world was washed away.

And the rage came back, howling its fury.

Sabin flexed, the tension in his body continued to tighten. He'd have to release some of his building rage soon.

A knock occurred at the door. He glanced at the mirror for the first time, inspecting his appearance to make sure he was indeed fully covered, then answered the door while choking back his rage.

* * *

Chito gave another vicious tug on her hair, bringing her back into the

747

painful present and out of the embarrassing past. Tullia bit her lip to stop the swear words from pouring out and barely managed to control her hand movement from whacking him with her elbow.

Five silent, torturous minutes Chito stopped tugging and stepped back with a little flourish.

"Done! Your hair is beautiful now." He sang, with a few claps. Clearly pleased with his brutalizing session.

Tullia looked in the mirror and was slightly impressed by the volume he managed to get, and the level of intricacy with the braids. However, her scalp throbbed hotly, diminishing any enthusiasm, and lessening any wow factor.

Screw pretty hair if it was going to cause pain.

"It's super pretty, thanks Chito." Tullia turned and smiled at him, sliding out of the chair and away from his torturous hands.

Chito flipped his long black hair over his shoulder, clearly delighted. "You're welcome, I can braid your hair anytime. Just ask."

She would never ask unless she needed to be in extreme pain. Which would never be.

A tinkling sound occurred, then a giant multicolored bubble appeared in the middle of the room.

"Please report to the meeting room in the next ten minutes. Thank you." A small chirping like voice said, then the bubble popped with a small sound.

"Meeting room?" Chito looked at Tullia, she just shrugged. She had been in a few rooms, but she didn't pay attention in any way, shape, or form to the maze-like hallways or rooms in the Grand High's mansion. She honestly did not think it would be important.

"Sabin probably knows where it is." She responded, after all he got them in the bunk room, he could navigate them to the meeting room. Touching the zipper on her hoodie, she looked at the bathroom door, expecting Sabin to be done and appear in front of them.

He didn't, the jerk. Can't he sense that they need him with his ninja mercenary senses or whatever?

"How does Sabin know his way around the Grand High's house so well?" Chito sat on the bottom bunk and began to fuss with his own hair. Gently, she noticed with an edge of irritation, he was ever so gentle with his own hair.

"He's…a contractor for the Grand High." Tullia said, hesitantly. She remembered Sabin saying he often did jobs for Cliona, and he also saved her while on a job for the Grand High as well.

But she didn't quite know his role in those jobs. An exterminator of the bad guys? A vampire hunter?

"Like a contract killer?" Chito's offhand question, made Tullia start. She stared at him with wide eyes.

Contract killer?

She didn't see Sabin in that light. She didn't want to see him that way. He was once a mercenary…but he wasn't anymore. He killed the bad guys, like the vampires that were running a live human blood bank.

Doubt crept in, fogging her golden glow she held around Sabin. She shook her head, that was her BFF, she was going to be a ride or die dammit. Ride or dies don't doubt.

Tullia shrugged, uncomfortable with her thoughts and slightly agitated. "Don't know." She then narrowed her eyes at Chito, she just remembered she had beef with this pretty boy. "Speaking of the dragon," Chito frowned, confused, but Tullia mowed right along, "Could you please not use me as a physical shield in front of Jiang Li? Or at the very least can you not make it so obvious that you're avoiding him." Tullia huffed, crossing her arms.

"Easy for you to say. He's giving me these looks that make me want to crawl out of my skin. It's unsettling." Chito folded his arms too, his pouting face was both childish and endearingly cute.

"Dude, his looks give me a brain freeze and heartburn, okay?"

Chito rolled his eyes but sighed in defeat.

Tullia felt her lips tilt up in the corners. She flounced over to him and sat down really close. She nudged him with her shoulder. "Maybe, he's really only looking at you and thinks you're a whole meal."

At Chito's flat look, Tullia raised an eyebrow. "What'd I say?"

"He's a very, very, very old dragon. I doubt he sees me in that way. He is probably considering me as a *literal* meal."

Tullia had a niggling feeling that he was wrong, but she kept quiet. Instead, she shrugged, "Well, he obviously had enough of a thing to want to keep looking at your cute ass. Why not try to find out? It may clear up the weird vibe that has been happening."

"Why on earth would I want to speak with him voluntarily?" The utter disgust in his tone was dramatic, and the gritty sourness that coated her palate really pissed her off.

"Cause he glares at me every time he remembers my existence because you cling to me when you avoid him!" She burst, "And I don't like that! That makes me uncomfortable!"

Chito leaned away from her, his lips pursed, and his eyebrow raised. "What's this outburst?"

Tullia forced herself to calm down. "Look, all I'm saying is, we are all on the same team now. Maybe, our first impression of him was skewed. Maybe he had a reason for acting the way he did. Like you said, he's a time capsule." Tullia said, forcing the other words to stay unsaid.

Chito made a soft sound of disbelief, turning his head away from her with a snappy flourish, but he didn't say anything because he knew she was right.

They both lounged around for a couple of minutes, before Chito nudged her with his ridiculously pretty foot.

"What's taking Sabin so long? Should I go ask him if he needs any help?"

A prickly sensation scraped up her spine and rejection to his suggestion was hot on her tongue. "No." She said far too quickly, then forced herself to smile nonchalantly at Chito. "He likes his private time. Like a diva." Tullia bounced up from her seat. "I'll endure his wrath."

Tullia made her way quickly to the bathroom door, irritated by the fact that Chito seemed to cleave onto Sabin. And irritated that Chito called Sabin a killer. How dare he get all slinky with Sabin then call him a killer, that was her BFF. Then she became irritated at her irritation, because it was ridiculous. She knocked a bit harder on the door than she intended. She looked down at her hands, they *were* on the thicker, sturdier side…

But they still weren't man hands. Screw whatever Chito said.

* * *

When Sabin opened the door Tullia was standing there, her small form swallowed by a giant sweatshirt, it was a style she seemed to favor, and her silky black hair was tamed back into two braids that ended right at her jaw. It really brought attention to her smooth face that was supple with youth and her silver eyes.

She seemed to be born of the moon on a still night. Tullia looked up at him, her eyes serious and glinted. The expression was fleeting, but he'd seen enough to know she was bothered about something. Her face then morphed, her lips tilting up and her eyes crinkling at the corners as the apples of her cheeks turned pink.

"Hi ya."

Sabin cocked his head to the side as his stomach seemed to quiver and his heartbeats became unsteady.

"Your hair is different." He said in lieu of greeting.

Her brows furrowed and a thunderous expression darkened her face. "Do you know what this hairstyle is called?" Before Sabin could even give a reaction, Tullia charged on. "It's called 'torturous hair techniques from a pretty boy shifter'. One-star service. I don't recommend."

Chito's indignant call in the room made Tullia roll her eyes.

Sabin felt his lips curve up, thankfully he was hidden behind a mask.

"I see. It looks nice." He said, amused by the way her face transformed into exaggerated aggrieved.

"Okay, well thank you. Are you ready? A giant bubble told us we are needed in the meeting room in ten minutes." She clasped her hands behind her back and rocked back on her heels, looking guilty. "And that may have been ten minutes ago."

Sabin nodded, noting the way Tullia's silvery eyes seemed to shine under the fluorescent light of the bathroom. The way the light caresses her face, highlighted her feminine features, and caused a sensation within Sabin that he couldn't identify. If he could die and wasn't magic resistant, he might've been concerned that Tullia's lost magic was harmful to him. But he was more confused than worried, she seemed to tug at Sabin effortlessly, muddling up his rage and his thoughts.

Which could be dangerous, but the care to worry would not form.

Sabin cleared his throat, mostly to distract himself from his pointless thoughts. "Alright, let's go."

Tullia smiled and twirled on her foot, striding into the bedroom with her usual careless prance. Sabin glanced back at the mirror, analyzing himself swiftly and critically.

Good.

None of his skin was showing.

He then strode out into the bedroom, the dark fog that had begun to creep in his mind dissipating under the light banter between Tullia and Chito.

His rage prowled deeper within him, crouching low in wait. It cackled, sending a shot of ice in Sabin's stomach.

He would need to expel his build up *very* soon.

* * *

"'Bout time you half-baked runts showed up." The Grand High was floating above a chair, her dark hair was in an afro, with glittering gold studs enmeshed within. She was wearing a gold, shimmery wrapped dress that made the melanin areas on her exposed skin simply glow with a divinity sort of sheen. She thrusted out a bangled covered arm to motion for them to sit with her long fingers. "Asses in the seats, so we can finally start." Though she sounded irritated, Tullia tasted exhaustion from the Grand High, a flat peppery flavor.

Tullia and Chito skittered over, while Sabin strode in casually.

Tullia glanced at Jiang Li, his face was smooth, though his eyes, a deep blue, were trained on Chito in an inquisitive way. A slight bubble and a little sweetness flitted on and disappeared from her palette. Tullia pursed her lips and looked at Chito. His eyes were riveted on the Grand High.

"Begin." Cliona commanded.

"Your highness," One witch with her highlight game strong, addressed politely, "We found possible locations based upon the details provided in the folklore."

A world map appeared in the middle of the table that they all sat around.

"There are many ancient cities around the world, however based upon the faun's assumed homeland, somewhere in either Greece or Rome, we have ruled out the North and South American continents entirely." The little witch shifted. Tullia could taste her nerves, they fizzed and had a flat flavor. The entire left hemisphere of the world map disappeared and only Asia, Europe and Africa were left to float.

"We've researched the ancient cities where Judas trees inhabit naturally, however, due to the means in which the Judas trees were grown, we have hypothesized the possibility that those trees were not inhabited to the land and therefore holds no bearing on location potential."

"The cities." Cliona demanded; she tilted her head to the side, looking at the map with a frown.

"Yes, Grand High." Then a few red arrows popped up in certain places. "We have compiled a list of ancient cities that would be prime candidates to consider."

The names of the cities and countries appeared neatly in list formation.

Faiyum, Egypt
  Argos, Greece
  Aleppo, Syria
  Jericho, West Bank
  Damascus, Syria
  Plovdiv, Bulgaria
  Byblos, Lebanon

Sidon, Lebanon
Luoyang, China
Jerusalem, Israel
Varanasi, India

"All of these locations have a wealth of history, age and resilience. They are cities that have high magic remnants in their soils and their MRS's were all well above average range."

Tullia shot her hand up in the air. The shiny witch, Tullia noticed, eyed her nervously and glanced at Cliona, as if asking for permission to interact with her. Cliona raised her eyebrow at Tullia.

"What, petal?" Her tone was amused.

"What's MRS?"

The Grand High sighed. "Magic Reading Score."

Tullia nodded. She didn't know exactly what that was, but at least she had the name.

"Any other questions thus far?" Cliona asked out. "I forgot that normies like you lot don't undergo witch terminology or Aged magical remnants courses."

"How do we know what your servants have pulled is accurate?" Jiang Li's light, smooth voice sounded like chimes in a light autumn breeze.

The Grand High clicked her tongue. "Well, I don't see anyone else coming up with ideas or having a well-balanced team of highly educated, highly skill, and highly training doctorates researching and hypothesizing vague ass myths that no one has heard of except an old, worn out piece of leather, all within a ten-hour time frame." Tullia was impressed, the Grand High said all of that in one breath. "So, if you wanna throw out ideas, we're all ears."

Jiang Li, to his credit, didn't bat an eye at the Grand High's viciousness, he merely said. "You have a few valid points. You may continue."

"Oh may I? Thank you so much." The sarcasm was thick in her falsetto voice. She then turned to look at the list for a moment. Her obsidian eyes restless. The silence dragged on for a few minutes, Chito and Tullia were shooting each other confused looks.

"You know what?" Cliona murmured. "We are going to let the lost magic decide." She looked at Tullia and smiled. "Which place, petal?"

Tullia blinked confused and simply stared at the Grand High like an idiot.

"Pick a place." She made a grand gesture at the list. Tullia became hugely nervous to the point where her palms started sweating. She pointed to herself. "Me?"

The Grand High shrugged. "Why not? You may feel...*drawn* to a place. We can go there first. I think it's our best bet besides merely guessing where to go." Her head slumped to the side, making her appear unstable. "Magic does not follow statistics nor logic all the time."

Tullia licked her lips and looked at the list of potential places again. She straightened in her seat, then focused on them intently.

Faiyum, Egypt
  Argos, Greece
  Aleppo, Syria

Jericho, West Bank
Damascus, Syria
Plovdiv, Bulgaria
Byblos, Lebanon
Sidon, Lebanon
Luoyang, China
Jerusalem, Israel
Varanasi, India

She looked at the countries austerely, willing a feeling, an intuition, a niggling….

A freaking flashing light or something to indicate something!

She felt her shoulders sag and looked at the Grand High. "I have no idea."

Cliona was lazily spinning in a circle. "Doesn't matter. Just pick."

She glanced at the list again, intimidated by the length and all the letters. "But maybe we can use some more facts instead—"

"Pick!" The Grand High shouted, her face never losing its blankness. It was unsettling to see her beautiful face so still. Her visage was like a sudden summer storm, constantly flashing with emotion and turbulence.

Sighing, Tullia closed her eyes and went to point at any random place. After all, she didn't know, despite Cliona's conviction that she'd pick the place where they were meant to go via the lost magic that was in her. She didn't feel anything, nor did she feel anything with her intuition. She raised her arm up, pausing, then she felt her arm become heavy, sagging suddenly, as if her arms could not bear its own weight, before abruptly stilling.

Tullia frowned, opening her eyes to look at her arm in confusion. Who moved her?

"Bulgaria," The Grand High's face cracked an empty grin, "Well then, I guess we should pack for colder weather. It'll be chilly in October this time of year."

Chapter Twenty-Six

Sabin had met many nobles in his life. From the corrupt, to the humble, to the disillusioned and to the arrogant. Jiang Li, for all his elegance, managed to prick Sabin's irritation quite frequently, and the man barely opened his mouth to speak. His rage rose in waves around the dragon. Managing it had fatigued him greatly and he had only been in his presence for barely an hour.

They boarded a jet, a rented charter flight, as the witch had said multiple times in an aggrieved tone with a hostile glare at the dragon.

"The Bulgarian witches are traditional; they like to keep to the…formal traditions of magic use and are quite conservative. So, teleportation is, unfortunately, out of the question." The witch's tone was hissing, like a cat that became soaked with icy water. "And some dumb ass dragon decided to take a bite out of my jet, which was the top of the line in speed, agility, and commodities." Her ebony eyes shot daggers at the dragon, who was sitting primly. He gave no reaction and met the fiery glare with an icy one and a stalemate ensued.

Now they all were flying to Bulgaria.

The dragon sat strait-laced in his chair, back straight and arms folded. He was also far too close to Sabin for his comfort, and he was eight feet away. The air was stale between them and Sabin wanted to escape the suffocating air. Tullia sat next to Sabin and was pressed close, even though the seats were spacious. Sabin glanced down at her when he felt her stir, though she was not touching him, he could perceive her soft heat even through his layered clothes. He watched her slight fidgets and rub the cuffs of her sweatshirt in-between her fingers nervously. She kept glancing up in the direction of where the dragon sat.

His rage twitched, and Sabin followed where her eyes were looking. Then his rage surged up.

The dragon's eyes, cold and blue like the deepest part of the sea, were glaring at Tullia relentlessly. Sabin glanced down at Tullia again. Her hair, that she had assured Sabin was torture, was glossy and from the angle of her face, she showed no outward discomfort or even notice of Jiang Li's hostility.

But Sabin did. And he didn't like that the dragon's eyes were constantly watching her. His eyes should not look upon her.

"Eyes over here, dragon." He said, watching the way the reptile in human guise shifted his cold eyes over. The frosted eyes shot icicles at Sabin. "Focus on the person that'll rip you in half within a heartbeat."

His eyebrow rose, clear disbelief and contempt, but the dragon's gaze, though straying from Sabin, did not return to bully Tullia.

Good. His rage was calmed a bit, but it jerked with a violent force, wanting to

maim the pretty man's face. Sabin flexed his chest, trying to alleviate the tension.

He forcefully brought up his calming, sunrise drenched lake image, searching for peace within the memory. A soft touch had Sabin opening his eyes, he hadn't realized he had shut them, and saw Tullia's small hand had come up to rest on Sabin's covered forearm.

She smiled and mouthed a "thank you". Sabin winked and his rage *purred* and tucked itself away. It was not out of sight, but it was certainly…tamed for the moment. Sabin forced his eyes away from Tullia, he found he did not tire of the sight of her and feared his lingering look would unsettle her.

The plane ride was estimated to be a grueling sixteen hours. Usually, Sabin would have rejected the idea of flying on a small plane with a handful of other people. His rage did not have tolerance for enclosed spaces, it took Sabin decades to force himself to not go into an uncontrollable anger when he sat inside a car. Modern conveniences were great, but the planes…Sabin found his mind couldn't accept the notion, and his being preferred to remain earthbound.

Sabin would never admit it, but the witch's jet was much better than a mere charter plane and he now understood why she became so enraged when the dragon destroyed it. Though, a part of him was glad it was destroyed, simply because he thought she had far too many spoils and acted far too greedy.

"Sabin," Tullia's voice was soft and a bit hesitant. He turned to her, looking down into pools of pure moonlight. "Do you think you could tell me a story?" The request had Sabin blinking in surprise. She pointed two tiny fingers at him. "Like you did in the forest in the Philippines?"

Sabin rubbed his jaw, the fabric abrasive over his skin, thinking back over the story he told her in the forest.

"A story?" He mused, he wasn't a bard and the stories he told her was when they were alone and lacked the flourish of a good story.

"Yeah, like something that you went through or an urban tale you heard or something." Her fingers went to work again, worrying about the cuffs of her sweater.

He watched her action for a moment, then gave a slow nod. "Hm, I suppose I could tell you a tale."

She bounced excitedly next to him and gave two small, happy claps. He watched as she then wiggled close to him and looked up with bright eyes and pink cheeks.

Yes, he did not tire of her image in front of his eyes.

A story…what would entertain her?

Images of wild limbs, aghast faces and frantic musicians infiltrated his mind. He felt a smile curl his lips.

Tullia liked humor, there were very few funny incidents that were innocent. Oftentimes, his tales ended up with someone broken or dead.

This memory, however, left no one dead and may make a decent story.

"Have you heard of the dancing plagues?"

Tullia wrinkled her nose and shook her head.

Perfect.

"Well, nowadays it may be medically defined, or given a name, but back a few hundred years, it was…disturbing to people. If not sinful."

Though Sabin found the ancient people's views on dancing being a sinful pagan practice was exaggerated. Though he had found himself prejudiced against them and their own practices.

However, the entire situation of the 'Dancing Plague' is the very reason he distrusted and disliked witches immensely.

Sabin crossed his arms over his chest, dusting the webs from his memory. "I was in Aachen at the time, employed by the Holy Roman Empire's emperor…" Sabin paused, thinking, what was that pompous ass's name? "Charles… IV, I believe. He was a…selfish man, jaded by life and blinded by the riches that came with his title. I had done a job for him and was in the main market area, sitting in the shade between two covered shops."

The market was bustling with merchants, thieves and gruff working women.

"You were in one of the cities of the Holy Roman Empire during the *Holy Roman Empire?*" Her tone was marvelous. "What was it like?"

Sabin paused, thinking back over his long life to that short span of time. The dirt, the blood, the corruption…

"It was a very brutal place." Sabin said simply, it was far too complex delving into just what was wrong with that time frame and, more particularly, that empire.

Tullia pursed her lips, making her look like she was pouting. Sabin felt himself almost smile, but it died when Chito asked, "How was it brutal?" He poked his head out from beside Tullia. His smooth brown face was intensely focused.

A very innocent question. A very loaded question.

Sabin inhaled. "There was no justice system, people would take matters of revenge into their own hands." Which always ended in innocent blood being spilled needlessly. "There were a lot of...slaves from war, forced to work and they were treated badly." Sabin found that humans openly owning other humans did not change until recent years, even then the descendants of slaves were still treated very differently. Sabin had watched the world's empires trade, enslave, and end human lives as easily as they breathed. It was the way of the ancient world. Slowly, as the dawning of new ideas came to become popular opinion, the necessity of slavery became a cruel concept rather than a commodity.

"Death was frequent and common. Anyone could die within an hour or a day or a week."

Sabin had seen the haggard and unsurprised looks of another child dying, or another husband not returning for years, of people dropping like flies due to illnesses.

Reflecting on it, it was a very different time with different problems than modern times.

Sabin was pulled from his brief musing with the stillness and the silence next to him. Tullia and Chito were staring at him with eyes wide and reevaluating faces.

Sabin shook his head, dispelling the darker remnants, and cleared his throat, continuing his story. "The sun was high, and the weather was sweltering. I was sitting in-between stands, under a drooping shade when a flashy group came...stumbling about." He still remembered that day, the dusty ground, the smell of overripe fruits and animals, all marinating under the heat.

He was grateful for modern times, they smelled much better, and it was much more sanitary. He no longer needed to smell animal feces when picking up pears from a sweaty fruit seller that coughed over the fruits.

"I could tell they were magic wielders, by the way they did not fear the eyes of the guards."

Everyone was jumpy, except the rich, but the peasants and lower merchants were meek, if not subservient when they were near the royal guards. There were particular guards that Sabin had taken note of that enjoyed intimidating free items from vendors and being aggressive towards women. Though they were merely for riot control, they acted as though the law was formed and enforced by them.

Sabin didn't particularly care at the time, if it didn't involve him, he would remain uninvolved. His mind was swathed in the darkness of what the Romans had called melancholia. Some days he was barely aware of his actions and years faded away as the minutes did to mortals.

"The group of witches were heavily intoxicated from opium and wine. I could smell the drug and alcohol coming off them from a distance." Sabin thought that they bathed in it, the smell was rancid, and their voices were obnoxiously overbearing in volume.

"They were laughing, and one was playing the tibia, very badly."

Sabin had watched their drunken stumbles, their faces flushed, their gazes glazed with disgusted remembrance. He had been a witness and a participant of many drunken stupors in his younger, ignorant days. He glanced at Tullia's face, then at Chito's. They both were looking at him with rapt attention. Sabin fought the urge to check to make sure he was completely covered. He knew he was, none of his shameful ugly was exposed.

He continued on, detailing what he remembered. "They stumbled into people, knocking over some merchant goods, spilling their drinks…" Sabin shook his head, "People were cursing them, but that was all they did. It wasn't until they banged into a particularly cruel merchant, causing him to drop his bloody piece of meat, that they were violently confronted."

The merchant was an unsightly man, his features were crudely carved into a face of scars and lines that spoke of a foul temperament rather than age. He was holding a large haunch of meat that must have been fresh from the rivulets of blood that still dripped from the flesh in his arms.

"Many wealthy merchants had guards around them for protection." He explained, "And the merchant was furious that his expensive meat was now dirty." The man's face turned the most unique shade of purple. "He swore and had ordered his guard to avenge his meat by taking their money and their lives."

Chito gasped audibly and Tullia had a hand pressed to her lips.

"Very dramatic." She murmured, Chito nodded in agreement.

"Indeed. However, when the guards grabbed the witches, they became sober enough to become offended."

Sabin had never met a humble witch. They were mortals that became entitled with their perceived elevation through their manipulation of the immortal essence.

"When a witch becomes offended, they become aggressive with their magic use." Sabin had usually purposely offended witches to get them to use their magic against him just to see their confused rage when they were powerless against him.

It never failed to amuse him.

"They tried to aim their magic at the guards…" Sabin paused, "However, they were still uncoordinated from their intoxication and missed. Several times. Instead, their magic shots ended up hitting the bystanders and their spell…" He paused again, looking at Tullia's and Chito's face, seeing the interest, "Their spell caused the peasants to dance."

There was a silence, and Sabin waited for the inevitable question.

"Why did the witches cast a spell to make people dance?" Tullia asked, confused, she propped her face up on one of her hands.

Sabin shrugged. "They were drunk and high, I don't think they were aware of much that was going on, let alone what they were doing. But when people started dancing, it took a strange turn."

Tullia leaned closer, he could smell her sweet gale scent and the soft, faded emotions of his youth washed over him. It wasn't unpleasant.

"How?" Chito asked, he too was leaning in closer, hovering over Tullia.

Sabin rubbed his jaw to expel some of the excess energy that seemed to pile up inside. "Back then, when people started spontaneously dancing many cried possession, others merely watched on in horror, some joined in voluntarily and many started to pray for their salvation and for forgiveness." It was only a few peasants that had actually been spellbound, but soon it became a riot of writhing bodies that were shouting pleads of confusion, anger, and fear.

Sabin wasn't bothered by their dances, it was odd, but he had been raised within a culture that did dance for worship and celebration. The Roman people were…stiff due to the rigid Christianity that swept the land like an obsession. Anything not related to the one God was a sin, and the one God was a very jealous, cruel God as the ancient people understood him to be.

Sabin continued. "After a few bad aims, they finally managed to hit their targets, and then the guards started dancing as well as the merchant too."

"Were they mad?"

Sabin thought back for a moment. "The merchant wept, the meat that had fallen was now being danced upon by himself and his guards."

Tullia flung her head back and gave a short bark of laughter. "And the witches? Did they bolt?"

Sabin shook his head. "They joined in."

Chito giggled. "I suppose that would be appropriate if you're intoxicated."

"And what did you do?" Tullia asked, silver eyes glimmered up at him.

He shrugged. "I simply watched."

She waited, Sabin said nothing more. She huffed a little. "You didn't join in or try to stop the witches?"

"Sweetness, I was on break, and it was a comedy scene that I enjoyed until my lunch was over." While he was amused at the sight, he was still wary of the witches and wanted to keep himself out of their sight. Especially witches that did not have their wits or brains about them. They always caused trouble, he preferred to stay out of their kind of trouble. It was always dramatic.

Tullia watched him for a moment. A twinkle of humor in her dove gray eyes brightening. "So, a random dance pandemic, which freaked the highly religious people of that time out, started when a bunch of drunk witches got into a fight, but were so drunk that their spells were wonky and they ended up infecting innocent people with magic and were forced to dance?"

Good summary. Sabin nodded. "Yes."

She hit her legs with her hands, a sharp sound filled the air in a burst of noise. "Wow. I bet historians and researchers don't have that written down as one possible hypothesis, huh?"

Chito laughed and Tullia giggled, covering her mouth. Sabin noticed out of the corner of his eye that the dragon's eyes were watching them. Well, he was mostly tracking Chito's motions.

Good. The reptile had better keep his eyes off Tullia. Or else he'd remove his eyes. His rage cackled happily and flexed within him. His chest tightened in a mild panic; his possessiveness ran deeper towards Tullia than he initially thought.

"Do you have any more tales to tell, Sabin?" Tullia's vivacious voice called out to him, he slid his eyes back to her upturned face.

"I may have a bit more." His voice was light, but he began to bury his panic, bury his fully formed thoughts, bury his budding emotions.

Her smile was painful and cleansing. "Do you have any more involving witches?" He would need to rid himself of this infliction whenever Tullia was concerned.

"Troves." He murmured, moving his eyes away from her innocence. "Troves."

* * *

The city of Plovdiv, looking at it from the international airport, was barren. There were fields of tall ashy blond grass on both sides of where Tullia looked. She inhaled, the air was tinged with a real promise of cold, but it was merely sweater weather…for now. The daylight was just kissing the sky, pretty hues of pink, gold and orange chased away the dark of the night.

Tullia snuggled down into her thick sweatshirt, pulling her hands in for ultimate warmth and creating sweater paws. Chito stood beside her, his dark eyes scanning the surroundings then a frown marred his pretty face.

"This is…Plovdiv?" He asked hesitantly.

"Yes." The Grand High said swiftly, snapping her fingers and pointing to her two servants. They quickly scurried away in the direction of the jet. "This is just the international airport, we're about twenty minutes away from the heart of the city." Cliona was in an all-white tracksuit with the classic Gucci stripes running down her sides. The color in her delicate mix of dark and light skin was brought out. Her hair, now in the color of a warm brown, stood fluffy and curly in a full afro. She popped her gum, her glossed lips catching the gleam of the fluorescent lights above, as did the gold on her cheeks and Tullia found her heart skipping a beat.

She was gorgeous. Stunning. Impossible to comprehend.

"You're so beautiful," Her mouth formed the words, before she could stifle them, "how on earth do you manage to be so beautiful?" Tullia asked, still dazed from the reality that was Cliona.

The Grand High looked over to her and smiled a Hollywood smile. "Baby girl, all of this…" She dragged her fingers over her hair, down her neck, outlined her figure, then flicked her fingers up. "Is all black girl magic. No one, but us black girls can do it just like this."

"That's some powerful magic." She had never seen a more beautiful person than the Grand High yet to date.

"Oh honey, it's the most powerful." She tilted her big sunglasses down and winked.

Tullia felt the urge to swoon. Was this what fangirls felt like? She pulled at her sweatshirt as her face reddened and had to turn away or else she'd embarrass herself. It was then she spied Sabin, standing a bit apart from everyone. His outline was tall and dark against the bright sunrise. Tullia stared at his profile for a long moment. It struck her that he looked really good against the blossoming day and the yellow grass. Strong, virile…though with him standing by his lonesome against the brightening sky, he looked burdened and utterly weary. She didn't like that and the urge to go stand with him was such a tangible feeling that she took two steps toward him before remembering his emotions on the plane. They were sour, tangy and bitter, at first, she thought he was upset at her for asking for stories. His gold eyes would not look at her and she felt a type of coolness radiating from him when she came too close.

Tullia forced herself to look away from Sabin, swallowing down a stupid type of hurt. She doubted he wanted her for comfort, he probably wanted space. Thinking back over the past few days, she had been clinging to him like a baby monkey to a mother monkey. Which made her entire body tighten with embarrassment. Even BFF's need space from each other. She would allow him a few more moments to himself. She looked around, noticing Chito was not beside her, and found him leaning casually against a pillar, looking around with an unimpressed face at the tall yellow grass. His warm brown skin was loved by the awakening sun rays and his smooth hair was a waterfall down his back. He wore a fluffy dark green teddy coat that was made for him. She then glanced at Jiang Li, who was standing coolly off to the side. His sharp eyes were trained on Chito. He had adopted a modern style of dress after the Grand High shoved a laptop at him with an hour-long video of Chinese Tik Tok fashion trends.

"Modern up, you sad sack of scales." She had sneered disdainfully at him.

Now Jiang Li wore very flowy dress pants and a stylish oversized coat. He looked even more stunning than Tullia could comprehend, and her eyes began to throb painfully. She wasn't meant to see that much mythical beauty, she supposed.

Tullia looked around at everyone again, then sighed in dismay. How in the hell could she ever even be in the same league with these people? She adjusted her hood on her head and pulled the strings tight so that her entire face was covered, except for her eyes. It was noticeably clear that she was the token ugly group member with the personality.

A car pulled up then, and the Grand High's two servants appeared, ushering them inside the spacious car.

Before entering the car, Sabin took out his magic vape pen and inhaled deeply from the tip. She watched as he held the magic smoke within him for a moment, before he exhaled and a thick cloud of white smoke bloomed from his lips...

Then Sabin was covered by a stranger's face and swathed in a painful disguise that seemed to shrink him in multiple ways. She never noticed before, but in the new light of day on foreign soil she was taken out of her familiarity and her eyes saw even the ordinary differently.

Then they were chugging away from the airport and towards Plovdiv.

The scenery outside the car window did not vary from the wheat-colored grass for the first couple of minutes. There were only street lights lining the two-way road and a few random green trees. Then the backroad morphed into a highway and Tullia's eyes soaked up the scenery.

There were other cars driving on the road, looking straight out of the 1990's and early 2000's. Tullia saw an all-white building with a golden dome cap and two blue Bulgarian words. She glanced at Cliona, who lounged regally in the passenger's seat with her head tilted back and her eyes closed. She wondered if the Grand High would give her the gift to understand Bulgarian. She made a mental note to ask her later.

Tullia's eyes stayed glued to the window for the remainder of the drive, absorbing in the scenery from a land that was so far away from her home. They passed what looked like a gas station, a used car lot, more blonde grass, an industrial center, various, random shops on the side of the road before the buildings morphed and became more consistent, shrubbery was more manicured and there were more advertisements. The advertisements were fascinating, the structure was the same, but it was done in a completely different way than what she was used to.

Then they passed under a blue sign with abstract figures on it that said, "Welcome! Let's create together!" in English.

Everything Tullia saw was familiar but foreign at the same time. The advertisements were different, the language was different, the models were different… Her eyes soaked up the scene, her entire being shaking with excitement. This was different than when they went to the Philippines, probably because the whole build up from the teleporter was a huge letdown for her and marred her whole experience. That and having to camp in the jungle was fun for the first night, after that it just sucked. Also, the whole tikbalang violence, hidden city being really hard to find, and the heartbreaking funeral with heavy ass emotions that were really taxing…it didn't leave much room to admire the gorgeous lushness. Also, going to China to climb up a stupid mountain while it was freezing, was not exactly her idea of an exciting trip that she wanted to remember.

This, however, with air conditioning and reasonable weather conditions, she was jittery with excitement. The buildings grew around them, streets became antique and greenery was lush. Though Tullia was surprised to see the colorful graffiti covering a lot of the buildings and the walls, it somehow blended with the cityscape instead of being an eyesore.

They drove on and buildings that looked like cutely aged town homes continued to sit alongside the road, with narrow spaces beside them that were packed full of cars. They passed a giant building with the name Princess Casino on the top with a restaurant beneath it named Victoria. Tullia's stomach growled just at that time.

She turned, looking away from the window for the first time since she entered the car, and began to ask, "Cliona can we—"

"Get coffee and snacks?" She said without looking back or moving an inch from her lounged position. "You bet, petal."

Tullia clapped her hands happily, then returned to gobble up the scenery with her eyes. Twenty minutes later they arrived as far as the car could go to a cobbled wide path flanked by stores and an old-world charm.

"This way." Cliona motioned them forward, taking long strides on the path.

They all started walking in silence, the city sounds of cars and people were soothing to Tullia. She liked the noise that cities brought, liked knowing that there were people around living their own lives as she was living hers.

It was a coping method to feel less lonely by absorbing the crowds at a distance.

Tullia noticed that Jiang Li was walking behind them, his hands clasped behind his back and his face tilted up to the sky. He seemed at ease, looking around casually at the surroundings. Tullia bit her lower lip as a thought popped inside her mind. She shrugged, knowing that the dragon couldn't physically hurt her or mentally, and slowed her pace to walk next to Jiang Li. Instantly, his ease vanished, and he glared down at her, clearly displeased that she was next to him.

Tullia just raised her eyebrow at him, his hostility was becoming hugely unnecessary and a bit exasperating. "No need to openly hate me, I'm just existing, you know."

He didn't say anything, merely shifted his eyes away from her to look forward. He then pretended she didn't exist, it was the same technique her parents used on her all the time, before they simply believed she was truly non-existent.

A small pang occurred in her heart, but Tullia brushed it away. That mattered then, but it had lost most of its importance now.

"I think," She began, knowing full well that he could smack her into the bushes for her nettling, but it would be eons before any type of progress would be made between Chito and Jiang Li if she left it to them, "that with Chito," Jiang Li jerked at the name slightly, though he still did not look at her.

Bingo.

"You need to take a very slow and soft approach." Tullia looked up to see hanging tree branches with lush green leaves offering sparse pockets of shade. She knew full well that his whole attention was on her, even if he refused to acknowledge her. "You offended him deeply in your cave. So, for him to not dislike you anymore, you need to be gentle and actually talk to him." She side eyed him. "Don't just stare. It's creepy."

His face was perfectly smooth, and it seemed as though he wasn't even listening to her. Tullia might have believed he was, but his emotions tasted like a blend of complex savory and sweet flavors. He was thinking about what she said and now his thoughts were evoking emotions.

Good. Then he better do something about it and stop glaring at her all the time. Because she didn't know what she would do next, but it wouldn't be pretty for anyone.

"If you like someone, you have to let them know you like them. Like…"

What would she like?

"…sweet words, or consideration, or books." She rambled, her mind trying to paste an image of a certain tall ex-Viking, but she kept washing it away so she couldn't see it clearly. Though it did give her tummy a few jittery butterflies. Which was weird.

A small silence, and Tullia had the feeling that any more words that she spoke would be ignored. Her time had expired with Jiang Li. But… "Also, stop openly hating me so hard. It scares Chito." She added in quickly before jogging ahead to walk next to Sabin for protection.

Sabin glanced down at her, she smiled up at him innocently.

"Hi ya."

"You look like an imp that has just caused mischief." He commented, his gold eyes light and his demeanor welcoming.

Tullia felt her smile widen. "I am an angel. I don't cause mischief, I initiate peace." She cupped her face innocently, blinking up at him purely.

Sabin chuckled, the barest hint of untamed emotion in the small sound. He ruffled her hair, making Tullia swat at him wildly.

"The heck." She hissed, but her smile ruined any type of true annoyance. She had damned the braids and now her hair was a wild, wavy mess of onyx.

Tullia felt the bubbles as sweetness from Sabin's amusement coated her tongue. She fixed her hair, by ruffling it back into place, then tilted her head towards the sky. The sunshine on her face, the lazy frost in the air, the bubbles in her soul, the silent echo of ancient feet marching along the cobbled road…she had never felt as light as she had in that moment.

It was freeing.

Ten minutes later, they made it to the amphitheater. There were bars around the entire perimeter of the ancient structure, which, sadly, made sense. It was eight fifteen am, the amphitheater didn't open until nine am. Which means they had time to kill.

So, they stopped in front of a cute little storefront that was framed with deep browns and a giant blue and yellow sign in the shape of the amphitheater right above. There were many tables and chairs as well as some umbrellas with lounging chairs right up against white bars. It was a super cute little layout.

"Alright, talk amongst yourself. Decide what you'll have when I come back. I need to use the restroom." Cliona said, clicking her nails together. A menu appeared in Tullia's hand, surprising her into dropping it. Quickly, she picked it up and looked up at the Grand High. She fluffed her afro, the sun adoring her at every angle. The Grand High shot a sideways look to Sabin. "I'm feeling generous, I'll get you a drink too, meathead."

Sabin didn't react, but Tullia tasted the faint surprise on her tongue.

Cliona pushed her sunglasses up higher on the bridge of her nose, movie star like, and snapped her fingers. Two of her servants appeared instantly. Tullia blinked in disbelief, where did they come from?

"Bathroom." She said sharply, the two witches nodded, then began to smoke a pale blue color that enveloped them entirely…then the three were gone once the smoke dissipated.

"Wow." Chito said, his tone one of wonder.

Tullia nodded, curious as to why Cliona needed two servants to escort her to the bathroom? She shrugged off her question and looked down at the menu. "Okay, what do you want, Chito?"

Chito looked over his shoulder, his long black hair smelling of coconut and flowers. "I just want a fruit cup. I'm not in the mood for a drink."

Tullia nodded, shifting from side to side in contemplation. "I think I'll get a mocha frappe." She said, knowing it was chilly and that a frappe was not the best idea, but she didn't really care. She also wasn't really that hungry anymore, her excitement smothered any and all hunger.

"You're pretty stupid." Chito commented.

"Yeah, well, sticks and stones." Tullia shot back, she turned to look at Sabin. "Do you want to see the menu Sabin?"

He shook his head. "I'll just have a hot black coffee."

Tullia made a face at him, impressed and disgusted by the fact that he could drink straight up black coffee. She looked around for Jiang Li and found him standing apart, analyzing his surroundings with a very judging look on his pretty face. She went to call out to him, paused, looked at Chito, looked back at the dragon, then looked at Chito again and smiled.

"Hey, Chito," She sang sweetly. His pretty brown eyes furrowed slightly with distrust. "Can you go ask Jiang Li what he wants from the cafe?"

"No." He answered instantly. Tullia elbowed Chito hard, Chito glared at her, rubbing his rib. She then widened her eyes and dramatically looked at the coffee place, then looked at Jiang Li and repeated the eye movement three times until he groaned.

"You're so weird and annoying." Chito hissed, grabbing the menu from Tullia's hands. "Fine. I'll ask the stupid lizard." He all but snarled before stomping over to where Jiang Li was.

Tullia smiled, pleased with herself. They would become amicable dammit. She'd force them to so the scary beautiful dragon would stop seeing her as competition and stop trying to melt her face off with the intensity of his glare.

* * *

Chito felt his heart race within his chest with soul shaking anxiety. He walked over to where Jiang Li was staring at the amphitheater through the metal bars.

His hair was loose around him, only the top portion twisted up into a very messy bun, it was at odds with his nearly flawless appearance. Besides his hair, the dragon was glamoured in an ultra-flashy outfit. He was wearing oversized white slack looking pants, a shiny black belt, a tight-fitting white turtleneck, and a flowy gray suit jacket. There was a shimmery aura around him that caused the people's eyes to linger on him for longer than what was polite.

He was art, Chito concluded, ancient art and as much as he hated it, he liked the dragon's style. Chito liked pretty things and pretty people, even if they were jerks.

"Jiang Li," Chito addressed, his soft voice firm and light. Jiang Li's deep blue eyes slid to his, the churning emotion a forceful beam that Chito did not want to be under, "What would you like?" His voice came out squeakier than the gentle inquisitive tone he was striving for. He felt his face become flushed with embarrassment.

Jiang Li looked puzzled by the question; his thin eyebrows furrowed over magical eyes.

Chito felt his body heat up with the gaze of an attractive person focused on him. Even though the attractive person was a huge jerk, he still felt the urge to preen. Instead, Chito held out the menu towards him and cleared his throat. "Would you like something to eat or drink from the cafe?"

A slight tilt of his head. "Cafe?" He didn't make any attempt to grab the menu.

Chito found himself mimicking his confusion. "Yeah, the cafe," He hiked his thumb over his shoulder towards the little building, "it's where drinks and food are sold. This is the menu."

"Ah," He didn't bother looking over to where Chito had pointed nor at the menu. His gaze never wavered from Chito. The pressure of that heavy gaze made Chito's legs tremble. "I see. I will have hot green tea then." Chito found his eyes flitting from bushes, the ground, and everywhere in-between to break up the intensity of meeting Jiang Li's stare.

Chito nodded, then turned to leave, but paused, weren't they supposed to get him acclimated to the modern times? He turned back to the dragon. "Why don't you try coffee?'

Jiang Li, he noticed, did not fiddle, he remained perfectly motionless and completely rapt. "Coffee? I do not know what that is."

A small shot of excitement jolted through Chito, he loved to try new things and he loved introducing new things to people. Even crusty people like Jiang Li.

"All the more reason to try it." Chito's tone became higher with the enthusiasm, he looked over his shoulder at the cafe and saw Tullia talking with Sabin with a lot of hand gestures and facial expressions. Chito wanted to shake his head at her in an amused way, she had no control over her movements. He turned back to the dragon; his piercing eyes were still looking at him.

Chito gripped a hunk of his hair and began to play with it nervously. "I think you may like it." That was a lie, Chito was clueless about what he liked, but a lot of people loved coffee and since the giant time capsule didn't know what coffee was...

"I am not in favor of trying this coffee. I'd still prefer tea." Jiang Li said lowly, his voice smooth and silky like a cat's fur coat.

Chito shrugged, turned his back on the dragon and strode back to stand next to Tullia in measured steps. Though he wanted to run, he still felt the burning pressure of the dragon's weighted eyes on his back the entire way.

"—And that's why you should never ask a postman about the size of his pant pockets." Tullia's black hair flitted around her pretty face in crinkly curls. She had, at some point, undid all of Chito's hard work and now her hair was kinked and wild.

She turned to look at him, her big gray eyes shining with a brilliance that made Chito feel giddy at times.

"Did you ask him what he wanted?" Her tone was impeccably naive.

"The dumb lizard wants green tea." Chito muttered, irritated that he had to interact with the dragon at all, let alone take his stupid order.

Tullia raised her eyebrow at Chito. "I see the Grand High's sass is rubbing off on you."

He shrugged, pleased that his nerves and rapid-fire heartbeat weren't apparent. The dragon looked like he'd spirit him away and lock him up like an exotic pet at any given moment, which increased Chito's anxiety.

Tullia grinned a knowing smile, her face, small and delicately wrought, had a wicked, wicked gleam to them.

Chito's stomach sank at the thought of Tullia continuously pairing him with the dragon throughout this trip.

* * *

"One mocha frappe, one hot green tea, one hot black coffee and a fruit cup please." Tullia said, as she stood on the balls of her feet, her excitement simply too much to contain in stillness.

The Grand High nodded regally, she had returned from her magical restroom two minutes before. "I'll order it. I know anyone else will screw it up." She glanced to the seating area and flicked her glamoured fingers towards them in a sharp gesture. "Find a table and wait for me." She then sauntered away, the lusty eyes of the sparse pedestrians glued to her figure.

Tullia scoped out the seating options, then walked over to claim a table that was situated right next to the iron bars that overlooked the amphitheater and had a big enough table for everyone to sit at. The morning chill was thawing out into a comfortable cool with sunshine drenched skies and no wayward breezes. Sabin, Chito and Jiang Li had followed behind her, Sabin sat next to her, Chito across from her and (much to Chito's obvious displeasure) Jiang Li sat right next to him. The sounds of rustling leaves and soft foreign chattering was pleasing as it was exhilarating.

Tullia soaked in the scenery, she looked at the ancient amphitheater, at its well maintained but crumbling stone seats, the ancient layout, the still regal stage and the weathered, but glorious backdrop.

She sighed internally; she was actually looking at this view. Not through a computer or a book or a stupid lake…she was looking directly at it. It was like an utter dream come true.

What would it have been like to see something like this built new and glossy under an ancient sun? It must have been a wonder. She glanced over at Sabin. Was there a wonder that he witnessed in its creation that is now an ancient ruin? If he claims to be as old as dirt, then surely there must be…

"Hey Sabin, have you ever seen an amphitheater being built?" Tullia asked, slouching her body on top of the table.

Sabin, in his plain "John Doe" get up, rubbed his jaw thoughtfully. Such a masculine motion, she thought absentmindedly.

"If I have, I don't remember." Sabin paused. "Though I have seen a few castles and mounds made."

Tullia faced him, interest twisting inside her and riling up her excitement even more. Curling one leg up on her chair and gripping the arm rest to lean closer to him, she asked. "Are they still standing today?"

Sabin shrugged his bulky shoulders. "I don't know. Though, perhaps some of them are."

Tullia frowned. "How do you not know?"

A smile with teeth that wasn't all…*humor.* "I haven't been back in ages, sweetness. I don't know where anything would be in the new world's layout." Sabin crossed his arms, his glamoured arms that were still just as buff as his original form advertised them to be, which Tullia wholeheartedly approved of.

He seemed nonchalant about the demographics of his world, a world that was now extinct. Though the slightly bitter and salty flavor on her palate told her more than he probably wanted anyone to know.

"Doesn't that make you sad?" She asked softly, Sabin didn't taste of sadness per-se, but he tasted of something soft and something slightly bitter. He shook his head. "Aye," a small hint at a tilting accent, "well I lived it. I try to forget it. Can't dwell on what has already happened if you plan to move forward."

Tullia thought that those words should've been a quote pinned up somewhere for a moody teen. However, she clicked her tongue. "I'm going to have to show you a bunch of pictures then and we're going to play a game of 'guess this historic site.'"

He shrugged, again. Was that the only motion he knew of during conversation? "If you wish , I may not recognize them if they're in ruins though."

"Well, we're gonna try anyway." She vowed, determined. Tullia was certain there was something from his past still intact somewhere. And who knows, maybe they'd find something amazing, and Sabin wouldn't feel sad about the changing world. Maybe he'd feel lighter knowing that something from his past was still standing.

Or maybe she was being a busybody.

The Grand High appeared then, the drinks floating beside her. She clicked her nails twice and their drinks were dispersed to them neatly in front of them on the table. Cliona then reclined in the air like an Egyptian queen under the adoring morning sun. Chito was looking around at the other pedestrians, eyes wide and nervous.

"Relax, Cheeto Puff, I am glamoured. People only see me sitting in a chair." Cliona said, taking a sip of her hot drink, undisturbed and majestic.

They all sipped their drinks in silence, but it was a comfortable quiet amongst them. There wasn't a need to speak, instead it felt as though this was a moment of silence for the task ahead that would surely be a pain in the ass.

Tullia thought over the plan that the Grand High had outlined to them as she stared through the bars to the ancient amphitheater.

Cliona had her minions research where there were strong magical signatures in Plovdiv. Turns out many of the historic sites were at the top of the list. So, the plan was to explore the sites thoroughly and see if they could find the hidden portal amongst the remaining rubble.

The part that would be tricky would be the actual finding of the portal. Since the portal is juiced by nearly ancient, invisible magic, Cliona would try to "take" the magic that lingered in the ancient sites. Cliona's researcher hypothesized three possible situations will occur. The first and most ideal is that the portal guardian will jump out, pissed that Cliona was trying to take the magic of its territory, then badda bing, badda boom they found it. The second occurrence that could happen is that Cliona could get a snapshot of an ancient past occurrence from the magic, and it may show the goat dude or another helpful piece of information. Maybe. The last situation is that nothing happens. Which was the likeliest possibility.

Tullia cupped her frappe, pleased by the sweetness and the coolness. Her impatience to explore was keening, needing to be satisfied through action, but she squashed the urge by really absorbing the moment. She willed her mind to lock the taste of the frappe away, to remember the chill, the sunshine peeking through the trees, the feeling of, for once, not being all alone…

She wanted to burn the sensation of companionship into her mind the most. It would hopefully inspire her in the dark moments after…

She paused, shying away from the inevitable future of being all alone again. Maybe she wouldn't be all alone though, maybe they would all be friends.

They will leave, all of them. She disrupted their lives and they were only sticking around because of the lost magic; it would only be natural for them to go back to their own lives once the lost magic was gone.

She just…didn't have a life.

And she would be alone, like she always was.

Shoving the thought away violently, Tullia glanced secretly at everyone. Chito was neatly eating his fruit with dainty bites. Jiang Li was drinking his tea with clear dissatisfaction, sneaking glances at Chito multiple times out of the corner of his eye. Cliona had her eyes closed and her gorgeous face tilted towards the sun with her drink floating next to her, it looked to be a latte of sorts by its light tan color. Tullia then glanced at Sabin, his big body sprawled out in the chair, one hand clasping his coffee cup, ignoring the handle entirely, and sipping it while surveying the area with dark gold eyes.

The tastes in her mouth were sweet, light and slightly bubbly, a perfect mood.

Tullia's mind wandered back to her thoughts about companionship. They'd at least be friends after all this was over, right?

Well, maybe not Jiang Li, he didn't like her. Chito was planning to travel the world, and while Tullia was 85% sure that he wouldn't mind having her go with him, she didn't have any money. And she was not going to be a leach, that would be a sure-fire way to kill any type of friendship. The Grand High was royalty, Tullia didn't think Cliona disliked her, but they were of two different worlds. Though, perhaps that Grand High would drop by every now and again when she was bored.

And Sabin…

Tullia's thoughts stalled and then shut down entirely. She looked down at her half-drunk frappe, thinking about her non-life after the adventure of a lifetime was done.

Her life seemed pretty bleak and dull afterwards.

Tullia shook her head slightly, trying to dispel the heavy forming cloud that was depression.

Positivity, positivity, positivity…

Okay, well she was used to being alone, so that wouldn't be a big adjustment.

The dark cloud within her became thicker. Tullia sipped her frosty drink. She wouldn't be crazy anymore, at least not in the way that would be super noticeable, so maybe she could get a normal job. Tullia perked up a little. Yeah, she would get a better paying job, move into a cute apartment, and save up for a little house…then get a dog! No, definitely she would get dogs!

Yes!

And she could have a library, she could actually buy books instead of just renting them. And pillows! She could buy a ton of fancy pillows for her full-sized bed.

A bubbly and warm type of feeling enveloped her and the budding brightness within shoved the darkness away.

Tullia sipped the last bit of her frappe, slightly cheered. She now developed a goal for the future. For *her* future that she could possibly start to build. For a future she could think about now. And she may be alone in the future, but at least she could start her future now instead of merely surviving day to day. Peaceful minutes drifted by and the sun seemed to strengthen its beams, chasing the icy grip out of the air, but leaving enough chill to be pretty damn nippy.

"Alright, let's get this going." The Grand High said suddenly, she clicked her nails together, making all of their cups disappear without anyone's consent, then she stopped floating. When her heels touched the ground, she put her hands on her hips. "Plovdiv is a large city, we need to get a move on so that we can meet today's quota. We are aiming for six sites today, people. Six."

Tullia wiggled in her seat then stood up, excitement threading through-out her blood once more. She was going to enjoy every single freaking second of this exploration. She looked through the bars encasing the amphitheater. She made the 'I'm watching you motion' with her hand towards the ancient stage, then grinned.

This would be fun.

* * *

Chito tugged at his sweater self-consciously. The hairs on the back of his neck standing up from the stupid lizard's stare. He had tried so hard to ignore the burden of his eyes on him, but it seemed to become heavier and heavier as the minutes passed. The only time Chito was given relief from the weighted gaze was when he clung to Tullia.

He glanced at Tullia, her midnight hair was still kinked and fluffy around her now slightly red face. Her oversized sweatshirt gave her a shapeless appearance, but she looked…cuddly he supposed. Like you could pick her up and give her a hug and be comforted.

That thought, and Tullia's possible affronted reaction made Chito's lips twitch in amusement.

A shiver shot down through his spine as they walked through the entrance of the amphitheater. He forced his eyes forward; he did not want to accidentally meet the dark blue depths that were the dragon's eyes. He swallowed thickly, resisting the urge to cower or transform into something small and hide.

"Chito! Look. At. These. *Stones!*" Tullia's voice, excited and light, cried out to him. He looked over to where she was and spied her couching down motioning with both hands at one of the stone seats. "They're so old!" She cried, a smile making her cute face into something warm and unpretentious.

"Wow. You're very easily impressed." He called but sped his pace up so that he could be next to her warmth that melted the ice from the

791

dragon's cold, cold stare. Chito glanced at Sabin, he was standing next to Tullia as usual, looking around with a face that was very plain and forgettable. It was difficult to look at Sabin like that. He was a man swathed in blackness and had a very brooding aura. If it wasn't for Tullia's sunshine, Chito would have never, ever, ever been able to be near him. No matter how physically alluring and mysterious he was. Nor how kind his actions were. Darkness clung to him and made Chito's nerves stand on edge.

When Chito reached Tullia, she looked up at him, the smile still in place on her pink tinted face. "You came from a magical hidden city, so I don't expect you to understand human accomplishments, but see this?" She motioned all around them to the amphitheater. "This was done by humans and has endured for centuries." She seemed proud.

Chito looked around, it was impressive that ancient humans accomplished this. "Are you sure humans made it?" He teased.

Tullia seemed to pause, she thought for a moment, then added. "At least from what I know it was built by humans, but now that I actually think about it, this might not have been," Her brows furrowed as she dropped her hands down in deflation. "Crap." She stood up and stomped her foot once. "That thought just killed my vibe. Thanks, Chito." Chito chuckled, then ice trailed up his spine again and sat heavy at the back of his neck.

Those eyes were on him again. Watching him, like a predator would his prey.

He suppressed a shiver, focusing back on Tullia. She was theatrical at times and Chito found her to be too funny. Especially when he mentioned her hands. He shrugged casually. "Well, if the humans who built this had extremely burly hands like yours then I suppose it is possible for a structure to withstand time."

Her face reddened deeper with indignation. "You're the biggest brat to ever slink onto the planet." She snapped, then her eyes flickered behind him, a wicked gleamed entered in the gray depths when she looked back at him. "Jiang Li!" She called out, and Chito stiffened, horrified that Tullia would interact with the lizard. "I have a question, please answer honestly. Do I have burly man hands?" She held up her hands, flipping her fingers around in the air to show off her palms and the backs of her hands.

Chito refused to turn around and look at the lizard. He was afraid that if he looked, if he acknowledged…the dragon would close the distance between them and Chito's instincts would force him to flee, like prey.

Jiang Li was silent, but Tullia only raised her eyebrows at him, waiting. "Don't look away from me." She called out, a very small smile on her lips.

Chito didn't need to see the dragon's face to know he was glaring ice darts at Tullia, annoyed at being spoken to by her. However, Sabin was next to her, big and protective, his eyes, the color of a simmering fire, watching the dragon.

A heavy sigh that was far closer than Chito thought. "They are average human hands."

Tullia made a weird groaning sound, her head slumped back, making her silky hair bounce. She jerked her head up and the silver of her eyes glinted metallically. "Female or male hands?" She demanded.

Chito shifted slightly, glancing over his shoulder. Jiang Li was bathed in sunlight and glittering. His dark blues were narrowed, and his brow was raised in arrogance.

Gorgeous. So flawless it was almost painful to admire him directly.

"They are indistinguishable between the genders." The dragon said curtly.

Tullia clicked her tongue, Chito looked back at her to see her face set in a pout and her arms crossed like a two year old.

"Screw you, you ancient sack of scales." Her voice was petulant, like a sulky child being denied a toy.

Chito's eyes widened at her insult, then a laugh bubbled up and overflowed from his mouth. Tullia's eyes shot daggers at him, but Chito couldn't stop laughing. It was too much, everyone seemed to go along with the whole 'man hand' joke. And it was the first time Tullia called Jiang Li something else besides his name. He hunched a little as his laughter shook his entire frame.

"Screw you both." She muttered darkly then flounced away, though Chito was pretty sure she intended to 'stomp', but her bouncy steps did not allow for that. It made him laugh harder.

"Your laugh is pleasant." A mellifluous murmur, a warm breath at the back of his nape. Chito jerked in fright, his mirth dying quickly as he spun to face Jiang Li.

His lungs compressed under the force of his beauty. His sharp features were highlighted under the bright sun and all his attention was focused directly on Chito. Swallowing nervously, stuffing down his instinct to run far and fast, Chito nodded at the dragon and shuffled away a bit.

Jiang Li raised a thin brow. "I am not interested in harming you." His voice was amused, his face was thawed a bit.

Chito pressed his hands to his stomach, willing the butterflies to settle down. "That's good to know." He stammered, interlacing his fingers to pin the flutters down.

Jiang Li leaned in closer, only bending his upper body and stopped about a foot away from Chito's face. His scent of ice and herbs washed over Chito's senses, making his heart race and his mouth go dry.

"Walk with me, Chito. Let us converse." Jiang Li paused, as if he were choosing his words carefully. "I fear our initial meeting was…less than ideal. I would like to make up for that." The invitation caused Chito's stomach to twist and his legs to quiver.

But warmth also bloomed, just a bit, in his chest. Chito didn't quite know how to respond to the dragon's eloquent invitation. However, it was obvious he was waiting for a response.

Chito swallowed thickly against the dryness in his mouth, wishing he had Tullia's nonchalance and quick wit or the Grand High's arrogance and sass.

"That would be…okay." He mumbled, squeezing his hands nervously.

Jiang Li then smiled, it wasn't a toothy grin, just a small curve of his lips and Chito felt his face flush deeply.

This dragon was indeed breathtaking and wrecked Chito's composure. He wasn't used to this.

"Wonderful." The dragon said softly and reached forward with one pale hand towards Chito. Stunned from the unexpected smile, Chito didn't move when Jiang Li's cold, long fingers touched his interlaced hands. Gently tugging one hand free and lacing their fingers together in a fluid motion, Jiang Li then tugged Chito with him as he strode forward.

Chito's heart froze at the sensation of the dragon holding his hand. It was the first time anyone besides his family and maybe Tullia held his hand. Then his heart tripped and slammed hard against his chest. The dragon was speaking, his soft, lyrical voice was brushing against Chito's ears, but he couldn't decipher the language, the roaring of blood racing in his veins and his heart thundering deafened him.

When the dragon looked back at him, looking for a response, Chito found his head bobbing in agreement. Jiang Li did that small smile again, then turned forward, his grip still firm on Chito's hand.

He looked down at their hands, seeing his brown skin against alabaster white was a stark contrast that looked very, very pretty together. Chito was helpless in the situation, his confusion too great to make sense of.

This was not good for his heart, Chito thought slightly dizzy as he tried to even out his breathing.

What in the hell was happening right now?

* * *

The amphitheater up close was awesome. Just knowing that the weathering centuries took its toll on the structure, yet it continues to defy age and still stand strong was mind boggling. Especially since everything was being made so cheaply today. She doubted anything made in today's time would endure like some of the ancient structures. After inspecting the stone seats, examining the stone pillars, walking all along the stage, looking through the bars to the modern shopping district and a solid five minutes of Tullia mimicking a monkey and climbing on nearly every surface that could be climbed, the historic luster dulled, and her enthusiasm diminished.

So much for soaking up every single moment, she thought with some ruefulness. It got boring faster than she thought, which made Tullia want to smack herself.

Tullia glanced around and spotted Jiang Li and Chito walking around hand in hand. Though Jiang Li looked expressionless and Chito's face was heavily flushed and confused, they looked so beautiful together.

Like models. A model couple.

Her advice must have worked then on Jiang Li. She flipped her hair, feeling a sense of accomplishment and pride. She could possibly start up her own matchmaking business at this rate. She looked at Sabin, he was examining a stone step with a deep look of concentration.

"See that." She said to him, pointing to where Jiang Li and Chito slowly ambled along, still holding hands and talking. She squinted, well maybe not talking, no one's lips are moving…perhaps they spoke via telepathy. "I assisted in that." Tullia boasted placing her hands on her hips.

Sabin glanced at Tullia, his gold eyes the only recognizable feature on his painfully plain face. He then followed her finger to look where Chito and Jiang Li walked. He watched them for a moment, his face blank and his emotions tasteless.

Then the bubbles began to generate along her tongue. "Poor Chito." He said, then resumed his study of the stair brick.

Tullia frowned, then folded her arms. "No, there is no victim here. They are simply getting along better."

Sabin glanced up at her, his gold eyes shining. "I'm sure they are."

Her frown deepened and was about to speak when Cliona's crystal smooth voice rang out.

"Alright then. Let's see if momma gets some good juice." Cliona stood in the middle of the stage, tall and elegant. The Grand High inhaled deeply then raised her arms up in a grand, encompassing motion before placing her palms face up towards the sky. Her lips were moving slowly, and deep blue smoke wafted lightly around her figure. Her black eyes were hooded as she continued to wordlessly chant. Then her eyes closed, and her stunning face, a bloomed perfection of cream and coffee, was serene as the sun kissed the gold highlights on her face.

Tullia glanced over at Chito, he was staring at the Grand High, clearly appreciating her beauty in an awe-struck way as Tullia was. She slid her eyes to the right and saw that Jiang Li was looking around with very little interest, though he was taking deep breaths through his mouth.

Tullia had the impression that he was 'tasting' the air.

Tullia looked back to the Grand High, then jolted back in fright. Cliona's mouth was inhumanly wide as she sucked in air.

Tullia shuddered slightly and bumped into Sabin's broad chest. He wrapped one arm around her shoulders, giving her stability and comfort. Tullia huddled back into Sabin as dark blue tendrils webbed out from around the Grand High's mouth and eyes.

Seconds scraped by slowly until Cliona's mouth suddenly shut with an audible snap and the blue smoke evaporated instantly. She lowered her arms and adjusted her clothes casually.

"Well, there was some backwater magic, though I didn't get anything good or relevant." She said, fluffing her afro, a small smile twisted her lips. "It turns out this spot was a make out joint for ancient witches."

Tullia giggled at that.

Cliona put her hands on her hips. "Well, let's go. There is nothing here for us."

And thus began the intense site hopping.

Chapter Twenty-Seven

From the amphitheater, they traveled to the Stadium of Philippopolis that was sitting beneath a bridge and smack dab in the middle of a busy shopping district. Tullia was impressed by not only how well the buildings were placed around the stadium, but the size of the stadium itself.

It was massive.

After walking around the entire stadium for about an hour, nothing was gathered, not even an impression of a memory. The only interesting thing that occurred was the Grand High being hit on by two very pretty Bulgarian boys, to which she winked at and shot them down gracefully.

After the stadium, they walked all throughout old town Plovdiv. Tullia adored this place. She adored the way in which the streets were narrow, the roads were cobbled and the old-world style of the buildings crowding up next to the street. It was a beautiful blend of preserved history with modern times. Sadly, while the shops and sights were enjoyable, after two hours of not finding a single trace of magic, the Grand High dramatically threw her hands up and announced, "Shopping break. I want souvenirs."

They then sauntered into a little shop that held a bunch of touristy shirts exclaiming: "I heart Plovdiv" or "I Came, I Saw, I Plovdiv". There were postcards, mugs, little figurines, basically everything a tourist would want was crowded in that one shop.

Tullia clapped her hands and bounced off to look at the wall that contained stuffed toys.

After a few moments of looking, picking out a frog stuffy to hold on to cause it was so cute, Chito came over to Tullia. He seemed to slouch into her, resting his head on her shoulder and wrapping his arms around her waist from the side.

"Oh no, what happened go-go boy?" Tullia asked in a sing-song voice, making her froggy give Chito a kiss on the top of his silky head.

"I'm going to have a heart attack by the end of the day." He muttered and Tullia blinked, surprised.

"Why?"

"He's way too beautiful. Up close he's even *more* beautiful. And he constantly keeps *touching* me, with his *beautiful* hands. My eyes are stinging under his glory and my heart is trying to break my ribs." He all but wailed.

Tullia smiled and gave Chito's head another kiss using her stuffed frog. "Poor Chito."

"You're mocking me." His tone indicated irritation.

"No, being around beautiful people is tiring." She would know, she was the one with 'personality' in their little group. "Sometimes, you gotta just put it at rest."

Chito sighed, still clinging to her in a way that made Tullia feel special. They have only known each other for a few days, but already she felt as though Chito had been a part of her life for a decade. She felt comfortable with him, she'd even go as far to say that she felt as though they had long lost friend vibes. However, that was Tullia getting ahead of herself. She never really had any friends, so it may just be her inexperience doing all the conjuring and feeling.

The side of her face suddenly felt as though an arctic ice block was pressing against her roughly. She looked over to see Jiang Li standing by the candles and incense. His dark blue gaze was stone cold on Tullia, his displeasure clearly lined on his otherwise smooth face.

She raised an eyebrow, hoping it conveyed that she was an innocent bystander in this situation. However, Jiang Li either ignored her message or didn't receive it, for his gaze became even more wintery than before.

Tullia swiveled her head back towards the dolls, pursing her lips and putting the stuffed frog back on the shelf.

She reached up and tugged one of Chito's loose locks. "Come on now, there's nothing a little retail therapy can't fix." She cheered, sliding out of his hold. "Let's find a cute hat for you or a belt."

She then tugged Chito towards the small section that had a bunch of random merchandise that was stamped with Plovdiv's name in every type of font. They looked at calendars, shirts, snow globes, more stuffed animals, and finally they browsed through the 'survival section' as Tullia liked to call it. There were tiny first aid kits, compasses, backpacks, key chains, headphones, and a colorful assortment of lighters.

A glimmer, then a small internal tug had Tullia lingering over the lighter section, picking one up to inspect it.

Tullia became hypnotized by the lighter in her hand. It was so cute, all decorated in rhinestones and a small little depiction of the amphitheater. She rolled it in her hand, knowing that it was a dumb souvenir since she literally had no use for a lighter, but wanting it all the same. Shaking her head, she went to put it back then paused. Her hand retained a tight grip on it.

A large shadow occupied her peripheral space on the right, and Tullia turned to look at Sabin. "Hey, perfect timing. Sabin, do you think they accept an American visa card here?"

Sabin's glamoured face, a face Tullia did not like Sabin to assume, raised an eyebrow at her. "Show me what you want." She opened her palm to show him the sparkly lighter.

He didn't say anything, but Tullia had a disorder where she liked to over explain everything and anything she did to everyone.

"You see, not only is it useful, in case I need to burn a bitch, but it can also be used to schmooze someone." She held up the lighter and spun the silver thing, pretending to light it. "Oh, do you need a light? I happen to have a lighter just for you, good lookin'." She said in her best seductress voice and held up the lighter as she wiggled her eyebrows enticingly.

Sabin's body stiffened, but a small smile curved his lips as he looked down at her. The sweet bubbles of amusement that popped along her palate had a sour taste undertone.

"Valid points." He murmured, his gold eyes wandering over the lighter section.

She lifted her hands up, palms to the ceiling and shrugged. His reaction was a bit…odd. But Sabin was a little odd in general. "So I think it's pretty necessary." She concluded.

"Agreed." He took the lighter from her hand and began to walk over to the cashier.

"Hey, I can pay for it." Tullia said, jogging to keep up with his long strides, her arms half extended to try and grab back her lighter. Not that she'd have a chance in hell to be able to reach it. Sabin was built like a great oak tree; tall, thick and solid.

Sabin ignored her and held the lighter up to the cashier. Even though Tullia protested the entire time, he purchased the lighter and handed her the bag with a smirking grin on his face.

Tullia huffed, taking the bag. "Well, thank you. I will treasure it."

Sabin nodded, seemingly satisfied.

"Let's get a move on you lazy louts!" Cliona's voice boomed from the outside. She had various bags hanging on her arms. "We're done here."

Tullia, with her gifted lighter, and Sabin followed the Grand High out, Chito came prancing next her and Jiang Li was strolling next to Chito, seemingly eager to leave.

Before continuing on their historic magic hunt, they ate at an uppity looking restaurant and had a host of the most amazing foods such as Shopska salad, Sarma, a pork and vegetable stew, and Banitsa (since the Grand High said this was a special occasion). Tullia had never tasted anything like the food served to them before, but she certainly would order it again if she had the chance.

After lunch they traveled to the ancient bath turned art museum. Tullia thought it was fun as did Chito, turns out they both enjoyed art galleries, commenting on the artwork, and standing close together since it was a bit frosty in the ancient bath house. The Grand High was not in the least bit impressed. After looking around for exactly five minutes she hurriedly ushered them out and off to the next location.

The Bachkovo Monastery was far grander than Tullia had first assumed it to be from the rather plain looking exterior. The wall murals inside were bright and colorful, though the inside was heavily shaded due to the small and deep-set windows. They seemed to travel all over the monastery for hours, before (finally) the Grand High concluded that there was nothing abnormal about the church. Sabin was tense and quiet the entire time in the monastery. His glamour, usually a nice tan color, was ashened and his jaw was clenched tight. The taste on Tullia's palate was one of salty sadness, spicy anger, and bitter regret. Tullia didn't ask him anything, but the urge to comfort him, even knowing it wouldn't be accepted, was a nearly painful urge.

Their next stop was the ancient Roman Theater and Asen's Fortress that were both well preserved and slightly crumbling ruins that spoke of times long ago…and both turned out to be a bust. Thankfully, between those two locations Sabin recovered his good humor and even made a passing remark on how the fortresses had too many flaws in the security department.

The sun crept all along the sky, before lowering, and allowing the shadows to stretch out across the earth.

The newest bust of a location was Nebet Tepe. It was a hill that overlooked the city, and consisted of remaining ruins of walls that were from the founding days back in the 4000 B.C.E. (at least that's what one tourist said). The site itself was not impressive, but the view was enough to make you sigh. The tops of the red roofs and with bushy patches of autumn kissed treetops and rolling hills in the distance was as scenic as it was picturesque.

Nebet Tepe was now swathed in patches of shadows and dimming sunlight that made the ancient, crumbling walls look lonely and enduring. But the lights on the city began to glow and increase in intensity as the darkness grew.

"Nothing, not a single damn thing in all the locations we searched and now the sun is setting." The Grand High huffed, crossing her arms. She looked off into the distance for a moment, her complexion dewy and her profile was all heavenly angles. "I think we can squeeze in one more site before it gets completely dark. In fact, perhaps we should visit the next places at night. The veil is thinnest during the witching hours." She tapped her chin thoughtfully. "I might be able to get impressions faster."

Sabin shook his head. "I'd rather not trespass."

"Boo." She said, though it sounded as though Cliona was still deep in thought. "Like they'd detain us."

"Such a rash idea, from an undignified witch." Jiang Li chided; his hands were folded delicately in front of him. "It is not wise for us to push beyond what we are capable of." Jiang Li stated.

Cliona stared at him with a look of disgust. "Boy, does it look like I can't handle anything?"

Jiang Li glanced over at Chito, then back at the Grand High. "It would be wiser to stop here for now and recover our strength, then resume tomorrow."

"I agree with the dragon." Sabin rumbled. His glamour was now gone, which Tullia was happy about. She was beginning to really dislike whenever he wore it. He looked so much more…like Sabin when his ninja garb was on rather than a stranger's bland face hiding him. "We have been nonstop all day."

"Big, strong berserker tired already?" She mocked, a sneer on her beautiful face. "Pathetic."

"You are looking for speed in this search. It is foolish of you to think that this hunt is to be quick." He shot back; the prickly frozen pickle flavor told her that he was irritated at the Grand High. "It will take several days of searching, witch. One more location today will not change that fact."

Tullia saw Cliona bare her teeth at him in a savage manner. "I don't think you comprehend the need for speed in this mission. This could last years if we do not work with haste and I do not have years to waste on this."

Sabin's demeanor tensed. "You're the one who wants the lost magic. That is your aim in this whole escapade. You do not have the right to abuse others simply because you have the means to do so."

Cliona's pitch-black eyes glowed an ominous dark blue. "Berserker, you are a mere tag along to this expedition that was approved of by the vessel of lost magic. I am not abusing anyone; I am taking care of everyone." She turned her nose up at him. "It would be wise of you to remember that even though you are magic proof, I can still make it so that you are out of this equation."

A sour, pepper spice flavor occurred and then Sabin said something else, but Tullia stopped listening. They were going in circles and honestly, she wasn't against going to another location or going to rest and eat. Her excitement at being in a foreign country and seeing so many sights with people she was beginning to become really fond of, she didn't think this was ever going to happen again. So, she was down for anything as long as she wasn't alone.

She let her eyes roam over the landscape again, lingering on the half-crumbled stone walls and the happy little weeds wiggling in the small breeze. She wandered about the landscape, picking her way through, glancing at the sparkling town spread below them. Then she tripped, nearly sending herself sprawling out onto the dirt floor. Luckily, she was just nimble enough to catch herself and not fall, but she decided to focus on where her feet were going instead of being distracted.

It was then Tullia noticed a glimmer near the ground. She wandered further away from the group, they were still discussing, well more like arguing, where they needed to go next or if they should call it a night.

Tullia kept her eyes on the glimmering something that seemed to wink at her brightly. The closer she wandered towards it, the brighter it blinked at her. When she was nearly upon it, the shiny thing disappeared. She backed away, and it reappeared, when she went closer, it winked out and she could find nothing that would make a glimmer that bright in dim moonlight. She backed up again, studying the bright shiny something on the ground.

Crawl in it.

Tullia tilted her head at the barely formed words that twisted an idea in her mind.

It was nice to be reminded that, clinically, she was insane.

Crawl....

She looked down at the rough, uneven, dirty, cold ground.

Crawl…

No.

Crawl…

The ground was littered with tiny and not so tiny rocks and other things that are jagged. Those could very likely destroy her knees.

Crawl…

It was also cold so she would be even colder than she was now.

Crawl…

Plus her poor hands would be torn up…

Crawl…

She threw her head back and let out a sigh, then she dropped to her knees and began to crawl towards the shiny thing. Rocks dug into her knees through her yoga pants and the ground was icy just as she had thought it would be. Gently and as lightly as possible she began to crawl.

This sucked. When she got rid of the lost magic, she better be rid of her crazies too. 'Cause she didn't like crawling on the cold ground because the voices wouldn't shut up.

"What are you up to, little one?" Sabin's voice sounded above her head, startling her into putting her palm down too hard on the ground. A little rock jabbed her palm and she winced. Tullia twisted her head to see Sabin's big form half squatting, his gold eyes confused and by the bubbles and sweetness along on her palate, he was amused by her.

Stupid man, of course he was, he didn't have a voice telling him what to do in his head.

"Well," She said in an irritated sigh, "I saw something shiny, so I wanted to get a closer look. However, every time I tried to get it, it wasn't there."

"A shiny something?"

"Right," She confirmed, not bothering to explain it, because shiny something is all the description she had, "then I thought, why don't I crawl towards it? I think it may work better to catch the shiny something from the ground level, you know?"

Sabin was silent as he watched her face for a long moment. Her neck started to get a cramp and her confidence began to shrink as embarrassment crept in.

"…or something like that." She muttered, looking away.

Crawl…

Yeah, working on it, she thought back to the voice with some heat. Stupid insanity, making her look crazy.

Suddenly, Sabin got down on his knees next to her.

"Where's the shiny something?" He asked, his gold eyes scanning the ground, looking for it.

Stupid tears rushed to her eyes and she blinked them away so as not to make it awkward. She pointed to the very small glimmering thing, flickering wildly, almost like it was waving.

Sabin's sun rich eyes followed her finger and crinkled in the corners in concentration. "I believe I see it. Lead the way, I will follow behind you."

Tullia nodded, started to crawl forward then stopped, she turned to look at Sabin over her shoulder. "Don't judge my butt."

An impression of a smile. "Never. I will only look at the shiny something."

She turned back around allowing a goofy smile to consume her face. She then focused on the glimmer and crawled towards it, minding her punctured hand. This time, the shiny something did not move and the closer Tullia got, the more details she was able to see. It looked…like a part of a flower? Tullia frowned as she came right in front of the shiny something. It flickered or moved and Tullia reached out a finger to touch it…and her entire hand disappeared into the shiny something.

She gave a squeak, yanking her hand back forcefully. Luckily, her hand returned to her, causing her to sigh in relief. Okay, from now on when reaching for something she was going to use her left hand, she would be doomed if her right hand went MIA. Sabin's bulk and heat suddenly surrounded her.

"What happened?" The rumbling of his voice and the bulk of his body reminded Tullia that her heart seemed to overreact near him. Swallowing against the rising awareness, she shook her head.

"Look." She went to touch the shiny something again, this time with her left hand, and again her hand disappeared. She stuck it in and out, in and out, in and out…

Sabin grabbed her hand; his black gloved hand consumed hers. She looked up at him, he was staring at the shiny something, his eyebrows furrowed with concentration and the flavor of baked Brussels sprouts filled her mouth.

Ugh. That was a new one.

Sabin let go of her hand and seemed to fold his big body down, compressing so that he could get closer to the ground. "Looks like this is something more than a mere shiny something."

"Good deduction." Tullia murmured, swallowing against the urge to cuddle into his warmth. With the sun practically gone from the sky and the darkness thickening over the land, it was becoming more and more cold. She could smell his woodsy scent and wanted to roll around in it like a dog would in grass.

Unless Sabin didn't like dogs. But that would be awful, 'cause dogs are awesome.

She frowned. "Do you like dogs?" She asked suddenly.

Sabin glanced at her, surprised by the seemingly random question.

"I do not mind dogs." He said slowly, confused and a sweet and sour flavor entered her mouth.

Awesome, she liked dogs too. Tullia nodded. "Okay, you go first and I will follow right behind you."

"No," Sabin said instantly, the confusion dissipating. "You will wait right here, until I come and get you."

It took Tullia a moment to process just what Sabin was ordering her to do. "Excuse me?" Her irritation rose sharply. "I found the shiny something first, you're a tag along to my discovery. I think I have a right to be included in the said discovery."

Sabin's gold eyes seemed to narrow as he looked at her. "No. I will not be moved from this. You will stay and wait here until I make sure the area is safe."

Tullia glared at him, she had forgotten he was a relic too. So, he did have the tendency to behave like that, though his rusty side did not show often, it was still there.

The taste of steel and ice infiltrated her mouth. Tullia flexed her jaw, wholeheartedly against being told what to do in this situation.

She thought for a moment, the cold ground under her palms biting her, then she smiled. "Fine. Whatever. You'll come and get me when it's safe?"

Sabin stared at her for a moment, a searching look. Tullia knew she looked irritated, but innocent. Sabin nodded. "Yes. I promise."

She nodded and scuttled out of his way. She watched as he crawled into the shiny something and then just disappeared, just like her hand did. Tullia glanced back at the rest of her group. The Grand High was smoking a fiery blue as she pointed at Jiang Li, clearly, she was arguing with him about something. The dragon stood, stone faced and clearly not listening as he stared at Chito, who was examining a half-crumbled wall with interest.

Okay, so they were all preoccupied.

Tullia turned back towards the shiny something and smiled. What Sabin misjudged about Tullia is that she could play the game of command and obey, but she'd do what she wanted in the end. She learned that faux obedience at the asylum when she was young. Just tell them what they want to hear.

She quickly crawled into the shiny something, ignoring the stinging in her palm. The ground underneath her shimmered and became thick, green grass and the night was nonexistent under the sunshine. Tullia looked up and had to squint under the full force of the sun rays that illuminated everything to a brilliant level.

When her eyes finally adjusted to the brightness she stood and soaked up the beauty. Judas trees, pink and full and large clustered in a rough circle. The grass was a lush green, except for the patches near the center of the tree circle. That grass was brown and looked withered. Tullia did a slow circle, the air was fresh, seemingly untainted and the sky was a ripe blue without a trace of a single cloud and framed by the fully bloomed Judas trees.

It was beautiful, but there was something very wrong. A slimy feeling slithered up her spine and the idea that something was watching her made her skin feel sticky. Tullia took a few steps forward, staring at the brown grass with curiosity. Everything was vibrant and lush, it seemed so odd that a patch near the center would be dead…

A giant shadow engulfed her as hard hands landed on her shoulders.

Tullia gave a shrill scream of fright, and her body curled into herself as she whirled around. However, her feet were clumsy and tangled together, she found herself being pulled down by gravity.

Large, hard hands snatched her up at the waist and hip, catching her before she met the dirt. Tullia's wide eyes met a pair of stern gold ones.

"Sabin!" Tullia sang in relief, to which a crease formed between his eyes.

Uh-oh. That was a new expression.

"You did not listen to me." He bit out, spicy pickles raced along her tongue.

"To be fair, I rarely listen to anyone." She defended.

Sabin seemed to eye her, then sighed, hoisting her up on her two feet once more.

"What would you have done if I wasn't here and something attacked you?" He asked, his tone still hard.

"Died." She said instantly, as she looked around at the pink trees.

She heard another sigh, and a slight taste of flat exasperation, but Sabin didn't say anything more.

"This place is beautiful," She said slowly, "And creepy."

"Agreed." Sabin's rumbling voice seemed very out of place in this brightly lit space with stale air.

Tullia shivered as the feeling of eyes watching her slid along her spine intimately.

"We should…get the others. This has to be the place from Jiang Li's fable." It wouldn't make any sense, if this wasn't the place.

"If it's not, I'll be a Roman." Sabin's tone was deadpan, and his tawny eyes were alert as they scanned the area. "Go get the others, I'll remain here."

Tullia nodded, turned, then turned back to Sabin, "This is one of those rare instances where I am following instructions. Just an FYI. Don't get used to it."

Sabin shook his head but didn't look at her. Which was fine, she could taste the sweet bubbles of amusement with a tart flavor. Smiling, she turned around again, and the once shiny something that she had crawled through became a smudged spot. Dropping to her hands and knees on the soft grass, she crawled towards the smudged spot…

Rough rocks and dirt welcomed her in an abrasive way that had Tullia cursing as she stood up. She brushed the dirt from her palms and looked around. It was now completely dark out, the moon was a pale, pale spot in the black kissed sky. Her eyes, used to the sun drench space, slowly adjusted to the dark rich area.

Where the Grand High, Jiang Li and Chito once were when she went into the shiny something, they were no longer there anymore.

Frick.

"Chito?" Tullia called out tentatively. "Cliona?" She shuffled two steps forward, the darkness seemed really thick….

"There you are, petal." The Grand High's voice sounded right behind her causing Tullia to jump in fright. Cliona laughed out loud, amused by Tullia's fright. "And where did you run off too? I couldn't sense you anywhere."

Tullia's heart was thudding in her chest and her bladder trembled, on the brink of releasing everything. She inhaled deeply; the crisp night air was an effective cleansing agent for her temporary fright.

"We found the Judas trees." She stated, grinning.

Chapter Twenty-Eight

Tullia showed the Grand High the shiny something and then showed her how to enter by getting on her hands and knees and sticking her arms through.

Cliona looked disgruntled by the fact that she had to get lower to the ground, but she nodded in understanding. She clicked her nails twice and Chito popped up right next to her, looking stunned and slightly smoking with blue smoke.

Tullia repeated the same instructions to Chito. Just when she finished, Jiang Li swooped in, looking utterly peeved.

"Do not pull Chito around on your whim, witch." His voice was rough, as though he swallowed a handful of little pebbles. She waved away his words, clearly not going to offer a rebuttal.

"Tell him, petal."

So, for the third time, Tullia told Jiang Li how to enter the shiny something.

But this time instead of just demonstrating by sticking her arm into the shiny something, she crawled through it. She waited about three minutes, then they all came through too. First The Grand High, then Chito and lastly, Jiang Li.

They stood and stared at the new surroundings, taking in the picturesque view.

The Grand High groaned. "Oh my hell, by my ancestors, how many bloody portals and hidden shit are we gonna have to go through, just to get where we need to go?" She turned to glare at the dragon. "You didn't say anything about it being hidden? What if we missed it!"

Jiang Li was serene and still so handsomely beautiful, even in the face of Cliona's dangerous rage he was cool as a cucumber. He glanced at Cliona. "I recited a folklore, not a documented historical event."

She flipped him off in a few different ways.

"It doesn't matter." Sabin said briskly. "What matters is that we are surrounded by Judas trees and there is supposed to be a hostile portal guardian." He was withdrawing his black axes. "Now is not the time to be distracted."

Tullia looked up at the bright sun that seemed frozen in place. "This place seems…suspended."

"Oh, it is. This place has not aged in hundreds of years." The Grand High confirmed, her hands were on her hips and she took in the area with her onyx eyes. "This place is saturated in magic. It's so thick and so *old*…" She cleared her throat, "It's not quite lost magic, but it's certainly something."

The Grand High held out her hand, her long, long fingers slowly curled up and thick wafts of blue smoke stretched out into the air, before a lightning flash hit her palms. Tullia jerked in surprise and jerked again when Cliona swore and shook her hands out violently.

A gust of wind roared around them, but the Judas trees did not move.

"Foolish witch. You try to take what is not yours." A whispering of voices surrounded them.

Everyone's heads swiveled, searching for the source of the sound, but Tullia found herself looking up at the pink treetops.

Sabin flexed his arms. "Nice work, witch." His tone was sarcastic and edgy.

"I always get results." She snapped back, her feet leaving the ground and blue smoke seeping out from her pores.

"You have angered the demon. Offer your sincerest apologies." Tullia squinted over at Jiang Li, he was shielding Chito from the heavy winds as it tore at his body and face.

Hala...

"No." The Grand High said her tone was petulant, like that of a child knowing they did wrong, but would not admit it to their sibling.

Hala...

"You all have trespassed." The whispering voices were rusty, almost as if they have not spoken in a long, long time.

Hala...

Tullia looked up once again through crinkled eyes, the voices were back and this time they said a name.

Hala...

"We beseech you to stop...*please Hala.*" Tullia yelled through the screaming wind and into the open space. The sunshine darkened and ice frosted the winds that now picked up speed in their fury. Tullia was jostled around, before Sabin's strong arm hooked her at the waist and pressed her tight against him. Tullia buried her face into his chest, shuddering at the cold. Suddenly it all ceased. Tullia peeked to see the sunshine back and the air still and warm.

She also saw a woman with iced blue eyes, long brown hair and red lips glaring at them from the center of the Judas tree circle. Her face was round and lightly tanned, with a pouty mouth and high cheekbones. She wore a white shapeless dress that concealed her entire body, limbs and all, from the neck down. She was ethereal, neither beautiful nor ugly.

Hala.

This must be Hala.

Tullia swallowed nervously as Hala tilted her head to the side, in a very slow and very unnatural manner.

"What do you think you are doing?" Her voice was husky and thick with a Romanian accent. Tullia blinked in surprise, she did not think that Hala would speak to them in English.

Hala was only staring at Tullia, with eyes that were void of human emotions. "Who are you?" She repeated, harsher this time.

"We are—" Hala hissed at the Grand High when she tried to speak. A sharp gust of wind slammed Cliona face down onto the grass.

Cliona was silent for a moment, before she started to giggle darkly… insanely.

Hala opened her mouth and inhaled deeply. Tullia had the strong urge that the demon was tasting them.

"Hala does not care about them." A sneer and a condemning look. "Who are you, girl?"

"We are visitors." Tullia said quickly, swallowing as the rot of insanity grew thicker in her mouth.

Hala stared at her, a frown twisting her lips down harshly. "You. Who are *you.*"

"A visitor." Tullia repeated nervously, she bit the inside of her cheek.

Hala suddenly was right in front of Tullia, bare inches away from her face. She was so close that Tullia could smell the wind and decay wafting from Hala's breath. "Who. Are. You." A hiss from a twisted voice that did not come from any human.

Sabin's hard arm jerked her away and he swung down one of his black axes in a blurred motion…into soft earth. The wind howled, laughing and Hala appeared in the center once more.

"It seems to Hala, you do not know who you are. But Hala knows. Hala knows." She held out her hand, her face a perfect glacier, void of emotion and frozen. "Come here. Hala needs to take you to the other one. What is apart must be put back together."

Sabin shifted, his muscles flexing tight underneath the fabric that shrouded him. Tullia realized she was gripping his ninja shirt with both of her fists. She hastily let go, her palms damp and her heart in her throat. She leaned around Sabin, who shoved his arm out to keep her back, and asked, "The other one?"

Hala tilted her head. "You reek of the magic that was before. You must go back to the other magic."

"You mean lost magic?" Chito asked excitedly, Tullia turned to see that Chito was standing very close to Jiang Li, his usually sleek hair was wind blown and mussed. He looked like a nervous puppy who peed in the house and is now waiting for their mom to find out.

Hala seemed to sneer. "Magic is never lost. Magic hides and waits." She put out the other hand. "Come, human."

Tullia hesitated. "We *all* need to go…to the other magic."

Hala looked around at her group, the Grand High was no longer pinned to the ground, and it looked as though she was never placed there, save for the viciousness in her deep abyss eyes and the taste of cayenne doused rot that smothered Tullia's palette. Jiang Li stood tall and completely unfazed. And then her gaze rested on Sabin, both axes drawn, and his big frame tensed and ready for violence.

"No." She said finally, her inhuman gaze lying on Sabin with obvious disdain. "They are not permitted to go to the other magic. They are tarnished by the new age magic."

"You don't understand—" Tullia began but a loud crack of thunder deafened the space, and the sunshine began to bruise as thick, ominous clouds rolled over them.

Wind gathered around Tullia and swirled violently around her ankles. The force was strong enough to feel as though a large animal was shoving into her.

Tullia stumbled against the force, Sabin snagged her around the waist, squeezing her to him so tight it hurt to breathe.

Hala watched them, and a smile stretched over her face. It was the most horrible, inhuman smile, void of any type of emotion and more of a bearing of the teeth than anything.

She raised her arms, her lower body fading away as she rose high into the air.

"Come to Hala." She cried, and visible winds swirled down to her, heading her call gleefully.

Tullia shivered and felt the sharp threads of wind whip her face. Hala never broke eye contact with Sabin and her strangled smile never wavered either.

Mini tornadoes darted forward and raced towards them…then they seemed to hit an invisible wall, twirling apart effortlessly.

"It seems you've been living by yourself for far too long." The Grand High's voice was cracking with power. Tullia glanced over her shoulder to see Cliona smoking blue and her eyes a cold, cold sapphire. "You don't recognize powerful beings and pay your respect to them. You fool. You'll now have to be crushed beneath my foot for the lack of self-preservation."

Oh snap, Tullia thought, shit might have just gotten real.

Hala didn't seem bothered in fact she seemed more amused than anything. "Mortals are the weakest race. Mortals are nothing but lowly creatures, expendable wastes of space. Like mosquitoes, they suck the life essence, get fat, then die."

"Did this bitch just call me fat?" Cliona asked, laughing, clearly amused. "The only thing fat on me, honey, is my ass and yes, it is fat." Her eyes flashed with white lightning. "You're an expired demon, guarding a portal long after you have been forgotten." The Grand High sneered. "We can simply remove you. After all, you're only a peon of a demon."

Hala's face that was once smooth and seamless, twisted into something unholy.

"Die."

She swiped her hands down and faded entirely as golf ball sized hail hammered down. Tullia gave a cry when one struck her shoulder with bruising force. She heard Chito cry out too but the hail ceased. Tullia opened her eyes to see the hail hitting another invisible force.

"Ha!" The Grand High screamed.

But the hail seemed to push down on the barrier.

"We need a plan now." Cliona's teeth were gritted. "Her magic is laced with some lost magic, making it a bit more…robust than mine."

"Can you even slay an elemental demon?" Jiang Li asked, his hands shrinking back to normal from his dragon form.

Tullia rubbed her shoulder that throbbed smartly.

"Surely there must be? Like killing them with the opposite element?" Chito said, nimbly braiding his hair back.

"Is Hala even an elemental? I think it's a weather demon." Tullia said.

The Grand High stared at her barrier bending under the weight of the piled-up hail. "I do not know how to kill a weather demon."

"I do." Sabin rumbled darkly, "We need them to appear before us and lobe off their head."

"Just like that?" Cliona asked, her eyebrows raising in disbelief.

"Just like that." Sabin affirmed grimly.

"Have you killed one before?" She asked, flexing her inhumanly long fingers.

"Once, back in Macedonia. Took a few years, but I finally discovered its weakness."

"It *would* take you years to figure anything out." She remarked snidely, her eyes still on the barrier ceiling.

"Your barrier is breaking, witch." A multitude of voices whispered around them.

"Shut the hell up, ugly!" Cliona shouted over the clunking sounds of the oversized hail.

"We need her to manifest then, for us to kill her." Jiang Li murmured. His face was smooth and untroubled, they might as well have been talking about something pleasant like literature or flower arrangements.

"How?" Chito asked, his pretty face was tense.

"Baiting." Sabin said. "Enough insults the demon is going to want to watch you suffer and make sure they are the last thing you see."

"Makes sense." Tullia said, the throbbing in her shoulder numbing under the cold that seemed to intensify by the minute.

"I'll shield Chito and Tullia." Cliona glanced at Jiang Li. "Good at insults?"

Jiang Li raised one perfect eyebrow. "I have perfected the craft. Lowly beings are often quite abysmal and require to be reminded of their status every now and again."

Tullia nodded, impressed by how snobby he sounded and how confident. So, did he make it a sport as to which peasant he could insult the most? What was the point system based on, who cried first?

"I think that is the best answer I've ever heard come out of your handsome mouth." The Grand High laughed, then looked to Sabin. "Be ready with your lumber slicers, berserker."

Sabin nodded, and nudged Tullia toward Chito. They both huddled together. There was a small crack then the hail poured in.

Jiang Li snarled in anger, one of his hands rose, and the hail was soon sliding off a small round barrier above his head. Sabin used one of his ax blades to cover his head, but the ice chunks still battered down on his body. However, he showed no reaction.

"A lowly being indeed." Jiang Li's voice was scoffing and demeaning. "Hiding and using cheap tricks to defeat their opponent. This creature is worthless, their honor is nonexistent as is any type of intelligence."

The hail slowed and thrashes of wind began to come in succession.

"While I will admit, your insults were very…insulting, I think this demon requires them to be more forward." Cliona yelled over the howling winds.

"You're a pitiable demon! You have to hide in order to actually put up a fight! *Lame*! You suck!" The Grand High yelled loudly.

A vicious laugh from a distortion of multiple voices.

"You are the ones that are truly pitiful. This is Hala's domain! Here, you are *nothing*."

A sharp blast of wind shoved everyone but Tullia down to the ground.

"Chito!" Tullia cried, but before she could help him up, she was picked up off the ground by a whirl of tumbling wind, her arms and legs were pushed up by the wind and she was carried towards the center of the Judas tree circle, where Hala had stood.

She screamed, struggling to break free of the caging winds, thrashing wildly. She shuddered as ice consumed her from the coldness of the gusts. She flipped onto her stomach, and shoved her hands out towards Sabin, who was running through the heavy hail downpour.

She was nearly at the center of the circle, and fear engulfed her, she kicked and struggled to move, willing the stupid wind to drop her. She looked behind her and felt horror seize her heart. The portal was open and visible. It was a giant black hole. There was a glimmering darkness swirling within and it seemed to wink at her from its center. Fear unlike any that she has felt consumed her and ravaged her mind with terror.

She began to contort her body and screech, clawing at nothing but empty space as she was pulled towards the frightening portal.

She looked back, to see Sabin a few feet from her, his gold eyes churning like melted gold. She felt tears come to her eyes as she strained towards him. He threw one of his black axes down and stretched one of his arms out towards her.

Their fingers brushed lightly, nearly touching, before he was flung back as though hit in the chest by a speeding car.

"Sabin!" She screamed, terror overtaking her as the wind shoved her into the portal. Blackness engulfed her vision and the sensation of free falling stole her breath and took her consciousness away.

* * *

Tullia's wide gray eyes, scared and panicked, had pleaded silently for him to help her. And the damned demon had pelted him with tennis ball sized hail and vicious winds to keep his body back. He struggled against the demon's weather, absorbing the hits, and pushing against the winds…

But he couldn't reach her.

When she screamed his name, terror filled and shrill, a sound of pure desperation, a voice that called out to him for help. A sound she had not made, a tone she did not make, until this demon came.

She had called for him to save her, and he had failed. The demon had casted her into the portal and Tullia had been swallowed easily, disappearing, leaving the clearing deadened with the remnants of her screams.

Snap.

His rage, snapping and snarling, rose swiftly within and raced through his blood. Heating it and searing his control entirely. Sabin slammed his foot down in the ground encasing it two inches deep to gain stability in the whipping winds and stared at the demon with fanatical focus.

Kill.

Kill.

Slay!

He felt every muscle, every blood cell, every fiber of his being honed in on the demon. His rage curled his remaining lips back underneath his mask in a challenging snarl as he lifted both his arms up. The hail he no longer felt, it was no longer there to Sabin. He launched *slatra* with his entire raging might at the still demon.

Sabin never removed his gaze from her and felt an intoxicating shot of pleasure when his ax struck the demon's left side. The blank shock and the wavering of its form pleased Sabin, it made him hungrier for its death.

The demon's body became nonexistent, *slatra* falling to the ground silently. Hail began to fall again, hitting his body with sharp, stinging slaps. Sabin let the pain fuel his rage. "Wretched demon." He snarled into the clearing. "Face me." He walked towards the demon. It vanished and lightning struck the ground before him.

Sabin no longer carried the capability to fear anything. He no longer processed pain, he merely would endure it, but he would always survive it.

He continued towards his discarded ax and picked up his weapon. Both of his hands felt heavy with his blades. "Miserable demon that can do nothing but throw ice balls and blow wind at us." He inhaled deeply, the cold seeping through his clothes and into every pore. But he was on fire, his rage was the flames that overtook everything and spared no one.

"A pitiful demon like you, it's no wonder you were left to rot in this tiny space."

The hail ceased and the frost in the air thickened. Sabin exhaled slowly, seeing his breath in a thick lingering fog.

"Hala will display your bones in this clearing. Hala will take delight in ending your existence with physical hands as you so desire." Then it appeared, the creature with the long hair and pale face.

Sabin did not hesitate, he threw *snubba* towards the demon. It dodged his blade, a smirk on its mouth, its cold eyes flickering to *snubba*. His rage laughed, a flicker was all he needed, as he sprinted forward and leapt high, *slatra* raised high above his head. His existence for that moment was to slay the demon, nothing else mattered. *Slatra* came down hard…into earth. He slanted his gaze to the side, seeing the demon standing there with a gash down the side of its face and fresh blood oozing out, dripping onto the grass in thick globs.

He liked that sight.

Sabin felt himself smile, yanking *slatra* out of the ground and standing upright.

"Be prepared for your end, demon." Sabin murmured. Stalking towards it, he saw nothing but its melting form. He would not stop until he held its head in his grasp, detached from its body.

"Your insolence is grating." The layering voices screeched as its claws shot up into the air. A heavy curtain of rain slammed down on him, obscuring his view of the demon.

No matter. He would kill it. He wouldn't stop until he killed it. He'd never stop until the blood drained from the demon's corpse and each and every bone was splintered underneath his boots and grated into fine powder.

His rage screamed, and his world was tinted red.

* * *

He snapped. His rage was out, and his berserker mode was in full swing. Cliona stared at the scene before her, protection shields were over her and Chito's head to keep the rain from dousing them. The dragon had supplied his own cover from the dowsing rain. As he should since he boasted enough about his magic and title as the 'great river dragon'.

She had watched Tullia be sucked into the portal and witnessed Sabin's rage consume him, turning him into the berserker he once was in ancient times. There would be no reasoning with him until he had cooled down.

And while she was not opposed to a good bloody fight especially with an annoying, stupid man, Sabin was in a different category.

Take him on, bury him alive....Splatter paint the tree with a pretty red.

Cliona rolled her neck, her muscles were bunched up from the creeping insanity within her. Her odds of winning were slim to none, especially with her little gray eyed magic battery now MIA. She curled her lips in distaste of the thought, but her remaining sanity that utilized logic was right. He was magic resistant and unable to die. You kill him once, the bastard just pops right back up, like a weed. Cliona had heard several rumors on the berserker, though she wasn't sure if they were exaggerated facts or pure fiction.

One particular rumor was that he had strangled a man with his own entrails, then hung him in his mother's house with said entrails. When she found him, she dropped dead with fright.

Cliona couldn't see Sabin doing that, but she had sensed a deep, prowling darkness within him and he was the most feared and revered mercenary for centuries.

"We need to help him!" Chito cried, taking a few steps forward, only to smack his face against her barrier.

"He's in an uncontrollable state right now." She said to Chito, her eyes searching through the rain. "He cannot distinguish between friend or foe." She looked down at the cutie pie shifter, whose face was creased with stress and fear. "Best not to intervene until Sabin kills the demon."

Chito bit his lip and looked out towards the rain where they could faintly see Sabin and Hala. He pressed his hands to the barrier.

"Dragon." Cliona addressed, not taking her eye off the shadowed figures in the rain. "Be ready when the rain ceases."

He said nothing, but Cliona didn't need his response. The dragon was an old being, sensitive to magic and power. Sabin was imbued with both, that spoke of olden times long forgotten. Sabin was powerful, even though he slinked around trying to act like a non-existent wallflower. But he was far too damn big and imposing to ever be overlooked. He was also oozing with power, tightly leashed power, but power, nonetheless. However, Cliona never forgot what he was, a cursed killer, forever doomed to linger on the earth until the end of time. She didn't know why, but to be cursed with such cruel magic, he must have screwed over one of the gods of old.

She was only brazen with him for his control was impeccable. He was far stronger than her, a fact she disliked immensely and would never share with anyone.

She folded her arms, waiting for him to kill the demon. As she waited, she began to think. Sabin went ballistic when Tullia was shoved into the portal. It seemed he had a chink in his armor. She tapped her fingers against her arm.

Where did the girl go, and just what is she a part of? Where was the other half hiding? What was the other half?

A small smile curled her lips. Either way, Cliona would get both parts of that lost magic.

Then she could put her plan into action.

* * *

Sabin opened his senses. Scents became stronger, he could smell the unnatural rot in the rain as it fell. He could hear each and every raindrop hit the grass. He could see each droplet fall past his eyes and he saw the demon. Standing long, tall and distorted. Looking nothing like the woman that had first appeared in the clearing. Sabin stalked over to where *snubba* was laying, his eyes fastened obsessively on the demon. He picked up *snubba*, then tightened his grip on both axes, not daring to blink.

And then he ran, full throttle towards the demon's form. His heart thundering, his blood liquid fire in his veins and his rage a consuming force.

Sabin's mind dimmed as his rage swathed his thoughts in a red fog. He dimly heard himself scream, a sound he had not made in ages, as his limbs once more performed the dance of death.

Each swing of his blade the red fog soaked deeper into his mind. Each sound of rage emitted from Sabin further enhanced and excited his wrath. Sabin swung madly at the weather demon, the bolts of lightning, the now pumpkin sized hail, the blistering wind, he felt none of it. He stalked the wounded demon, watching with glee as the demon's distorted face morphed into a sloppy mess of terror as it tried to scuttle back from him.

Sabin crossed *snubba* and *slatra* in front of the demon's throat. Then he jerked his hands violently and the hail stopped, the rain ceased, and the sky lightened. Sabin grunted, searching the area around him, looking for the demon.

He looked down to see a crumpled lump that was once Hala, now headless and dead on the grass in front of him. A surge of newly heated rage tore through him.

He was not done! He was not done fighting the demon! It died far too readily! Where was his victory? Giving a shout of pure anger, Sabin rose his axes above his head and slammed them down on the demon's body. He gave a shout each time his axes made contact, cursing the demon for dying too quickly and being a weak opponent.

He slammed his axes into the corpse of the demon again and again, feeling his rage increase under the action, feeling no relief at the wet meaty sounds or the crispy bone snapping sounds that his axes made.

His rage was howling, his rage was too wild, his rage was now in control for the first time in a century.

Sabin threw his head back, a gush of noise clawing out of his mouth, and he screamed. It was a scream that was dragged up bloody, raw and mangled from the deepest part of him. It was a scream that he heard nightly and suffocated daily. It was a scream of release…and his rage pulled his sanity deep under its gore infested lake, drowning him until his vision swam red and his thoughts died away to only a single mantra.

Kill.

Kill.

Kill.

"Sabin?" A voice.

He snapped his head around; he saw a slender frame and long black hair.

"Are…a-are you okay?" The timid voice was shaking, it made his rage hungry.

He jerked *slatra* and *snubba* from the mangled corpse of the now unrecognizable demon and turned to the slender form. The face was dim, but it mattered not, they wouldn't be needing their face in death.

"Shit." He heard from beyond his sight, but he would get to them. First the slender one would taste his blades.

Sabin exhaled a roar of fury and darted towards the slender figure. He ate up the scream of fear, his rage reveling in the sound. His vision soaked in blood and his stomach tightened in the anticipation of more bones shattering, blood spilling, life draining…

A flash of dull blue and a heavy weight slammed into his side, causing him to fly and hit one of the Judas trees hard. Sabin grunted, the pain a sweet addition to his rage. He looked up, stilled momentarily then Sabin threw his head back and laughed wildly, his rage seeping out from his mouth. He fixed his eyes on the massive blue beast, protectively encircling the slender figure and emitting a loud, thrumming growl.

A beast worthy of slaying, his rage whispered to him.

"I shall wear your scales, beast." Sabin uttered low, his voice tight and cascading in the language of his homeland. "I shall eat your heart before your dying eyes. I shall bath my axes in your blood."

Sabin stood and gripped *snubba* and *slatra* tightly. He felt his mouth stretch wide and felt his heart pump wildly with exaltation as his breathing turned ragged from the thrill. A beast worthy to feed his blades, it had been too long since he gave it all in a battle.

"Hey, berserker." A feminine voice, arrogant and loud, called to him. Sabin only slid his eyes to glance at the voice, his entire body remained focused on the dragon. "Now is not the time to get crazy on us."

Witch, he determined with amusement. They posed no threat, their magic as useful as a feathered sword against him.

"You demolished the portal guardian and made the stupid portal collapse." Her voice seemed to be increasing in volume, raising his ire. A cocky stance. He'd chop her legs off first, then beat her with them.

"If you ever want to see your girl again, you better snap the hell out of it."

Sabin decided to ignore the witch, he'd slay the dragon first and then slay her.

An exaggerated sigh when Sabin scraped his blades together, his eyes going back to the dragon. "We need to find Tullia. Remember her? White girl, black short hair, pretty enough face? Gray eyes?"

A pair of bright gray eyes, laughing and light, framed by thick black lashes consumed his vision. Sabin shook his head, a searing throb started to grow on the sides of his head.

"She was dragged through the portal. She's most likely scared and calling out for you." The annoying voice was conjuring images of a woman small and bouncy, chattering and sweet.

It conjured images…memories of how she spoke, her little actions, her smile…

A smile that cooled his rage down enough for Sabin's mind to clear. He dropped his blades to cradle his throbbing head, as he wrestled with his rage, shoving it down deep, back into its cage. His breathing turned labored as his rage fought viciously. Sabin clenched his teeth as he wrestled his rage down. Water dripped from him as he held himself perfectly still, tucking away the remaining remnants of rage from his system.

When he was confident he was no longer under his rage's thrall, Sabin looked up. The witch was staring at him, her face indiscernible. She glanced at the dragon and shifter. Chito looked scared and concerned, though he did not move from the dragon's protective embrace. Jiang Li looked on guard, his massive teeth were still displayed in warning.

Sabin sighed shakily, his body throbbing and his rage screaming within him. He rolled his shoulders and bent down slowly, feeling his rage as he picked up and sheathed both *snubba* and *slatra*.

"You good?" The witch asked, still staring at him with those dark, ominous eyes.

"Yes." He said hoarsely. He wasn't good, but his rage was contained once more, shredding his insides with its restlessness and its vehemence at him contained once more. But he was sane and in control, that mattered more than how he felt.

"Alright then." She said then turned to the other two. "He's back. He won't try to kill us anymore. Let's get going." Her voice was hard and dared anyone to argue with her decision.

No one did. The Grand High strode up to where the portal once was and put her hand out. There was a giant pulse that radiated throughout the area.

"Oh," She purred, her pure white tracksuit, crinkled and stained in a few places. She turned to look over her shoulder, her smile wide, "Well, looks like this baddie didn't collapse as I thought it did. And it tastes of lost magic."

Sabin watched as the cold seeped deep into his bones. The witch wiggled her fingers and a pop of smoke and roaring mist of blackness swirled angrily. She gave a sharp laugh then pushed through and disappeared. Sabin moved his eyes to the shifter and the dragon, he motioned for them to go first. The dragon had a firm hold on the shifter, pressing him tightly to his side as he passed Sabin. Chito did not look at Sabin, his brown skin ashened and his brown eyes red. They too disappeared into the portal, leaving Sabin alone with the demon body and blood fed trees.

He looked back at the slabs of meat that used to be a demon and stiffened. When he thought he had moved on from his barbaric habits, it is proven to him that he has not changed in the least bit.

Guilt choked him as he looked at the once green grass splattered with blood. He swallowed, forcing the emotion down with his rage.

He was a fool to be shocked over his actions. He was a monster. A fact that he had forgotten when he was with Tullia.

A fact that reminded him that he was irredeemable and cursed.

He would always be nothing but a monster.

Sabin turned away from the mangled demon's corpse and strode through the portal.

He was going to see Tullia safe through this travel and he was going to make sure she succeeded in her life. He'd give her everything she needed. So that in her future, he could be warmed by the memory that he had helped at least one person thrive in his never-ending curse.

It was more for him than for her but, after all, monsters are supposed to be selfish.

***

Tullia slowly came awake to nothing but darkness. Fear consumed her as she remembered being shoved through the portal then passing out. Was this just like what Cierico experienced, total nothingness before complete madness? She gasped and heard her voice echo out as well as her heart throbbing loudly in her ears. Shifting sounds, like sand falling through cracks hissed around her, both relieving her and renewing her fear in a different way. The darkness was thick, but not oppressive.

She jerked up from the altar type slab of stone and fumbled a bit in the dark. Then a mental light bulb went off in her head. She dug around in her hoodie pocket, looking for her decorative lighter that Sabin bought, hoping that it didn't fall out and that it actually worked.

She fumbled in her pocket for a long ass time and when she found her lighter it took a few clicks for the flame to jump to life, cutting dimly through the darkness. She looked around, seeing weathered stones, sand and…blackness around her.

Tullia listened, but she only heard hisses from the sand and her own petrified heartbeat. She looked over her shoulder and, surprise, more unseeable darkness. The flame shook in her hand, jumping along the walls and creating shadows that seemed to laugh at Tullia.

Swallowing against the nearly overwhelming fear, she inhaled deeply, and sneezed hugely, winking out her light.

Shit.

Slightly panicked, she clicked the lighter again and the flame came alive once more. Tullia held her arm out and slowly walked forward, noticing that underneath her feet was…limestone? She held the flame out around her, trying to find something, anything but sand and darkness.

She saw stones stacked on top of one another and she came across a pillar with very primitive pictures of what looked like…

Tullia tilted her head and held the light up closer to the pillar, it looked like a cat with very, very, very large teeth and no eyes and not a lot of details. She frowned, it didn't look like hieroglyphics, but it certainly looked old…

A soft hiss made Tullia tense and spin too fast around, causing her fragile little light to be blown out again. Cursing and sweating enough to cause her hoodie to become damp, Tullia snapped at her lighter, her fingers slippery and clumsy.

Her dim light wiggled up and stayed small, but at least it was something for the darkness. Swallowing, Tullia looked up and noticed that the pillar was actually in the shape of a T.

Huh.

She moved on from the T-pillar and carefully walked forward then noticed a step that led up to a slab of limestone. Scampering over, Tullia inspected a carving on the slab. It was a very crude, very rough design of what looked like a woman with something protruding out of her center.

Wait.

Tullia stared at it with relief…where had she seen this before?

A prickly feeling of eyes ripped her from her study as a tickle went up her spine sending chills throughout her body.

Tullia nervously looked up and froze in suspended horror filled disbelief.

There was a figure, standing a few feet away from where she stood. It wasn't there before. Tullia stopped breathing from fright, her heart stuttered, before pounding in her chest, urging her to run away.

Run away to where? The never ending darkness?

The flame in her hand began to shake violently and sweat formed, then rolled down her face. Her thumb that was pressing down the lighter became raw and stung as she pressed down even harder.

The figure didn't move, but she knew, knew all its attention was on *her*. She felt it, she felt the eyes. Trembling, Tullia opened her mouth, trying to call out to it, but her throat choked off the words before they could escape.

What does she do?

Time dripped by as Tullia stared at the figure, hoping it was only her mind going bonkers again.

"*Tullia.*" It said, the voice a velvety symphony of voices, yet funneled as one. Neither feminine nor masculine, a purely androgynous voice. "You have finally arrived." The figure leaned closer, its face was vague in the darkness, even under the weak flame light, Tullia saw nothing.

"*Welcome young one. We finally meet at last.*"

Her lighter's flame winked out and darkness swallowed her whole.

About the Author

Victoria Kasminoff is an introverted, old-soul foodie that likes to spend half her day in the kitchen cooking recipes that tickle her pickle. She, a dyslexic hyper individual, loves to read, write, and watch anime all simultaneously while looking at her phone periodically. She practices yoga consistently to help ease the busyness that is her mind palace. She has a fluffy dog by the name of Layla, whom is snooty and old money pretty. When she's not at home, which is 99% of the time, she enjoys going for short drives to her favorite tea spot and sometimes, if she dares to be wild, explore different grocery stores.